# Little Lulu ®

D1603257

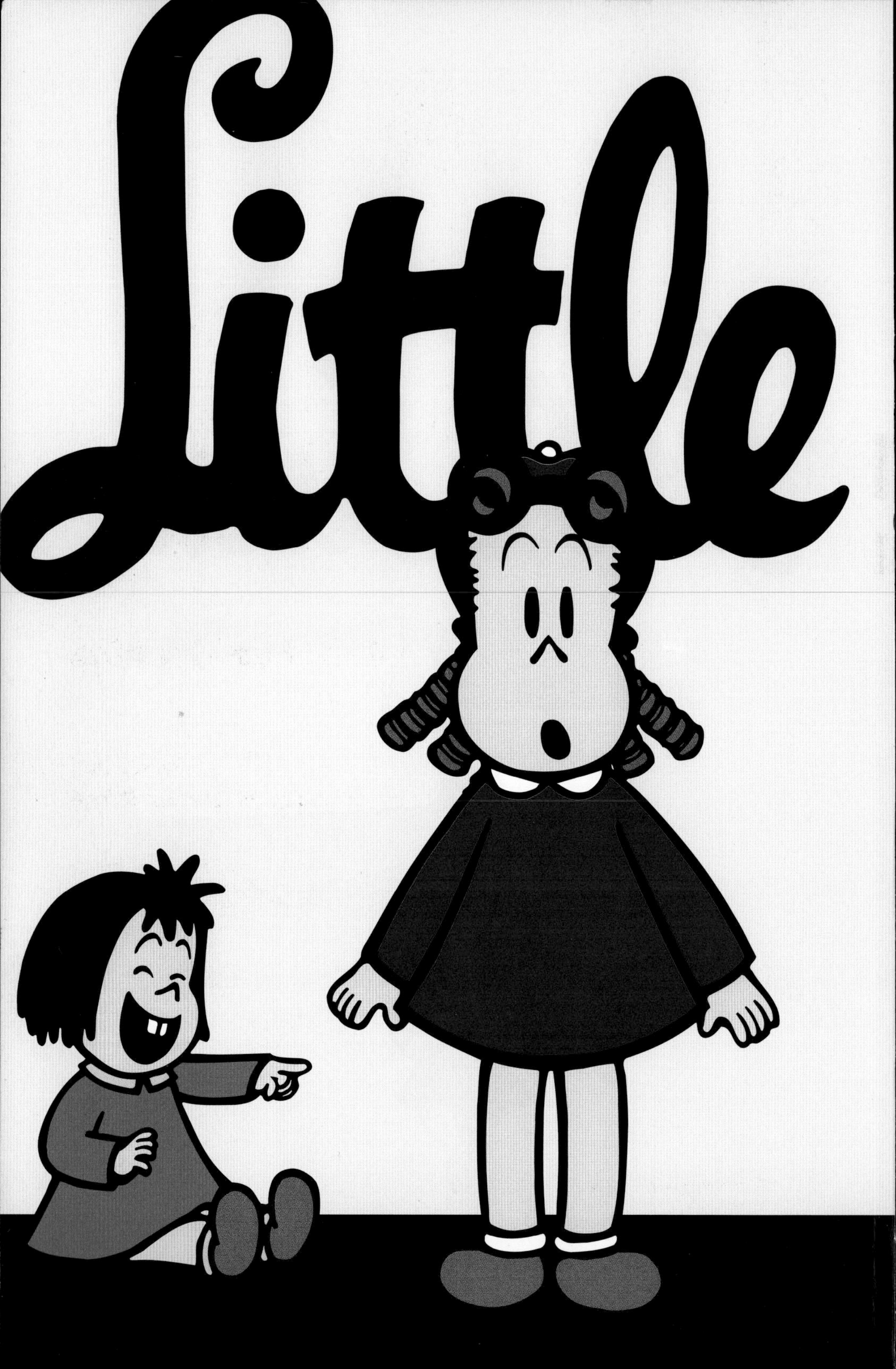
Little

# The Alamo and Other Stories

Story and Art
**John Stanley & Irving Tripp**

Based on the character created by
**Marge Buell**

Dark Horse Books®

Publisher **Mike Richardson**

Editor **Dave Marshall**

Assistant Editor **Brendan Wright**

Collection Designer **Krystal Hennes**


Published by Dark Horse Books

A division of Dark Horse Comics, Inc.

10956 SE Main Street

Milwaukie, Oregon 97222


First edition: May 2009

ISBN: 978-1-59582-293-2

# Little Lulu® Volume 19: The Alamo and Other Stories

This volume contains every comic from issues eighty-eight through ninety-three of
*Marge's Little Lulu*, originally published by Dell Comics.

© 2009 Classic Media, Inc. LITTLE LULU character names and images are trademarks of and copyrighted by Classic Media, Inc., an Entertainment Rights group company. All rights reserved. Dark Horse Books® and the Dark Horse logo are registered trademarks of Dark Horse Comics, Inc. All rights reserved. No portion of this publication may be reproduced or transmitted, in any form or by any means, without the express written permission of Dark Horse Comics, Inc. Names, characters, places, and incidents featured in this publication either are the product of the author's imagination or are used fictitiously. Any resemblance to actual persons (living or dead), events, institutions, or locales, without satiric intent, is coincidental.

Mike Richardson, President and Publisher • Neil Hankerson, Executive Vice President • Tom Weddle, Chief Financial Officer • Randy Stradley, Vice President of Publishing • Michael Martens, Vice President of Business Development • Anita Nelson, Vice President of Marketing, Sales, and Licensing • David Scroggy, Vice President of Product Development • Dale LaFountain, Vice President of Information Technology • Darlene Vogel, Director of Purchasing • Ken Lizzi, General Counsel • Davey Estrada, Editorial Director • Scott Allie, Senior Managing Editor • Chris Warner, Senior Books Editor, Dark Horse Books • Rob Simpson, Senior Books Editor, M Press/DH Press • Diana Schutz, Executive Editor • Cary Grazzini, Director of Design and Production • Lia Ribacchi, Art Director • Cara Niece, Director of Scheduling

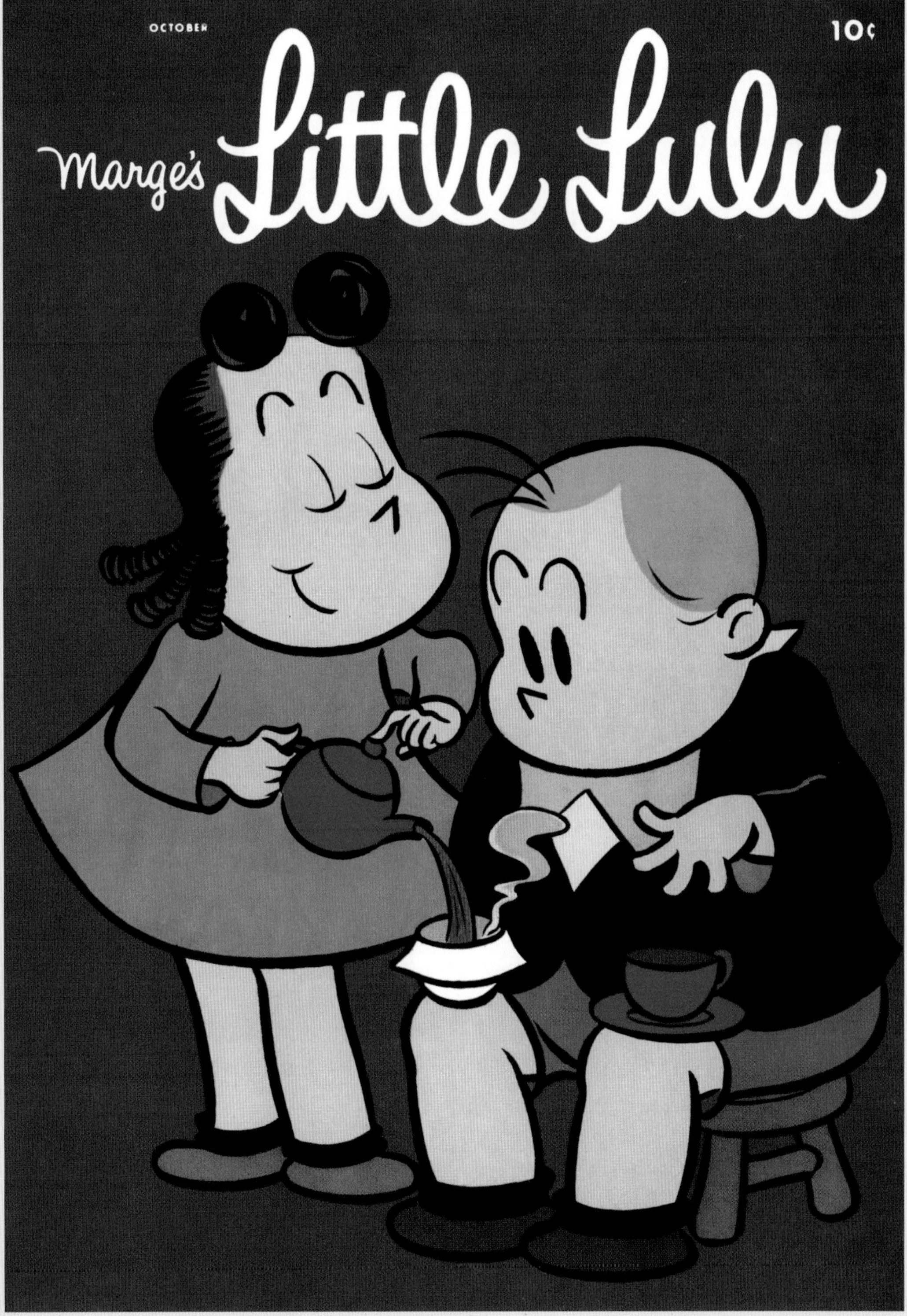
OCTOBER
10¢
Marge's Little Lulu

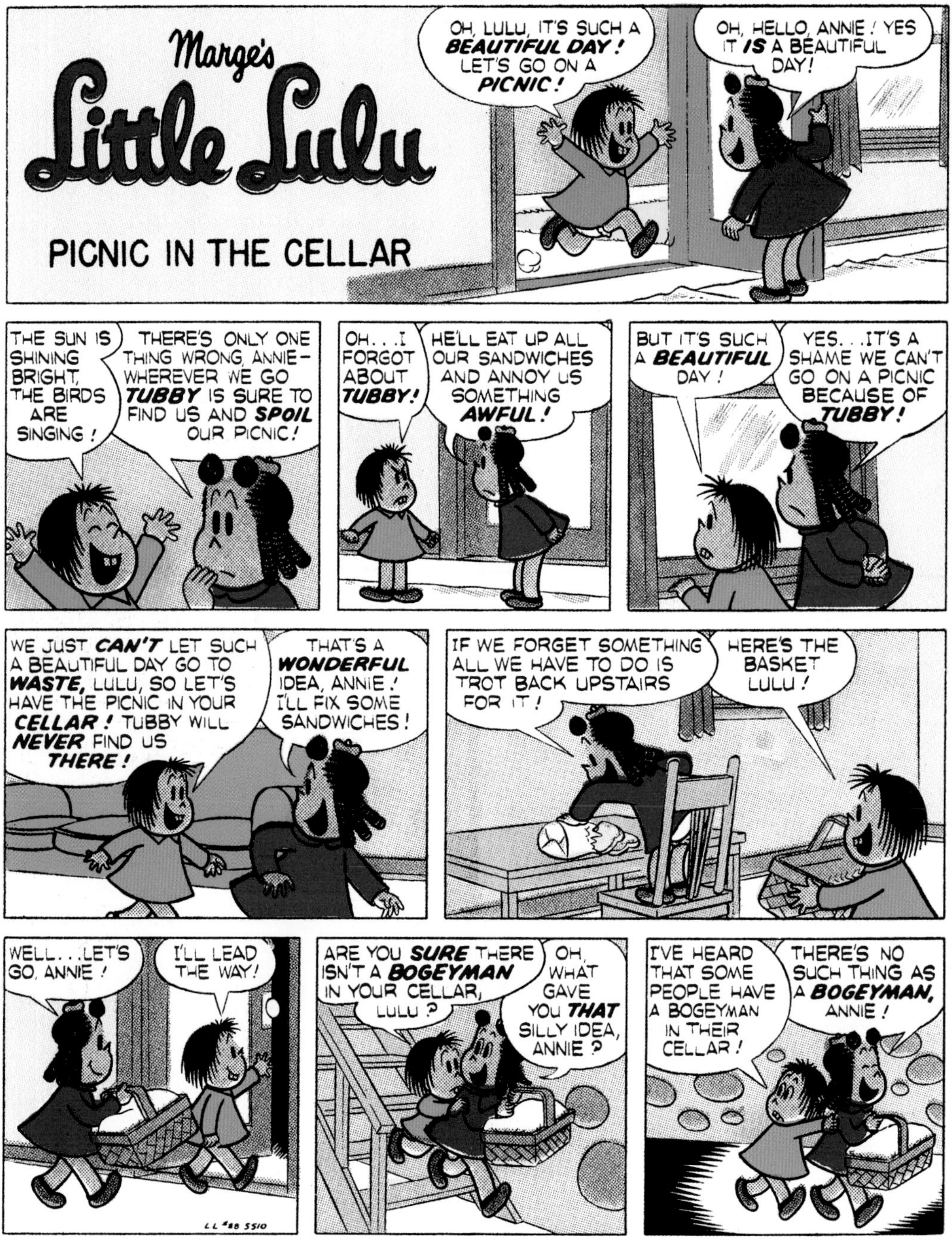
Marge's Little Lulu
PICNIC IN THE CELLAR
OH, LULU, IT'S SUCH A BEAUTIFUL DAY! LET'S GO ON A PICNIC!
OH, HELLO, ANNIE! YES IT IS A BEAUTIFUL DAY!
THE SUN IS SHINING BRIGHT, THE BIRDS ARE SINGING!
THERE'S ONLY ONE THING WRONG, ANNIE– WHEREVER WE GO TUBBY IS SURE TO FIND US AND SPOIL OUR PICNIC!
OH. . .I FORGOT ABOUT TUBBY!
HE'LL EAT UP ALL OUR SANDWICHES AND ANNOY US SOMETHING AWFUL!
BUT IT'S SUCH A BEAUTIFUL DAY!
YES. . .IT'S A SHAME WE CAN'T GO ON A PICNIC BECAUSE OF TUBBY!
WE JUST CAN'T LET SUCH A BEAUTIFUL DAY GO TO WASTE, LULU, SO LET'S HAVE THE PICNIC IN YOUR CELLAR! TUBBY WILL NEVER FIND US THERE!
THAT'S A WONDERFUL IDEA, ANNIE! I'LL FIX SOME SANDWICHES!
IF WE FORGET SOMETHING ALL WE HAVE TO DO IS TROT BACK UPSTAIRS FOR IT!
HERE'S THE BASKET LULU!
WELL. . .LET'S GO, ANNIE!
I'LL LEAD THE WAY!
LL #88 5510
ARE YOU SURE THERE ISN'T A BOGEYMAN IN YOUR CELLAR, LULU?
OH, WHAT GAVE YOU THAT SILLY IDEA, ANNIE?
I'VE HEARD THAT SOME PEOPLE HAVE A BOGEYMAN IN THEIR CELLAR!
THERE'S NO SUCH THING AS A BOGEYMAN, ANNIE!

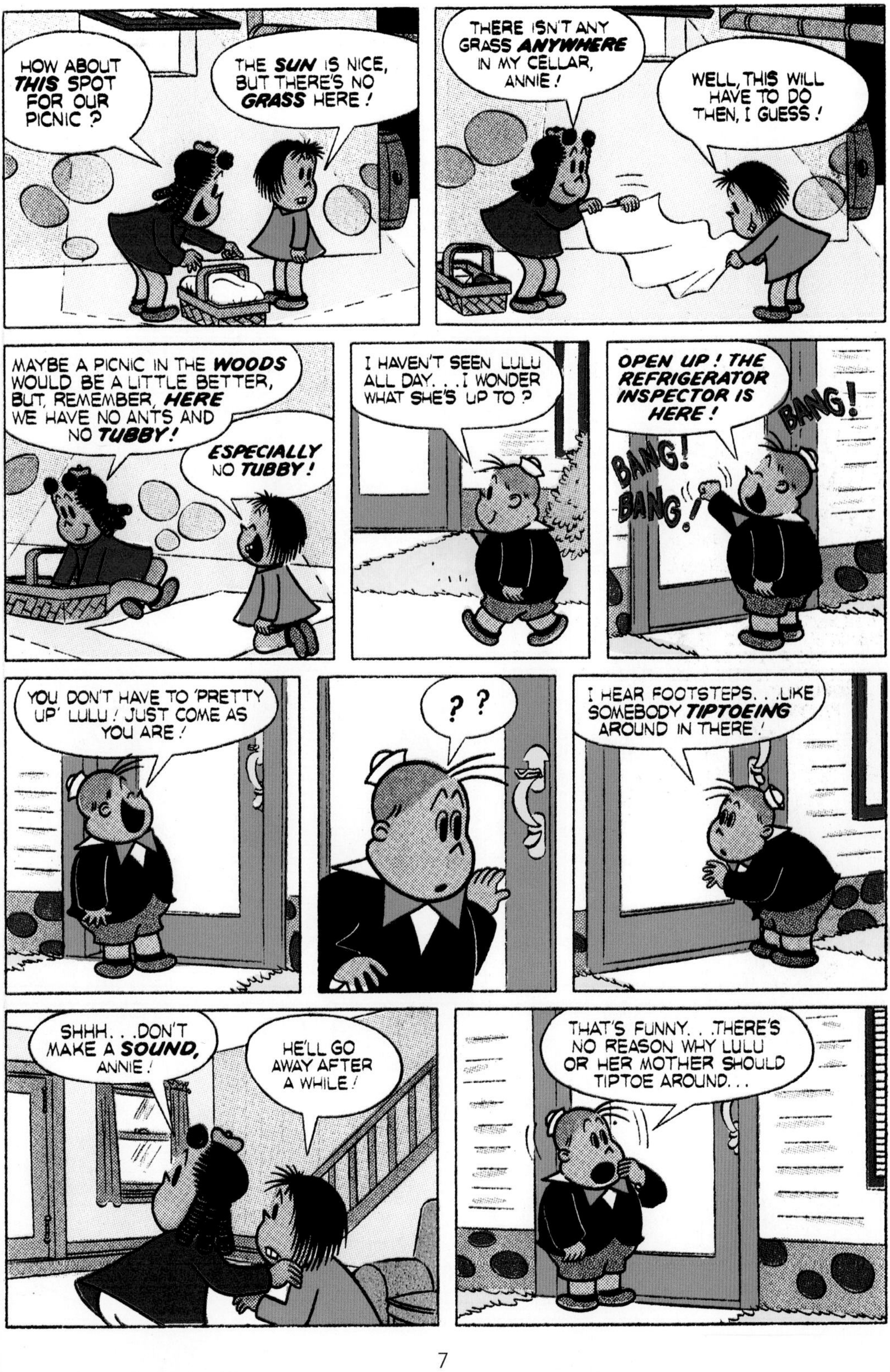
HOW ABOUT THIS SPOT FOR OUR PICNIC ?
THE SUN IS NICE, BUT THERE'S NO GRASS HERE !
THERE ISN'T ANY GRASS ANYWHERE IN MY CELLAR, ANNIE !
WELL, THIS WILL HAVE TO DO THEN, I GUESS !
MAYBE A PICNIC IN THE WOODS WOULD BE A LITTLE BETTER, BUT, REMEMBER, HERE WE HAVE NO ANTS AND NO TUBBY !
ESPECIALLY NO TUBBY !
I HAVEN'T SEEN LULU ALL DAY. . . I WONDER WHAT SHE'S UP TO ?
OPEN UP ! THE REFRIGERATOR INSPECTOR IS HERE !
BANG!
BANG!
BANG!
YOU DON'T HAVE TO 'PRETTY UP' LULU ! JUST COME AS YOU ARE !
? ?
I HEAR FOOTSTEPS. . .LIKE SOMEBODY TIPTOEING AROUND IN THERE !
SHHH. . .DON'T MAKE A SOUND, ANNIE !
HE'LL GO AWAY AFTER A WHILE !
THAT'S FUNNY. . .THERE'S NO REASON WHY LULU OR HER MOTHER SHOULD TIPTOE AROUND. . .

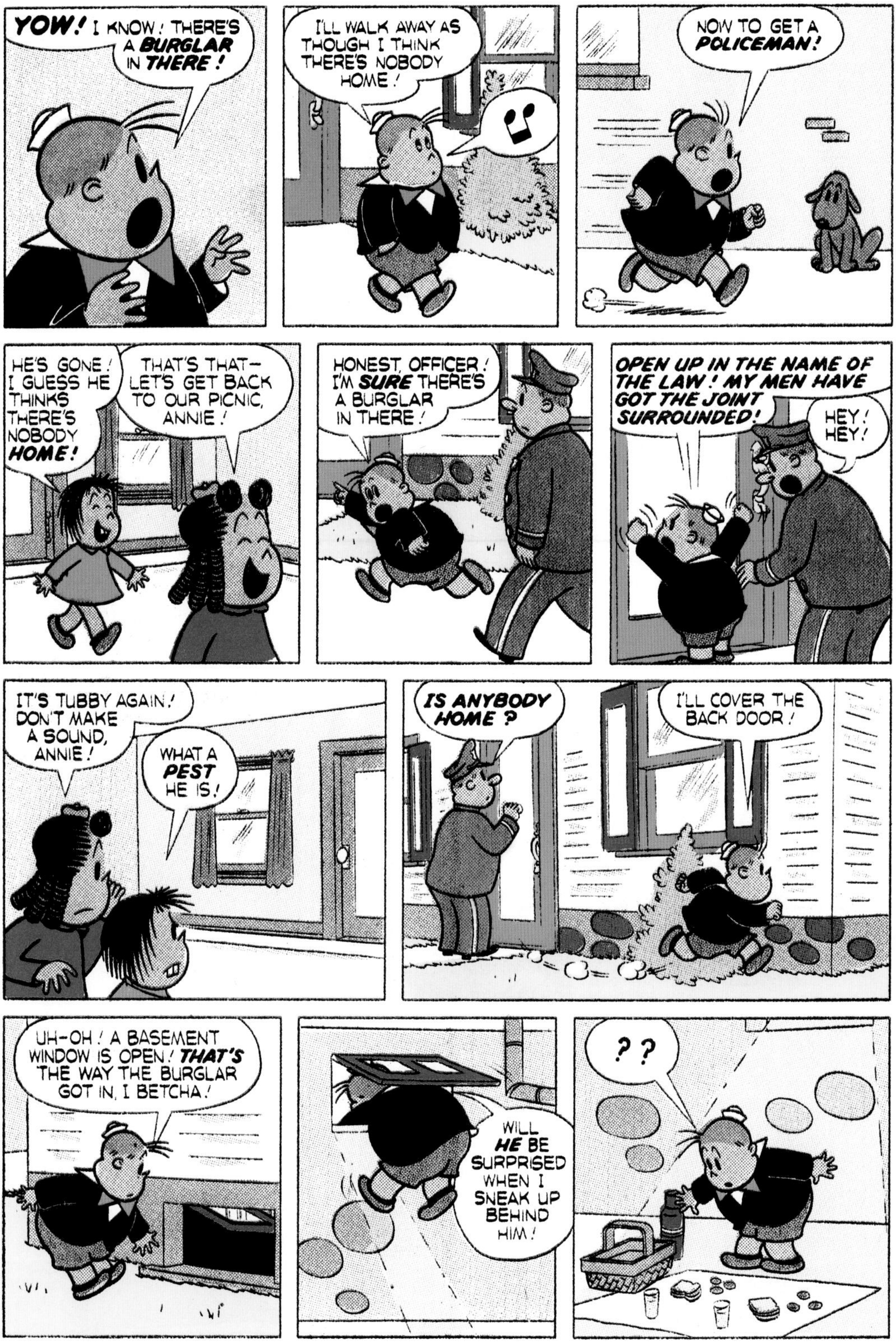
YOW! I KNOW! THERE'S A BURGLAR IN THERE!
I'LL WALK AWAY AS THOUGH I THINK THERE'S NOBODY HOME!
NOW TO GET A POLICEMAN!
HE'S GONE! I GUESS HE THINKS THERE'S NOBODY HOME!
THAT'S THAT— LET'S GET BACK TO OUR PICNIC, ANNIE!
HONEST, OFFICER! I'M SURE THERE'S A BURGLAR IN THERE!
OPEN UP IN THE NAME OF THE LAW! MY MEN HAVE GOT THE JOINT SURROUNDED!
HEY! HEY!
IT'S TUBBY AGAIN! DON'T MAKE A SOUND, ANNIE!
WHAT A PEST HE IS!
IS ANYBODY HOME?
I'LL COVER THE BACK DOOR!
UH-OH! A BASEMENT WINDOW IS OPEN! THAT'S THE WAY THE BURGLAR GOT IN, I BETCHA!
WILL HE BE SURPRISED WHEN I SNEAK UP BEHIND HIM!
??

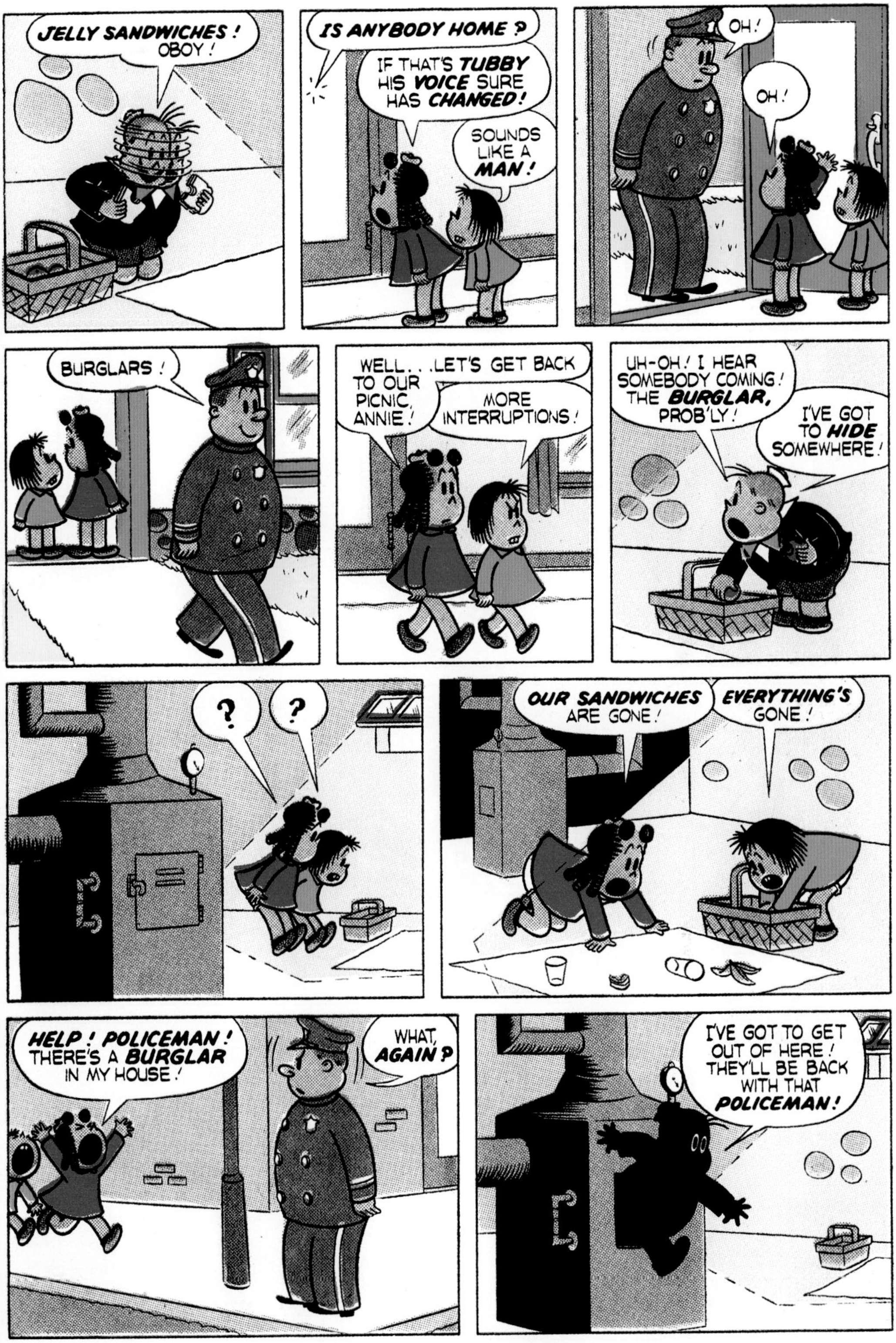
JELLY SANDWICHES! OBOY!
IS ANYBODY HOME?
IF THAT'S TUBBY HIS VOICE SURE HAS CHANGED!
SOUNDS LIKE A MAN!
OH!
OH!
BURGLARS!
WELL. . .LET'S GET BACK TO OUR PICNIC, ANNIE!
MORE INTERRUPTIONS!
UH-OH! I HEAR SOMEBODY COMING! THE BURGLAR, PROB'LY!
I'VE GOT TO HIDE SOMEWHERE!
?
?
OUR SANDWICHES ARE GONE!
EVERYTHING'S GONE!
HELP! POLICEMAN! THERE'S A BURGLAR IN MY HOUSE!
WHAT, AGAIN?
I'VE GOT TO GET OUT OF HERE! THEY'LL BE BACK WITH THAT POLICEMAN!

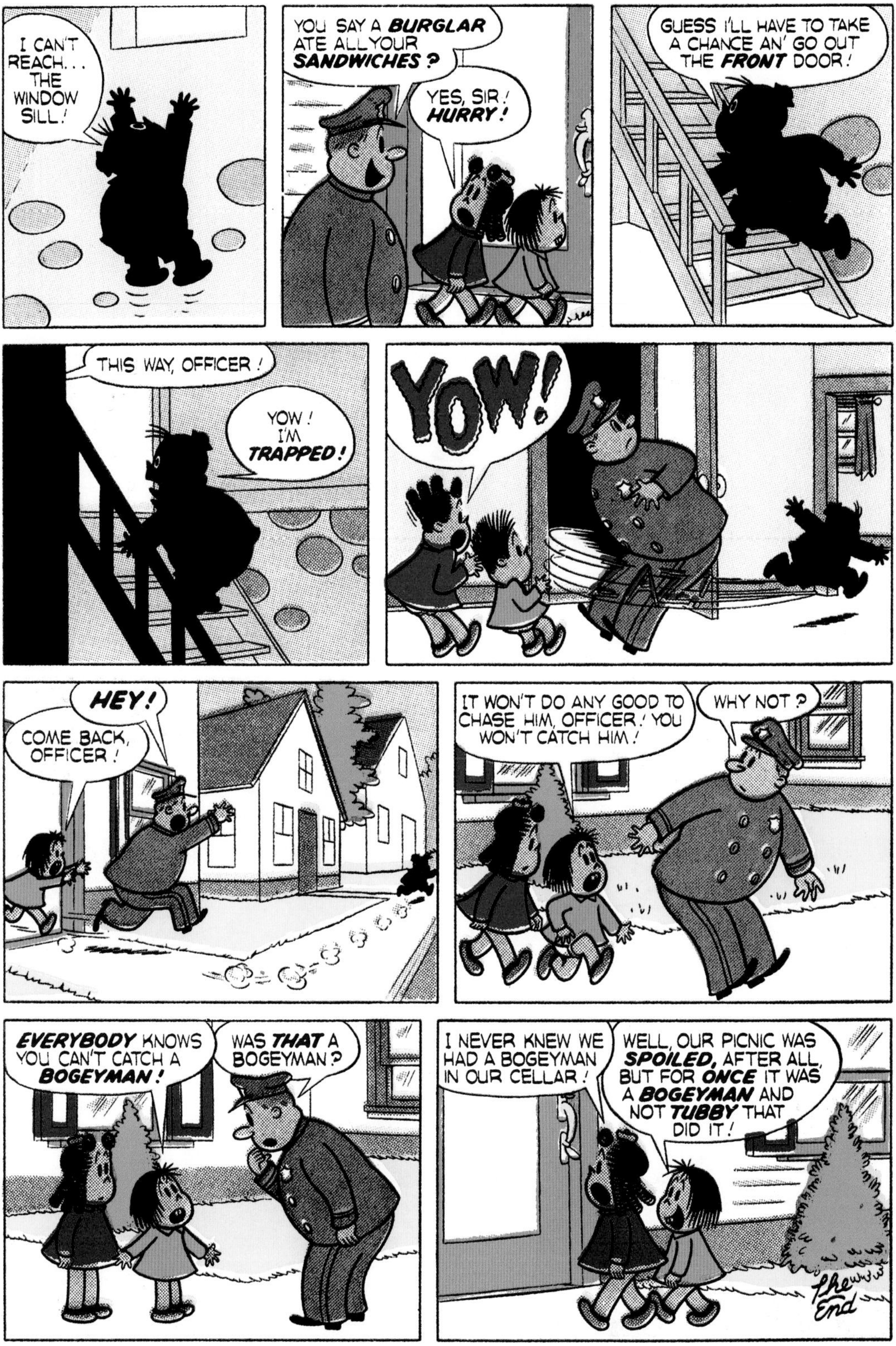
I CAN'T REACH... THE WINDOW SILL!
YOU SAY A BURGLAR ATE ALL YOUR SANDWICHES?
YES, SIR! HURRY!
GUESS I'LL HAVE TO TAKE A CHANCE AN' GO OUT THE FRONT DOOR!
THIS WAY, OFFICER!
YOW! I'M TRAPPED!
YOW!
HEY!
COME BACK, OFFICER!
IT WON'T DO ANY GOOD TO CHASE HIM, OFFICER! YOU WON'T CATCH HIM!
WHY NOT?
EVERYBODY KNOWS YOU CAN'T CATCH A BOGEYMAN!
WAS THAT A BOGEYMAN?
I NEVER KNEW WE HAD A BOGEYMAN IN OUR CELLAR!
WELL, OUR PICNIC WAS SPOILED, AFTER ALL, BUT FOR ONCE IT WAS A BOGEYMAN AND NOT TUBBY THAT DID IT!
The End

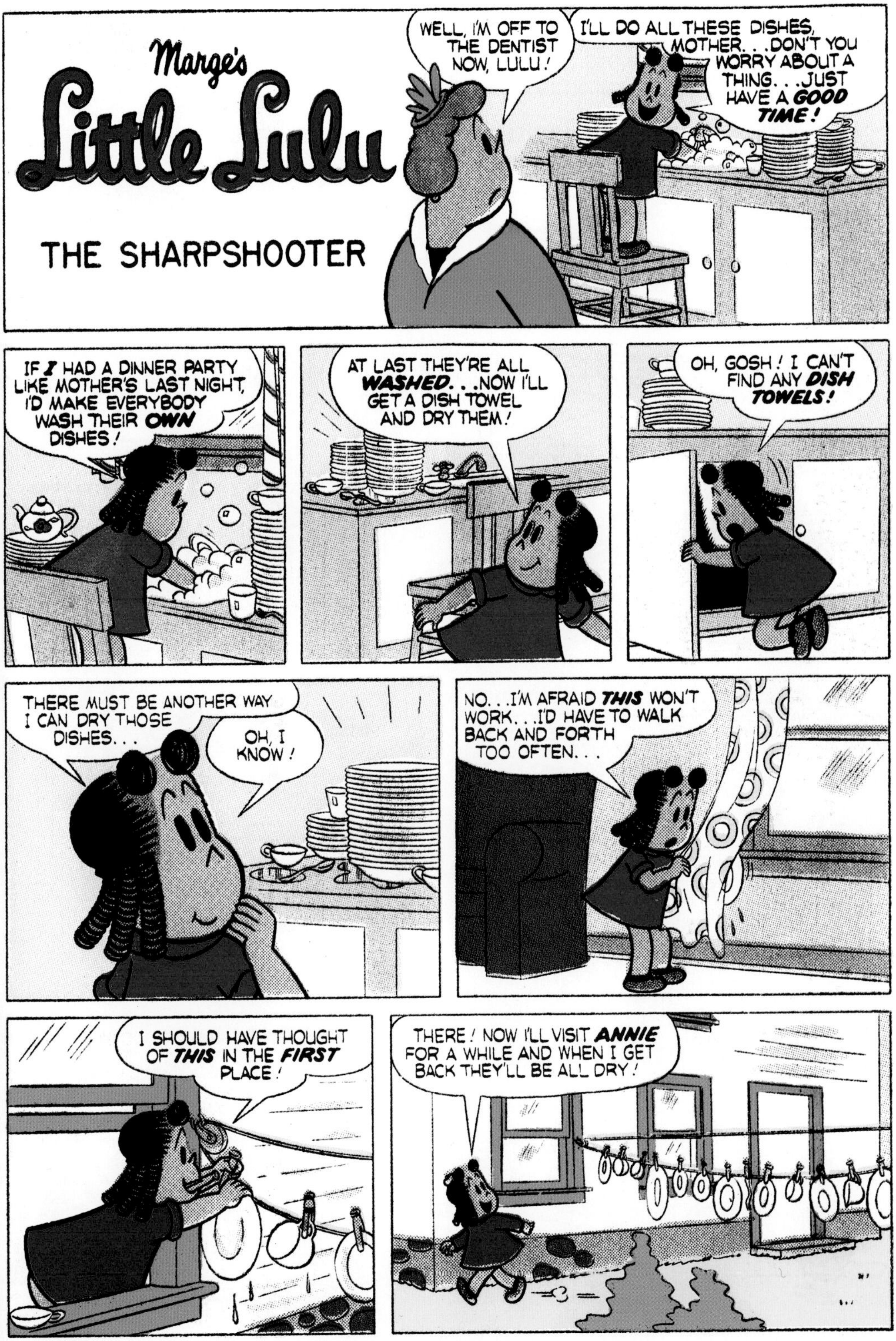
Marge's Little Lulu
THE SHARPSHOOTER
WELL, I'M OFF TO THE DENTIST NOW, LULU!
I'LL DO ALL THESE DISHES, MOTHER. . .DON'T YOU WORRY ABOUT A THING. . .JUST HAVE A GOOD TIME!
IF I HAD A DINNER PARTY LIKE MOTHER'S LAST NIGHT, I'D MAKE EVERYBODY WASH THEIR OWN DISHES!
AT LAST THEY'RE ALL WASHED. . .NOW I'LL GET A DISH TOWEL AND DRY THEM!
OH, GOSH! I CAN'T FIND ANY DISH TOWELS!
THERE MUST BE ANOTHER WAY I CAN DRY THOSE DISHES. . .
OH, I KNOW!
NO. . .I'M AFRAID THIS WON'T WORK. . .I'D HAVE TO WALK BACK AND FORTH TOO OFTEN. . .
I SHOULD HAVE THOUGHT OF THIS IN THE FIRST PLACE!
THERE! NOW I'LL VISIT ANNIE FOR A WHILE AND WHEN I GET BACK THEY'LL BE ALL DRY!

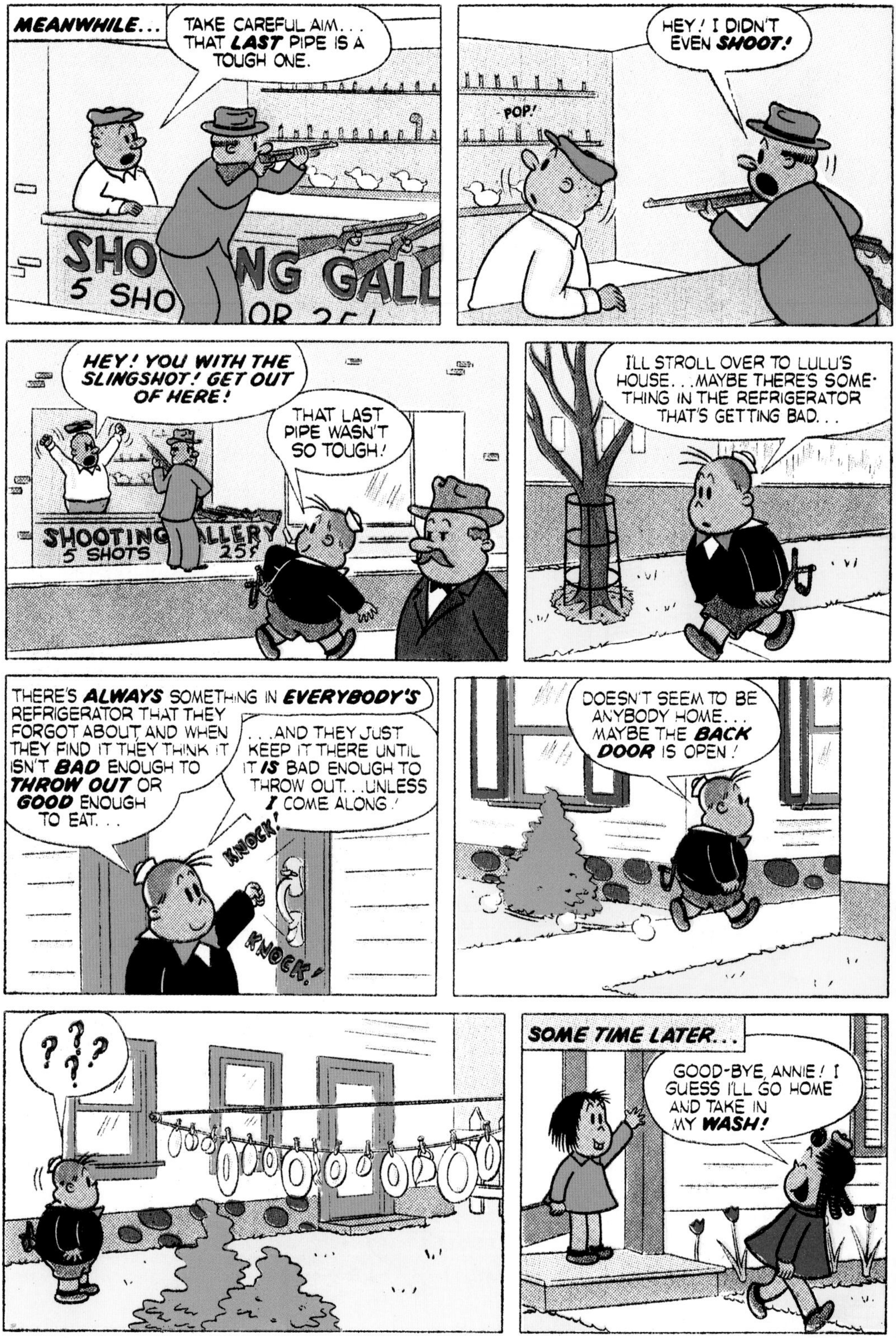
MEANWHILE...
TAKE CAREFUL AIM... THAT LAST PIPE IS A TOUGH ONE.
SHOOTING GALLERY
5 SHOTS FOR 25¢
POP!
HEY! I DIDN'T EVEN SHOOT!
HEY! YOU WITH THE SLINGSHOT! GET OUT OF HERE!
THAT LAST PIPE WASN'T SO TOUGH!
SHOOTING GALLERY 5 SHOTS 25¢
I'LL STROLL OVER TO LULU'S HOUSE...MAYBE THERE'S SOMETHING IN THE REFRIGERATOR THAT'S GETTING BAD...
THERE'S ALWAYS SOMETHING IN EVERYBODY'S REFRIGERATOR THAT THEY FORGOT ABOUT AND WHEN THEY FIND IT THEY THINK IT ISN'T BAD ENOUGH TO THROW OUT OR GOOD ENOUGH TO EAT...
...AND THEY JUST KEEP IT THERE UNTIL IT IS BAD ENOUGH TO THROW OUT...UNLESS I COME ALONG!
KNOCK!
KNOCK!
DOESN'T SEEM TO BE ANYBODY HOME... MAYBE THE BACK DOOR IS OPEN!
????
SOME TIME LATER...
GOOD-BYE, ANNIE! I GUESS I'LL GO HOME AND TAKE IN MY WASH!

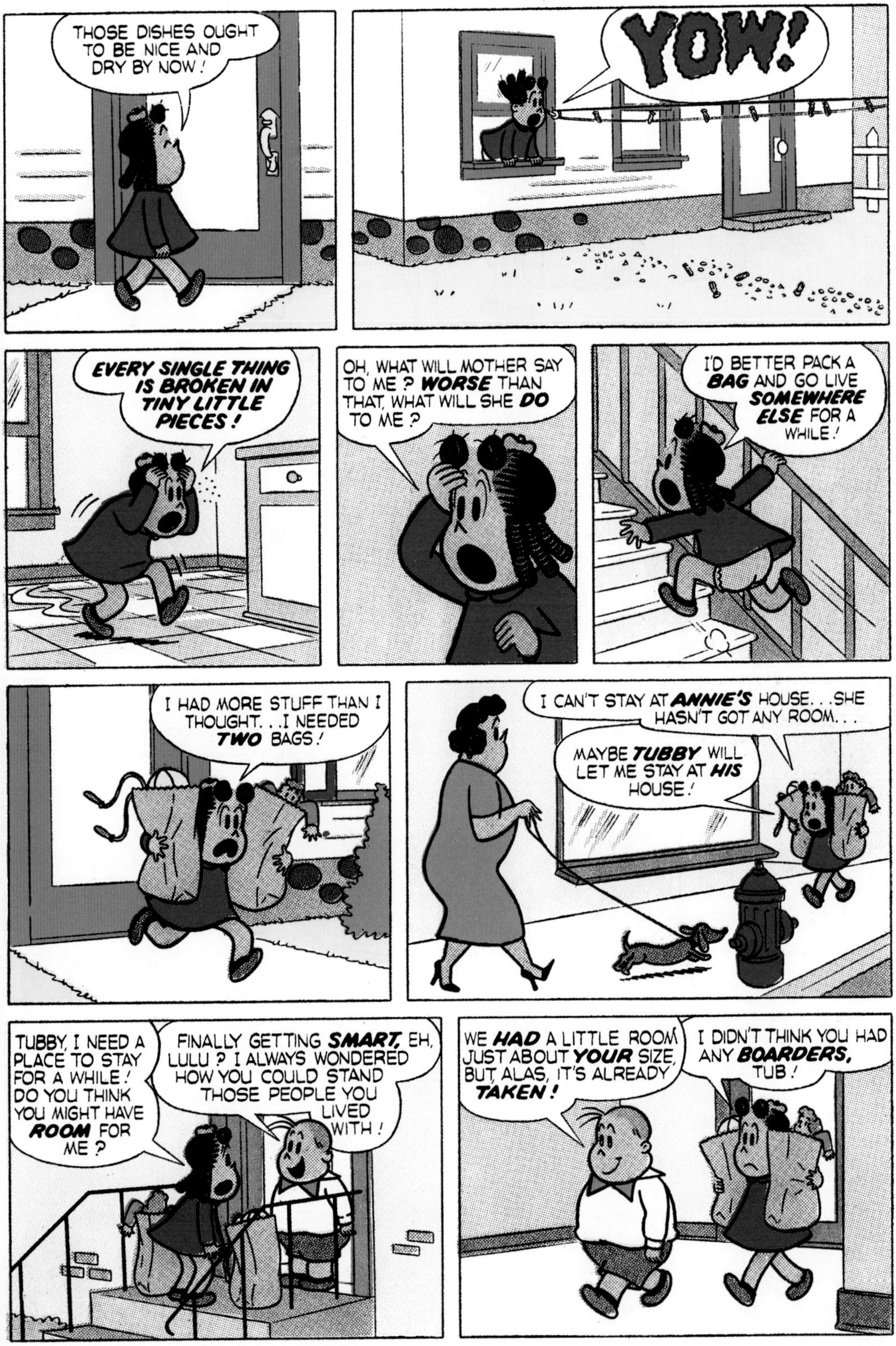

THOSE DISHES OUGHT TO BE NICE AND DRY BY NOW!
YOW!
EVERY SINGLE THING IS BROKEN IN TINY LITTLE PIECES!
OH, WHAT WILL MOTHER SAY TO ME? WORSE THAN THAT, WHAT WILL SHE DO TO ME?
I'D BETTER PACK A BAG AND GO LIVE SOMEWHERE ELSE FOR A WHILE!
I HAD MORE STUFF THAN I THOUGHT...I NEEDED TWO BAGS!
I CAN'T STAY AT ANNIE'S HOUSE...SHE HASN'T GOT ANY ROOM...
MAYBE TUBBY WILL LET ME STAY AT HIS HOUSE!
TUBBY, I NEED A PLACE TO STAY FOR A WHILE! DO YOU THINK YOU MIGHT HAVE ROOM FOR ME?
FINALLY GETTING SMART, EH, LULU? I ALWAYS WONDERED HOW YOU COULD STAND THOSE PEOPLE YOU LIVED WITH!
I DIDN'T THINK YOU HAD ANY BOARDERS, TUB!
WE HAD A LITTLE ROOM JUST ABOUT YOUR SIZE, BUT, ALAS, IT'S ALREADY TAKEN!

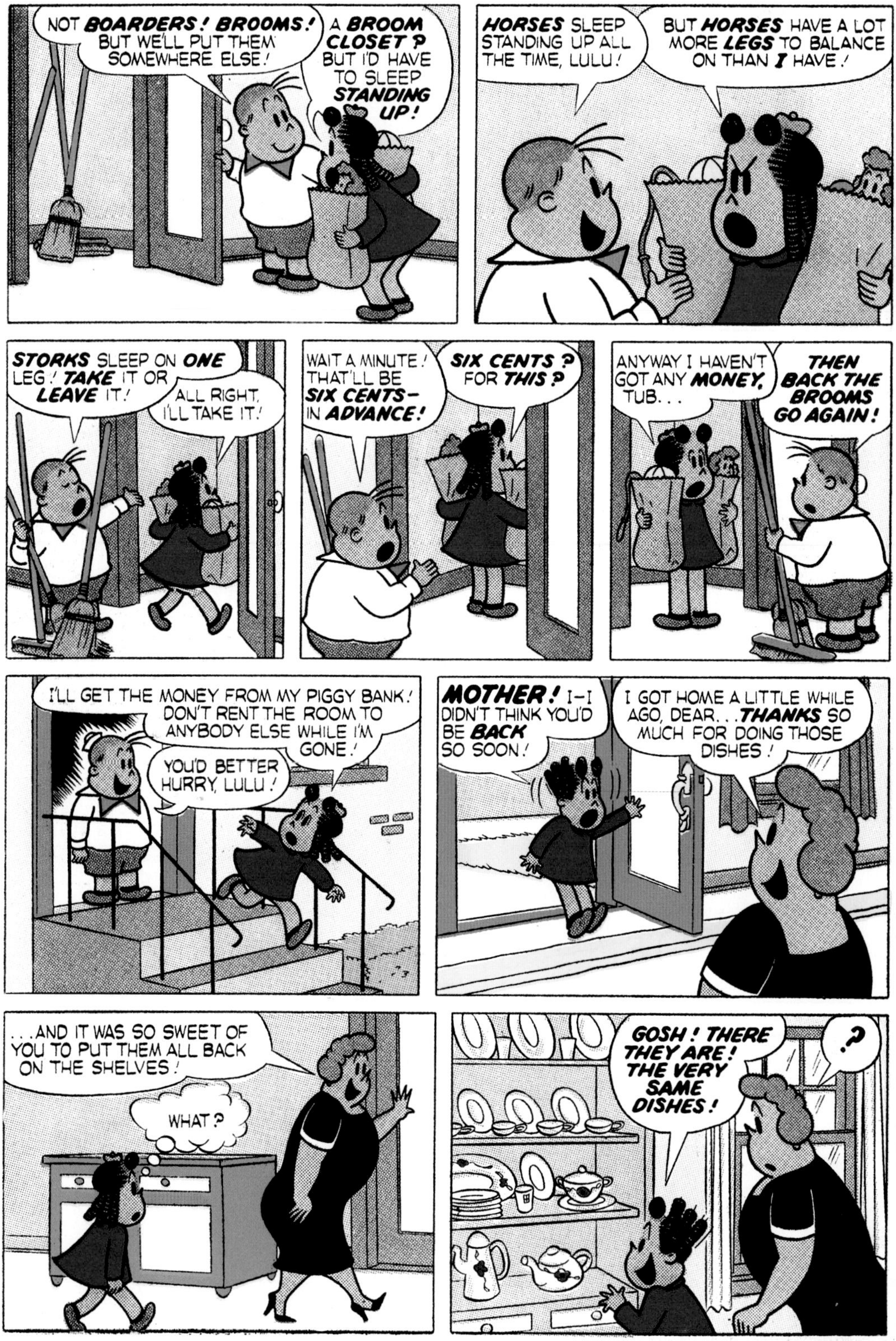
NOT BOARDERS! BROOMS! BUT WE'LL PUT THEM SOMEWHERE ELSE!
A BROOM CLOSET? BUT I'D HAVE TO SLEEP STANDING UP!
HORSES SLEEP STANDING UP ALL THE TIME, LULU!
BUT HORSES HAVE A LOT MORE LEGS TO BALANCE ON THAN I HAVE!
STORKS SLEEP ON ONE LEG! TAKE IT OR LEAVE IT!
ALL RIGHT, I'LL TAKE IT!
WAIT A MINUTE! THAT'LL BE SIX CENTS— IN ADVANCE!
SIX CENTS? FOR THIS?
ANYWAY I HAVEN'T GOT ANY MONEY, TUB...
THEN BACK THE BROOMS GO AGAIN!
I'LL GET THE MONEY FROM MY PIGGY BANK! DON'T RENT THE ROOM TO ANYBODY ELSE WHILE I'M GONE!
YOU'D BETTER HURRY, LULU!
MOTHER! I—I DIDN'T THINK YOU'D BE BACK SO SOON!
I GOT HOME A LITTLE WHILE AGO, DEAR...THANKS SO MUCH FOR DOING THOSE DISHES!
...AND IT WAS SO SWEET OF YOU TO PUT THEM ALL BACK ON THE SHELVES!
WHAT?
GOSH! THERE THEY ARE! THE VERY SAME DISHES!
?

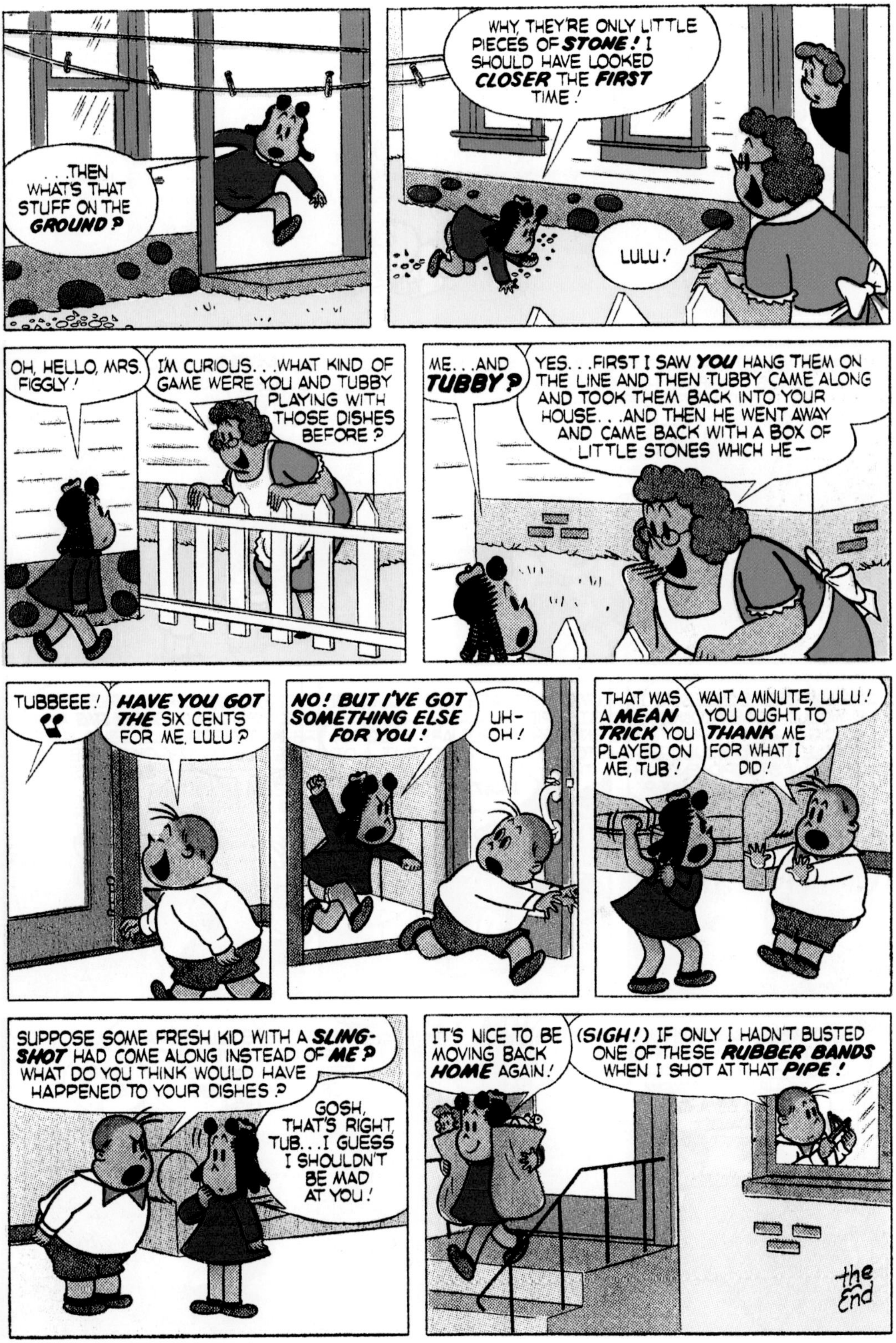

. . .THEN WHAT'S THAT STUFF ON THE GROUND?
WHY, THEY'RE ONLY LITTLE PIECES OF STONE! I SHOULD HAVE LOOKED CLOSER THE FIRST TIME!
LULU!
OH, HELLO, MRS. FIGGLY!
I'M CURIOUS. . .WHAT KIND OF GAME WERE YOU AND TUBBY PLAYING WITH THOSE DISHES BEFORE?
ME. . .AND TUBBY?
YES. . .FIRST I SAW YOU HANG THEM ON THE LINE AND THEN TUBBY CAME ALONG AND TOOK THEM BACK INTO YOUR HOUSE. . .AND THEN HE WENT AWAY AND CAME BACK WITH A BOX OF LITTLE STONES WHICH HE—
TUBBEEE!
HAVE YOU GOT THE SIX CENTS FOR ME, LULU?
NO! BUT I'VE GOT SOMETHING ELSE FOR YOU!
UH-OH!
THAT WAS A MEAN TRICK YOU PLAYED ON ME, TUB!
WAIT A MINUTE, LULU! YOU OUGHT TO THANK ME FOR WHAT I DID!
SUPPOSE SOME FRESH KID WITH A SLING-SHOT HAD COME ALONG INSTEAD OF ME? WHAT DO YOU THINK WOULD HAVE HAPPENED TO YOUR DISHES?
GOSH, THAT'S RIGHT, TUB. . .I GUESS I SHOULDN'T BE MAD AT YOU!
IT'S NICE TO BE MOVING BACK HOME AGAIN!
(SIGH!) IF ONLY I HADN'T BUSTED ONE OF THESE RUBBER BANDS WHEN I SHOT AT THAT PIPE!
the End

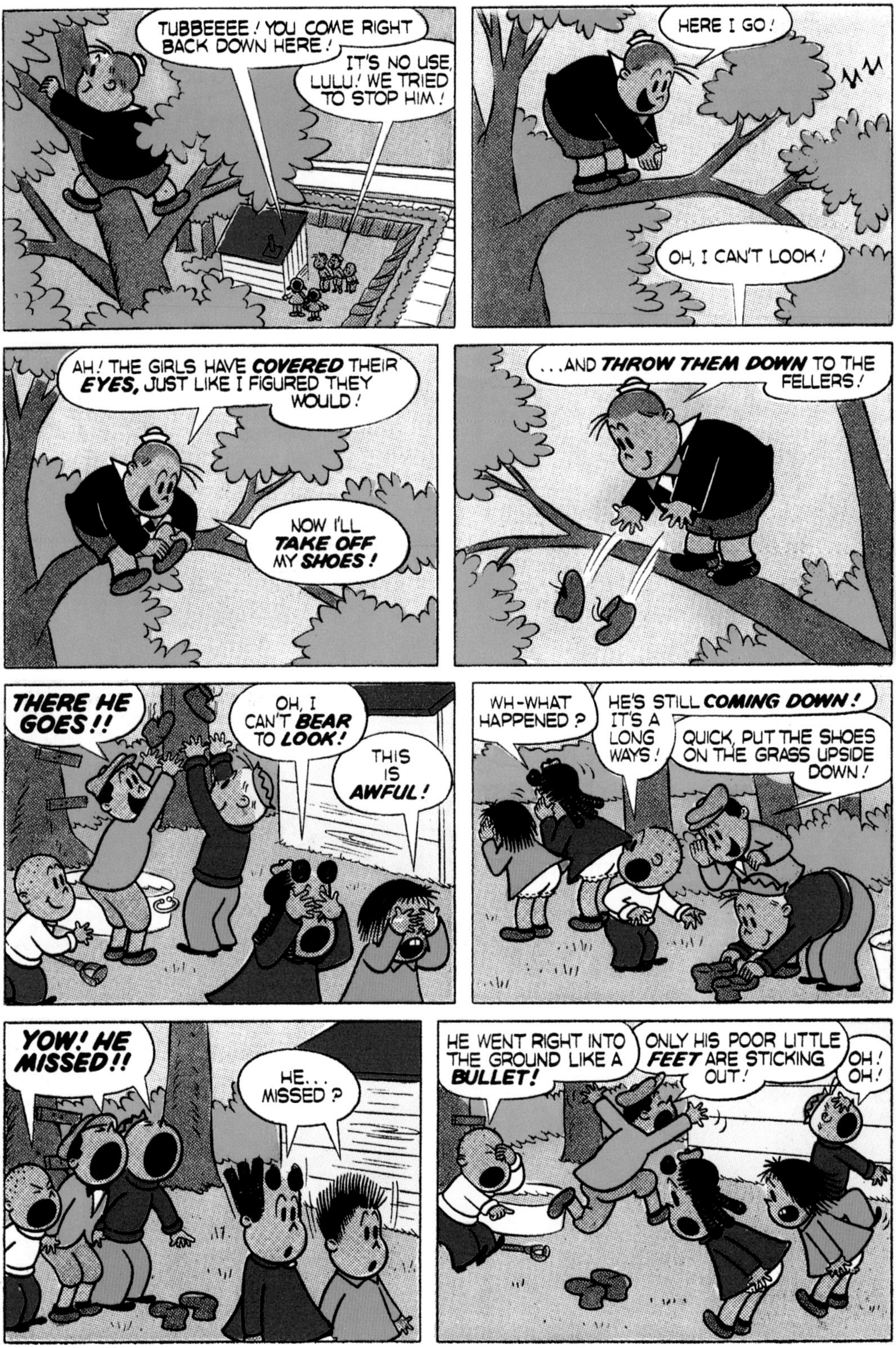
TUBBEEEE! YOU COME RIGHT BACK DOWN HERE!
IT'S NO USE, LULU! WE TRIED TO STOP HIM!
HERE I GO!
OH, I CAN'T LOOK!
AH! THE GIRLS HAVE COVERED THEIR EYES, JUST LIKE I FIGURED THEY WOULD!
NOW I'LL TAKE OFF MY SHOES!
...AND THROW THEM DOWN TO THE FELLERS!
THERE HE GOES!!
OH, I CAN'T BEAR TO LOOK!
THIS IS AWFUL!
WH-WHAT HAPPENED?
HE'S STILL COMING DOWN! IT'S A LONG WAYS!
QUICK, PUT THE SHOES ON THE GRASS UPSIDE DOWN!
YOW! HE MISSED!!
HE... MISSED?
HE WENT RIGHT INTO THE GROUND LIKE A BULLET!
ONLY HIS POOR LITTLE FEET ARE STICKING OUT!
OH! OH!

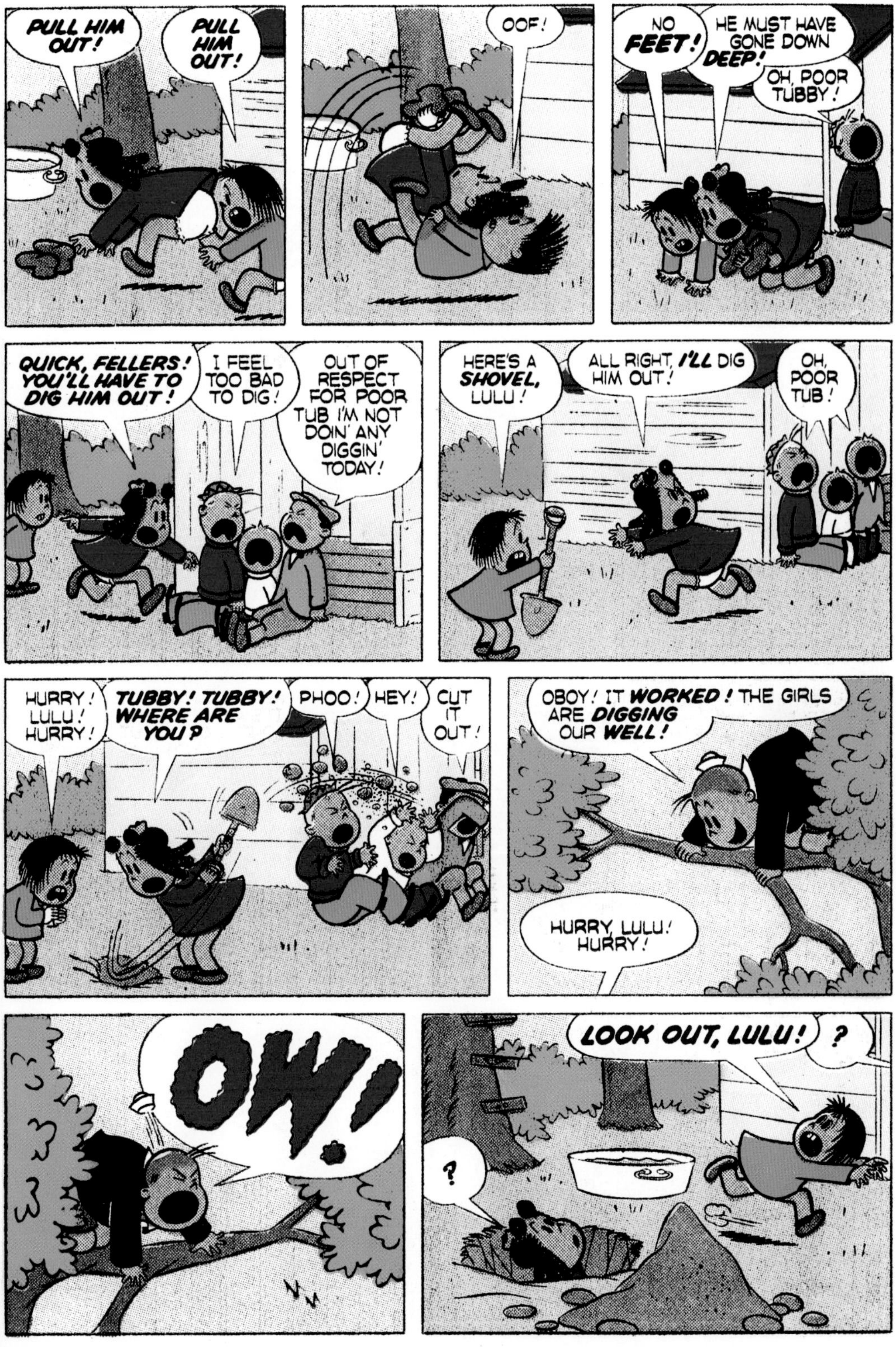
PULL HIM OUT!
PULL HIM OUT!
OOF!
NO FEET!
HE MUST HAVE GONE DOWN DEEP!
OH, POOR TUBBY!
QUICK, FELLERS! YOU'LL HAVE TO DIG HIM OUT!
I FEEL TOO BAD TO DIG!
OUT OF RESPECT FOR POOR TUB I'M NOT DOIN' ANY DIGGIN' TODAY!
HERE'S A SHOVEL, LULU!
ALL RIGHT, I'LL DIG HIM OUT!
OH, POOR TUB!
HURRY! LULU! HURRY!
TUBBY! TUBBY! WHERE ARE YOU?
PHOO!
HEY!
CUT IT OUT!
OBOY! IT WORKED! THE GIRLS ARE DIGGING OUR WELL!
HURRY, LULU! HURRY!
OW!
LOOK OUT, LULU!
?
?

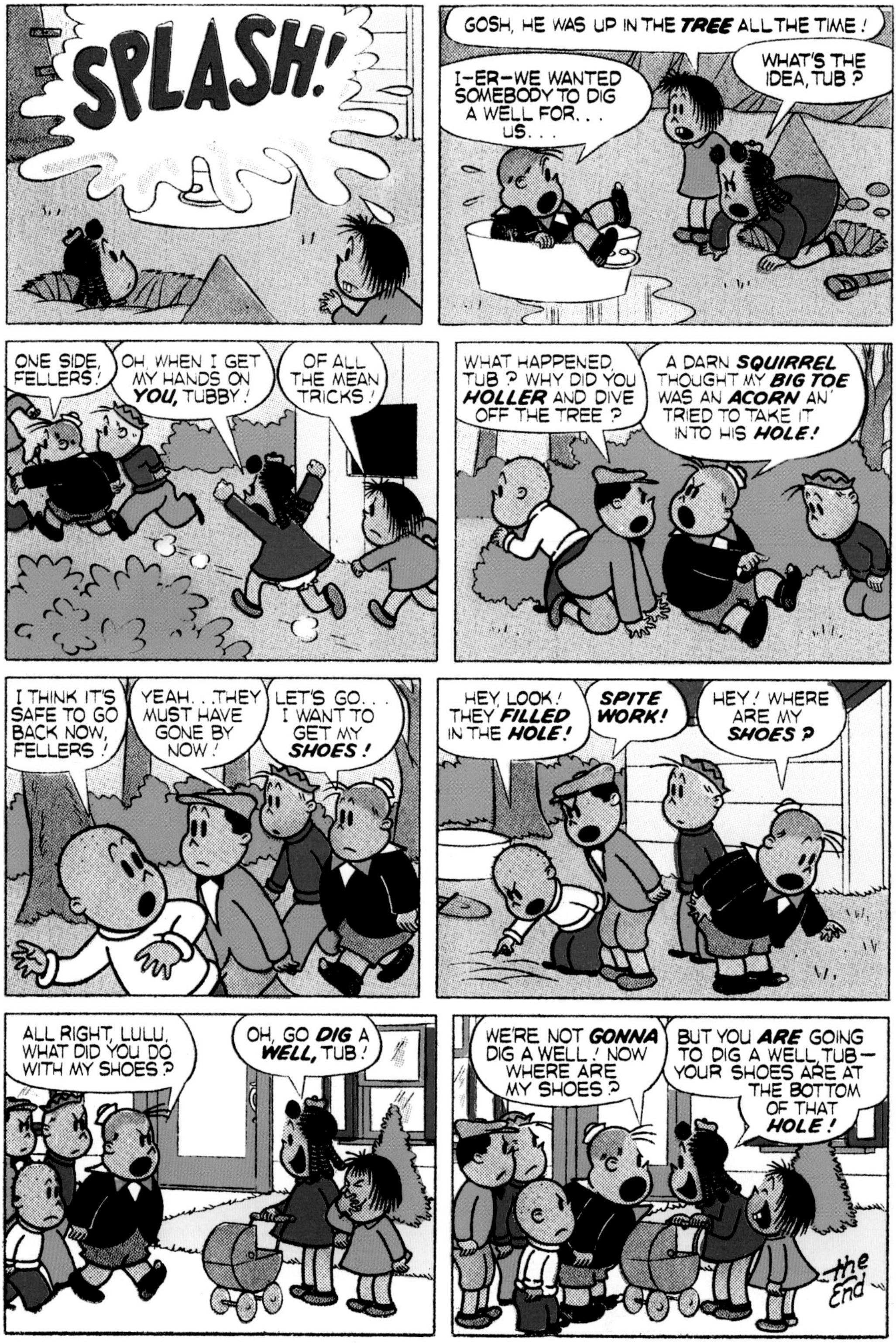
SPLASH!
GOSH, HE WAS UP IN THE TREE ALL THE TIME!
I-ER-WE WANTED SOMEBODY TO DIG A WELL FOR... US...
WHAT'S THE IDEA, TUB?
ONE SIDE, FELLERS!
OH, WHEN I GET MY HANDS ON YOU, TUBBY!
OF ALL THE MEAN TRICKS!
WHAT HAPPENED, TUB? WHY DID YOU HOLLER AND DIVE OFF THE TREE?
A DARN SQUIRREL THOUGHT MY BIG TOE WAS AN ACORN AN' TRIED TO TAKE IT INTO HIS HOLE!
I THINK IT'S SAFE TO GO BACK NOW, FELLERS!
YEAH...THEY MUST HAVE GONE BY NOW!
LET'S GO... I WANT TO GET MY SHOES!
HEY, LOOK! THEY FILLED IN THE HOLE!
SPITE WORK!
HEY! WHERE ARE MY SHOES?
ALL RIGHT, LULU, WHAT DID YOU DO WITH MY SHOES?
OH, GO DIG A WELL, TUB!
WE'RE NOT GONNA DIG A WELL! NOW WHERE ARE MY SHOES?
BUT YOU ARE GOING TO DIG A WELL, TUB— YOUR SHOES ARE AT THE BOTTOM OF THAT HOLE!
the End

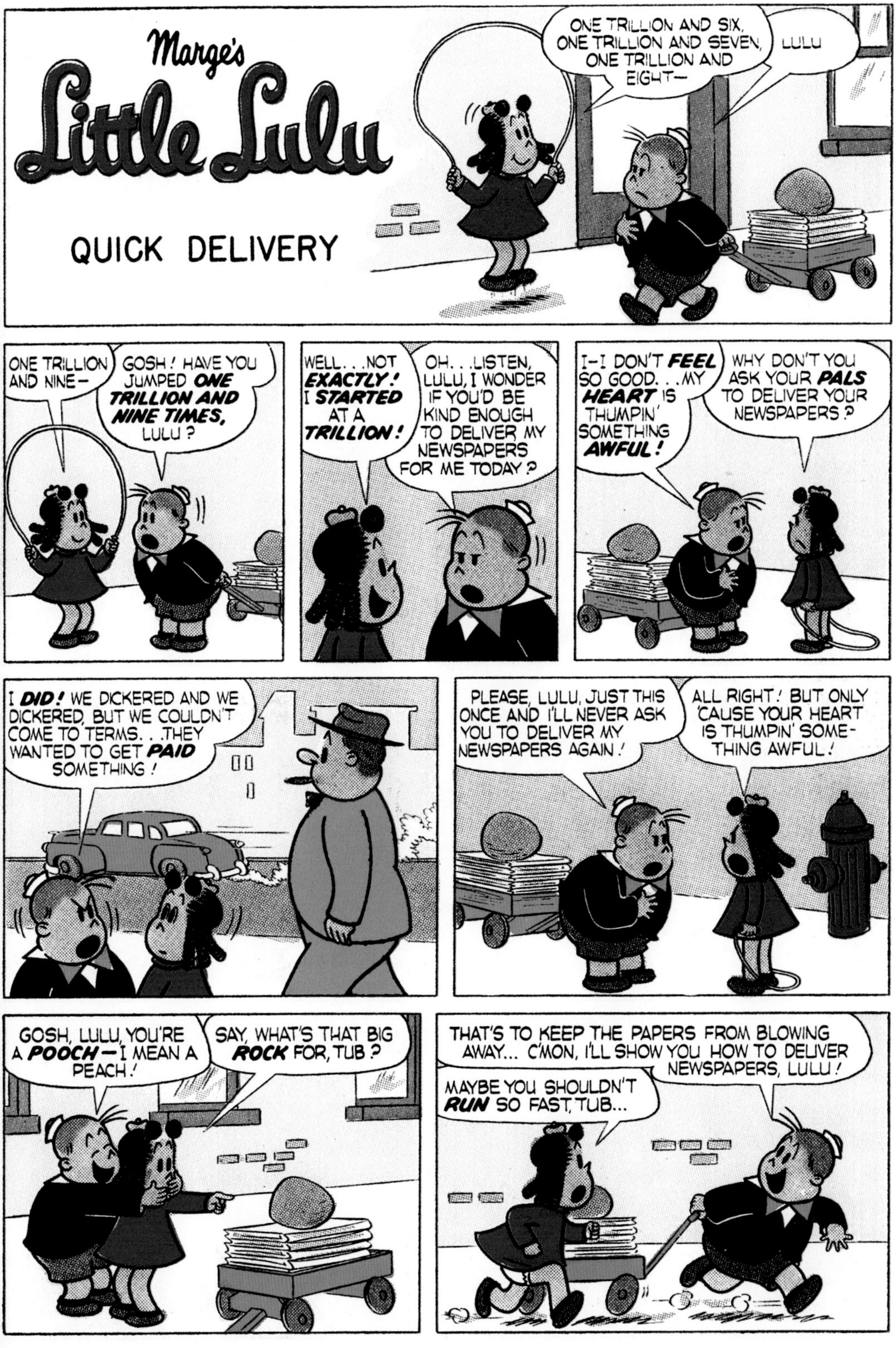
Marge's Little Lulu
QUICK DELIVERY
ONE TRILLION AND SIX, ONE TRILLION AND SEVEN, ONE TRILLION AND EIGHT—
LULU
ONE TRILLION AND NINE—
GOSH! HAVE YOU JUMPED ONE TRILLION AND NINE TIMES, LULU?
WELL...NOT EXACTLY! I STARTED AT A TRILLION!
OH...LISTEN, LULU, I WONDER IF YOU'D BE KIND ENOUGH TO DELIVER MY NEWSPAPERS FOR ME TODAY?
I-I DON'T FEEL SO GOOD...MY HEART IS THUMPIN' SOMETHING AWFUL!
WHY DON'T YOU ASK YOUR PALS TO DELIVER YOUR NEWSPAPERS?
I DID! WE DICKERED AND WE DICKERED, BUT WE COULDN'T COME TO TERMS...THEY WANTED TO GET PAID SOMETHING!
PLEASE, LULU, JUST THIS ONCE AND I'LL NEVER ASK YOU TO DELIVER MY NEWSPAPERS AGAIN!
ALL RIGHT! BUT ONLY 'CAUSE YOUR HEART IS THUMPIN' SOMETHING AWFUL!
GOSH, LULU, YOU'RE A POOCH—I MEAN A PEACH!
SAY, WHAT'S THAT BIG ROCK FOR, TUB?
THAT'S TO KEEP THE PAPERS FROM BLOWING AWAY... C'MON, I'LL SHOW YOU HOW TO DELIVER NEWSPAPERS, LULU!
MAYBE YOU SHOULDN'T RUN SO FAST, TUB...

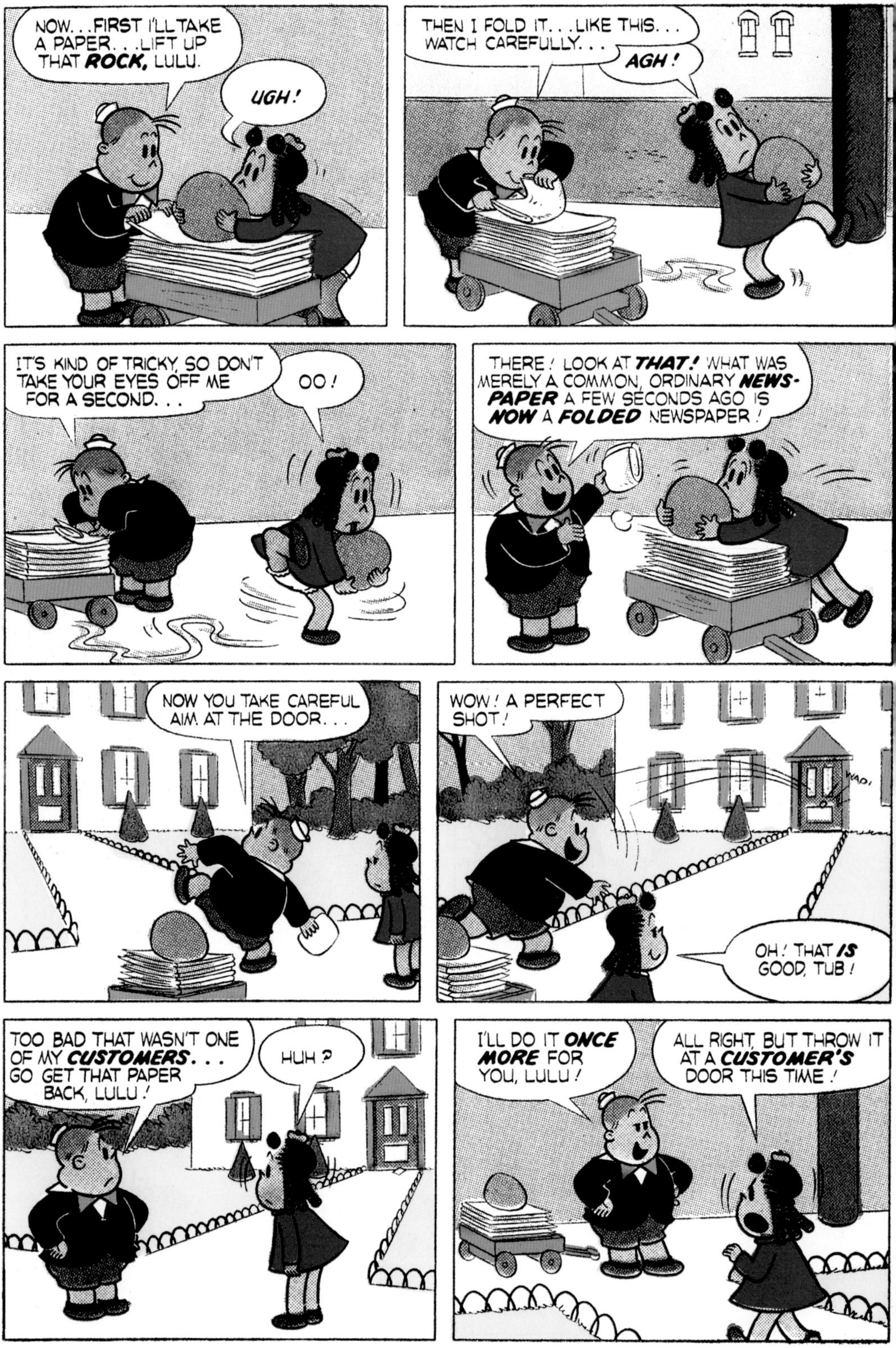
NOW. . .FIRST I'LL TAKE A PAPER. . .LIFT UP THAT **ROCK,** LULU.
**UGH!**
THEN I FOLD IT. . .LIKE THIS. . . WATCH CAREFULLY. . .
**AGH!**
IT'S KIND OF TRICKY, SO DON'T TAKE YOUR EYES OFF ME FOR A SECOND. . .
OO!
THERE! LOOK AT **THAT!** WHAT WAS MERELY A COMMON, ORDINARY **NEWS-PAPER** A FEW SECONDS AGO IS **NOW** A **FOLDED** NEWSPAPER!
NOW YOU TAKE CAREFUL AIM AT THE DOOR. . .
WOW! A PERFECT SHOT!
OH! THAT **IS** GOOD, TUB!
TOO BAD THAT WASN'T ONE OF MY **CUSTOMERS**. . . GO GET THAT PAPER BACK, LULU!
HUH?
I'LL DO IT **ONCE MORE** FOR YOU, LULU!
ALL RIGHT, BUT THROW IT AT A **CUSTOMER'S** DOOR THIS TIME!

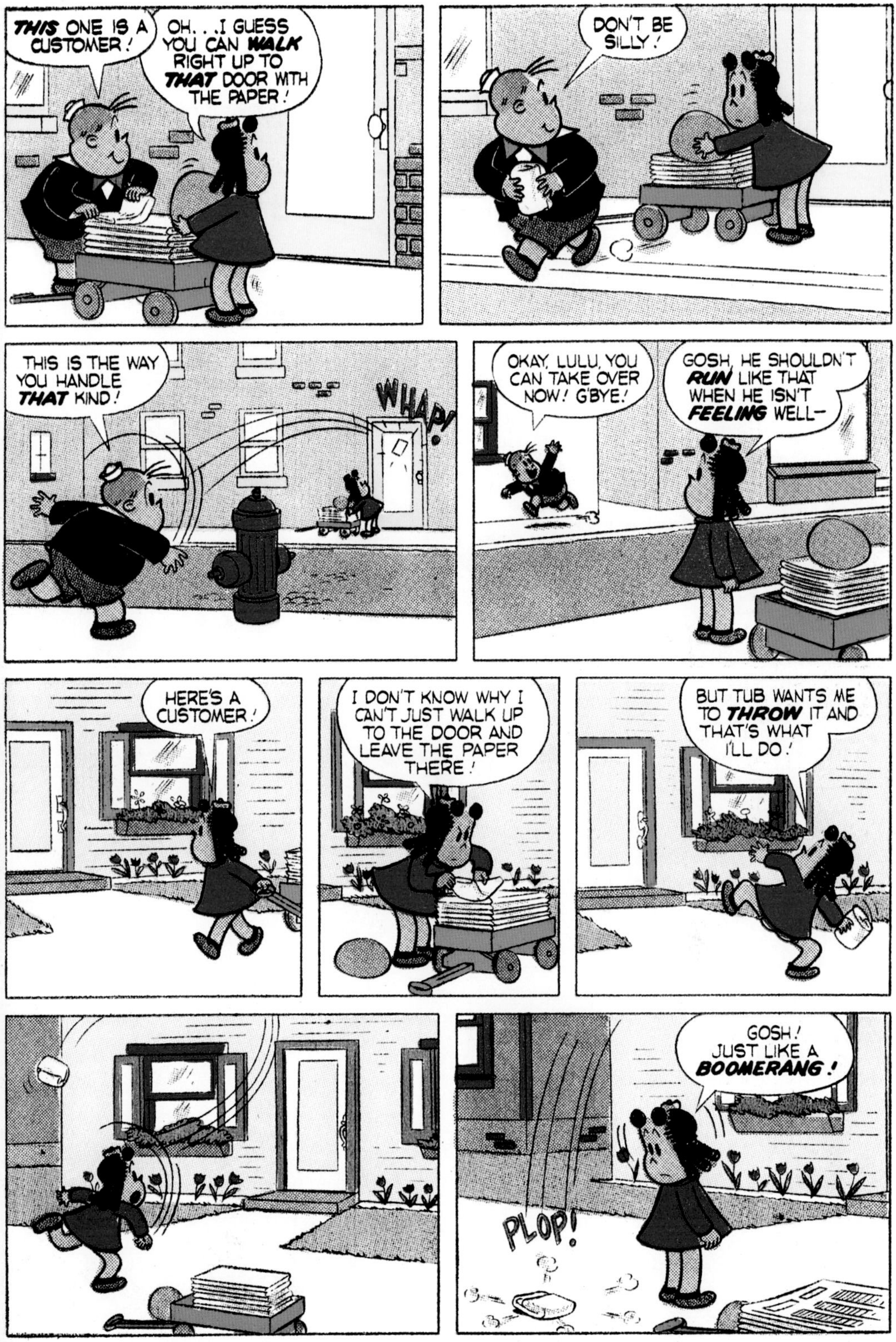
THIS ONE IS A CUSTOMER!
OH. . .I GUESS YOU CAN WALK RIGHT UP TO THAT DOOR WITH THE PAPER!
DON'T BE SILLY!
THIS IS THE WAY YOU HANDLE THAT KIND!
WHAP!
OKAY, LULU, YOU CAN TAKE OVER NOW! G'BYE!
GOSH, HE SHOULDN'T RUN LIKE THAT WHEN HE ISN'T FEELING WELL—
HERE'S A CUSTOMER!
I DON'T KNOW WHY I CAN'T JUST WALK UP TO THE DOOR AND LEAVE THE PAPER THERE!
BUT TUB WANTS ME TO THROW IT AND THAT'S WHAT I'LL DO!
GOSH! JUST LIKE A BOOMERANG!
PLOP!

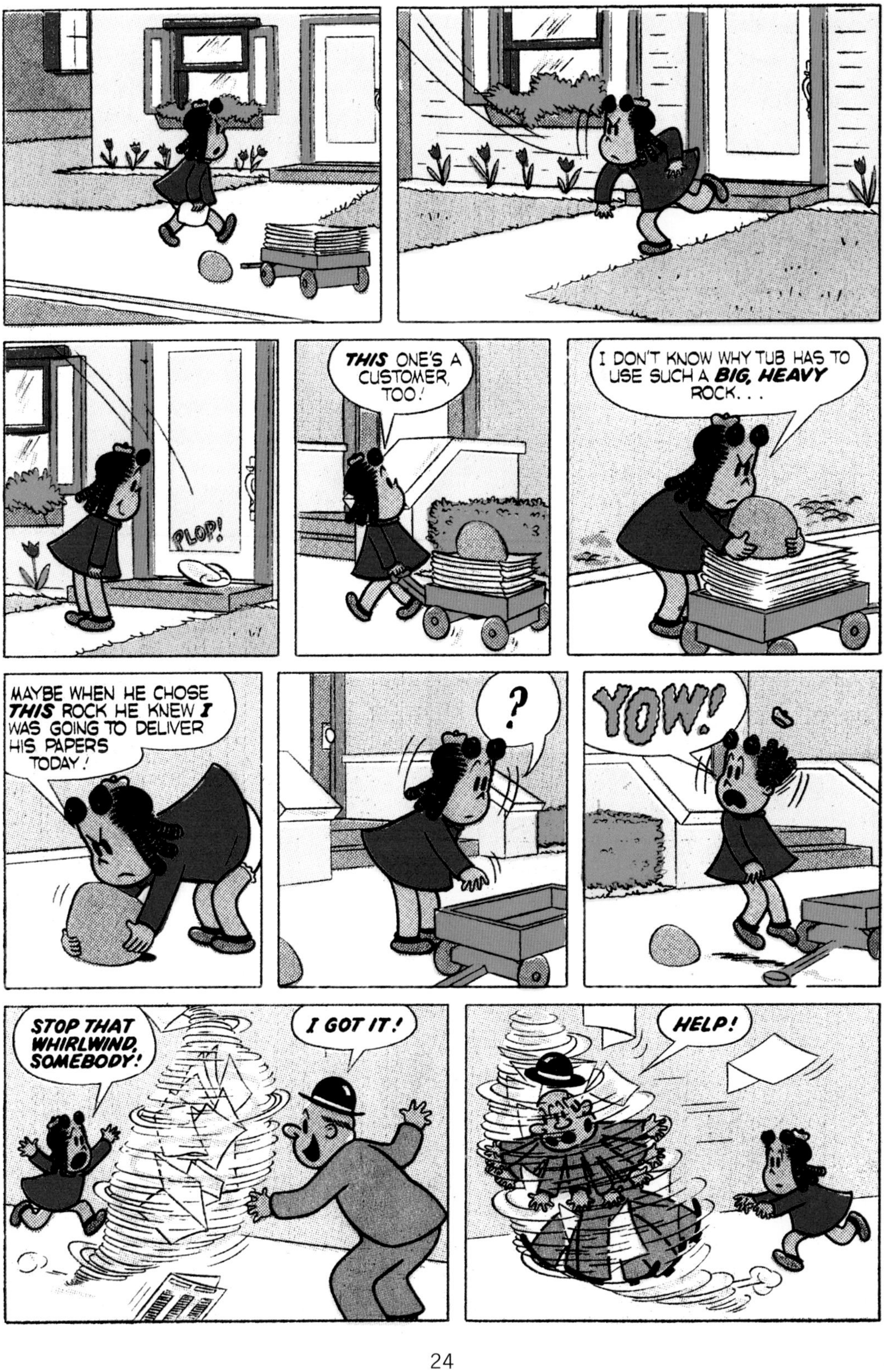
PLOP!
THIS ONE'S A CUSTOMER, TOO!
I DON'T KNOW WHY TUB HAS TO USE SUCH A BIG, HEAVY ROCK. . .
MAYBE WHEN HE CHOSE THIS ROCK HE KNEW I WAS GOING TO DELIVER HIS PAPERS TODAY!
?
YOW!
STOP THAT WHIRLWIND, SOMEBODY!
I GOT IT!
HELP!

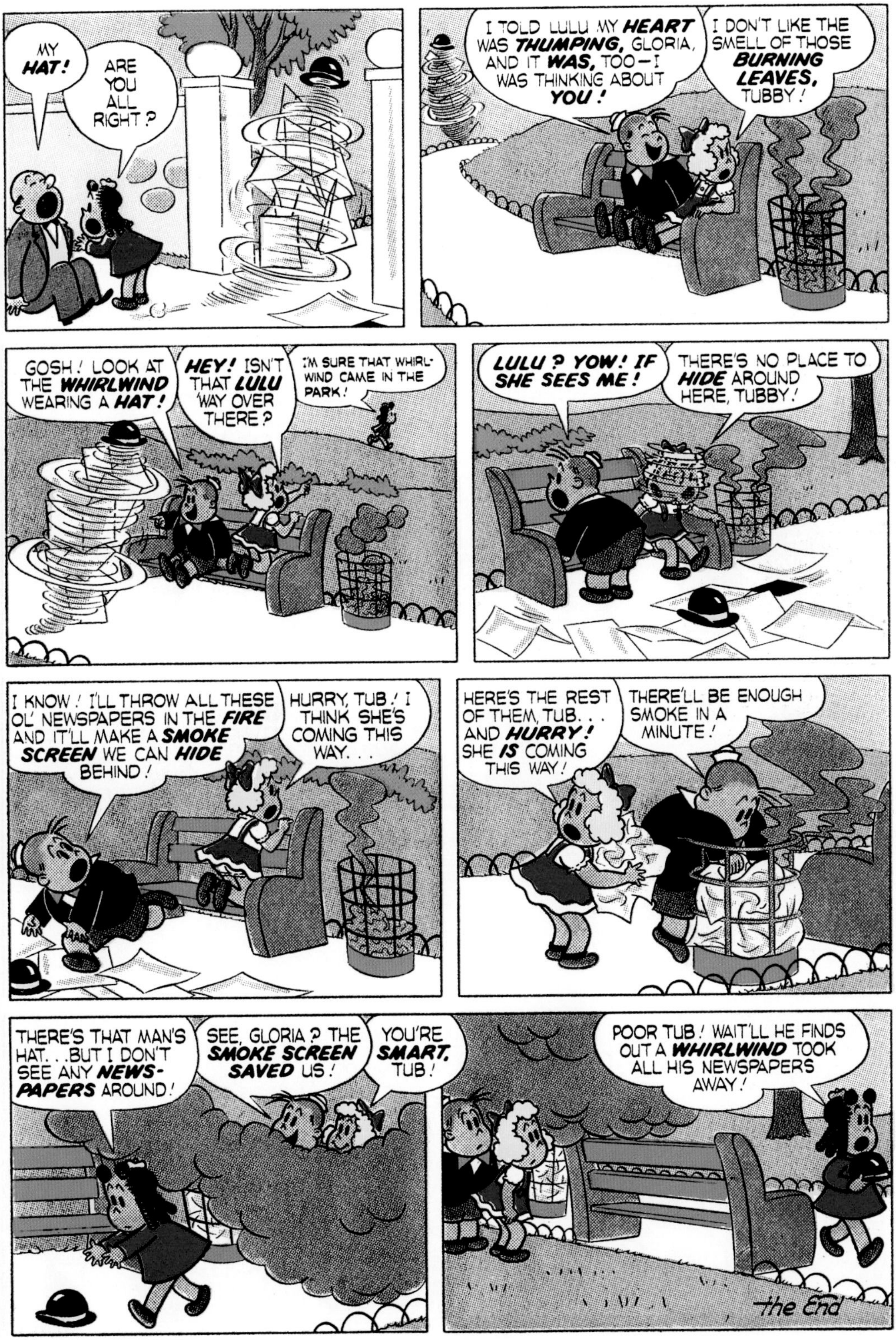
MY HAT!
ARE YOU ALL RIGHT?
I TOLD LULU MY HEART WAS THUMPING, GLORIA, AND IT WAS, TOO—I WAS THINKING ABOUT YOU!
I DON'T LIKE THE SMELL OF THOSE BURNING LEAVES, TUBBY!
GOSH! LOOK AT THE WHIRLWIND WEARING A HAT!
HEY! ISN'T THAT LULU 'WAY OVER THERE?
I'M SURE THAT WHIRLWIND CAME IN THE PARK!
LULU? YOW! IF SHE SEES ME!
THERE'S NO PLACE TO HIDE AROUND HERE, TUBBY!
I KNOW! I'LL THROW ALL THESE OL' NEWSPAPERS IN THE FIRE AND IT'LL MAKE A SMOKE SCREEN WE CAN HIDE BEHIND!
HURRY, TUB! I THINK SHE'S COMING THIS WAY...
HERE'S THE REST OF THEM, TUB... AND HURRY! SHE IS COMING THIS WAY!
THERE'LL BE ENOUGH SMOKE IN A MINUTE!
THERE'S THAT MAN'S HAT...BUT I DON'T SEE ANY NEWSPAPERS AROUND!
SEE, GLORIA? THE SMOKE SCREEN SAVED US!
YOU'RE SMART, TUB!
POOR TUB! WAIT'LL HE FINDS OUT A WHIRLWIND TOOK ALL HIS NEWSPAPERS AWAY!
the End

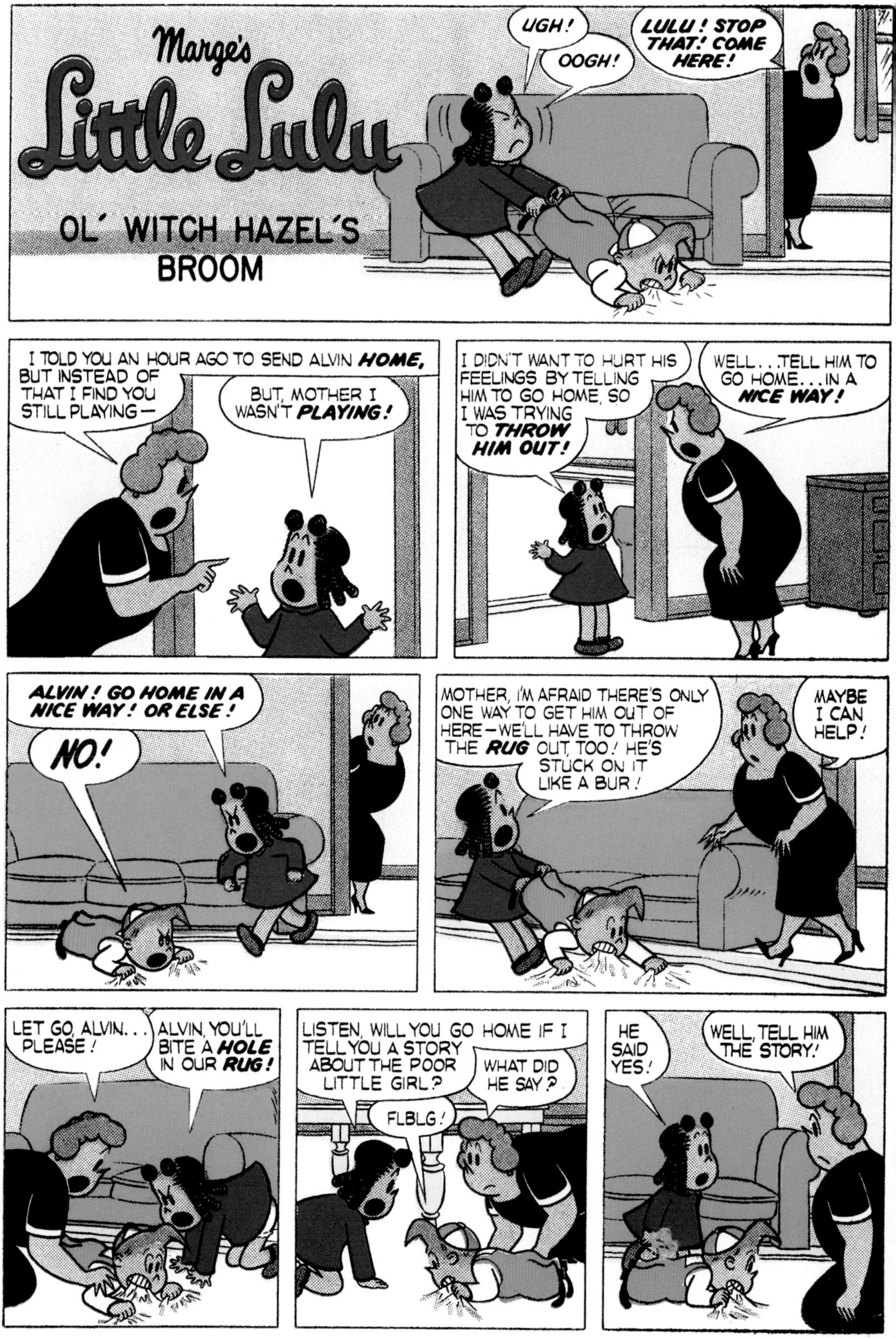
Marge's Little Lulu
OL' WITCH HAZEL'S BROOM
UGH!
OOGH!
LULU! STOP THAT! COME HERE!
I TOLD YOU AN HOUR AGO TO SEND ALVIN HOME, BUT INSTEAD OF THAT I FIND YOU STILL PLAYING—
BUT, MOTHER I WASN'T PLAYING!
I DIDN'T WANT TO HURT HIS FEELINGS BY TELLING HIM TO GO HOME, SO I WAS TRYING TO THROW HIM OUT!
WELL...TELL HIM TO GO HOME...IN A NICE WAY!
ALVIN! GO HOME IN A NICE WAY! OR ELSE!
NO!
MOTHER, I'M AFRAID THERE'S ONLY ONE WAY TO GET HIM OUT OF HERE—WE'LL HAVE TO THROW THE RUG OUT, TOO! HE'S STUCK ON IT LIKE A BUR!
MAYBE I CAN HELP!
LET GO, ALVIN... PLEASE!
ALVIN, YOU'LL BITE A HOLE IN OUR RUG!
LISTEN, WILL YOU GO HOME IF I TELL YOU A STORY ABOUT THE POOR LITTLE GIRL?
FLBLG!
WHAT DID HE SAY?
HE SAID YES!
WELL, TELL HIM THE STORY!

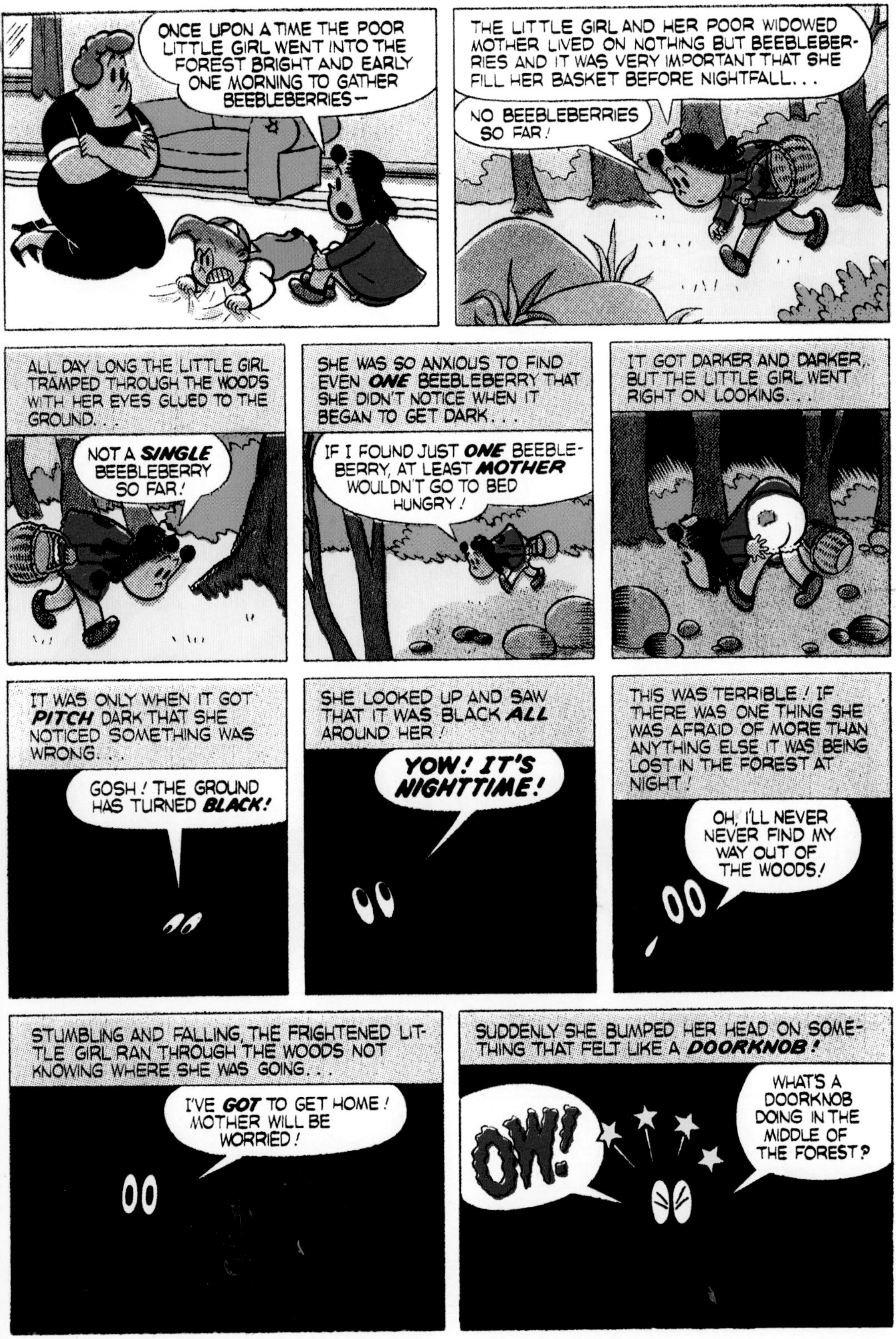
ONCE UPON A TIME THE POOR LITTLE GIRL WENT INTO THE FOREST BRIGHT AND EARLY ONE MORNING TO GATHER BEEBLEBERRIES—
THE LITTLE GIRL AND HER POOR WIDOWED MOTHER LIVED ON NOTHING BUT BEEBLEBERRIES AND IT WAS VERY IMPORTANT THAT SHE FILL HER BASKET BEFORE NIGHTFALL...
NO BEEBLEBERRIES SO FAR!
ALL DAY LONG THE LITTLE GIRL TRAMPED THROUGH THE WOODS WITH HER EYES GLUED TO THE GROUND...
NOT A SINGLE BEEBLEBERRY SO FAR!
SHE WAS SO ANXIOUS TO FIND EVEN ONE BEEBLEBERRY THAT SHE DIDN'T NOTICE WHEN IT BEGAN TO GET DARK...
IF I FOUND JUST ONE BEEBLEBERRY, AT LEAST MOTHER WOULDN'T GO TO BED HUNGRY!
IT GOT DARKER AND DARKER, BUT THE LITTLE GIRL WENT RIGHT ON LOOKING...
IT WAS ONLY WHEN IT GOT PITCH DARK THAT SHE NOTICED SOMETHING WAS WRONG...
GOSH! THE GROUND HAS TURNED BLACK!
SHE LOOKED UP AND SAW THAT IT WAS BLACK ALL AROUND HER!
YOW! IT'S NIGHTTIME!
THIS WAS TERRIBLE! IF THERE WAS ONE THING SHE WAS AFRAID OF MORE THAN ANYTHING ELSE IT WAS BEING LOST IN THE FOREST AT NIGHT!
OH, I'LL NEVER NEVER FIND MY WAY OUT OF THE WOODS!
STUMBLING AND FALLING, THE FRIGHTENED LITTLE GIRL RAN THROUGH THE WOODS NOT KNOWING WHERE SHE WAS GOING...
I'VE GOT TO GET HOME! MOTHER WILL BE WORRIED!
SUDDENLY SHE BUMPED HER HEAD ON SOMETHING THAT FELT LIKE A DOORKNOB!
OW!
WHAT'S A DOORKNOB DOING IN THE MIDDLE OF THE FOREST?

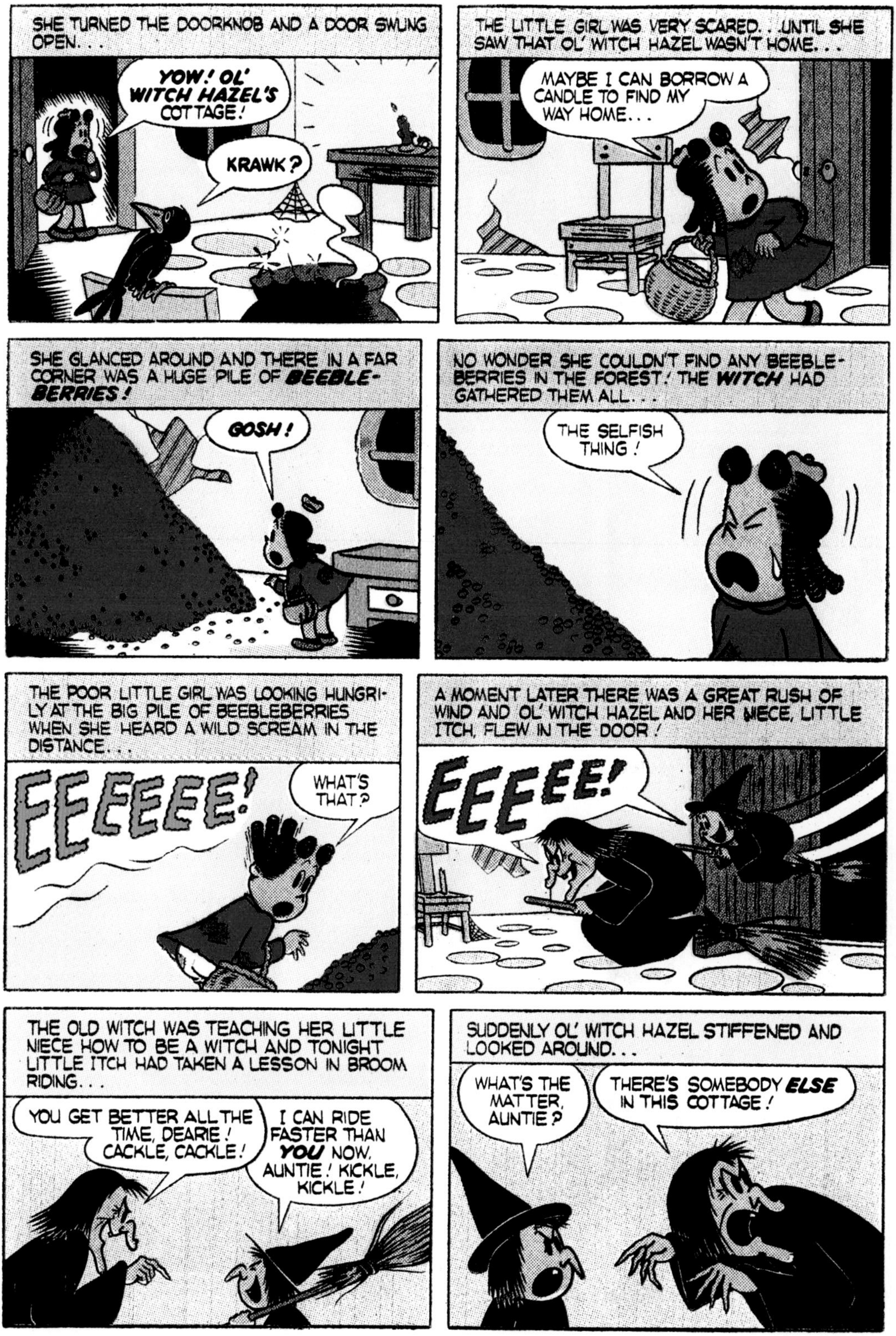
SHE TURNED THE DOORKNOB AND A DOOR SWUNG OPEN. . .
YOW! OL' WITCH HAZEL'S COTTAGE!
KRAWK?
THE LITTLE GIRL WAS VERY SCARED. . . UNTIL SHE SAW THAT OL' WITCH HAZEL WASN'T HOME. . .
MAYBE I CAN BORROW A CANDLE TO FIND MY WAY HOME. . .
SHE GLANCED AROUND AND THERE IN A FAR CORNER WAS A HUGE PILE OF BEEBLE-BERRIES!
GOSH!
NO WONDER SHE COULDN'T FIND ANY BEEBLE-BERRIES IN THE FOREST! THE WITCH HAD GATHERED THEM ALL. . .
THE SELFISH THING!
THE POOR LITTLE GIRL WAS LOOKING HUNGRILY AT THE BIG PILE OF BEEBLEBERRIES WHEN SHE HEARD A WILD SCREAM IN THE DISTANCE. . .
EEEEEE!
WHAT'S THAT?
A MOMENT LATER THERE WAS A GREAT RUSH OF WIND AND OL' WITCH HAZEL AND HER NIECE, LITTLE ITCH, FLEW IN THE DOOR!
EEEEEE!
THE OLD WITCH WAS TEACHING HER LITTLE NIECE HOW TO BE A WITCH AND TONIGHT LITTLE ITCH HAD TAKEN A LESSON IN BROOM RIDING. . .
YOU GET BETTER ALL THE TIME, DEARIE! CACKLE, CACKLE!
I CAN RIDE FASTER THAN YOU NOW, AUNTIE! KICKLE, KICKLE!
SUDDENLY OL' WITCH HAZEL STIFFENED AND LOOKED AROUND. . .
WHAT'S THE MATTER, AUNTIE?
THERE'S SOMEBODY ELSE IN THIS COTTAGE!

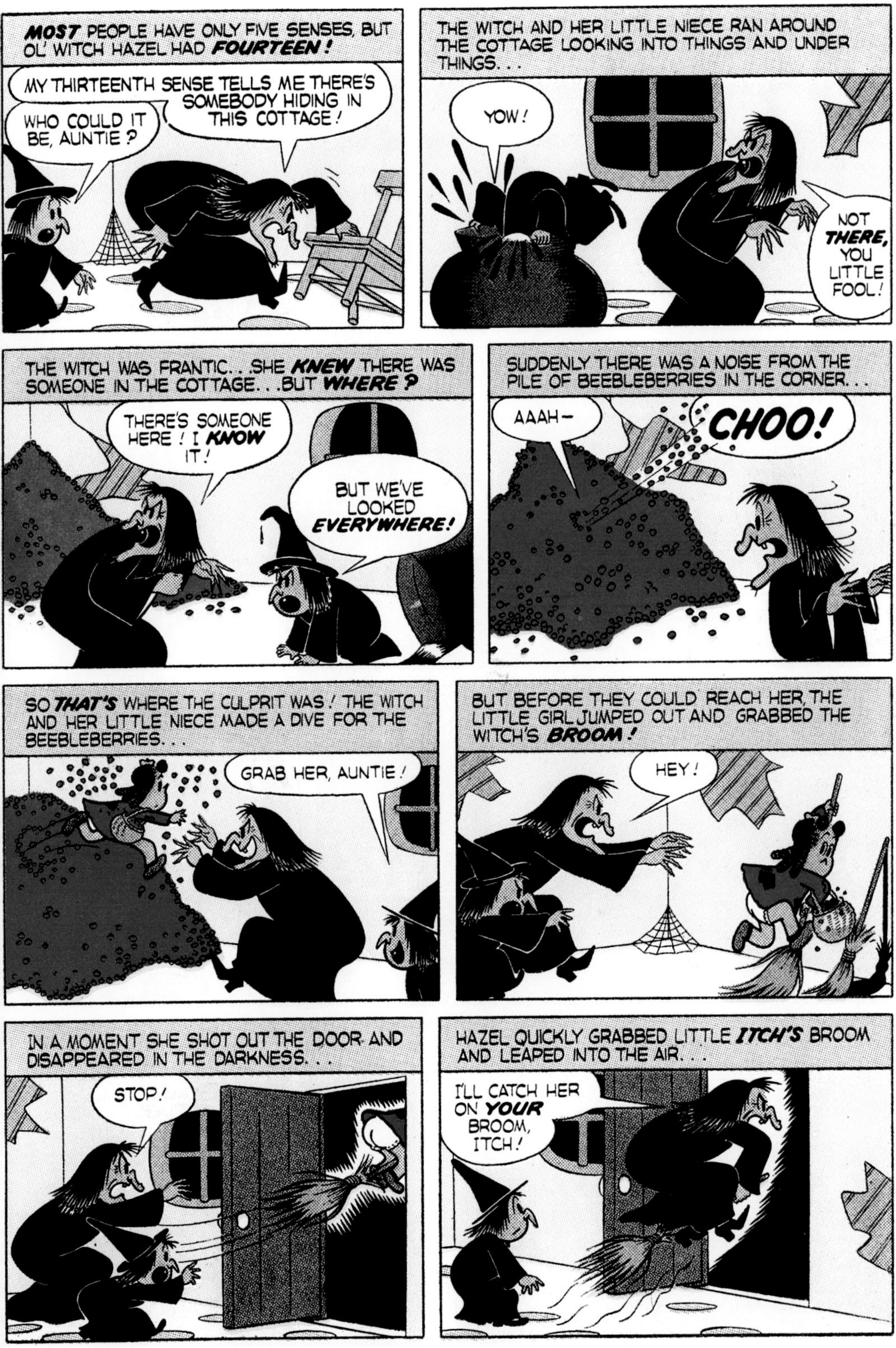

MOST PEOPLE HAVE ONLY FIVE SENSES, BUT OL' WITCH HAZEL HAD FOURTEEN!
MY THIRTEENTH SENSE TELLS ME THERE'S SOMEBODY HIDING IN THIS COTTAGE!
WHO COULD IT BE, AUNTIE?
THE WITCH AND HER LITTLE NIECE RAN AROUND THE COTTAGE LOOKING INTO THINGS AND UNDER THINGS. . .
YOW!
NOT THERE, YOU LITTLE FOOL!
THE WITCH WAS FRANTIC. . .SHE KNEW THERE WAS SOMEONE IN THE COTTAGE. . .BUT WHERE?
THERE'S SOMEONE HERE! I KNOW IT!
BUT WE'VE LOOKED EVERYWHERE!
SUDDENLY THERE WAS A NOISE FROM THE PILE OF BEEBLEBERRIES IN THE CORNER. . .
AAAH–
CHOO!
SO THAT'S WHERE THE CULPRIT WAS! THE WITCH AND HER LITTLE NIECE MADE A DIVE FOR THE BEEBLEBERRIES. . .
GRAB HER, AUNTIE!
BUT BEFORE THEY COULD REACH HER, THE LITTLE GIRL JUMPED OUT AND GRABBED THE WITCH'S BROOM!
HEY!
IN A MOMENT SHE SHOT OUT THE DOOR AND DISAPPEARED IN THE DARKNESS. . .
STOP!
HAZEL QUICKLY GRABBED LITTLE ITCH'S BROOM AND LEAPED INTO THE AIR. . .
I'LL CATCH HER ON YOUR BROOM, ITCH!

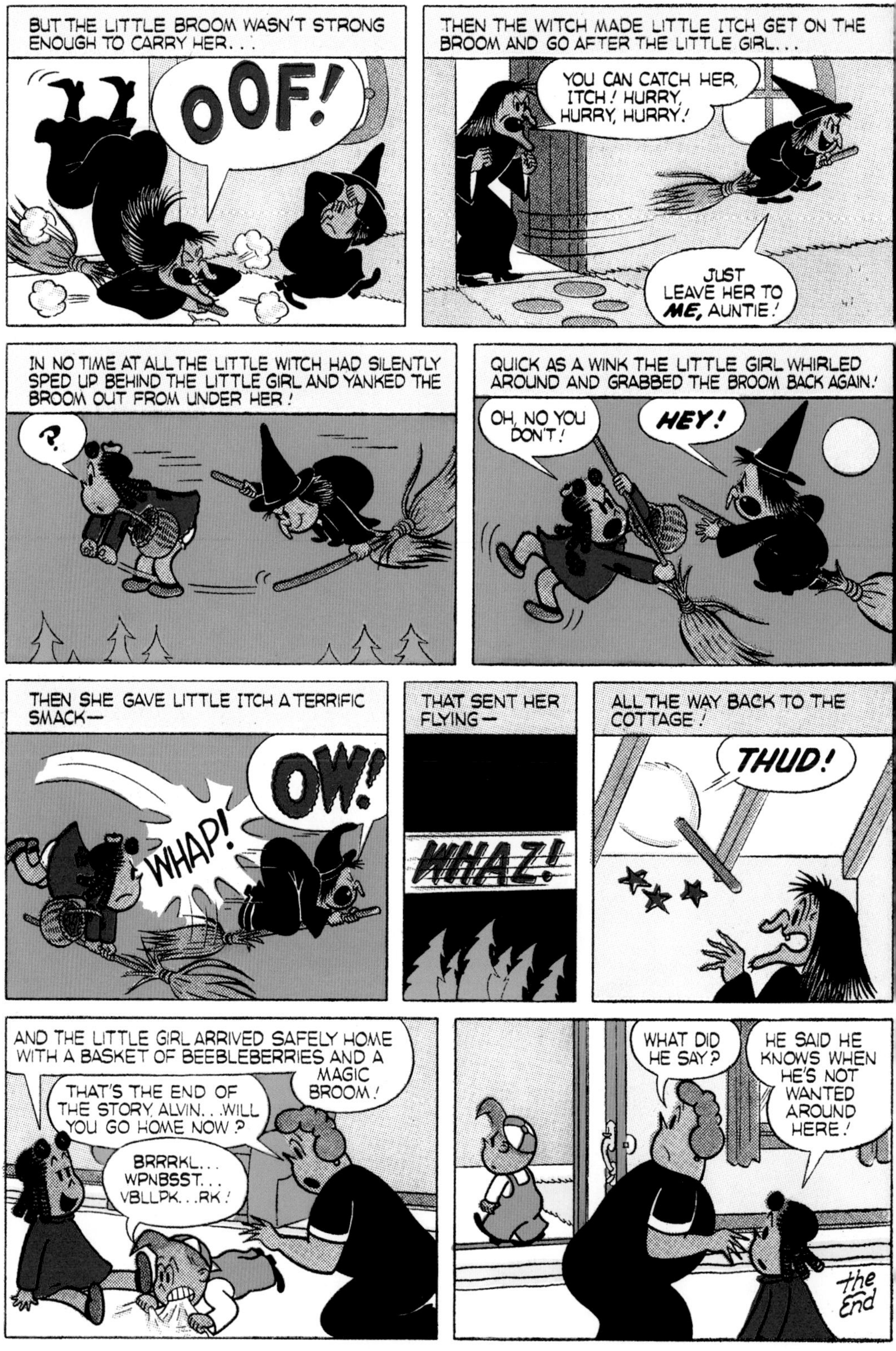
BUT THE LITTLE BROOM WASN'T STRONG ENOUGH TO CARRY HER...
OOF!
THEN THE WITCH MADE LITTLE ITCH GET ON THE BROOM AND GO AFTER THE LITTLE GIRL...
YOU CAN CATCH HER, ITCH! HURRY, HURRY, HURRY!
JUST LEAVE HER TO ME, AUNTIE!
IN NO TIME AT ALL THE LITTLE WITCH HAD SILENTLY SPED UP BEHIND THE LITTLE GIRL AND YANKED THE BROOM OUT FROM UNDER HER!
?
QUICK AS A WINK THE LITTLE GIRL WHIRLED AROUND AND GRABBED THE BROOM BACK AGAIN!
OH, NO YOU DON'T!
HEY!
THEN SHE GAVE LITTLE ITCH A TERRIFIC SMACK—
OW!
WHAP!
THAT SENT HER FLYING—
WHAZ!
ALL THE WAY BACK TO THE COTTAGE!
THUD!
AND THE LITTLE GIRL ARRIVED SAFELY HOME WITH A BASKET OF BEEBLEBERRIES AND A MAGIC BROOM!
THAT'S THE END OF THE STORY, ALVIN... WILL YOU GO HOME NOW?
BRRRKL... WPNBSST... VBLLPK...RK!
WHAT DID HE SAY?
HE SAID HE KNOWS WHEN HE'S NOT WANTED AROUND HERE!
the End

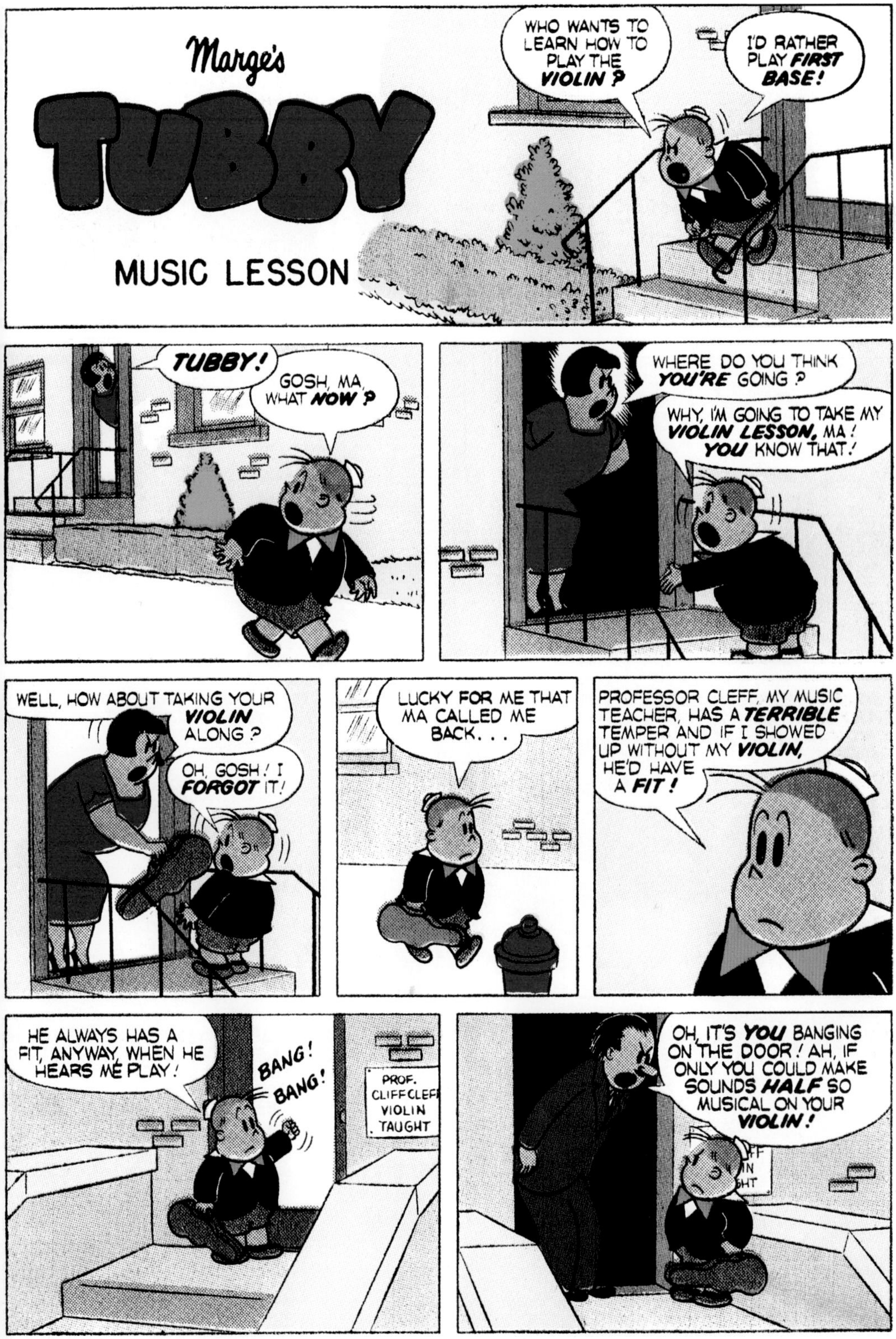
Marge's
TUBBY
MUSIC LESSON
WHO WANTS TO LEARN HOW TO PLAY THE VIOLIN ?
I'D RATHER PLAY FIRST BASE!
TUBBY!
GOSH, MA, WHAT NOW ?
WHERE DO YOU THINK YOU'RE GOING ?
WHY, I'M GOING TO TAKE MY VIOLIN LESSON, MA! YOU KNOW THAT!
WELL, HOW ABOUT TAKING YOUR VIOLIN ALONG ?
OH, GOSH! I FORGOT IT!
LUCKY FOR ME THAT MA CALLED ME BACK. . .
PROFESSOR CLEFF, MY MUSIC TEACHER, HAS A TERRIBLE TEMPER AND IF I SHOWED UP WITHOUT MY VIOLIN, HE'D HAVE A FIT!
HE ALWAYS HAS A FIT, ANYWAY, WHEN HE HEARS ME PLAY!
BANG! BANG!
PROF. CLIFFCLEFF VIOLIN TAUGHT
OH, IT'S YOU BANGING ON THE DOOR! AH, IF ONLY YOU COULD MAKE SOUNDS HALF SO MUSICAL ON YOUR VIOLIN!

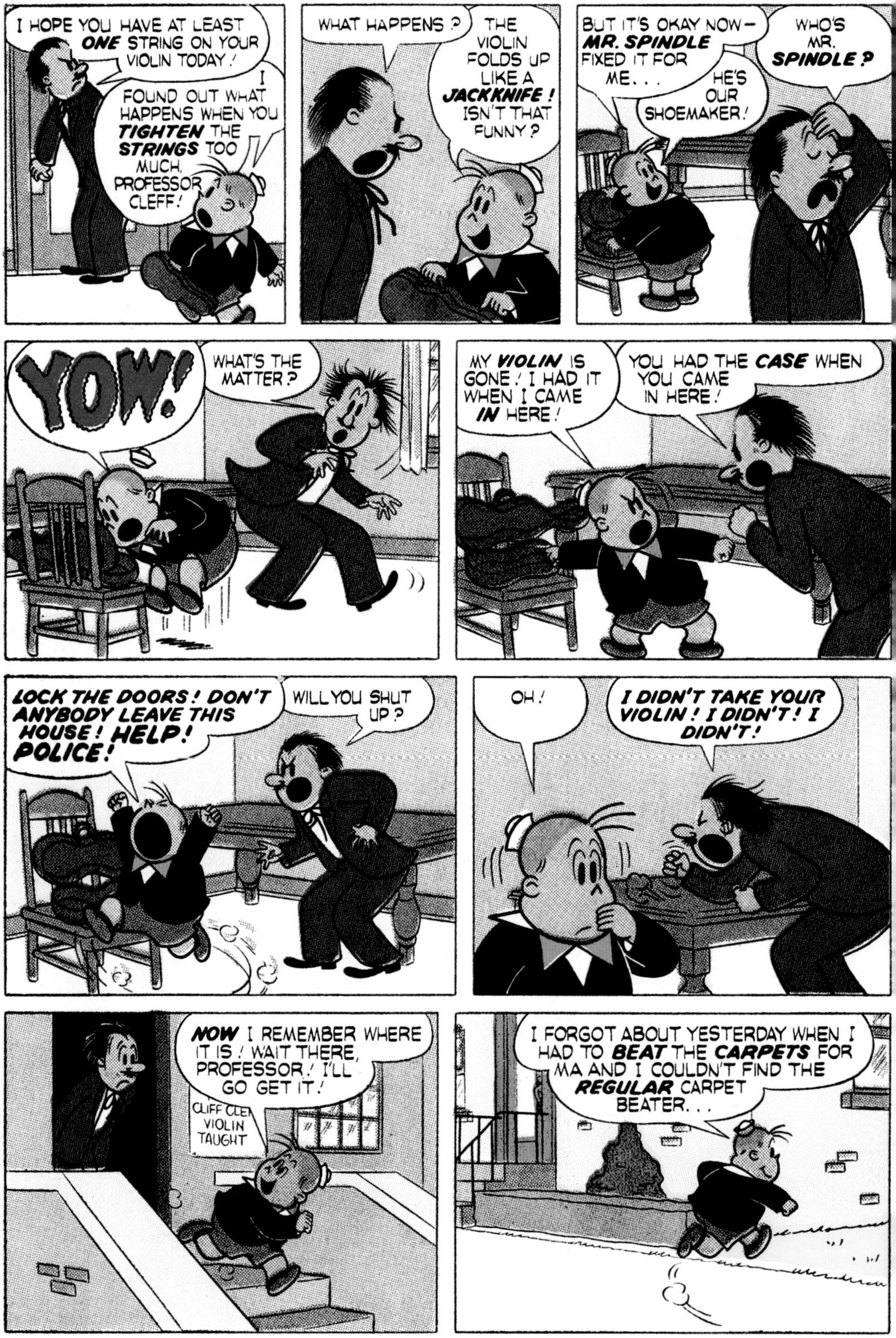
I HOPE YOU HAVE AT LEAST ONE STRING ON YOUR VIOLIN TODAY!
I FOUND OUT WHAT HAPPENS WHEN YOU TIGHTEN THE STRINGS TOO MUCH, PROFESSOR CLEFF!
WHAT HAPPENS?
THE VIOLIN FOLDS UP LIKE A JACKKNIFE! ISN'T THAT FUNNY?
BUT IT'S OKAY NOW— MR. SPINDLE FIXED IT FOR ME...
WHO'S MR. SPINDLE?
HE'S OUR SHOEMAKER!
YOW!
WHAT'S THE MATTER?
MY VIOLIN IS GONE! I HAD IT WHEN I CAME IN HERE!
YOU HAD THE CASE WHEN YOU CAME IN HERE!
LOCK THE DOORS! DON'T ANYBODY LEAVE THIS HOUSE! HELP! POLICE!
WILL YOU SHUT UP?
OH!
I DIDN'T TAKE YOUR VIOLIN! I DIDN'T! I DIDN'T!
NOW I REMEMBER WHERE IT IS! WAIT THERE, PROFESSOR! I'LL GO GET IT!
CLIFF CLEF VIOLIN TAUGHT
I FORGOT ABOUT YESTERDAY WHEN I HAD TO BEAT THE CARPETS FOR MA AND I COULDN'T FIND THE REGULAR CARPET BEATER...

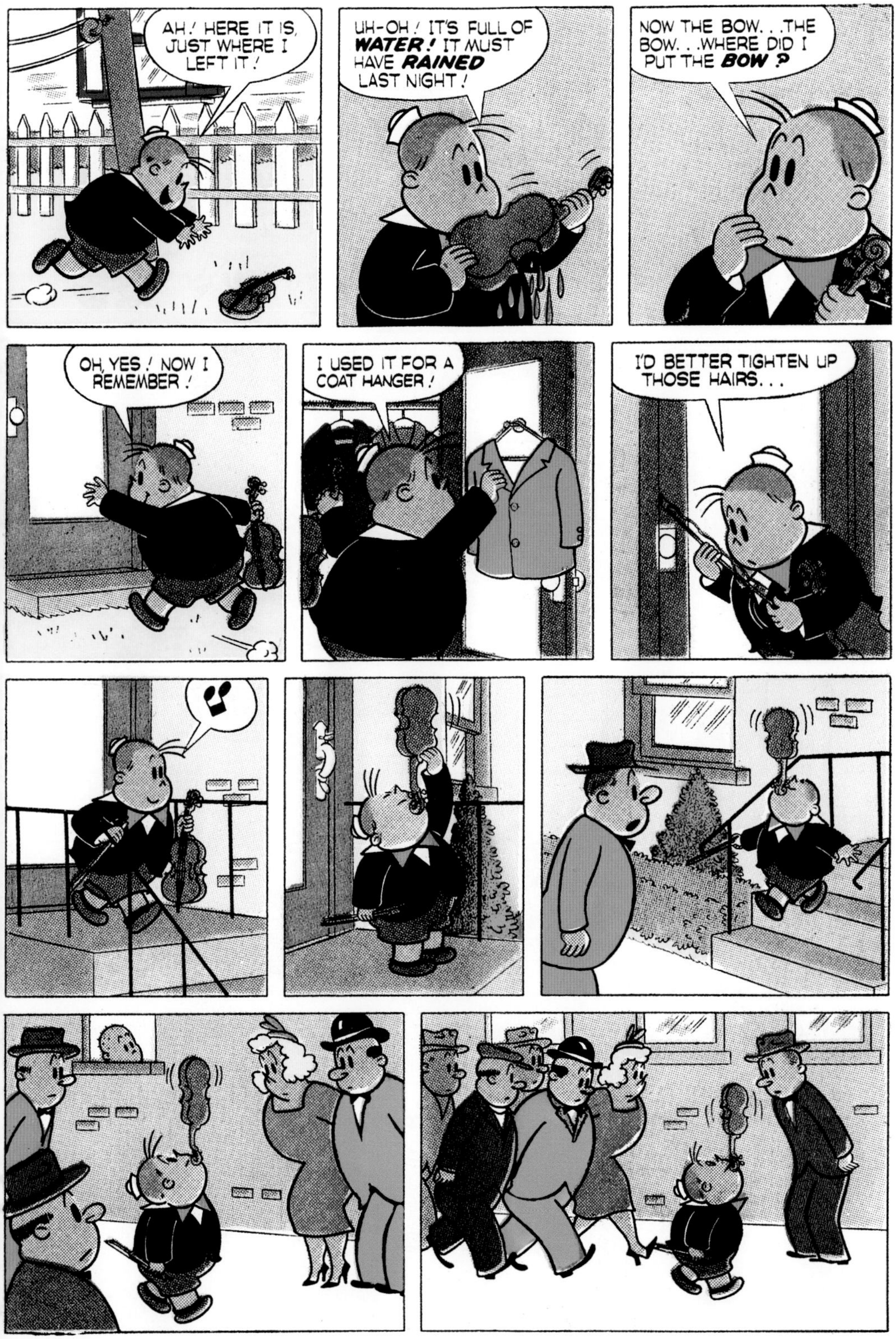
AH! HERE IT IS, JUST WHERE I LEFT IT!
UH-OH! IT'S FULL OF **WATER!** IT MUST HAVE **RAINED** LAST NIGHT!
NOW THE BOW. . .THE BOW. . .WHERE DID I PUT THE **BOW ?**
OH, YES! NOW I REMEMBER!
I USED IT FOR A COAT HANGER!
I'D BETTER TIGHTEN UP THOSE HAIRS. . .

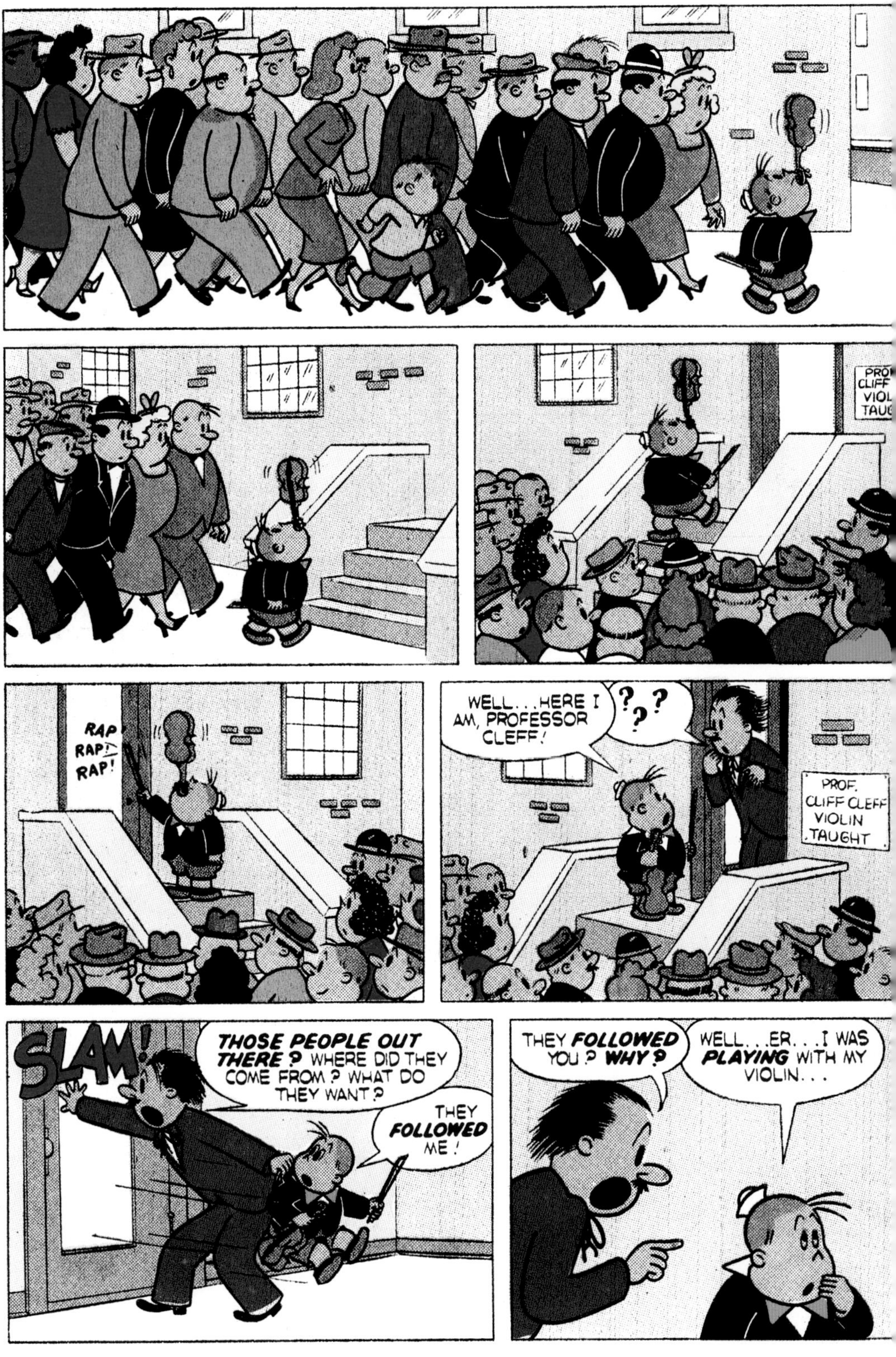
RAP
RAP!
RAP!
WELL...HERE I AM, PROFESSOR CLEFF!
???
PROF. CLIFF CLEFF VIOLIN TAUGHT
SLAM!
**THOSE PEOPLE OUT THERE?** WHERE DID THEY COME FROM? WHAT DO THEY WANT?
THEY **FOLLOWED** ME!
THEY **FOLLOWED** YOU? **WHY?**
WELL...ER...I WAS **PLAYING** WITH MY VIOLIN...

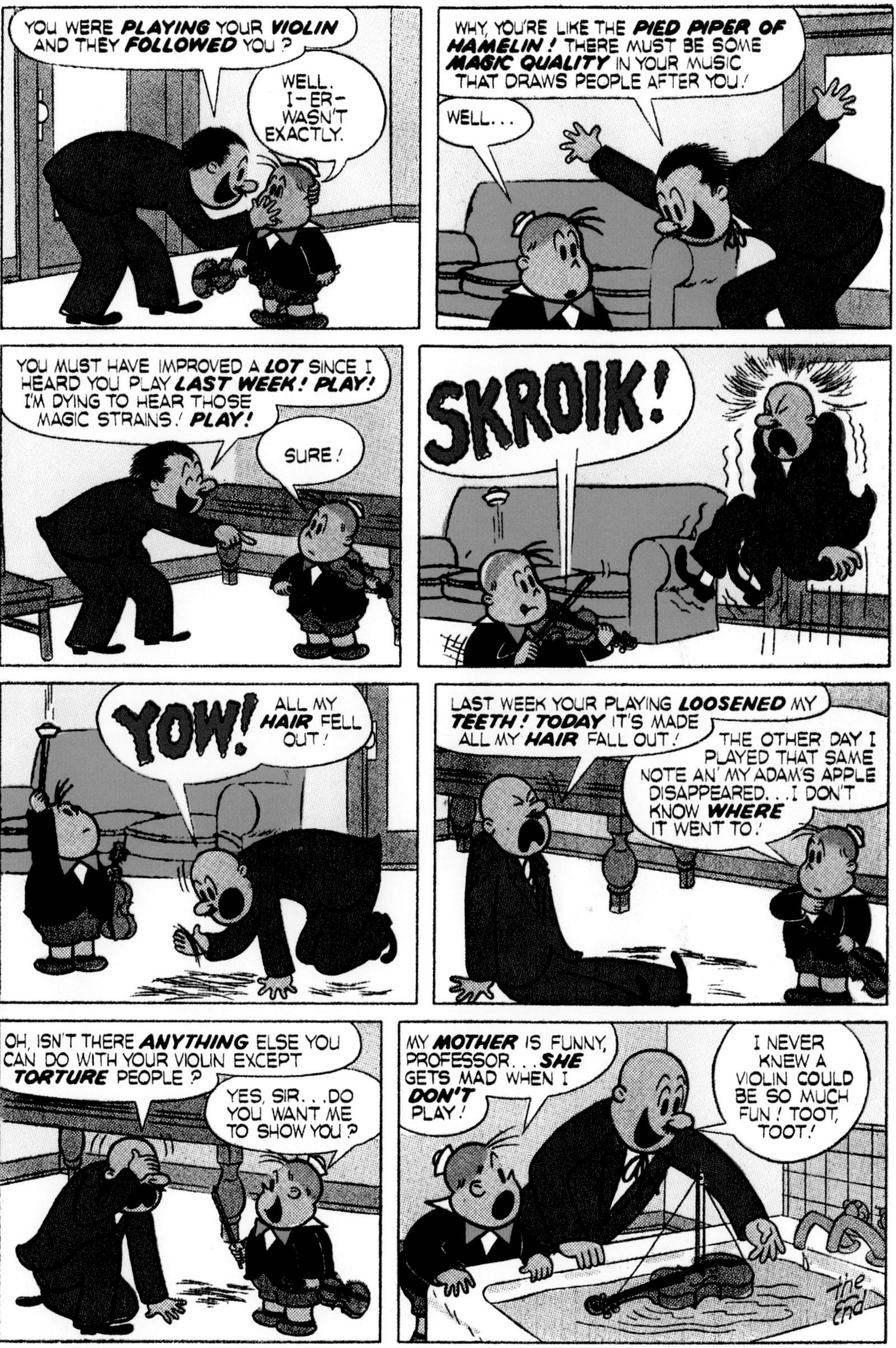
YOU WERE PLAYING YOUR VIOLIN AND THEY FOLLOWED YOU?
WELL. I-ER- WASN'T EXACTLY.
WHY, YOU'RE LIKE THE PIED PIPER OF HAMELIN! THERE MUST BE SOME MAGIC QUALITY IN YOUR MUSIC THAT DRAWS PEOPLE AFTER YOU!
WELL...
YOU MUST HAVE IMPROVED A LOT SINCE I HEARD YOU PLAY LAST WEEK! PLAY! I'M DYING TO HEAR THOSE MAGIC STRAINS! PLAY!
SURE!
SKROIK!
YOW!
ALL MY HAIR FELL OUT!
LAST WEEK YOUR PLAYING LOOSENED MY TEETH! TODAY IT'S MADE ALL MY HAIR FALL OUT!
THE OTHER DAY I PLAYED THAT SAME NOTE AN' MY ADAM'S APPLE DISAPPEARED...I DON'T KNOW WHERE IT WENT TO!
OH, ISN'T THERE ANYTHING ELSE YOU CAN DO WITH YOUR VIOLIN EXCEPT TORTURE PEOPLE?
YES, SIR...DO YOU WANT ME TO SHOW YOU?
MY MOTHER IS FUNNY, PROFESSOR...SHE GETS MAD WHEN I DON'T PLAY!
I NEVER KNEW A VIOLIN COULD BE SO MUCH FUN! TOOT, TOOT!
the End

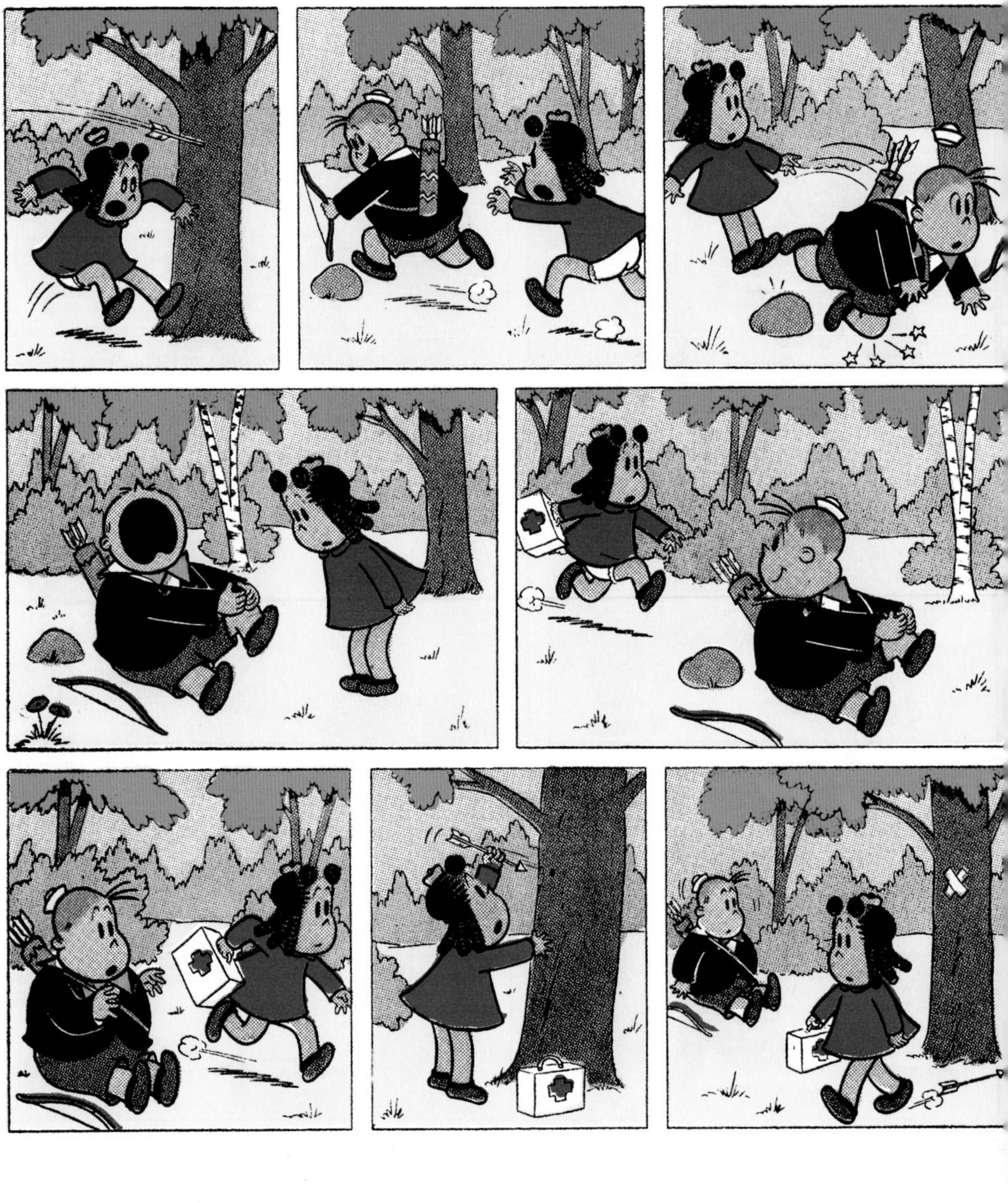

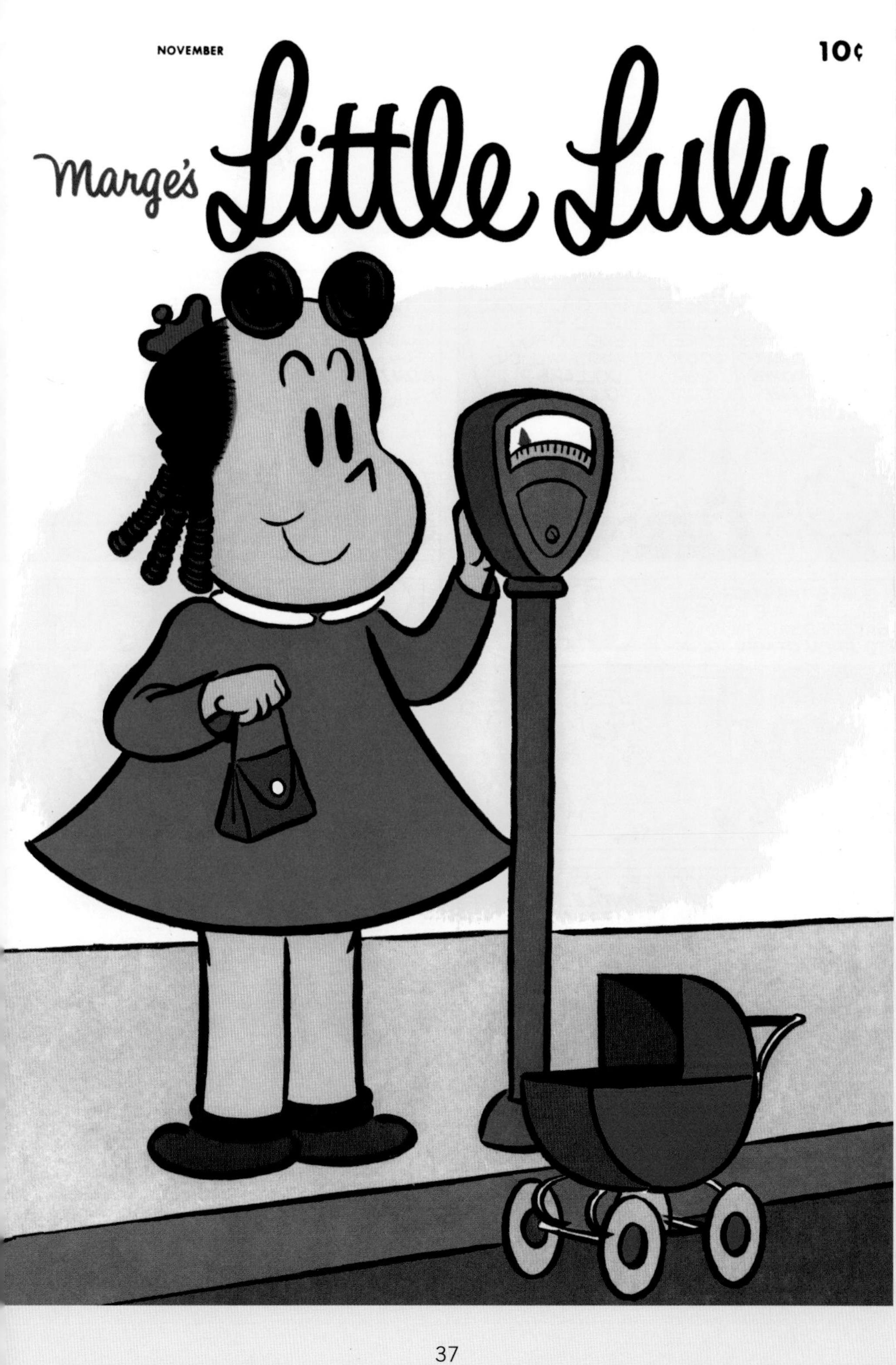
NOVEMBER
10¢
Marge's Little Lulu

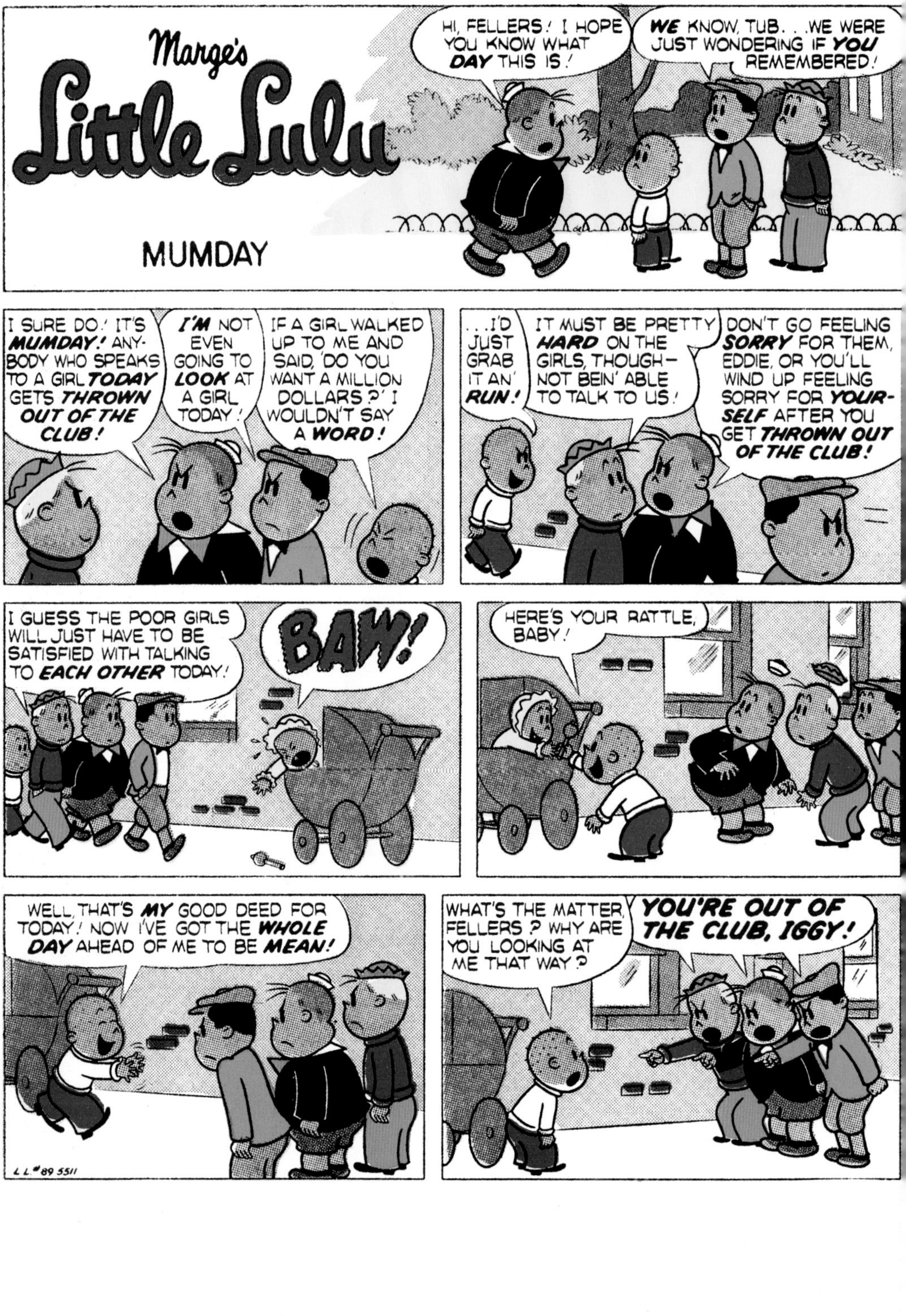
Marge's Little Lulu
MUMDAY
HI, FELLERS! I HOPE YOU KNOW WHAT DAY THIS IS!
WE KNOW, TUB. . .WE WERE JUST WONDERING IF YOU REMEMBERED!
I SURE DO! IT'S MUMDAY! ANYBODY WHO SPEAKS TO A GIRL TODAY GETS THROWN OUT OF THE CLUB!
I'M NOT EVEN GOING TO LOOK AT A GIRL TODAY!
IF A GIRL WALKED UP TO ME AND SAID, 'DO YOU WANT A MILLION DOLLARS?' I WOULDN'T SAY A WORD!
. . .I'D JUST GRAB IT AN' RUN!
IT MUST BE PRETTY HARD ON THE GIRLS, THOUGH— NOT BEIN' ABLE TO TALK TO US!
DON'T GO FEELING SORRY FOR THEM, EDDIE, OR YOU'LL WIND UP FEELING SORRY FOR YOURSELF AFTER YOU GET THROWN OUT OF THE CLUB!
I GUESS THE POOR GIRLS WILL JUST HAVE TO BE SATISFIED WITH TALKING TO EACH OTHER TODAY!
BAW!
HERE'S YOUR RATTLE, BABY!
WELL, THAT'S MY GOOD DEED FOR TODAY! NOW I'VE GOT THE WHOLE DAY AHEAD OF ME TO BE MEAN!
WHAT'S THE MATTER, FELLERS? WHY ARE YOU LOOKING AT ME THAT WAY?
YOU'RE OUT OF THE CLUB, IGGY!
L.L.#89 5511

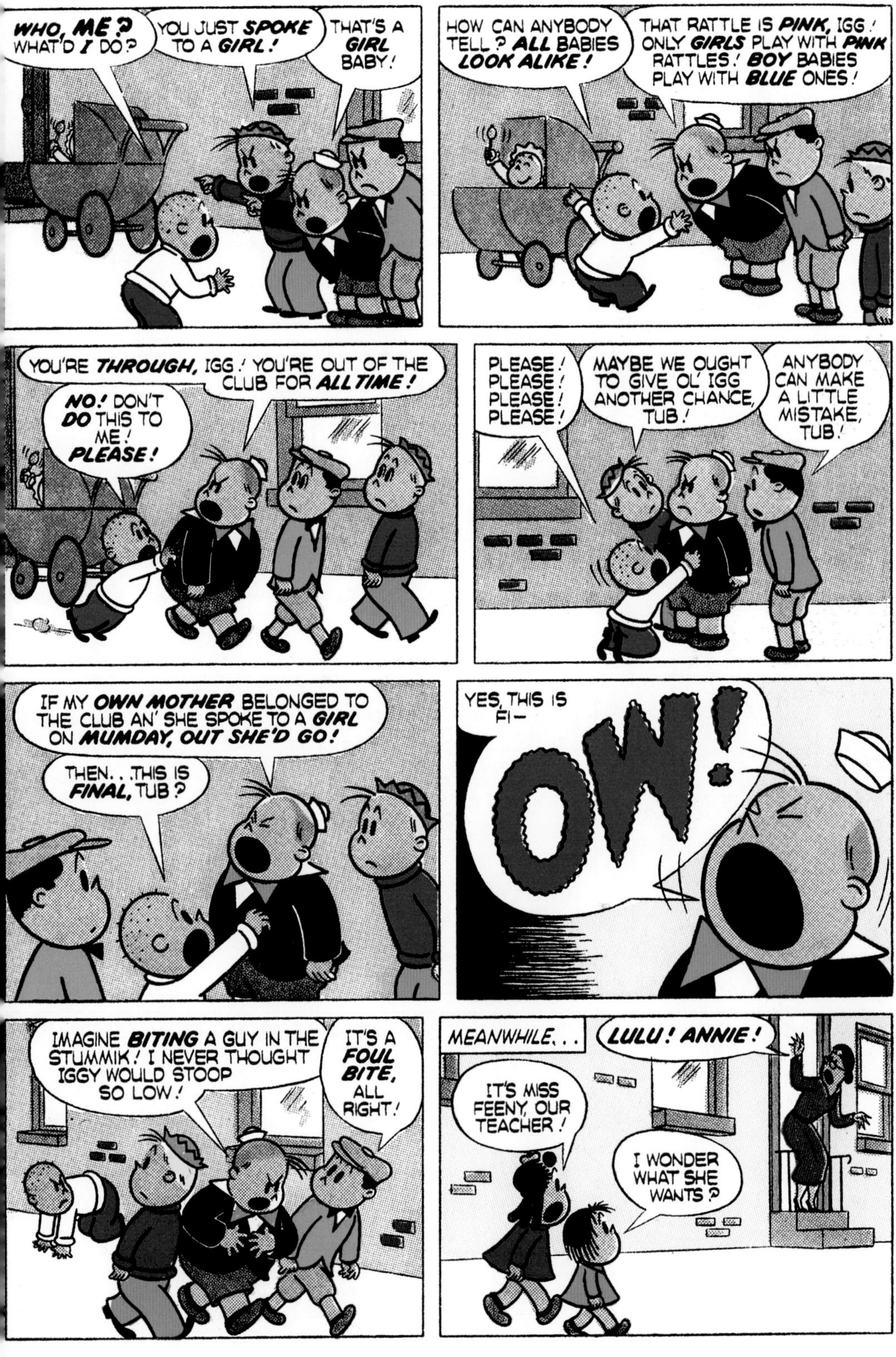
WHO, ME? WHAT'D I DO?
YOU JUST SPOKE TO A GIRL!
THAT'S A GIRL BABY!
HOW CAN ANYBODY TELL? ALL BABIES LOOK ALIKE!
THAT RATTLE IS PINK, IGG! ONLY GIRLS PLAY WITH PINK RATTLES! BOY BABIES PLAY WITH BLUE ONES!
YOU'RE THROUGH, IGG! YOU'RE OUT OF THE CLUB FOR ALL TIME!
NO! DON'T DO THIS TO ME! PLEASE!
PLEASE! PLEASE! PLEASE! PLEASE!
MAYBE WE OUGHT TO GIVE OL' IGG ANOTHER CHANCE, TUB!
ANYBODY CAN MAKE A LITTLE MISTAKE, TUB!
IF MY OWN MOTHER BELONGED TO THE CLUB AN' SHE SPOKE TO A GIRL ON MUMDAY, OUT SHE'D GO!
THEN...THIS IS FINAL, TUB?
YES, THIS IS FI—
OW!
IMAGINE BITING A GUY IN THE STUMMIK! I NEVER THOUGHT IGGY WOULD STOOP SO LOW!
IT'S A FOUL BITE, ALL RIGHT!
MEANWHILE...
LULU! ANNIE!
IT'S MISS FEENY, OUR TEACHER!
I WONDER WHAT SHE WANTS?

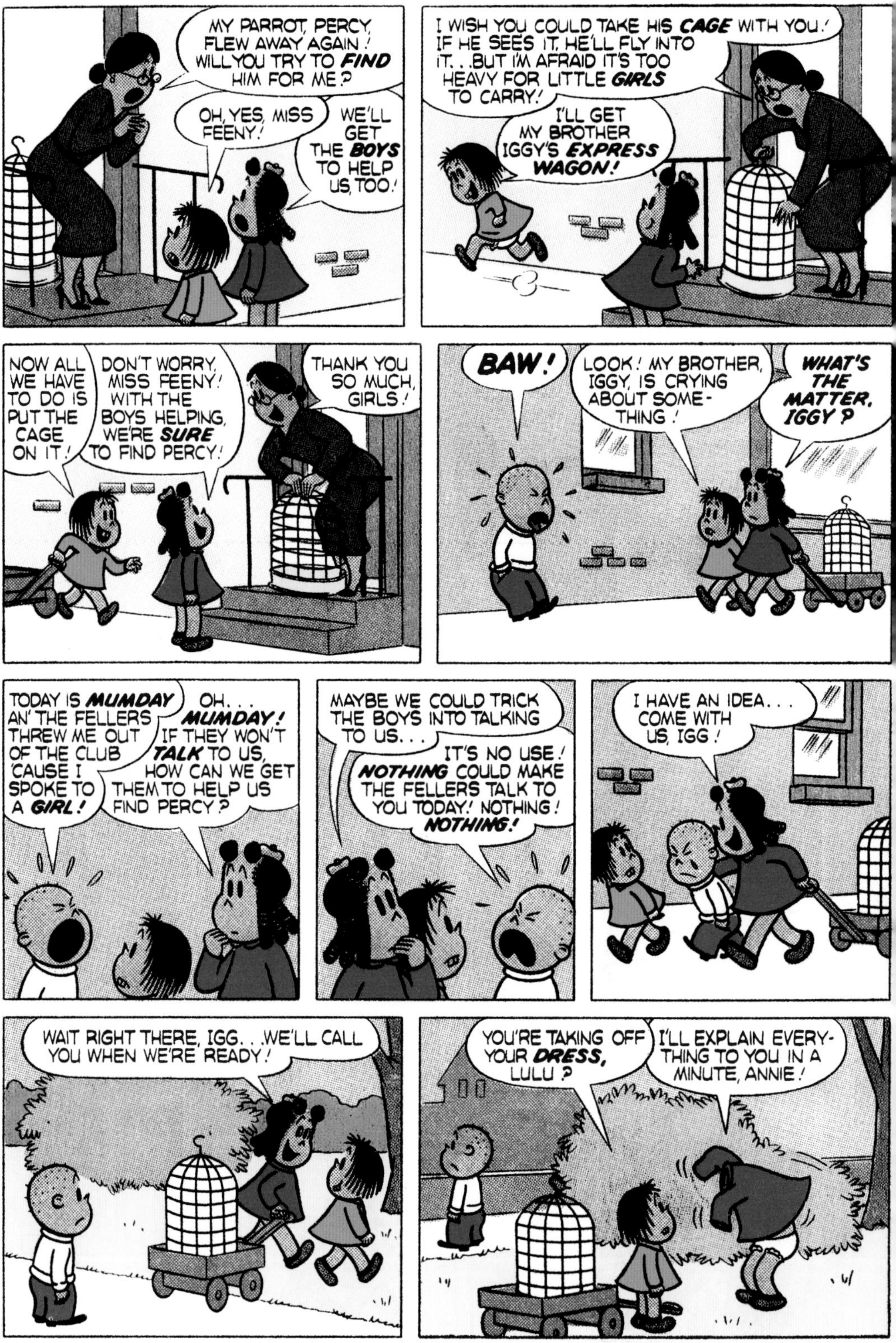
MY PARROT, PERCY, FLEW AWAY AGAIN! WILL YOU TRY TO FIND HIM FOR ME?
OH, YES, MISS FEENY!
WE'LL GET THE BOYS TO HELP US, TOO!
I WISH YOU COULD TAKE HIS CAGE WITH YOU! IF HE SEES IT, HE'LL FLY INTO IT. . .BUT I'M AFRAID IT'S TOO HEAVY FOR LITTLE GIRLS TO CARRY!
I'LL GET MY BROTHER IGGY'S EXPRESS WAGON!
NOW ALL WE HAVE TO DO IS PUT THE CAGE ON IT!
DON'T WORRY, MISS FEENY! WITH THE BOYS HELPING, WE'RE SURE TO FIND PERCY!
THANK YOU SO MUCH, GIRLS!
BAW!
LOOK! MY BROTHER, IGGY, IS CRYING ABOUT SOME-THING!
WHAT'S THE MATTER, IGGY?
TODAY IS MUMDAY AN' THE FELLERS THREW ME OUT OF THE CLUB 'CAUSE I SPOKE TO A GIRL!
OH. . . MUMDAY! IF THEY WON'T TALK TO US, HOW CAN WE GET THEM TO HELP US FIND PERCY?
MAYBE WE COULD TRICK THE BOYS INTO TALKING TO US. . .
IT'S NO USE! NOTHING COULD MAKE THE FELLERS TALK TO YOU TODAY! NOTHING! NOTHING!
I HAVE AN IDEA. . . COME WITH US, IGG!
WAIT RIGHT THERE, IGG. . .WE'LL CALL YOU WHEN WE'RE READY!
YOU'RE TAKING OFF YOUR DRESS, LULU?
I'LL EXPLAIN EVERY-THING TO YOU IN A MINUTE, ANNIE!

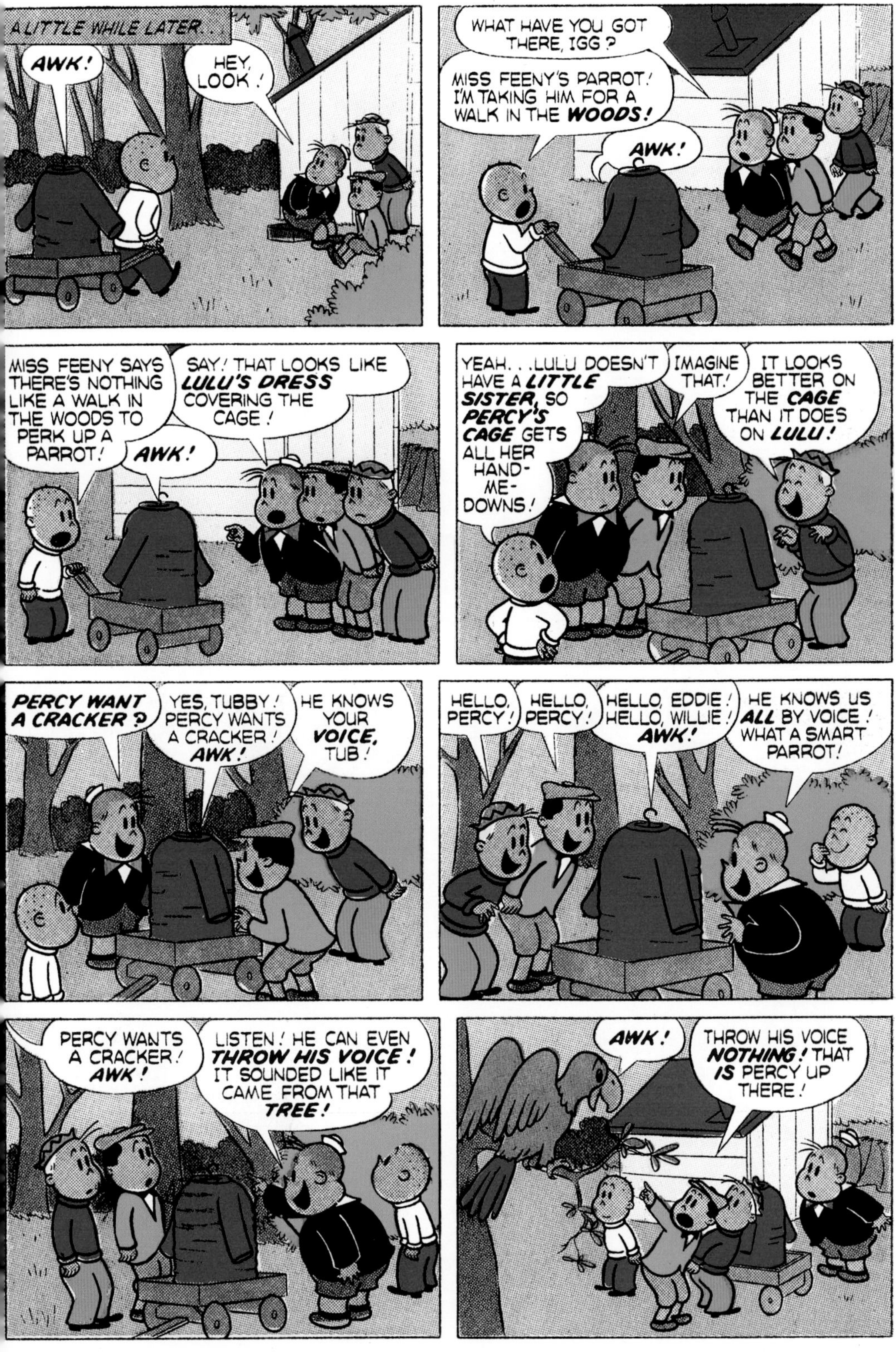
A LITTLE WHILE LATER...
AWK!
HEY, LOOK!
WHAT HAVE YOU GOT THERE, IGG?
MISS FEENY'S PARROT! I'M TAKING HIM FOR A WALK IN THE WOODS!
AWK!
MISS FEENY SAYS THERE'S NOTHING LIKE A WALK IN THE WOODS TO PERK UP A PARROT!
AWK!
SAY! THAT LOOKS LIKE LULU'S DRESS COVERING THE CAGE!
YEAH...LULU DOESN'T HAVE A LITTLE SISTER, SO PERCY'S CAGE GETS ALL HER HAND-ME-DOWNS!
IMAGINE THAT!
IT LOOKS BETTER ON THE CAGE THAN IT DOES ON LULU!
PERCY WANT A CRACKER?
YES, TUBBY! PERCY WANTS A CRACKER! AWK!
HE KNOWS YOUR VOICE, TUB!
HELLO, PERCY!
HELLO, PERCY!
HELLO, EDDIE! HELLO, WILLIE! AWK!
HE KNOWS US ALL BY VOICE! WHAT A SMART PARROT!
PERCY WANTS A CRACKER! AWK!
LISTEN! HE CAN EVEN THROW HIS VOICE! IT SOUNDED LIKE IT CAME FROM THAT TREE!
AWK!
THROW HIS VOICE NOTHING! THAT IS PERCY UP THERE!

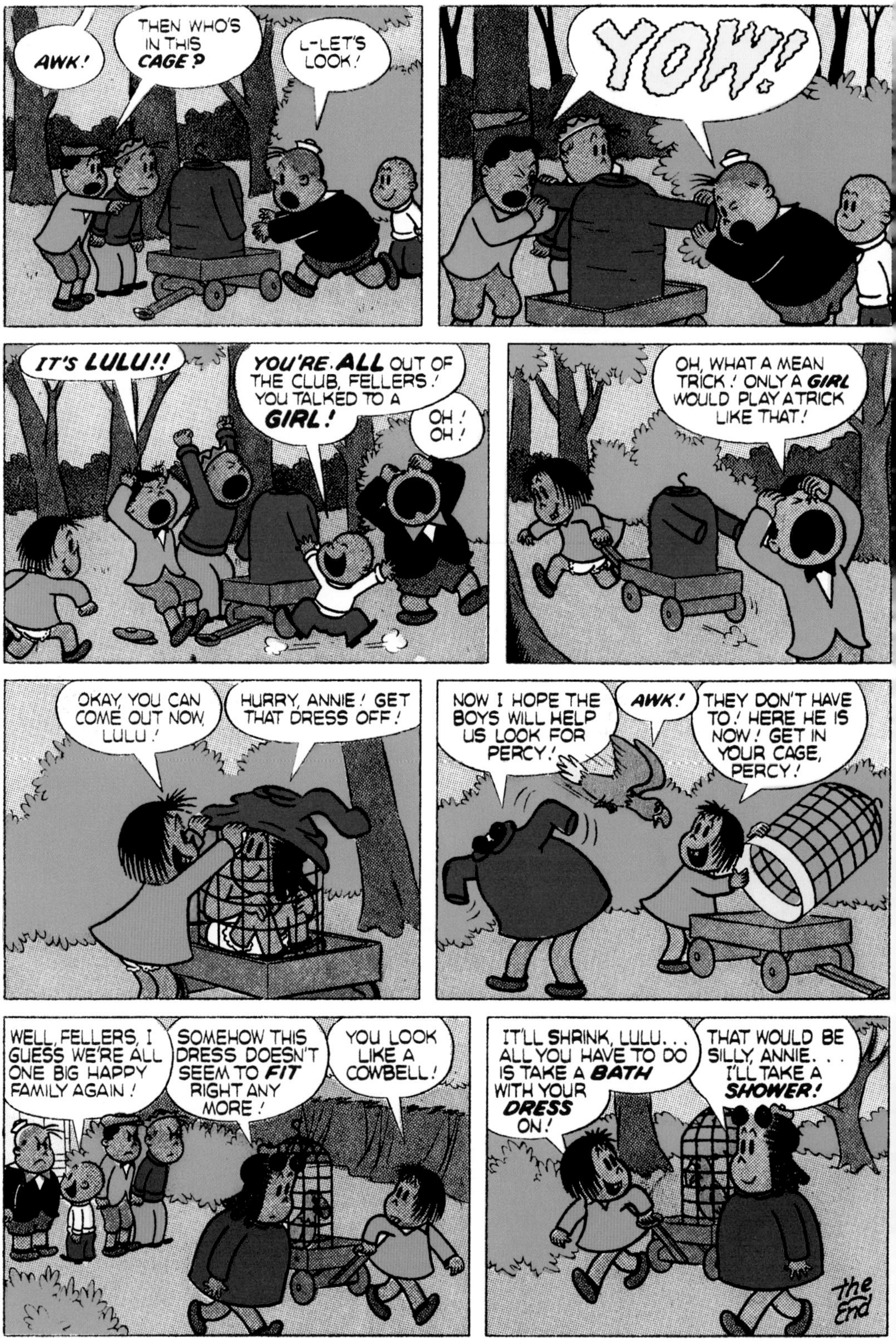
AWK!
THEN WHO'S IN THIS CAGE?
L-LET'S LOOK!
YOW!
IT'S LULU!!
YOU'RE ALL OUT OF THE CLUB, FELLERS! YOU TALKED TO A GIRL!
OH! OH!
OH, WHAT A MEAN TRICK! ONLY A GIRL WOULD PLAY A TRICK LIKE THAT!
OKAY, YOU CAN COME OUT NOW, LULU!
HURRY, ANNIE! GET THAT DRESS OFF!
NOW I HOPE THE BOYS WILL HELP US LOOK FOR PERCY!
AWK!
THEY DON'T HAVE TO! HERE HE IS NOW! GET IN YOUR CAGE, PERCY!
WELL, FELLERS, I GUESS WE'RE ALL ONE BIG HAPPY FAMILY AGAIN!
SOMEHOW THIS DRESS DOESN'T SEEM TO FIT RIGHT ANY MORE!
YOU LOOK LIKE A COWBELL!
IT'LL SHRINK, LULU... ALL YOU HAVE TO DO IS TAKE A BATH WITH YOUR DRESS ON!
THAT WOULD BE SILLY, ANNIE... I'LL TAKE A SHOWER!
the End

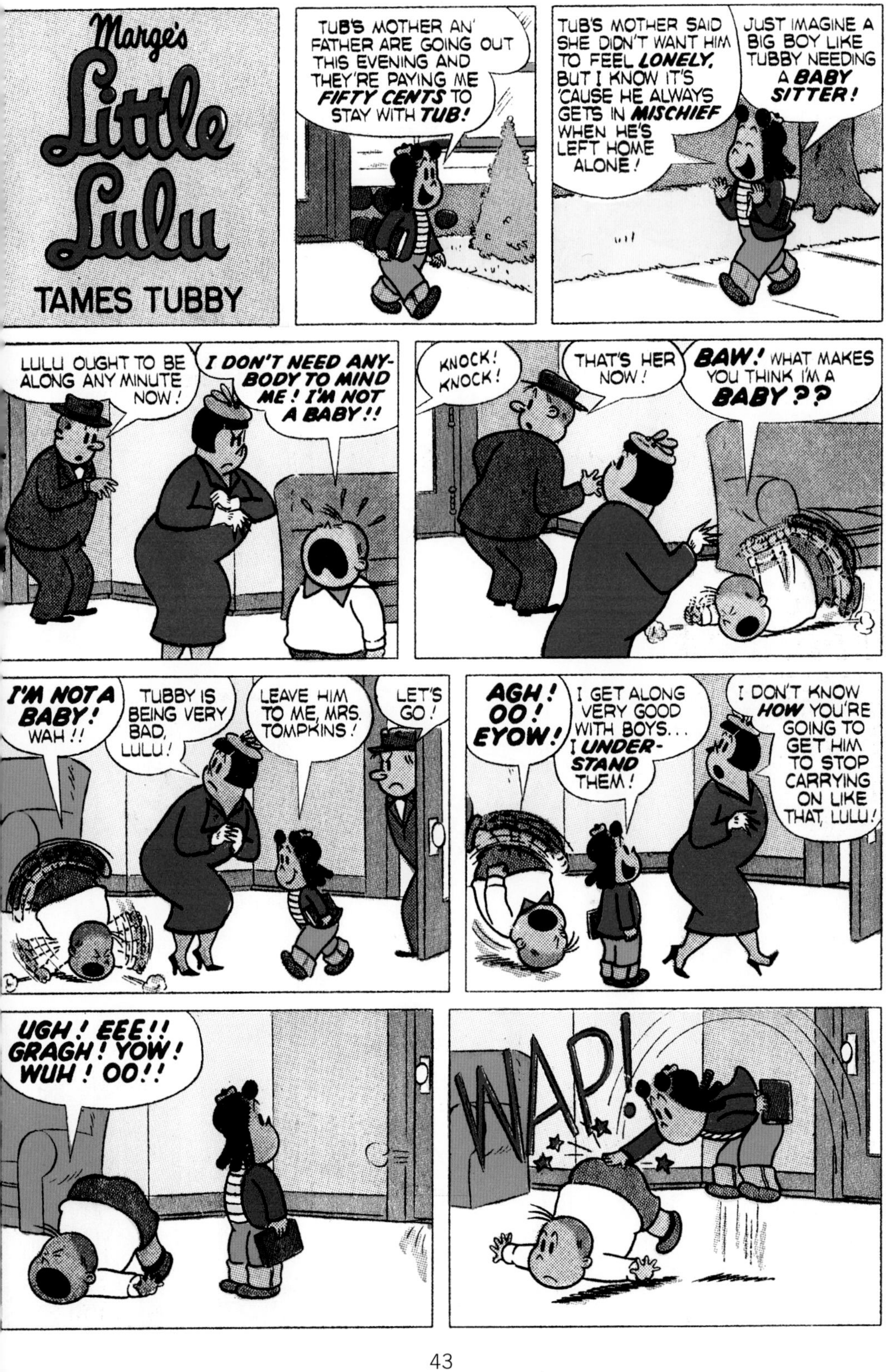
Marge's Little Lulu
TAMES TUBBY
TUB'S MOTHER AN' FATHER ARE GOING OUT THIS EVENING AND THEY'RE PAYING ME FIFTY CENTS TO STAY WITH TUB!
TUB'S MOTHER SAID SHE DIDN'T WANT HIM TO FEEL LONELY, BUT I KNOW IT'S 'CAUSE HE ALWAYS GETS IN MISCHIEF WHEN HE'S LEFT HOME ALONE!
JUST IMAGINE A BIG BOY LIKE TUBBY NEEDING A BABY SITTER!
LULU OUGHT TO BE ALONG ANY MINUTE NOW!
I DON'T NEED ANY-BODY TO MIND ME! I'M NOT A BABY!!
KNOCK! KNOCK!
THAT'S HER NOW!
BAW! WHAT MAKES YOU THINK I'M A BABY??
I'M NOT A BABY! WAH!!
TUBBY IS BEING VERY BAD, LULU!
LEAVE HIM TO ME, MRS. TOMPKINS!
LET'S GO!
AGH! OO! EYOW!
I GET ALONG VERY GOOD WITH BOYS... I UNDER-STAND THEM!
I DON'T KNOW HOW YOU'RE GOING TO GET HIM TO STOP CARRYING ON LIKE THAT, LULU!
UGH! EEE!! GRAGH! YOW! WUH! OO!!
WAP!

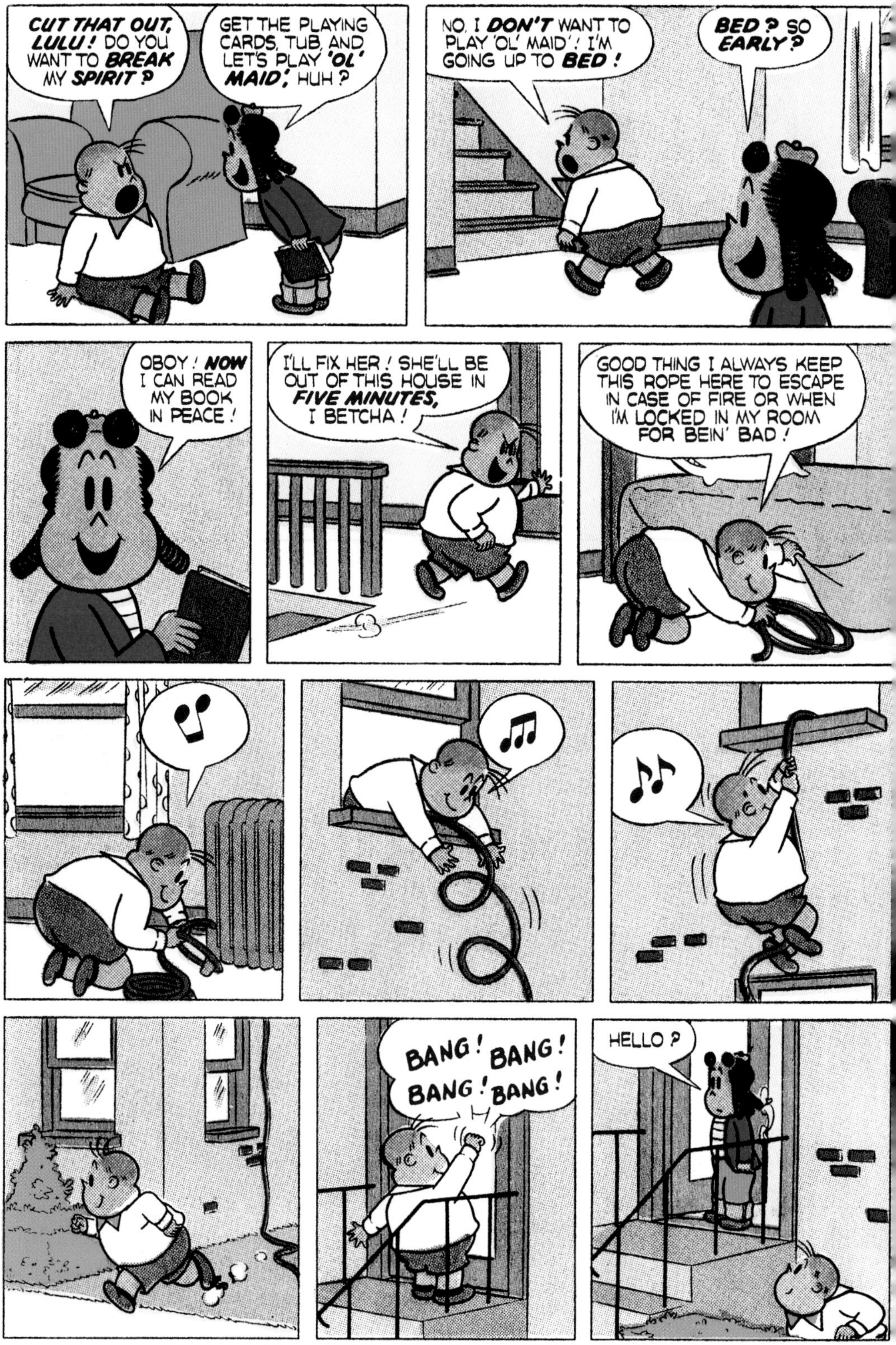
CUT THAT OUT, LULU! DO YOU WANT TO BREAK MY SPIRIT?
GET THE PLAYING CARDS, TUB, AND LET'S PLAY 'OL' MAID', HUH?
NO, I DON'T WANT TO PLAY 'OL' MAID'! I'M GOING UP TO BED!
BED? SO EARLY?
OBOY! NOW I CAN READ MY BOOK IN PEACE!
I'LL FIX HER! SHE'LL BE OUT OF THIS HOUSE IN FIVE MINUTES, I BETCHA!
GOOD THING I ALWAYS KEEP THIS ROPE HERE TO ESCAPE IN CASE OF FIRE OR WHEN I'M LOCKED IN MY ROOM FOR BEIN' BAD!
BANG! BANG! BANG! BANG!
HELLO?

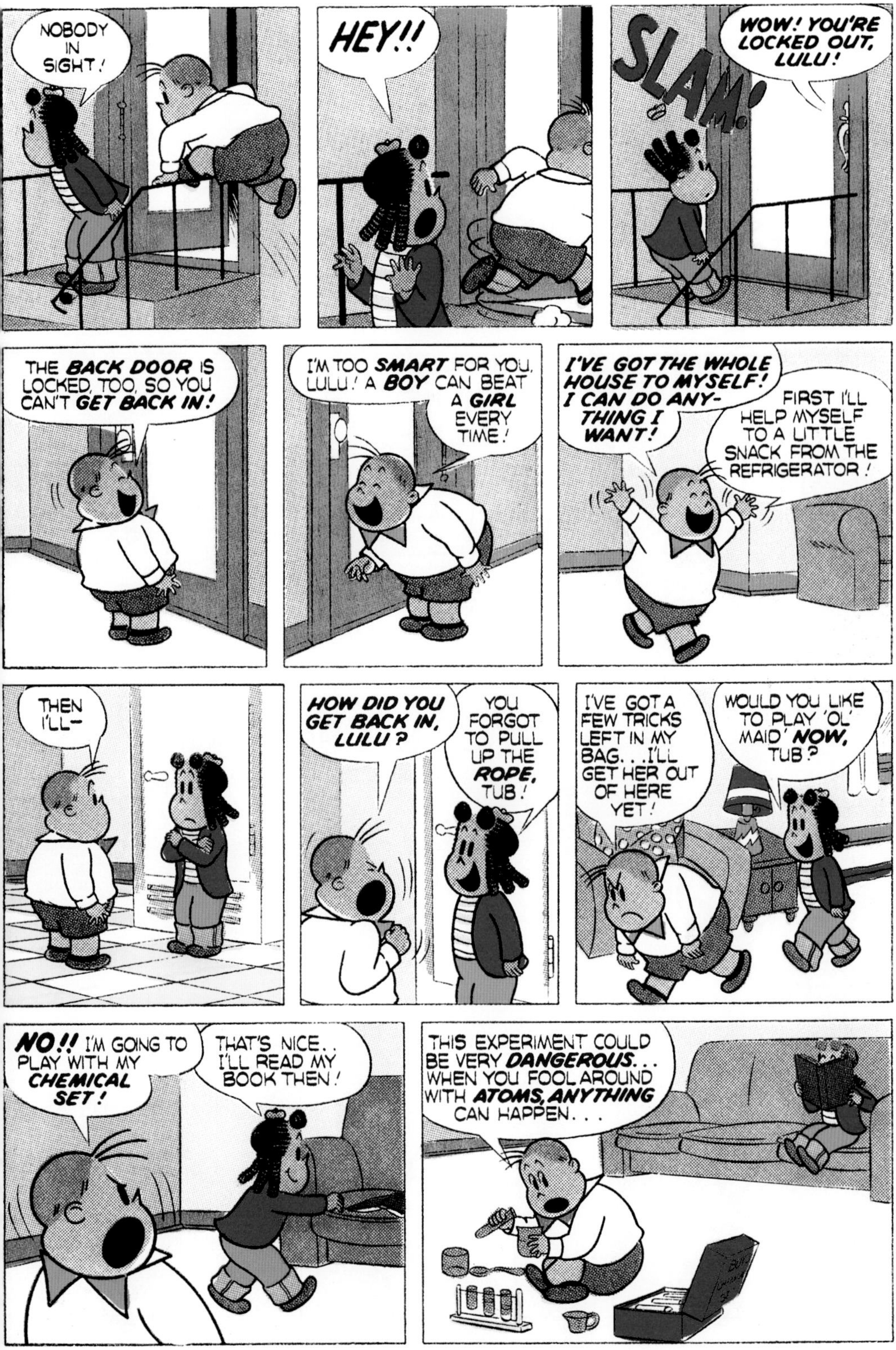
NOBODY IN SIGHT!
HEY!!
SLAM!
WOW! YOU'RE LOCKED OUT, LULU!
THE BACK DOOR IS LOCKED, TOO, SO YOU CAN'T GET BACK IN!
I'M TOO SMART FOR YOU, LULU! A BOY CAN BEAT A GIRL EVERY TIME!
I'VE GOT THE WHOLE HOUSE TO MYSELF! I CAN DO ANYTHING I WANT!
FIRST I'LL HELP MYSELF TO A LITTLE SNACK FROM THE REFRIGERATOR!
THEN I'LL—
HOW DID YOU GET BACK IN, LULU?
YOU FORGOT TO PULL UP THE ROPE, TUB!
I'VE GOT A FEW TRICKS LEFT IN MY BAG. . .I'LL GET HER OUT OF HERE YET!
WOULD YOU LIKE TO PLAY 'OL' MAID' NOW, TUB?
NO!! I'M GOING TO PLAY WITH MY CHEMICAL SET!
THAT'S NICE.. I'LL READ MY BOOK THEN!
THIS EXPERIMENT COULD BE VERY DANGEROUS... WHEN YOU FOOL AROUND WITH ATOMS, ANYTHING CAN HAPPEN. . .

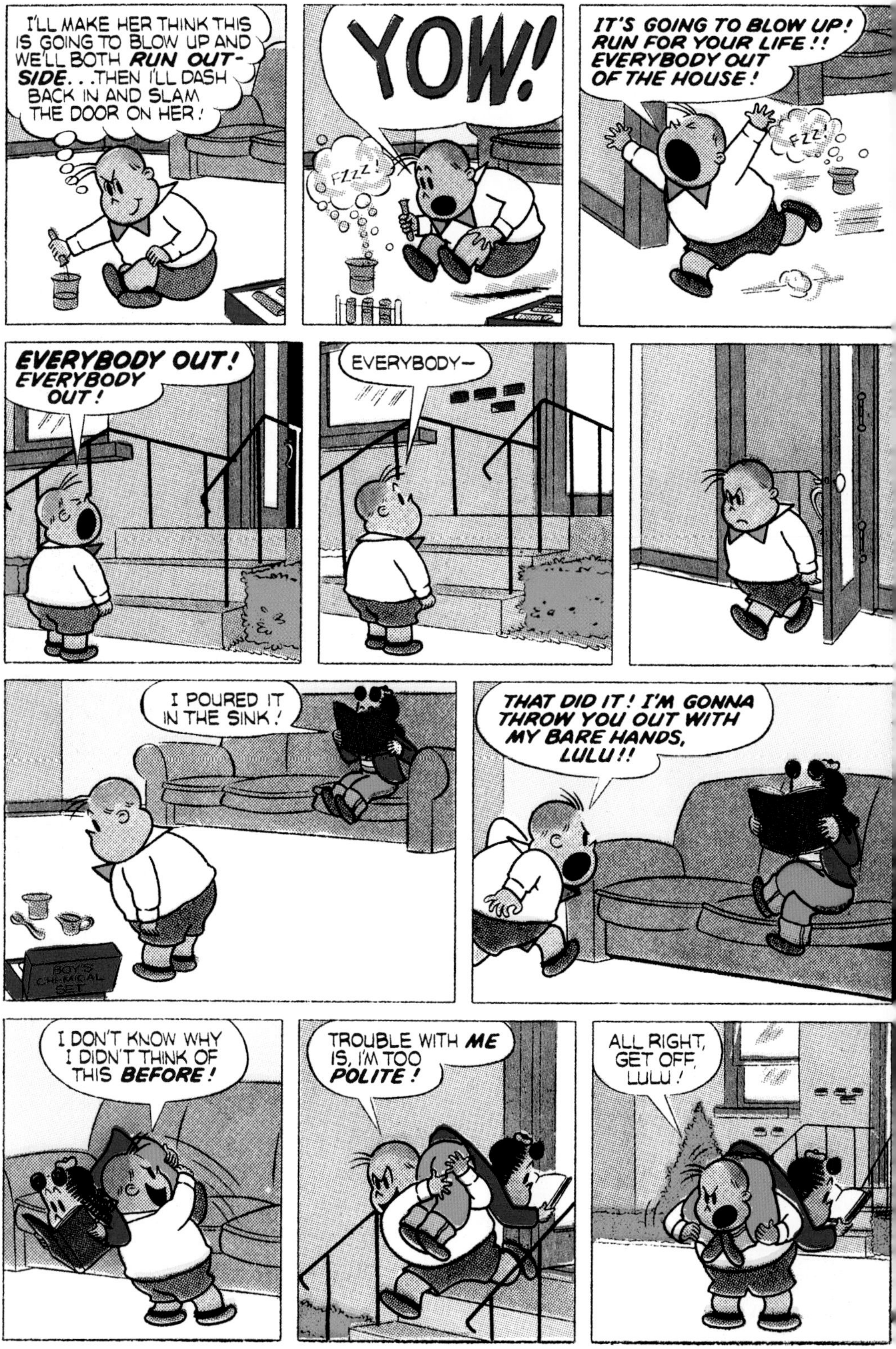
I'LL MAKE HER THINK THIS IS GOING TO BLOW UP AND WE'LL BOTH RUN OUT-SIDE. . .THEN I'LL DASH BACK IN AND SLAM THE DOOR ON HER!
YOW!
FZZZ!
IT'S GOING TO BLOW UP! RUN FOR YOUR LIFE!! EVERYBODY OUT OF THE HOUSE!
FZZ!
EVERYBODY OUT! EVERYBODY OUT!
EVERYBODY—
I POURED IT IN THE SINK!
BOY'S CHEMICAL SET
THAT DID IT! I'M GONNA THROW YOU OUT WITH MY BARE HANDS, LULU!!
I DON'T KNOW WHY I DIDN'T THINK OF THIS BEFORE!
TROUBLE WITH ME IS, I'M TOO POLITE!
ALL RIGHT, GET OFF, LULU!

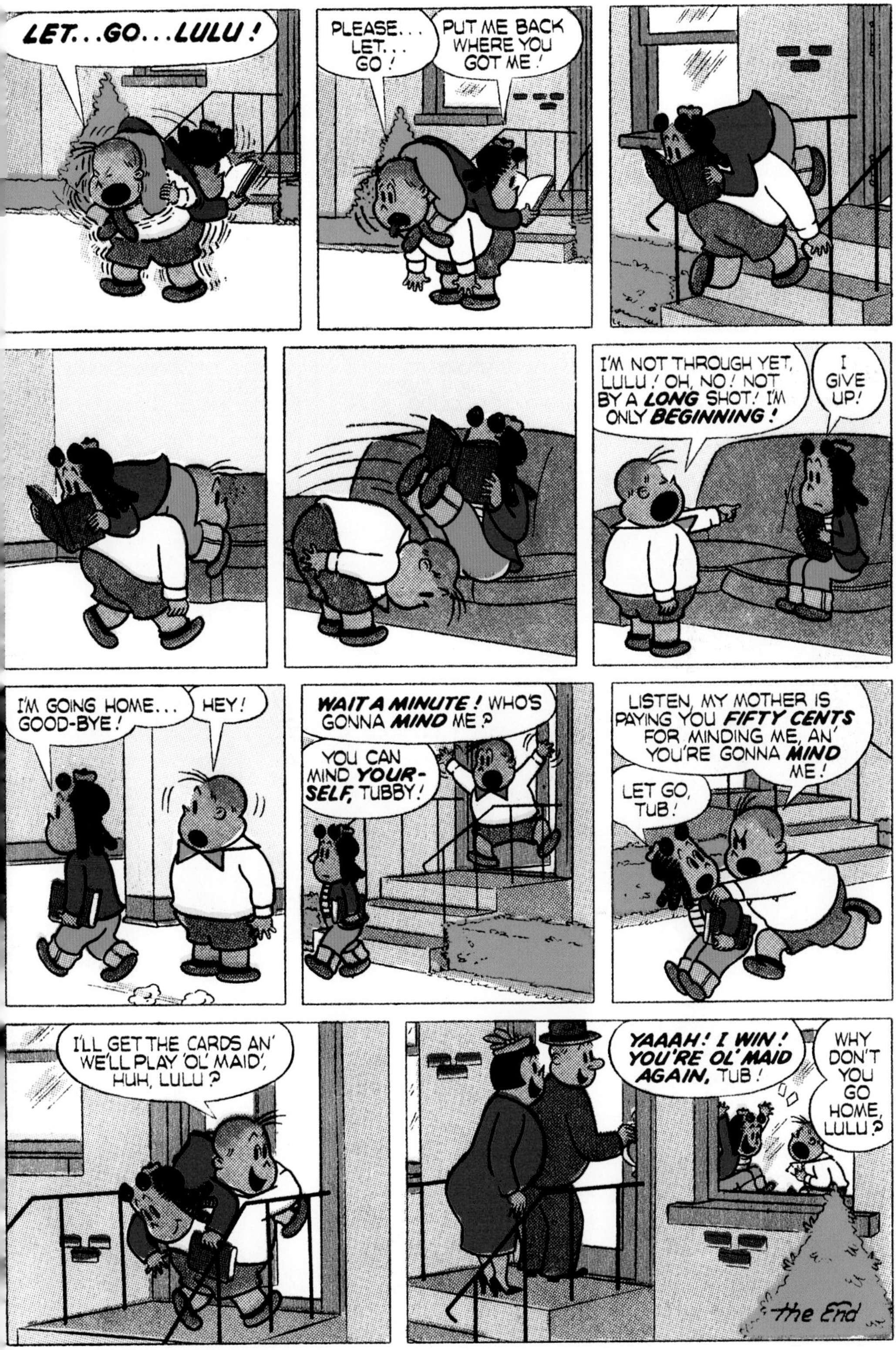
LET...GO...LULU!
PLEASE... LET... GO!
PUT ME BACK WHERE YOU GOT ME!
I'M NOT THROUGH YET, LULU! OH, NO! NOT BY A LONG SHOT! I'M ONLY BEGINNING!
I GIVE UP!
I'M GOING HOME... GOOD-BYE!
HEY!
WAIT A MINUTE! WHO'S GONNA MIND ME?
YOU CAN MIND YOURSELF, TUBBY!
LISTEN, MY MOTHER IS PAYING YOU FIFTY CENTS FOR MINDING ME, AN' YOU'RE GONNA MIND ME!
LET GO, TUB!
I'LL GET THE CARDS AN' WE'LL PLAY 'OL' MAID', HUH, LULU?
YAAAH! I WIN! YOU'RE OL' MAID AGAIN, TUB!
WHY DON'T YOU GO HOME, LULU?
The End

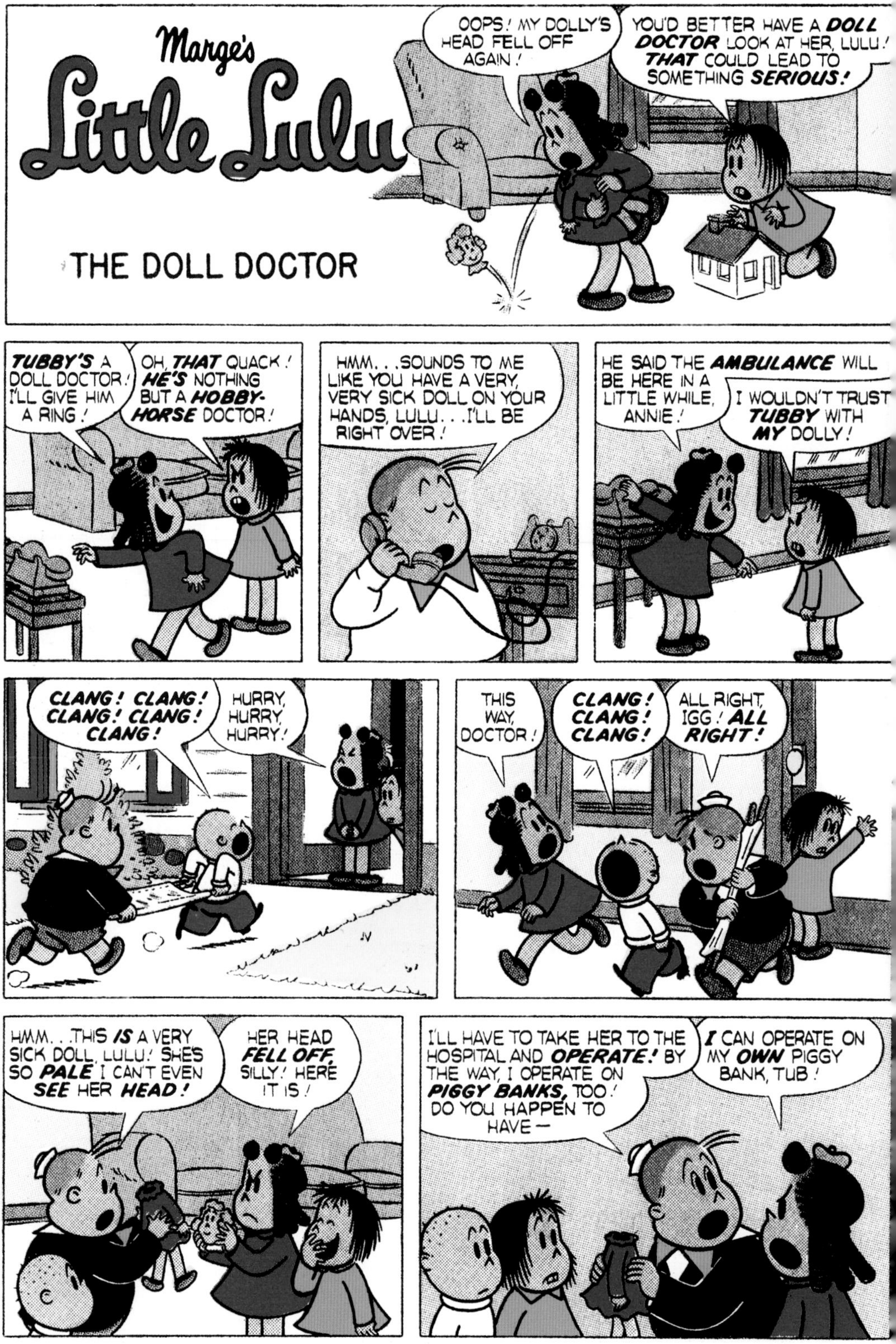
Marge's
Little Lulu
THE DOLL DOCTOR
OOPS! MY DOLLY'S HEAD FELL OFF AGAIN!
YOU'D BETTER HAVE A DOLL DOCTOR LOOK AT HER, LULU! THAT COULD LEAD TO SOMETHING SERIOUS!
TUBBY'S A DOLL DOCTOR! I'LL GIVE HIM A RING!
OH, THAT QUACK! HE'S NOTHING BUT A HOBBY-HORSE DOCTOR!
HMM. . .SOUNDS TO ME LIKE YOU HAVE A VERY, VERY SICK DOLL ON YOUR HANDS, LULU. . .I'LL BE RIGHT OVER!
HE SAID THE AMBULANCE WILL BE HERE IN A LITTLE WHILE, ANNIE!
I WOULDN'T TRUST TUBBY WITH MY DOLLY!
CLANG! CLANG! CLANG! CLANG! CLANG!
HURRY, HURRY, HURRY!
THIS WAY, DOCTOR!
CLANG! CLANG! CLANG!
ALL RIGHT, IGG! ALL RIGHT!
HMM. . .THIS IS A VERY SICK DOLL, LULU! SHE'S SO PALE I CAN'T EVEN SEE HER HEAD!
HER HEAD FELL OFF, SILLY! HERE IT IS!
I'LL HAVE TO TAKE HER TO THE HOSPITAL AND OPERATE! BY THE WAY, I OPERATE ON PIGGY BANKS, TOO! DO YOU HAPPEN TO HAVE —
I CAN OPERATE ON MY OWN PIGGY BANK, TUB!

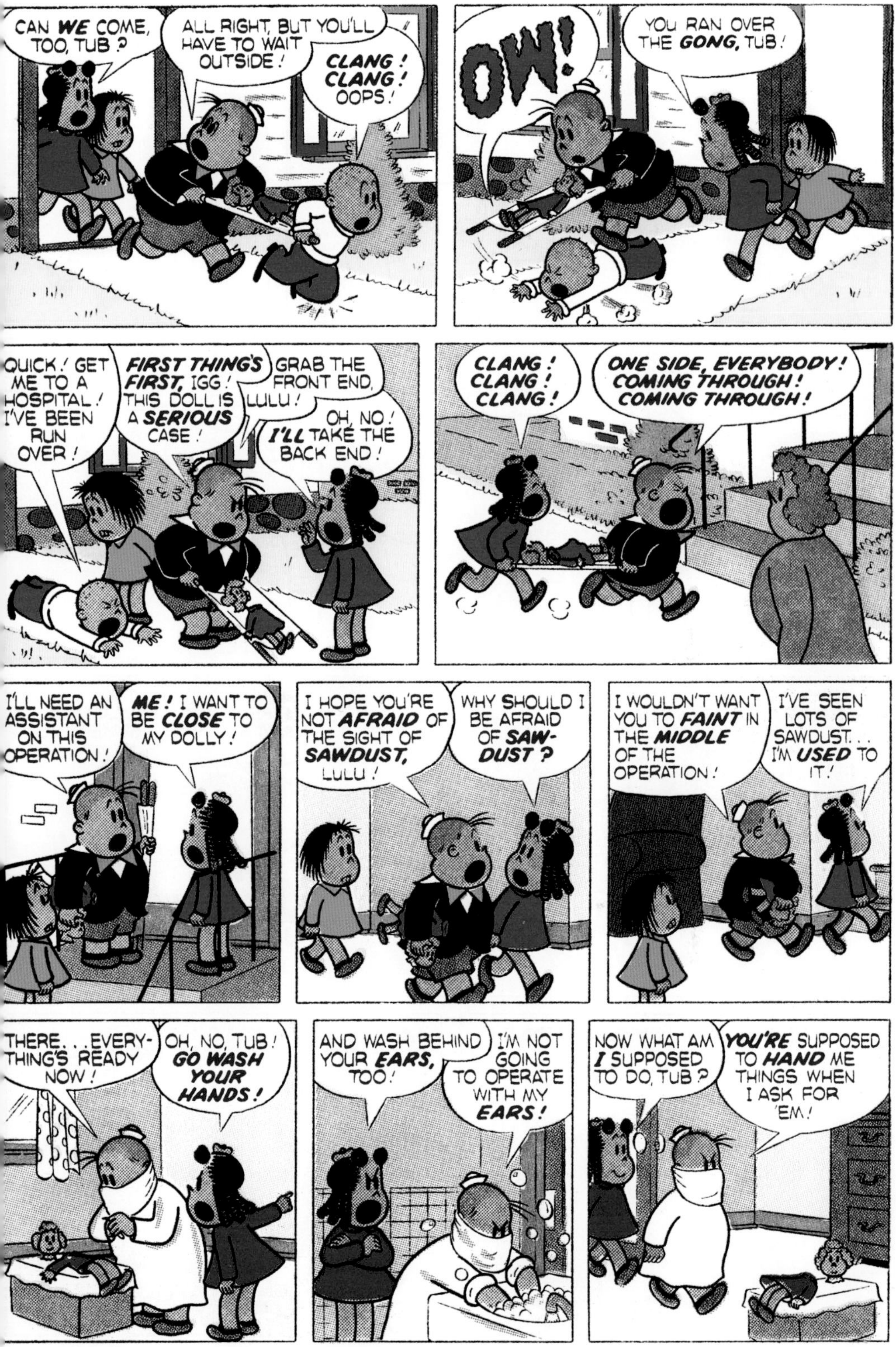
CAN WE COME, TOO, TUB ?
ALL RIGHT, BUT YOU'LL HAVE TO WAIT OUTSIDE!
CLANG! CLANG! OOPS!
OW!
YOU RAN OVER THE GONG, TUB!
QUICK! GET ME TO A HOSPITAL! I'VE BEEN RUN OVER!
FIRST THING'S FIRST, IGG! THIS DOLL IS A SERIOUS CASE!
GRAB THE FRONT END, LULU!
OH, NO! I'LL TAKE THE BACK END!
CLANG! CLANG! CLANG!
ONE SIDE, EVERYBODY! COMING THROUGH! COMING THROUGH!
I'LL NEED AN ASSISTANT ON THIS OPERATION!
ME! I WANT TO BE CLOSE TO MY DOLLY!
I HOPE YOU'RE NOT AFRAID OF THE SIGHT OF SAWDUST, LULU!
WHY SHOULD I BE AFRAID OF SAW-DUST ?
I WOULDN'T WANT YOU TO FAINT IN THE MIDDLE OF THE OPERATION!
I'VE SEEN LOTS OF SAWDUST... I'M USED TO IT!
THERE...EVERY-THING'S READY NOW!
OH, NO, TUB! GO WASH YOUR HANDS!
AND WASH BEHIND YOUR EARS, TOO!
I'M NOT GOING TO OPERATE WITH MY EARS!
NOW WHAT AM I SUPPOSED TO DO, TUB ?
YOU'RE SUPPOSED TO HAND ME THINGS WHEN I ASK FOR 'EM!

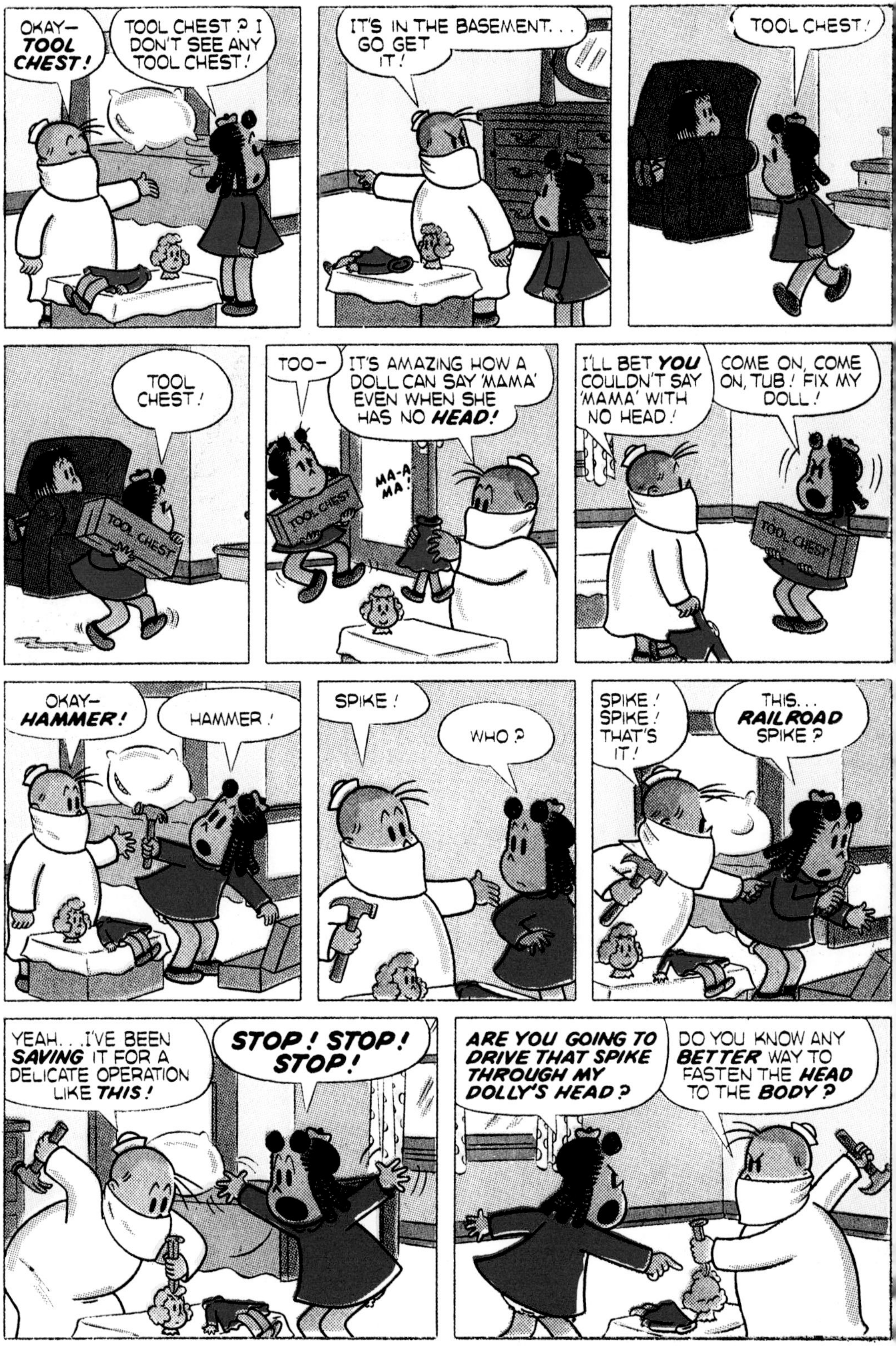

OKAY— TOOL CHEST!
TOOL CHEST? I DON'T SEE ANY TOOL CHEST!
IT'S IN THE BASEMENT... GO GET IT!
TOOL CHEST!
TOOL CHEST!
TOOL CHEST
TOO—
IT'S AMAZING HOW A DOLL CAN SAY 'MAMA' EVEN WHEN SHE HAS NO HEAD!
MA-A MA!
TOOL CHEST
I'LL BET YOU COULDN'T SAY 'MAMA' WITH NO HEAD!
COME ON, COME ON, TUB! FIX MY DOLL!
TOOL CHEST
OKAY— HAMMER!
HAMMER!
SPIKE!
WHO?
SPIKE! SPIKE! THAT'S IT!
THIS... RAILROAD SPIKE?
YEAH... I'VE BEEN SAVING IT FOR A DELICATE OPERATION LIKE THIS!
STOP! STOP! STOP!
ARE YOU GOING TO DRIVE THAT SPIKE THROUGH MY DOLLY'S HEAD?
DO YOU KNOW ANY BETTER WAY TO FASTEN THE HEAD TO THE BODY?

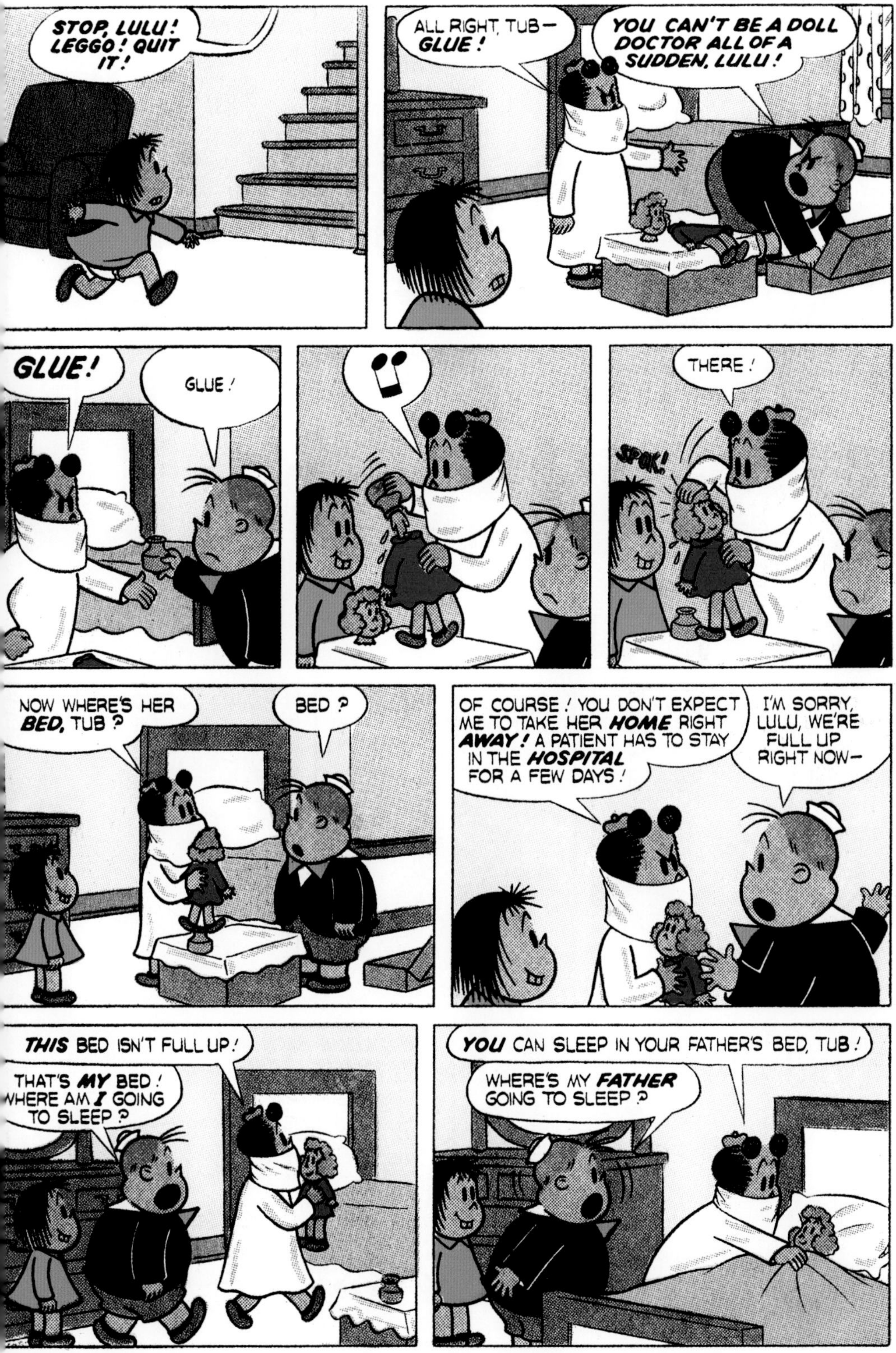
STOP, LULU! LEGGO! QUIT IT!
ALL RIGHT, TUB— GLUE!
YOU CAN'T BE A DOLL DOCTOR ALL OF A SUDDEN, LULU!
GLUE!
GLUE!
THERE!
SPOK!
NOW WHERE'S HER BED, TUB?
BED?
OF COURSE! YOU DON'T EXPECT ME TO TAKE HER HOME RIGHT AWAY! A PATIENT HAS TO STAY IN THE HOSPITAL FOR A FEW DAYS!
I'M SORRY, LULU, WE'RE FULL UP RIGHT NOW—
THIS BED ISN'T FULL UP!
THAT'S MY BED! WHERE AM I GOING TO SLEEP?
YOU CAN SLEEP IN YOUR FATHER'S BED, TUB!
WHERE'S MY FATHER GOING TO SLEEP?

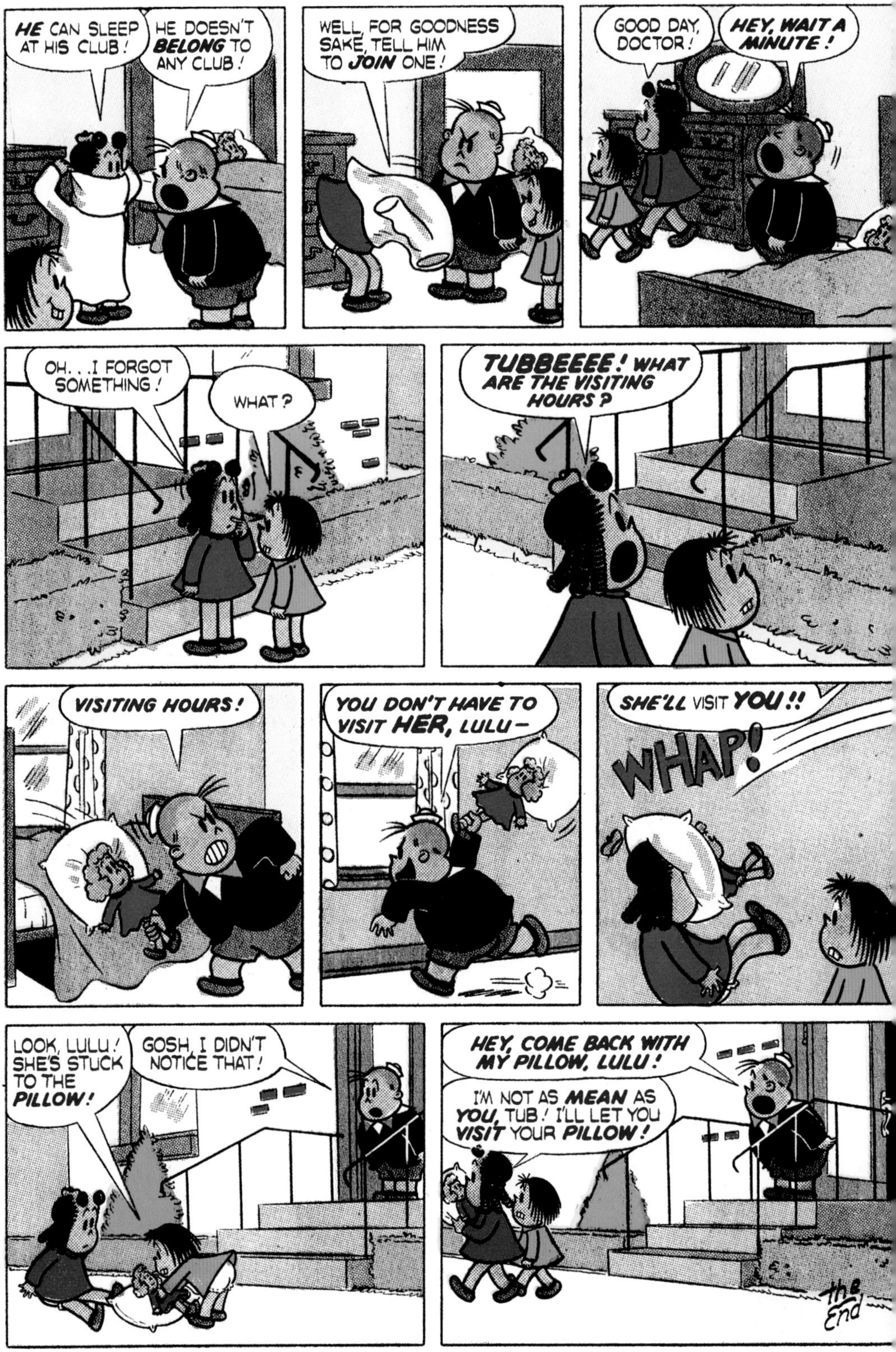

HE CAN SLEEP AT HIS CLUB!
HE DOESN'T BELONG TO ANY CLUB!
WELL, FOR GOODNESS SAKE, TELL HIM TO JOIN ONE!
GOOD DAY, DOCTOR!
HEY, WAIT A MINUTE!
OH...I FORGOT SOMETHING!
WHAT?
TUBBEEEE! WHAT ARE THE VISITING HOURS?
VISITING HOURS!
YOU DON'T HAVE TO VISIT HER, LULU—
SHE'LL VISIT YOU!!
WHAP!
LOOK, LULU! SHE'S STUCK TO THE PILLOW!
GOSH, I DIDN'T NOTICE THAT!
HEY, COME BACK WITH MY PILLOW, LULU!
I'M NOT AS MEAN AS YOU, TUB! I'LL LET YOU VISIT YOUR PILLOW!
the End

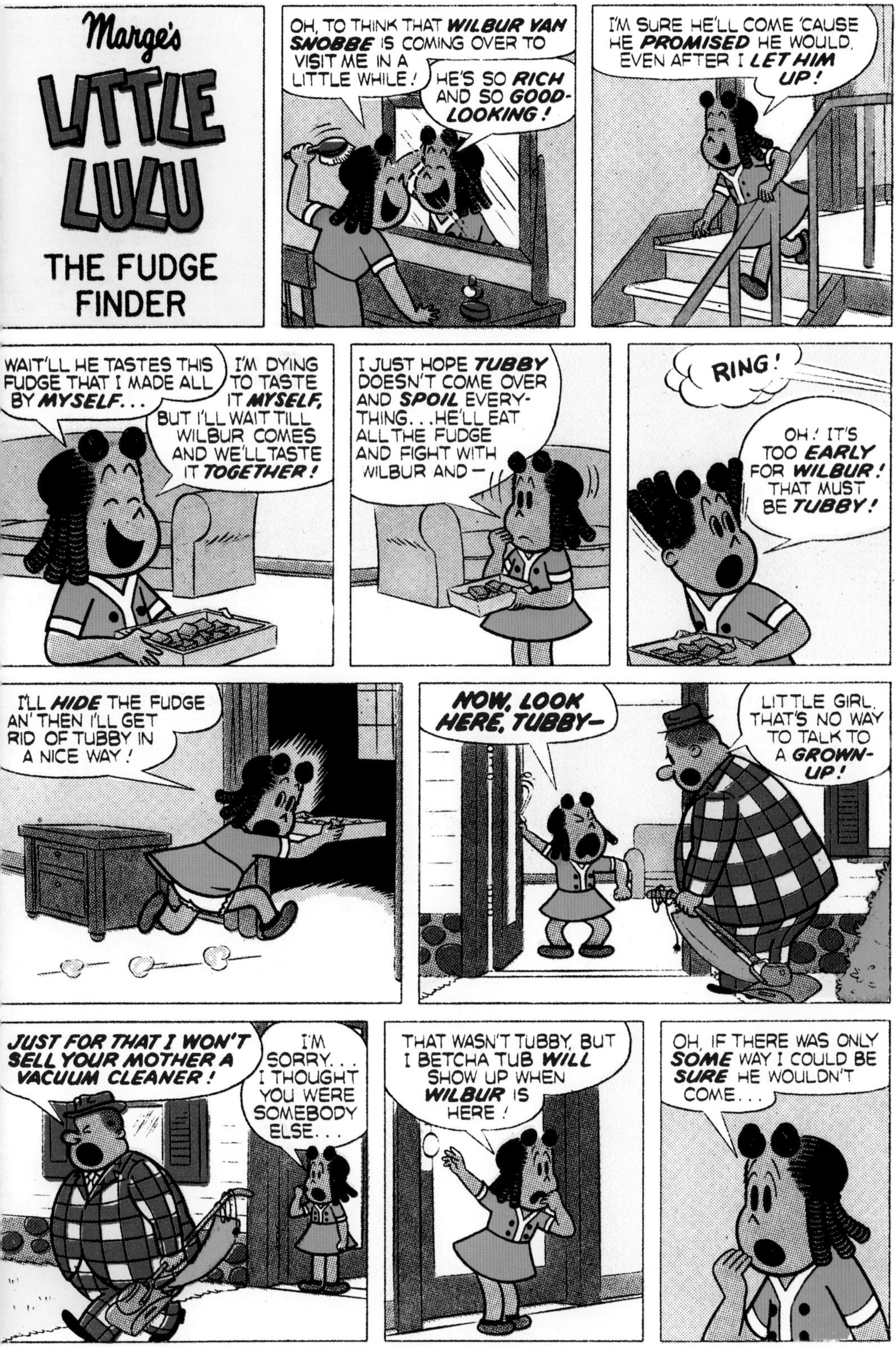
Marge's
LITTLE LULU
THE FUDGE FINDER
OH, TO THINK THAT WILBUR VAN SNOBBE IS COMING OVER TO VISIT ME IN A LITTLE WHILE!
HE'S SO RICH AND SO GOOD-LOOKING!
I'M SURE HE'LL COME 'CAUSE HE PROMISED HE WOULD, EVEN AFTER I LET HIM UP!
WAIT'LL HE TASTES THIS FUDGE THAT I MADE ALL BY MYSELF...
I'M DYING TO TASTE IT MYSELF, BUT I'LL WAIT TILL WILBUR COMES AND WE'LL TASTE IT TOGETHER!
I JUST HOPE TUBBY DOESN'T COME OVER AND SPOIL EVERYTHING...HE'LL EAT ALL THE FUDGE AND FIGHT WITH WILBUR AND—
RING!
OH! IT'S TOO EARLY FOR WILBUR! THAT MUST BE TUBBY!
I'LL HIDE THE FUDGE AN' THEN I'LL GET RID OF TUBBY IN A NICE WAY!
NOW, LOOK HERE, TUBBY—
LITTLE GIRL, THAT'S NO WAY TO TALK TO A GROWN-UP!
JUST FOR THAT I WON'T SELL YOUR MOTHER A VACUUM CLEANER!
I'M SORRY... I THOUGHT YOU WERE SOMEBODY ELSE...
THAT WASN'T TUBBY, BUT I BETCHA TUB WILL SHOW UP WHEN WILBUR IS HERE!
OH, IF THERE WAS ONLY SOME WAY I COULD BE SURE HE WOULDN'T COME...

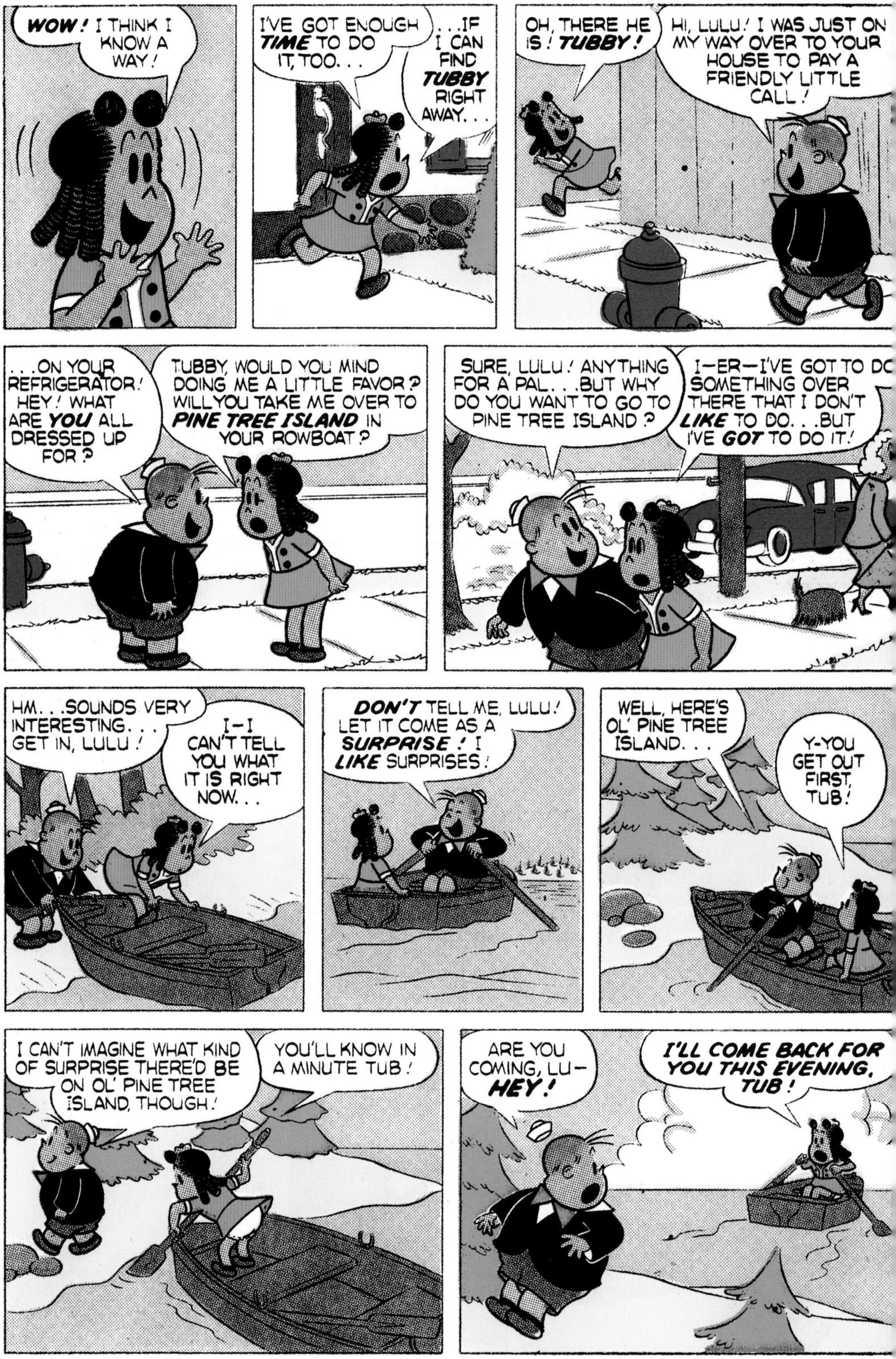
WOW! I THINK I KNOW A WAY!
I'VE GOT ENOUGH TIME TO DO IT, TOO...
...IF I CAN FIND TUBBY RIGHT AWAY...
OH, THERE HE IS! TUBBY!
HI, LULU! I WAS JUST ON MY WAY OVER TO YOUR HOUSE TO PAY A FRIENDLY LITTLE CALL!
...ON YOUR REFRIGERATOR! HEY! WHAT ARE YOU ALL DRESSED UP FOR?
TUBBY, WOULD YOU MIND DOING ME A LITTLE FAVOR? WILL YOU TAKE ME OVER TO PINE TREE ISLAND IN YOUR ROWBOAT?
SURE, LULU! ANYTHING FOR A PAL...BUT WHY DO YOU WANT TO GO TO PINE TREE ISLAND?
I—ER—I'VE GOT TO DO SOMETHING OVER THERE THAT I DON'T LIKE TO DO...BUT I'VE GOT TO DO IT!
HM...SOUNDS VERY INTERESTING... GET IN, LULU!
I—I CAN'T TELL YOU WHAT IT IS RIGHT NOW...
DON'T TELL ME, LULU! LET IT COME AS A SURPRISE! I LIKE SURPRISES!
WELL, HERE'S OL' PINE TREE ISLAND...
Y-YOU GET OUT FIRST, TUB!
I CAN'T IMAGINE WHAT KIND OF SURPRISE THERE'D BE ON OL' PINE TREE ISLAND, THOUGH!
YOU'LL KNOW IN A MINUTE TUB!
ARE YOU COMING, LU— HEY!
I'LL COME BACK FOR YOU THIS EVENING, TUB!

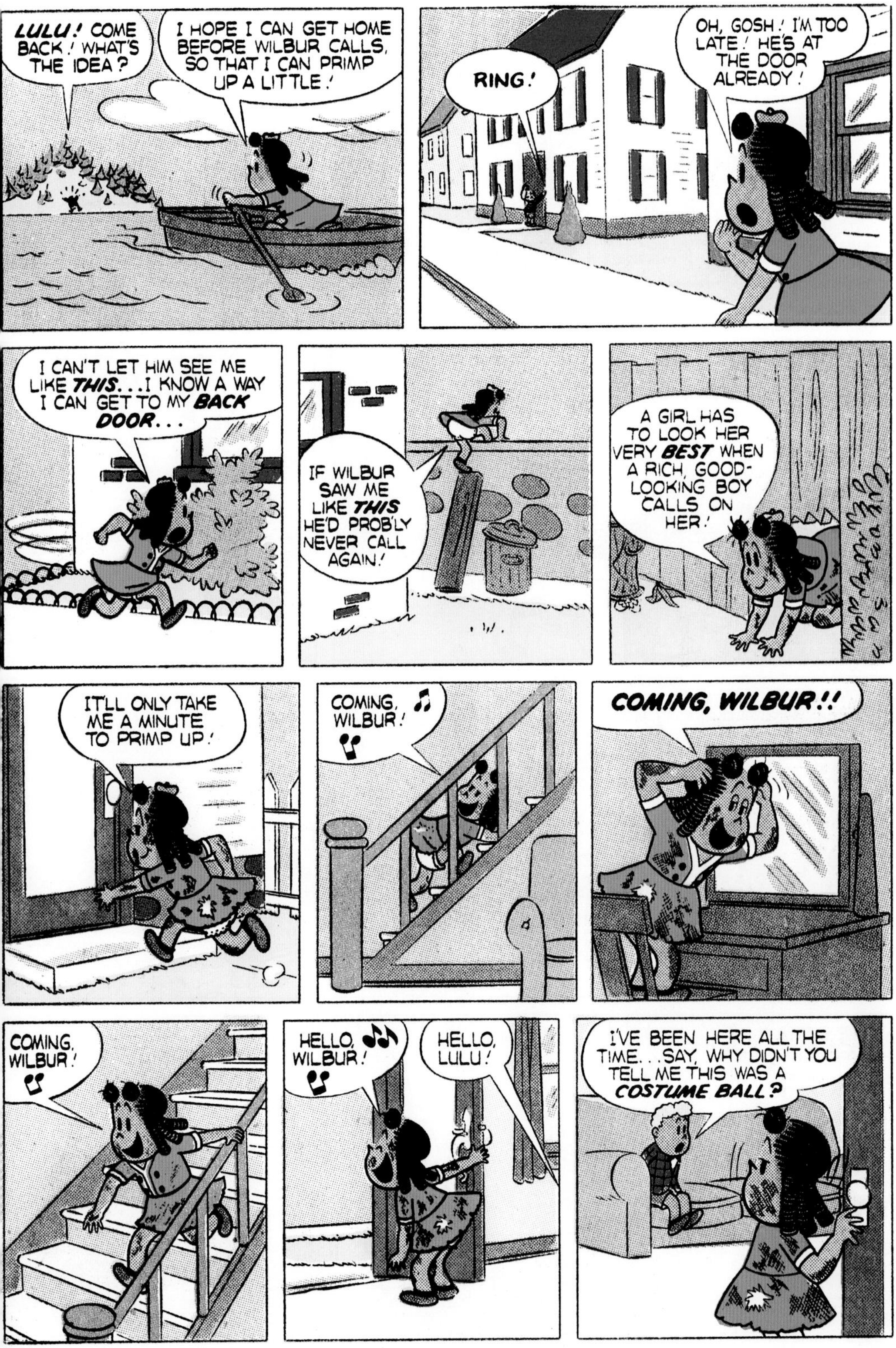
LULU! COME BACK! WHAT'S THE IDEA?
I HOPE I CAN GET HOME BEFORE WILBUR CALLS, SO THAT I CAN PRIMP UP A LITTLE!
RING!
OH, GOSH! I'M TOO LATE! HE'S AT THE DOOR ALREADY!
I CAN'T LET HIM SEE ME LIKE THIS...I KNOW A WAY I CAN GET TO MY BACK DOOR...
IF WILBUR SAW ME LIKE THIS HE'D PROB'LY NEVER CALL AGAIN!
A GIRL HAS TO LOOK HER VERY BEST WHEN A RICH, GOOD-LOOKING BOY CALLS ON HER!
IT'LL ONLY TAKE ME A MINUTE TO PRIMP UP!
COMING, WILBUR!
COMING, WILBUR!!
COMING, WILBUR!
HELLO, WILBUR!
HELLO, LULU!
I'VE BEEN HERE ALL THE TIME...SAY, WHY DIDN'T YOU TELL ME THIS WAS A COSTUME BALL?

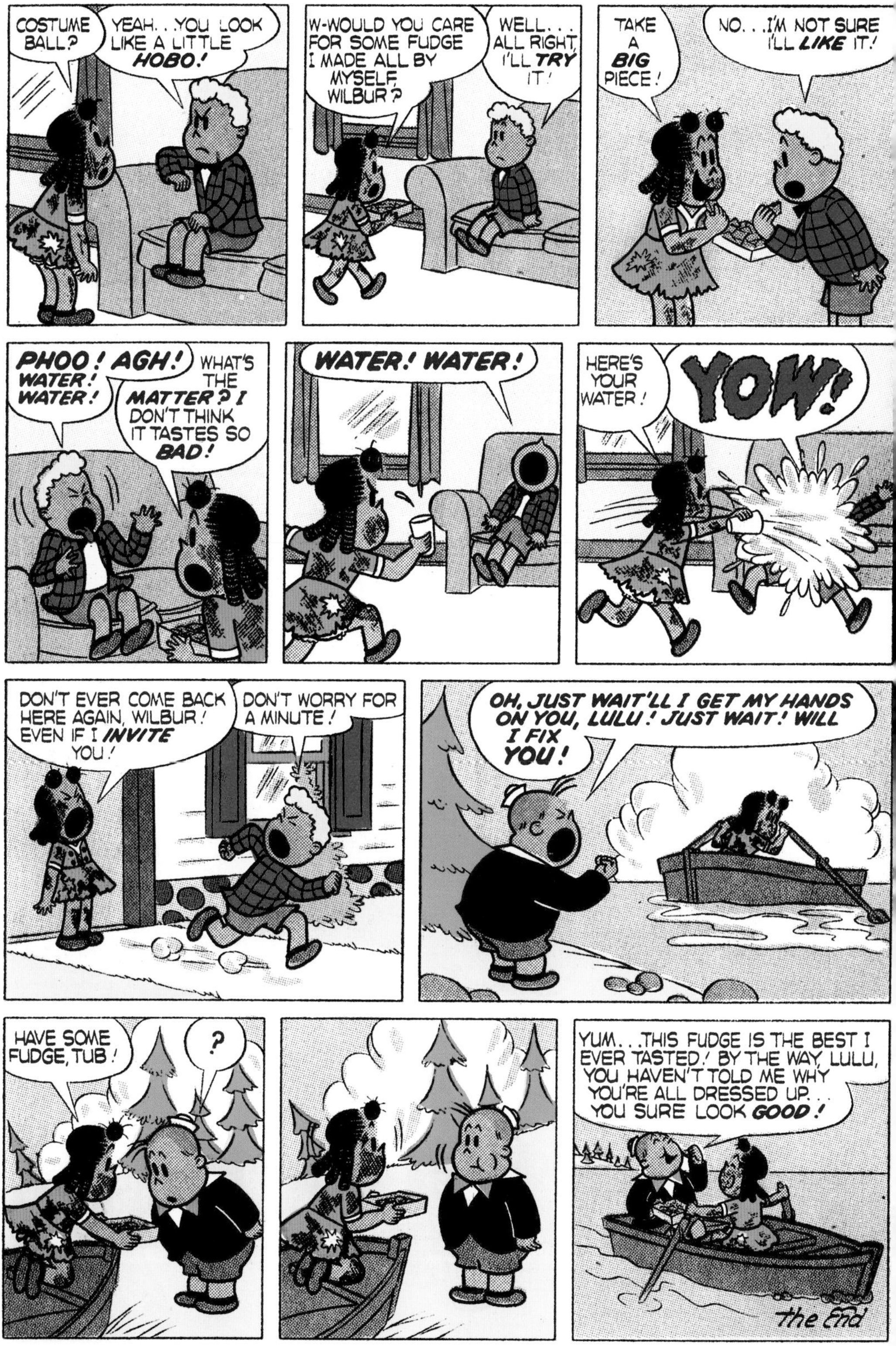

COSTUME BALL?
YEAH. . .YOU LOOK LIKE A LITTLE HOBO!
W-WOULD YOU CARE FOR SOME FUDGE I MADE ALL BY MYSELF, WILBUR?
WELL. . . ALL RIGHT, I'LL TRY IT!
TAKE A BIG PIECE!
NO. . .I'M NOT SURE I'LL LIKE IT!
PHOO! AGH! WATER! WATER!
WHAT'S THE MATTER? I DON'T THINK IT TASTES SO BAD!
WATER! WATER!
HERE'S YOUR WATER!
YOW!
DON'T EVER COME BACK HERE AGAIN, WILBUR! EVEN IF I INVITE YOU!
DON'T WORRY FOR A MINUTE!
OH, JUST WAIT'LL I GET MY HANDS ON YOU, LULU! JUST WAIT! WILL I FIX YOU!
HAVE SOME FUDGE, TUB!
?
YUM. . .THIS FUDGE IS THE BEST I EVER TASTED! BY THE WAY, LULU, YOU HAVEN'T TOLD ME WHY YOU'RE ALL DRESSED UP. . . YOU SURE LOOK GOOD!
the End

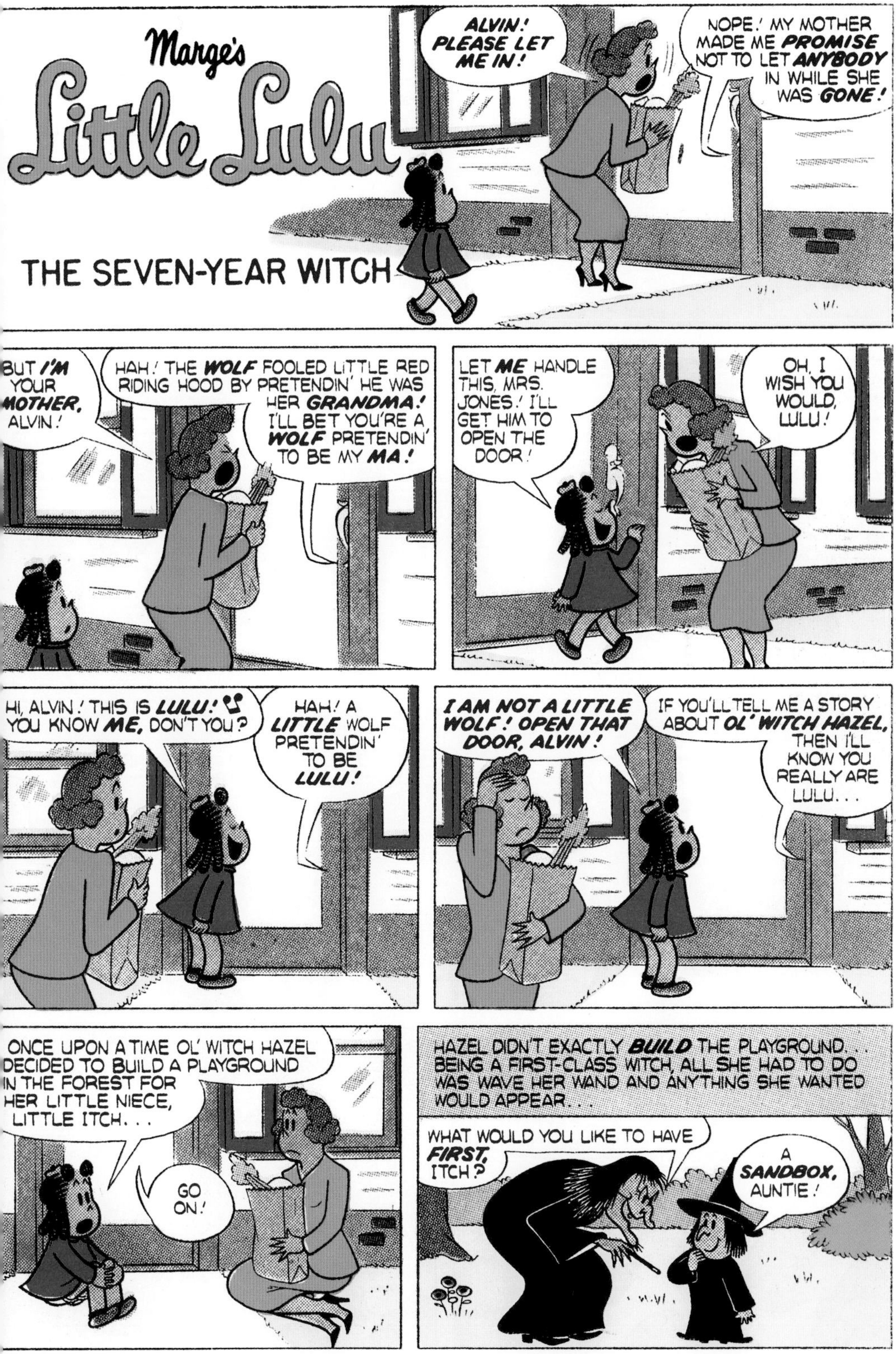
Marge's Little Lulu
THE SEVEN-YEAR WITCH
ALVIN! PLEASE LET ME IN!
NOPE! MY MOTHER MADE ME PROMISE NOT TO LET ANYBODY IN WHILE SHE WAS GONE!
BUT I'M YOUR MOTHER, ALVIN!
HAH! THE WOLF FOOLED LITTLE RED RIDING HOOD BY PRETENDIN' HE WAS HER GRANDMA! I'LL BET YOU'RE A WOLF PRETENDIN' TO BE MY MA!
LET ME HANDLE THIS, MRS. JONES! I'LL GET HIM TO OPEN THE DOOR!
OH, I WISH YOU WOULD, LULU!
HI, ALVIN! THIS IS LULU! YOU KNOW ME, DON'T YOU?
HAH! A LITTLE WOLF PRETENDIN' TO BE LULU!
I AM NOT A LITTLE WOLF! OPEN THAT DOOR, ALVIN!
IF YOU'LL TELL ME A STORY ABOUT OL' WITCH HAZEL, THEN I'LL KNOW YOU REALLY ARE LULU...
ONCE UPON A TIME OL' WITCH HAZEL DECIDED TO BUILD A PLAYGROUND IN THE FOREST FOR HER LITTLE NIECE, LITTLE ITCH...
GO ON!
HAZEL DIDN'T EXACTLY BUILD THE PLAYGROUND... BEING A FIRST-CLASS WITCH, ALL SHE HAD TO DO WAS WAVE HER WAND AND ANYTHING SHE WANTED WOULD APPEAR...
WHAT WOULD YOU LIKE TO HAVE FIRST, ITCH?
A SANDBOX, AUNTIE!

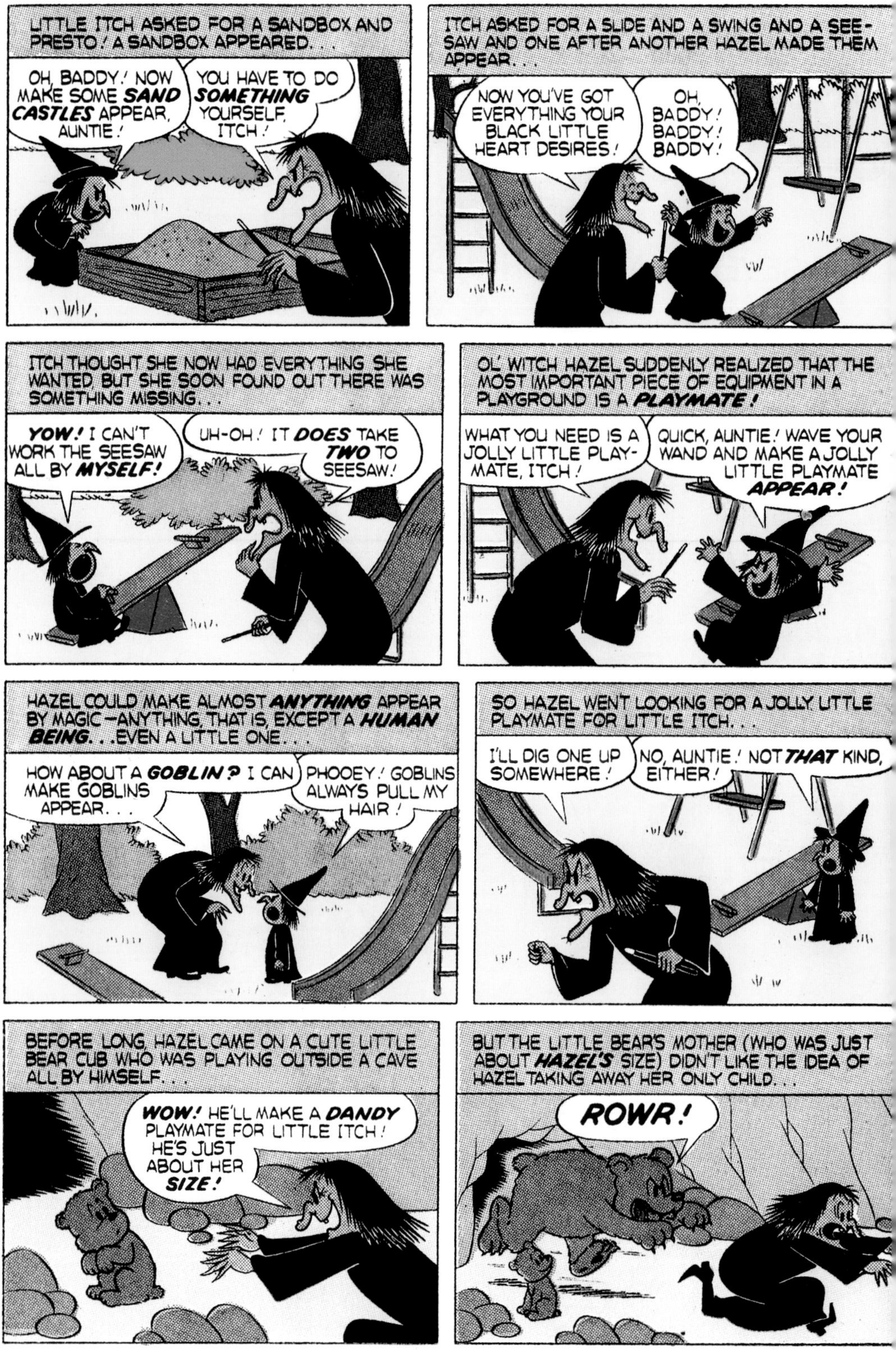
LITTLE ITCH ASKED FOR A SANDBOX AND PRESTO! A SANDBOX APPEARED. . .
OH, BADDY! NOW MAKE SOME SAND CASTLES APPEAR, AUNTIE!
YOU HAVE TO DO SOMETHING YOURSELF, ITCH!
ITCH ASKED FOR A SLIDE AND A SWING AND A SEE-SAW AND ONE AFTER ANOTHER HAZEL MADE THEM APPEAR. . .
NOW YOU'VE GOT EVERYTHING YOUR BLACK LITTLE HEART DESIRES!
OH, BADDY! BADDY! BADDY!
ITCH THOUGHT SHE NOW HAD EVERYTHING SHE WANTED, BUT SHE SOON FOUND OUT THERE WAS SOMETHING MISSING. . .
YOW! I CAN'T WORK THE SEESAW ALL BY MYSELF!
UH-OH! IT DOES TAKE TWO TO SEESAW!
OL' WITCH HAZEL SUDDENLY REALIZED THAT THE MOST IMPORTANT PIECE OF EQUIPMENT IN A PLAYGROUND IS A PLAYMATE!
WHAT YOU NEED IS A JOLLY LITTLE PLAY-MATE, ITCH!
QUICK, AUNTIE! WAVE YOUR WAND AND MAKE A JOLLY LITTLE PLAYMATE APPEAR!
HAZEL COULD MAKE ALMOST ANYTHING APPEAR BY MAGIC—ANYTHING, THAT IS, EXCEPT A HUMAN BEING. . . EVEN A LITTLE ONE. . .
HOW ABOUT A GOBLIN? I CAN MAKE GOBLINS APPEAR. . .
PHOOEY! GOBLINS ALWAYS PULL MY HAIR!
SO HAZEL WENT LOOKING FOR A JOLLY LITTLE PLAYMATE FOR LITTLE ITCH. . .
I'LL DIG ONE UP SOMEWHERE!
NO, AUNTIE! NOT THAT KIND, EITHER!
BEFORE LONG, HAZEL CAME ON A CUTE LITTLE BEAR CUB WHO WAS PLAYING OUTSIDE A CAVE ALL BY HIMSELF. . .
WOW! HE'LL MAKE A DANDY PLAYMATE FOR LITTLE ITCH! HE'S JUST ABOUT HER SIZE!
BUT THE LITTLE BEAR'S MOTHER (WHO WAS JUST ABOUT HAZEL'S SIZE) DIDN'T LIKE THE IDEA OF HAZEL TAKING AWAY HER ONLY CHILD. . .
ROWR!

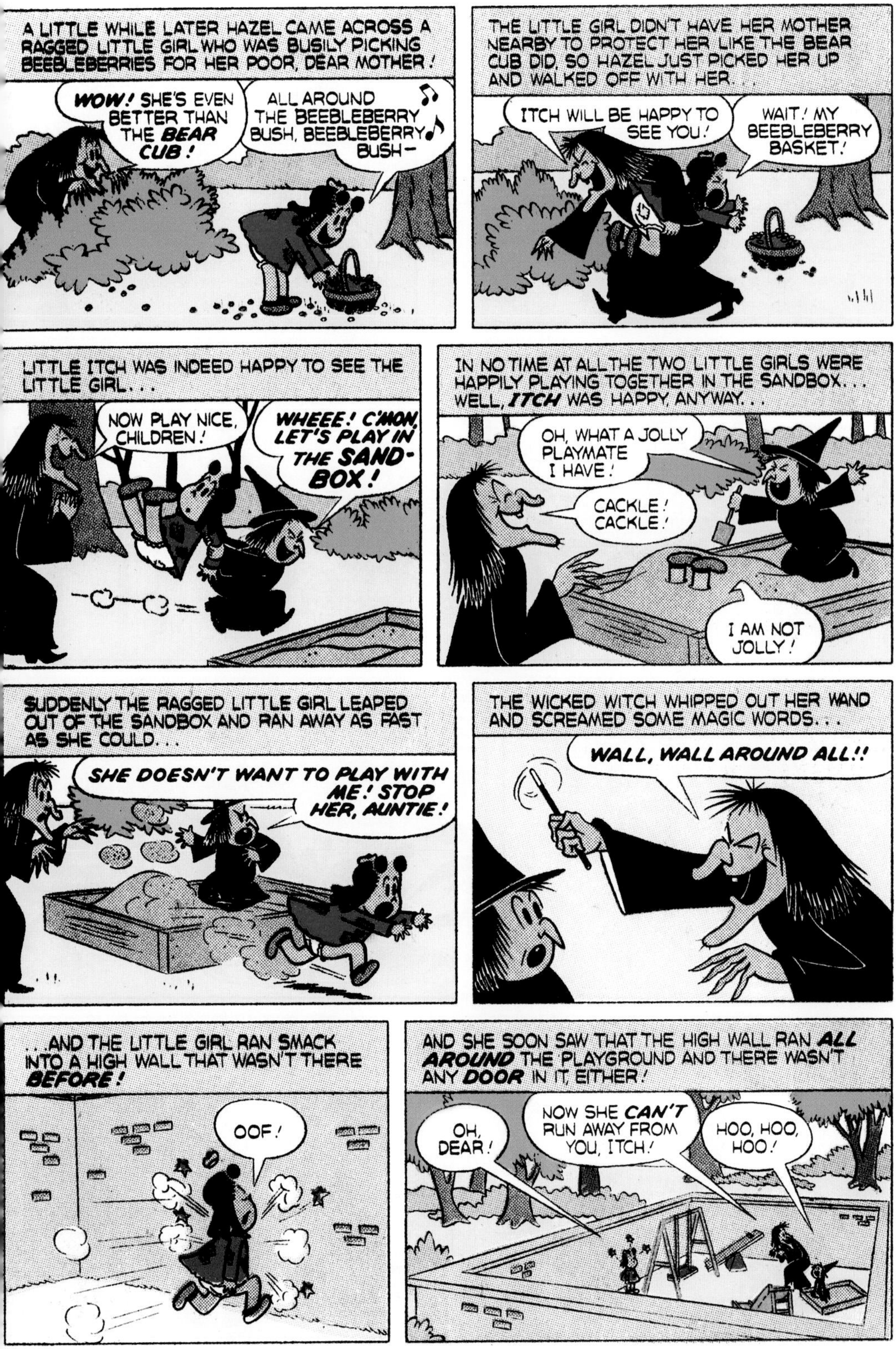
A LITTLE WHILE LATER HAZEL CAME ACROSS A RAGGED LITTLE GIRL WHO WAS BUSILY PICKING BEEBLEBERRIES FOR HER POOR, DEAR MOTHER!
WOW! SHE'S EVEN BETTER THAN THE BEAR CUB!
ALL AROUND THE BEEBLEBERRY BUSH, BEEBLEBERRY BUSH—
THE LITTLE GIRL DIDN'T HAVE HER MOTHER NEARBY TO PROTECT HER LIKE THE BEAR CUB DID, SO HAZEL JUST PICKED HER UP AND WALKED OFF WITH HER...
ITCH WILL BE HAPPY TO SEE YOU!
WAIT! MY BEEBLEBERRY BASKET!
LITTLE ITCH WAS INDEED HAPPY TO SEE THE LITTLE GIRL...
NOW PLAY NICE, CHILDREN!
WHEEE! C'MON, LET'S PLAY IN THE SAND-BOX!
IN NO TIME AT ALL THE TWO LITTLE GIRLS WERE HAPPILY PLAYING TOGETHER IN THE SANDBOX... WELL, ITCH WAS HAPPY, ANYWAY...
OH, WHAT A JOLLY PLAYMATE I HAVE!
CACKLE! CACKLE!
I AM NOT JOLLY!
SUDDENLY THE RAGGED LITTLE GIRL LEAPED OUT OF THE SANDBOX AND RAN AWAY AS FAST AS SHE COULD...
SHE DOESN'T WANT TO PLAY WITH ME! STOP HER, AUNTIE!
THE WICKED WITCH WHIPPED OUT HER WAND AND SCREAMED SOME MAGIC WORDS...
WALL, WALL AROUND ALL!!
...AND THE LITTLE GIRL RAN SMACK INTO A HIGH WALL THAT WASN'T THERE BEFORE!
OOF!
AND SHE SOON SAW THAT THE HIGH WALL RAN ALL AROUND THE PLAYGROUND AND THERE WASN'T ANY DOOR IN IT, EITHER!
OH, DEAR!
NOW SHE CAN'T RUN AWAY FROM YOU, ITCH!
HOO, HOO, HOO!

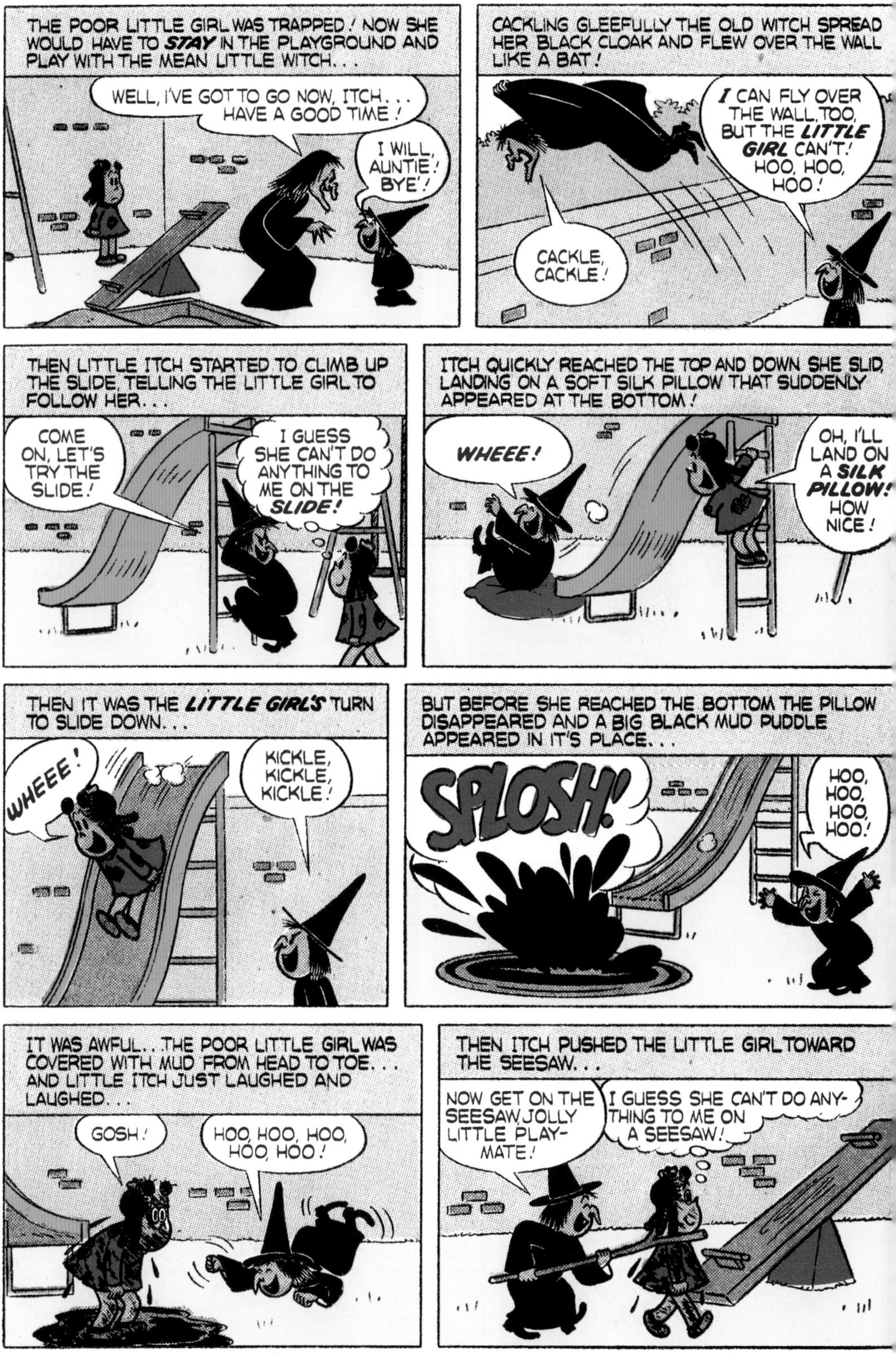

THE POOR LITTLE GIRL WAS TRAPPED! NOW SHE WOULD HAVE TO *STAY* IN THE PLAYGROUND AND PLAY WITH THE MEAN LITTLE WITCH. . .
WELL, I'VE GOT TO GO NOW, ITCH. . . HAVE A GOOD TIME!
I WILL, AUNTIE! BYE!
CACKLING GLEEFULLY THE OLD WITCH SPREAD HER BLACK CLOAK AND FLEW OVER THE WALL LIKE A BAT!
CACKLE, CACKLE!
*I* CAN FLY OVER THE WALL, TOO, BUT THE *LITTLE GIRL* CAN'T! HOO, HOO, HOO!
THEN LITTLE ITCH STARTED TO CLIMB UP THE SLIDE, TELLING THE LITTLE GIRL TO FOLLOW HER. . .
COME ON, LET'S TRY THE SLIDE!
I GUESS SHE CAN'T DO ANYTHING TO ME ON THE *SLIDE!*
ITCH QUICKLY REACHED THE TOP AND DOWN SHE SLID, LANDING ON A SOFT SILK PILLOW THAT SUDDENLY APPEARED AT THE BOTTOM!
*WHEEE!*
OH, I'LL LAND ON A *SILK PILLOW!* HOW NICE!
THEN IT WAS THE *LITTLE GIRL'S* TURN TO SLIDE DOWN. . .
WHEEE!
KICKLE, KICKLE, KICKLE!
BUT BEFORE SHE REACHED THE BOTTOM THE PILLOW DISAPPEARED AND A BIG BLACK MUD PUDDLE APPEARED IN IT'S PLACE. . .
SPLOSH!
HOO, HOO, HOO, HOO!
IT WAS AWFUL. . THE POOR LITTLE GIRL WAS COVERED WITH MUD FROM HEAD TO TOE. . . AND LITTLE ITCH JUST LAUGHED AND LAUGHED. . .
GOSH!
HOO, HOO, HOO, HOO, HOO!
THEN ITCH PUSHED THE LITTLE GIRL TOWARD THE SEESAW. . .
NOW GET ON THE SEESAW, JOLLY LITTLE PLAY-MATE!
I GUESS SHE CAN'T DO ANY-THING TO ME ON A SEESAW!

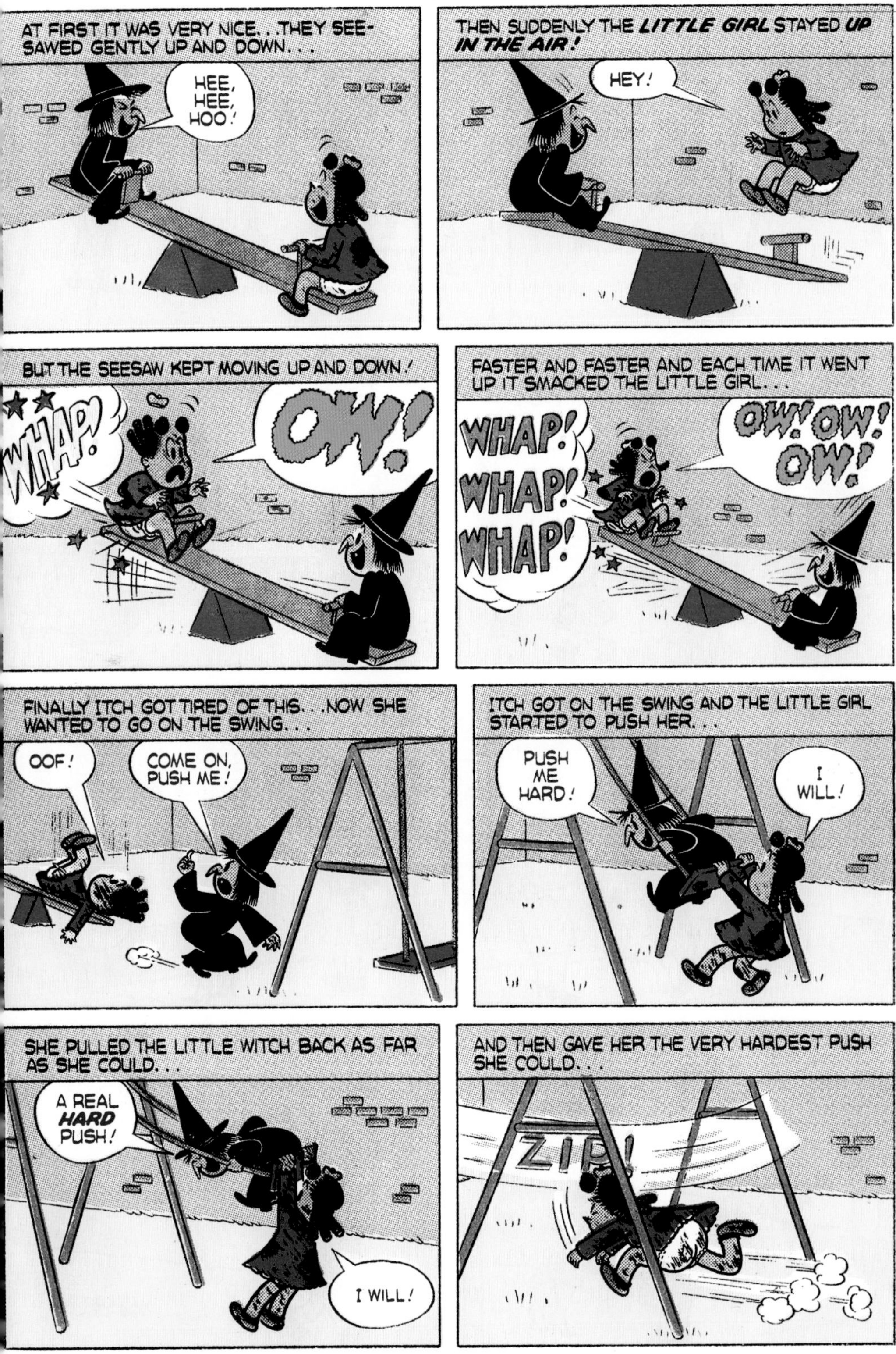
AT FIRST IT WAS VERY NICE. . .THEY SEE-SAWED GENTLY UP AND DOWN. . .
HEE, HEE, HOO!
THEN SUDDENLY THE LITTLE GIRL STAYED UP IN THE AIR!
HEY!
BUT THE SEESAW KEPT MOVING UP AND DOWN!
WHAP!
OW!
FASTER AND FASTER AND EACH TIME IT WENT UP IT SMACKED THE LITTLE GIRL. . .
WHAP! WHAP! WHAP!
OW! OW! OW!
FINALLY ITCH GOT TIRED OF THIS. . .NOW SHE WANTED TO GO ON THE SWING. . .
OOF!
COME ON, PUSH ME!
ITCH GOT ON THE SWING AND THE LITTLE GIRL STARTED TO PUSH HER. . .
PUSH ME HARD!
I WILL!
SHE PULLED THE LITTLE WITCH BACK AS FAR AS SHE COULD. . .
A REAL HARD PUSH!
I WILL!
AND THEN GAVE HER THE VERY HARDEST PUSH SHE COULD. . .
ZIP!

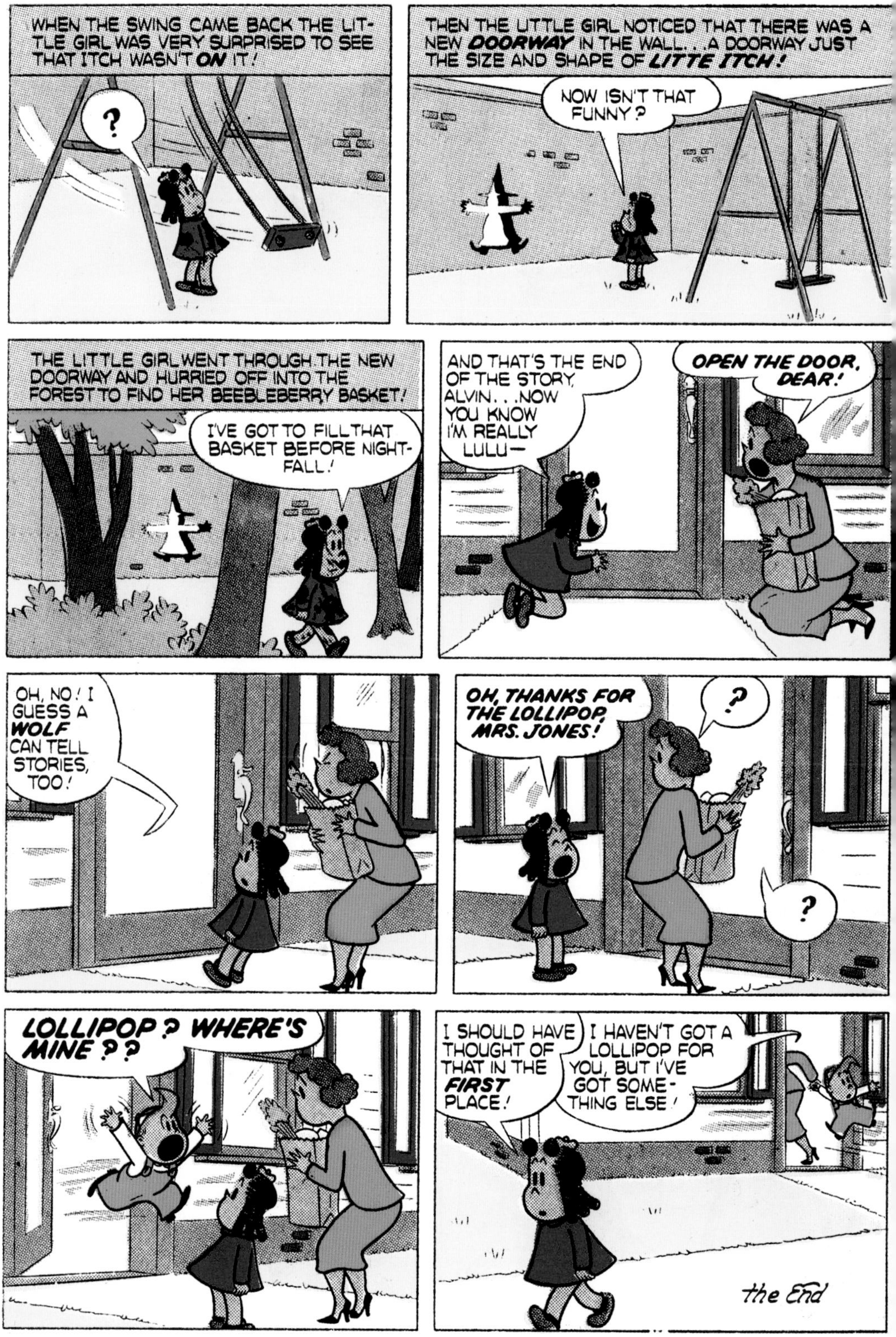
WHEN THE SWING CAME BACK THE LITTLE GIRL WAS VERY SURPRISED TO SEE THAT ITCH WASN'T ON IT!
?
THEN THE LITTLE GIRL NOTICED THAT THERE WAS A NEW DOORWAY IN THE WALL. . .A DOORWAY JUST THE SIZE AND SHAPE OF LITTE ITCH!
NOW ISN'T THAT FUNNY?
THE LITTLE GIRL WENT THROUGH THE NEW DOORWAY AND HURRIED OFF INTO THE FOREST TO FIND HER BEEBLEBERRY BASKET!
I'VE GOT TO FILL THAT BASKET BEFORE NIGHTFALL!
AND THAT'S THE END OF THE STORY, ALVIN. . .NOW YOU KNOW I'M REALLY LULU—
OPEN THE DOOR, DEAR!
OH, NO! I GUESS A WOLF CAN TELL STORIES, TOO!
OH, THANKS FOR THE LOLLIPOP, MRS. JONES!
?
?
LOLLIPOP? WHERE'S MINE??
I SHOULD HAVE THOUGHT OF THAT IN THE FIRST PLACE!
I HAVEN'T GOT A LOLLIPOP FOR YOU, BUT I'VE GOT SOMETHING ELSE!
the End

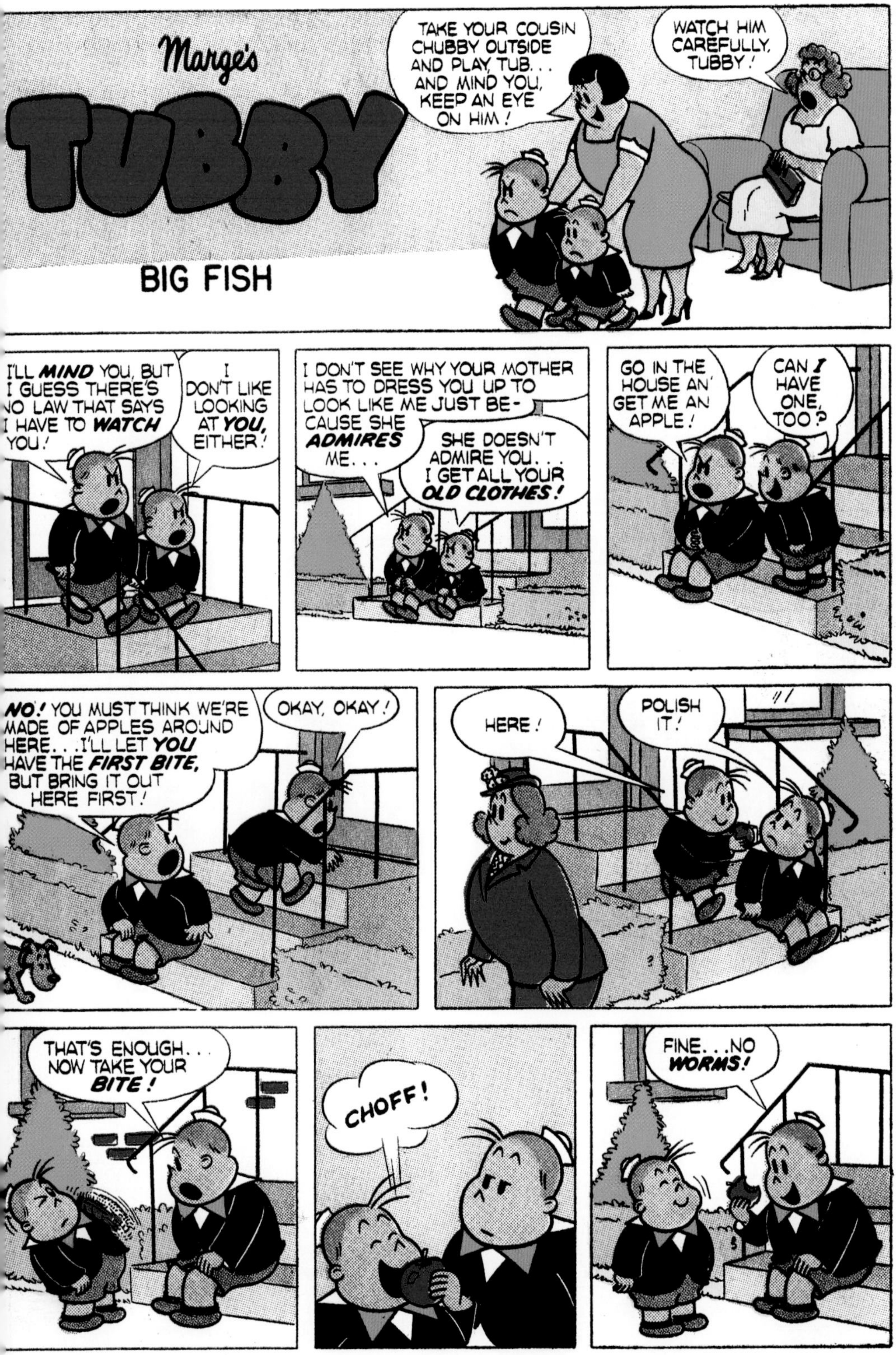
Marge's
TUBBY
BIG FISH
TAKE YOUR COUSIN CHUBBY OUTSIDE AND PLAY, TUB... AND MIND YOU, KEEP AN EYE ON HIM!
WATCH HIM CAREFULLY, TUBBY!
I'LL MIND YOU, BUT I GUESS THERE'S NO LAW THAT SAYS I HAVE TO WATCH YOU!
I DON'T LIKE LOOKING AT YOU, EITHER!
I DON'T SEE WHY YOUR MOTHER HAS TO DRESS YOU UP TO LOOK LIKE ME JUST BE-CAUSE SHE ADMIRES ME...
SHE DOESN'T ADMIRE YOU... I GET ALL YOUR OLD CLOTHES!
GO IN THE HOUSE AN' GET ME AN APPLE!
CAN I HAVE ONE, TOO?
NO! YOU MUST THINK WE'RE MADE OF APPLES AROUND HERE... I'LL LET YOU HAVE THE FIRST BITE, BUT BRING IT OUT HERE FIRST!
OKAY, OKAY!
HERE!
POLISH IT!
THAT'S ENOUGH... NOW TAKE YOUR BITE!
CHOFF!
FINE... NO WORMS!

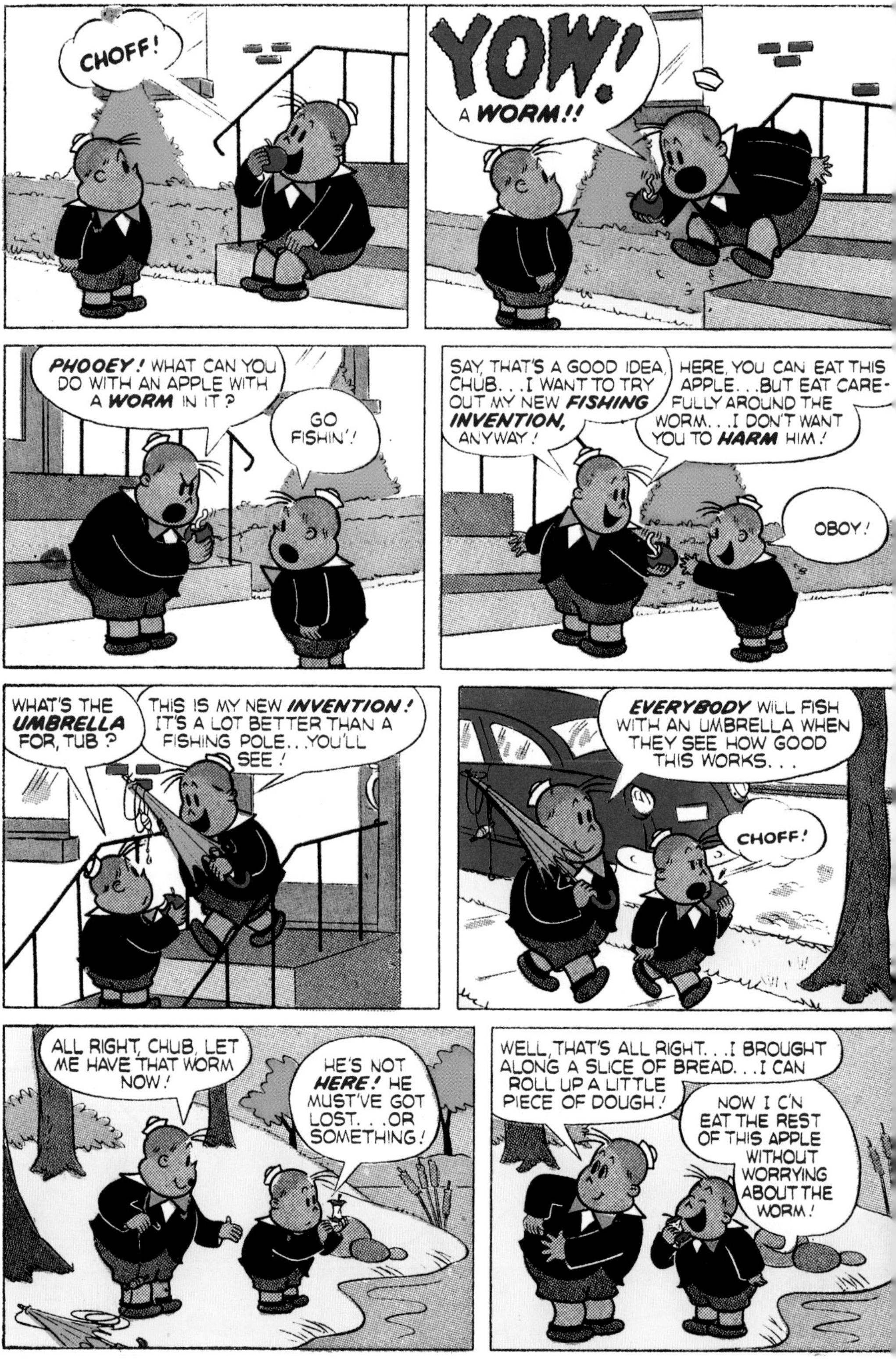
CHOFF!
YOW! A WORM!!
PHOOEY! WHAT CAN YOU DO WITH AN APPLE WITH A WORM IN IT?
GO FISHIN'!
SAY, THAT'S A GOOD IDEA, CHUB... I WANT TO TRY OUT MY NEW FISHING INVENTION, ANYWAY!
HERE, YOU CAN EAT THIS APPLE... BUT EAT CAREFULLY AROUND THE WORM... I DON'T WANT YOU TO HARM HIM!
OBOY!
WHAT'S THE UMBRELLA FOR, TUB?
THIS IS MY NEW INVENTION! IT'S A LOT BETTER THAN A FISHING POLE... YOU'LL SEE!
EVERYBODY WILL FISH WITH AN UMBRELLA WHEN THEY SEE HOW GOOD THIS WORKS...
CHOFF!
ALL RIGHT, CHUB, LET ME HAVE THAT WORM NOW!
HE'S NOT HERE! HE MUST'VE GOT LOST... OR SOMETHING!
WELL, THAT'S ALL RIGHT... I BROUGHT ALONG A SLICE OF BREAD... I CAN ROLL UP A LITTLE PIECE OF DOUGH!
NOW I C'N EAT THE REST OF THIS APPLE WITHOUT WORRYING ABOUT THE WORM!

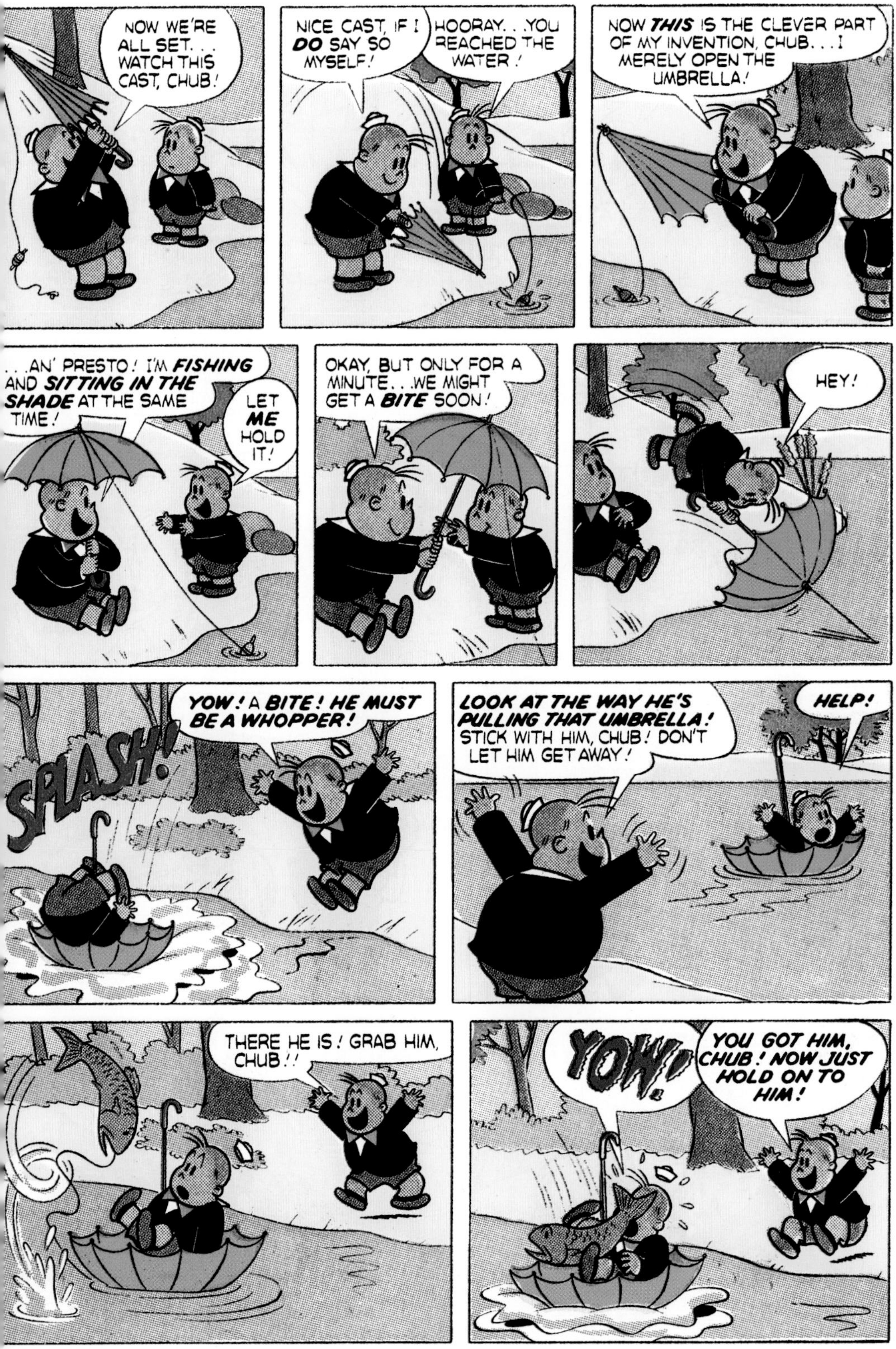
NOW WE'RE ALL SET. . . WATCH THIS CAST, CHUB!
NICE CAST, IF I DO SAY SO MYSELF!
HOORAY. . .YOU REACHED THE WATER!
NOW THIS IS THE CLEVER PART OF MY INVENTION, CHUB. . . I MERELY OPEN THE UMBRELLA!
. . .AN' PRESTO! I'M FISHING AND SITTING IN THE SHADE AT THE SAME TIME!
LET ME HOLD IT!
OKAY, BUT ONLY FOR A MINUTE. . .WE MIGHT GET A BITE SOON!
HEY!
SPLASH!
YOW! A BITE! HE MUST BE A WHOPPER!
LOOK AT THE WAY HE'S PULLING THAT UMBRELLA! STICK WITH HIM, CHUB! DON'T LET HIM GET AWAY!
HELP!
THERE HE IS! GRAB HIM, CHUB!!
YOW!
YOU GOT HIM, CHUB! NOW JUST HOLD ON TO HIM!

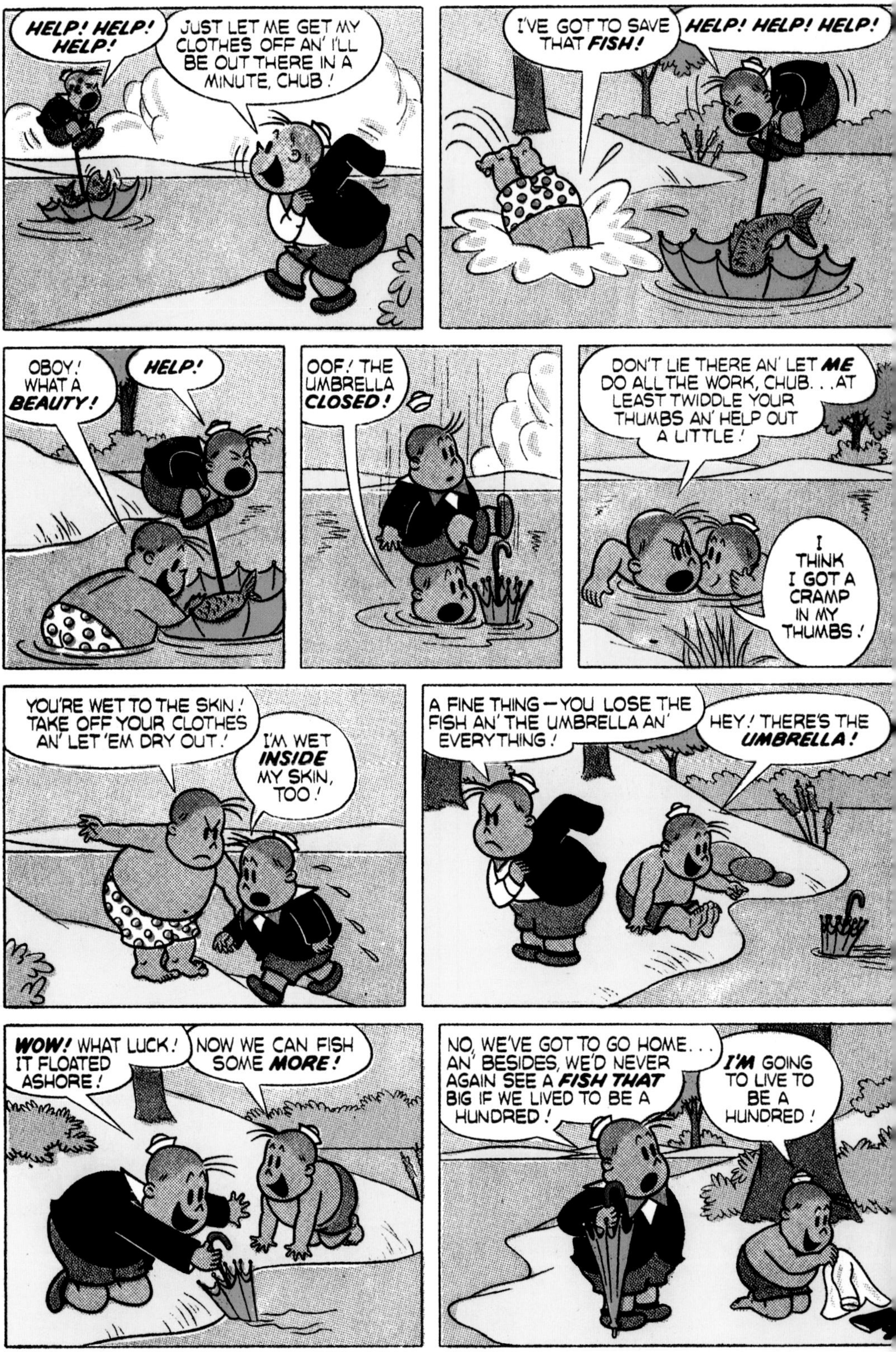
HELP! HELP! HELP!
JUST LET ME GET MY CLOTHES OFF AN' I'LL BE OUT THERE IN A MINUTE, CHUB!
I'VE GOT TO SAVE THAT FISH!
HELP! HELP! HELP!
OBOY! WHAT A BEAUTY!
HELP!
OOF! THE UMBRELLA CLOSED!
DON'T LIE THERE AN' LET ME DO ALL THE WORK, CHUB. . . AT LEAST TWIDDLE YOUR THUMBS AN' HELP OUT A LITTLE!
I THINK I GOT A CRAMP IN MY THUMBS!
YOU'RE WET TO THE SKIN! TAKE OFF YOUR CLOTHES AN' LET 'EM DRY OUT!
I'M WET INSIDE MY SKIN, TOO!
A FINE THING—YOU LOSE THE FISH AN' THE UMBRELLA AN' EVERYTHING!
HEY! THERE'S THE UMBRELLA!
WOW! WHAT LUCK! IT FLOATED ASHORE!
NOW WE CAN FISH SOME MORE!
NO, WE'VE GOT TO GO HOME. . . AN' BESIDES, WE'D NEVER AGAIN SEE A FISH THAT BIG IF WE LIVED TO BE A HUNDRED!
I'M GOING TO LIVE TO BE A HUNDRED!

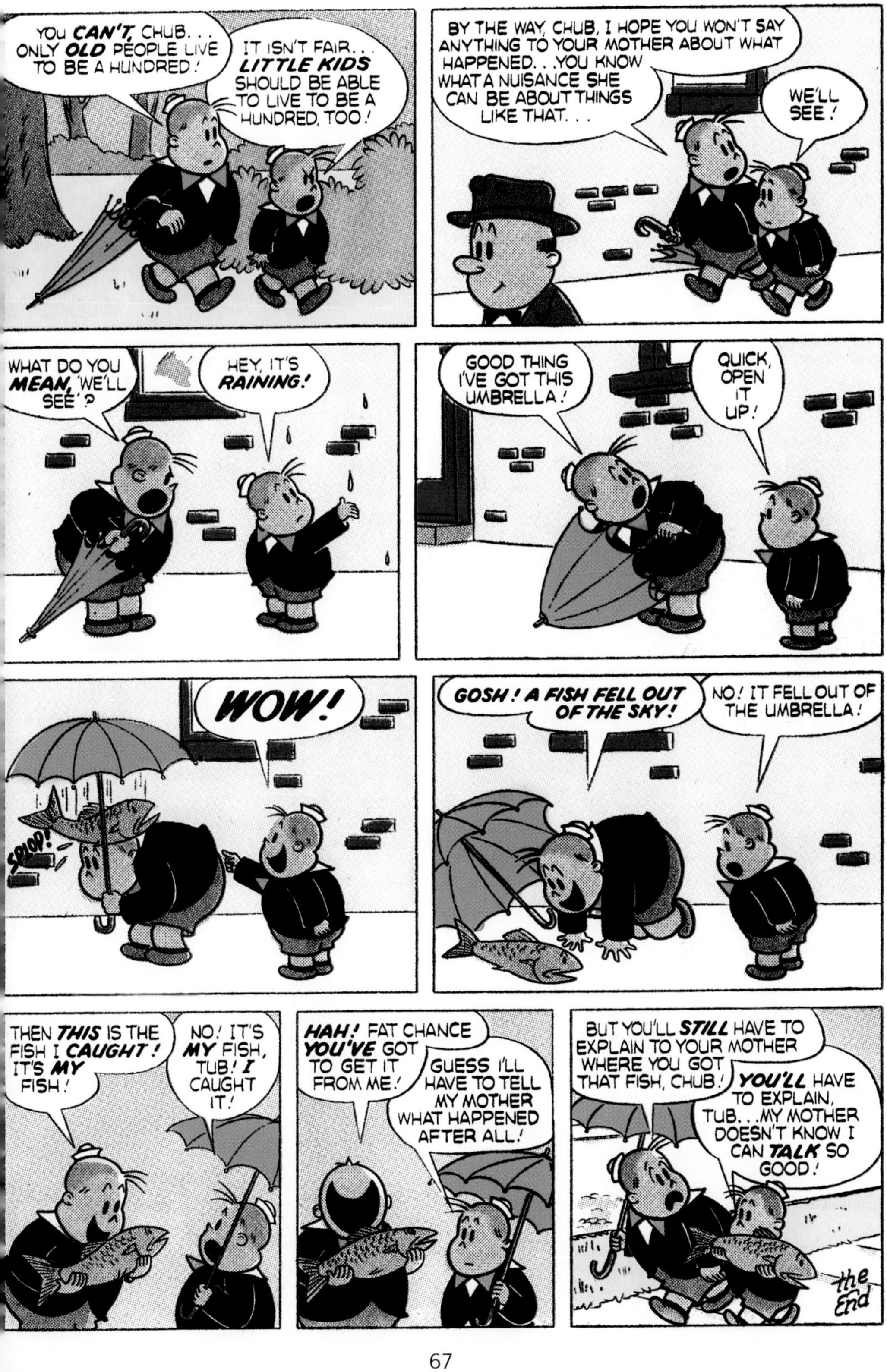
YOU CAN'T, CHUB... ONLY OLD PEOPLE LIVE TO BE A HUNDRED!
IT ISN'T FAIR... LITTLE KIDS SHOULD BE ABLE TO LIVE TO BE A HUNDRED, TOO!
BY THE WAY, CHUB, I HOPE YOU WON'T SAY ANYTHING TO YOUR MOTHER ABOUT WHAT HAPPENED...YOU KNOW WHAT A NUISANCE SHE CAN BE ABOUT THINGS LIKE THAT...
WE'LL SEE!
WHAT DO YOU MEAN, 'WE'LL SEE'?
HEY, IT'S RAINING!
GOOD THING I'VE GOT THIS UMBRELLA!
QUICK, OPEN IT UP!
WOW!
SPLOP!
GOSH! A FISH FELL OUT OF THE SKY!
NO! IT FELL OUT OF THE UMBRELLA!
THEN THIS IS THE FISH I CAUGHT! IT'S MY FISH!
NO! IT'S MY FISH, TUB! I CAUGHT IT!
HAH! FAT CHANCE YOU'VE GOT TO GET IT FROM ME!
GUESS I'LL HAVE TO TELL MY MOTHER WHAT HAPPENED AFTER ALL!
BUT YOU'LL STILL HAVE TO EXPLAIN TO YOUR MOTHER WHERE YOU GOT THAT FISH, CHUB!
YOU'LL HAVE TO EXPLAIN, TUB...MY MOTHER DOESN'T KNOW I CAN TALK SO GOOD!
the End

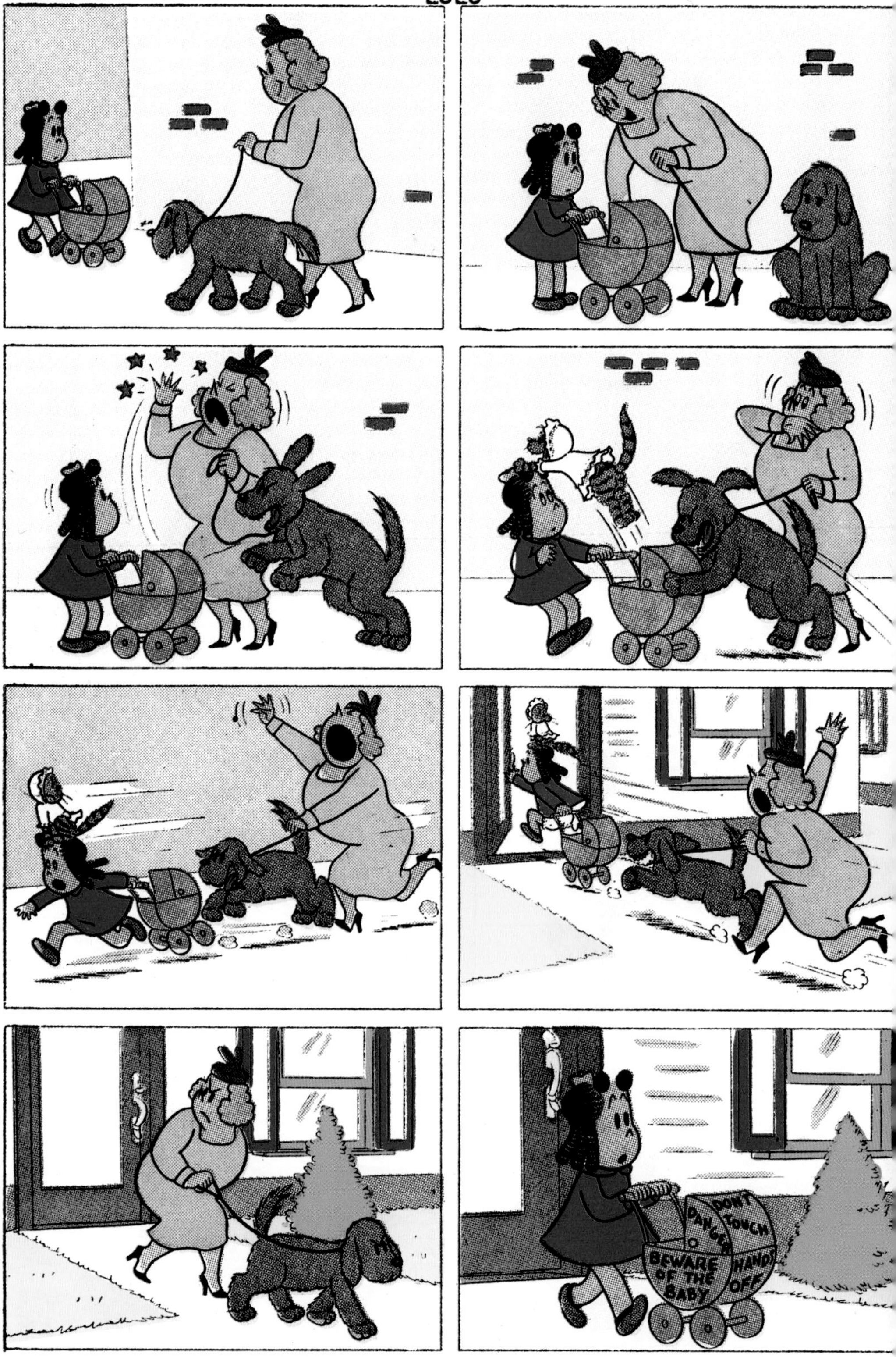
DON'T TOUCH
DANGER
BEWARE OF THE BABY
HANDS OFF

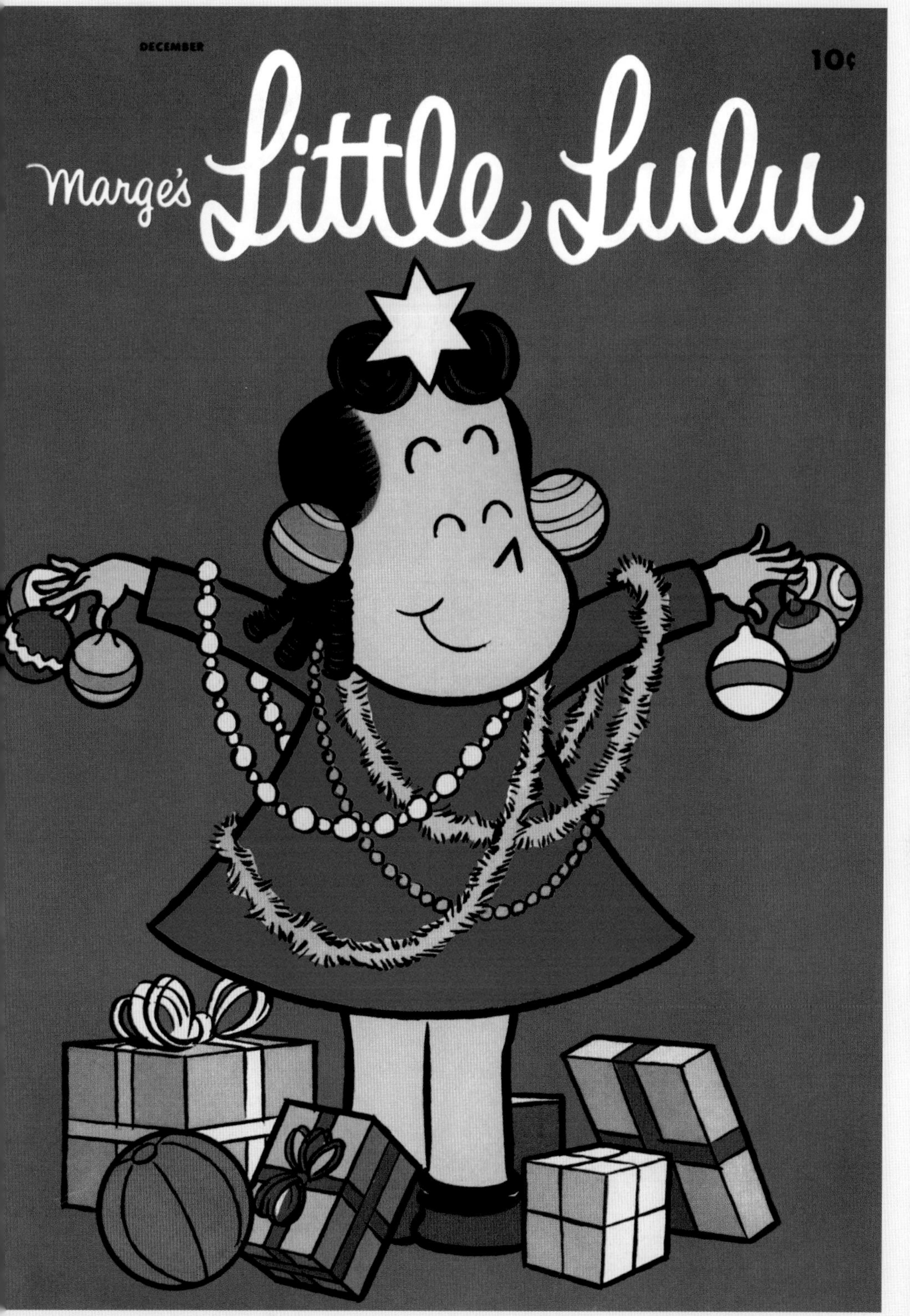
DECEMBER
10¢
Marge's Little Lulu

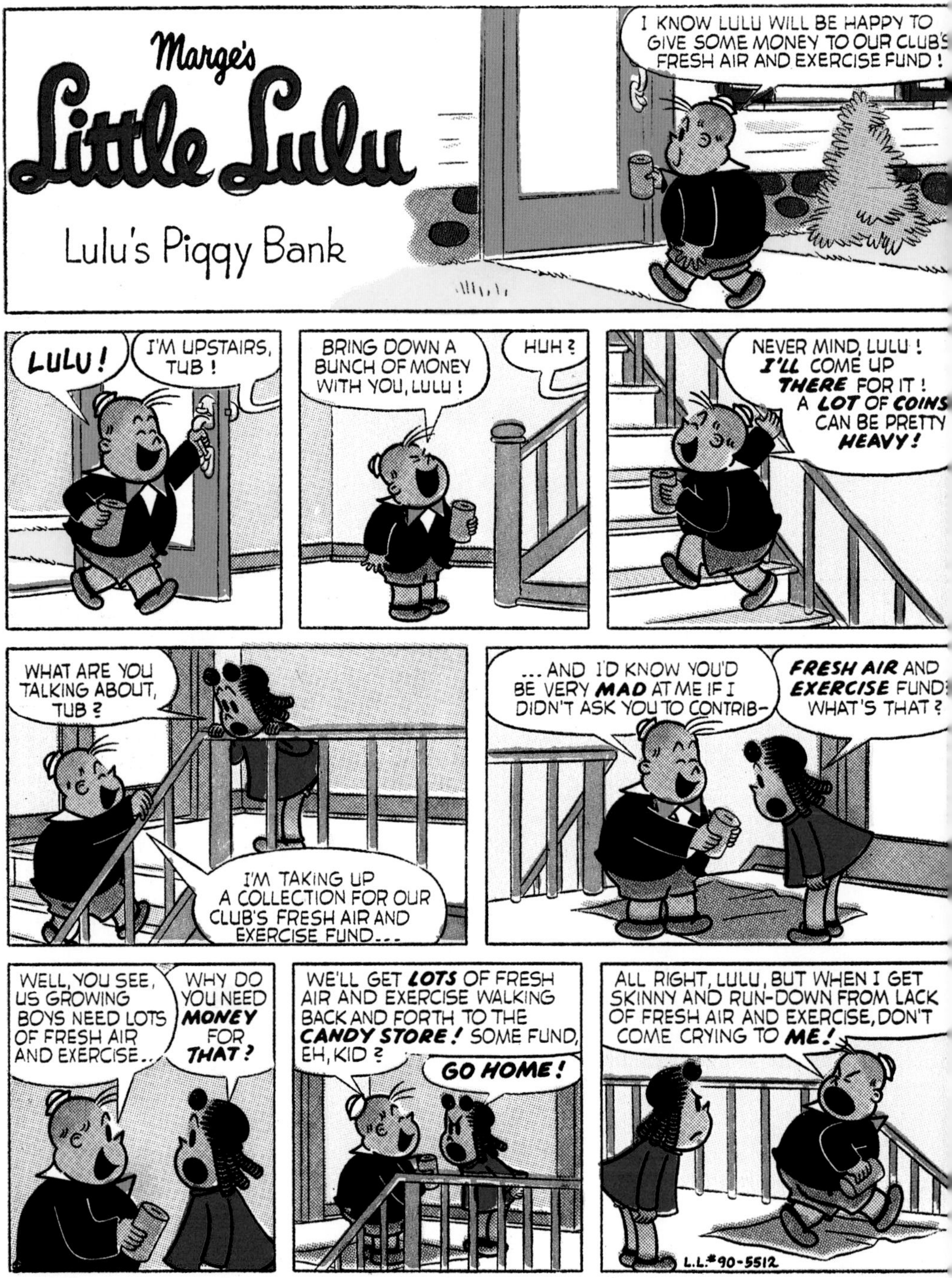
Marge's
Little Lulu
Lulu's Piggy Bank
I KNOW LULU WILL BE HAPPY TO GIVE SOME MONEY TO OUR CLUB'S FRESH AIR AND EXERCISE FUND!
LULU!
I'M UPSTAIRS, TUB!
BRING DOWN A BUNCH OF MONEY WITH YOU, LULU!
HUH?
NEVER MIND, LULU! I'LL COME UP THERE FOR IT! A LOT OF COINS CAN BE PRETTY HEAVY!
WHAT ARE YOU TALKING ABOUT, TUB?
I'M TAKING UP A COLLECTION FOR OUR CLUB'S FRESH AIR AND EXERCISE FUND...
...AND I'D KNOW YOU'D BE VERY MAD AT ME IF I DIDN'T ASK YOU TO CONTRIB-
FRESH AIR AND EXERCISE FUND? WHAT'S THAT?
WELL, YOU SEE, US GROWING BOYS NEED LOTS OF FRESH AIR AND EXERCISE..
WHY DO YOU NEED MONEY FOR THAT?
WE'LL GET LOTS OF FRESH AIR AND EXERCISE WALKING BACK AND FORTH TO THE CANDY STORE! SOME FUND, EH, KID?
GO HOME!
ALL RIGHT, LULU, BUT WHEN I GET SKINNY AND RUN-DOWN FROM LACK OF FRESH AIR AND EXERCISE, DON'T COME CRYING TO ME!
L.L.#90-5512

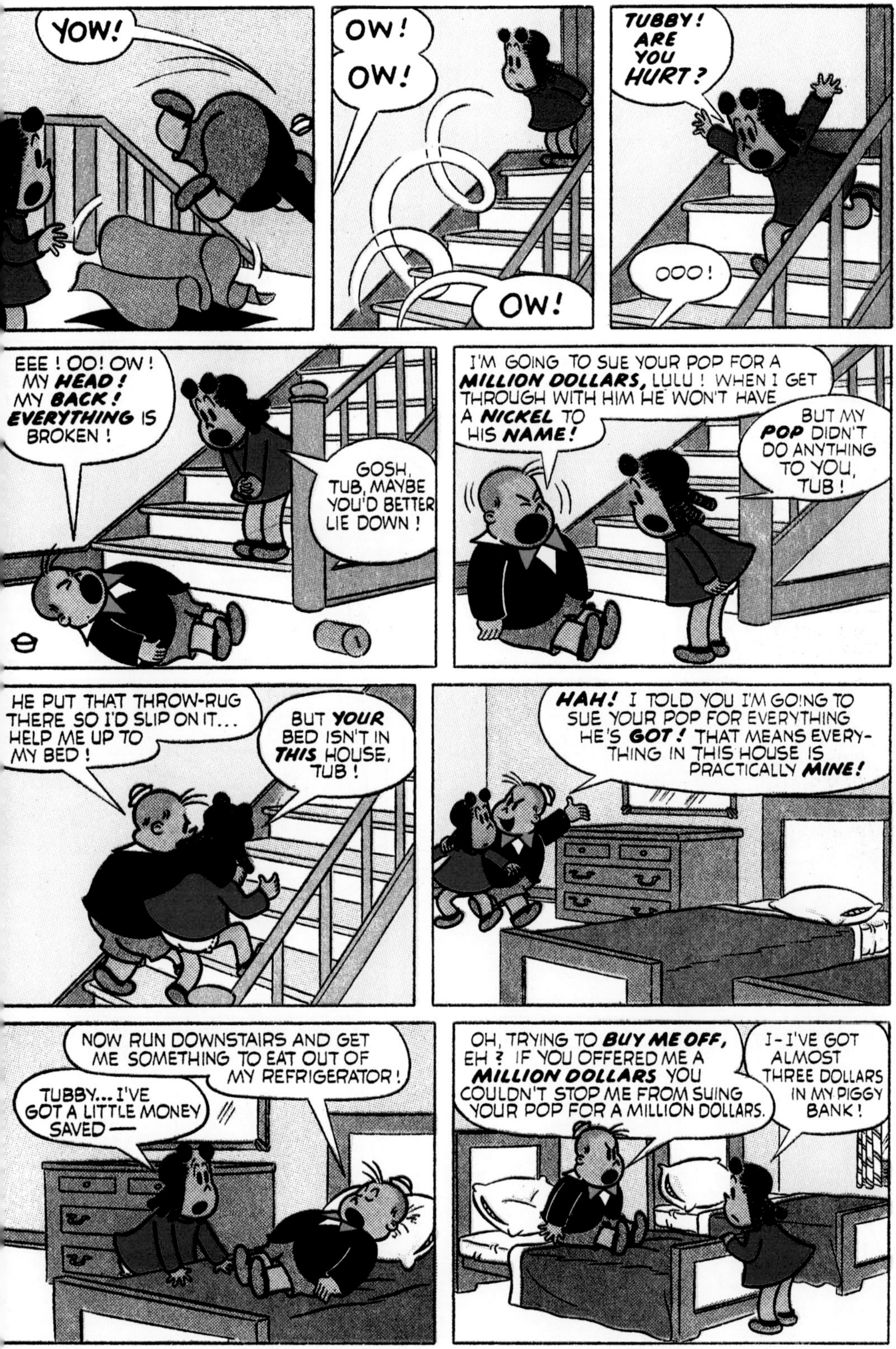
YOW!
OW!
OW!
OW!
TUBBY! ARE YOU HURT?
OOO!
EEE! OO! OW! MY HEAD! MY BACK! EVERYTHING IS BROKEN!
GOSH, TUB, MAYBE YOU'D BETTER LIE DOWN!
I'M GOING TO SUE YOUR POP FOR A MILLION DOLLARS, LULU! WHEN I GET THROUGH WITH HIM HE WON'T HAVE A NICKEL TO HIS NAME!
BUT MY POP DIDN'T DO ANYTHING TO YOU, TUB!
HE PUT THAT THROW-RUG THERE SO I'D SLIP ON IT... HELP ME UP TO MY BED!
BUT YOUR BED ISN'T IN THIS HOUSE, TUB!
HAH! I TOLD YOU I'M GOING TO SUE YOUR POP FOR EVERYTHING HE'S GOT! THAT MEANS EVERY-THING IN THIS HOUSE IS PRACTICALLY MINE!
NOW RUN DOWNSTAIRS AND GET ME SOMETHING TO EAT OUT OF MY REFRIGERATOR!
TUBBY... I'VE GOT A LITTLE MONEY SAVED—
I-I'VE GOT ALMOST THREE DOLLARS IN MY PIGGY BANK!
OH, TRYING TO BUY ME OFF, EH? IF YOU OFFERED ME A MILLION DOLLARS YOU COULDN'T STOP ME FROM SUING YOUR POP FOR A MILLION DOLLARS.

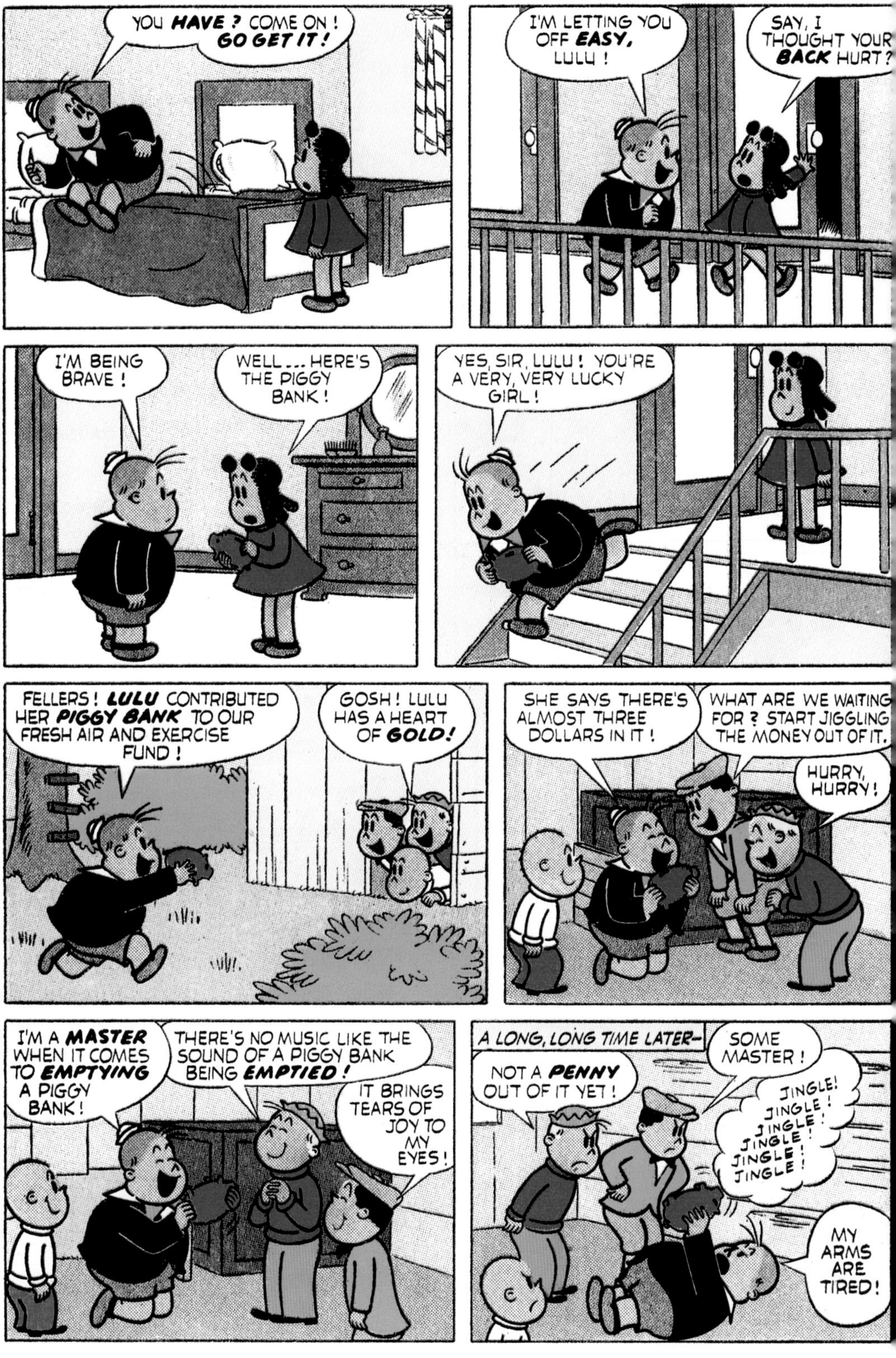

YOU HAVE? COME ON! GO GET IT!
I'M LETTING YOU OFF EASY, LULU!
SAY, I THOUGHT YOUR BACK HURT?
I'M BEING BRAVE!
WELL... HERE'S THE PIGGY BANK!
YES, SIR, LULU! YOU'RE A VERY, VERY LUCKY GIRL!
FELLERS! LULU CONTRIBUTED HER PIGGY BANK TO OUR FRESH AIR AND EXERCISE FUND!
GOSH! LULU HAS A HEART OF GOLD!
SHE SAYS THERE'S ALMOST THREE DOLLARS IN IT!
WHAT ARE WE WAITING FOR? START JIGGLING THE MONEY OUT OF IT.
HURRY, HURRY!
I'M A MASTER WHEN IT COMES TO EMPTYING A PIGGY BANK!
THERE'S NO MUSIC LIKE THE SOUND OF A PIGGY BANK BEING EMPTIED!
IT BRINGS TEARS OF JOY TO MY EYES!
A LONG, LONG TIME LATER—
NOT A PENNY OUT OF IT YET!
SOME MASTER!
JINGLE! JINGLE! JINGLE! JINGLE! JINGLE! JINGLE!
MY ARMS ARE TIRED!

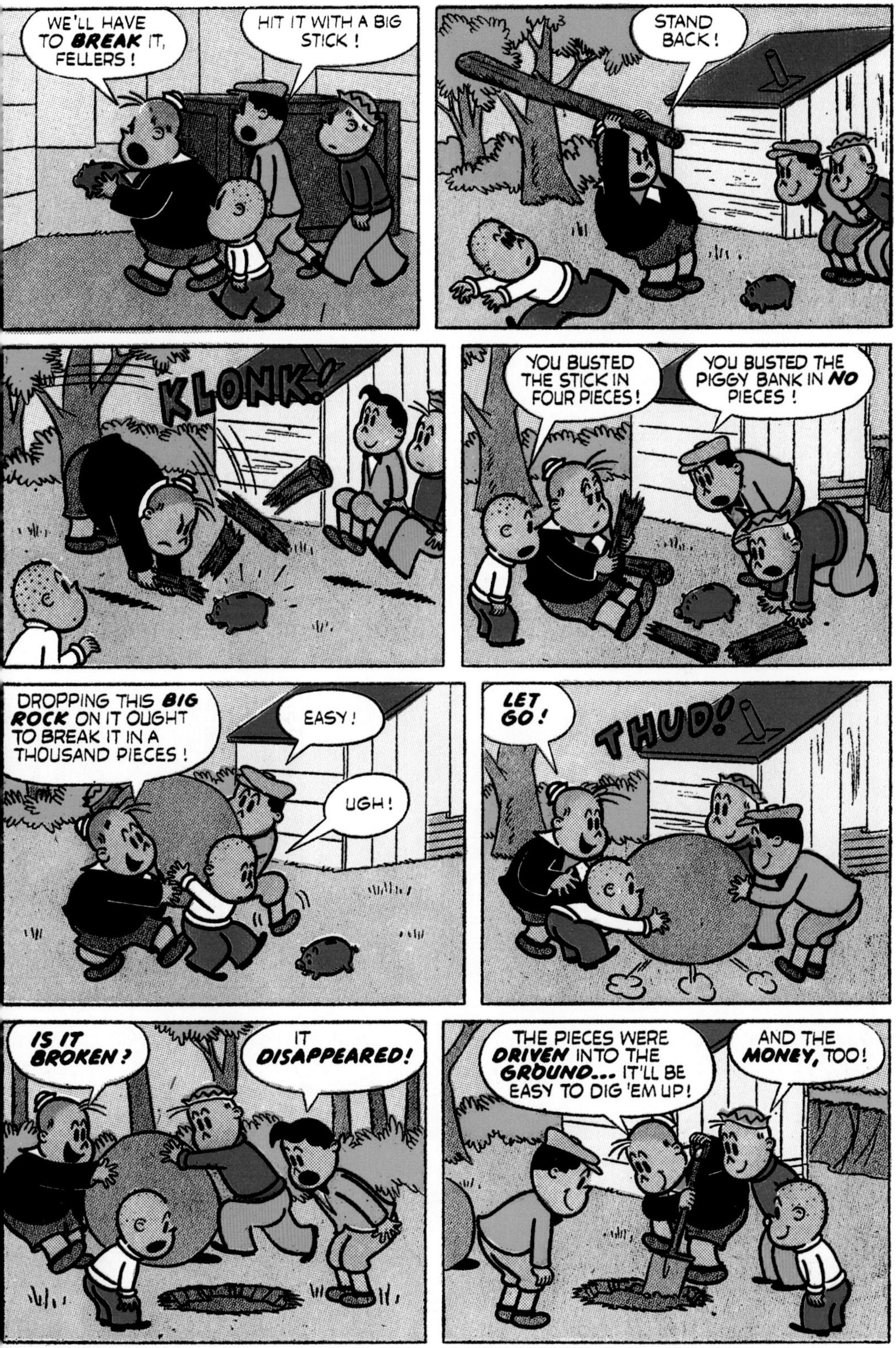
WE'LL HAVE TO BREAK IT, FELLERS!
HIT IT WITH A BIG STICK!
STAND BACK!
KLONK!
YOU BUSTED THE STICK IN FOUR PIECES!
YOU BUSTED THE PIGGY BANK IN NO PIECES!
DROPPING THIS BIG ROCK ON IT OUGHT TO BREAK IT IN A THOUSAND PIECES!
EASY!
UGH!
LET GO!
THUD!
IS IT BROKEN?
IT DISAPPEARED!
THE PIECES WERE DRIVEN INTO THE GROUND... IT'LL BE EASY TO DIG 'EM UP!
AND THE MONEY, TOO!

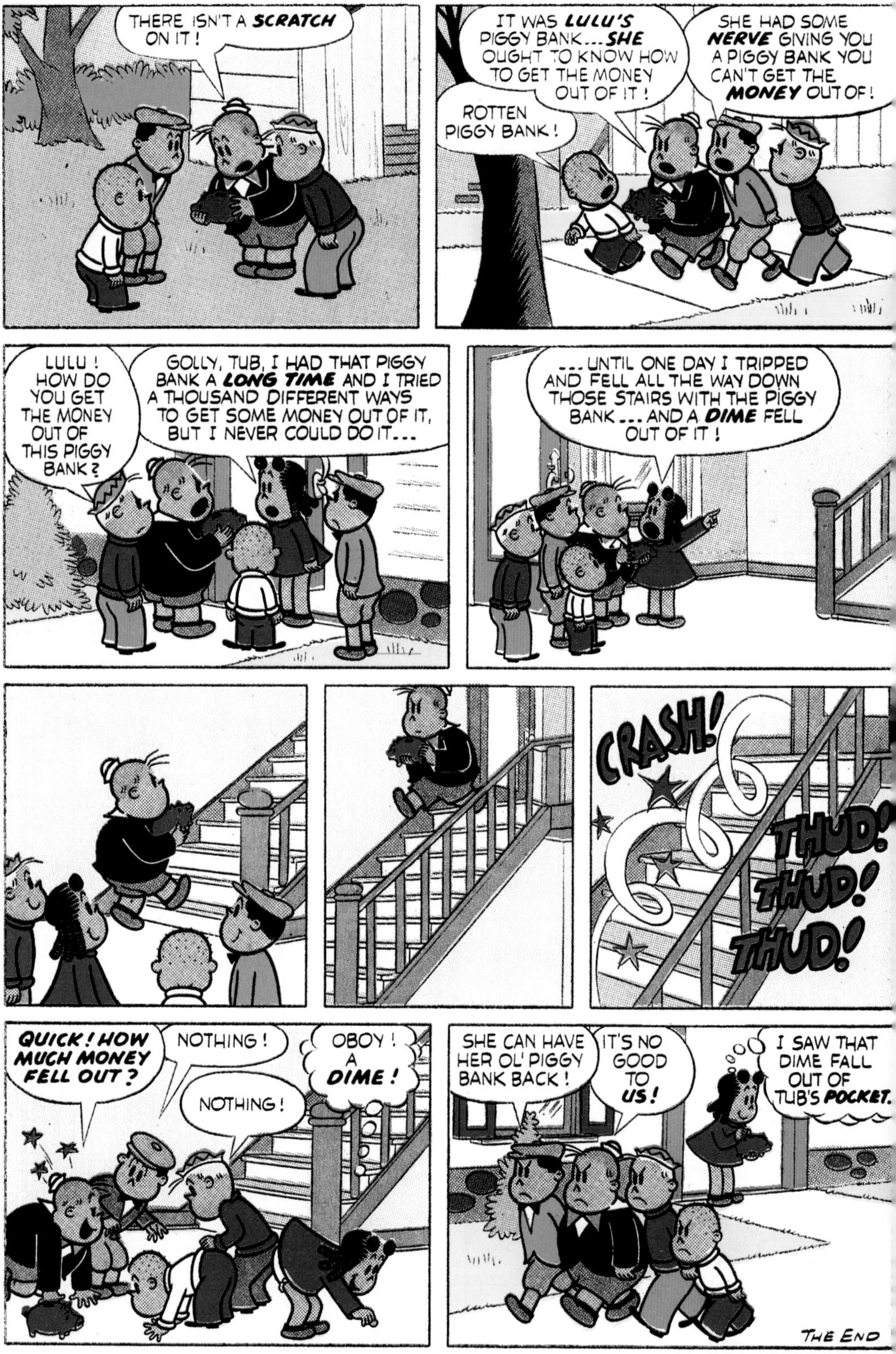
THERE ISN'T A SCRATCH ON IT!
IT WAS LULU'S PIGGY BANK... SHE OUGHT TO KNOW HOW TO GET THE MONEY OUT OF IT!
SHE HAD SOME NERVE GIVING YOU A PIGGY BANK YOU CAN'T GET THE MONEY OUT OF!
ROTTEN PIGGY BANK!
LULU! HOW DO YOU GET THE MONEY OUT OF THIS PIGGY BANK?
GOLLY, TUB, I HAD THAT PIGGY BANK A LONG TIME AND I TRIED A THOUSAND DIFFERENT WAYS TO GET SOME MONEY OUT OF IT, BUT I NEVER COULD DO IT...
...UNTIL ONE DAY I TRIPPED AND FELL ALL THE WAY DOWN THOSE STAIRS WITH THE PIGGY BANK... AND A DIME FELL OUT OF IT!
CRASH!
THUD!
THUD!
THUD!
QUICK! HOW MUCH MONEY FELL OUT?
NOTHING!
NOTHING!
OBOY! A DIME!
SHE CAN HAVE HER OL' PIGGY BANK BACK!
IT'S NO GOOD TO US!
I SAW THAT DIME FALL OUT OF TUB'S POCKET.
THE END

# Marge's Little Lulu

## The Dance

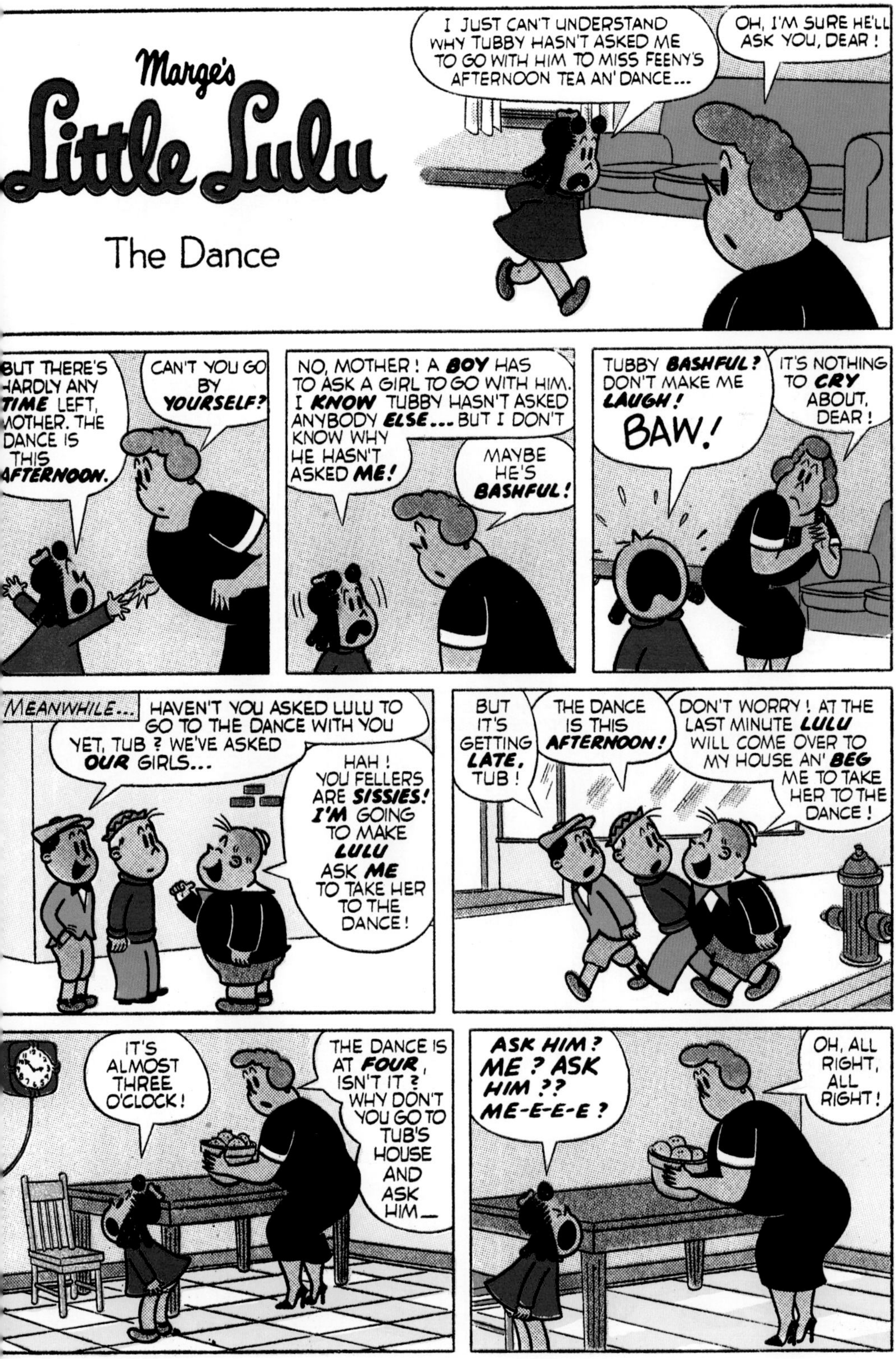
I JUST CAN'T UNDERSTAND WHY TUBBY HASN'T ASKED ME TO GO WITH HIM TO MISS FEENY'S AFTERNOON TEA AN' DANCE...
OH, I'M SURE HE'LL ASK YOU, DEAR!
BUT THERE'S HARDLY ANY TIME LEFT, MOTHER. THE DANCE IS THIS AFTERNOON.
CAN'T YOU GO BY YOURSELF?
NO, MOTHER! A BOY HAS TO ASK A GIRL TO GO WITH HIM. I KNOW TUBBY HASN'T ASKED ANYBODY ELSE... BUT I DON'T KNOW WHY HE HASN'T ASKED ME!
MAYBE HE'S BASHFUL!
TUBBY BASHFUL? DON'T MAKE ME LAUGH!
BAW!
IT'S NOTHING TO CRY ABOUT, DEAR!
MEANWHILE...
HAVEN'T YOU ASKED LULU TO GO TO THE DANCE WITH YOU YET, TUB? WE'VE ASKED OUR GIRLS...
HAH! YOU FELLERS ARE SISSIES! I'M GOING TO MAKE LULU ASK ME TO TAKE HER TO THE DANCE!
BUT IT'S GETTING LATE, TUB!
THE DANCE IS THIS AFTERNOON!
DON'T WORRY! AT THE LAST MINUTE LULU WILL COME OVER TO MY HOUSE AN' BEG ME TO TAKE HER TO THE DANCE!
IT'S ALMOST THREE O'CLOCK!
THE DANCE IS AT FOUR, ISN'T IT? WHY DON'T YOU GO TO TUB'S HOUSE AND ASK HIM —
ASK HIM? ME? ASK HIM?? ME-E-E-E?
OH, ALL RIGHT, ALL RIGHT!

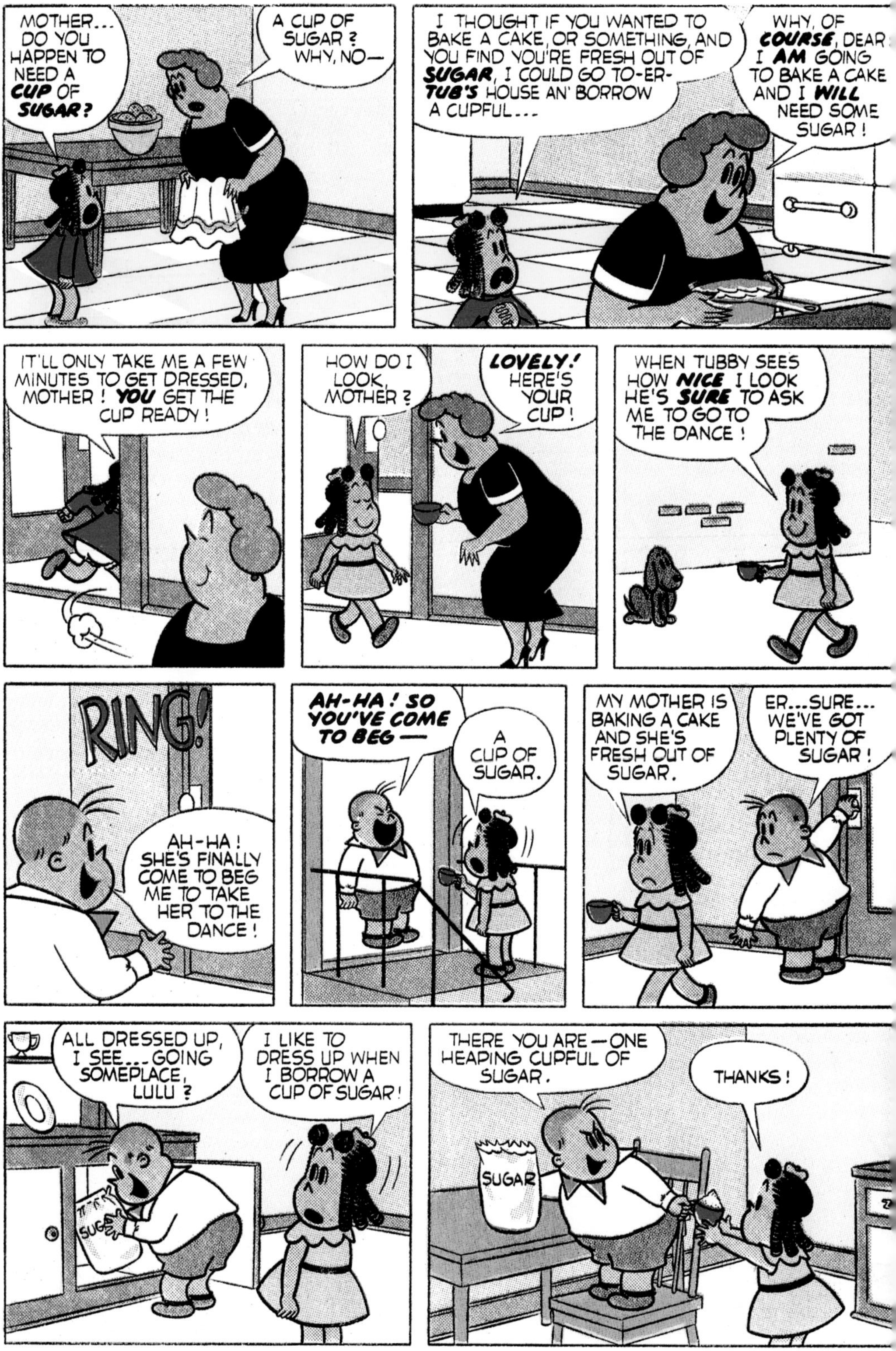

MOTHER... DO YOU HAPPEN TO NEED A CUP OF SUGAR?
A CUP OF SUGAR? WHY, NO—
I THOUGHT IF YOU WANTED TO BAKE A CAKE, OR SOMETHING, AND YOU FIND YOU'RE FRESH OUT OF SUGAR, I COULD GO TO-ER-TUB'S HOUSE AN' BORROW A CUPFUL...
WHY, OF COURSE, DEAR! I AM GOING TO BAKE A CAKE AND I WILL NEED SOME SUGAR!
IT'LL ONLY TAKE ME A FEW MINUTES TO GET DRESSED, MOTHER! YOU GET THE CUP READY!
HOW DO I LOOK, MOTHER?
LOVELY! HERE'S YOUR CUP!
WHEN TUBBY SEES HOW NICE I LOOK HE'S SURE TO ASK ME TO GO TO THE DANCE!
RING!
AH-HA! SHE'S FINALLY COME TO BEG ME TO TAKE HER TO THE DANCE!
AH-HA! SO YOU'VE COME TO BEG—
A CUP OF SUGAR.
MY MOTHER IS BAKING A CAKE AND SHE'S FRESH OUT OF SUGAR.
ER...SURE... WE'VE GOT PLENTY OF SUGAR!
ALL DRESSED UP, I SEE... GOING SOMEPLACE, LULU?
I LIKE TO DRESS UP WHEN I BORROW A CUP OF SUGAR!
THERE YOU ARE—ONE HEAPING CUPFUL OF SUGAR.
SUGAR
THANKS!

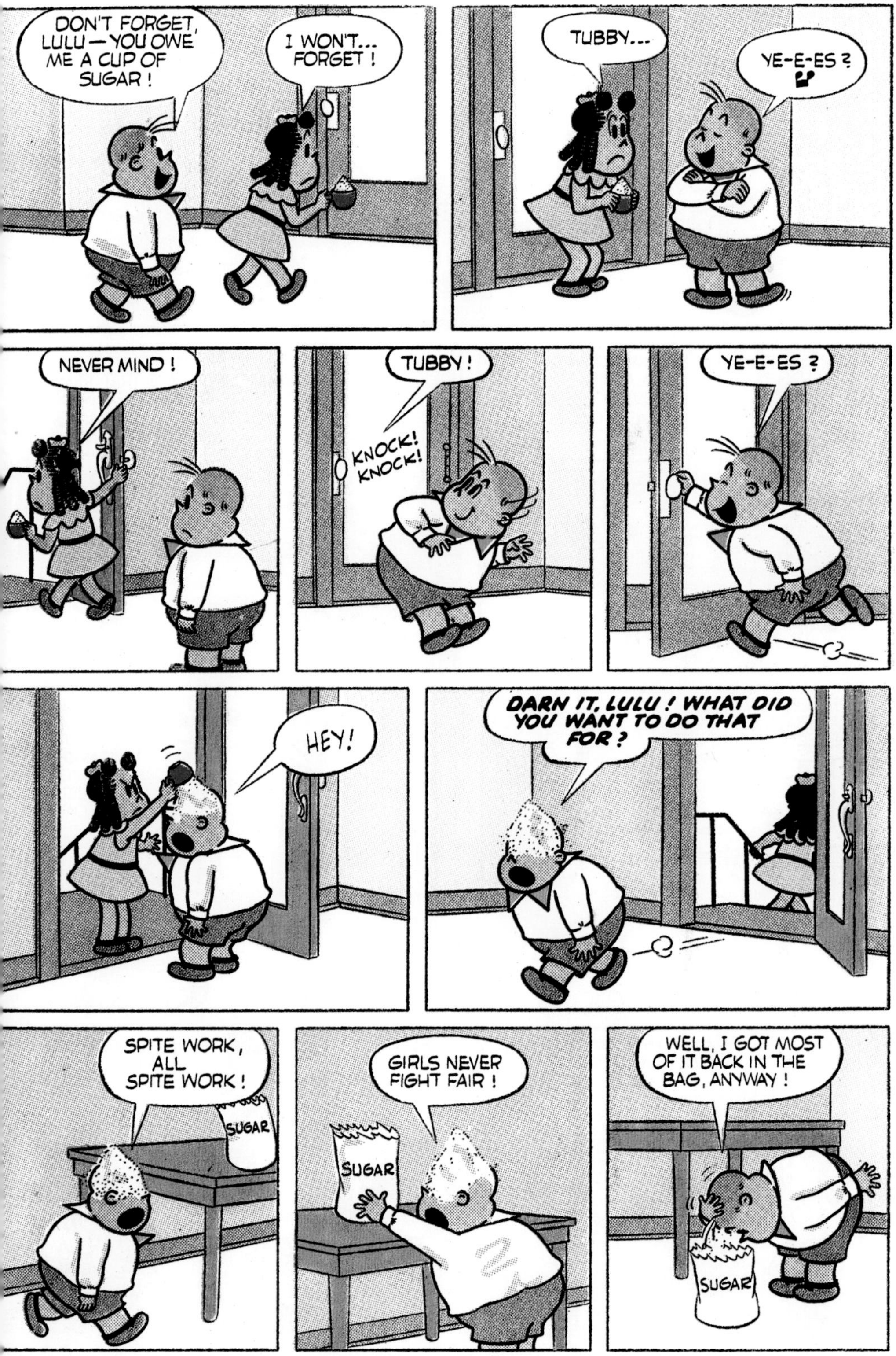
DON'T FORGET, LULU—YOU OWE ME A CUP OF SUGAR!
I WON'T... FORGET!
TUBBY...
YE-E-ES?
NEVER MIND!
TUBBY!
KNOCK! KNOCK!
YE-E-ES?
HEY!
DARN IT, LULU! WHAT DID YOU WANT TO DO THAT FOR?
SPITE WORK, ALL SPITE WORK!
SUGAR
GIRLS NEVER FIGHT FAIR!
SUGAR
WELL, I GOT MOST OF IT BACK IN THE BAG, ANYWAY!
SUGAR

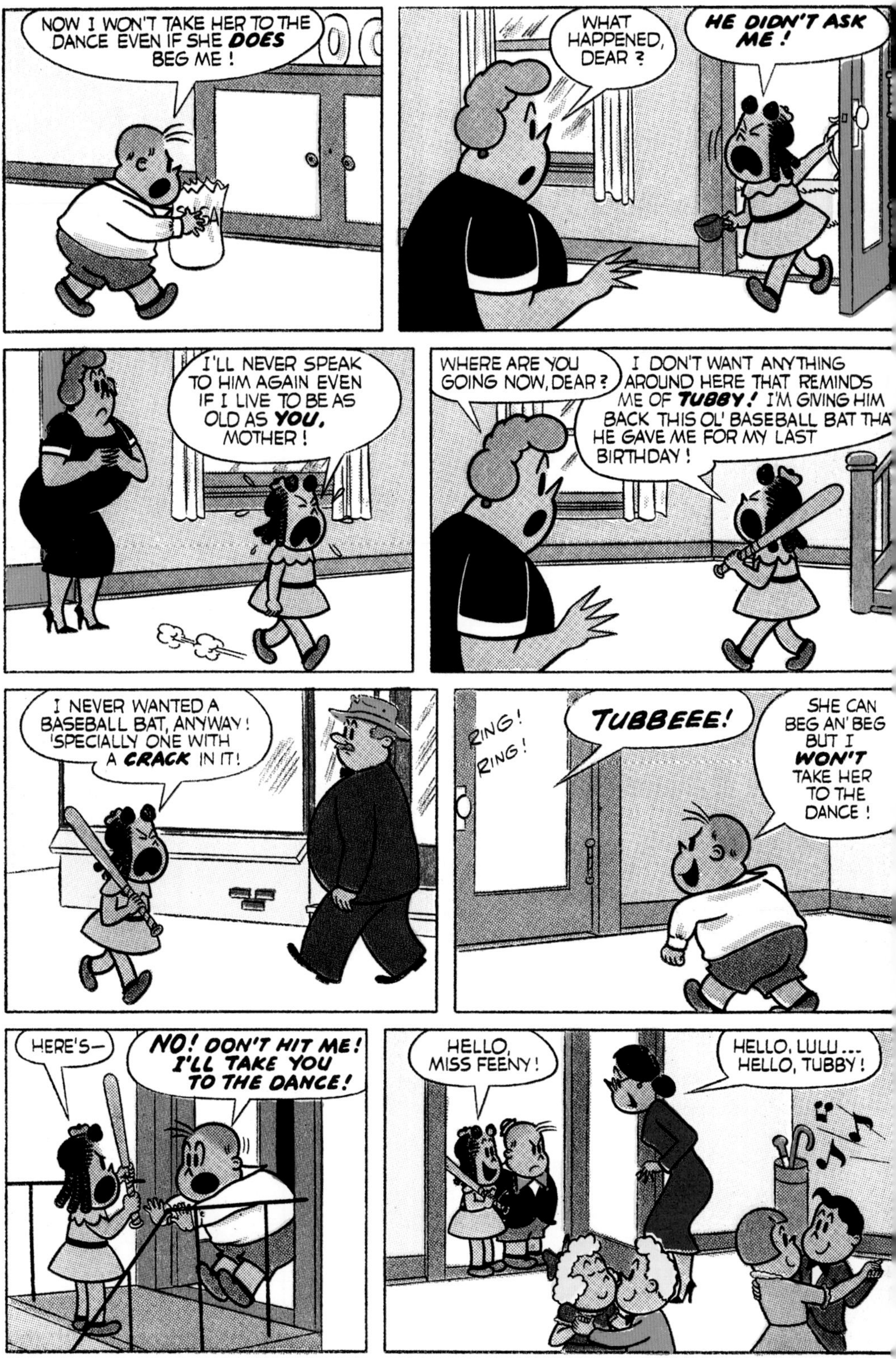
NOW I WON'T TAKE HER TO THE DANCE EVEN IF SHE DOES BEG ME !
WHAT HAPPENED, DEAR ?
HE DIDN'T ASK ME !
I'LL NEVER SPEAK TO HIM AGAIN EVEN IF I LIVE TO BE AS OLD AS YOU, MOTHER !
WHERE ARE YOU GOING NOW, DEAR ?
I DON'T WANT ANYTHING AROUND HERE THAT REMINDS ME OF TUBBY! I'M GIVING HIM BACK THIS OL' BASEBALL BAT THAT HE GAVE ME FOR MY LAST BIRTHDAY !
I NEVER WANTED A BASEBALL BAT, ANYWAY ! 'SPECIALLY ONE WITH A CRACK IN IT!
RING! RING!
TUBBEEE!
SHE CAN BEG AN' BEG BUT I WON'T TAKE HER TO THE DANCE !
HERE'S—
NO! DON'T HIT ME! I'LL TAKE YOU TO THE DANCE!
HELLO, MISS FEENY !
HELLO, LULU ... HELLO, TUBBY !

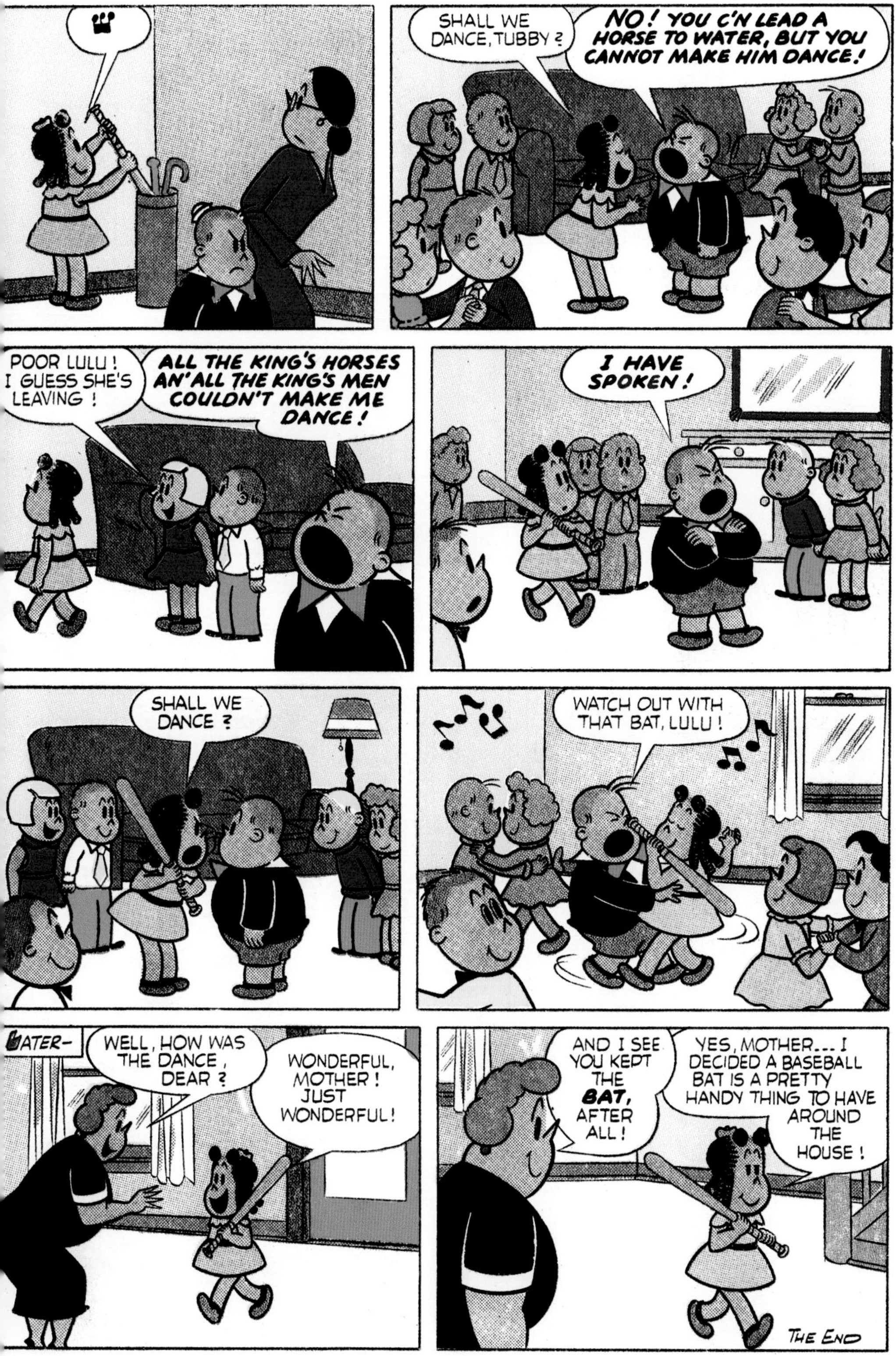
SHALL WE DANCE, TUBBY?
NO! YOU C'N LEAD A HORSE TO WATER, BUT YOU CANNOT MAKE HIM DANCE!
POOR LULU! I GUESS SHE'S LEAVING!
ALL THE KING'S HORSES AN' ALL THE KING'S MEN COULDN'T MAKE ME DANCE!
I HAVE SPOKEN!
SHALL WE DANCE?
WATCH OUT WITH THAT BAT, LULU!
LATER-
WELL, HOW WAS THE DANCE, DEAR?
WONDERFUL, MOTHER! JUST WONDERFUL!
AND I SEE YOU KEPT THE BAT, AFTER ALL!
YES, MOTHER... I DECIDED A BASEBALL BAT IS A PRETTY HANDY THING TO HAVE AROUND THE HOUSE!
THE END

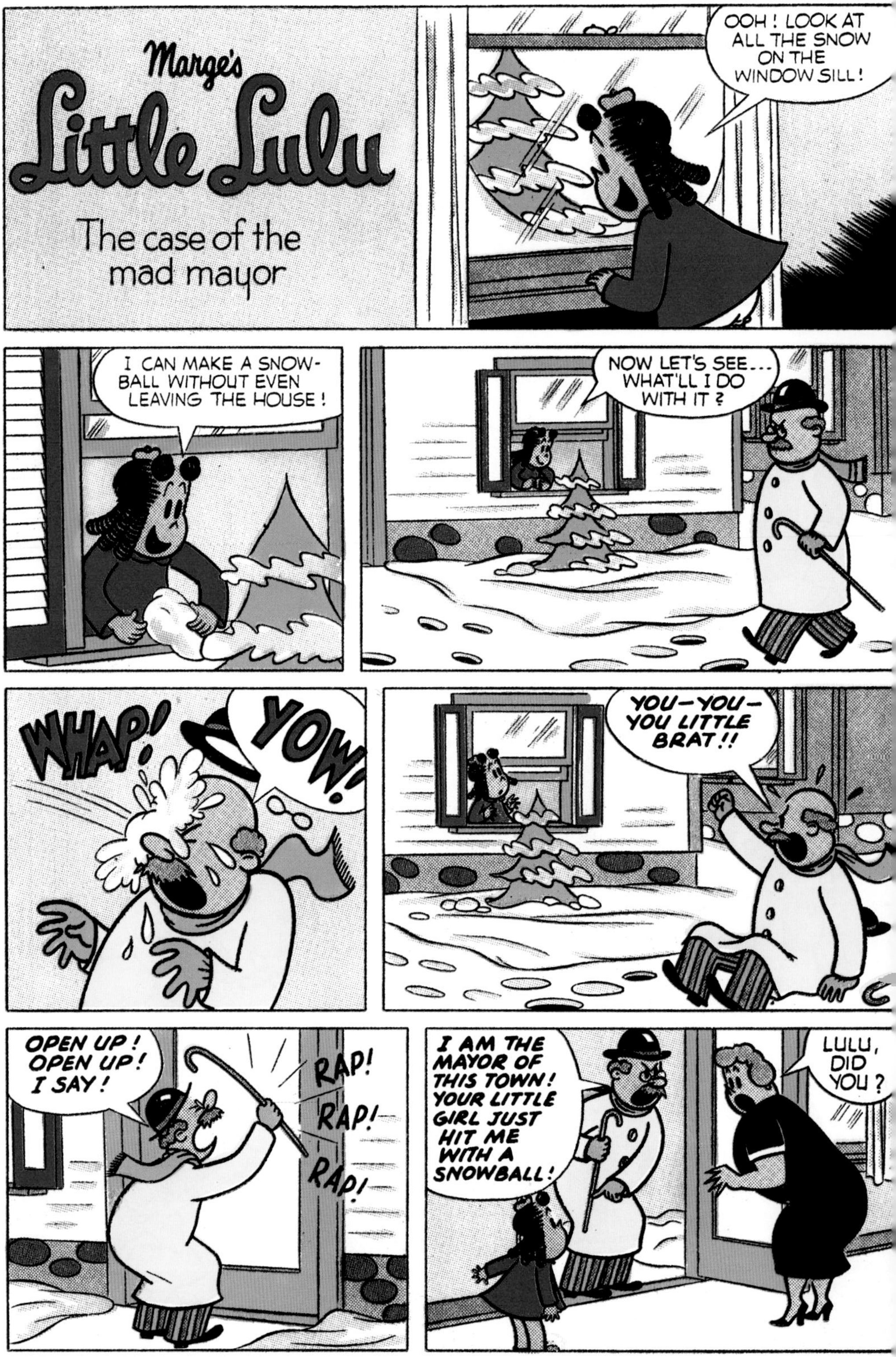
Marge's
Little Lulu
The case of the mad mayor
OOH! LOOK AT ALL THE SNOW ON THE WINDOW SILL!
I CAN MAKE A SNOW-BALL WITHOUT EVEN LEAVING THE HOUSE!
NOW LET'S SEE... WHAT'LL I DO WITH IT?
WHAP!
YOW!
YOU—YOU—YOU LITTLE BRAT!!
OPEN UP! OPEN UP! I SAY!
RAP!
RAP!
RAP!
I AM THE MAYOR OF THIS TOWN! YOUR LITTLE GIRL JUST HIT ME WITH A SNOWBALL!
LULU, DID YOU?

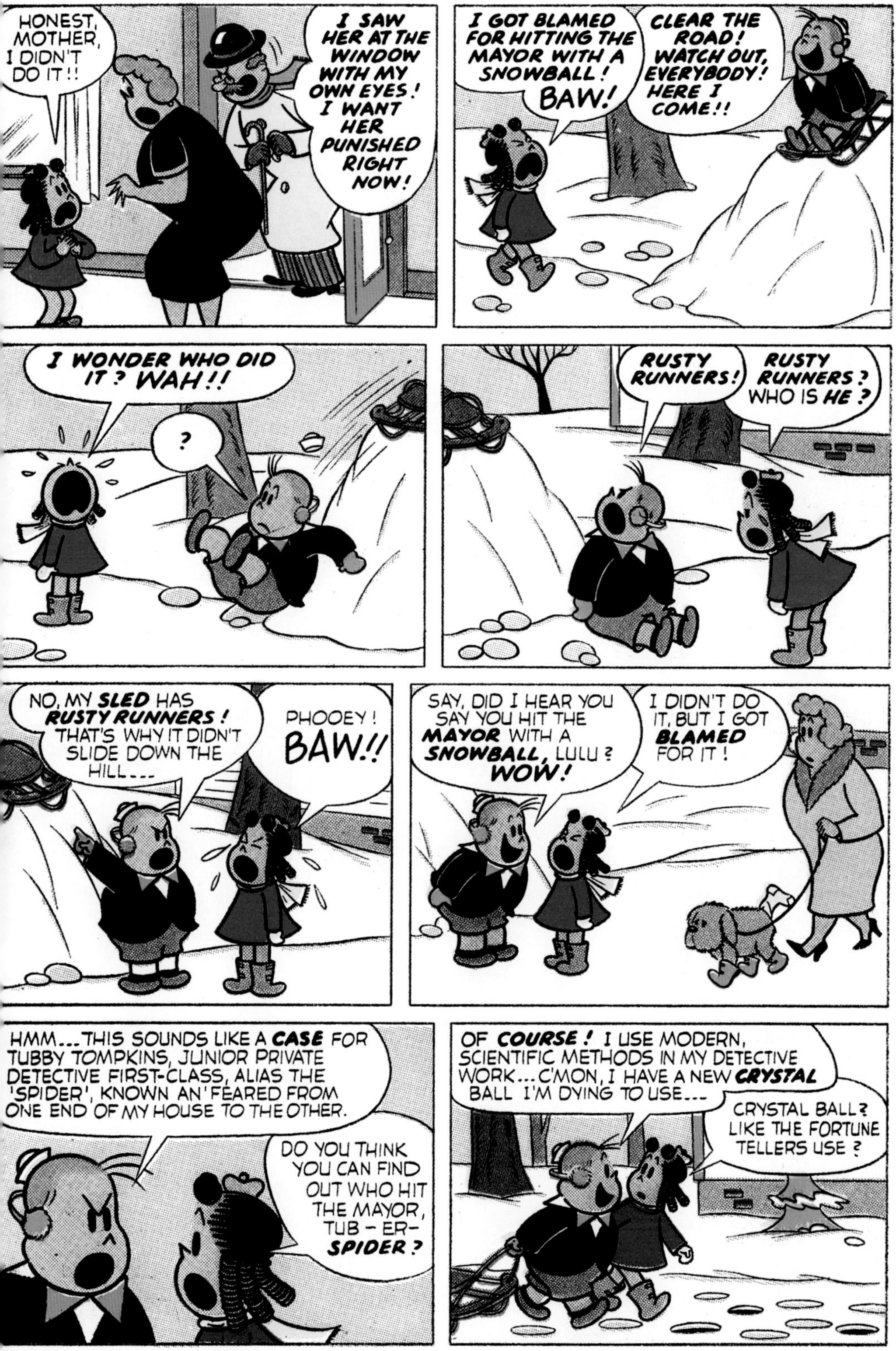
HONEST, MOTHER, I DIDN'T DO IT!!
I SAW HER AT THE WINDOW WITH MY OWN EYES! I WANT HER PUNISHED RIGHT NOW!
I GOT BLAMED FOR HITTING THE MAYOR WITH A SNOWBALL! BAW!
CLEAR THE ROAD! WATCH OUT, EVERYBODY! HERE I COME!!
I WONDER WHO DID IT? WAH!!
?
RUSTY RUNNERS!
RUSTY RUNNERS? WHO IS HE?
NO, MY SLED HAS RUSTY RUNNERS! THAT'S WHY IT DIDN'T SLIDE DOWN THE HILL...
PHOOEY! BAW!!
SAY, DID I HEAR YOU SAY YOU HIT THE MAYOR WITH A SNOWBALL, LULU? WOW!
I DIDN'T DO IT, BUT I GOT BLAMED FOR IT!
HMM...THIS SOUNDS LIKE A CASE FOR TUBBY TOMPKINS, JUNIOR PRIVATE DETECTIVE FIRST-CLASS, ALIAS THE 'SPIDER', KNOWN AN' FEARED FROM ONE END OF MY HOUSE TO THE OTHER.
DO YOU THINK YOU CAN FIND OUT WHO HIT THE MAYOR, TUB - ER- SPIDER?
OF COURSE! I USE MODERN, SCIENTIFIC METHODS IN MY DETECTIVE WORK...C'MON, I HAVE A NEW CRYSTAL BALL I'M DYING TO USE...
CRYSTAL BALL? LIKE THE FORTUNE TELLERS USE?

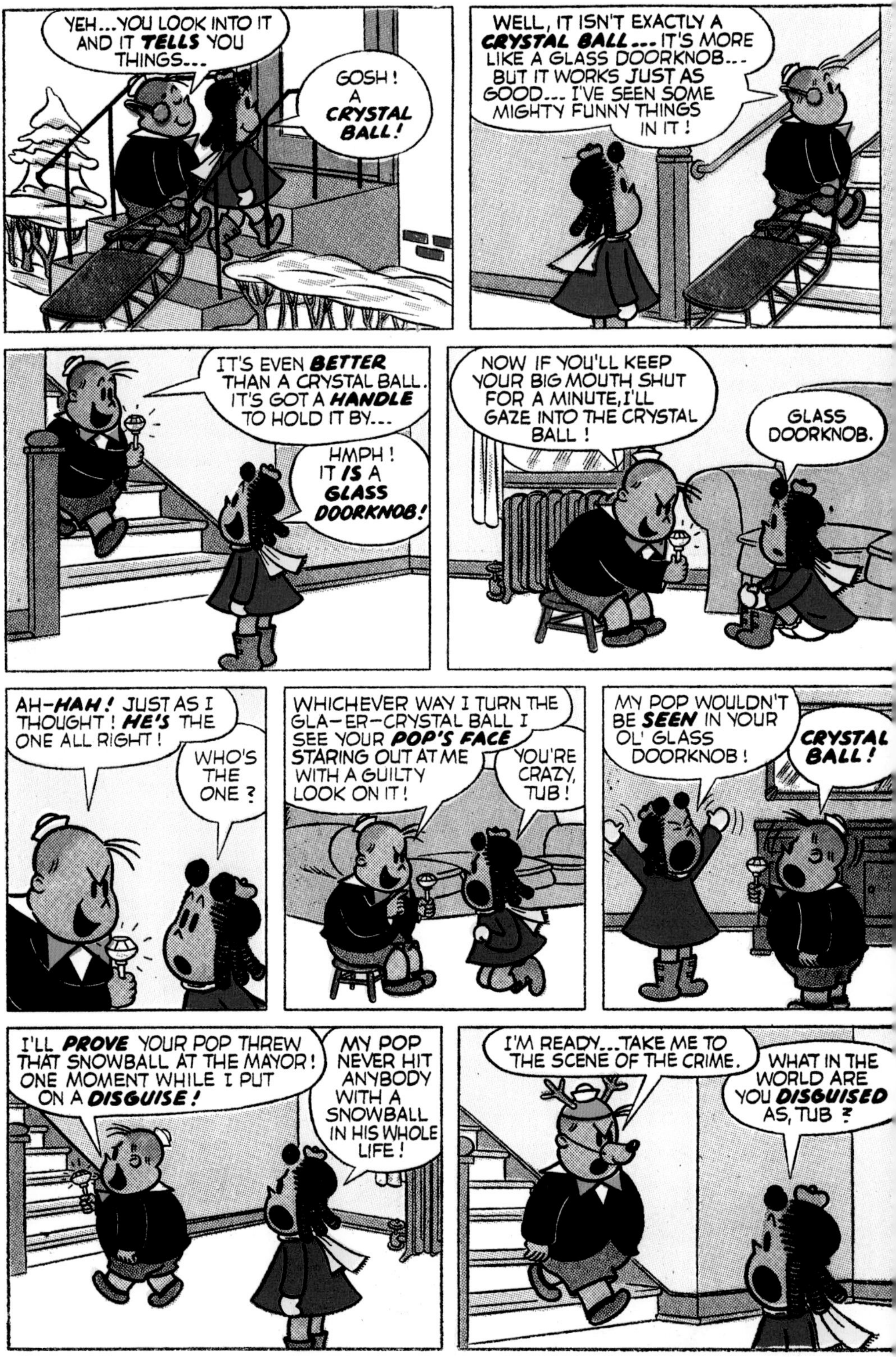
YEH...YOU LOOK INTO IT AND IT TELLS YOU THINGS...
GOSH! A CRYSTAL BALL!
WELL, IT ISN'T EXACTLY A CRYSTAL BALL... IT'S MORE LIKE A GLASS DOORKNOB... BUT IT WORKS JUST AS GOOD... I'VE SEEN SOME MIGHTY FUNNY THINGS IN IT!
IT'S EVEN BETTER THAN A CRYSTAL BALL. IT'S GOT A HANDLE TO HOLD IT BY...
HMPH! IT IS A GLASS DOORKNOB!
NOW IF YOU'LL KEEP YOUR BIG MOUTH SHUT FOR A MINUTE, I'LL GAZE INTO THE CRYSTAL BALL!
GLASS DOORKNOB.
AH-HAH! JUST AS I THOUGHT! HE'S THE ONE ALL RIGHT!
WHO'S THE ONE?
WHICHEVER WAY I TURN THE GLA-ER-CRYSTAL BALL I SEE YOUR POP'S FACE STARING OUT AT ME WITH A GUILTY LOOK ON IT!
YOU'RE CRAZY, TUB!
MY POP WOULDN'T BE SEEN IN YOUR OL' GLASS DOORKNOB!
CRYSTAL BALL!
I'LL PROVE YOUR POP THREW THAT SNOWBALL AT THE MAYOR! ONE MOMENT WHILE I PUT ON A DISGUISE!
MY POP NEVER HIT ANYBODY WITH A SNOWBALL IN HIS WHOLE LIFE!
I'M READY...TAKE ME TO THE SCENE OF THE CRIME.
WHAT IN THE WORLD ARE YOU DISGUISED AS, TUB?

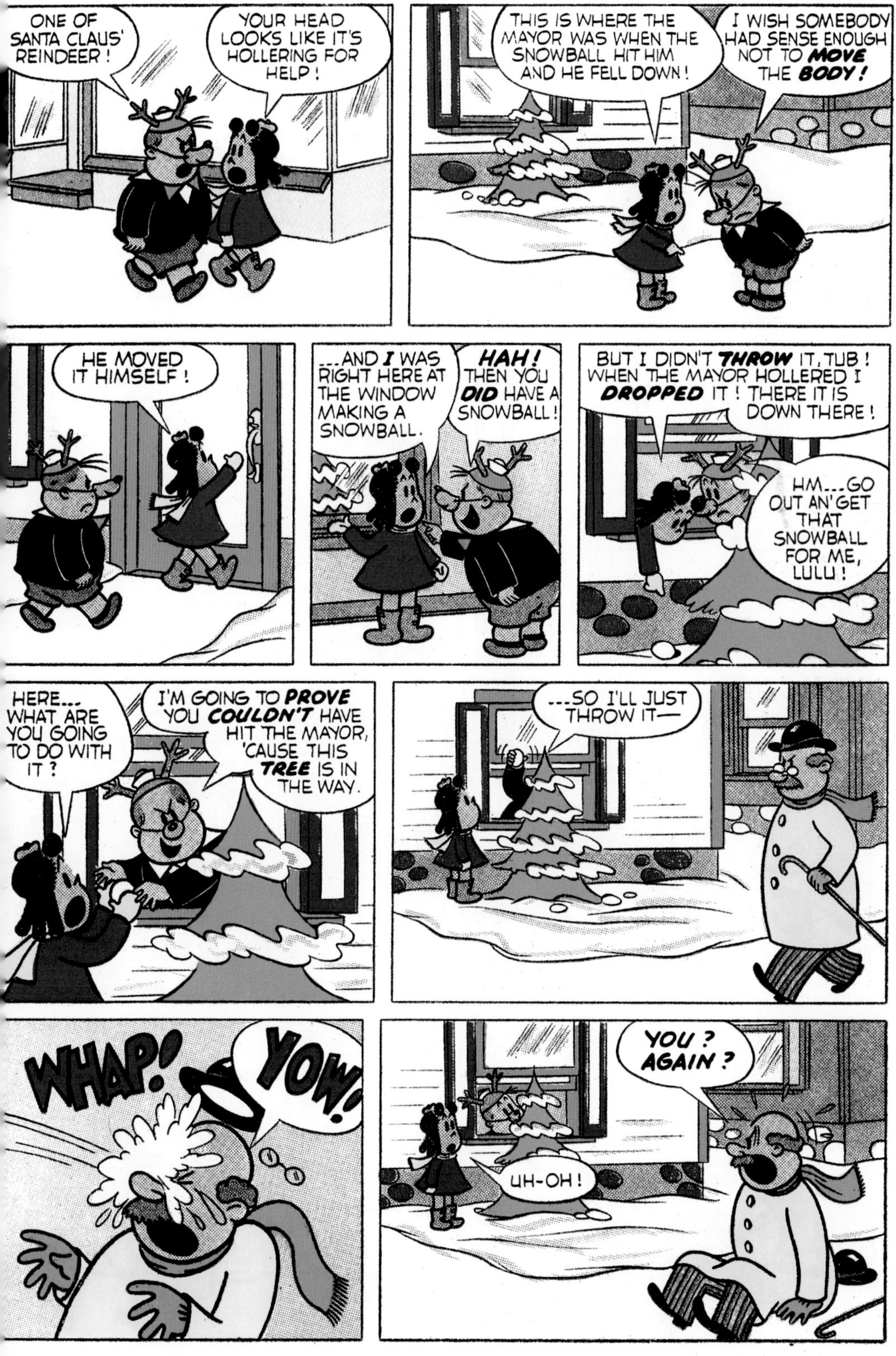
ONE OF SANTA CLAUS' REINDEER !
YOUR HEAD LOOKS LIKE IT'S HOLLERING FOR HELP !
THIS IS WHERE THE MAYOR WAS WHEN THE SNOWBALL HIT HIM AND HE FELL DOWN !
I WISH SOMEBODY HAD SENSE ENOUGH NOT TO **MOVE** THE **BODY !**
HE MOVED IT HIMSELF !
...AND **I** WAS RIGHT HERE AT THE WINDOW MAKING A SNOWBALL.
**HAH !** THEN YOU **DID** HAVE A SNOWBALL !
BUT I DIDN'T **THROW** IT, TUB ! WHEN THE MAYOR HOLLERED I **DROPPED** IT ! THERE IT IS DOWN THERE !
HM...GO OUT AN' GET THAT SNOWBALL FOR ME, LULU !
HERE... WHAT ARE YOU GOING TO DO WITH IT ?
I'M GOING TO **PROVE** YOU **COULDN'T** HAVE HIT THE MAYOR, 'CAUSE THIS **TREE** IS IN THE WAY.
...SO I'LL JUST THROW IT—
WHAP!
YOW!
YOU ? AGAIN ?
UH-OH !

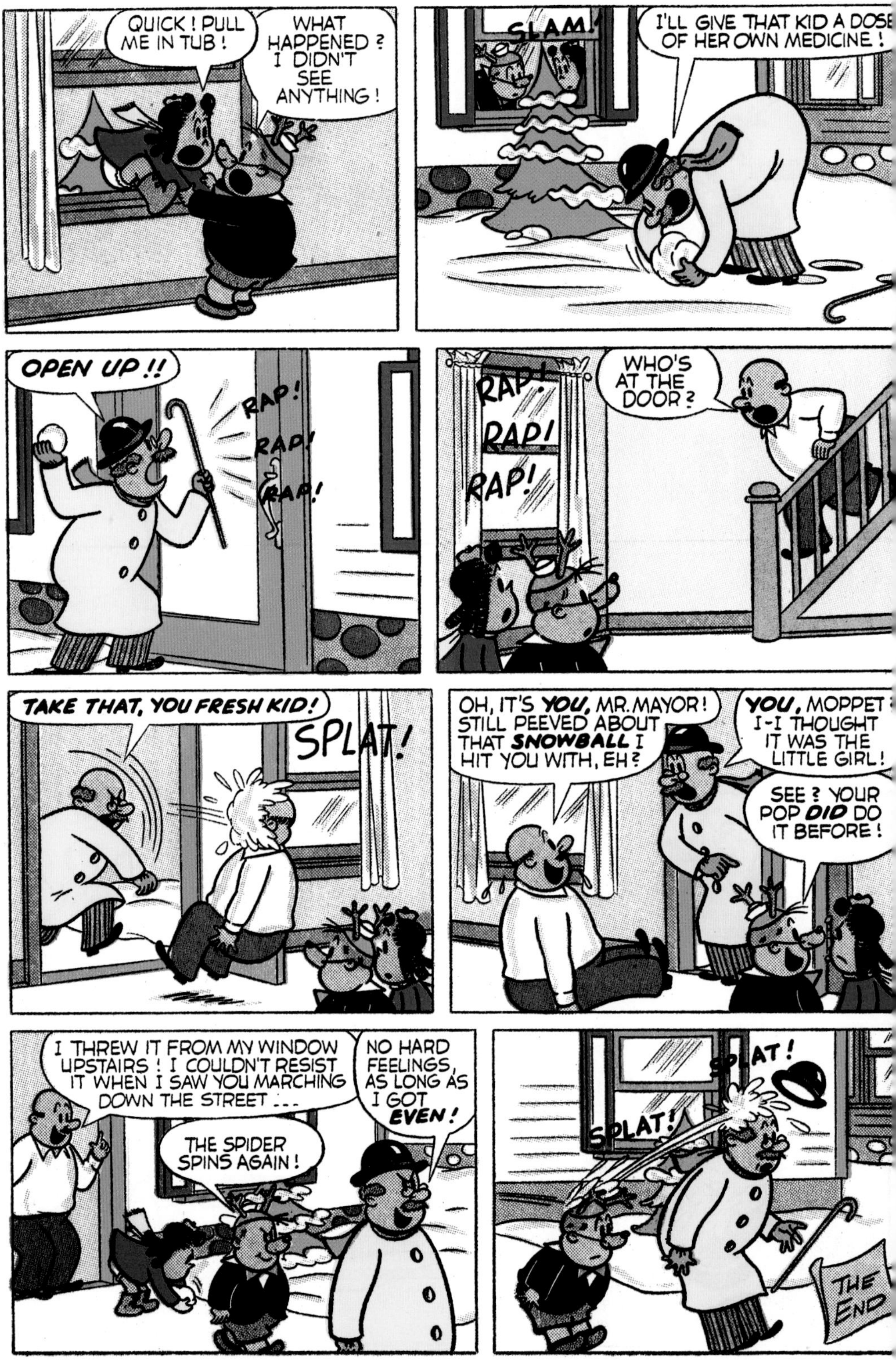
QUICK! PULL ME IN TUB!
WHAT HAPPENED? I DIDN'T SEE ANYTHING!
SLAM!
I'LL GIVE THAT KID A DOSE OF HER OWN MEDICINE!
OPEN UP!!
RAP! RAP! RAP!
RAP! RAP! RAP!
WHO'S AT THE DOOR?
TAKE THAT, YOU FRESH KID!
SPLAT!
OH, IT'S YOU, MR. MAYOR! STILL PEEVED ABOUT THAT SNOWBALL I HIT YOU WITH, EH?
YOU, MOPPET! I-I THOUGHT IT WAS THE LITTLE GIRL!
SEE? YOUR POP DID DO IT BEFORE!
I THREW IT FROM MY WINDOW UPSTAIRS! I COULDN'T RESIST IT WHEN I SAW YOU MARCHING DOWN THE STREET...
NO HARD FEELINGS, AS LONG AS I GOT EVEN!
THE SPIDER SPINS AGAIN!
SPLAT!
SPLAT!
THE END

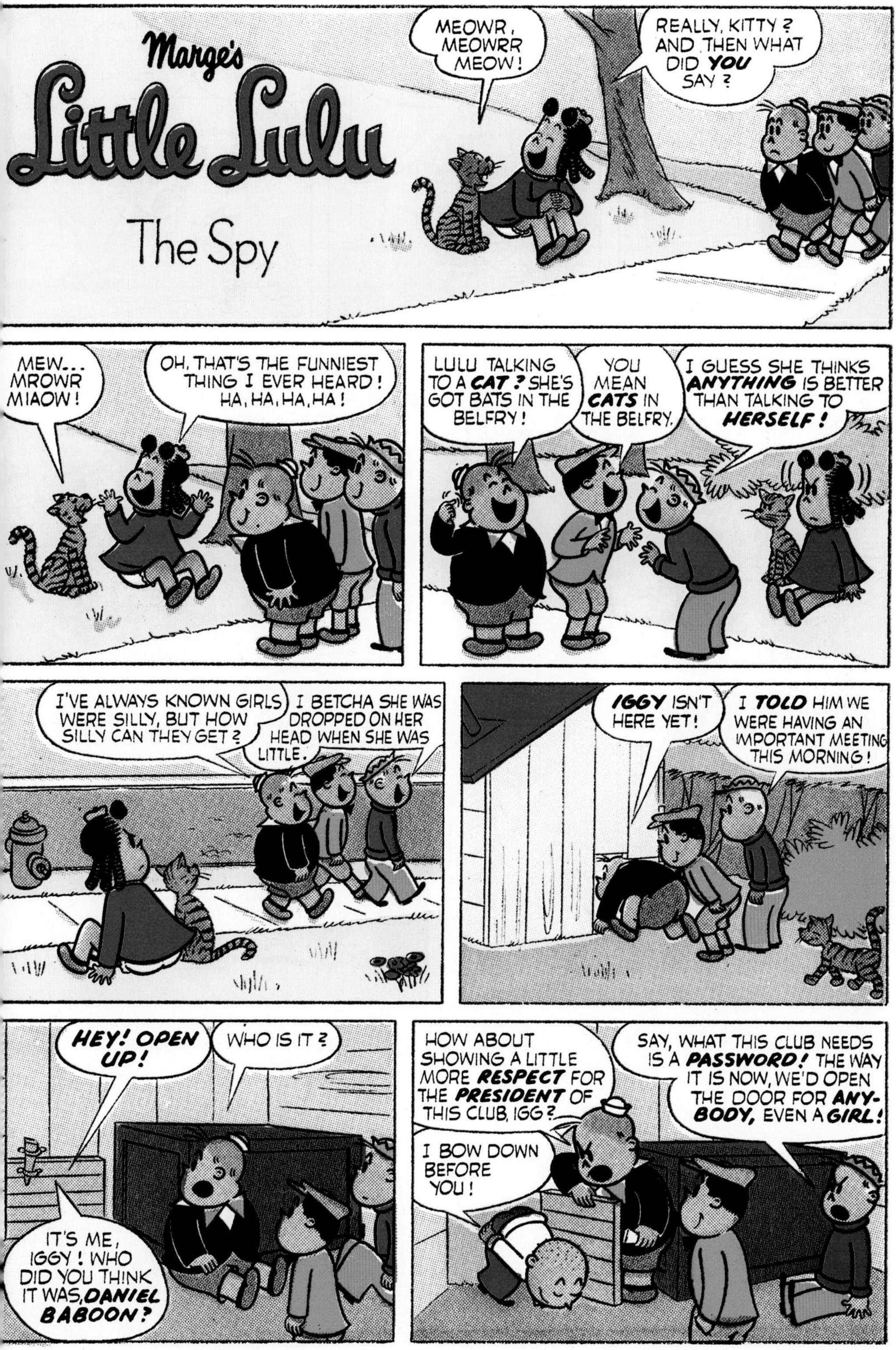
Marge's
Little Lulu
The Spy
MEOWR, MEOWRR MEOW!
REALLY, KITTY? AND THEN WHAT DID YOU SAY?
MEW... MROWR MIAOW!
OH, THAT'S THE FUNNIEST THING I EVER HEARD! HA, HA, HA, HA!
LULU TALKING TO A CAT? SHE'S GOT BATS IN THE BELFRY!
YOU MEAN CATS IN THE BELFRY.
I GUESS SHE THINKS ANYTHING IS BETTER THAN TALKING TO HERSELF!
I'VE ALWAYS KNOWN GIRLS WERE SILLY, BUT HOW SILLY CAN THEY GET?
I BETCHA SHE WAS DROPPED ON HER HEAD WHEN SHE WAS LITTLE.
IGGY ISN'T HERE YET!
I TOLD HIM WE WERE HAVING AN IMPORTANT MEETING THIS MORNING!
HEY! OPEN UP!
WHO IS IT?
IT'S ME, IGGY! WHO DID YOU THINK IT WAS, DANIEL BABOON?
HOW ABOUT SHOWING A LITTLE MORE RESPECT FOR THE PRESIDENT OF THIS CLUB, IGG?
I BOW DOWN BEFORE YOU!
SAY, WHAT THIS CLUB NEEDS IS A PASSWORD! THE WAY IT IS NOW, WE'D OPEN THE DOOR FOR ANYBODY, EVEN A GIRL!

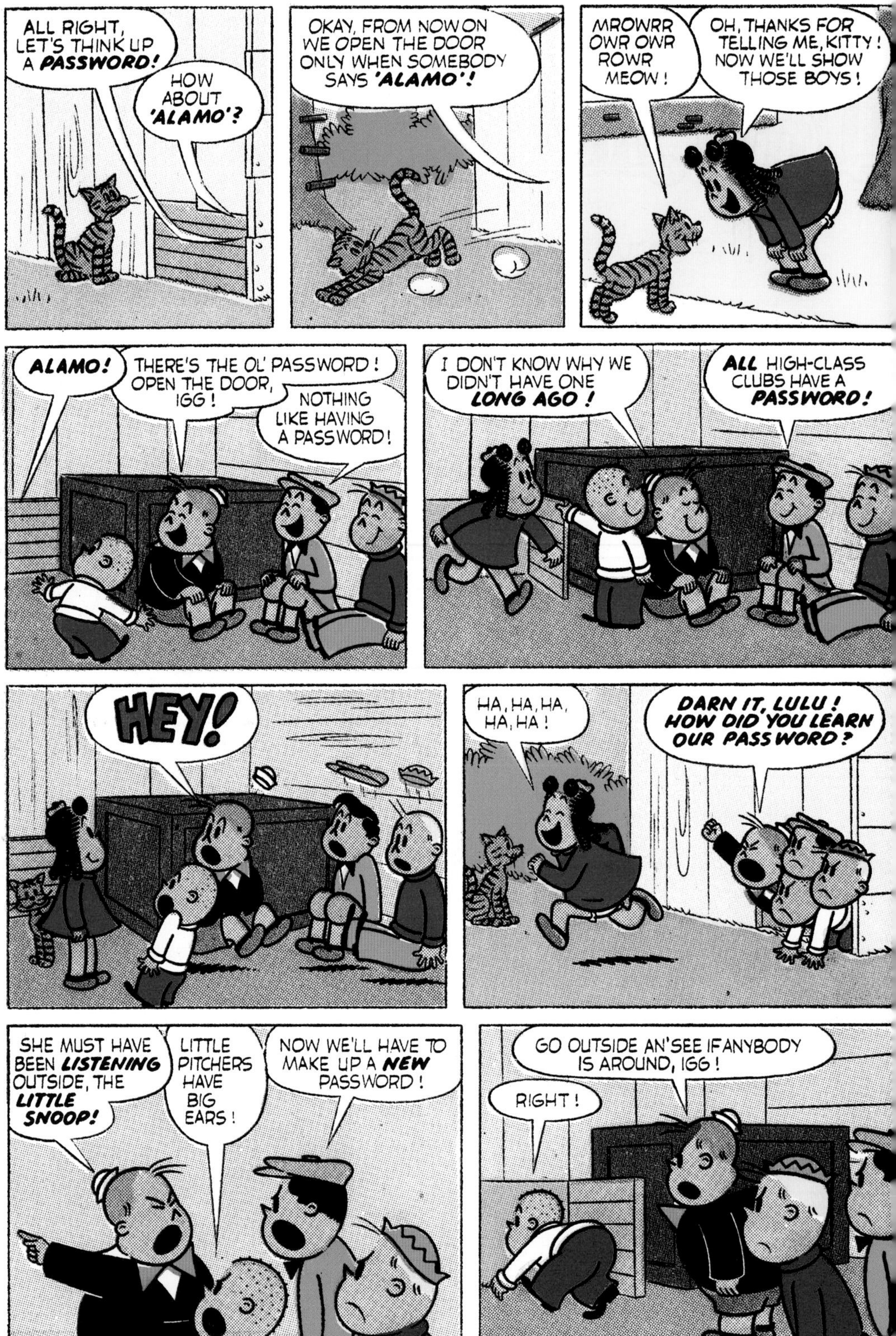
ALL RIGHT, LET'S THINK UP A PASSWORD!
HOW ABOUT 'ALAMO'?
OKAY, FROM NOW ON WE OPEN THE DOOR ONLY WHEN SOMEBODY SAYS 'ALAMO'!
MROWRR OWR OWR ROWR MEOW!
OH, THANKS FOR TELLING ME, KITTY! NOW WE'LL SHOW THOSE BOYS!
ALAMO!
THERE'S THE OL' PASSWORD! OPEN THE DOOR, IGG!
NOTHING LIKE HAVING A PASSWORD!
I DON'T KNOW WHY WE DIDN'T HAVE ONE LONG AGO!
ALL HIGH-CLASS CLUBS HAVE A PASSWORD!
HEY!
HA, HA, HA, HA, HA!
DARN IT, LULU! HOW DID YOU LEARN OUR PASSWORD?
SHE MUST HAVE BEEN LISTENING OUTSIDE, THE LITTLE SNOOP!
LITTLE PITCHERS HAVE BIG EARS!
NOW WE'LL HAVE TO MAKE UP A NEW PASSWORD!
GO OUTSIDE AN' SEE IF ANYBODY IS AROUND, IGG!
RIGHT!

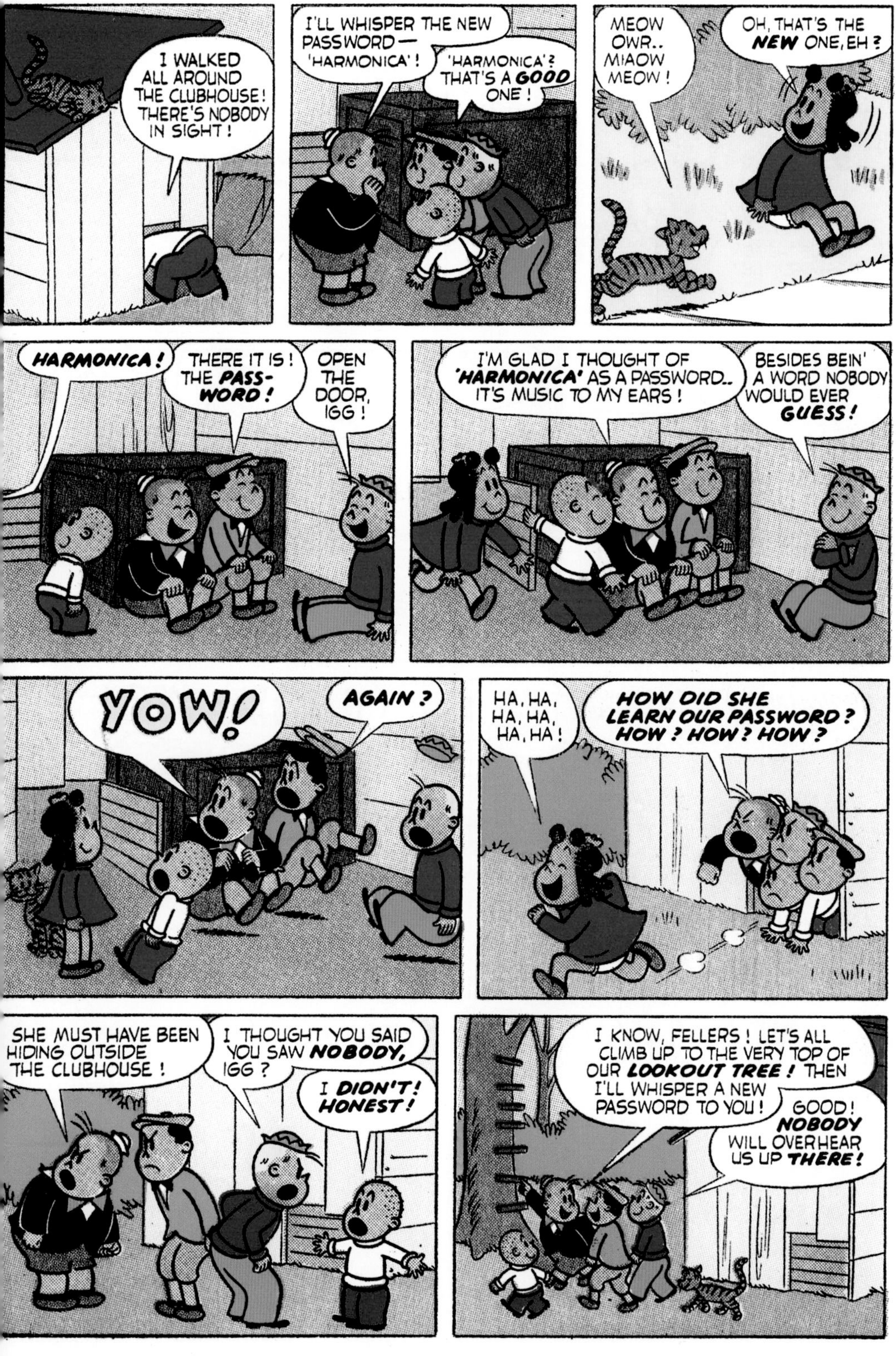
I WALKED ALL AROUND THE CLUBHOUSE! THERE'S NOBODY IN SIGHT!
I'LL WHISPER THE NEW PASSWORD — 'HARMONICA'!
'HARMONICA'? THAT'S A GOOD ONE!
MEOW OWR.. MIAOW MEOW!
OH, THAT'S THE NEW ONE, EH?
HARMONICA!
THERE IT IS! THE PASS-WORD!
OPEN THE DOOR, IGG!
I'M GLAD I THOUGHT OF 'HARMONICA' AS A PASSWORD.. IT'S MUSIC TO MY EARS!
BESIDES BEIN' A WORD NOBODY WOULD EVER GUESS!
YOW!
AGAIN?
HA, HA, HA, HA, HA, HA!
HOW DID SHE LEARN OUR PASSWORD? HOW? HOW? HOW?
SHE MUST HAVE BEEN HIDING OUTSIDE THE CLUBHOUSE!
I THOUGHT YOU SAID YOU SAW NOBODY, IGG?
I DIDN'T! HONEST!
I KNOW, FELLERS! LET'S ALL CLIMB UP TO THE VERY TOP OF OUR LOOKOUT TREE! THEN I'LL WHISPER A NEW PASSWORD TO YOU!
GOOD! NOBODY WILL OVERHEAR US UP THERE!

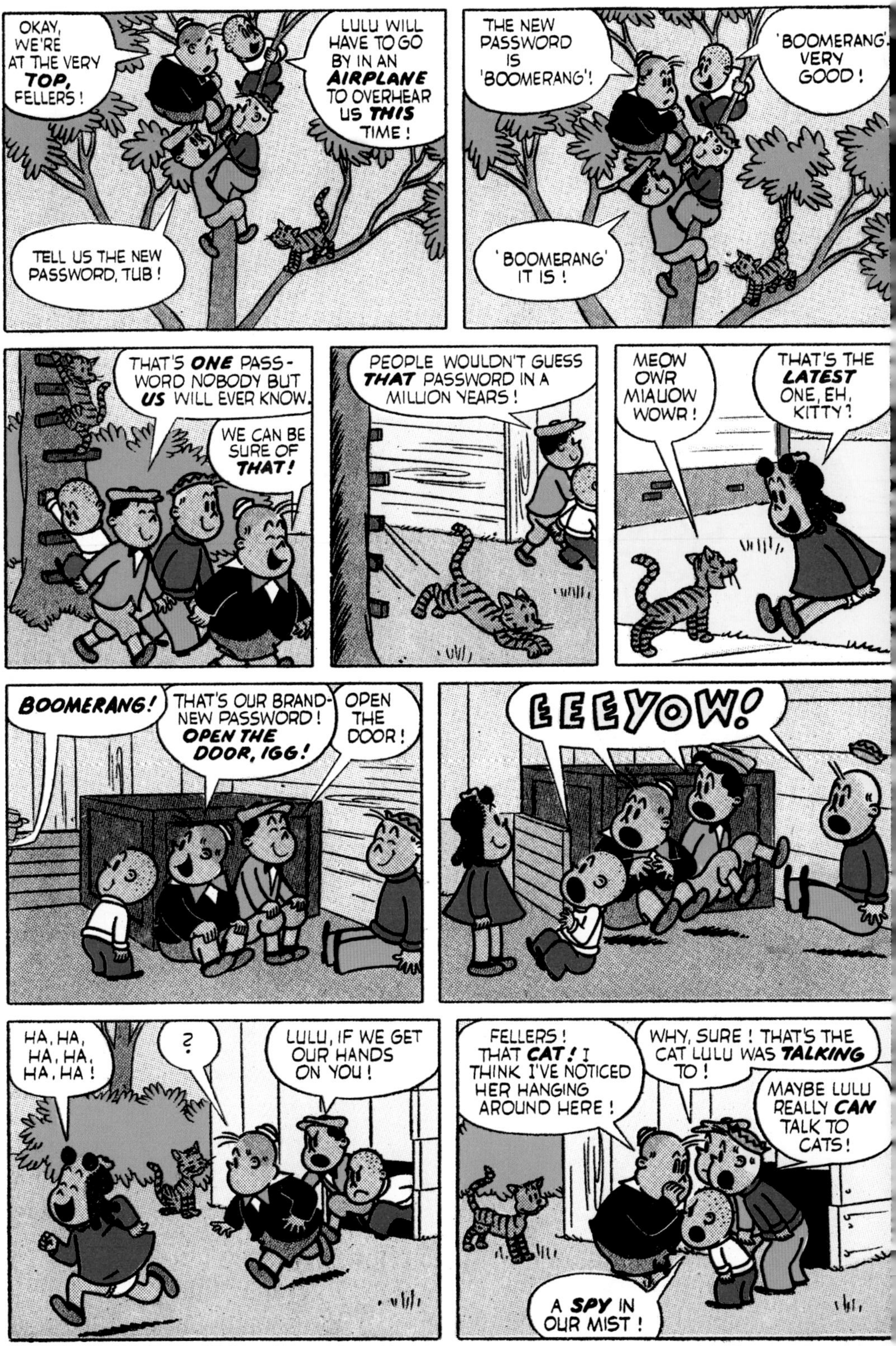

OKAY, WE'RE AT THE VERY TOP, FELLERS!
LULU WILL HAVE TO GO BY IN AN AIRPLANE TO OVERHEAR US THIS TIME!
TELL US THE NEW PASSWORD, TUB!
THE NEW PASSWORD IS 'BOOMERANG'!
'BOOMERANG'. VERY GOOD!
'BOOMERANG' IT IS!
THAT'S ONE PASS-WORD NOBODY BUT US WILL EVER KNOW.
WE CAN BE SURE OF THAT!
PEOPLE WOULDN'T GUESS THAT PASSWORD IN A MILLION YEARS!
MEOW OWR MIAUOW WOWR!
THAT'S THE LATEST ONE, EH, KITTY?
BOOMERANG!
THAT'S OUR BRAND-NEW PASSWORD! OPEN THE DOOR, IGG!
OPEN THE DOOR!
EEEYOW!
HA, HA, HA, HA, HA, HA!
?
LULU, IF WE GET OUR HANDS ON YOU!
FELLERS! THAT CAT! I THINK I'VE NOTICED HER HANGING AROUND HERE!
WHY, SURE! THAT'S THE CAT LULU WAS TALKING TO!
MAYBE LULU REALLY CAN TALK TO CATS!
A SPY IN OUR MIST!

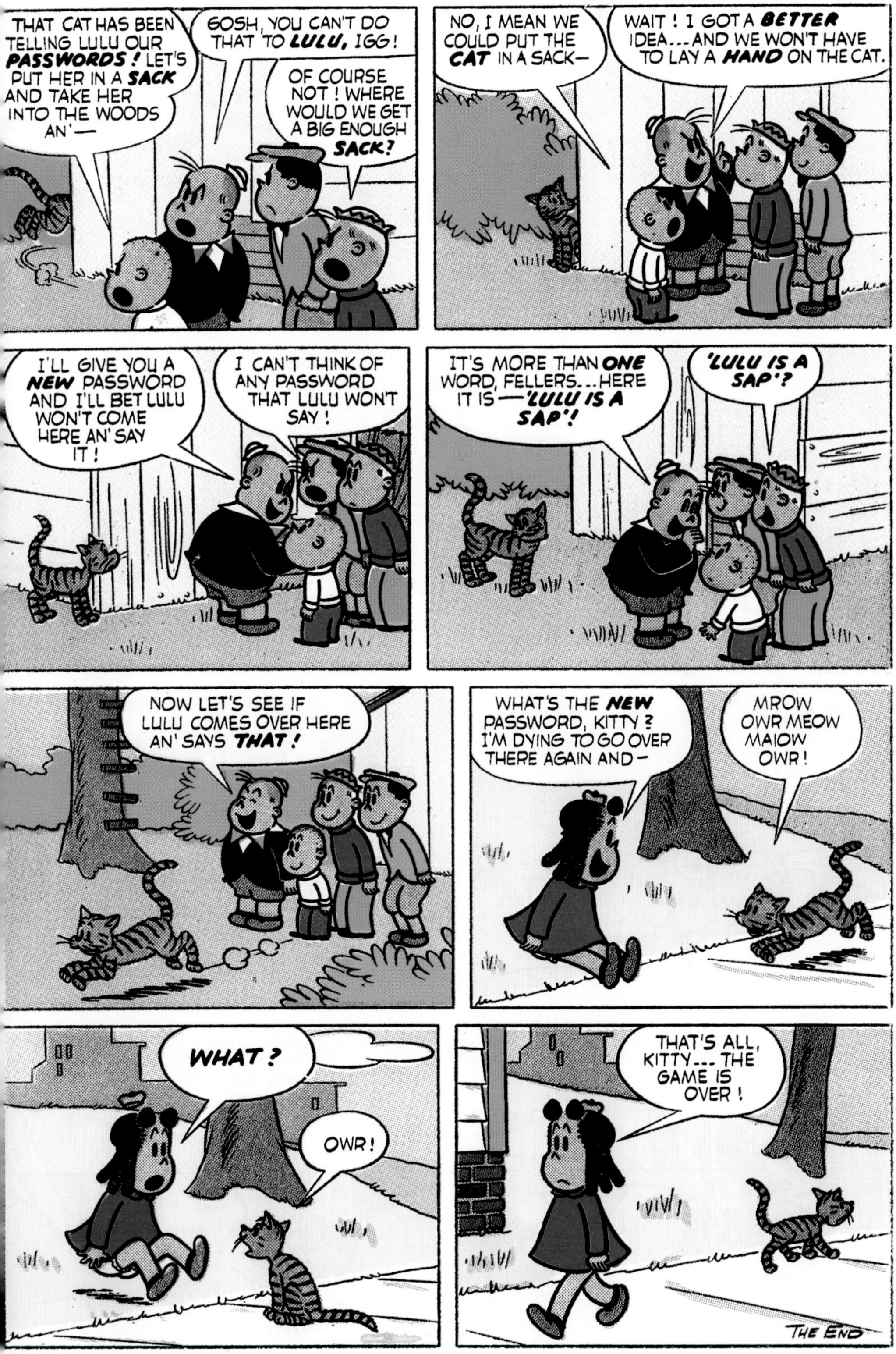
THAT CAT HAS BEEN TELLING LULU OUR PASSWORDS! LET'S PUT HER IN A SACK AND TAKE HER INTO THE WOODS AN'—
GOSH, YOU CAN'T DO THAT TO LULU, IGG!
OF COURSE NOT! WHERE WOULD WE GET A BIG ENOUGH SACK?
NO, I MEAN WE COULD PUT THE CAT IN A SACK—
WAIT! I GOT A BETTER IDEA...AND WE WON'T HAVE TO LAY A HAND ON THE CAT.
I'LL GIVE YOU A NEW PASSWORD AND I'LL BET LULU WON'T COME HERE AN' SAY IT!
I CAN'T THINK OF ANY PASSWORD THAT LULU WON'T SAY!
IT'S MORE THAN ONE WORD, FELLERS...HERE IT IS—'LULU IS A SAP'!
'LULU IS A SAP'?
NOW LET'S SEE IF LULU COMES OVER HERE AN' SAYS THAT!
WHAT'S THE NEW PASSWORD, KITTY? I'M DYING TO GO OVER THERE AGAIN AND—
MROW OWR MEOW MAIOW OWR!
WHAT?
OWR!
THAT'S ALL, KITTY... THE GAME IS OVER!
THE END

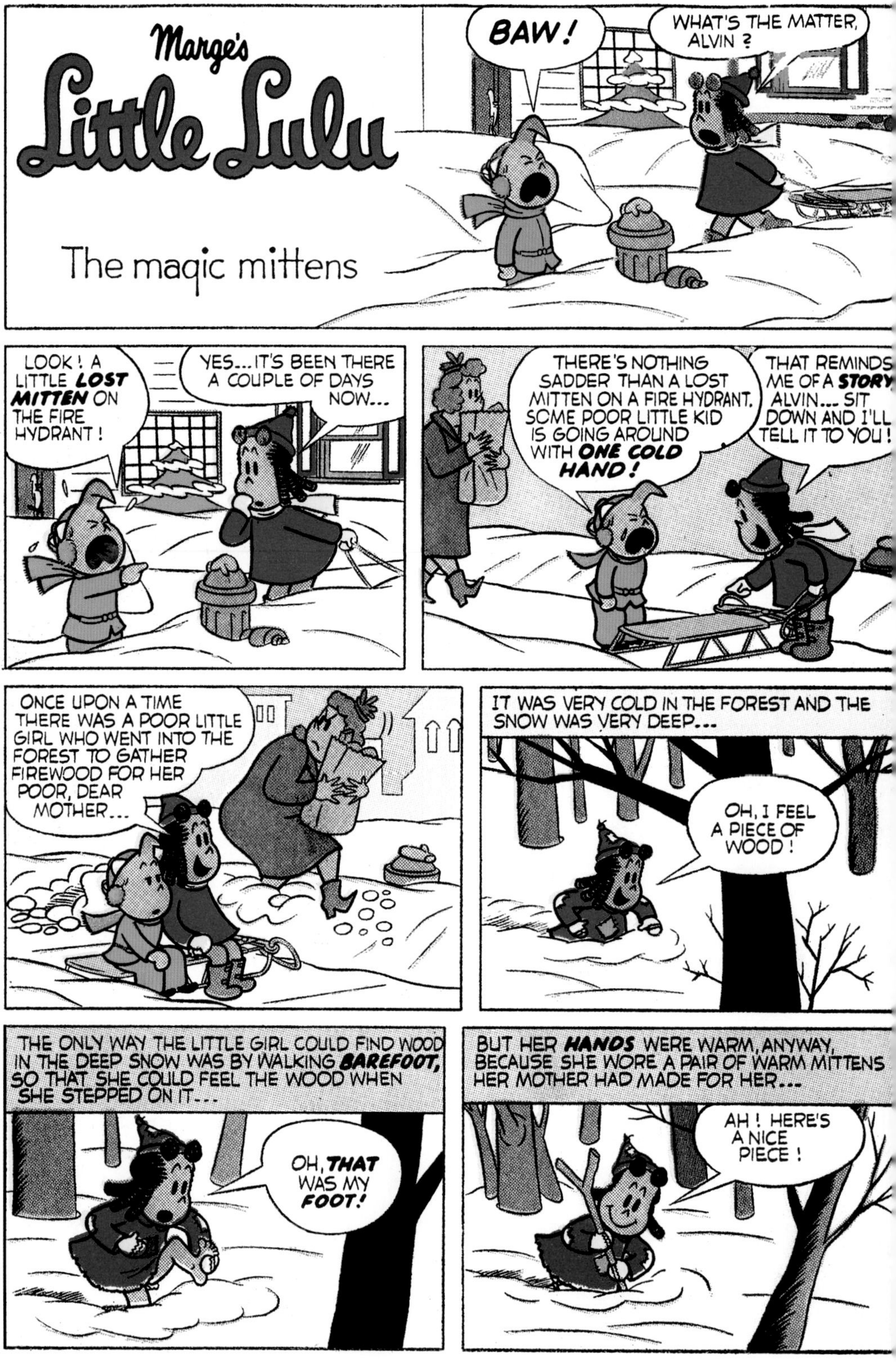
Marge's Little Lulu
The magic mittens
BAW!
WHAT'S THE MATTER, ALVIN ?
LOOK! A LITTLE LOST MITTEN ON THE FIRE HYDRANT!
YES... IT'S BEEN THERE A COUPLE OF DAYS NOW...
THERE'S NOTHING SADDER THAN A LOST MITTEN ON A FIRE HYDRANT. SOME POOR LITTLE KID IS GOING AROUND WITH ONE COLD HAND!
THAT REMINDS ME OF A STORY ALVIN... SIT DOWN AND I'LL TELL IT TO YOU!
ONCE UPON A TIME THERE WAS A POOR LITTLE GIRL WHO WENT INTO THE FOREST TO GATHER FIREWOOD FOR HER POOR, DEAR MOTHER...
IT WAS VERY COLD IN THE FOREST AND THE SNOW WAS VERY DEEP...
OH, I FEEL A PIECE OF WOOD!
THE ONLY WAY THE LITTLE GIRL COULD FIND WOOD IN THE DEEP SNOW WAS BY WALKING BAREFOOT, SO THAT SHE COULD FEEL THE WOOD WHEN SHE STEPPED ON IT...
OH, THAT WAS MY FOOT!
BUT HER HANDS WERE WARM, ANYWAY, BECAUSE SHE WORE A PAIR OF WARM MITTENS HER MOTHER HAD MADE FOR HER...
AH! HERE'S A NICE PIECE!

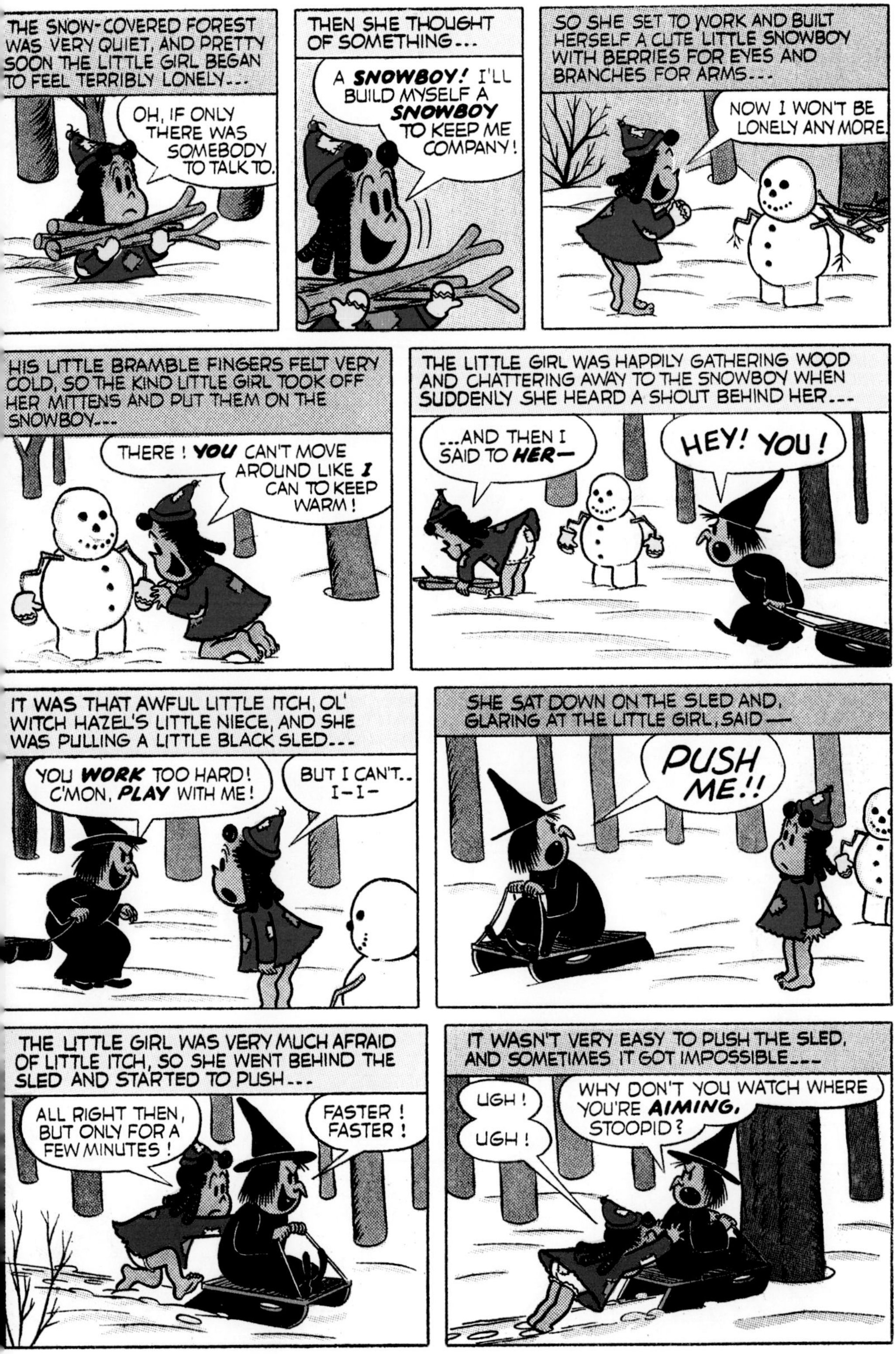
THE SNOW-COVERED FOREST WAS VERY QUIET, AND PRETTY SOON THE LITTLE GIRL BEGAN TO FEEL TERRIBLY LONELY...
OH, IF ONLY THERE WAS SOMEBODY TO TALK TO.
THEN SHE THOUGHT OF SOMETHING...
A SNOWBOY! I'LL BUILD MYSELF A SNOWBOY TO KEEP ME COMPANY!
SO SHE SET TO WORK AND BUILT HERSELF A CUTE LITTLE SNOWBOY WITH BERRIES FOR EYES AND BRANCHES FOR ARMS...
NOW I WON'T BE LONELY ANY MORE.
HIS LITTLE BRAMBLE FINGERS FELT VERY COLD, SO THE KIND LITTLE GIRL TOOK OFF HER MITTENS AND PUT THEM ON THE SNOWBOY...
THERE! YOU CAN'T MOVE AROUND LIKE I CAN TO KEEP WARM!
THE LITTLE GIRL WAS HAPPILY GATHERING WOOD AND CHATTERING AWAY TO THE SNOWBOY WHEN SUDDENLY SHE HEARD A SHOUT BEHIND HER...
...AND THEN I SAID TO HER—
HEY! YOU!
IT WAS THAT AWFUL LITTLE ITCH, OL' WITCH HAZEL'S LITTLE NIECE, AND SHE WAS PULLING A LITTLE BLACK SLED...
YOU WORK TOO HARD! C'MON, PLAY WITH ME!
BUT I CAN'T.. I-I-
SHE SAT DOWN ON THE SLED AND, GLARING AT THE LITTLE GIRL, SAID—
PUSH ME!!
THE LITTLE GIRL WAS VERY MUCH AFRAID OF LITTLE ITCH, SO SHE WENT BEHIND THE SLED AND STARTED TO PUSH...
ALL RIGHT THEN, BUT ONLY FOR A FEW MINUTES!
FASTER! FASTER!
IT WASN'T VERY EASY TO PUSH THE SLED, AND SOMETIMES IT GOT IMPOSSIBLE...
UGH!
UGH!
WHY DON'T YOU WATCH WHERE YOU'RE AIMING, STOOPID?

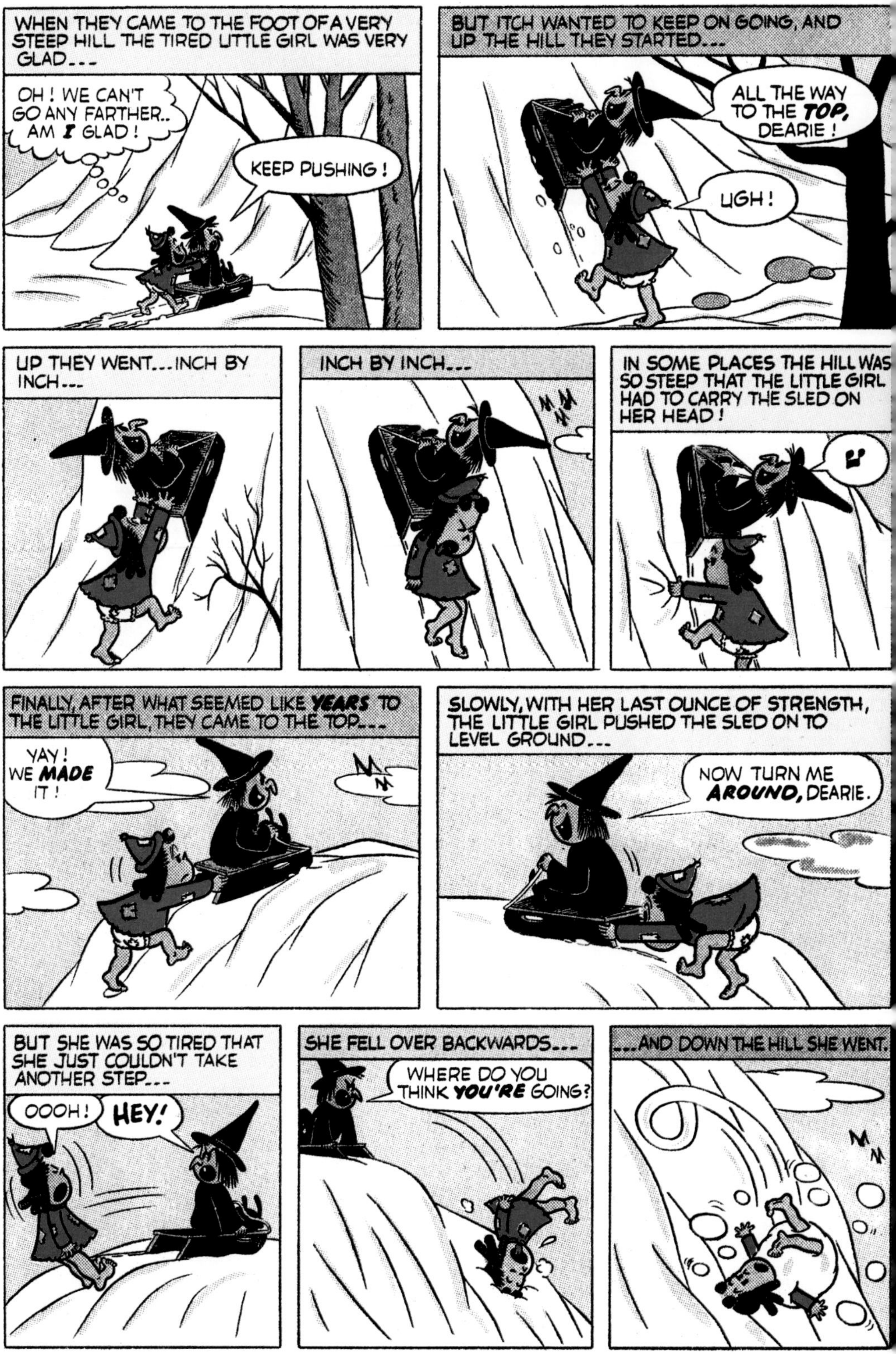

WHEN THEY CAME TO THE FOOT OF A VERY STEEP HILL THE TIRED LITTLE GIRL WAS VERY GLAD...
OH! WE CAN'T GO ANY FARTHER.. AM I GLAD!
KEEP PUSHING!
BUT ITCH WANTED TO KEEP ON GOING, AND UP THE HILL THEY STARTED...
ALL THE WAY TO THE TOP, DEARIE!
UGH!
UP THEY WENT... INCH BY INCH...
INCH BY INCH...
IN SOME PLACES THE HILL WAS SO STEEP THAT THE LITTLE GIRL HAD TO CARRY THE SLED ON HER HEAD!
FINALLY, AFTER WHAT SEEMED LIKE YEARS TO THE LITTLE GIRL, THEY CAME TO THE TOP...
YAY! WE MADE IT!
SLOWLY, WITH HER LAST OUNCE OF STRENGTH, THE LITTLE GIRL PUSHED THE SLED ON TO LEVEL GROUND...
NOW TURN ME AROUND, DEARIE.
BUT SHE WAS SO TIRED THAT SHE JUST COULDN'T TAKE ANOTHER STEP...
OOOH!
HEY!
SHE FELL OVER BACKWARDS...
WHERE DO YOU THINK YOU'RE GOING?
...AND DOWN THE HILL SHE WENT.

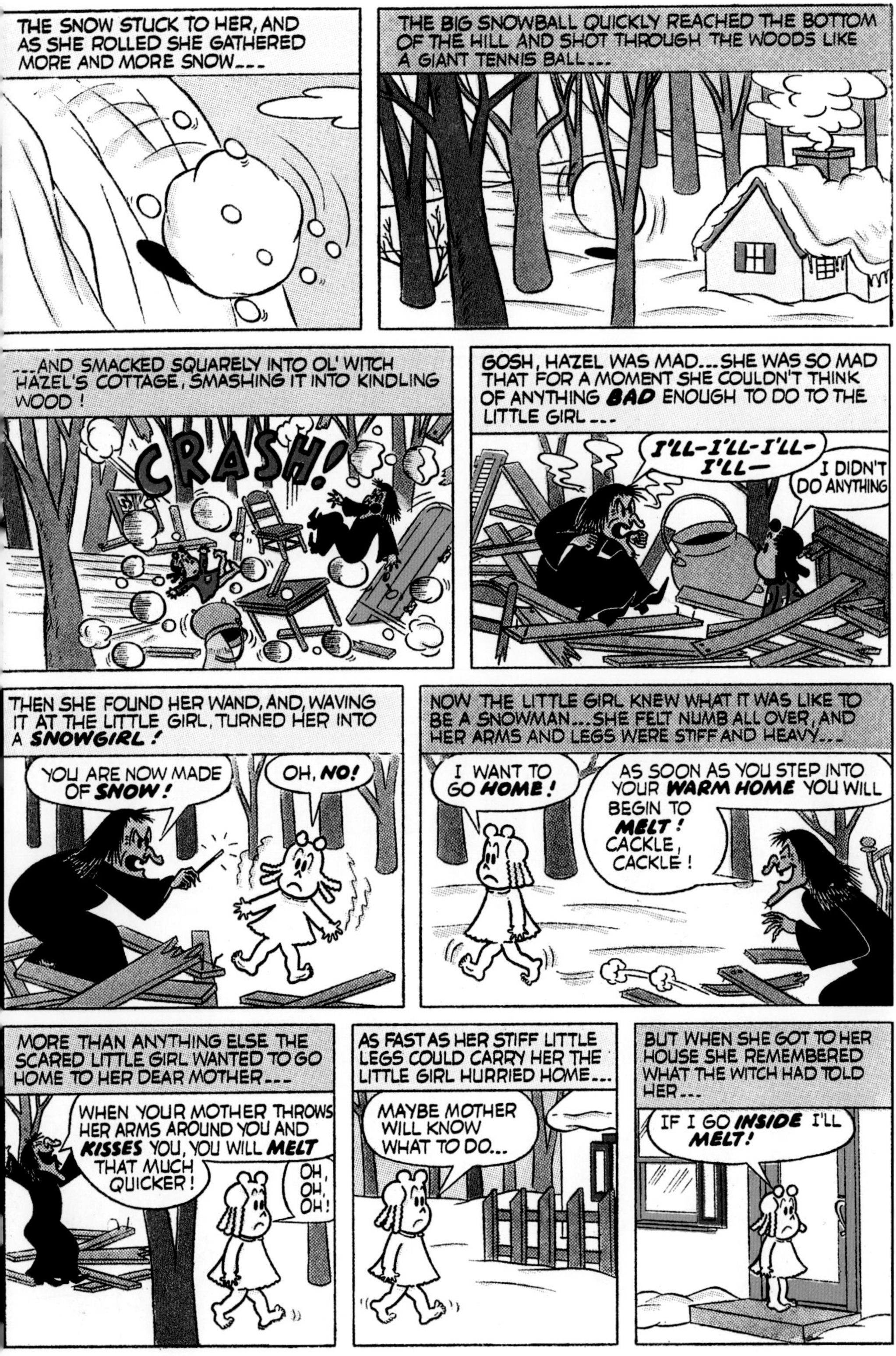
THE SNOW STUCK TO HER, AND AS SHE ROLLED SHE GATHERED MORE AND MORE SNOW...
THE BIG SNOWBALL QUICKLY REACHED THE BOTTOM OF THE HILL AND SHOT THROUGH THE WOODS LIKE A GIANT TENNIS BALL...
...AND SMACKED SQUARELY INTO OL' WITCH HAZEL'S COTTAGE, SMASHING IT INTO KINDLING WOOD!
CRASH!
GOSH, HAZEL WAS MAD...SHE WAS SO MAD THAT FOR A MOMENT SHE COULDN'T THINK OF ANYTHING BAD ENOUGH TO DO TO THE LITTLE GIRL...
I'LL-I'LL-I'LL-I'LL—
I DIDN'T DO ANYTHING
THEN SHE FOUND HER WAND, AND, WAVING IT AT THE LITTLE GIRL, TURNED HER INTO A SNOWGIRL!
YOU ARE NOW MADE OF SNOW!
OH, NO!
NOW THE LITTLE GIRL KNEW WHAT IT WAS LIKE TO BE A SNOWMAN...SHE FELT NUMB ALL OVER, AND HER ARMS AND LEGS WERE STIFF AND HEAVY...
I WANT TO GO HOME!
AS SOON AS YOU STEP INTO YOUR WARM HOME YOU WILL BEGIN TO MELT! CACKLE, CACKLE!
MORE THAN ANYTHING ELSE THE SCARED LITTLE GIRL WANTED TO GO HOME TO HER DEAR MOTHER...
WHEN YOUR MOTHER THROWS HER ARMS AROUND YOU AND KISSES YOU, YOU WILL MELT THAT MUCH QUICKER!
OH, OH, OH!
AS FAST AS HER STIFF LITTLE LEGS COULD CARRY HER THE LITTLE GIRL HURRIED HOME...
MAYBE MOTHER WILL KNOW WHAT TO DO...
BUT WHEN SHE GOT TO HER HOUSE SHE REMEMBERED WHAT THE WITCH HAD TOLD HER...
IF I GO INSIDE I'LL MELT!

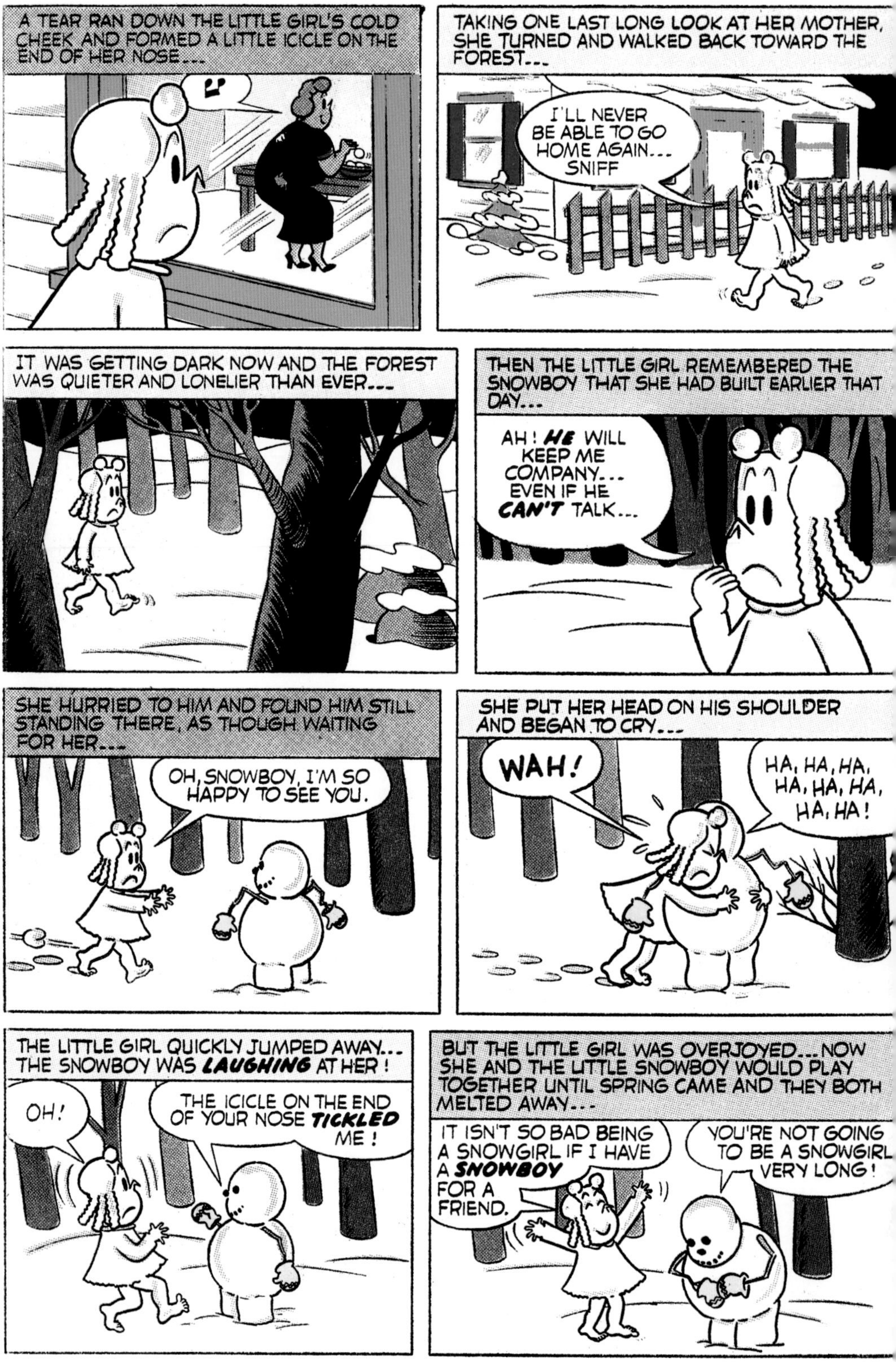
A TEAR RAN DOWN THE LITTLE GIRL'S COLD CHEEK AND FORMED A LITTLE ICICLE ON THE END OF HER NOSE...
TAKING ONE LAST LONG LOOK AT HER MOTHER, SHE TURNED AND WALKED BACK TOWARD THE FOREST...
I'LL NEVER BE ABLE TO GO HOME AGAIN... SNIFF
IT WAS GETTING DARK NOW AND THE FOREST WAS QUIETER AND LONELIER THAN EVER...
THEN THE LITTLE GIRL REMEMBERED THE SNOWBOY THAT SHE HAD BUILT EARLIER THAT DAY...
AH! HE WILL KEEP ME COMPANY... EVEN IF HE CAN'T TALK...
SHE HURRIED TO HIM AND FOUND HIM STILL STANDING THERE, AS THOUGH WAITING FOR HER...
OH, SNOWBOY, I'M SO HAPPY TO SEE YOU.
SHE PUT HER HEAD ON HIS SHOULDER AND BEGAN TO CRY...
WAH!
HA, HA, HA, HA, HA, HA, HA, HA!
THE LITTLE GIRL QUICKLY JUMPED AWAY... THE SNOWBOY WAS LAUGHING AT HER!
OH!
THE ICICLE ON THE END OF YOUR NOSE TICKLED ME!
BUT THE LITTLE GIRL WAS OVERJOYED... NOW SHE AND THE LITTLE SNOWBOY WOULD PLAY TOGETHER UNTIL SPRING CAME AND THEY BOTH MELTED AWAY...
IT ISN'T SO BAD BEING A SNOWGIRL IF I HAVE A SNOWBOY FOR A FRIEND.
YOU'RE NOT GOING TO BE A SNOWGIRL VERY LONG!

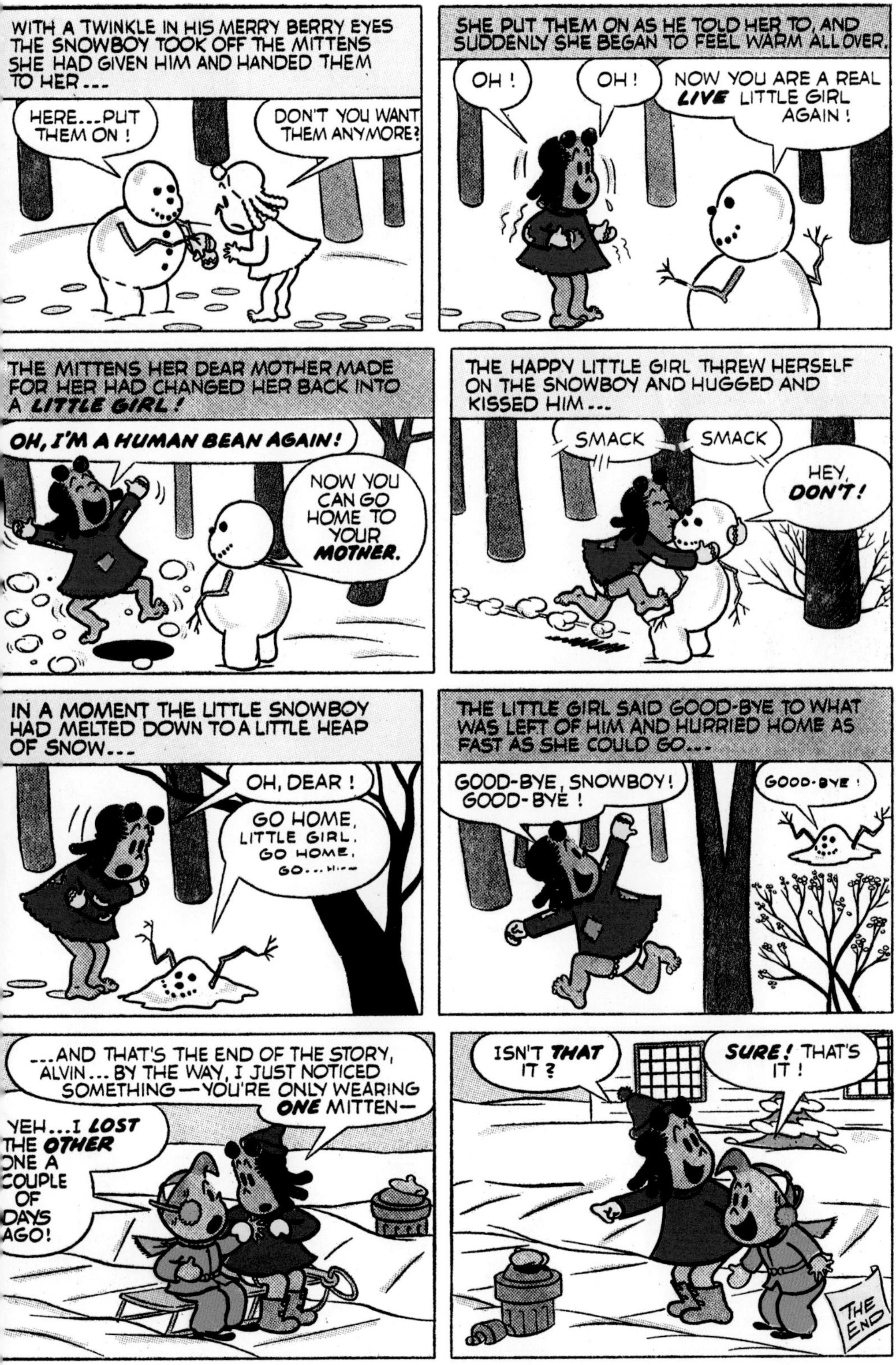
WITH A TWINKLE IN HIS MERRY BERRY EYES THE SNOWBOY TOOK OFF THE MITTENS SHE HAD GIVEN HIM AND HANDED THEM TO HER...
HERE...PUT THEM ON!
DON'T YOU WANT THEM ANYMORE?
SHE PUT THEM ON AS HE TOLD HER TO, AND SUDDENLY SHE BEGAN TO FEEL WARM ALL OVER.
OH!
OH!
NOW YOU ARE A REAL LIVE LITTLE GIRL AGAIN!
THE MITTENS HER DEAR MOTHER MADE FOR HER HAD CHANGED HER BACK INTO A LITTLE GIRL!
OH, I'M A HUMAN BEAN AGAIN!
NOW YOU CAN GO HOME TO YOUR MOTHER.
THE HAPPY LITTLE GIRL THREW HERSELF ON THE SNOWBOY AND HUGGED AND KISSED HIM...
SMACK
SMACK
HEY, DON'T!
IN A MOMENT THE LITTLE SNOWBOY HAD MELTED DOWN TO A LITTLE HEAP OF SNOW...
OH, DEAR!
GO HOME, LITTLE GIRL. GO HOME. GO...
THE LITTLE GIRL SAID GOOD-BYE TO WHAT WAS LEFT OF HIM AND HURRIED HOME AS FAST AS SHE COULD GO...
GOOD-BYE, SNOWBOY! GOOD-BYE!
GOOD-BYE!
...AND THAT'S THE END OF THE STORY, ALVIN... BY THE WAY, I JUST NOTICED SOMETHING—YOU'RE ONLY WEARING ONE MITTEN—
YEH...I LOST THE OTHER ONE A COUPLE OF DAYS AGO!
ISN'T THAT IT?
SURE! THAT'S IT!
THE END

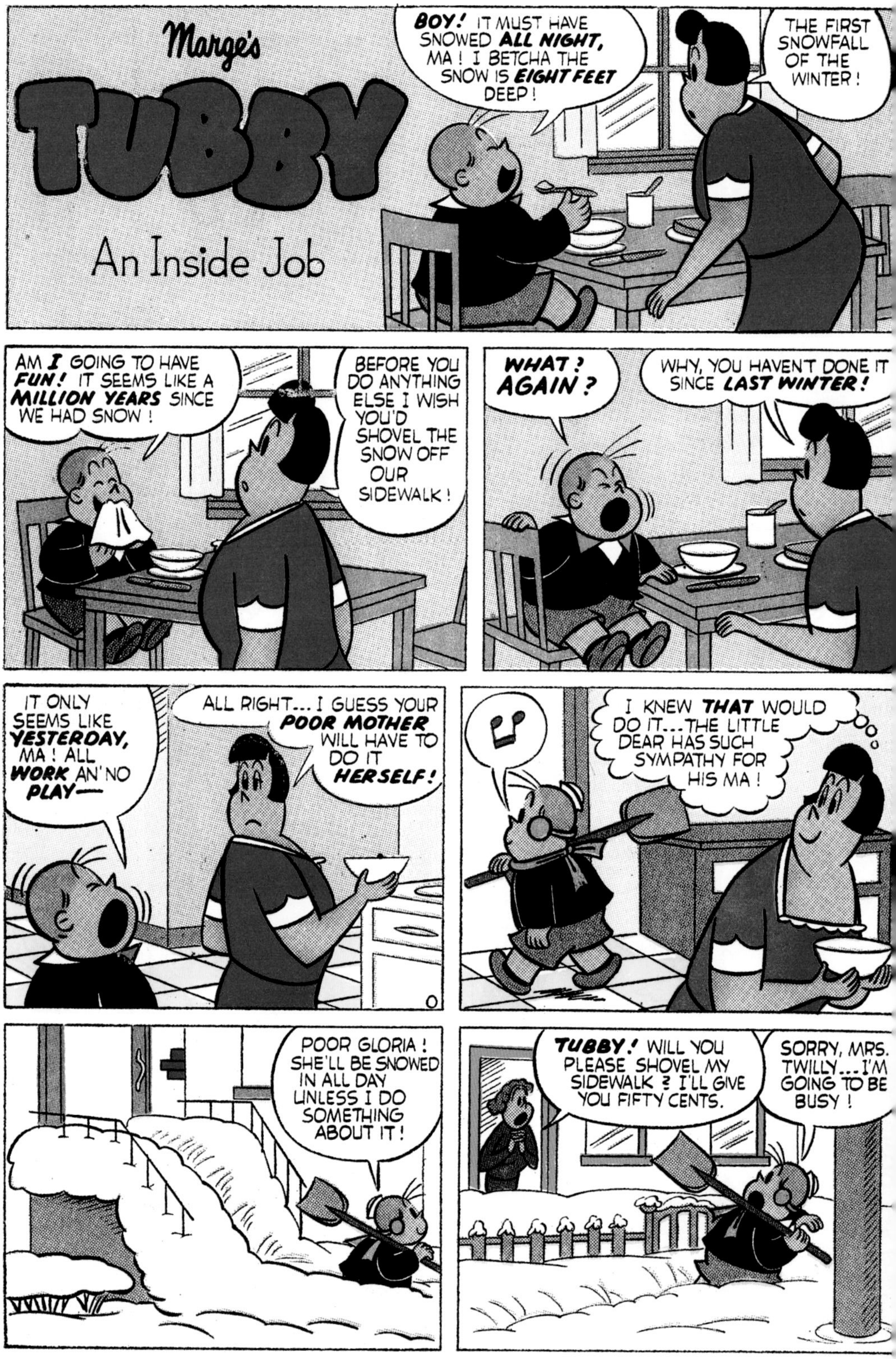
Marge's
TUBBY
An Inside Job
BOY! IT MUST HAVE SNOWED ALL NIGHT, MA! I BETCHA THE SNOW IS EIGHT FEET DEEP!
THE FIRST SNOWFALL OF THE WINTER!
AM I GOING TO HAVE FUN! IT SEEMS LIKE A MILLION YEARS SINCE WE HAD SNOW!
BEFORE YOU DO ANYTHING ELSE I WISH YOU'D SHOVEL THE SNOW OFF OUR SIDEWALK!
WHAT? AGAIN?
WHY, YOU HAVENT DONE IT SINCE LAST WINTER!
IT ONLY SEEMS LIKE YESTERDAY, MA! ALL WORK AN' NO PLAY—
ALL RIGHT... I GUESS YOUR POOR MOTHER WILL HAVE TO DO IT HERSELF!
I KNEW THAT WOULD DO IT... THE LITTLE DEAR HAS SUCH SYMPATHY FOR HIS MA!
POOR GLORIA! SHE'LL BE SNOWED IN ALL DAY UNLESS I DO SOMETHING ABOUT IT!
TUBBY! WILL YOU PLEASE SHOVEL MY SIDEWALK? I'LL GIVE YOU FIFTY CENTS.
SORRY, MRS. TWILLY... I'M GOING TO BE BUSY!

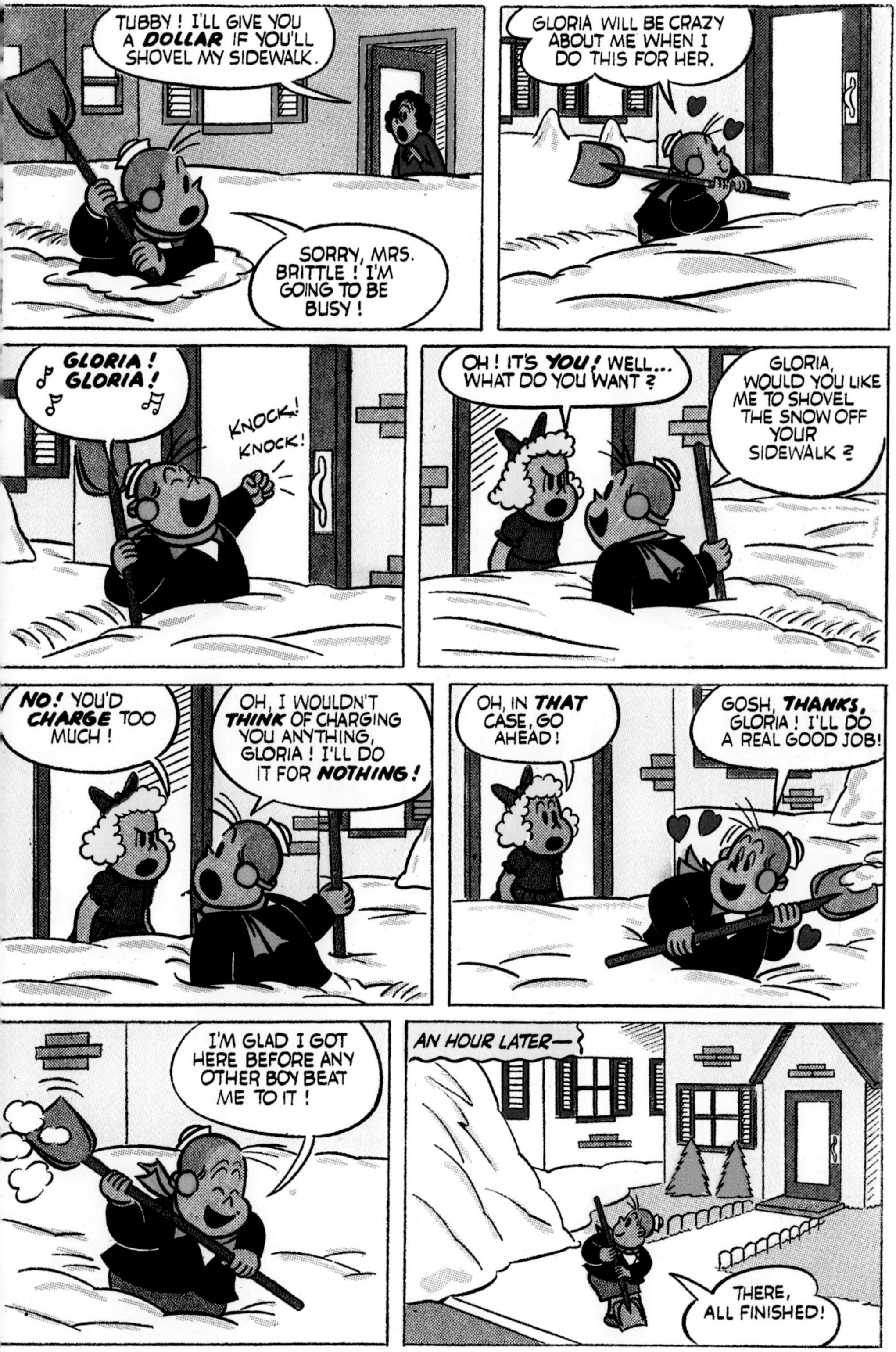
TUBBY ! I'LL GIVE YOU A DOLLAR IF YOU'LL SHOVEL MY SIDEWALK.
SORRY, MRS. BRITTLE ! I'M GOING TO BE BUSY !
GLORIA WILL BE CRAZY ABOUT ME WHEN I DO THIS FOR HER.
GLORIA ! GLORIA !
KNOCK ! KNOCK !
OH ! IT'S YOU ! WELL... WHAT DO YOU WANT ?
GLORIA, WOULD YOU LIKE ME TO SHOVEL THE SNOW OFF YOUR SIDEWALK ?
NO ! YOU'D CHARGE TOO MUCH !
OH, I WOULDN'T THINK OF CHARGING YOU ANYTHING, GLORIA ! I'LL DO IT FOR NOTHING !
OH, IN THAT CASE, GO AHEAD !
GOSH, THANKS, GLORIA ! I'LL DO A REAL GOOD JOB !
I'M GLAD I GOT HERE BEFORE ANY OTHER BOY BEAT ME TO IT !
AN HOUR LATER—
THERE, ALL FINISHED!

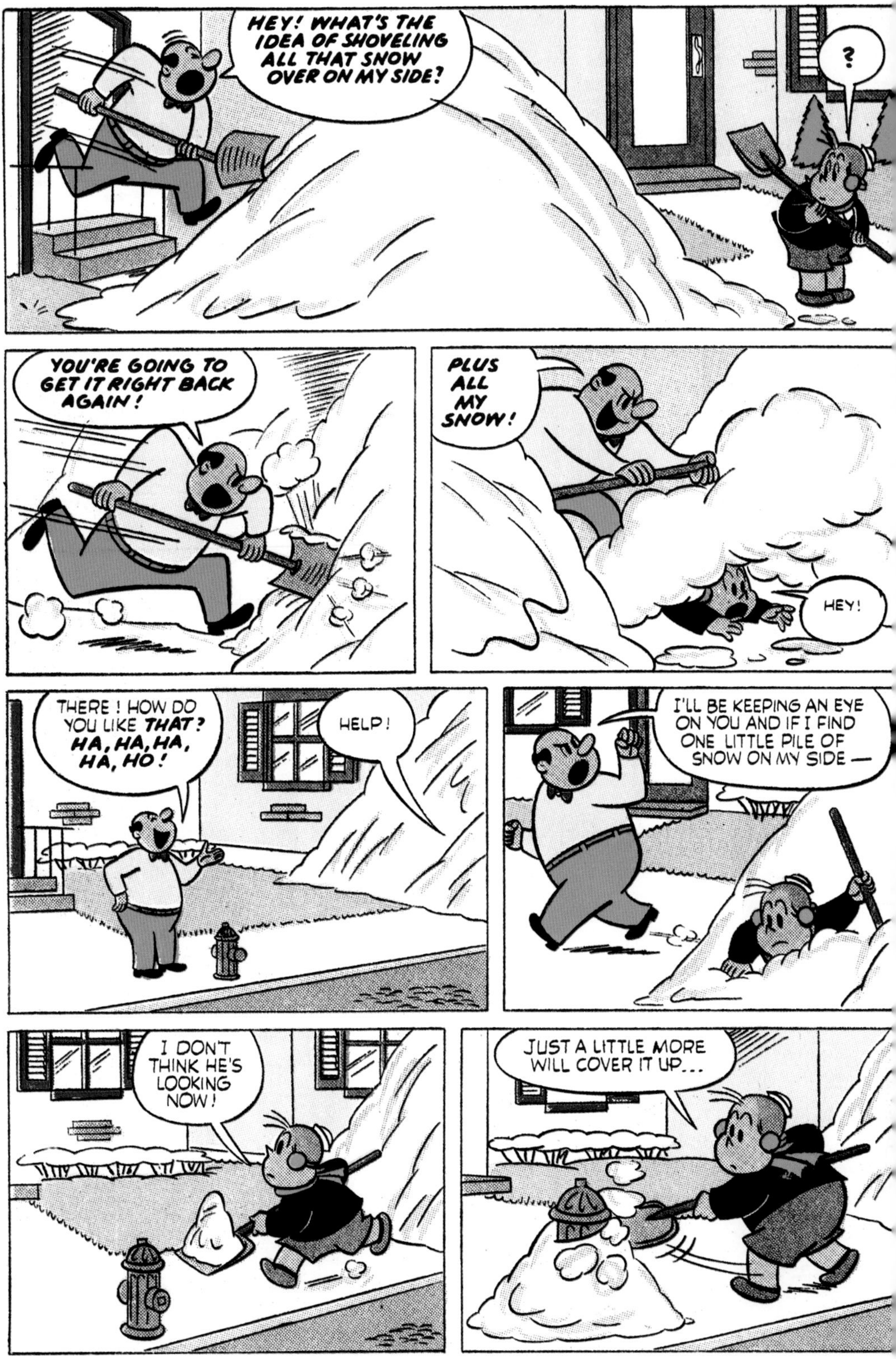
HEY! WHAT'S THE IDEA OF SHOVELING ALL THAT SNOW OVER ON MY SIDE?
?
YOU'RE GOING TO GET IT RIGHT BACK AGAIN!
PLUS ALL MY SNOW!
HEY!
THERE! HOW DO YOU LIKE THAT? HA, HA, HA, HA, HO!
HELP!
I'LL BE KEEPING AN EYE ON YOU AND IF I FIND ONE LITTLE PILE OF SNOW ON MY SIDE —
I DON'T THINK HE'S LOOKING NOW!
JUST A LITTLE MORE WILL COVER IT UP...

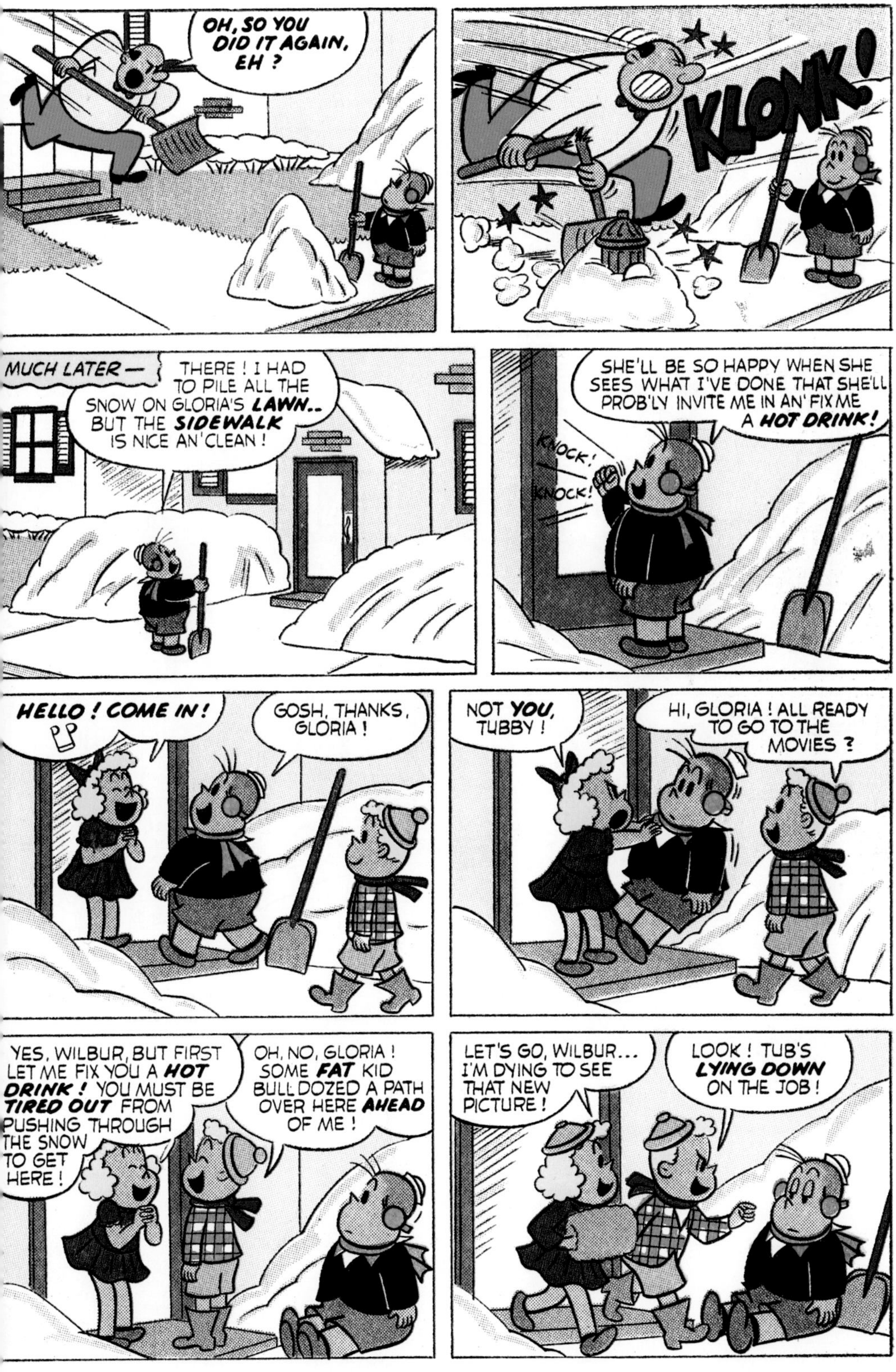
OH, SO YOU DID IT AGAIN, EH ?
KLONK!
MUCH LATER—
THERE ! I HAD TO PILE ALL THE SNOW ON GLORIA'S LAWN.. BUT THE SIDEWALK IS NICE AN' CLEAN !
SHE'LL BE SO HAPPY WHEN SHE SEES WHAT I'VE DONE THAT SHE'LL PROB'LY INVITE ME IN AN' FIX ME A HOT DRINK!
KNOCK!
KNOCK!
HELLO ! COME IN !
GOSH, THANKS, GLORIA !
NOT YOU, TUBBY !
HI, GLORIA ! ALL READY TO GO TO THE MOVIES ?
YES, WILBUR, BUT FIRST LET ME FIX YOU A HOT DRINK ! YOU MUST BE TIRED OUT FROM PUSHING THROUGH THE SNOW TO GET HERE !
OH, NO, GLORIA ! SOME FAT KID BULLDOZED A PATH OVER HERE AHEAD OF ME !
LET'S GO, WILBUR... I'M DYING TO SEE THAT NEW PICTURE !
LOOK ! TUB'S LYING DOWN ON THE JOB !

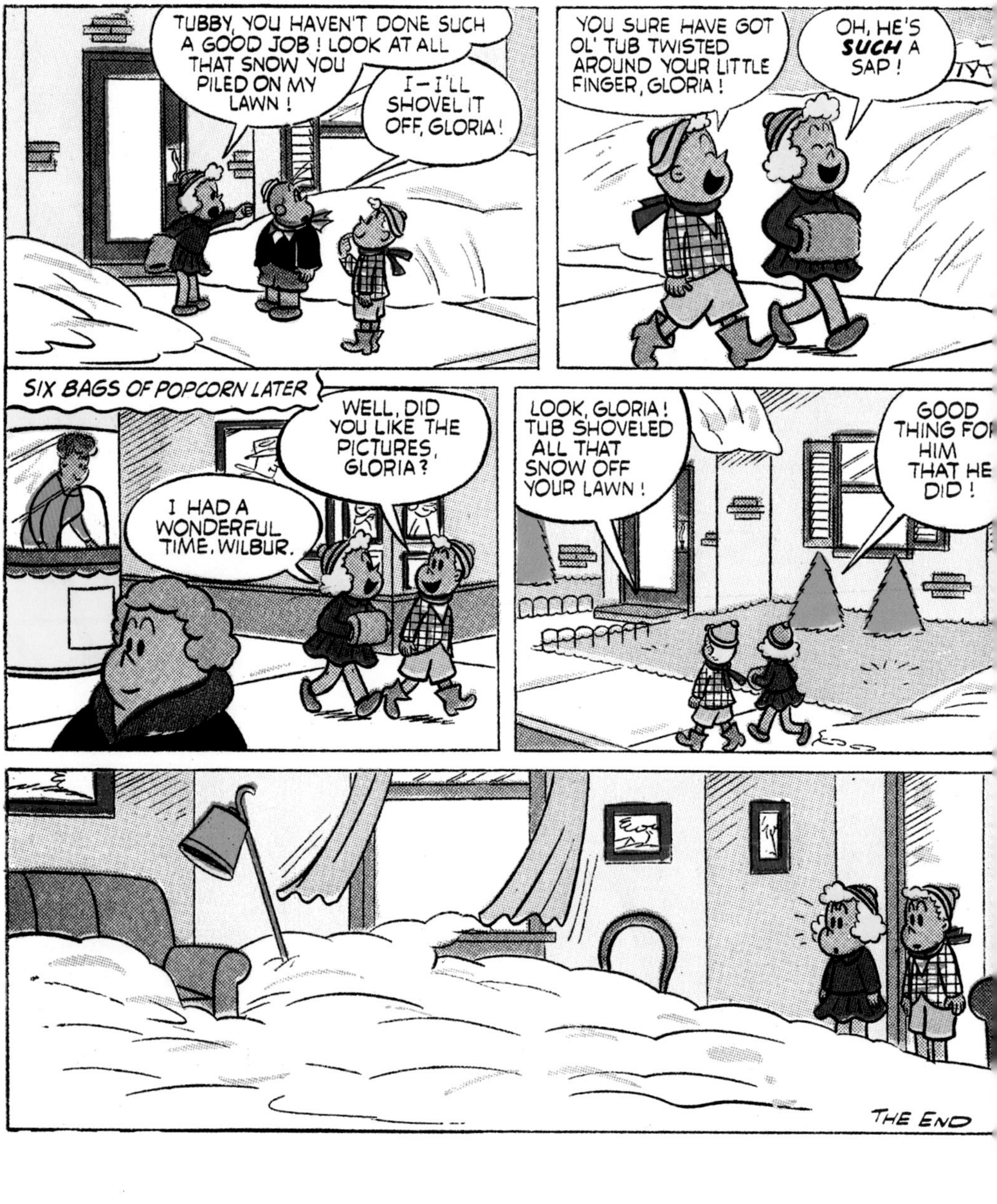
TUBBY, YOU HAVEN'T DONE SUCH A GOOD JOB ! LOOK AT ALL THAT SNOW YOU PILED ON MY LAWN !
I—I'LL SHOVEL IT OFF, GLORIA!
YOU SURE HAVE GOT OL' TUB TWISTED AROUND YOUR LITTLE FINGER, GLORIA !
OH, HE'S SUCH A SAP !
SIX BAGS OF POPCORN LATER
WELL, DID YOU LIKE THE PICTURES, GLORIA?
I HAD A WONDERFUL TIME, WILBUR.
LOOK, GLORIA ! TUB SHOVELED ALL THAT SNOW OFF YOUR LAWN !
GOOD THING FOR HIM THAT HE DID !
THE END

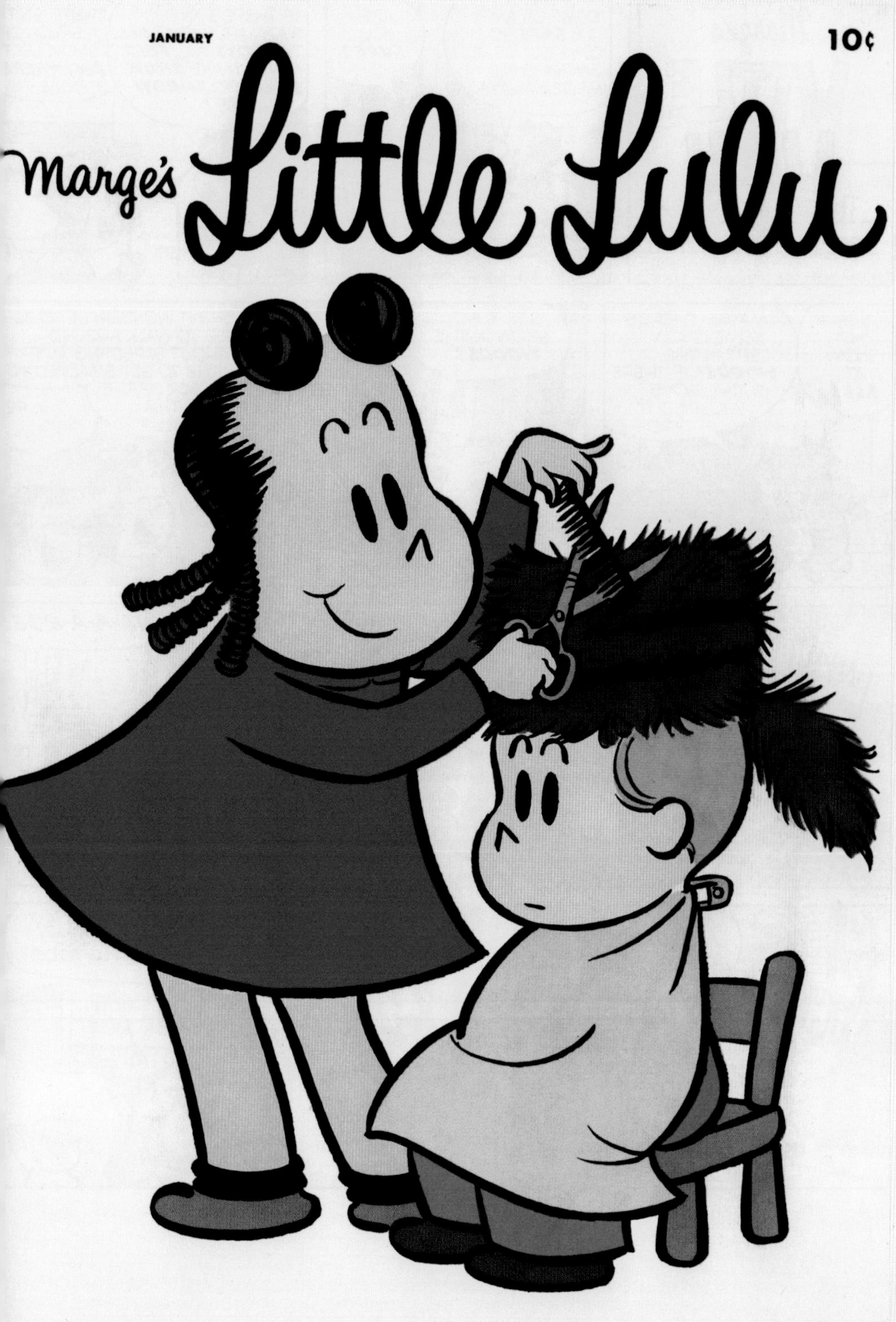
JANUARY
10¢
Marge's Little Lulu

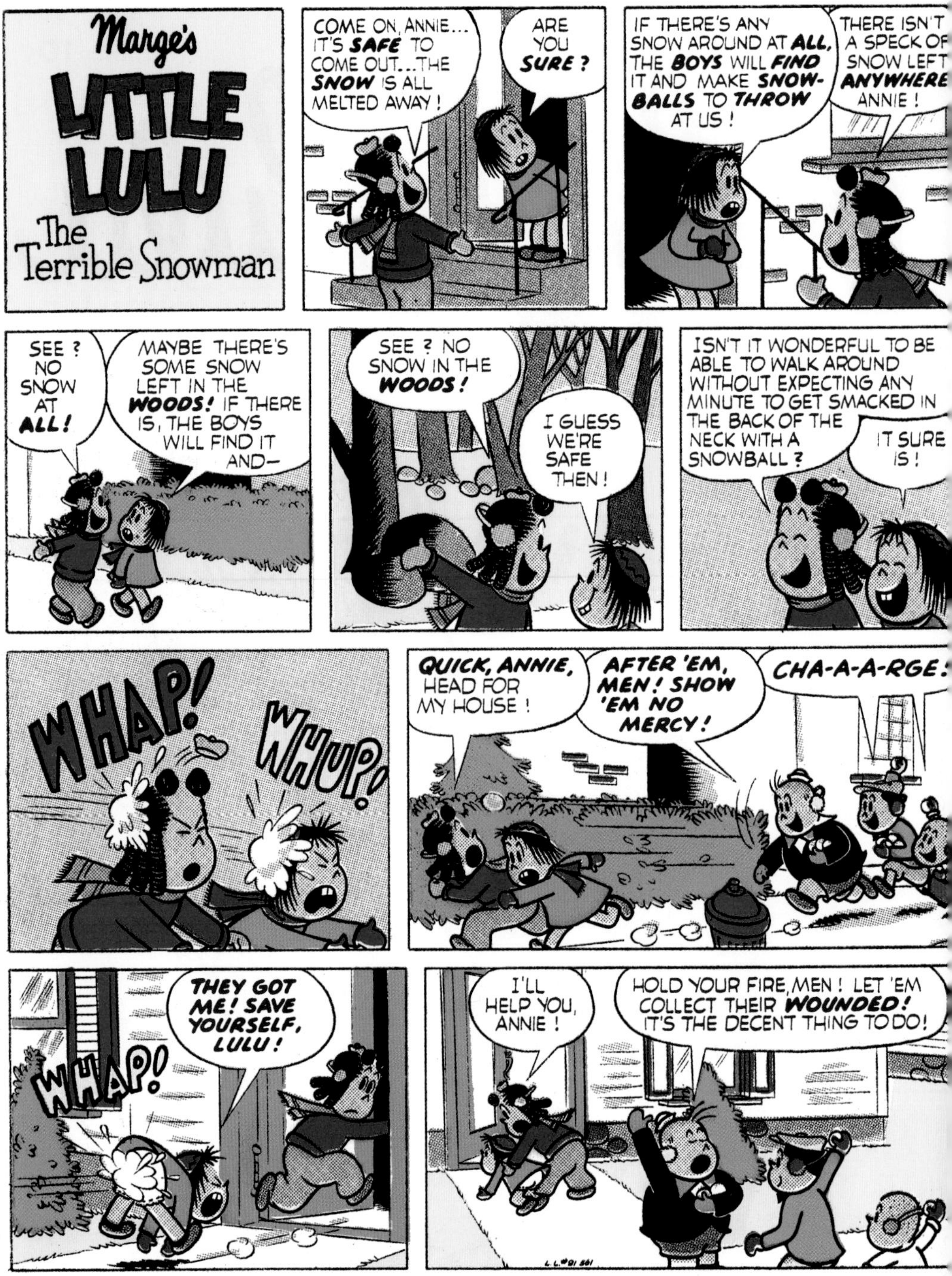
Marge's
LITTLE LULU
The Terrible Snowman
COME ON, ANNIE... IT'S SAFE TO COME OUT...THE SNOW IS ALL MELTED AWAY !
ARE YOU SURE ?
IF THERE'S ANY SNOW AROUND AT ALL, THE BOYS WILL FIND IT AND MAKE SNOW-BALLS TO THROW AT US !
THERE ISN'T A SPECK OF SNOW LEFT ANYWHERE ANNIE !
SEE ? NO SNOW AT ALL!
MAYBE THERE'S SOME SNOW LEFT IN THE WOODS! IF THERE IS, THE BOYS WILL FIND IT AND—
SEE ? NO SNOW IN THE WOODS!
I GUESS WE'RE SAFE THEN !
ISN'T IT WONDERFUL TO BE ABLE TO WALK AROUND WITHOUT EXPECTING ANY MINUTE TO GET SMACKED IN THE BACK OF THE NECK WITH A SNOWBALL ?
IT SURE IS !
WHAP!
WHUP!
QUICK, ANNIE, HEAD FOR MY HOUSE !
AFTER 'EM, MEN! SHOW 'EM NO MERCY!
CHA-A-A-RGE!
WHAP!
THEY GOT ME! SAVE YOURSELF, LULU!
I'LL HELP YOU, ANNIE !
HOLD YOUR FIRE, MEN ! LET 'EM COLLECT THEIR WOUNDED! IT'S THE DECENT THING TO DO!

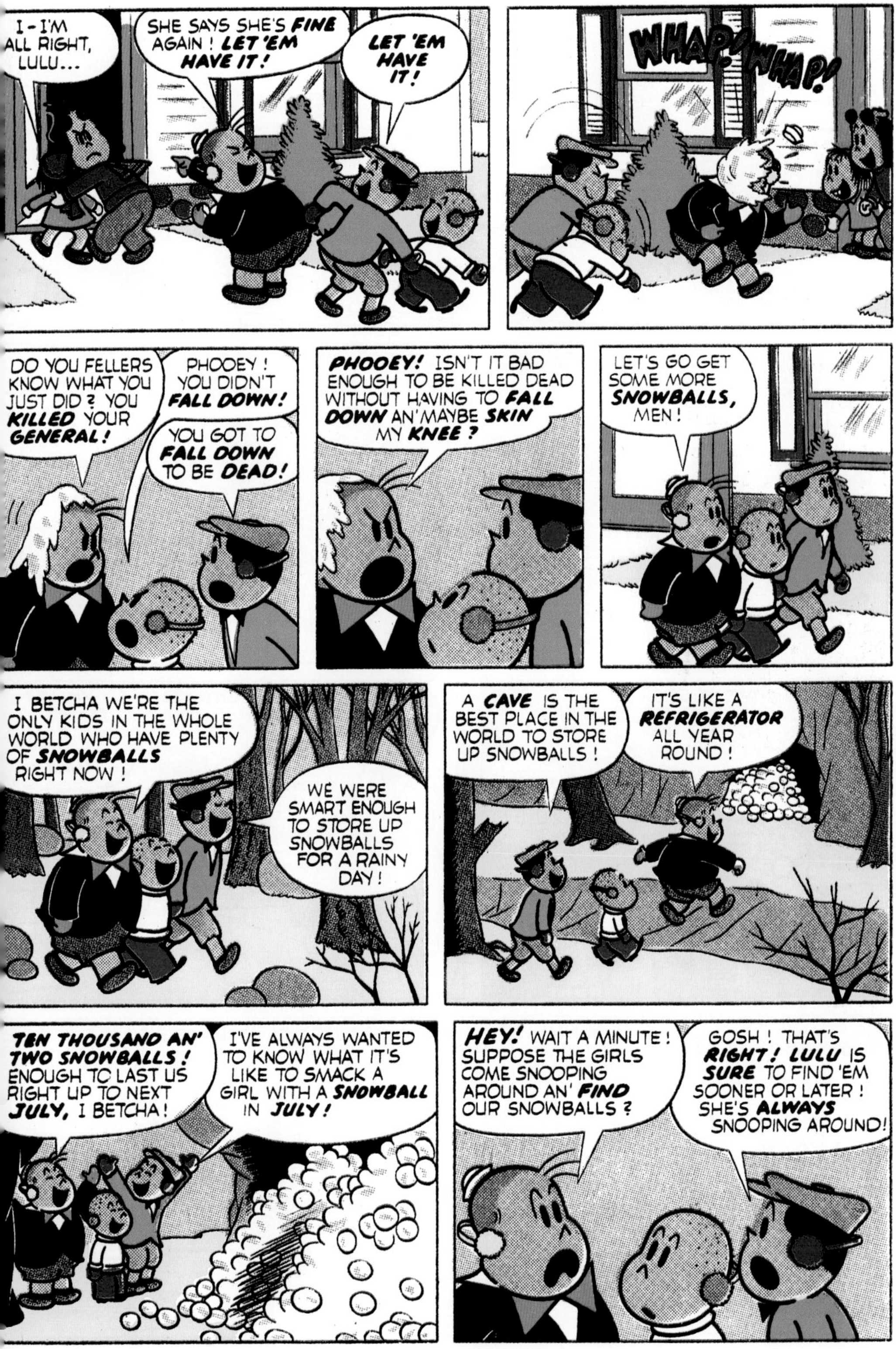
I-I'M ALL RIGHT, LULU...
SHE SAYS SHE'S FINE AGAIN! LET 'EM HAVE IT!
LET 'EM HAVE IT!
WHAP! WHAP!
DO YOU FELLERS KNOW WHAT YOU JUST DID? YOU KILLED YOUR GENERAL!
PHOOEY! YOU DIDN'T FALL DOWN!
YOU GOT TO FALL DOWN TO BE DEAD!
PHOOEY! ISN'T IT BAD ENOUGH TO BE KILLED DEAD WITHOUT HAVING TO FALL DOWN AN' MAYBE SKIN MY KNEE?
LET'S GO GET SOME MORE SNOWBALLS, MEN!
I BETCHA WE'RE THE ONLY KIDS IN THE WHOLE WORLD WHO HAVE PLENTY OF SNOWBALLS RIGHT NOW!
WE WERE SMART ENOUGH TO STORE UP SNOWBALLS FOR A RAINY DAY!
A CAVE IS THE BEST PLACE IN THE WORLD TO STORE UP SNOWBALLS!
IT'S LIKE A REFRIGERATOR ALL YEAR ROUND!
TEN THOUSAND AN' TWO SNOWBALLS! ENOUGH TO LAST US RIGHT UP TO NEXT JULY, I BETCHA!
I'VE ALWAYS WANTED TO KNOW WHAT IT'S LIKE TO SMACK A GIRL WITH A SNOWBALL IN JULY!
HEY! WAIT A MINUTE! SUPPOSE THE GIRLS COME SNOOPING AROUND AN' FIND OUR SNOWBALLS?
GOSH! THAT'S RIGHT! LULU IS SURE TO FIND 'EM SOONER OR LATER! SHE'S ALWAYS SNOOPING AROUND!

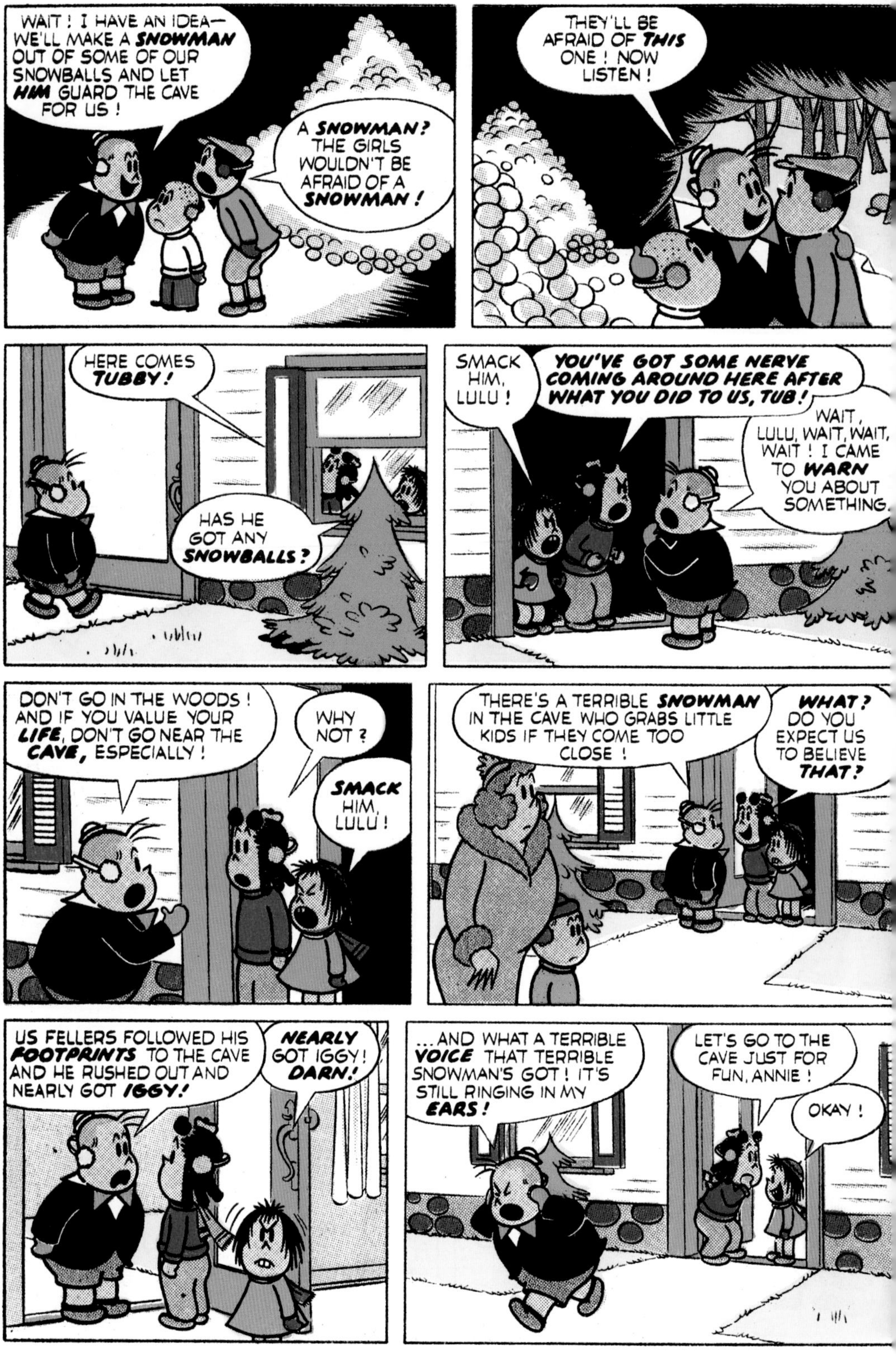
WAIT ! I HAVE AN IDEA— WE'LL MAKE A SNOWMAN OUT OF SOME OF OUR SNOWBALLS AND LET HIM GUARD THE CAVE FOR US !
A SNOWMAN? THE GIRLS WOULDN'T BE AFRAID OF A SNOWMAN !
THEY'LL BE AFRAID OF THIS ONE ! NOW LISTEN !
HERE COMES TUBBY !
HAS HE GOT ANY SNOWBALLS ?
SMACK HIM, LULU !
YOU'VE GOT SOME NERVE COMING AROUND HERE AFTER WHAT YOU DID TO US, TUB !
WAIT, LULU, WAIT, WAIT, WAIT ! I CAME TO WARN YOU ABOUT SOMETHING.
DON'T GO IN THE WOODS ! AND IF YOU VALUE YOUR LIFE, DON'T GO NEAR THE CAVE, ESPECIALLY !
WHY NOT ?
SMACK HIM, LULU !
THERE'S A TERRIBLE SNOWMAN IN THE CAVE WHO GRABS LITTLE KIDS IF THEY COME TOO CLOSE !
WHAT? DO YOU EXPECT US TO BELIEVE THAT?
US FELLERS FOLLOWED HIS FOOTPRINTS TO THE CAVE AND HE RUSHED OUT AND NEARLY GOT IGGY!
NEARLY GOT IGGY! DARN!
...AND WHAT A TERRIBLE VOICE THAT TERRIBLE SNOWMAN'S GOT! IT'S STILL RINGING IN MY EARS !
LET'S GO TO THE CAVE JUST FOR FUN, ANNIE !
OKAY !

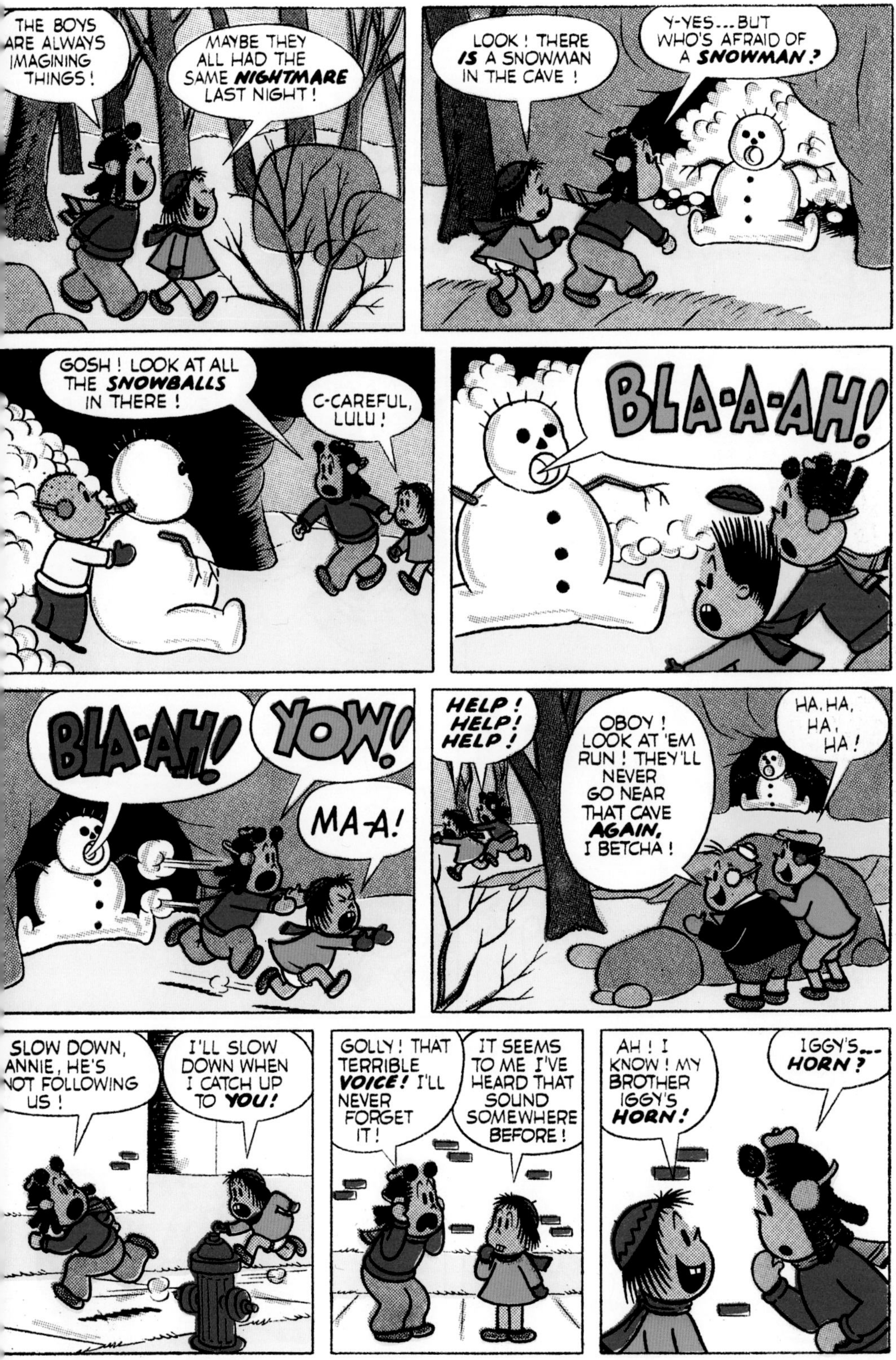
THE BOYS ARE ALWAYS IMAGINING THINGS!
MAYBE THEY ALL HAD THE SAME NIGHTMARE LAST NIGHT!
LOOK! THERE IS A SNOWMAN IN THE CAVE!
Y-YES... BUT WHO'S AFRAID OF A SNOWMAN?
GOSH! LOOK AT ALL THE SNOWBALLS IN THERE!
C-CAREFUL, LULU!
BLA-A-AH!
BLA-AH!
YOW!
MA-A!
HELP! HELP! HELP!
OBOY! LOOK AT 'EM RUN! THEY'LL NEVER GO NEAR THAT CAVE AGAIN, I BETCHA!
HA, HA, HA, HA!
SLOW DOWN, ANNIE, HE'S NOT FOLLOWING US!
I'LL SLOW DOWN WHEN I CATCH UP TO YOU!
GOLLY! THAT TERRIBLE VOICE! I'LL NEVER FORGET IT!
IT SEEMS TO ME I'VE HEARD THAT SOUND SOMEWHERE BEFORE!
AH! I KNOW! MY BROTHER IGGY'S HORN!
IGGY'S... HORN?

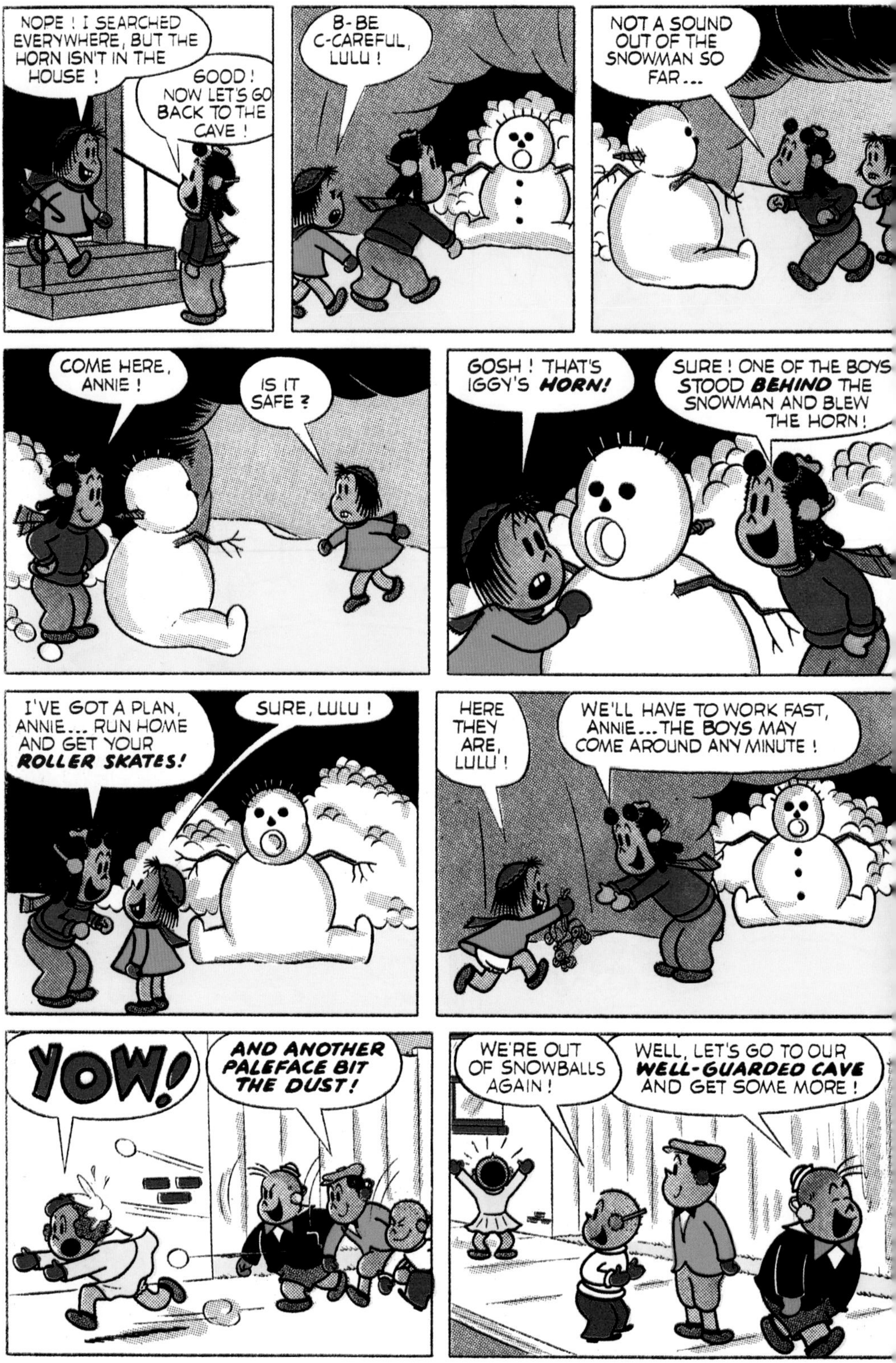
NOPE ! I SEARCHED EVERYWHERE, BUT THE HORN ISN'T IN THE HOUSE !
GOOD ! NOW LET'S GO BACK TO THE CAVE !
B-BE C-CAREFUL, LULU !
NOT A SOUND OUT OF THE SNOWMAN SO FAR...
COME HERE, ANNIE !
IS IT SAFE ?
GOSH ! THAT'S IGGY'S HORN!
SURE ! ONE OF THE BOYS STOOD BEHIND THE SNOWMAN AND BLEW THE HORN !
I'VE GOT A PLAN, ANNIE... RUN HOME AND GET YOUR ROLLER SKATES!
SURE, LULU !
HERE THEY ARE, LULU !
WE'LL HAVE TO WORK FAST, ANNIE...THE BOYS MAY COME AROUND ANY MINUTE !
YOW!
AND ANOTHER PALEFACE BIT THE DUST!
WE'RE OUT OF SNOWBALLS AGAIN !
WELL, LET'S GO TO OUR WELL-GUARDED CAVE AND GET SOME MORE !

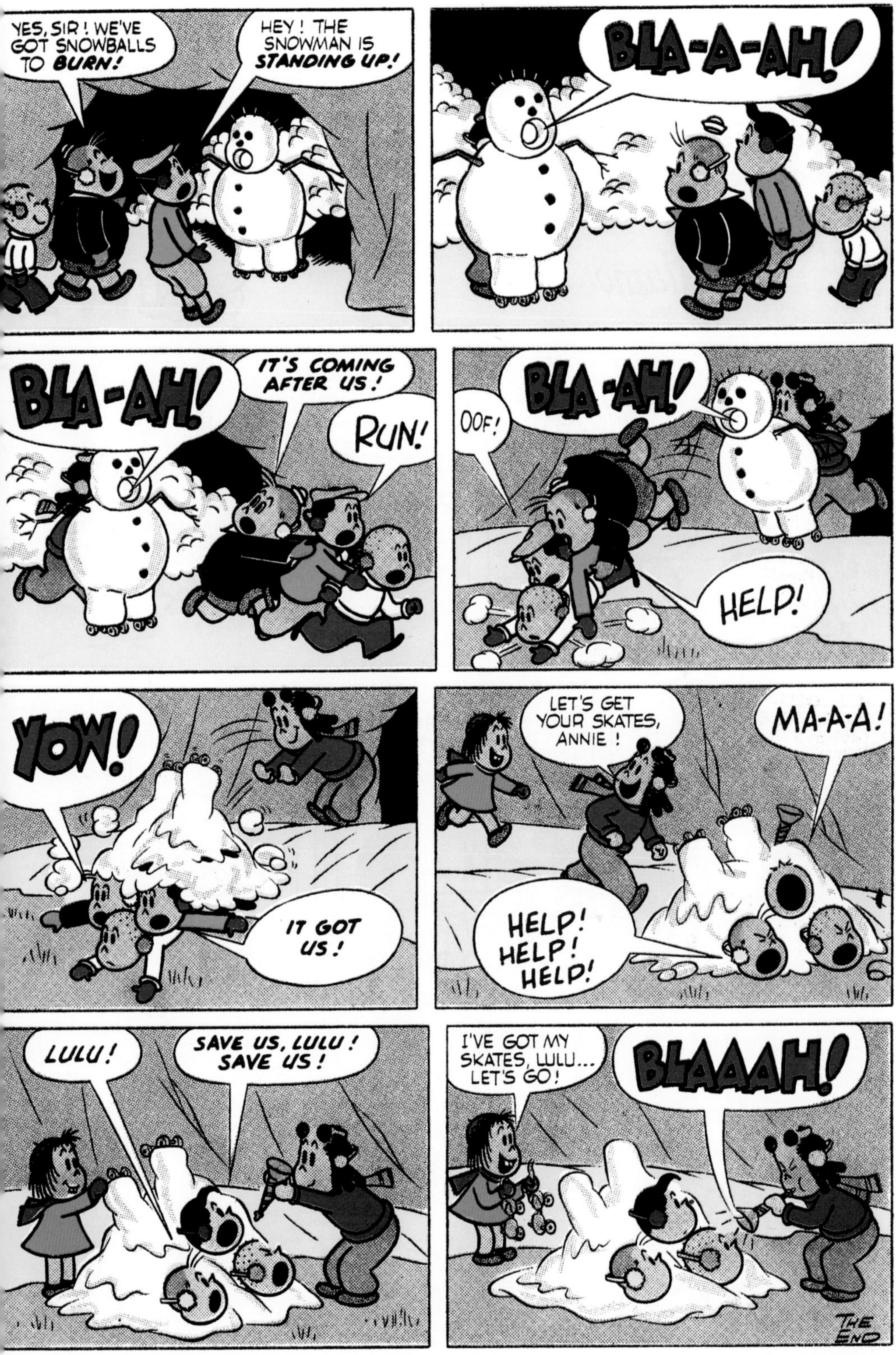
YES, SIR! WE'VE GOT SNOWBALLS TO BURN!
HEY! THE SNOWMAN IS STANDING UP!
BLA-A-AH!
BLA-AH!
IT'S COMING AFTER US!
RUN!
OOF!
BLA-AH!
HELP!
YOW!
IT GOT US!
LET'S GET YOUR SKATES, ANNIE!
MA-A-A!
HELP! HELP! HELP!
LULU!
SAVE US, LULU! SAVE US!
I'VE GOT MY SKATES, LULU... LET'S GO!
BLAAAH!
THE END

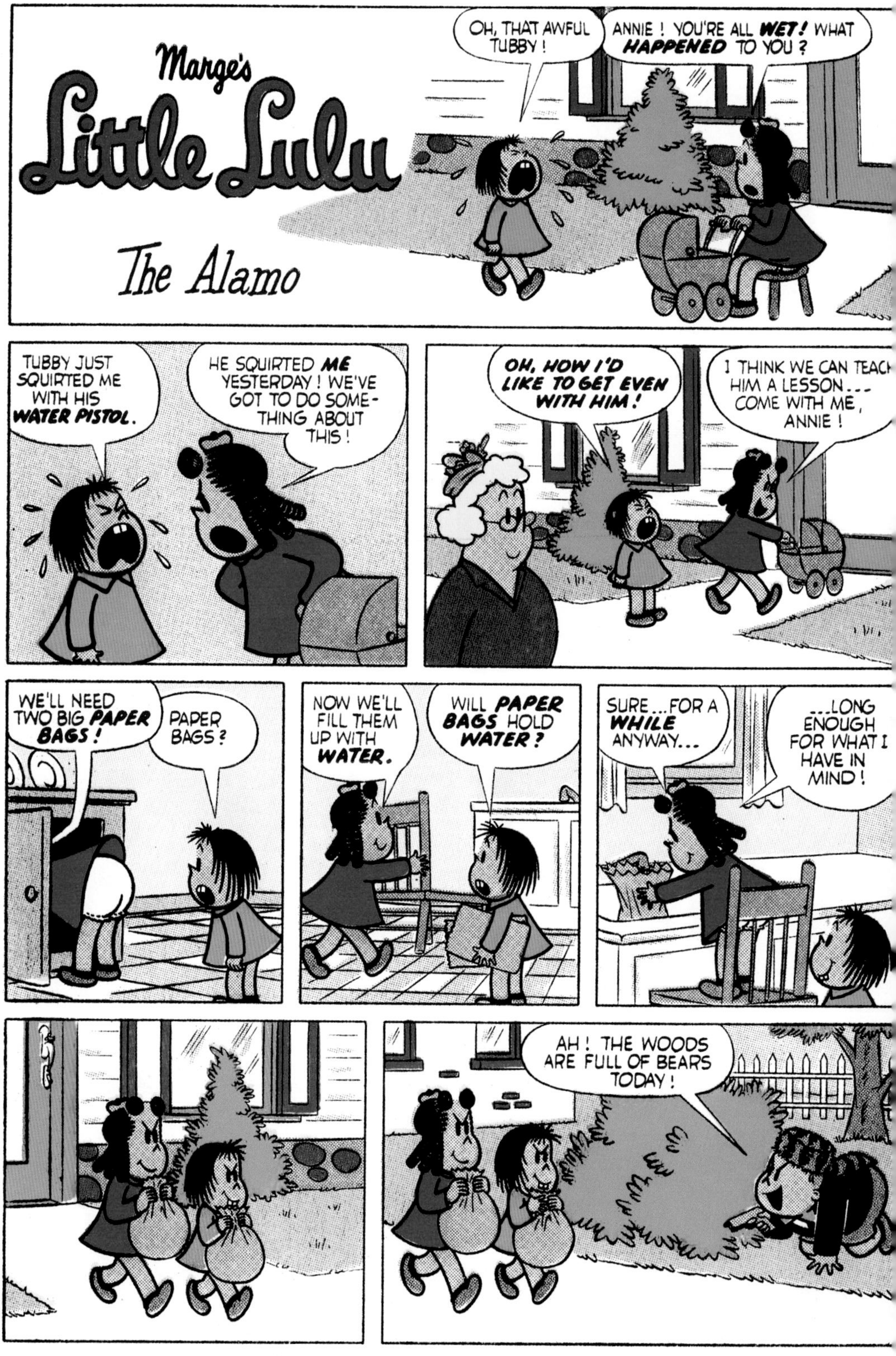
Marge's Little Lulu
The Alamo
OH, THAT AWFUL TUBBY!
ANNIE! YOU'RE ALL WET! WHAT HAPPENED TO YOU?
TUBBY JUST SQUIRTED ME WITH HIS WATER PISTOL.
HE SQUIRTED ME YESTERDAY! WE'VE GOT TO DO SOMETHING ABOUT THIS!
OH, HOW I'D LIKE TO GET EVEN WITH HIM!
I THINK WE CAN TEACH HIM A LESSON... COME WITH ME, ANNIE!
WE'LL NEED TWO BIG PAPER BAGS!
PAPER BAGS?
NOW WE'LL FILL THEM UP WITH WATER.
WILL PAPER BAGS HOLD WATER?
SURE...FOR A WHILE ANYWAY...
...LONG ENOUGH FOR WHAT I HAVE IN MIND!
AH! THE WOODS ARE FULL OF BEARS TODAY!

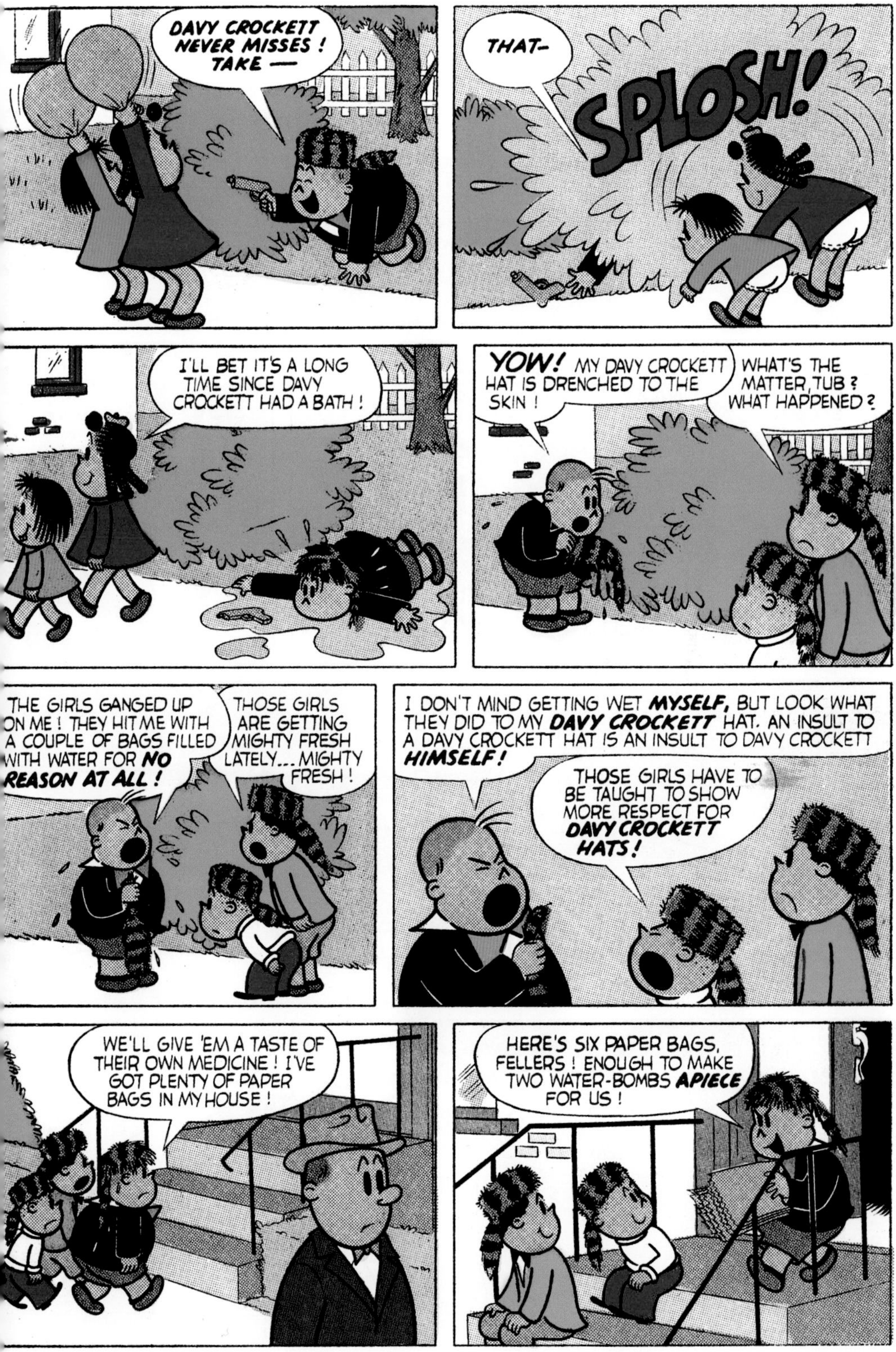
DAVY CROCKETT NEVER MISSES! TAKE —
THAT-
SPLOSH!
I'LL BET IT'S A LONG TIME SINCE DAVY CROCKETT HAD A BATH!
YOW! MY DAVY CROCKETT HAT IS DRENCHED TO THE SKIN!
WHAT'S THE MATTER, TUB? WHAT HAPPENED?
THE GIRLS GANGED UP ON ME! THEY HIT ME WITH A COUPLE OF BAGS FILLED WITH WATER FOR NO REASON AT ALL!
THOSE GIRLS ARE GETTING MIGHTY FRESH LATELY... MIGHTY FRESH!
I DON'T MIND GETTING WET MYSELF, BUT LOOK WHAT THEY DID TO MY DAVY CROCKETT HAT. AN INSULT TO A DAVY CROCKETT HAT IS AN INSULT TO DAVY CROCKETT HIMSELF!
THOSE GIRLS HAVE TO BE TAUGHT TO SHOW MORE RESPECT FOR DAVY CROCKETT HATS!
WE'LL GIVE 'EM A TASTE OF THEIR OWN MEDICINE! I'VE GOT PLENTY OF PAPER BAGS IN MY HOUSE!
HERE'S SIX PAPER BAGS, FELLERS! ENOUGH TO MAKE TWO WATER-BOMBS APIECE FOR US!

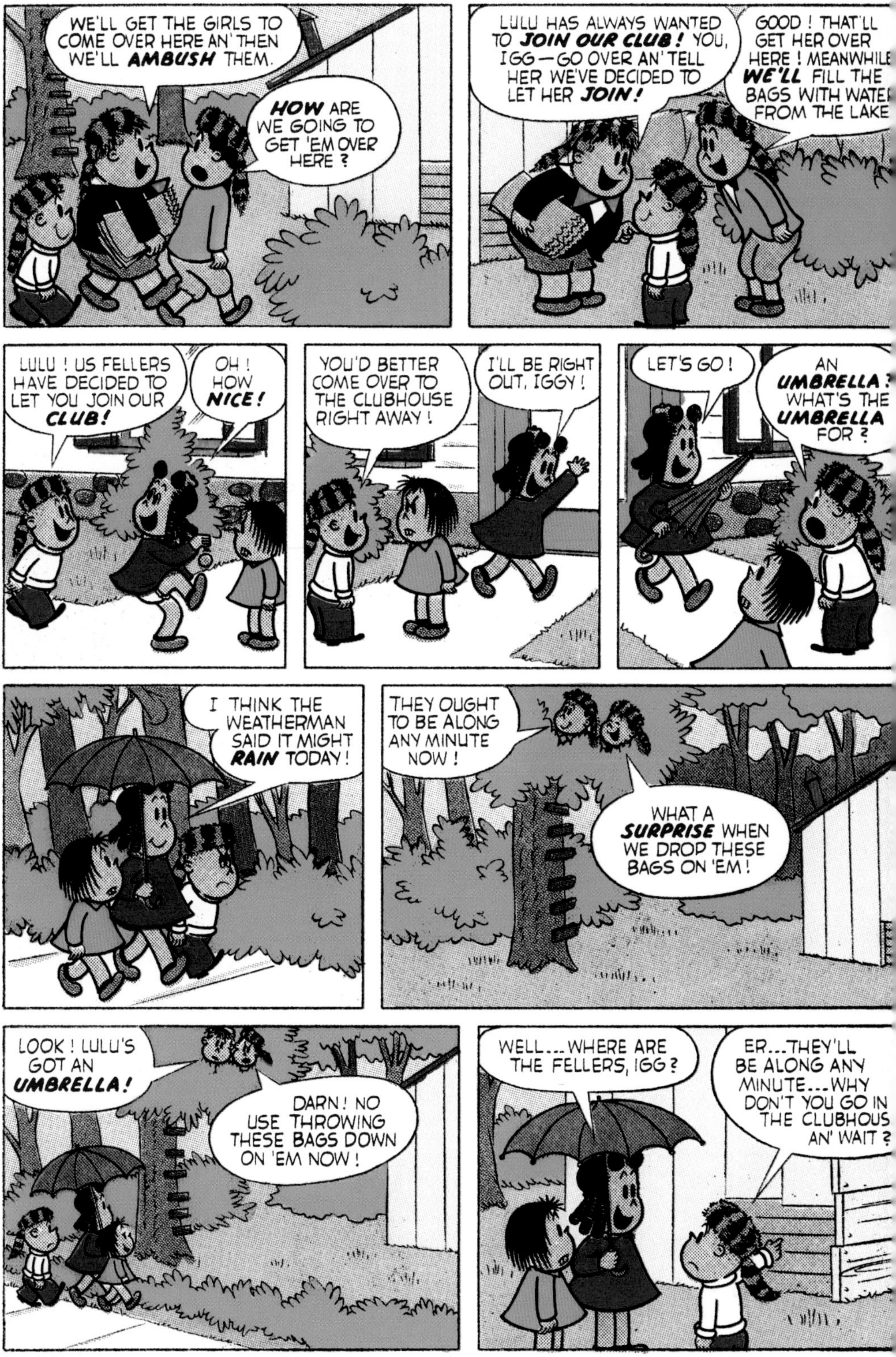
WE'LL GET THE GIRLS TO COME OVER HERE AN' THEN WE'LL AMBUSH THEM.
HOW ARE WE GOING TO GET 'EM OVER HERE ?
LULU HAS ALWAYS WANTED TO JOIN OUR CLUB ! YOU, IGG — GO OVER AN' TELL HER WE'VE DECIDED TO LET HER JOIN !
GOOD ! THAT'LL GET HER OVER HERE ! MEANWHILE WE'LL FILL THE BAGS WITH WATER FROM THE LAKE
LULU ! US FELLERS HAVE DECIDED TO LET YOU JOIN OUR CLUB !
OH ! HOW NICE !
YOU'D BETTER COME OVER TO THE CLUBHOUSE RIGHT AWAY !
I'LL BE RIGHT OUT, IGGY !
LET'S GO !
AN UMBRELLA ? WHAT'S THE UMBRELLA FOR ?
I THINK THE WEATHERMAN SAID IT MIGHT RAIN TODAY !
THEY OUGHT TO BE ALONG ANY MINUTE NOW !
WHAT A SURPRISE WHEN WE DROP THESE BAGS ON 'EM !
LOOK ! LULU'S GOT AN UMBRELLA !
DARN ! NO USE THROWING THESE BAGS DOWN ON 'EM NOW !
WELL... WHERE ARE THE FELLERS, IGG ?
ER... THEY'LL BE ALONG ANY MINUTE... WHY DON'T YOU GO IN THE CLUBHOUSE AN' WAIT ?

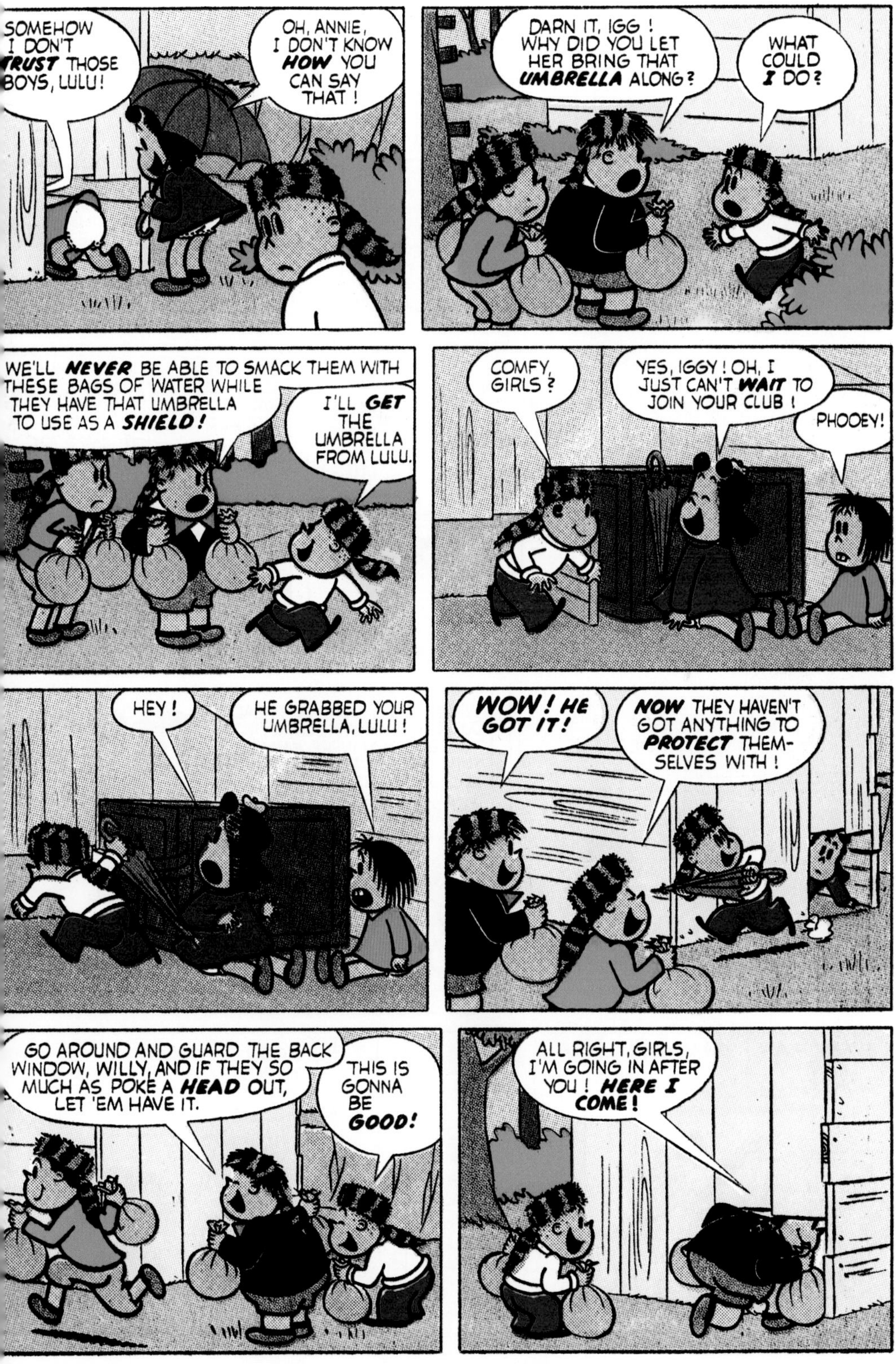

SOMEHOW I DON'T TRUST THOSE BOYS, LULU!
OH, ANNIE, I DON'T KNOW HOW YOU CAN SAY THAT!
DARN IT, IGG! WHY DID YOU LET HER BRING THAT UMBRELLA ALONG?
WHAT COULD I DO?
WE'LL NEVER BE ABLE TO SMACK THEM WITH THESE BAGS OF WATER WHILE THEY HAVE THAT UMBRELLA TO USE AS A SHIELD!
I'LL GET THE UMBRELLA FROM LULU.
COMFY, GIRLS?
YES, IGGY! OH, I JUST CAN'T WAIT TO JOIN YOUR CLUB!
PHOOEY!
HEY!
HE GRABBED YOUR UMBRELLA, LULU!
WOW! HE GOT IT!
NOW THEY HAVEN'T GOT ANYTHING TO PROTECT THEMSELVES WITH!
GO AROUND AND GUARD THE BACK WINDOW, WILLY, AND IF THEY SO MUCH AS POKE A HEAD OUT, LET 'EM HAVE IT.
THIS IS GONNA BE GOOD!
ALL RIGHT, GIRLS, I'M GOING IN AFTER YOU! HERE I COME!

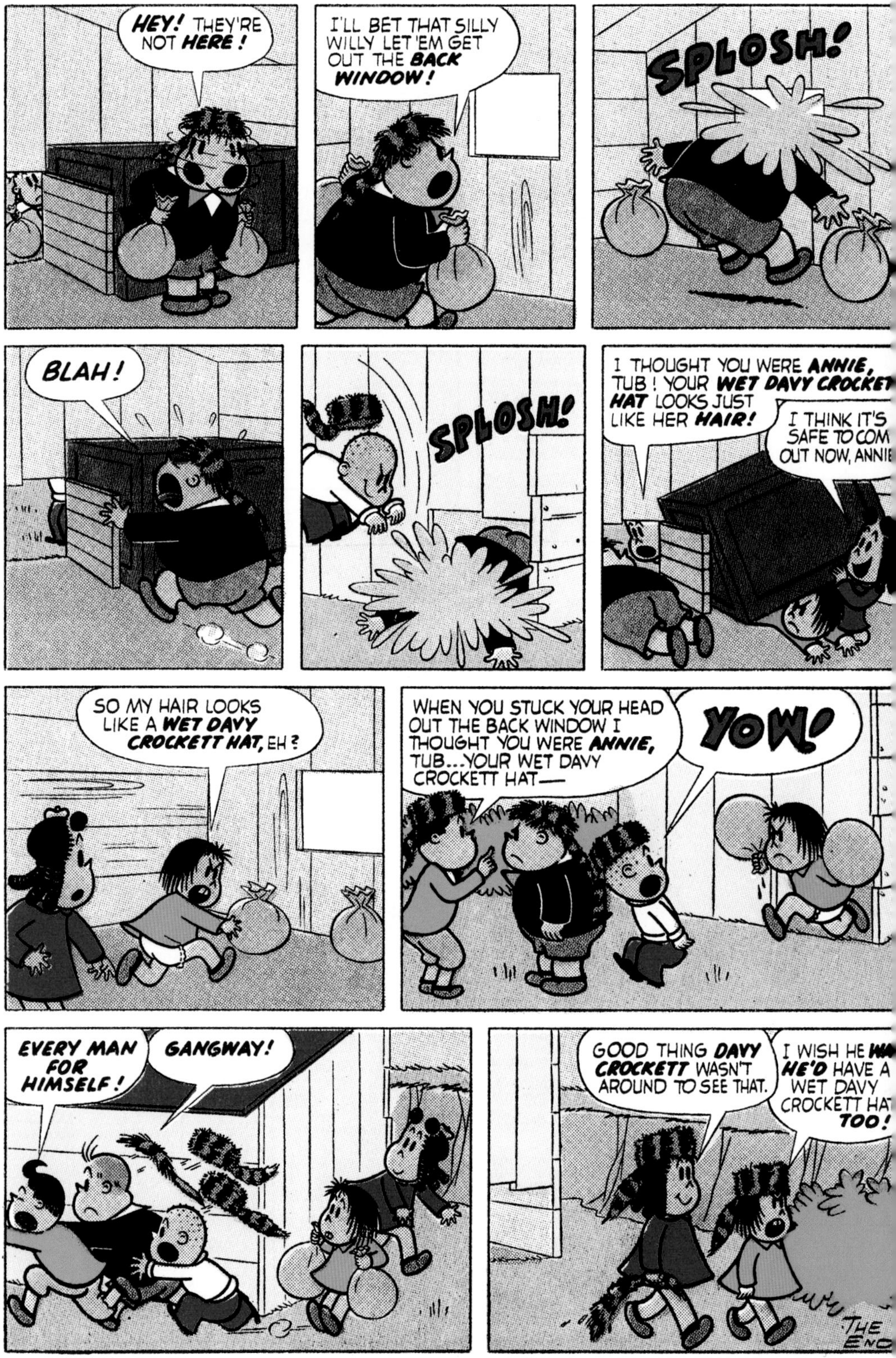
HEY! THEY'RE NOT HERE!
I'LL BET THAT SILLY WILLY LET 'EM GET OUT THE BACK WINDOW!
SPLOSH!
BLAH!
SPLOSH!
I THOUGHT YOU WERE ANNIE, TUB! YOUR WET DAVY CROCKET HAT LOOKS JUST LIKE HER HAIR!
I THINK IT'S SAFE TO COM OUT NOW, ANNI
SO MY HAIR LOOKS LIKE A WET DAVY CROCKETT HAT, EH?
WHEN YOU STUCK YOUR HEAD OUT THE BACK WINDOW I THOUGHT YOU WERE ANNIE, TUB...YOUR WET DAVY CROCKETT HAT—
YOW!
EVERY MAN FOR HIMSELF!
GANGWAY!
GOOD THING DAVY CROCKETT WASN'T AROUND TO SEE THAT.
I WISH HE HE'D HAVE A WET DAVY CROCKETT HA TOO!
THE END

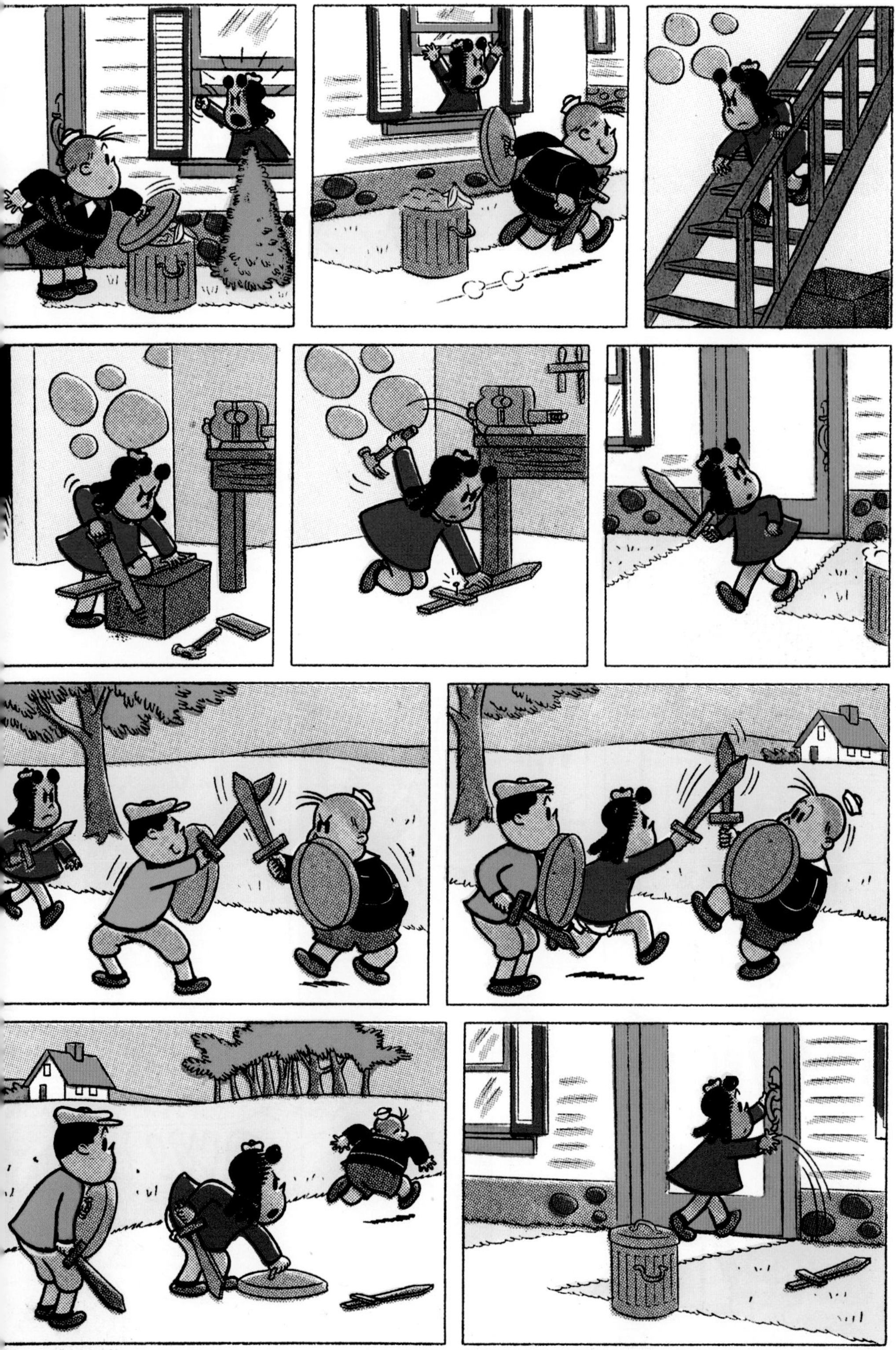

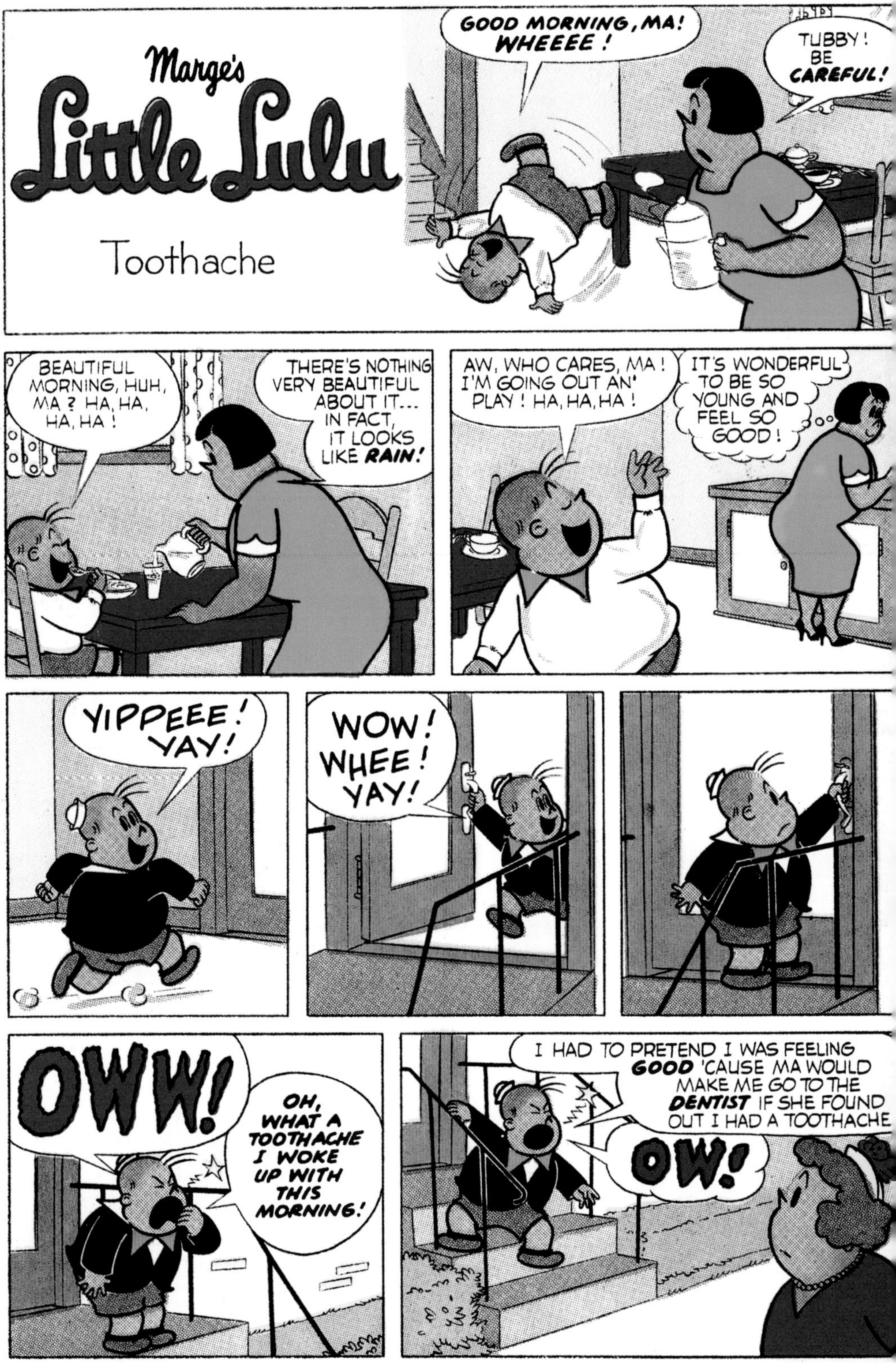
Marge's
Little Lulu
Toothache
GOOD MORNING, MA! WHEEEE!
TUBBY! BE CAREFUL!
BEAUTIFUL MORNING, HUH, MA? HA, HA, HA, HA!
THERE'S NOTHING VERY BEAUTIFUL ABOUT IT... IN FACT, IT LOOKS LIKE RAIN!
AW, WHO CARES, MA! I'M GOING OUT AN' PLAY! HA, HA, HA!
IT'S WONDERFUL TO BE SO YOUNG AND FEEL SO GOOD!
YIPPEEE! YAY!
WOW! WHEE! YAY!
OWW!
OH, WHAT A TOOTHACHE I WOKE UP WITH THIS MORNING!
I HAD TO PRETEND I WAS FEELING GOOD 'CAUSE MA WOULD MAKE ME GO TO THE DENTIST IF SHE FOUND OUT I HAD A TOOTHACHE
OW!

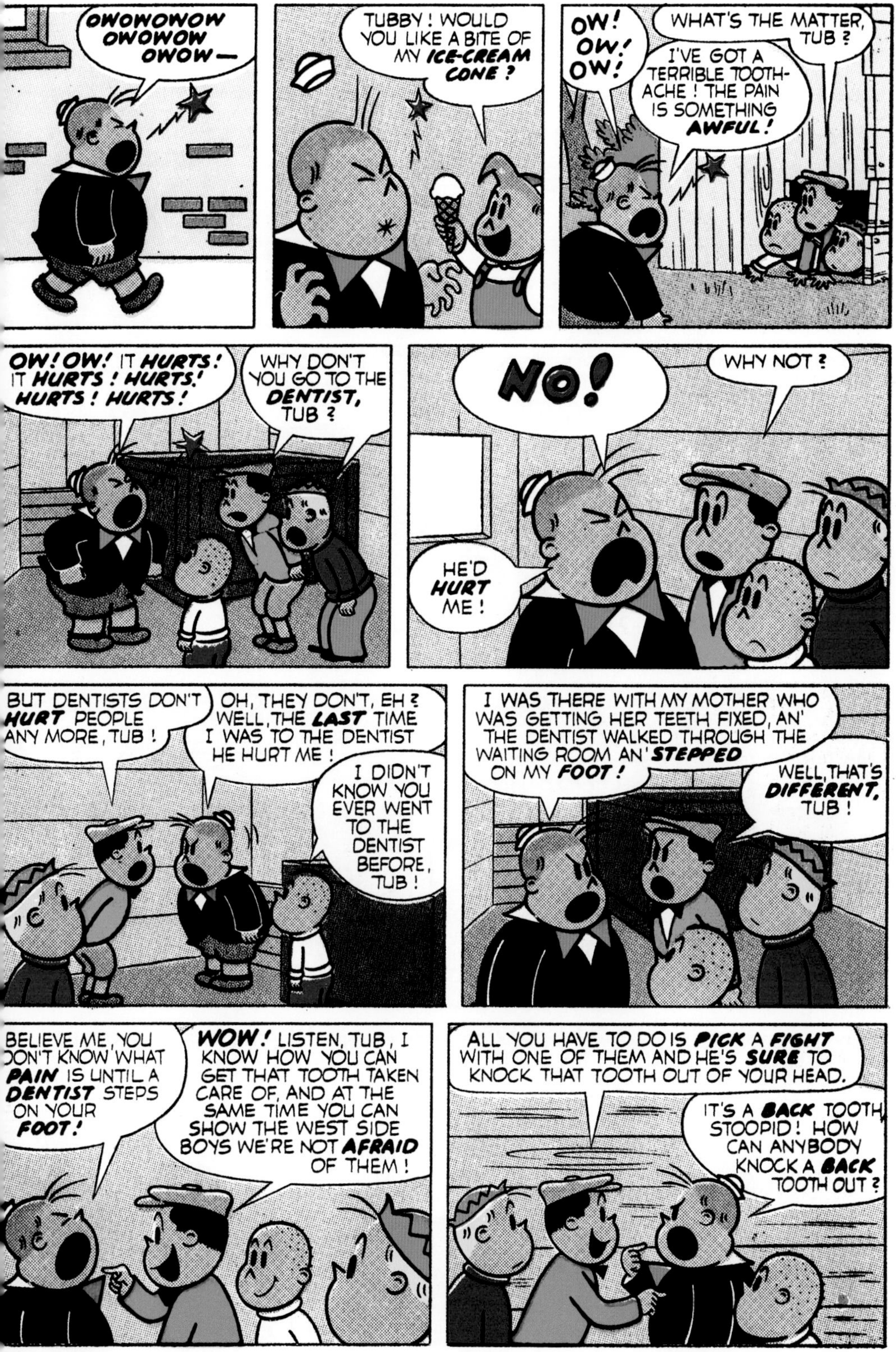
OWOWOWOW OWOWOW OWOW—
TUBBY! WOULD YOU LIKE A BITE OF MY ICE-CREAM CONE?
OW! OW! OW!
WHAT'S THE MATTER, TUB?
I'VE GOT A TERRIBLE TOOTH-ACHE! THE PAIN IS SOMETHING AWFUL!
OW! OW! IT HURTS! IT HURTS! HURTS! HURTS! HURTS!
WHY DON'T YOU GO TO THE DENTIST, TUB?
NO!
WHY NOT?
HE'D HURT ME!
BUT DENTISTS DON'T HURT PEOPLE ANY MORE, TUB!
OH, THEY DON'T, EH? WELL, THE LAST TIME I WAS TO THE DENTIST HE HURT ME!
I DIDN'T KNOW YOU EVER WENT TO THE DENTIST BEFORE, TUB!
I WAS THERE WITH MY MOTHER WHO WAS GETTING HER TEETH FIXED, AN' THE DENTIST WALKED THROUGH THE WAITING ROOM AN' STEPPED ON MY FOOT!
WELL, THAT'S DIFFERENT, TUB!
BELIEVE ME, YOU DON'T KNOW WHAT PAIN IS UNTIL A DENTIST STEPS ON YOUR FOOT!
WOW! LISTEN, TUB, I KNOW HOW YOU CAN GET THAT TOOTH TAKEN CARE OF, AND AT THE SAME TIME YOU CAN SHOW THE WEST SIDE BOYS WE'RE NOT AFRAID OF THEM!
ALL YOU HAVE TO DO IS PICK A FIGHT WITH ONE OF THEM AND HE'S SURE TO KNOCK THAT TOOTH OUT OF YOUR HEAD.
IT'S A BACK TOOTH, STOOPID! HOW CAN ANYBODY KNOCK A BACK TOOTH OUT?

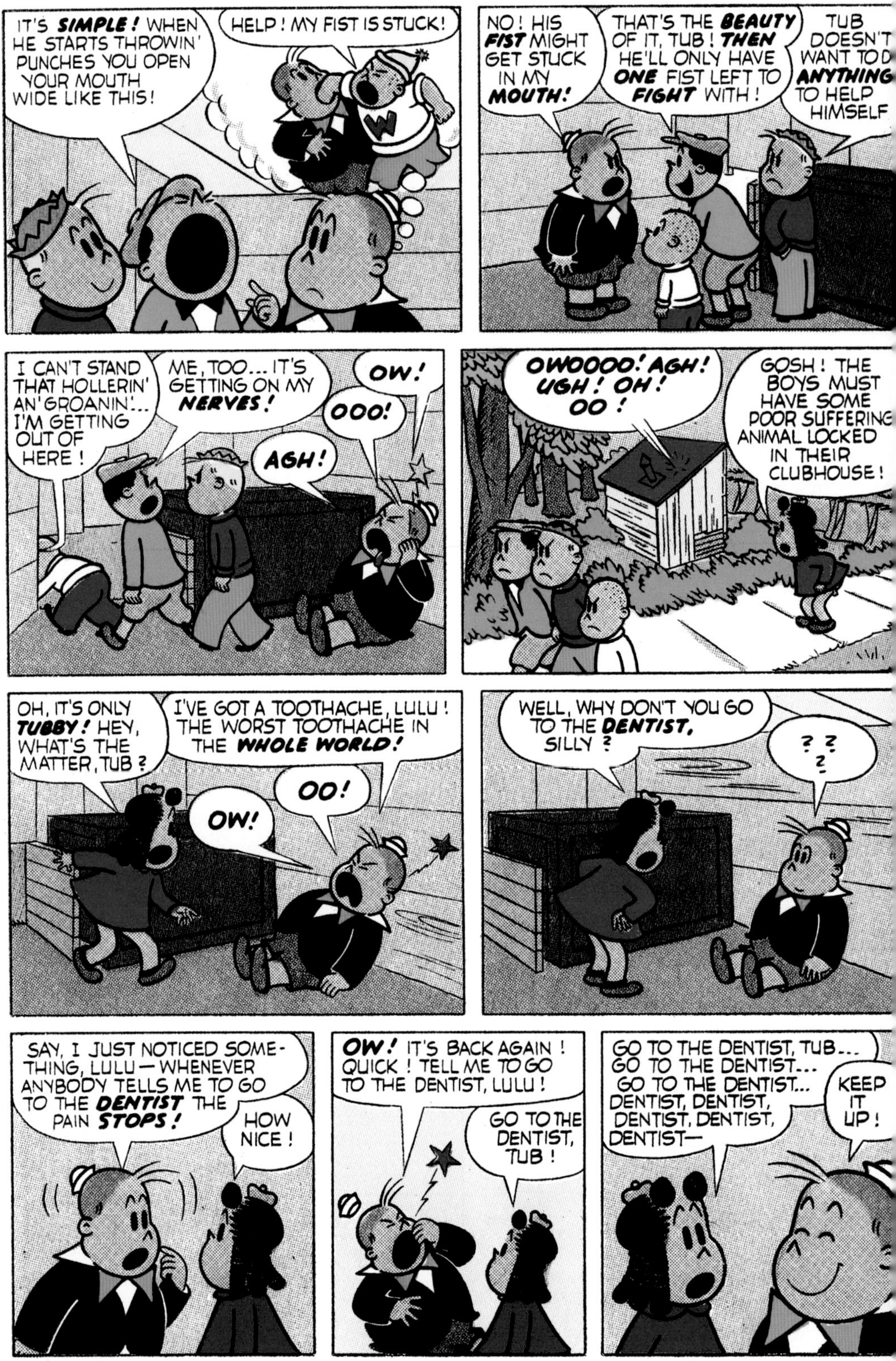
IT'S SIMPLE! WHEN HE STARTS THROWIN' PUNCHES YOU OPEN YOUR MOUTH WIDE LIKE THIS!
HELP! MY FIST IS STUCK!
NO! HIS FIST MIGHT GET STUCK IN MY MOUTH!
THAT'S THE BEAUTY OF IT, TUB! THEN HE'LL ONLY HAVE ONE FIST LEFT TO FIGHT WITH!
TUB DOESN'T WANT TO D ANYTHING TO HELP HIMSELF
I CAN'T STAND THAT HOLLERIN' AN' GROANIN'... I'M GETTING OUT OF HERE!
ME, TOO... IT'S GETTING ON MY NERVES!
OW!
OOO!
AGH!
OWOOOO! AGH! UGH! OH! OO!
GOSH! THE BOYS MUST HAVE SOME POOR SUFFERING ANIMAL LOCKED IN THEIR CLUBHOUSE!
OH, IT'S ONLY TUBBY! HEY, WHAT'S THE MATTER, TUB?
I'VE GOT A TOOTHACHE, LULU! THE WORST TOOTHACHE IN THE WHOLE WORLD!
OO!
OW!
WELL, WHY DON'T YOU GO TO THE DENTIST, SILLY?
? ? ?
SAY, I JUST NOTICED SOME-THING, LULU—WHENEVER ANYBODY TELLS ME TO GO TO THE DENTIST THE PAIN STOPS!
HOW NICE!
OW! IT'S BACK AGAIN! QUICK! TELL ME TO GO TO THE DENTIST, LULU!
GO TO THE DENTIST, TUB!
GO TO THE DENTIST, TUB... GO TO THE DENTIST... GO TO THE DENTIST... DENTIST, DENTIST, DENTIST, DENTIST, DENTIST—
KEEP IT UP!

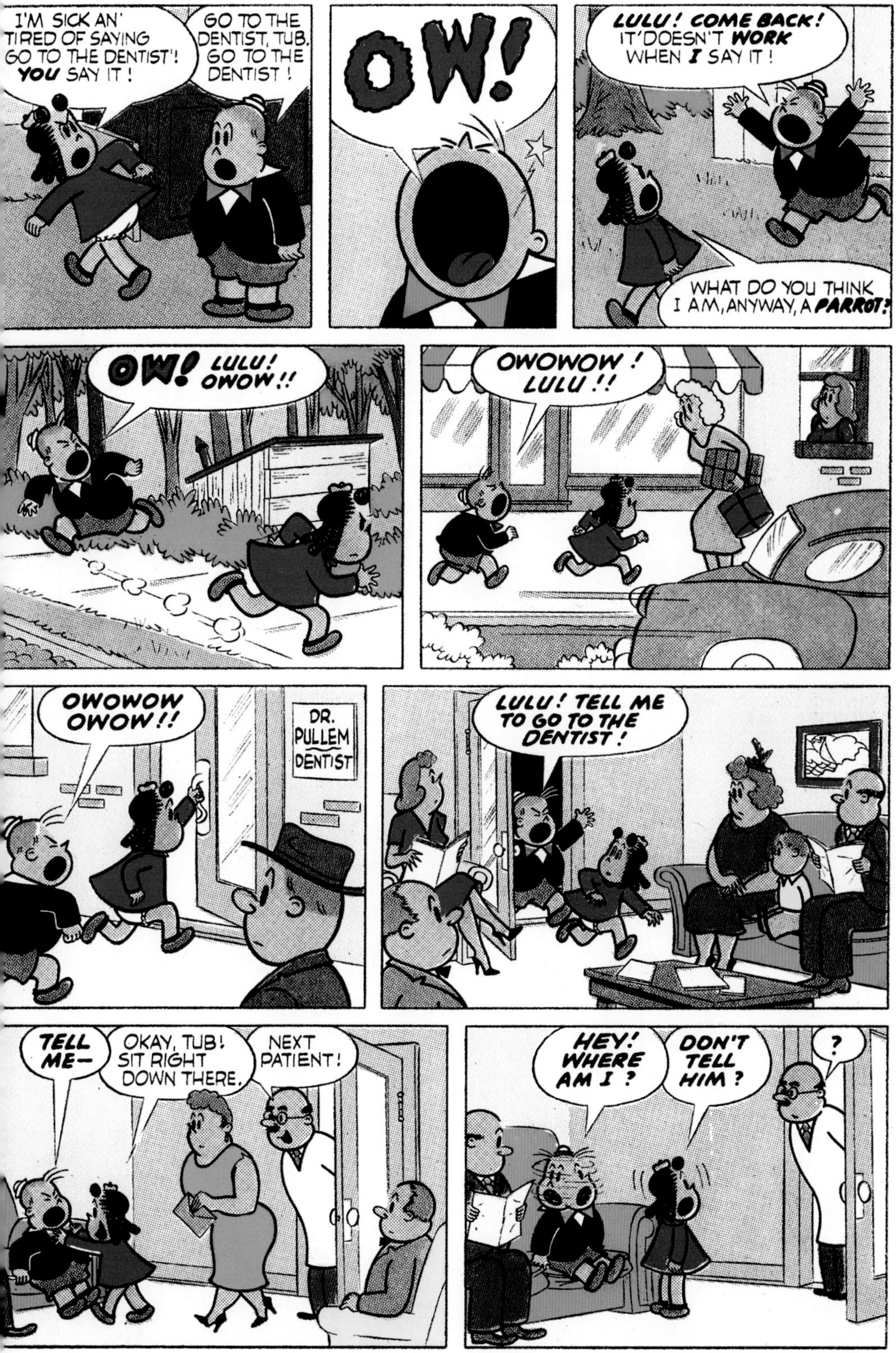
I'M SICK AN' TIRED OF SAYING 'GO TO THE DENTIST'! YOU SAY IT!
GO TO THE DENTIST, TUB. GO TO THE DENTIST!
OW!
LULU! COME BACK! IT DOESN'T WORK WHEN I SAY IT!
WHAT DO YOU THINK I AM, ANYWAY, A PARROT?
OW! LULU! OWOW!!
OWOWOW! LULU!!
OWOWOW OWOW!!
DR. PULLEM DENTIST
LULU! TELL ME TO GO TO THE DENTIST!
TELL ME—
OKAY, TUB! SIT RIGHT DOWN THERE.
NEXT PATIENT!
HEY! WHERE AM I?
DON'T TELL HIM?
?

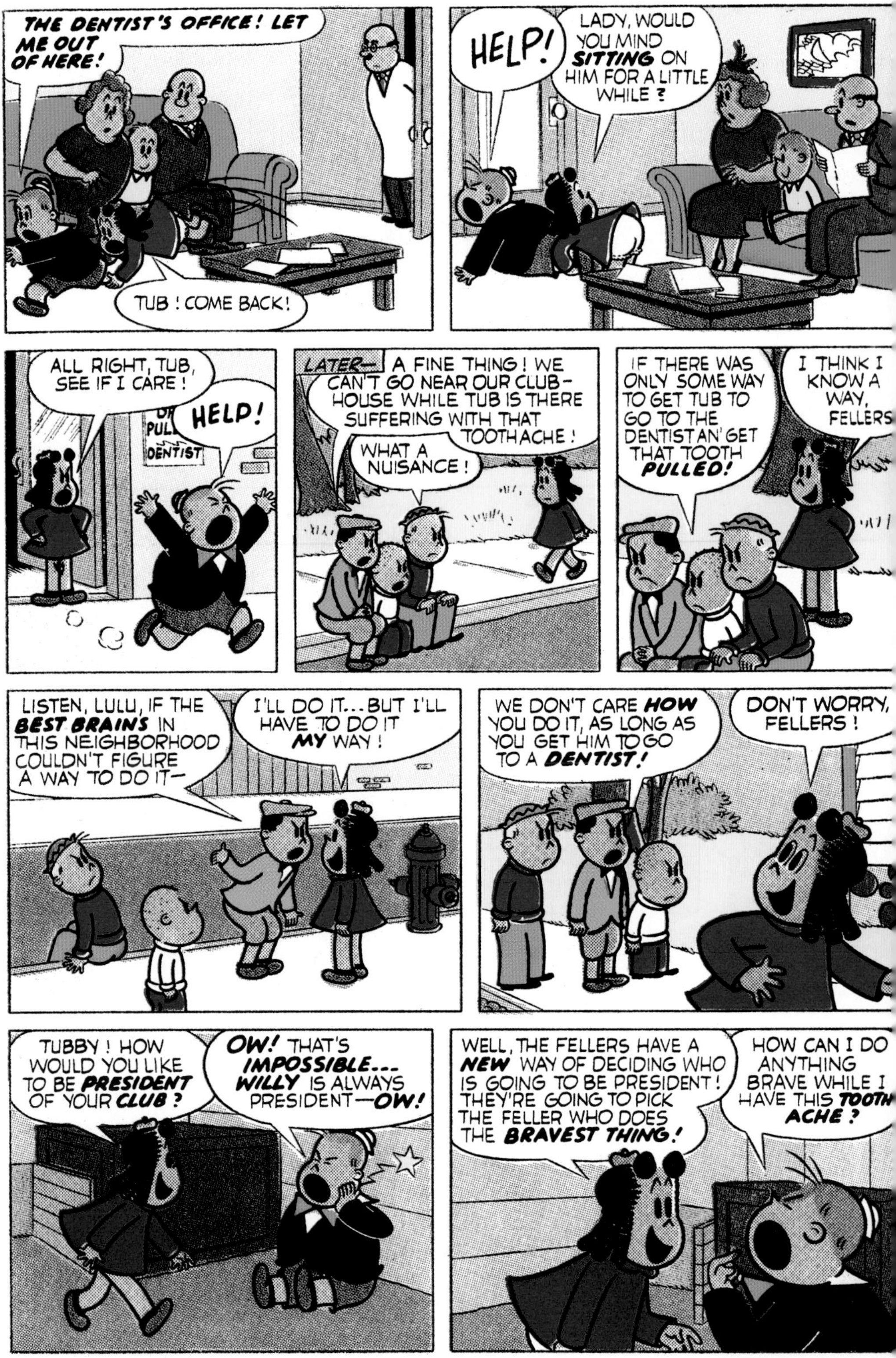
THE DENTIST'S OFFICE! LET ME OUT OF HERE!
TUB ! COME BACK!
HELP!
LADY, WOULD YOU MIND SITTING ON HIM FOR A LITTLE WHILE ?
ALL RIGHT, TUB, SEE IF I CARE !
HELP!
DENTIST
LATER—
A FINE THING ! WE CAN'T GO NEAR OUR CLUB-HOUSE WHILE TUB IS THERE SUFFERING WITH THAT TOOTHACHE !
WHAT A NUISANCE !
IF THERE WAS ONLY SOME WAY TO GET TUB TO GO TO THE DENTIST AN' GET THAT TOOTH PULLED!
I THINK I KNOW A WAY, FELLERS
LISTEN, LULU, IF THE BEST BRAINS IN THIS NEIGHBORHOOD COULDN'T FIGURE A WAY TO DO IT—
I'LL DO IT... BUT I'LL HAVE TO DO IT MY WAY !
WE DON'T CARE HOW YOU DO IT, AS LONG AS YOU GET HIM TO GO TO A DENTIST!
DON'T WORRY, FELLERS !
TUBBY ! HOW WOULD YOU LIKE TO BE PRESIDENT OF YOUR CLUB ?
OW! THAT'S IMPOSSIBLE... WILLY IS ALWAYS PRESIDENT—OW!
WELL, THE FELLERS HAVE A NEW WAY OF DECIDING WHO IS GOING TO BE PRESIDENT ! THEY'RE GOING TO PICK THE FELLER WHO DOES THE BRAVEST THING!
HOW CAN I DO ANYTHING BRAVE WHILE I HAVE THIS TOOTH ACHE ?

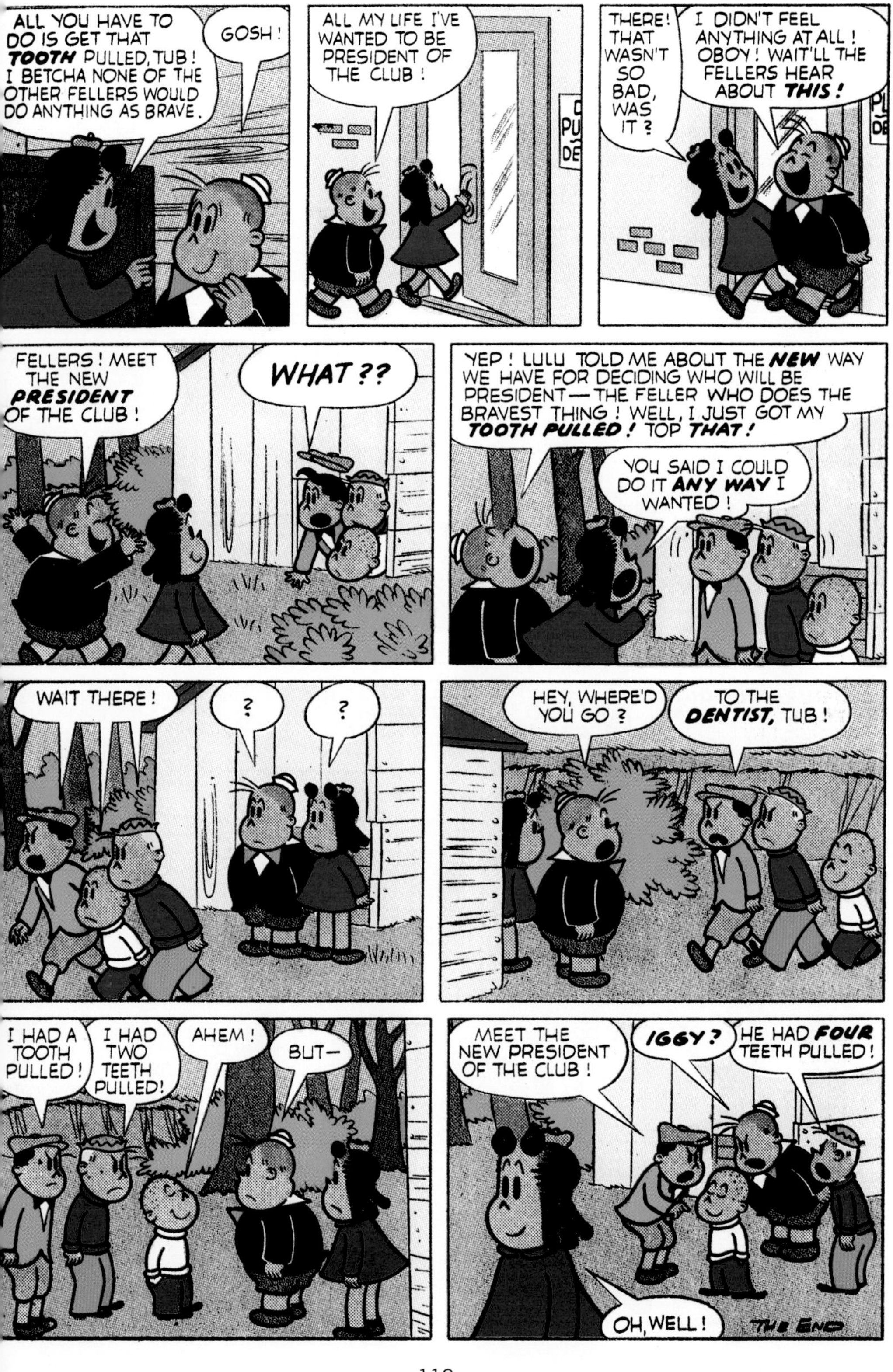
ALL YOU HAVE TO DO IS GET THAT TOOTH PULLED, TUB! I BETCHA NONE OF THE OTHER FELLERS WOULD DO ANYTHING AS BRAVE.
GOSH!
ALL MY LIFE I'VE WANTED TO BE PRESIDENT OF THE CLUB!
THERE! THAT WASN'T SO BAD, WAS IT?
I DIDN'T FEEL ANYTHING AT ALL! OBOY! WAIT'LL THE FELLERS HEAR ABOUT THIS!
FELLERS! MEET THE NEW PRESIDENT OF THE CLUB!
WHAT??
YEP! LULU TOLD ME ABOUT THE NEW WAY WE HAVE FOR DECIDING WHO WILL BE PRESIDENT—THE FELLER WHO DOES THE BRAVEST THING! WELL, I JUST GOT MY TOOTH PULLED! TOP THAT!
YOU SAID I COULD DO IT ANY WAY I WANTED!
WAIT THERE!
?
?
HEY, WHERE'D YOU GO?
TO THE DENTIST, TUB!
I HAD A TOOTH PULLED!
I HAD TWO TEETH PULLED!
AHEM!
BUT—
MEET THE NEW PRESIDENT OF THE CLUB!
IGGY?
HE HAD FOUR TEETH PULLED!
OH, WELL!
THE END

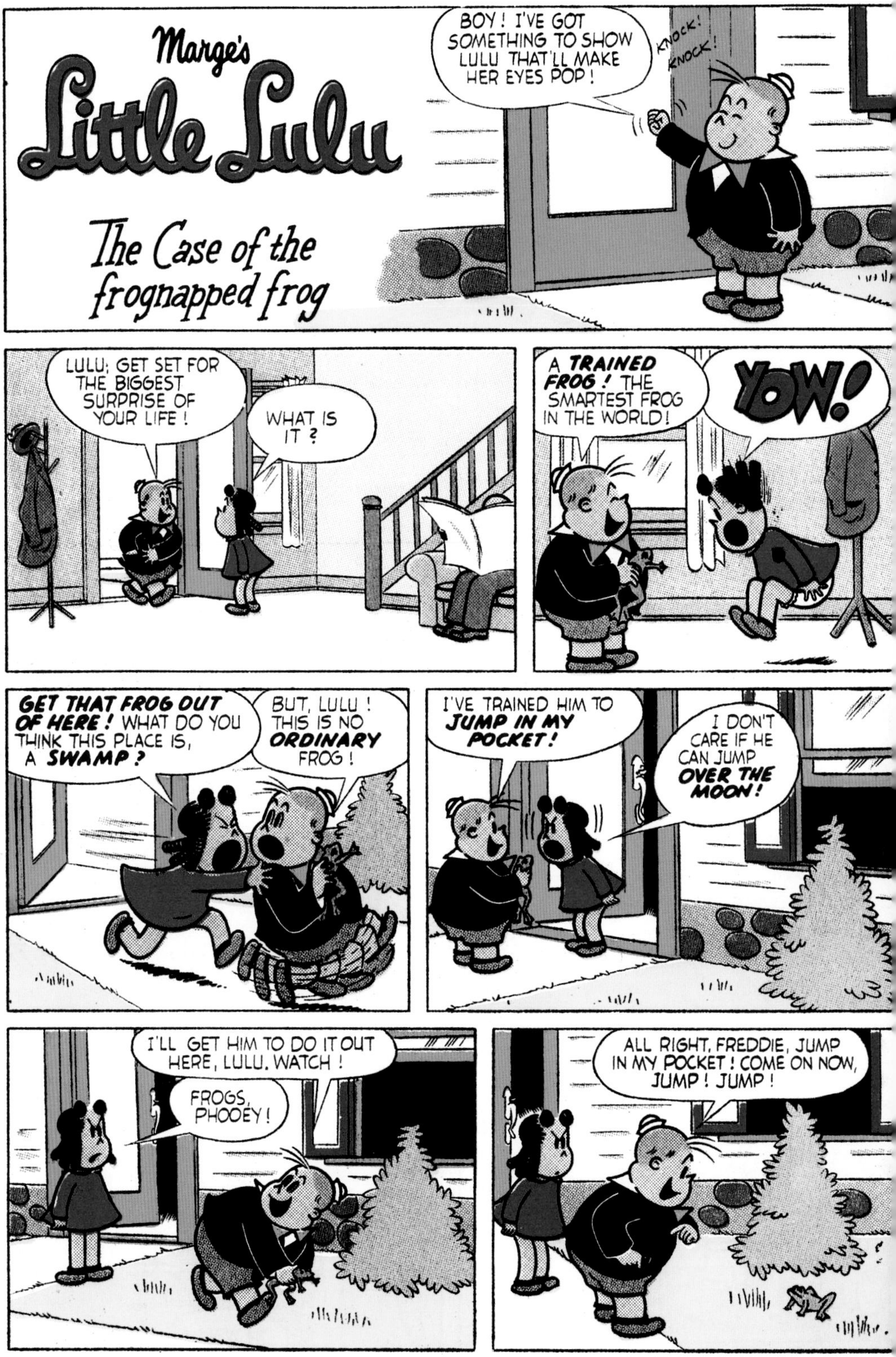
Marge's
Little Lulu
The Case of the frognapped frog
BOY! I'VE GOT SOMETHING TO SHOW LULU THAT'LL MAKE HER EYES POP!
KNOCK! KNOCK!
LULU; GET SET FOR THE BIGGEST SURPRISE OF YOUR LIFE!
WHAT IS IT?
A TRAINED FROG! THE SMARTEST FROG IN THE WORLD!
YOW!
GET THAT FROG OUT OF HERE! WHAT DO YOU THINK THIS PLACE IS, A SWAMP?
BUT, LULU! THIS IS NO ORDINARY FROG!
I'VE TRAINED HIM TO JUMP IN MY POCKET!
I DON'T CARE IF HE CAN JUMP OVER THE MOON!
I'LL GET HIM TO DO IT OUT HERE, LULU. WATCH!
FROGS, PHOOEY!
ALL RIGHT, FREDDIE, JUMP IN MY POCKET! COME ON NOW, JUMP! JUMP!

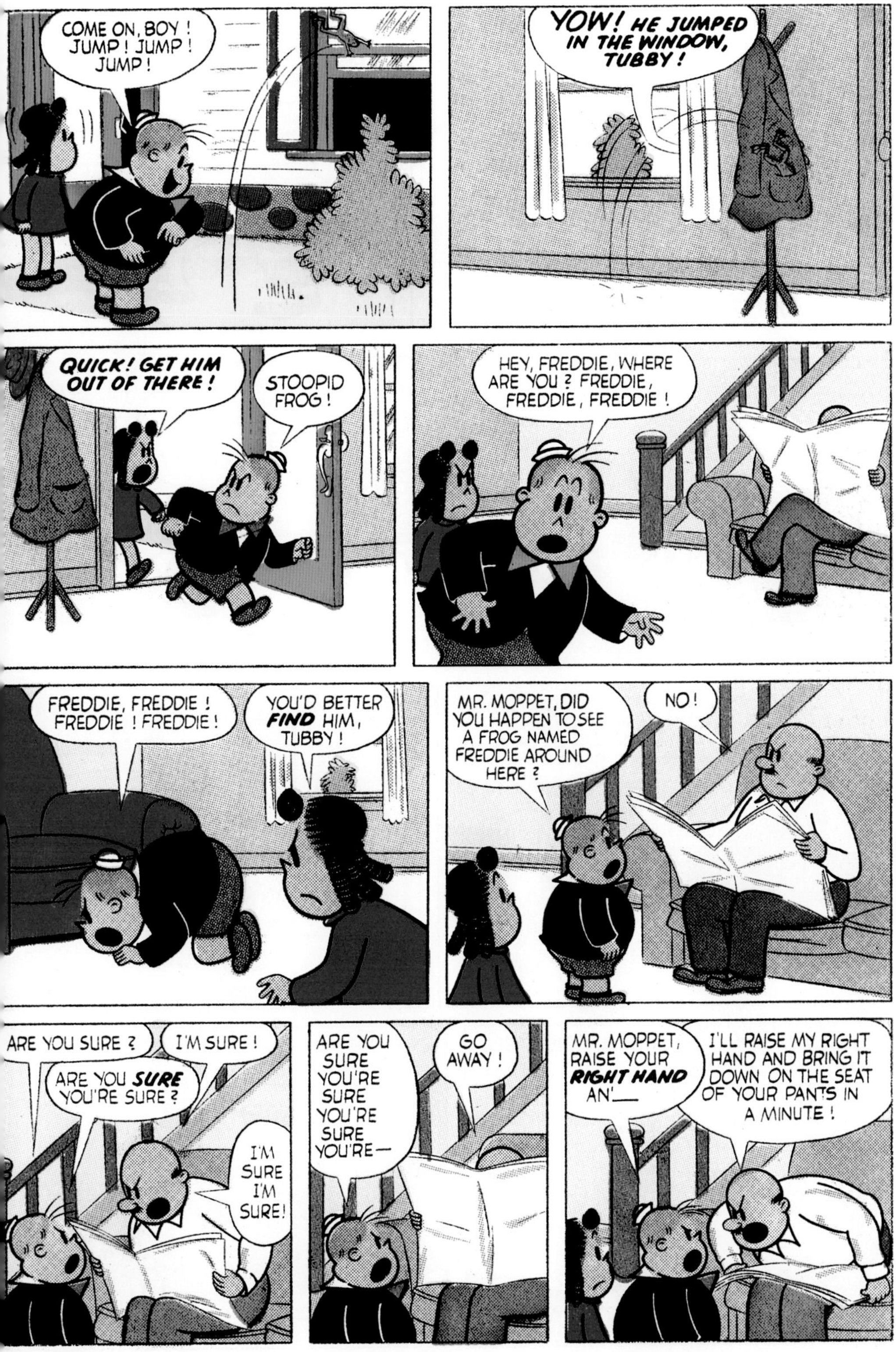
COME ON, BOY ! JUMP ! JUMP ! JUMP !
YOW! HE JUMPED IN THE WINDOW, TUBBY !
QUICK! GET HIM OUT OF THERE !
STOOPID FROG !
HEY, FREDDIE, WHERE ARE YOU ? FREDDIE, FREDDIE, FREDDIE !
FREDDIE, FREDDIE ! FREDDIE ! FREDDIE !
YOU'D BETTER FIND HIM, TUBBY !
MR. MOPPET, DID YOU HAPPEN TO SEE A FROG NAMED FREDDIE AROUND HERE ?
NO !
ARE YOU SURE ?
I'M SURE !
ARE YOU SURE YOU'RE SURE ?
I'M SURE I'M SURE!
ARE YOU SURE YOU'RE SURE YOU'RE SURE YOU'RE—
GO AWAY !
MR. MOPPET, RAISE YOUR RIGHT HAND AN'—
I'LL RAISE MY RIGHT HAND AND BRING IT DOWN ON THE SEAT OF YOUR PANTS IN A MINUTE !

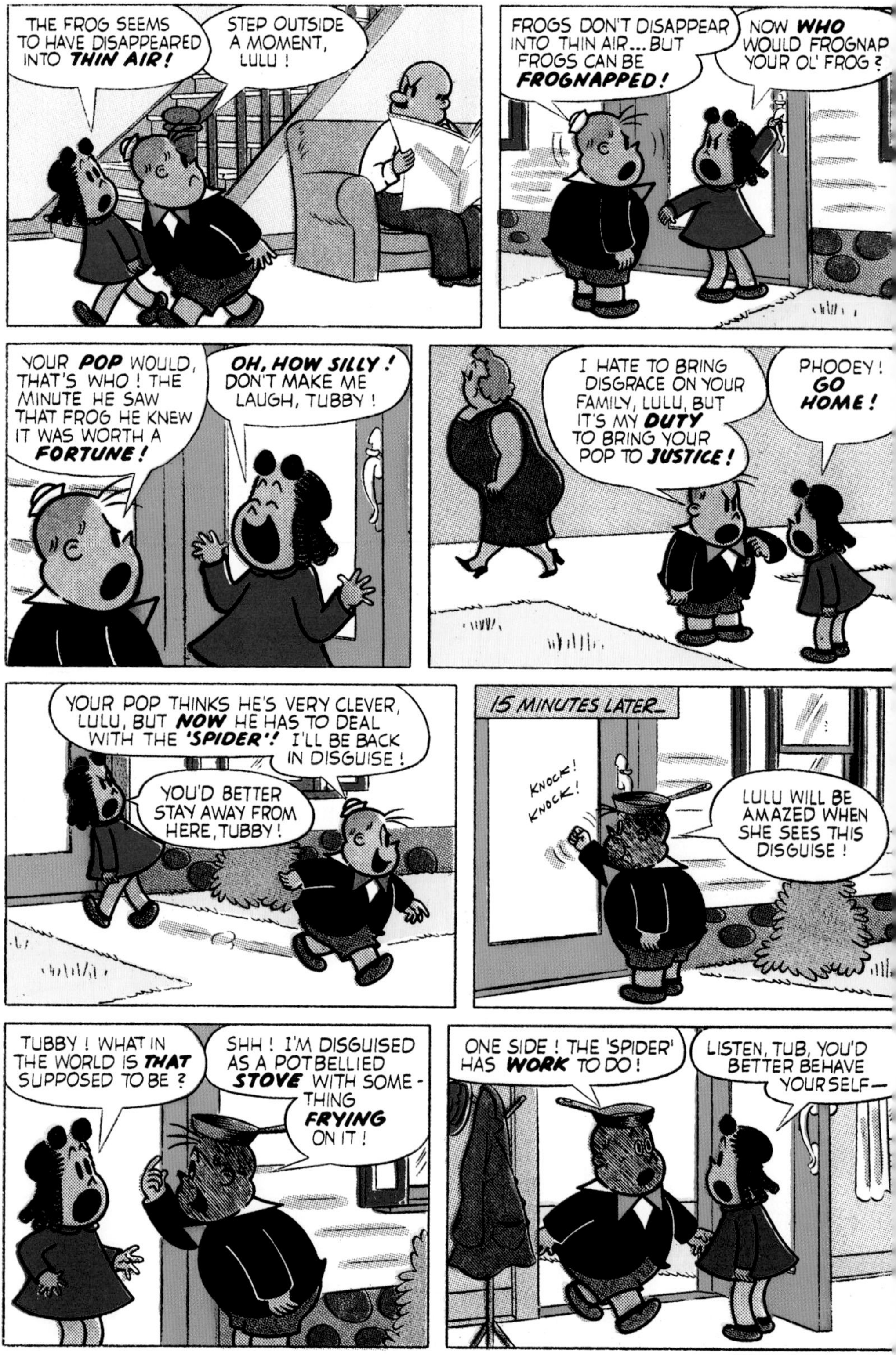
THE FROG SEEMS TO HAVE DISAPPEARED INTO THIN AIR!
STEP OUTSIDE A MOMENT, LULU!
FROGS DON'T DISAPPEAR INTO THIN AIR... BUT FROGS CAN BE FROGNAPPED!
NOW WHO WOULD FROGNAP YOUR OL' FROG?
YOUR POP WOULD, THAT'S WHO! THE MINUTE HE SAW THAT FROG HE KNEW IT WAS WORTH A FORTUNE!
OH, HOW SILLY! DON'T MAKE ME LAUGH, TUBBY!
I HATE TO BRING DISGRACE ON YOUR FAMILY, LULU, BUT IT'S MY DUTY TO BRING YOUR POP TO JUSTICE!
PHOOEY! GO HOME!
YOUR POP THINKS HE'S VERY CLEVER, LULU, BUT NOW HE HAS TO DEAL WITH THE 'SPIDER'! I'LL BE BACK IN DISGUISE!
YOU'D BETTER STAY AWAY FROM HERE, TUBBY!
15 MINUTES LATER
KNOCK! KNOCK!
LULU WILL BE AMAZED WHEN SHE SEES THIS DISGUISE!
TUBBY! WHAT IN THE WORLD IS THAT SUPPOSED TO BE?
SHH! I'M DISGUISED AS A POTBELLIED STOVE WITH SOME-THING FRYING ON IT!
ONE SIDE! THE 'SPIDER' HAS WORK TO DO!
LISTEN, TUB, YOU'D BETTER BEHAVE YOURSELF—

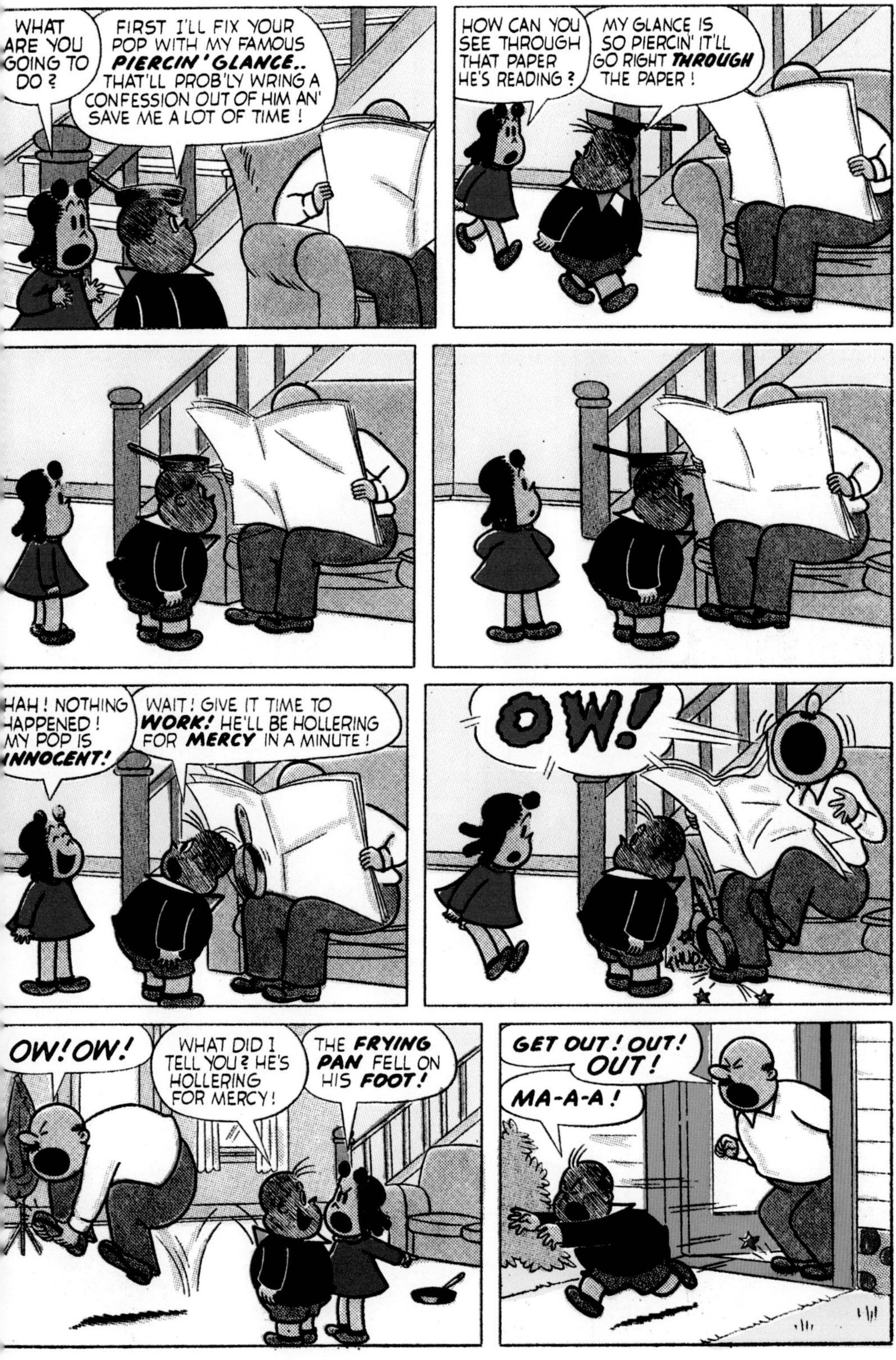

WHAT ARE YOU GOING TO DO?
FIRST I'LL FIX YOUR POP WITH MY FAMOUS PIERCIN' GLANCE.. THAT'LL PROB'LY WRING A CONFESSION OUT OF HIM AN' SAVE ME A LOT OF TIME!
HOW CAN YOU SEE THROUGH THAT PAPER HE'S READING?
MY GLANCE IS SO PIERCIN' IT'LL GO RIGHT THROUGH THE PAPER!
HAH! NOTHING HAPPENED! MY POP IS INNOCENT!
WAIT! GIVE IT TIME TO WORK! HE'LL BE HOLLERING FOR MERCY IN A MINUTE!
OW!
OW! OW!
WHAT DID I TELL YOU? HE'S HOLLERING FOR MERCY!
THE FRYING PAN FELL ON HIS FOOT!
GET OUT! OUT! OUT!
MA-A-A!

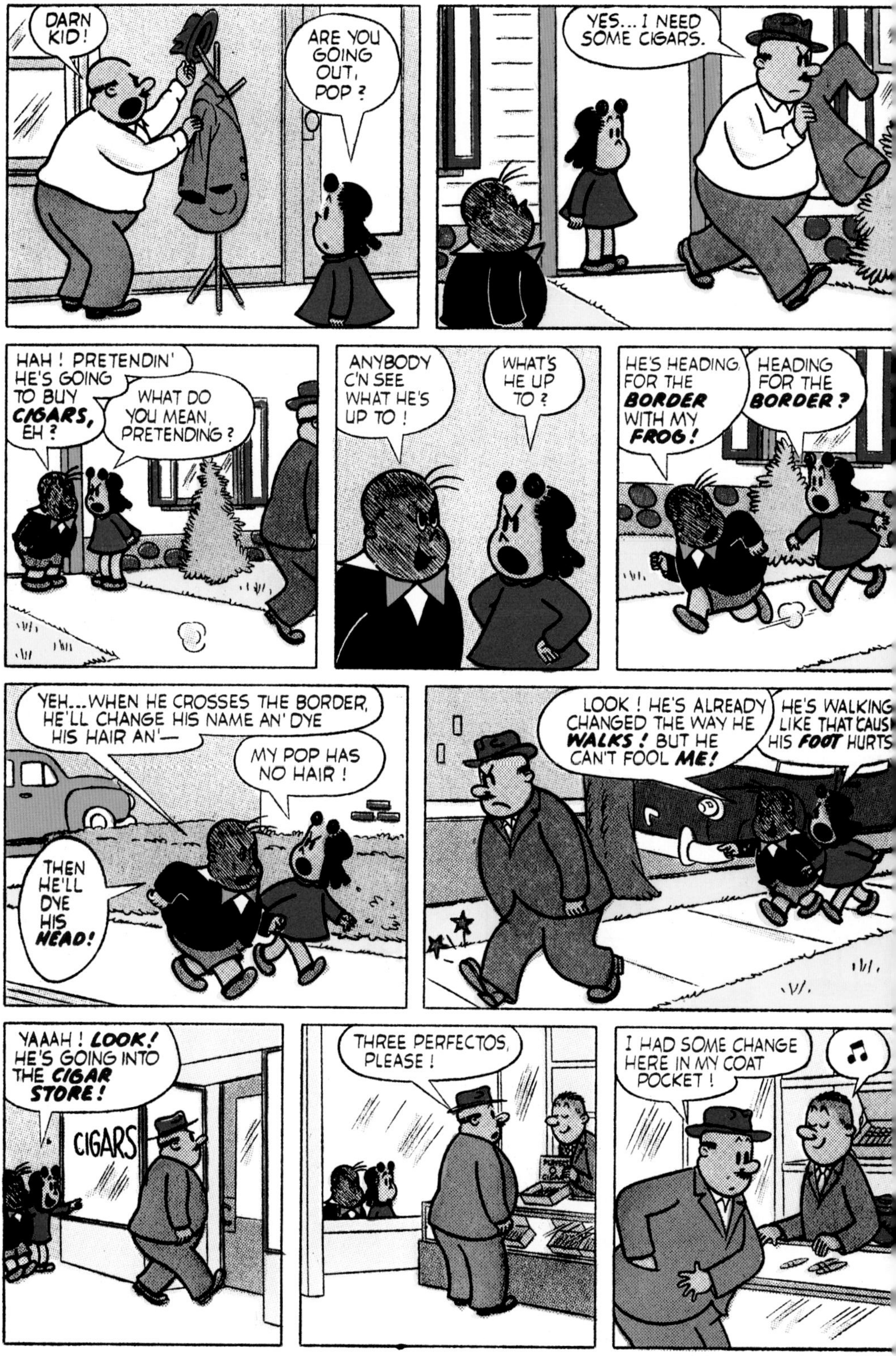
DARN KID!
ARE YOU GOING OUT, POP?
YES... I NEED SOME CIGARS.
HAH! PRETENDIN' HE'S GOING TO BUY CIGARS, EH?
WHAT DO YOU MEAN, PRETENDING?
ANYBODY C'N SEE WHAT HE'S UP TO!
WHAT'S HE UP TO?
HE'S HEADING FOR THE BORDER WITH MY FROG!
HEADING FOR THE BORDER?
YEH... WHEN HE CROSSES THE BORDER, HE'LL CHANGE HIS NAME AN' DYE HIS HAIR AN'—
MY POP HAS NO HAIR!
THEN HE'LL DYE HIS HEAD!
LOOK! HE'S ALREADY CHANGED THE WAY HE WALKS! BUT HE CAN'T FOOL ME!
HE'S WALKING LIKE THAT 'CAUS HIS FOOT HURTS
YAAAH! LOOK! HE'S GOING INTO THE CIGAR STORE!
CIGARS
THREE PERFECTOS, PLEASE!
I HAD SOME CHANGE HERE IN MY COAT POCKET!
♪

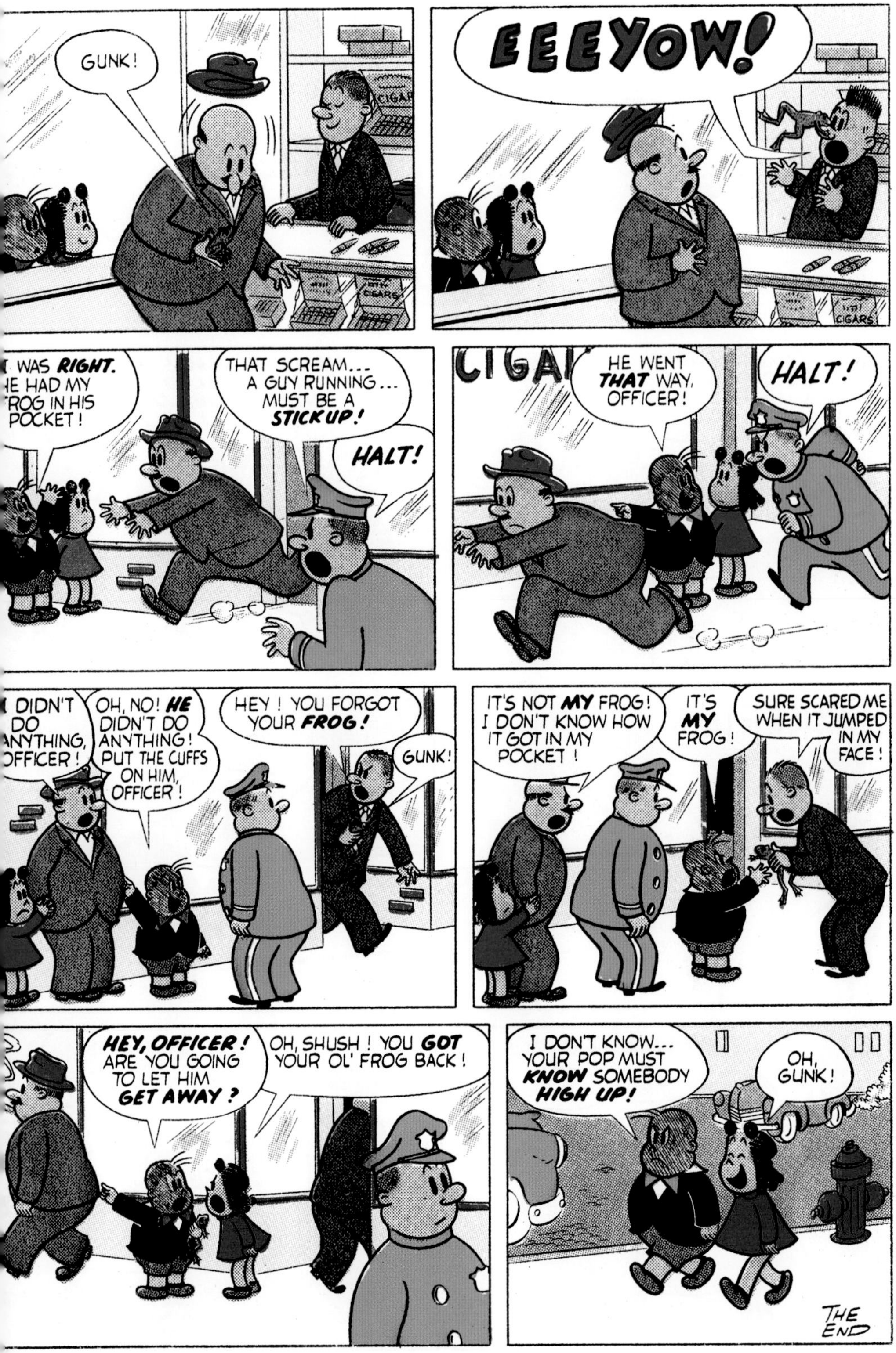
GUNK!
EEEYOW!
WAS RIGHT. HE HAD MY FROG IN HIS POCKET!
THAT SCREAM... A GUY RUNNING... MUST BE A STICKUP!
HALT!
HE WENT THAT WAY, OFFICER!
HALT!
DIDN'T DO ANYTHING, OFFICER!
OH, NO! HE DIDN'T DO ANYTHING! PUT THE CUFFS ON HIM, OFFICER!
HEY! YOU FORGOT YOUR FROG!
GUNK!
IT'S NOT MY FROG! I DON'T KNOW HOW IT GOT IN MY POCKET!
IT'S MY FROG!
SURE SCARED ME WHEN IT JUMPED IN MY FACE!
HEY, OFFICER! ARE YOU GOING TO LET HIM GET AWAY?
OH, SHUSH! YOU GOT YOUR OL' FROG BACK!
I DON'T KNOW... YOUR POP MUST KNOW SOMEBODY HIGH UP!
OH, GUNK!
THE END

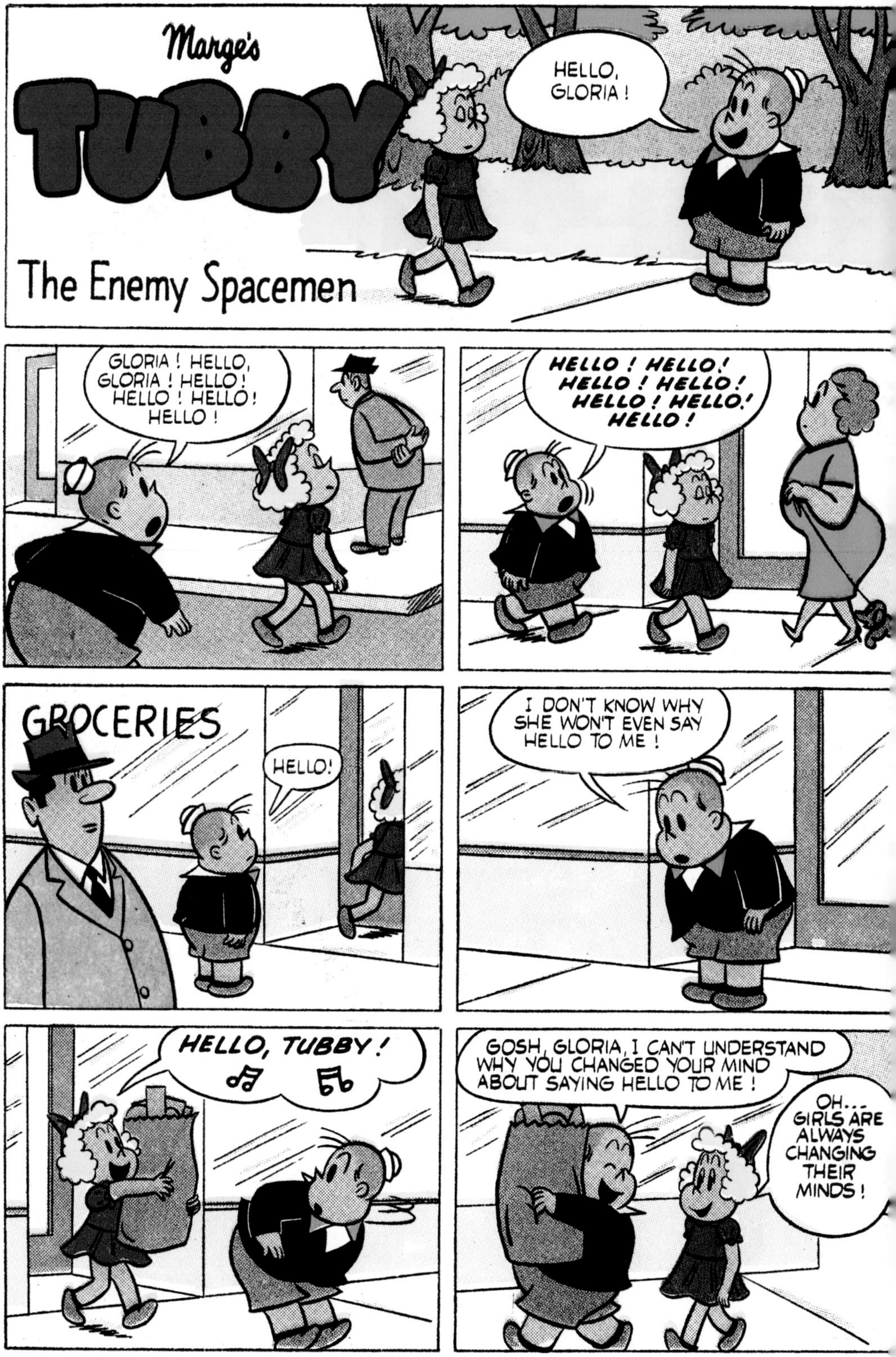
Marge's
TUBBY
The Enemy Spacemen
HELLO, GLORIA!
GLORIA! HELLO, GLORIA! HELLO! HELLO! HELLO! HELLO!
HELLO! HELLO! HELLO! HELLO! HELLO! HELLO! HELLO!
GROCERIES
HELLO!
I DON'T KNOW WHY SHE WON'T EVEN SAY HELLO TO ME!
HELLO, TUBBY!
GOSH, GLORIA, I CAN'T UNDERSTAND WHY YOU CHANGED YOUR MIND ABOUT SAYING HELLO TO ME!
OH... GIRLS ARE ALWAYS CHANGING THEIR MINDS!

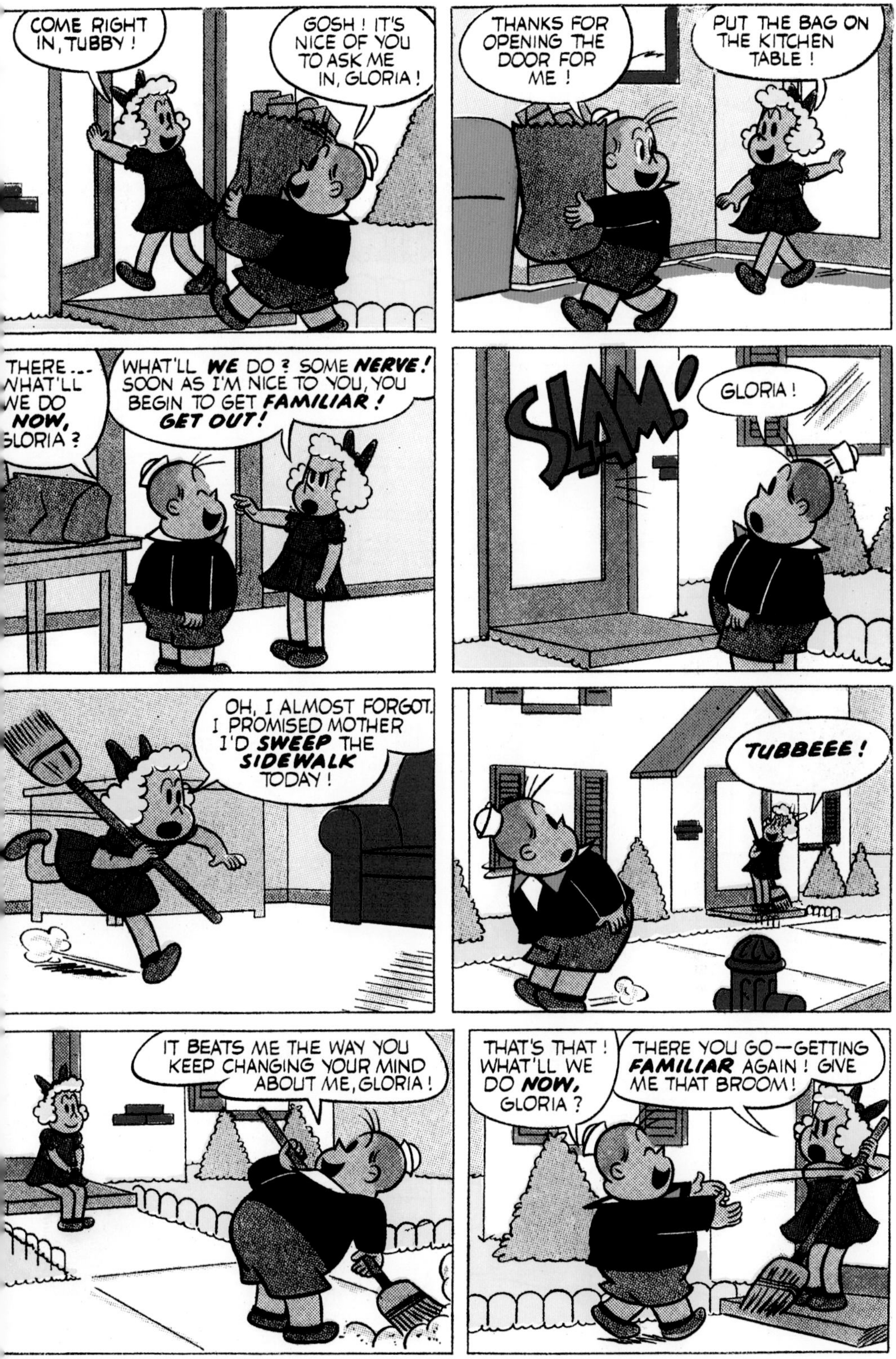
COME RIGHT IN, TUBBY!
GOSH! IT'S NICE OF YOU TO ASK ME IN, GLORIA!
THANKS FOR OPENING THE DOOR FOR ME!
PUT THE BAG ON THE KITCHEN TABLE!
THERE... WHAT'LL WE DO NOW, GLORIA?
WHAT'LL WE DO? SOME NERVE! SOON AS I'M NICE TO YOU, YOU BEGIN TO GET FAMILIAR! GET OUT!
SLAM!
GLORIA!
OH, I ALMOST FORGOT. I PROMISED MOTHER I'D SWEEP THE SIDEWALK TODAY!
TUBBEEE!
IT BEATS ME THE WAY YOU KEEP CHANGING YOUR MIND ABOUT ME, GLORIA!
THAT'S THAT! WHAT'LL WE DO NOW, GLORIA?
THERE YOU GO—GETTING FAMILIAR AGAIN! GIVE ME THAT BROOM!

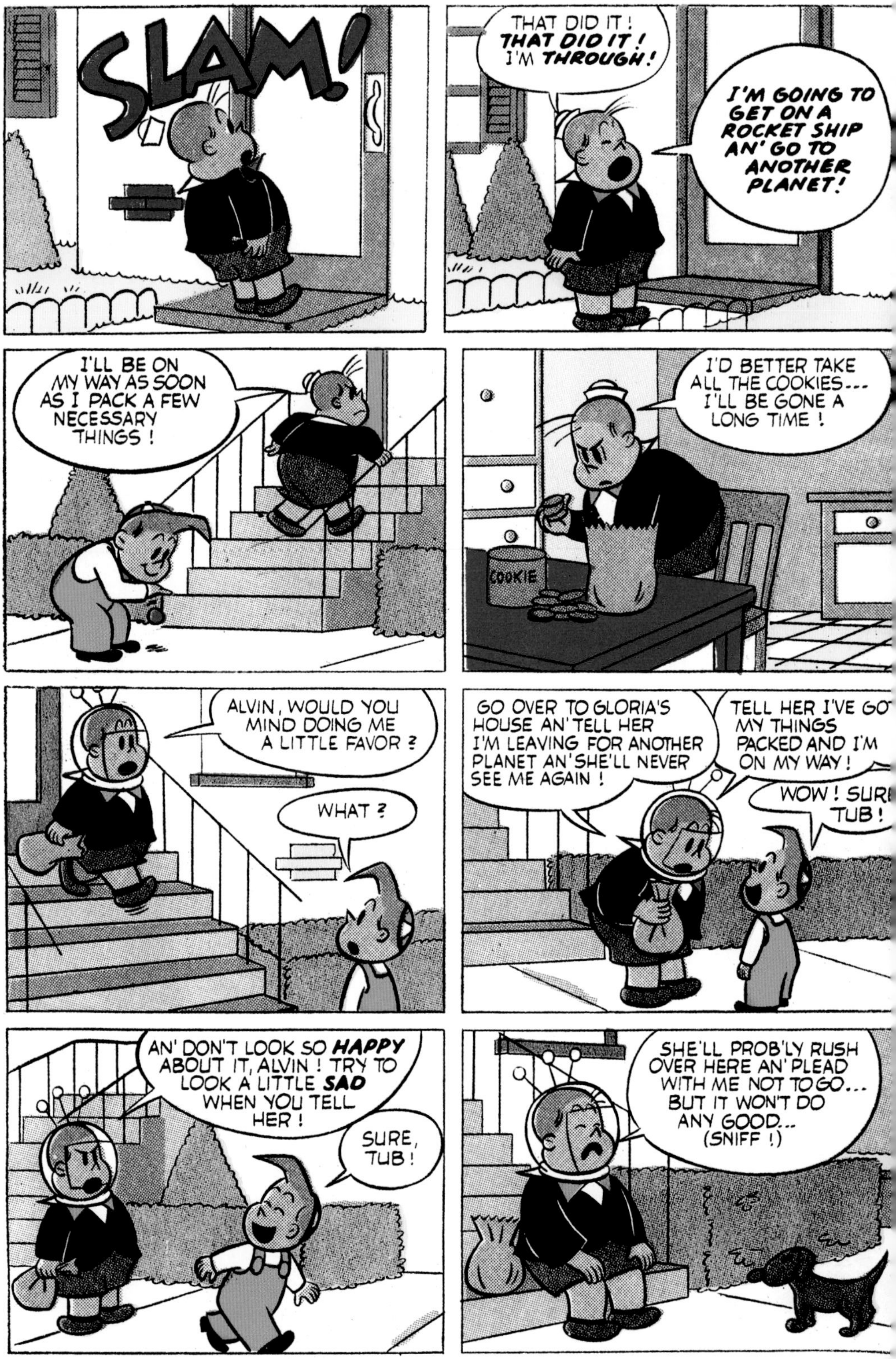
SLAM!
THAT DID IT! THAT DID IT! I'M THROUGH!
I'M GOING TO GET ON A ROCKET SHIP AN' GO TO ANOTHER PLANET!
I'LL BE ON MY WAY AS SOON AS I PACK A FEW NECESSARY THINGS!
I'D BETTER TAKE ALL THE COOKIES--- I'LL BE GONE A LONG TIME!
COOKIE
ALVIN, WOULD YOU MIND DOING ME A LITTLE FAVOR?
WHAT?
GO OVER TO GLORIA'S HOUSE AN' TELL HER I'M LEAVING FOR ANOTHER PLANET AN' SHE'LL NEVER SEE ME AGAIN!
AN' DON'T LOOK SO HAPPY ABOUT IT, ALVIN! TRY TO LOOK A LITTLE SAD WHEN YOU TELL HER!
SURE, TUB!
SHE'LL PROB'LY RUSH OVER HERE AN' PLEAD WITH ME NOT TO GO... BUT IT WON'T DO ANY GOOD... (SNIFF!)

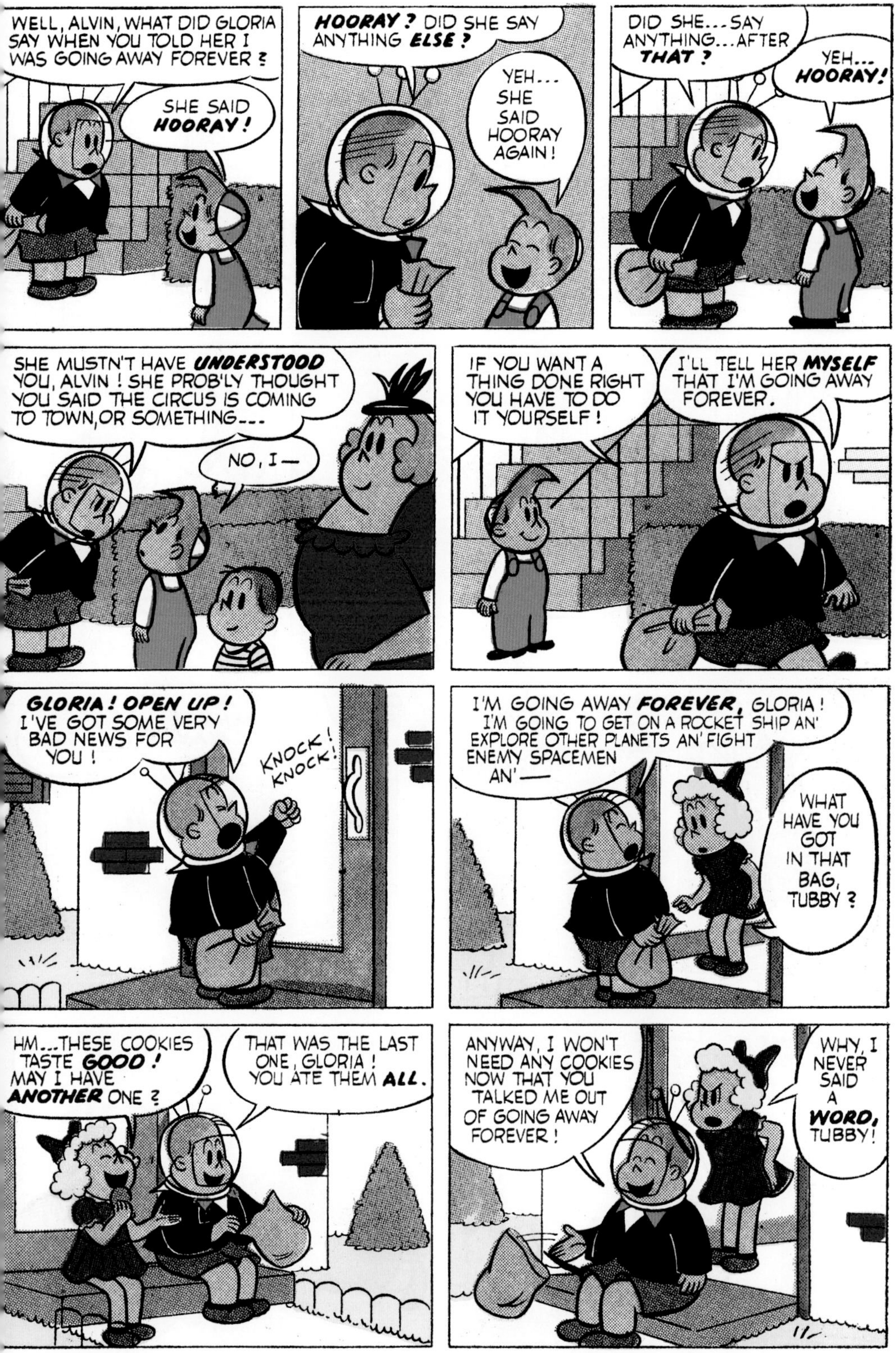
WELL, ALVIN, WHAT DID GLORIA SAY WHEN YOU TOLD HER I WAS GOING AWAY FOREVER ?
SHE SAID HOORAY !
HOORAY ? DID SHE SAY ANYTHING ELSE ?
YEH... SHE SAID HOORAY AGAIN !
DID SHE... SAY ANYTHING... AFTER THAT ?
YEH... HOORAY!
SHE MUSTN'T HAVE UNDERSTOOD YOU, ALVIN ! SHE PROB'LY THOUGHT YOU SAID THE CIRCUS IS COMING TO TOWN, OR SOMETHING...
NO, I—
IF YOU WANT A THING DONE RIGHT YOU HAVE TO DO IT YOURSELF !
I'LL TELL HER MYSELF THAT I'M GOING AWAY FOREVER.
GLORIA ! OPEN UP ! I'VE GOT SOME VERY BAD NEWS FOR YOU !
KNOCK ! KNOCK !
I'M GOING AWAY FOREVER, GLORIA ! I'M GOING TO GET ON A ROCKET SHIP AN' EXPLORE OTHER PLANETS AN' FIGHT ENEMY SPACEMEN AN'—
WHAT HAVE YOU GOT IN THAT BAG, TUBBY ?
HM... THESE COOKIES TASTE GOOD ! MAY I HAVE ANOTHER ONE ?
THAT WAS THE LAST ONE, GLORIA ! YOU ATE THEM ALL.
ANYWAY, I WON'T NEED ANY COOKIES NOW THAT YOU TALKED ME OUT OF GOING AWAY FOREVER !
WHY, I NEVER SAID A WORD, TUBBY!

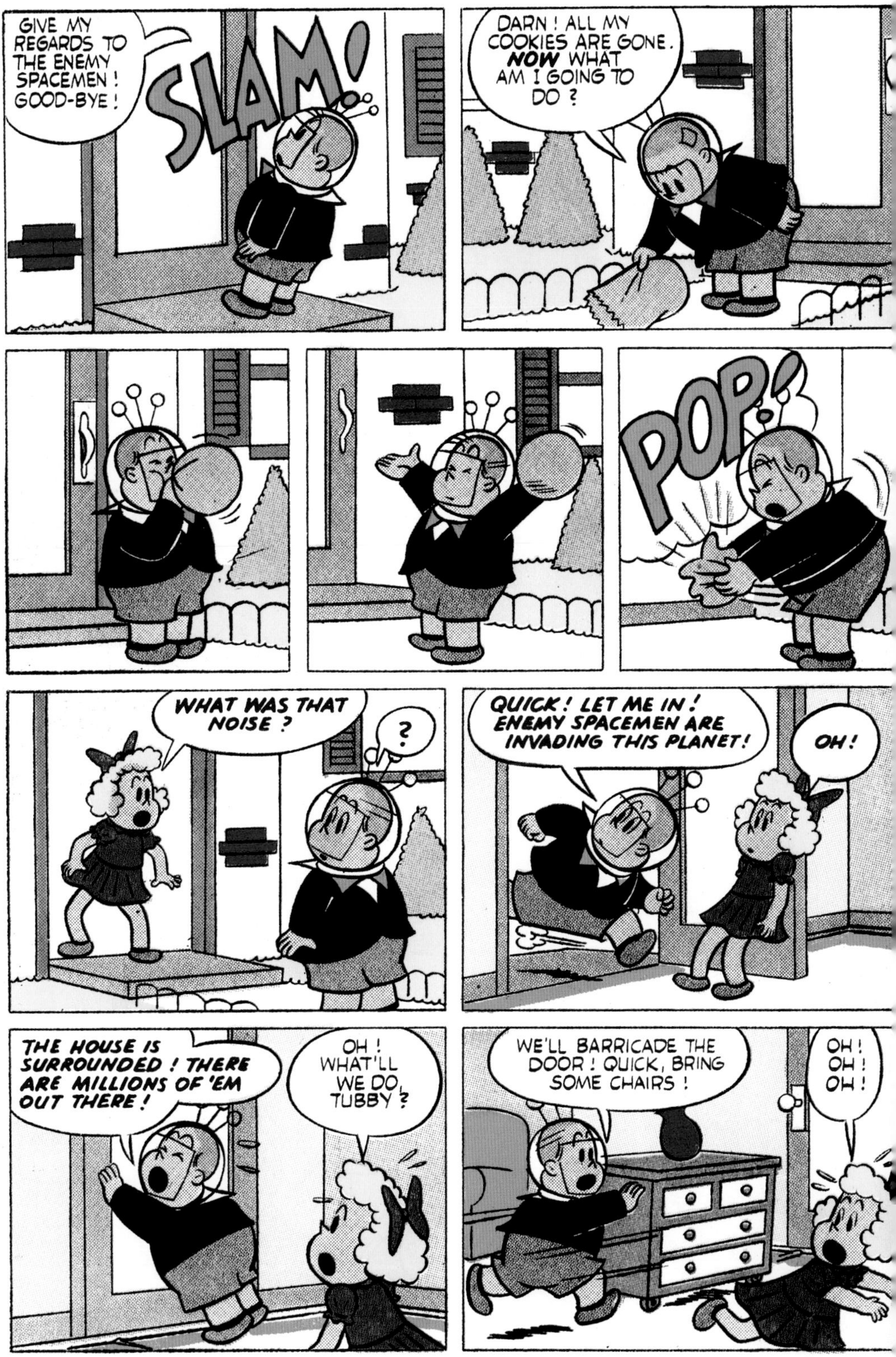
GIVE MY REGARDS TO THE ENEMY SPACEMEN! GOOD-BYE!
SLAM!
DARN! ALL MY COOKIES ARE GONE. NOW WHAT AM I GOING TO DO?
POP!
WHAT WAS THAT NOISE?
?
QUICK! LET ME IN! ENEMY SPACEMEN ARE INVADING THIS PLANET!
OH!
THE HOUSE IS SURROUNDED! THERE ARE MILLIONS OF 'EM OUT THERE!
OH! WHAT'LL WE DO, TUBBY?
WE'LL BARRICADE THE DOOR! QUICK, BRING SOME CHAIRS!
OH! OH! OH!

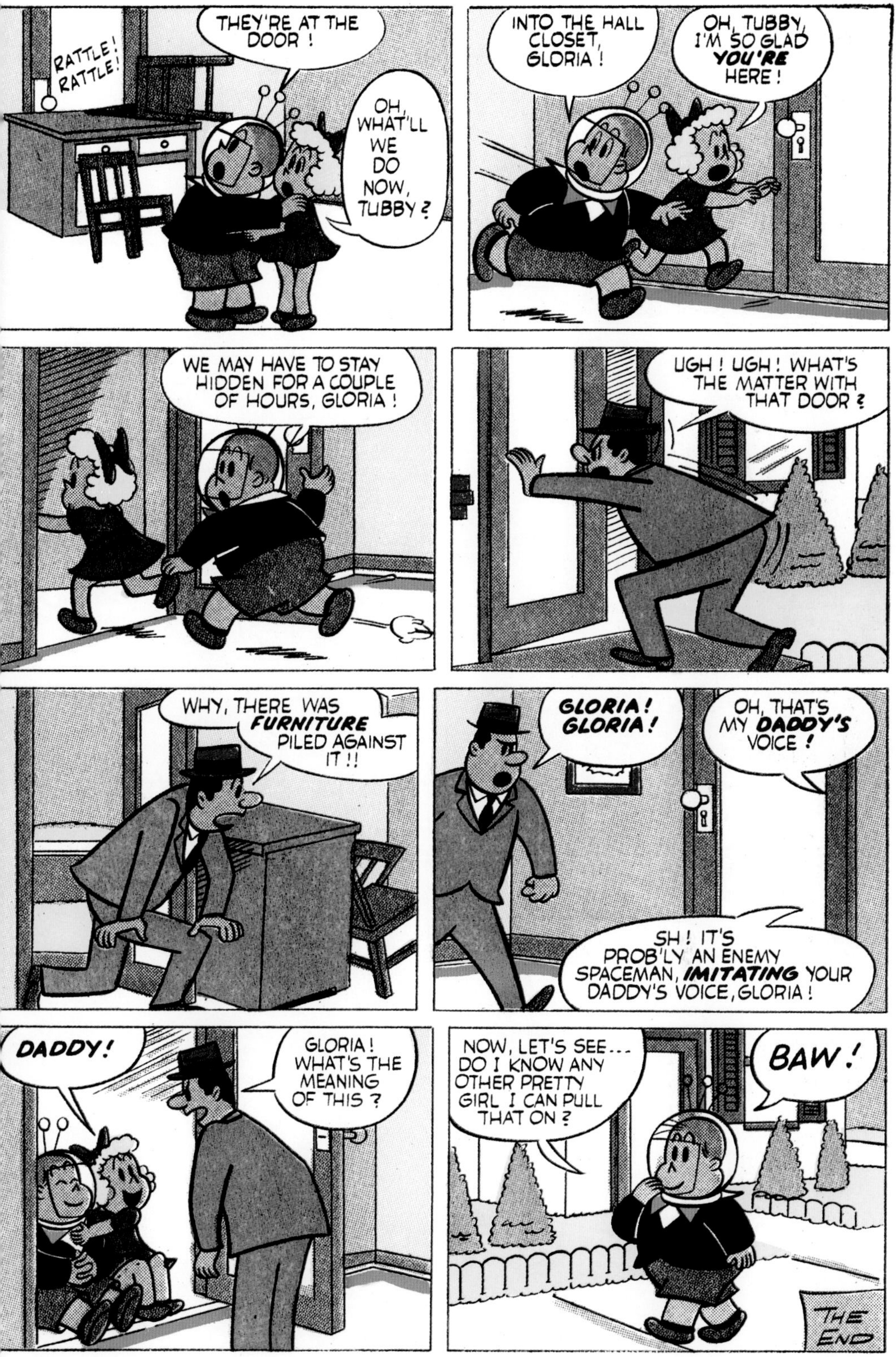

RATTLE! RATTLE!
THEY'RE AT THE DOOR!
OH, WHAT'LL WE DO NOW, TUBBY?
INTO THE HALL CLOSET, GLORIA!
OH, TUBBY, I'M SO GLAD YOU'RE HERE!
WE MAY HAVE TO STAY HIDDEN FOR A COUPLE OF HOURS, GLORIA!
UGH! UGH! WHAT'S THE MATTER WITH THAT DOOR?
WHY, THERE WAS FURNITURE PILED AGAINST IT!!
GLORIA! GLORIA!
OH, THAT'S MY DADDY'S VOICE!
SH! IT'S PROB'LY AN ENEMY SPACEMAN, IMITATING YOUR DADDY'S VOICE, GLORIA!
DADDY!
GLORIA! WHAT'S THE MEANING OF THIS?
NOW, LET'S SEE... DO I KNOW ANY OTHER PRETTY GIRL I CAN PULL THAT ON?
BAW!
THE END

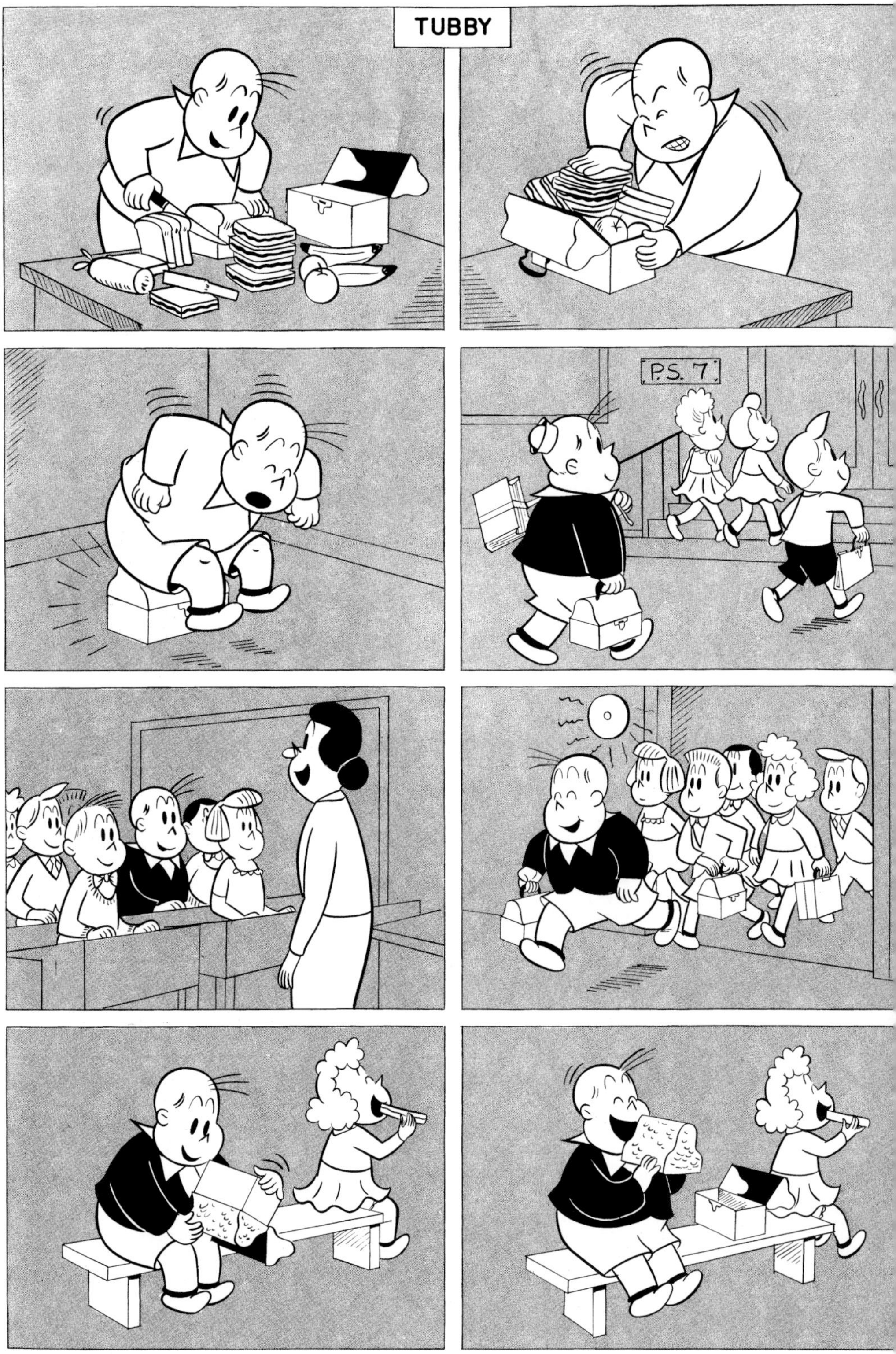
TUBBY
P.S. 7

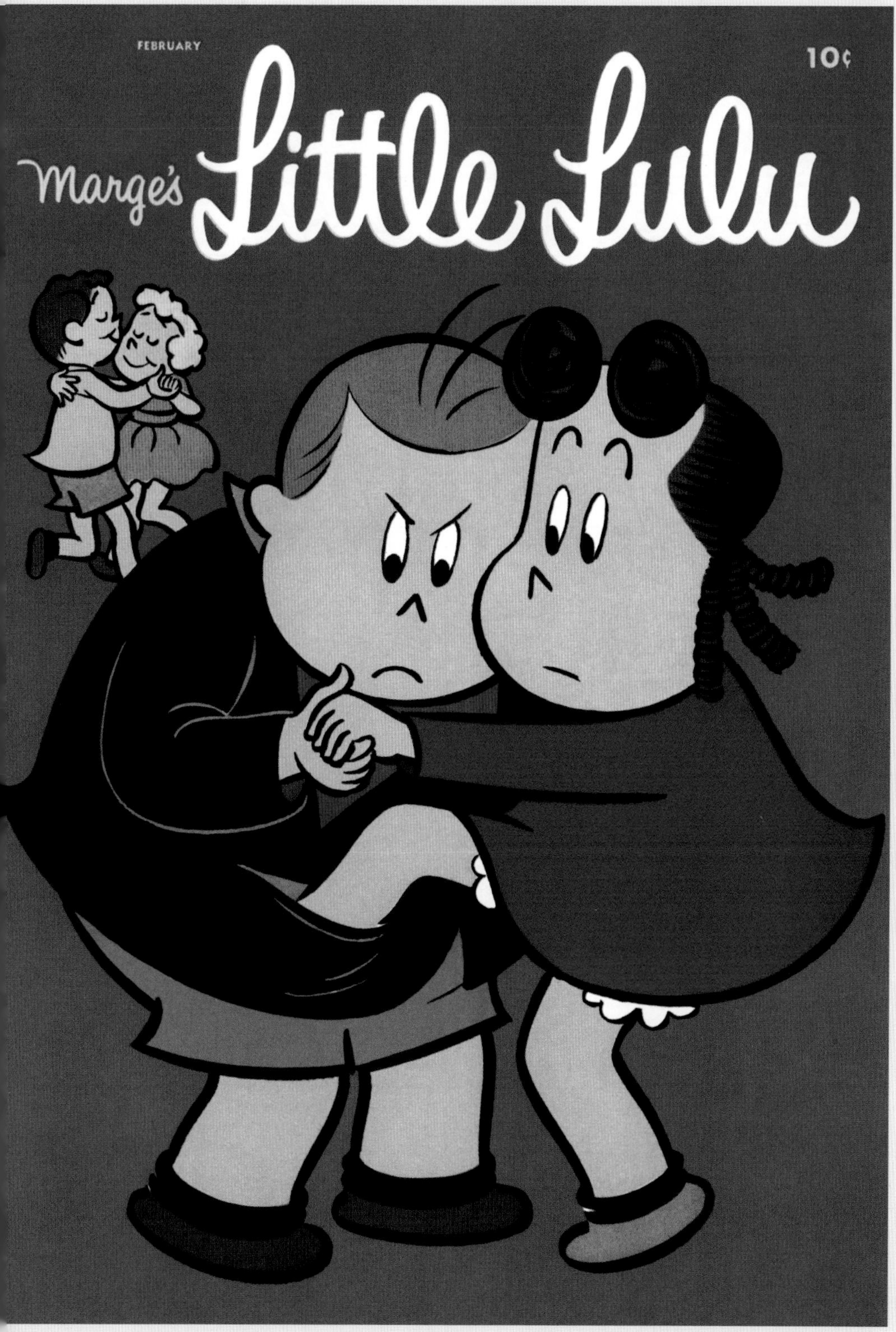
FEBRUARY
10¢
Marge's Little Lulu

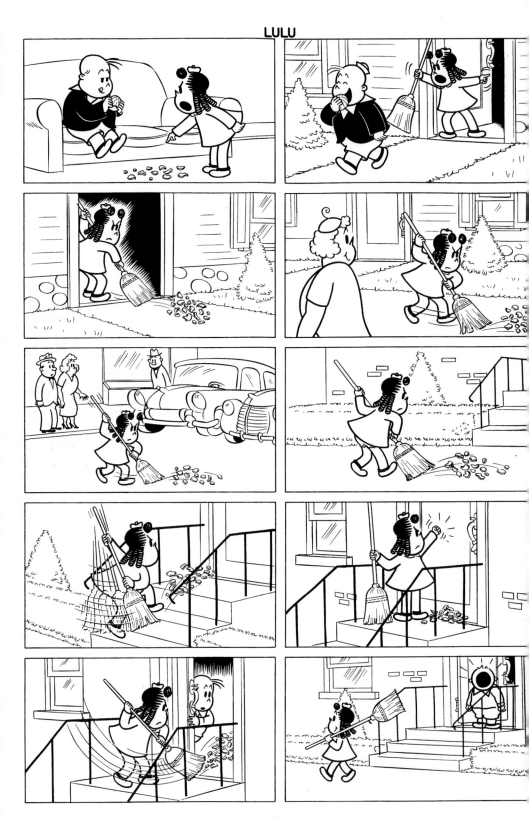

134

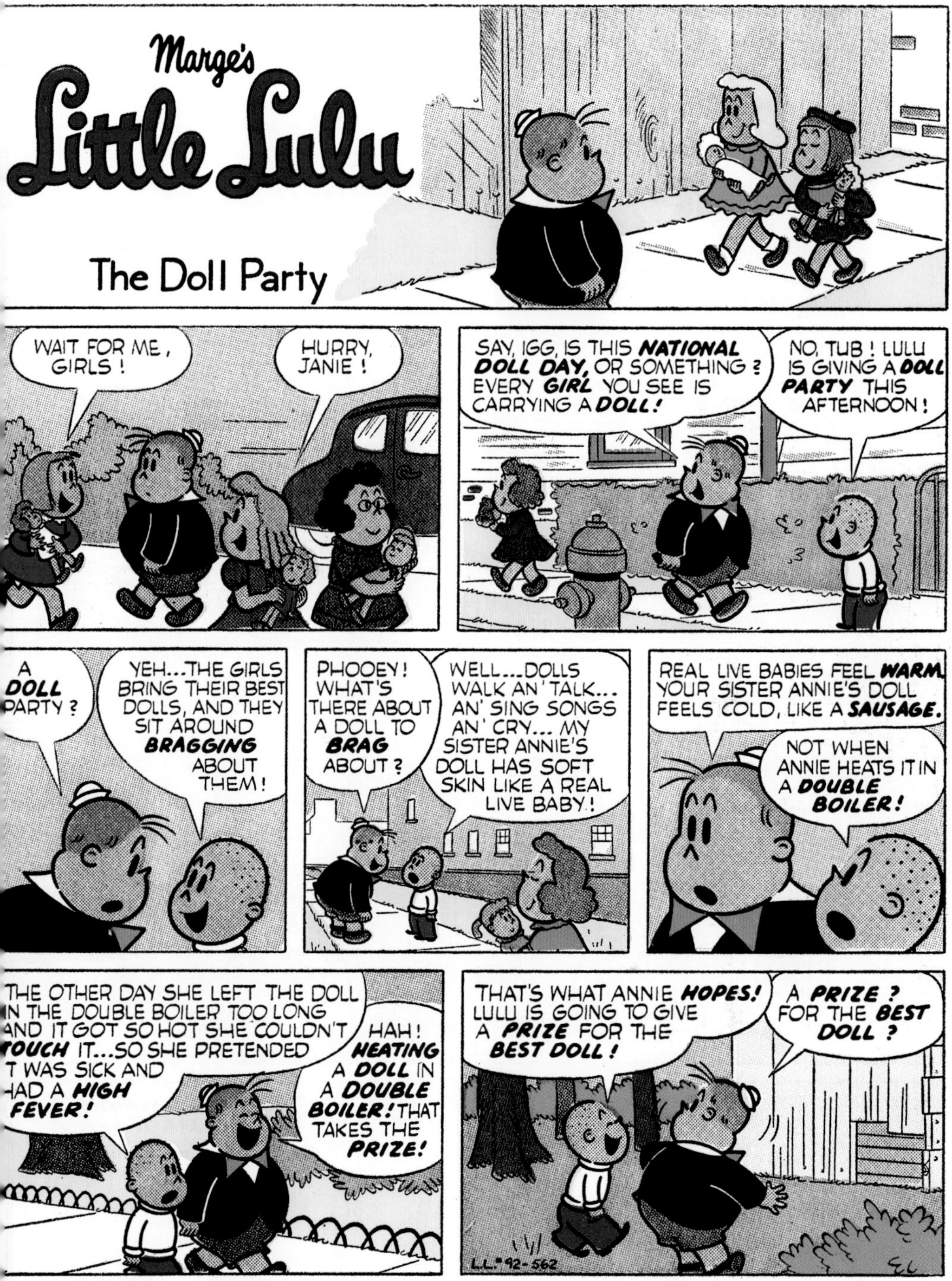
Marge's
Little Lulu
The Doll Party
WAIT FOR ME, GIRLS!
HURRY, JANIE!
SAY, IGG, IS THIS NATIONAL DOLL DAY, OR SOMETHING? EVERY GIRL YOU SEE IS CARRYING A DOLL!
NO, TUB! LULU IS GIVING A DOLL PARTY THIS AFTERNOON!
A DOLL PARTY?
YEH...THE GIRLS BRING THEIR BEST DOLLS, AND THEY SIT AROUND BRAGGING ABOUT THEM!
PHOOEY! WHAT'S THERE ABOUT A DOLL TO BRAG ABOUT?
WELL...DOLLS WALK AN' TALK... AN' SING SONGS AN' CRY... MY SISTER ANNIE'S DOLL HAS SOFT SKIN LIKE A REAL LIVE BABY!
REAL LIVE BABIES FEEL WARM. YOUR SISTER ANNIE'S DOLL FEELS COLD, LIKE A SAUSAGE.
NOT WHEN ANNIE HEATS IT IN A DOUBLE BOILER!
THE OTHER DAY SHE LEFT THE DOLL IN THE DOUBLE BOILER TOO LONG AND IT GOT SO HOT SHE COULDN'T TOUCH IT...SO SHE PRETENDED IT WAS SICK AND HAD A HIGH FEVER!
HAH! HEATING A DOLL IN A DOUBLE BOILER! THAT TAKES THE PRIZE!
THAT'S WHAT ANNIE HOPES! LULU IS GOING TO GIVE A PRIZE FOR THE BEST DOLL!
A PRIZE? FOR THE BEST DOLL?
L.L.#92-562

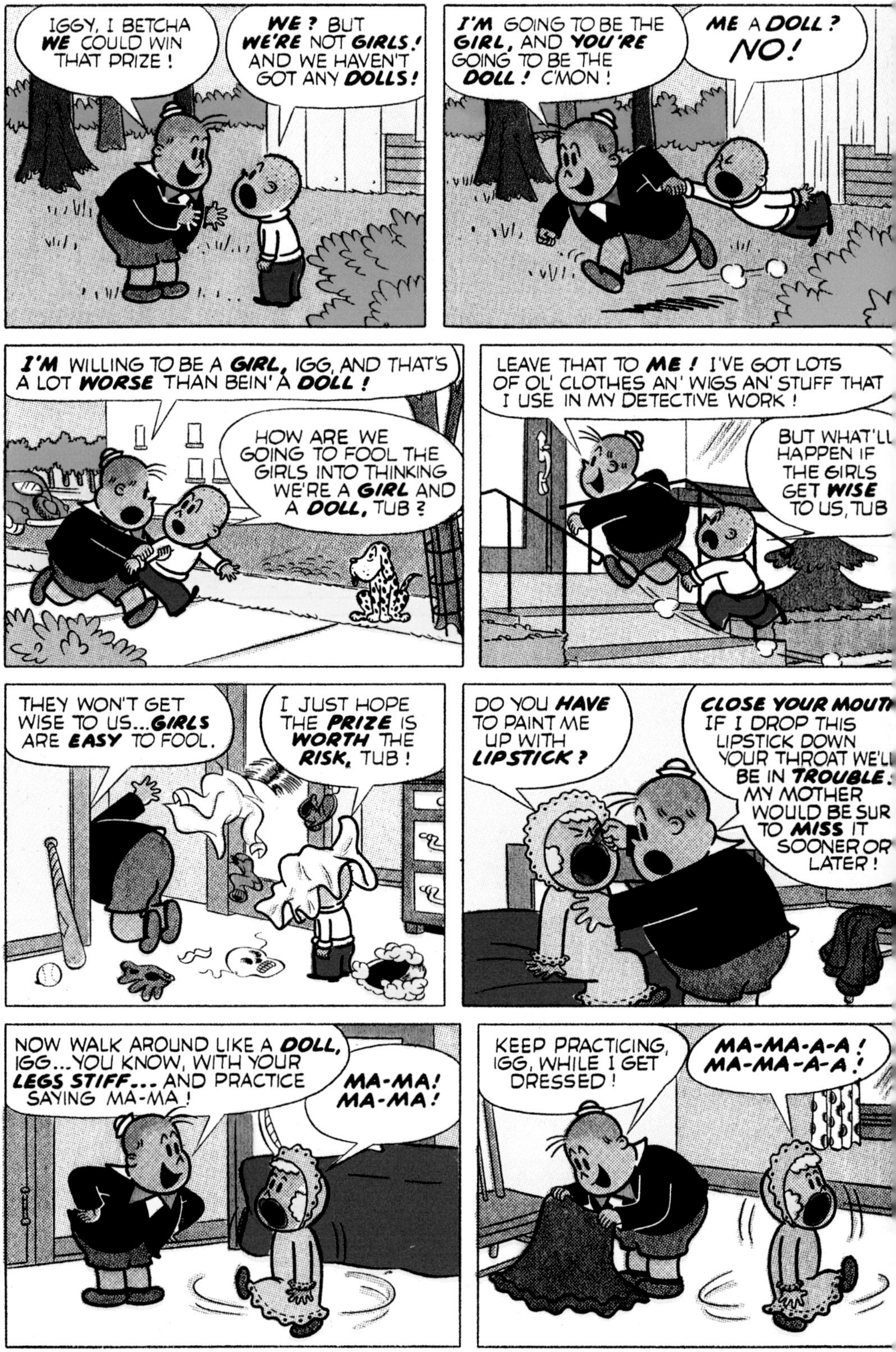

IGGY, I BETCHA WE COULD WIN THAT PRIZE!
WE? BUT WE'RE NOT GIRLS! AND WE HAVEN'T GOT ANY DOLLS!
I'M GOING TO BE THE GIRL, AND YOU'RE GOING TO BE THE DOLL! C'MON!
ME A DOLL? NO!
I'M WILLING TO BE A GIRL, IGG, AND THAT'S A LOT WORSE THAN BEIN' A DOLL!
HOW ARE WE GOING TO FOOL THE GIRLS INTO THINKING WE'RE A GIRL AND A DOLL, TUB?
LEAVE THAT TO ME! I'VE GOT LOTS OF OL' CLOTHES AN' WIGS AN' STUFF THAT I USE IN MY DETECTIVE WORK!
BUT WHAT'LL HAPPEN IF THE GIRLS GET WISE TO US, TUB
THEY WON'T GET WISE TO US... GIRLS ARE EASY TO FOOL.
I JUST HOPE THE PRIZE IS WORTH THE RISK, TUB!
DO YOU HAVE TO PAINT ME UP WITH LIPSTICK?
IF I DROP THIS LIPSTICK DOWN YOUR THROAT WE'LL BE IN TROUBLE! MY MOTHER WOULD BE SUR TO MISS IT SOONER OR LATER!
NOW WALK AROUND LIKE A DOLL, IGG... YOU KNOW, WITH YOUR LEGS STIFF... AND PRACTICE SAYING MA-MA!
MA-MA! MA-MA!
KEEP PRACTICING, IGG, WHILE I GET DRESSED!
MA-MA-A-A! MA-MA-A-A!

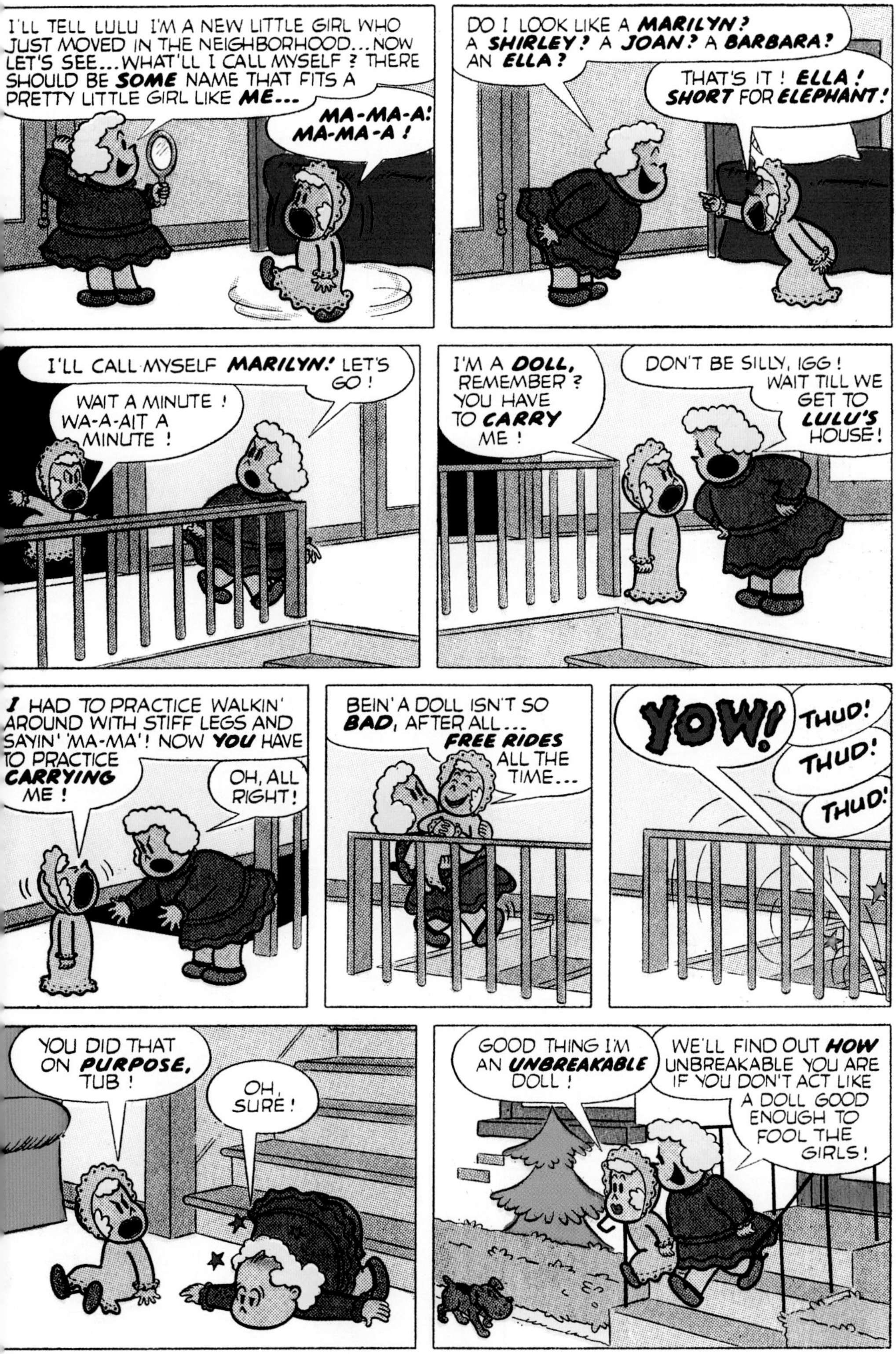
I'LL TELL LULU I'M A NEW LITTLE GIRL WHO JUST MOVED IN THE NEIGHBORHOOD... NOW LET'S SEE... WHAT'LL I CALL MYSELF ? THERE SHOULD BE SOME NAME THAT FITS A PRETTY LITTLE GIRL LIKE ME...
MA-MA-A! MA-MA-A !
DO I LOOK LIKE A MARILYN? A SHIRLEY? A JOAN? A BARBARA? AN ELLA?
THAT'S IT ! ELLA ! SHORT FOR ELEPHANT!
I'LL CALL MYSELF MARILYN! LET'S GO !
WAIT A MINUTE ! WA-A-AIT A MINUTE !
I'M A DOLL, REMEMBER ? YOU HAVE TO CARRY ME !
DON'T BE SILLY, IGG ! WAIT TILL WE GET TO LULU'S HOUSE!
I HAD TO PRACTICE WALKIN' AROUND WITH STIFF LEGS AND SAYIN' 'MA-MA'! NOW YOU HAVE TO PRACTICE CARRYING ME !
OH, ALL RIGHT!
BEIN' A DOLL ISN'T SO BAD, AFTER ALL... FREE RIDES ALL THE TIME...
YOW!
THUD!
THUD!
THUD!
YOU DID THAT ON PURPOSE, TUB !
OH, SURE !
GOOD THING I'M AN UNBREAKABLE DOLL !
WE'LL FIND OUT HOW UNBREAKABLE YOU ARE IF YOU DON'T ACT LIKE A DOLL GOOD ENOUGH TO FOOL THE GIRLS !

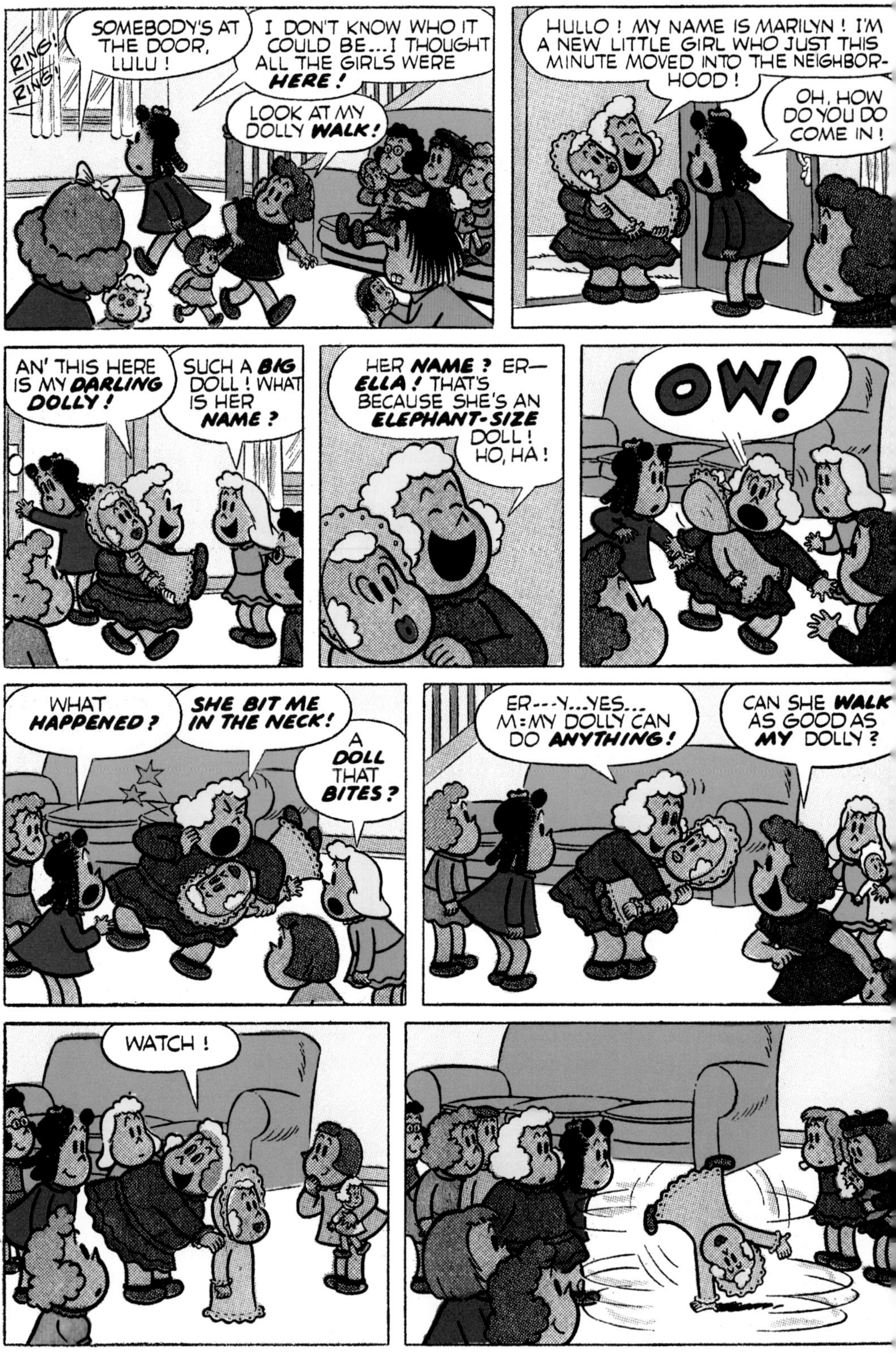
RING! RING!
SOMEBODY'S AT THE DOOR, LULU!
I DON'T KNOW WHO IT COULD BE... I THOUGHT ALL THE GIRLS WERE HERE!
LOOK AT MY DOLLY WALK!
HULLO! MY NAME IS MARILYN! I'M A NEW LITTLE GIRL WHO JUST THIS MINUTE MOVED INTO THE NEIGHBOR-HOOD!
OH, HOW DO YOU DO COME IN!
AN' THIS HERE IS MY DARLING DOLLY!
SUCH A BIG DOLL! WHAT IS HER NAME?
HER NAME? ER— ELLA! THAT'S BECAUSE SHE'S AN ELEPHANT-SIZE DOLL! HO, HA!
OW!
WHAT HAPPENED?
SHE BIT ME IN THE NECK!
A DOLL THAT BITES?
ER---Y...YES... M=MY DOLLY CAN DO ANYTHING!
CAN SHE WALK AS GOOD AS MY DOLLY?
WATCH!

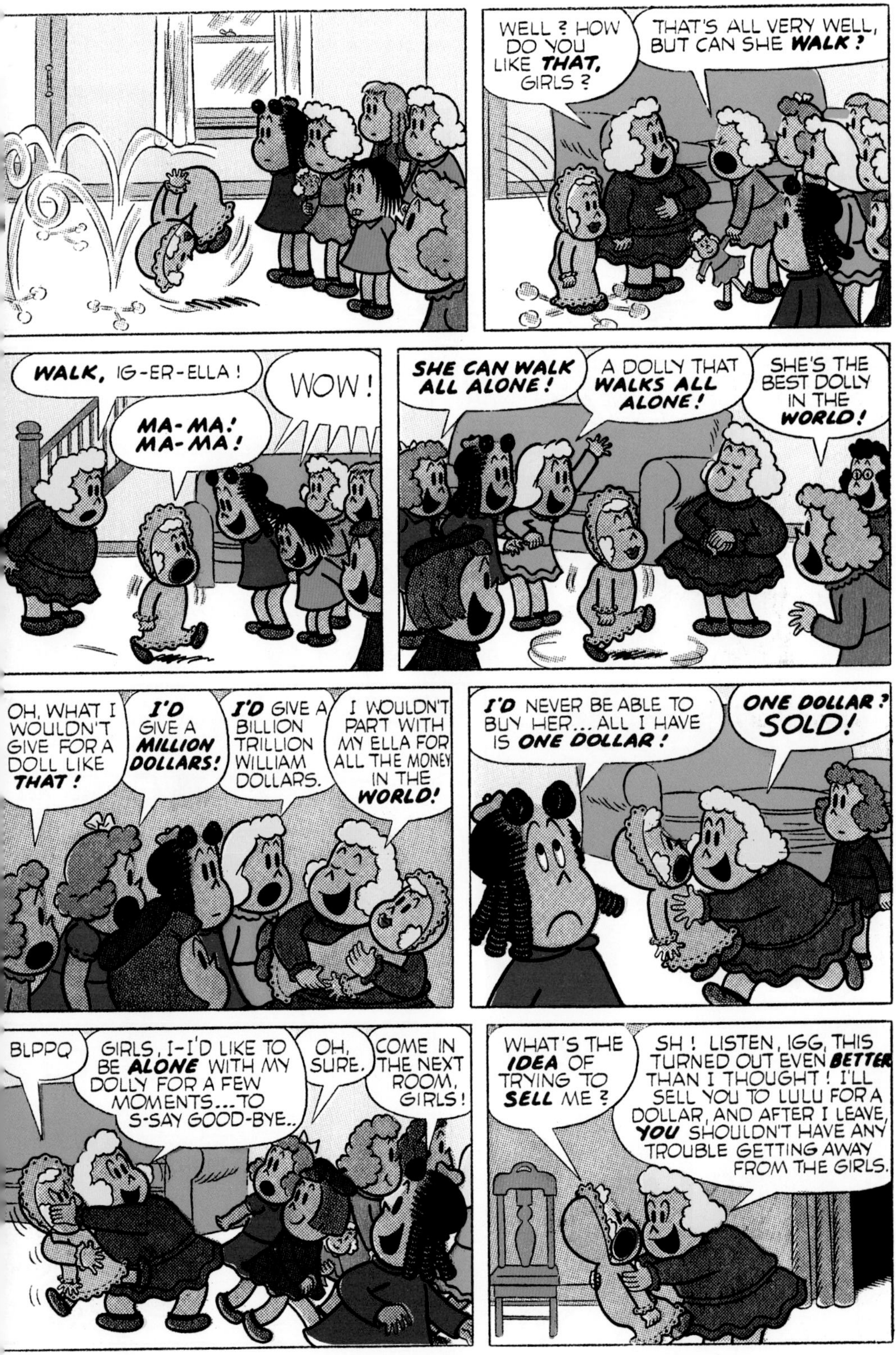
WELL ? HOW DO YOU LIKE **THAT,** GIRLS ?
THAT'S ALL VERY WELL, BUT CAN SHE **WALK ?**
**WALK,** IG-ER-ELLA !
**MA-MA! MA-MA!**
WOW!
**SHE CAN WALK ALL ALONE!**
A DOLLY THAT **WALKS ALL ALONE!**
SHE'S THE BEST DOLLY IN THE **WORLD!**
OH, WHAT I WOULDN'T GIVE FOR A DOLL LIKE **THAT!**
**I'D** GIVE A **MILLION DOLLARS!**
**I'D** GIVE A BILLION TRILLION WILLIAM DOLLARS.
I WOULDN'T PART WITH MY ELLA FOR ALL THE MONEY IN THE **WORLD!**
**I'D** NEVER BE ABLE TO BUY HER... ALL I HAVE IS **ONE DOLLAR!**
**ONE DOLLAR? SOLD!**
BLPPQ
GIRLS, I-I'D LIKE TO BE **ALONE** WITH MY DOLLY FOR A FEW MOMENTS...TO S-SAY GOOD-BYE..
OH, SURE.
COME IN THE NEXT ROOM, GIRLS!
WHAT'S THE **IDEA** OF TRYING TO **SELL** ME ?
SH ! LISTEN, IGG, THIS TURNED OUT EVEN **BETTER** THAN I THOUGHT ! I'LL SELL YOU TO LULU FOR A DOLLAR, AND AFTER I LEAVE, **YOU** SHOULDN'T HAVE ANY TROUBLE GETTING AWAY FROM THE GIRLS.

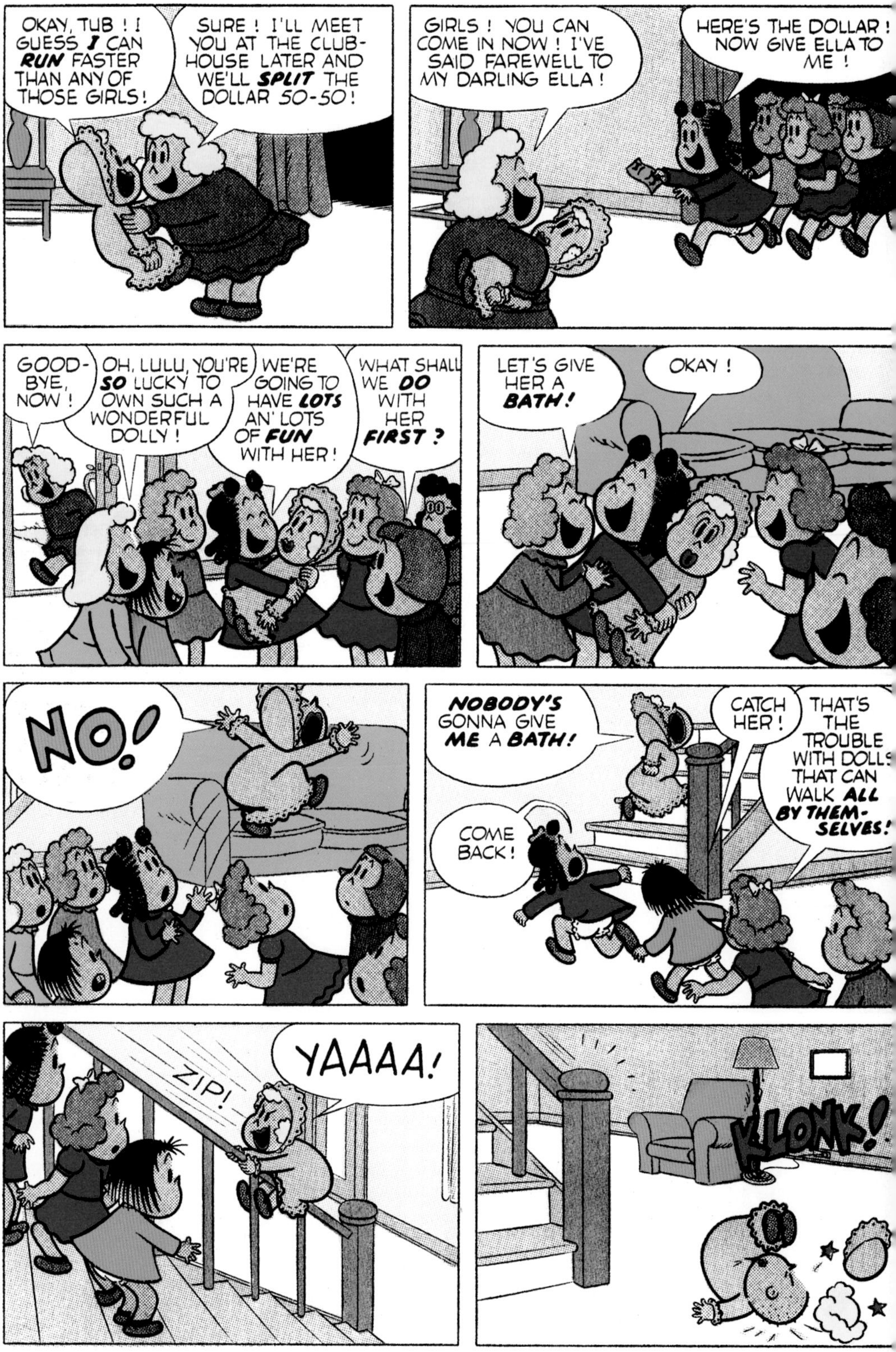
OKAY, TUB ! I GUESS I CAN RUN FASTER THAN ANY OF THOSE GIRLS !
SURE ! I'LL MEET YOU AT THE CLUB-HOUSE LATER AND WE'LL SPLIT THE DOLLAR 50-50 !
GIRLS ! YOU CAN COME IN NOW ! I'VE SAID FAREWELL TO MY DARLING ELLA !
HERE'S THE DOLLAR ! NOW GIVE ELLA TO ME !
GOOD-BYE, NOW !
OH, LULU, YOU'RE SO LUCKY TO OWN SUCH A WONDERFUL DOLLY !
WE'RE GOING TO HAVE LOTS AN' LOTS OF FUN WITH HER !
WHAT SHALL WE DO WITH HER FIRST ?
LET'S GIVE HER A BATH !
OKAY !
NO!
NOBODY'S GONNA GIVE ME A BATH!
CATCH HER !
THAT'S THE TROUBLE WITH DOLLS THAT CAN WALK ALL BY THEM-SELVES!
COME BACK!
YAAAA!
ZIP!
KLONK!

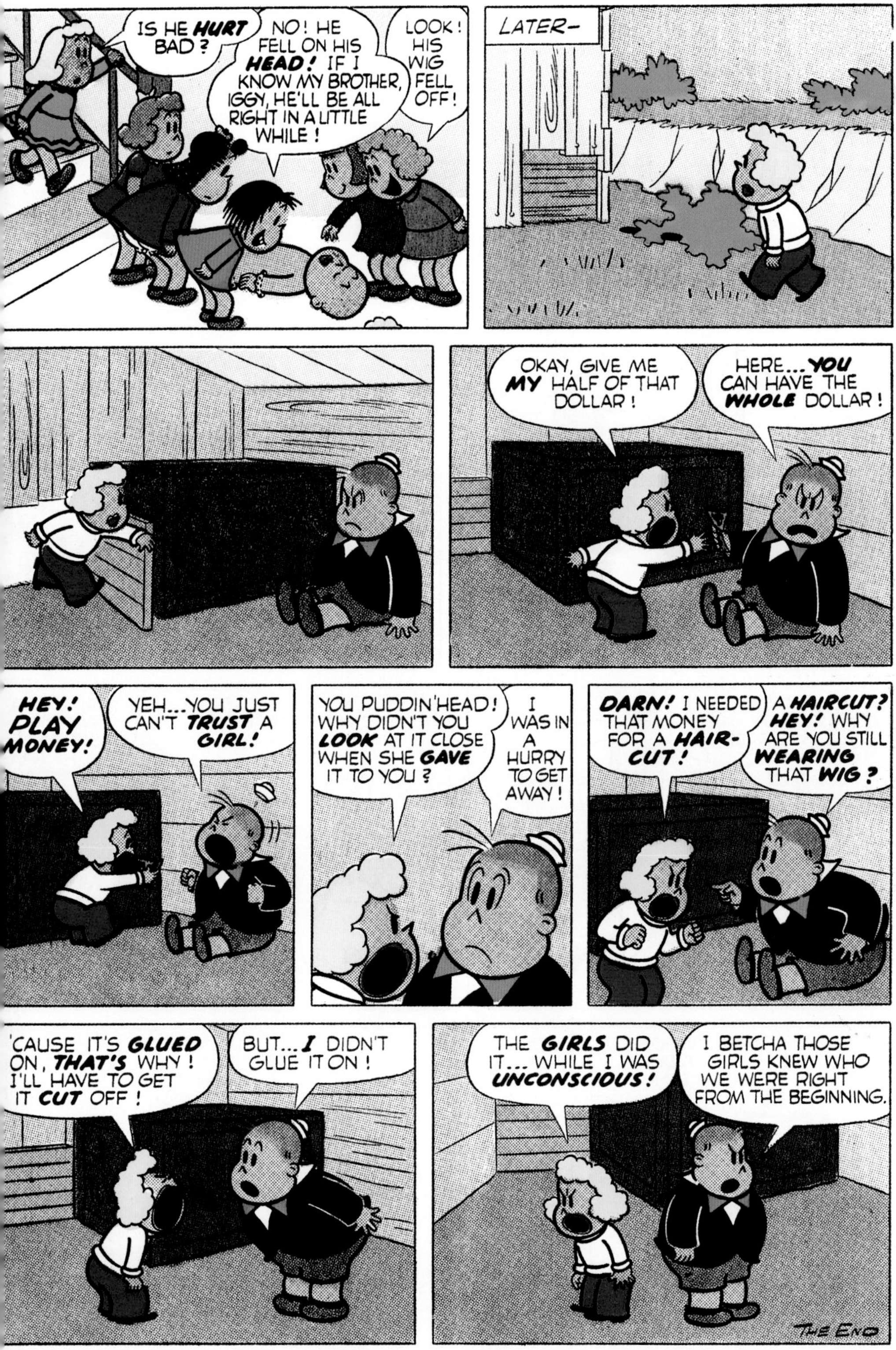
IS HE HURT BAD?
NO! HE FELL ON HIS HEAD! IF I KNOW MY BROTHER, IGGY, HE'LL BE ALL RIGHT IN A LITTLE WHILE!
LOOK! HIS WIG FELL OFF!
LATER-
OKAY, GIVE ME MY HALF OF THAT DOLLAR!
HERE... YOU CAN HAVE THE WHOLE DOLLAR!
HEY! PLAY MONEY!
YEH...YOU JUST CAN'T TRUST A GIRL!
YOU PUDDIN'HEAD! WHY DIDN'T YOU LOOK AT IT CLOSE WHEN SHE GAVE IT TO YOU?
I WAS IN A HURRY TO GET AWAY!
DARN! I NEEDED THAT MONEY FOR A HAIR-CUT!
A HAIRCUT? HEY! WHY ARE YOU STILL WEARING THAT WIG?
'CAUSE IT'S GLUED ON, THAT'S WHY! I'LL HAVE TO GET IT CUT OFF!
BUT...I DIDN'T GLUE IT ON!
THE GIRLS DID IT... WHILE I WAS UNCONSCIOUS!
I BETCHA THOSE GIRLS KNEW WHO WE WERE RIGHT FROM THE BEGINNING.
THE END

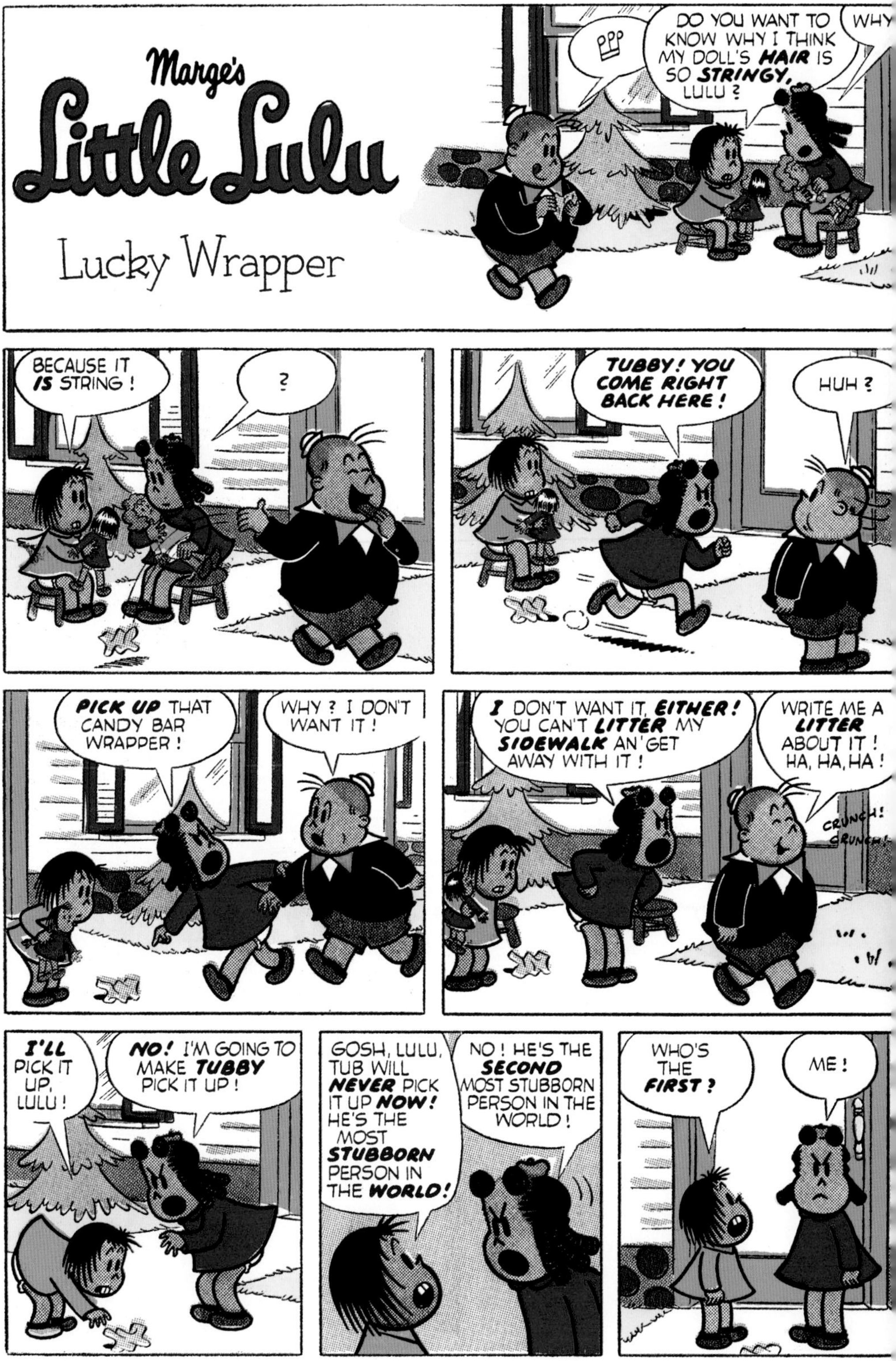

Marge's Little Lulu
Lucky Wrapper
PPP
DO YOU WANT TO KNOW WHY I THINK MY DOLL'S HAIR IS SO STRINGY, LULU ?
WHY
BECAUSE IT IS STRING !
?
TUBBY! YOU COME RIGHT BACK HERE!
HUH ?
PICK UP THAT CANDY BAR WRAPPER !
WHY ? I DON'T WANT IT !
I DON'T WANT IT, EITHER! YOU CAN'T LITTER MY SIDEWALK AN' GET AWAY WITH IT !
WRITE ME A LITTER ABOUT IT ! HA, HA, HA !
CRUNCH! CRUNCH!
I'LL PICK IT UP, LULU !
NO! I'M GOING TO MAKE TUBBY PICK IT UP !
GOSH, LULU, TUB WILL NEVER PICK IT UP NOW! HE'S THE MOST STUBBORN PERSON IN THE WORLD!
NO ! HE'S THE SECOND MOST STUBBORN PERSON IN THE WORLD !
WHO'S THE FIRST ?
ME !

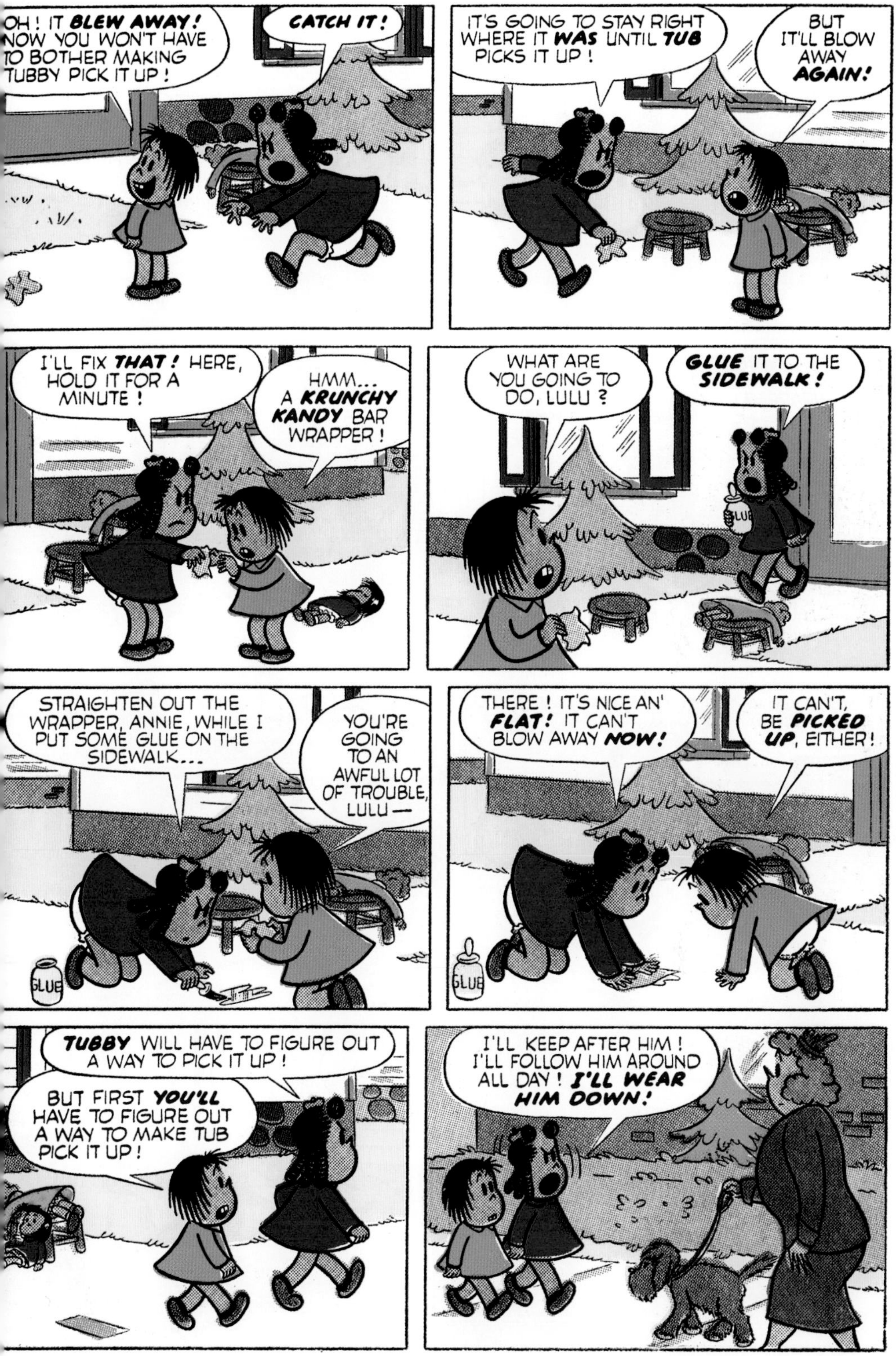
OH! IT BLEW AWAY! NOW YOU WON'T HAVE TO BOTHER MAKING TUBBY PICK IT UP!
CATCH IT!
IT'S GOING TO STAY RIGHT WHERE IT WAS UNTIL TUB PICKS IT UP!
BUT IT'LL BLOW AWAY AGAIN!
I'LL FIX THAT! HERE, HOLD IT FOR A MINUTE!
HMM... A KRUNCHY KANDY BAR WRAPPER!
WHAT ARE YOU GOING TO DO, LULU?
GLUE IT TO THE SIDEWALK!
GLUE
STRAIGHTEN OUT THE WRAPPER, ANNIE, WHILE I PUT SOME GLUE ON THE SIDEWALK...
YOU'RE GOING TO AN AWFUL LOT OF TROUBLE, LULU—
GLUE
THERE! IT'S NICE AN' FLAT! IT CAN'T BLOW AWAY NOW!
IT CAN'T BE PICKED UP, EITHER!
GLUE
TUBBY WILL HAVE TO FIGURE OUT A WAY TO PICK IT UP!
BUT FIRST YOU'LL HAVE TO FIGURE OUT A WAY TO MAKE TUB PICK IT UP!
I'LL KEEP AFTER HIM! I'LL FOLLOW HIM AROUND ALL DAY! I'LL WEAR HIM DOWN!

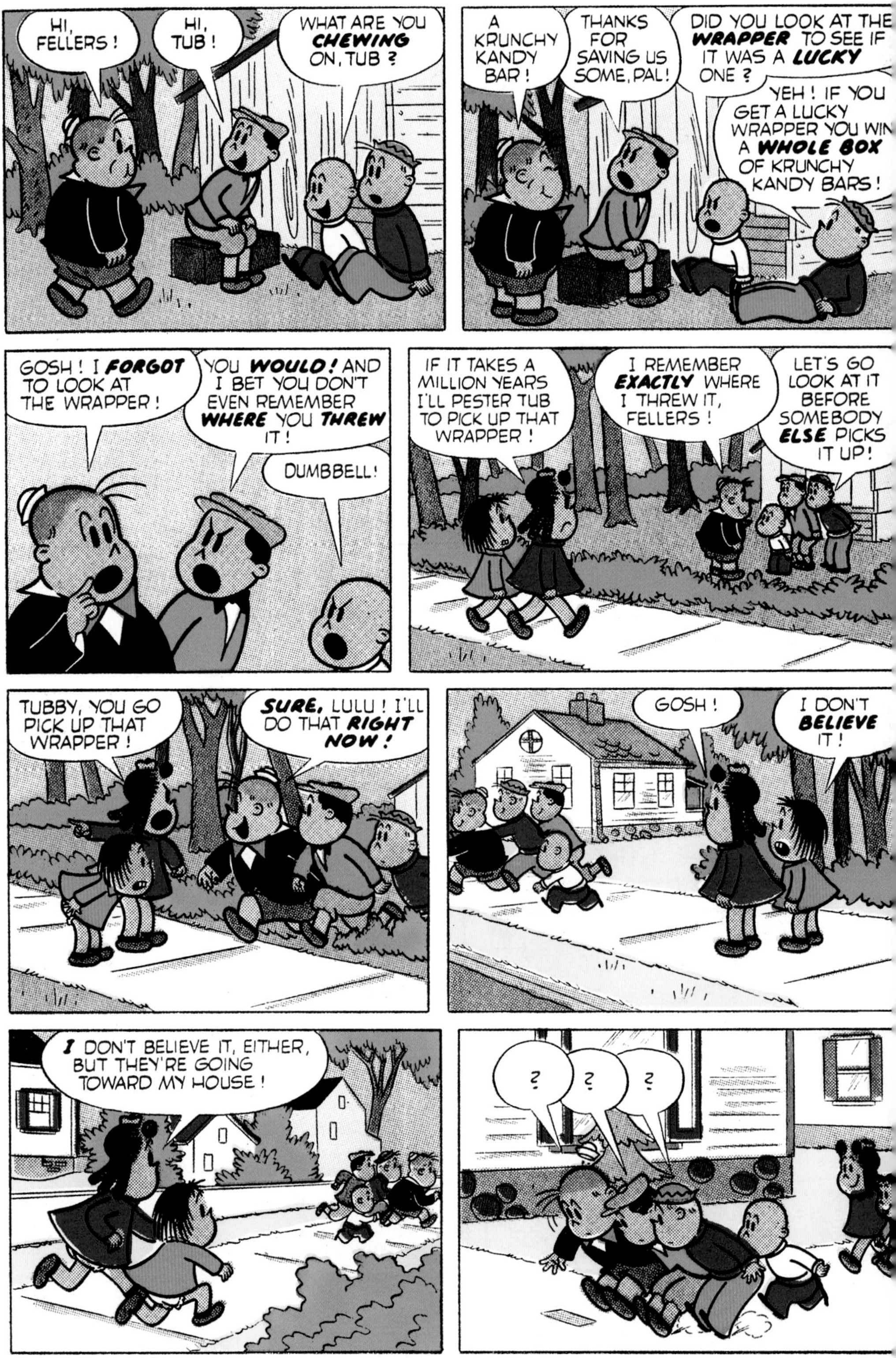
HI, FELLERS!
HI, TUB!
WHAT ARE YOU CHEWING ON, TUB?
A KRUNCHY KANDY BAR!
THANKS FOR SAVING US SOME, PAL!
DID YOU LOOK AT THE WRAPPER TO SEE IF IT WAS A LUCKY ONE?
YEH! IF YOU GET A LUCKY WRAPPER YOU WIN A WHOLE BOX OF KRUNCHY KANDY BARS!
GOSH! I FORGOT TO LOOK AT THE WRAPPER!
YOU WOULD! AND I BET YOU DON'T EVEN REMEMBER WHERE YOU THREW IT!
DUMBBELL!
IF IT TAKES A MILLION YEARS I'LL PESTER TUB TO PICK UP THAT WRAPPER!
I REMEMBER EXACTLY WHERE I THREW IT, FELLERS!
LET'S GO LOOK AT IT BEFORE SOMEBODY ELSE PICKS IT UP!
TUBBY, YOU GO PICK UP THAT WRAPPER!
SURE, LULU! I'LL DO THAT RIGHT NOW!
GOSH!
I DON'T BELIEVE IT!
I DON'T BELIEVE IT, EITHER, BUT THEY'RE GOING TOWARD MY HOUSE!
?
?
?

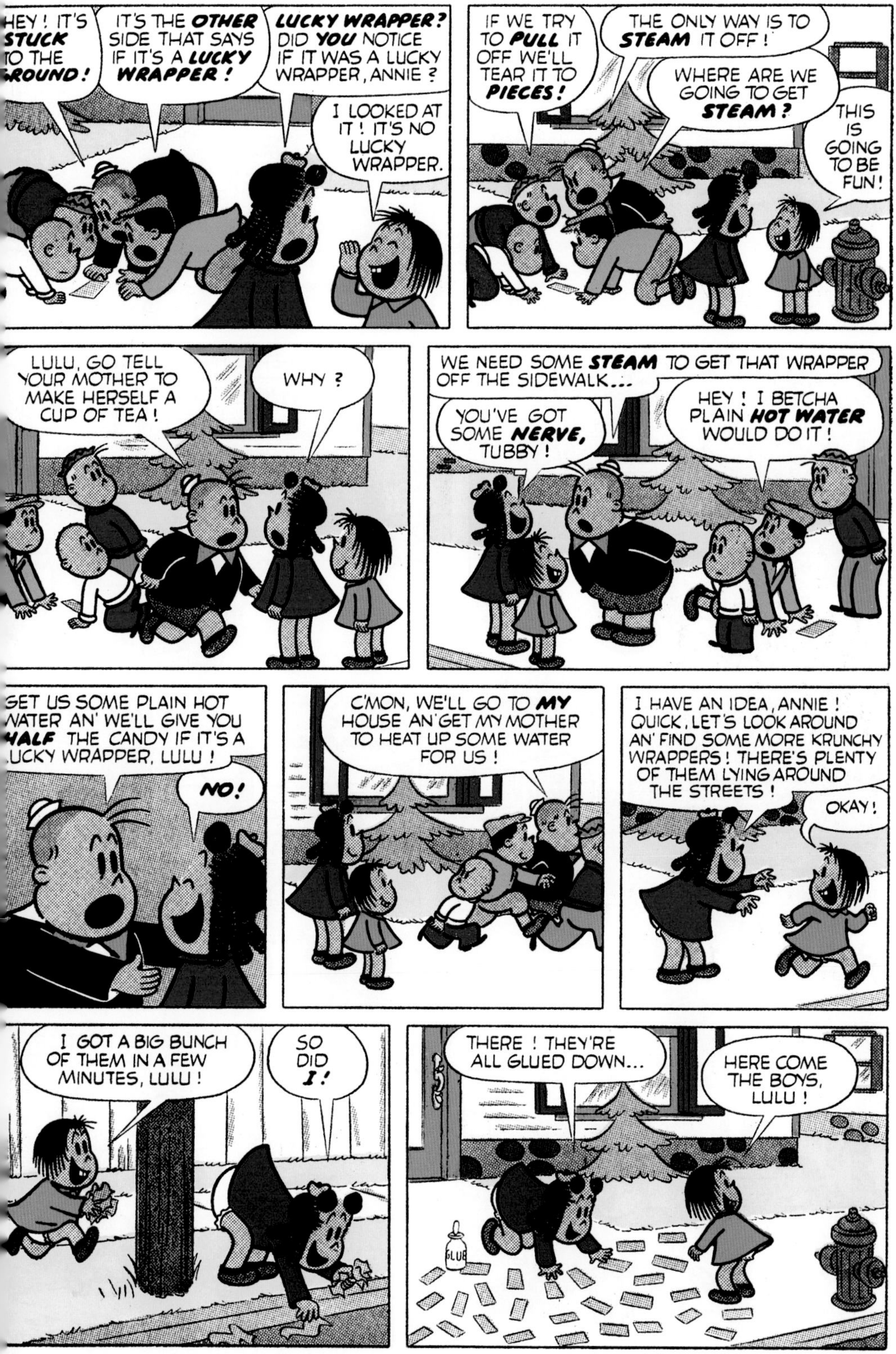
HEY! IT'S STUCK TO THE GROUND!
IT'S THE OTHER SIDE THAT SAYS IF IT'S A LUCKY WRAPPER!
LUCKY WRAPPER? DID YOU NOTICE IF IT WAS A LUCKY WRAPPER, ANNIE?
I LOOKED AT IT! IT'S NO LUCKY WRAPPER.
IF WE TRY TO PULL IT OFF WE'LL TEAR IT TO PIECES!
THE ONLY WAY IS TO STEAM IT OFF!
WHERE ARE WE GOING TO GET STEAM?
THIS IS GOING TO BE FUN!
LULU, GO TELL YOUR MOTHER TO MAKE HERSELF A CUP OF TEA!
WHY?
WE NEED SOME STEAM TO GET THAT WRAPPER OFF THE SIDEWALK...
YOU'VE GOT SOME NERVE, TUBBY!
HEY! I BETCHA PLAIN HOT WATER WOULD DO IT!
GET US SOME PLAIN HOT WATER AN' WE'LL GIVE YOU HALF THE CANDY IF IT'S A LUCKY WRAPPER, LULU!
NO!
C'MON, WE'LL GO TO MY HOUSE AN' GET MY MOTHER TO HEAT UP SOME WATER FOR US!
I HAVE AN IDEA, ANNIE! QUICK, LET'S LOOK AROUND AN' FIND SOME MORE KRUNCHY WRAPPERS! THERE'S PLENTY OF THEM LYING AROUND THE STREETS!
OKAY!
I GOT A BIG BUNCH OF THEM IN A FEW MINUTES, LULU!
SO DID I!
THERE! THEY'RE ALL GLUED DOWN...
HERE COME THE BOYS, LULU!
GLUE

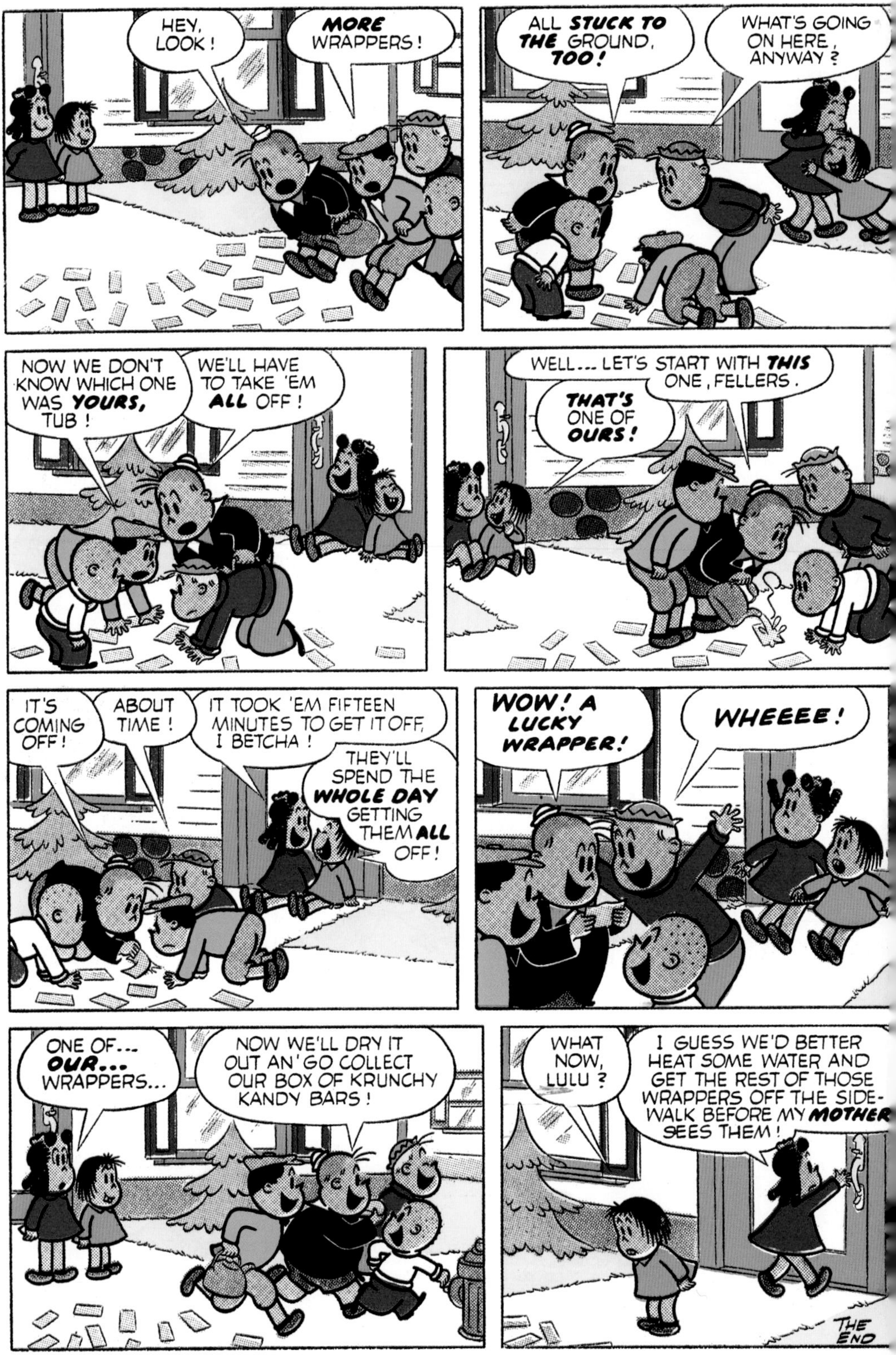
HEY, LOOK!
MORE WRAPPERS!
ALL STUCK TO THE GROUND, TOO!
WHAT'S GOING ON HERE, ANYWAY?
NOW WE DON'T KNOW WHICH ONE WAS YOURS, TUB!
WE'LL HAVE TO TAKE 'EM ALL OFF!
WELL... LET'S START WITH THIS ONE, FELLERS.
THAT'S ONE OF OURS!
IT'S COMING OFF!
ABOUT TIME!
IT TOOK 'EM FIFTEEN MINUTES TO GET IT OFF, I BETCHA!
THEY'LL SPEND THE WHOLE DAY GETTING THEM ALL OFF!
WOW! A LUCKY WRAPPER!
WHEEEE!
ONE OF... OUR... WRAPPERS...
NOW WE'LL DRY IT OUT AN' GO COLLECT OUR BOX OF KRUNCHY KANDY BARS!
WHAT NOW, LULU?
I GUESS WE'D BETTER HEAT SOME WATER AND GET THE REST OF THOSE WRAPPERS OFF THE SIDE-WALK BEFORE MY MOTHER SEES THEM!
THE END

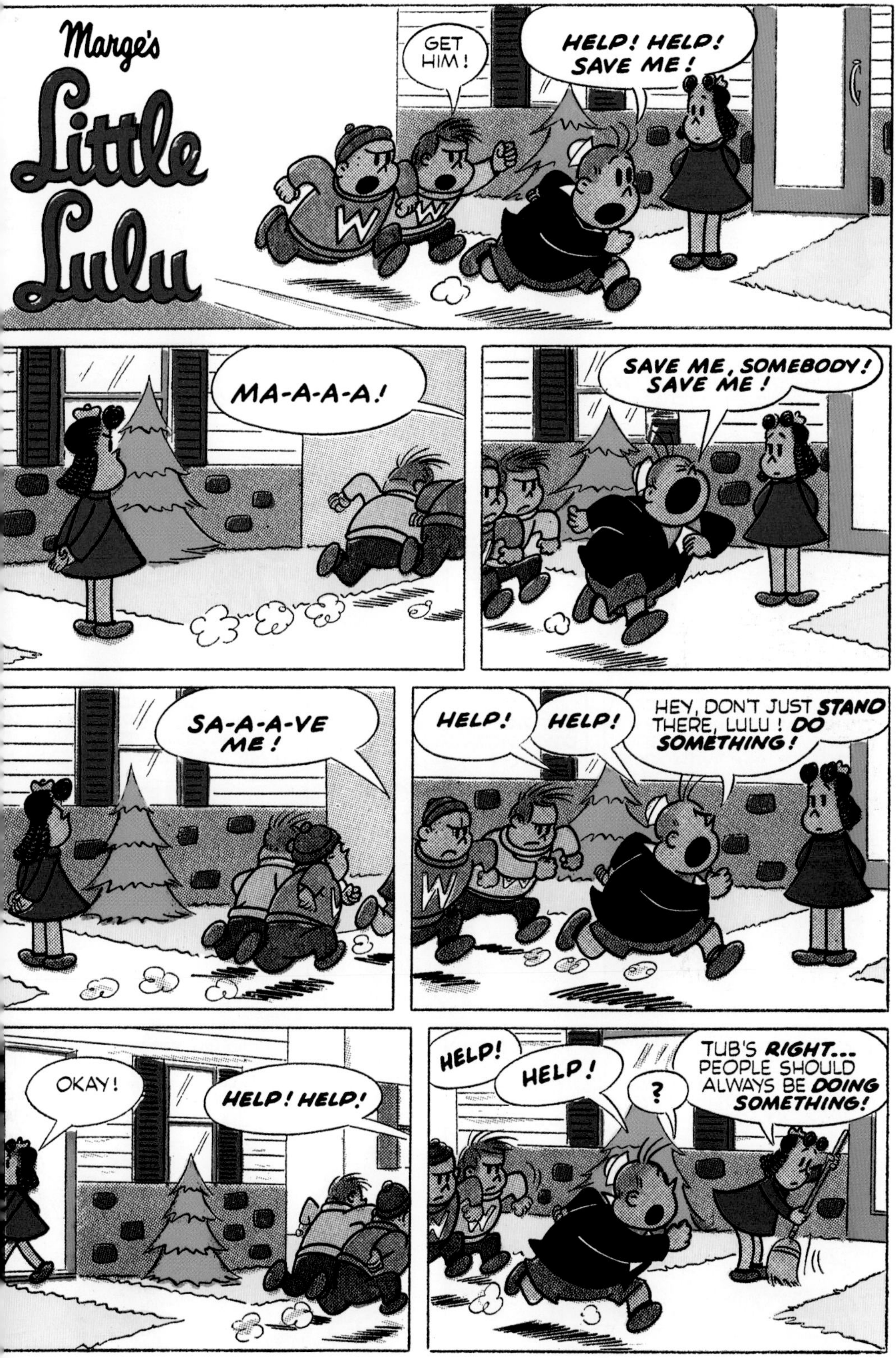

Marge's Little Lulu
GET HIM!
HELP! HELP! SAVE ME!
MA-A-A-A!
SAVE ME, SOMEBODY! SAVE ME!
SA-A-A-VE ME!
HELP!
HELP!
HEY, DON'T JUST STAND THERE, LULU! DO SOMETHING!
OKAY!
HELP! HELP!
HELP!
HELP!
?
TUB'S RIGHT... PEOPLE SHOULD ALWAYS BE DOING SOMETHING!

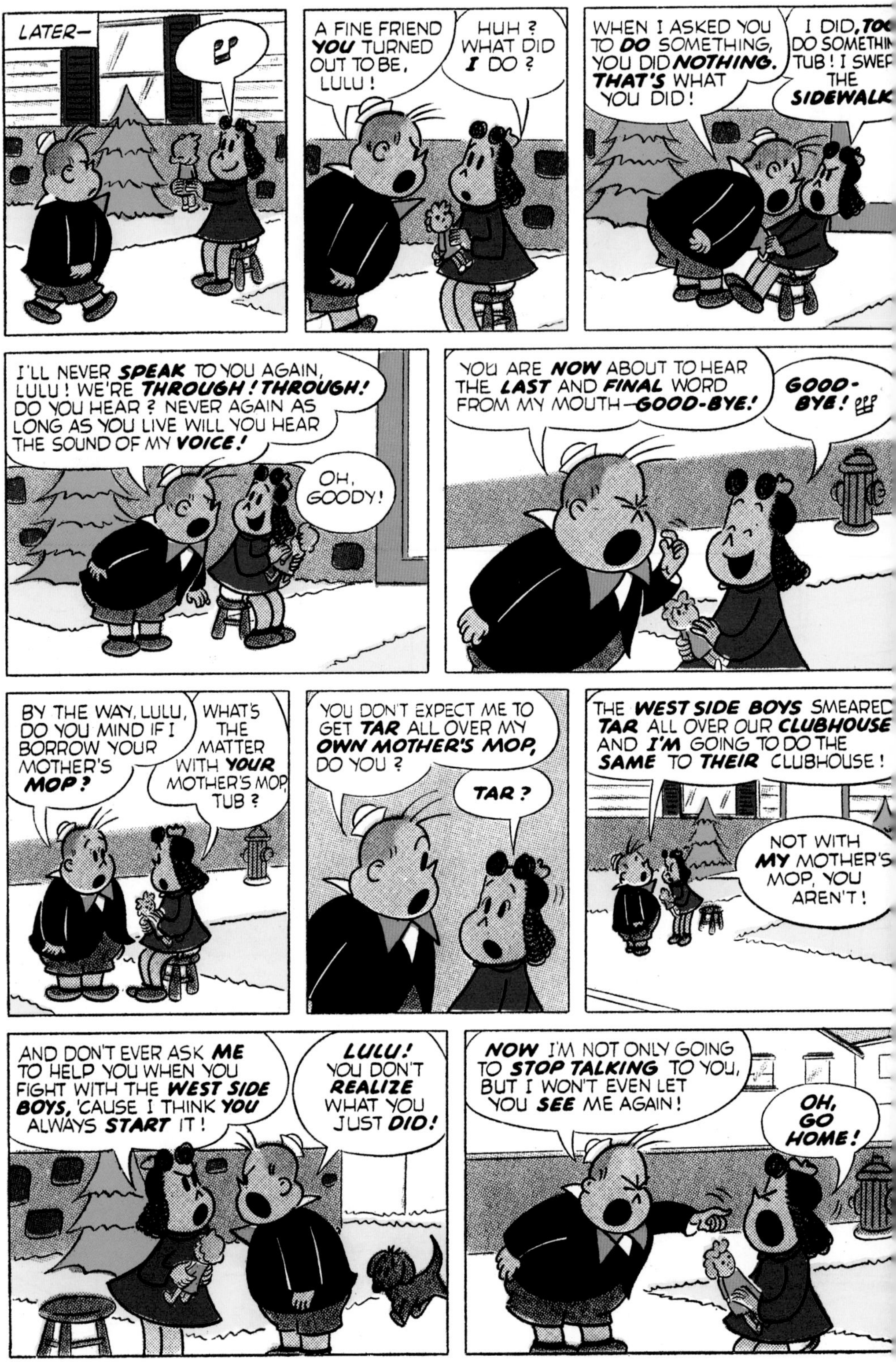
LATER—
A FINE FRIEND YOU TURNED OUT TO BE, LULU!
HUH? WHAT DID I DO?
WHEN I ASKED YOU TO DO SOMETHING, YOU DID NOTHING. THAT'S WHAT YOU DID!
I DID, TOO DO SOMETHIN TUB! I SWEP THE SIDEWALK
I'LL NEVER SPEAK TO YOU AGAIN, LULU! WE'RE THROUGH! THROUGH! DO YOU HEAR? NEVER AGAIN AS LONG AS YOU LIVE WILL YOU HEAR THE SOUND OF MY VOICE!
OH, GOODY!
YOU ARE NOW ABOUT TO HEAR THE LAST AND FINAL WORD FROM MY MOUTH—GOOD-BYE!
GOOD-BYE!
BY THE WAY, LULU, DO YOU MIND IF I BORROW YOUR MOTHER'S MOP?
WHAT'S THE MATTER WITH YOUR MOTHER'S MOP, TUB?
YOU DON'T EXPECT ME TO GET TAR ALL OVER MY OWN MOTHER'S MOP, DO YOU?
TAR?
THE WEST SIDE BOYS SMEARED TAR ALL OVER OUR CLUBHOUSE AND I'M GOING TO DO THE SAME TO THEIR CLUBHOUSE!
NOT WITH MY MOTHER'S MOP, YOU AREN'T!
AND DON'T EVER ASK ME TO HELP YOU WHEN YOU FIGHT WITH THE WEST SIDE BOYS, 'CAUSE I THINK YOU ALWAYS START IT!
LULU! YOU DON'T REALIZE WHAT YOU JUST DID!
NOW I'M NOT ONLY GOING TO STOP TALKING TO YOU, BUT I WON'T EVEN LET YOU SEE ME AGAIN!
OH, GO HOME!

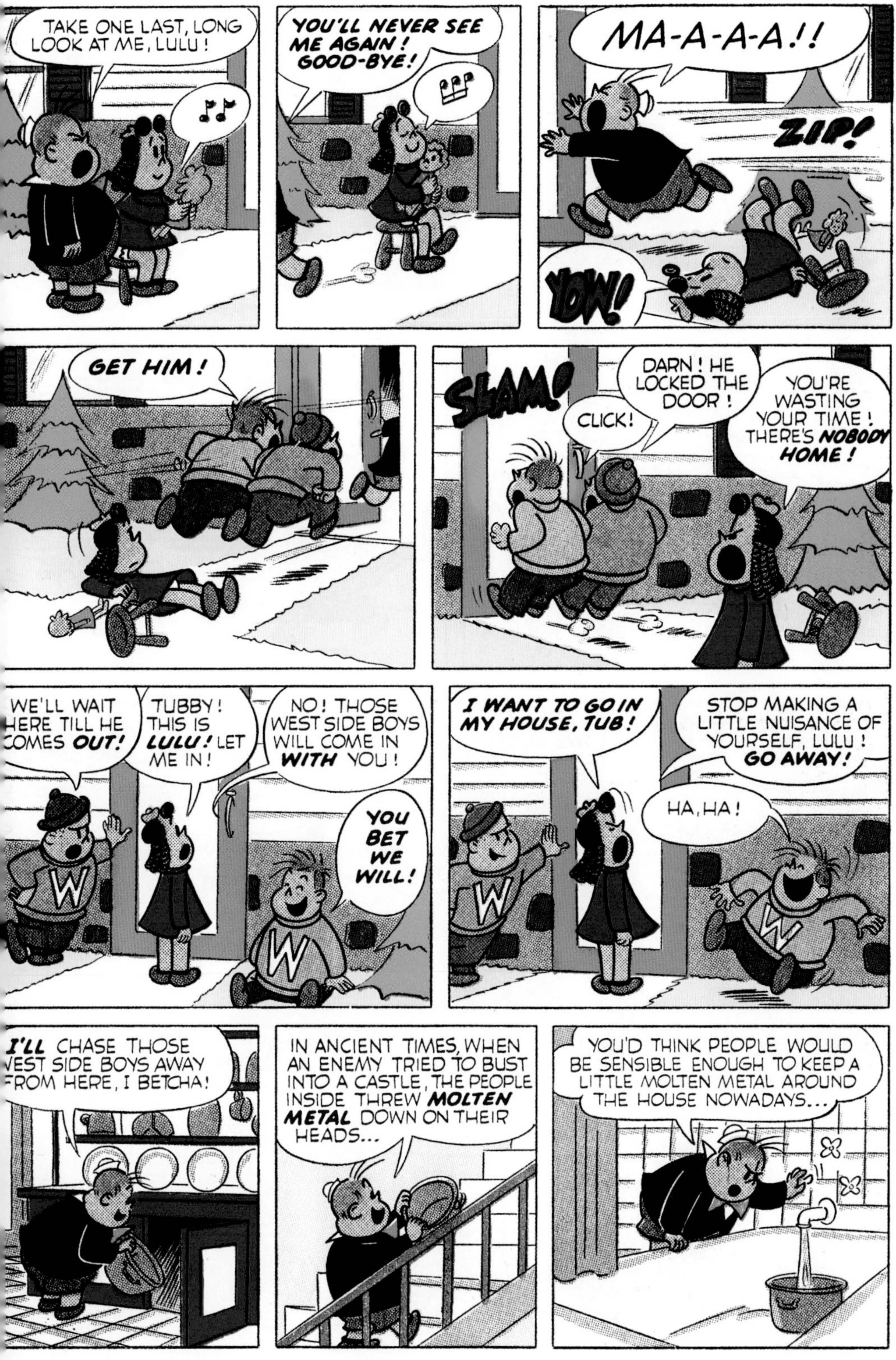
TAKE ONE LAST, LONG LOOK AT ME, LULU!
YOU'LL NEVER SEE ME AGAIN! GOOD-BYE!
MA-A-A-A!!
ZIP!
YOW!
GET HIM!
SLAM!
CLICK!
DARN! HE LOCKED THE DOOR!
YOU'RE WASTING YOUR TIME! THERE'S NOBODY HOME!
WE'LL WAIT HERE TILL HE COMES OUT!
TUBBY! THIS IS LULU! LET ME IN!
NO! THOSE WEST SIDE BOYS WILL COME IN WITH YOU!
YOU BET WE WILL!
I WANT TO GO IN MY HOUSE, TUB!
STOP MAKING A LITTLE NUISANCE OF YOURSELF, LULU! GO AWAY!
HA, HA!
I'LL CHASE THOSE WEST SIDE BOYS AWAY FROM HERE, I BETCHA!
IN ANCIENT TIMES, WHEN AN ENEMY TRIED TO BUST INTO A CASTLE, THE PEOPLE INSIDE THREW MOLTEN METAL DOWN ON THEIR HEADS...
YOU'D THINK PEOPLE WOULD BE SENSIBLE ENOUGH TO KEEP A LITTLE MOLTEN METAL AROUND THE HOUSE NOWADAYS...

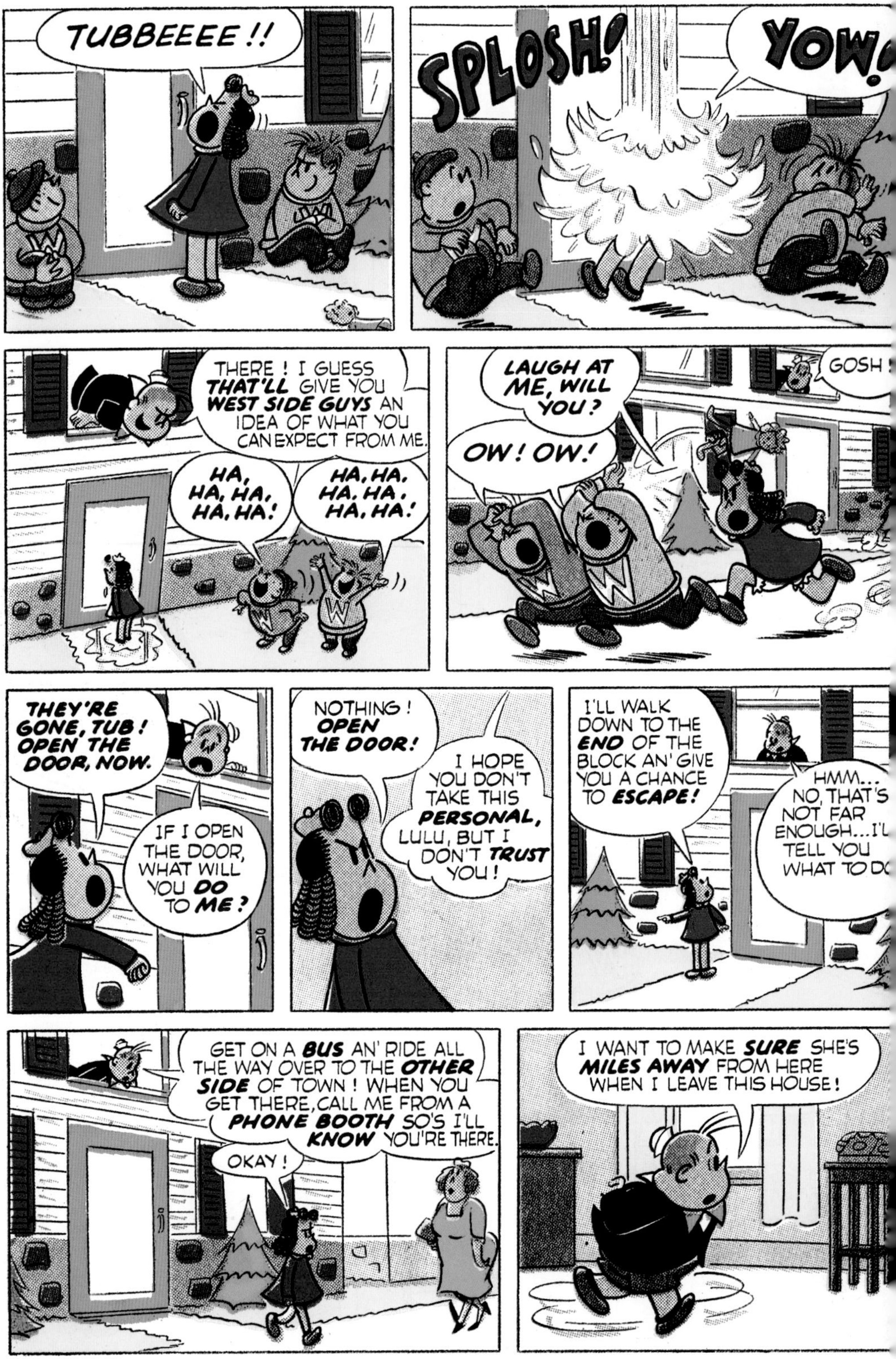
TUBBEEEE !!
SPLOSH!
YOW!
THERE ! I GUESS THAT'LL GIVE YOU WEST SIDE GUYS AN IDEA OF WHAT YOU CAN EXPECT FROM ME.
HA, HA, HA, HA, HA!
HA, HA, HA, HA, HA, HA!
LAUGH AT ME, WILL YOU?
OW! OW!
GOSH
THEY'RE GONE, TUB! OPEN THE DOOR, NOW.
IF I OPEN THE DOOR, WHAT WILL YOU DO TO ME?
NOTHING ! OPEN THE DOOR!
I HOPE YOU DON'T TAKE THIS PERSONAL, LULU, BUT I DON'T TRUST YOU!
I'LL WALK DOWN TO THE END OF THE BLOCK AN' GIVE YOU A CHANCE TO ESCAPE!
HMM... NO, THAT'S NOT FAR ENOUGH...I'L TELL YOU WHAT TO D
GET ON A BUS AN' RIDE ALL THE WAY OVER TO THE OTHER SIDE OF TOWN ! WHEN YOU GET THERE, CALL ME FROM A PHONE BOOTH SO'S I'LL KNOW YOU'RE THERE.
OKAY !
I WANT TO MAKE SURE SHE'S MILES AWAY FROM HERE WHEN I LEAVE THIS HOUSE !

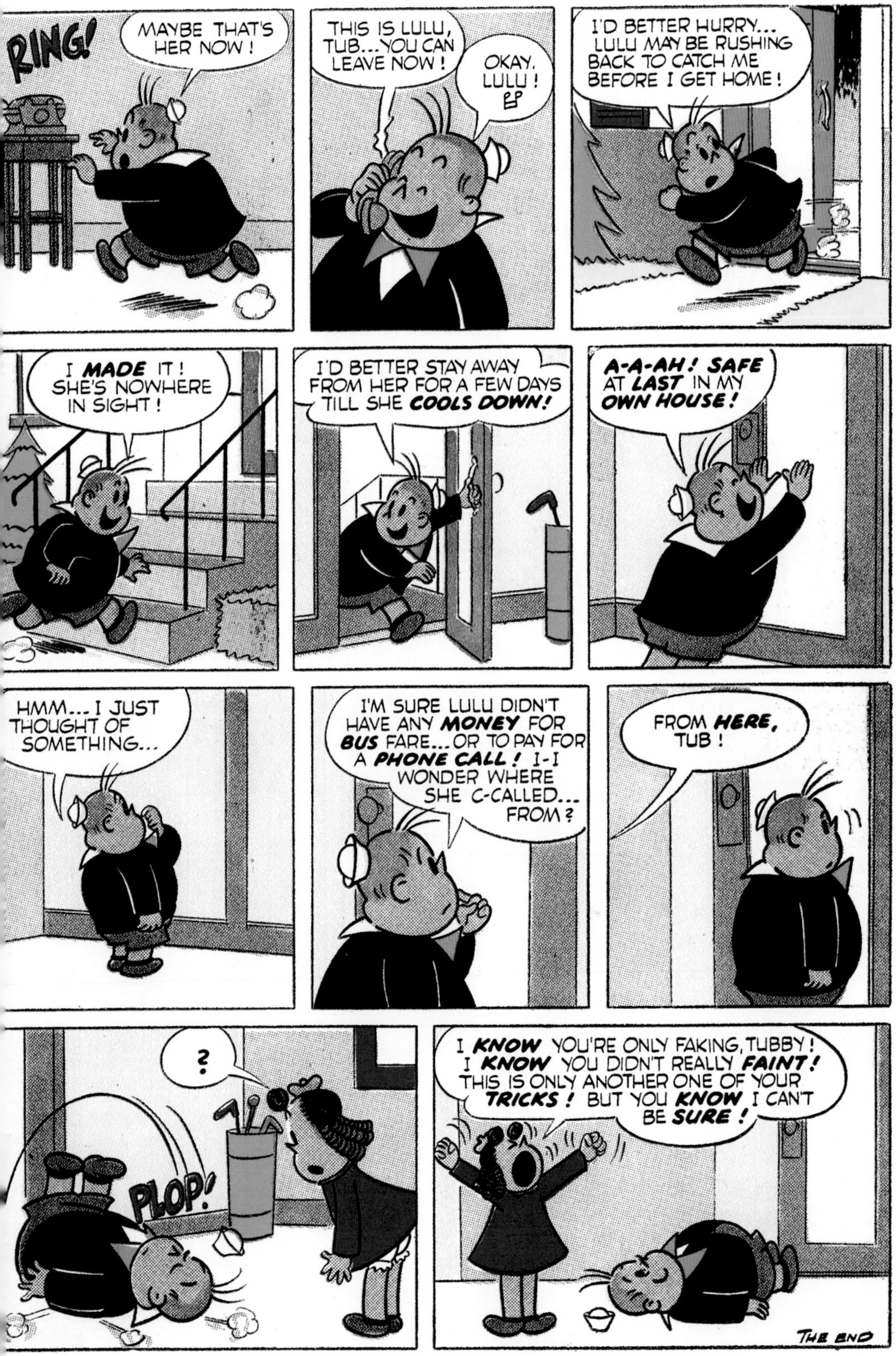
RING!
MAYBE THAT'S HER NOW!
THIS IS LULU, TUB...YOU CAN LEAVE NOW!
OKAY, LULU!
I'D BETTER HURRY... LULU MAY BE RUSHING BACK TO CATCH ME BEFORE I GET HOME!
I MADE IT! SHE'S NOWHERE IN SIGHT!
I'D BETTER STAY AWAY FROM HER FOR A FEW DAYS TILL SHE COOLS DOWN!
A-A-AH! SAFE AT LAST IN MY OWN HOUSE!
HMM... I JUST THOUGHT OF SOMETHING...
I'M SURE LULU DIDN'T HAVE ANY MONEY FOR BUS FARE...OR TO PAY FOR A PHONE CALL! I-I WONDER WHERE SHE C-CALLED... FROM?
FROM HERE, TUB!
?
PLOP!
I KNOW YOU'RE ONLY FAKING, TUBBY! I KNOW YOU DIDN'T REALLY FAINT! THIS IS ONLY ANOTHER ONE OF YOUR TRICKS! BUT YOU KNOW I CAN'T BE SURE!
THE END

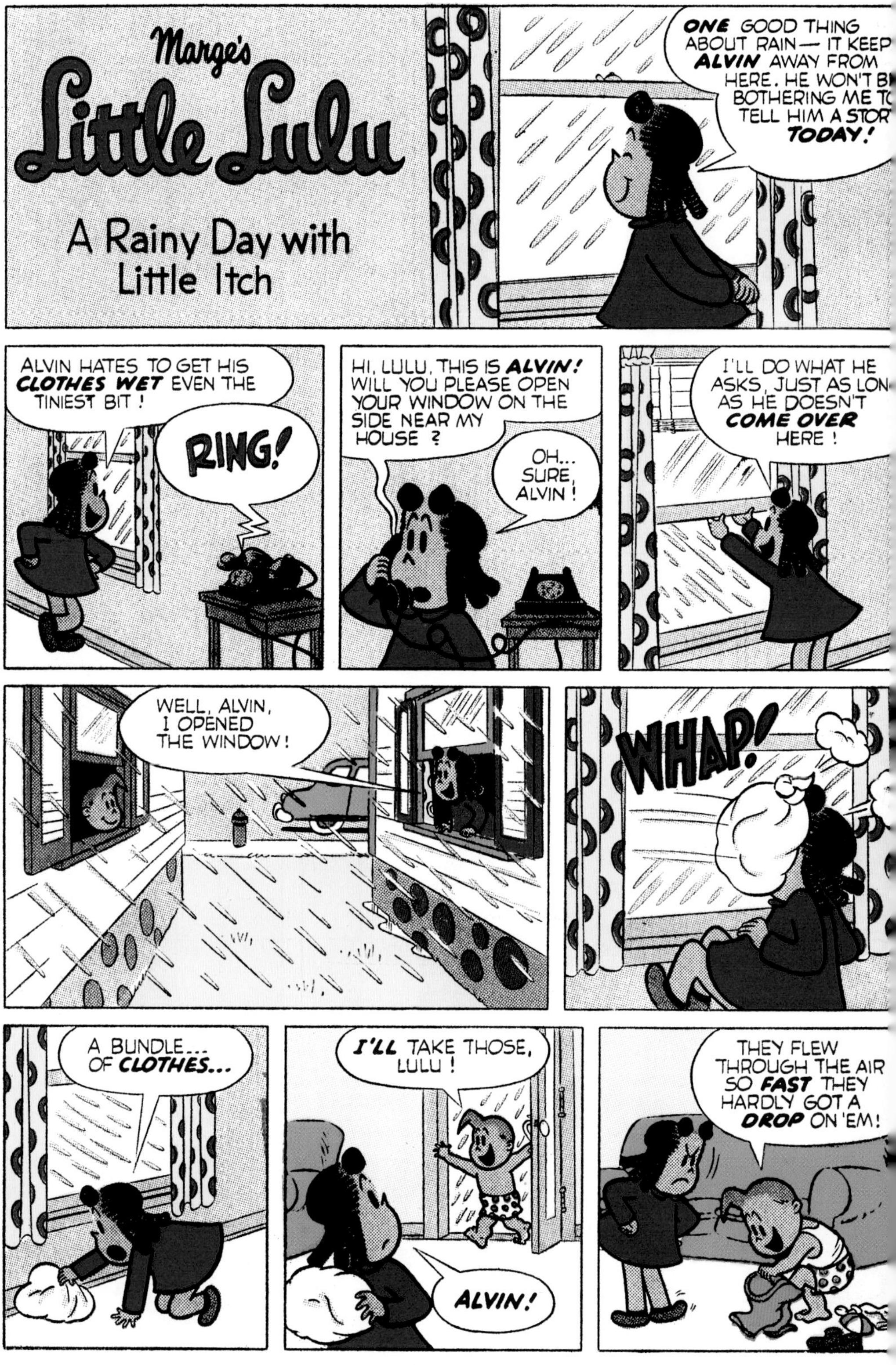

Marge's
Little Lulu
A Rainy Day with Little Itch
ONE GOOD THING ABOUT RAIN— IT KEEP ALVIN AWAY FROM HERE. HE WON'T B BOTHERING ME T TELL HIM A STOR TODAY!
ALVIN HATES TO GET HIS CLOTHES WET EVEN THE TINIEST BIT!
RING!
HI, LULU, THIS IS ALVIN! WILL YOU PLEASE OPEN YOUR WINDOW ON THE SIDE NEAR MY HOUSE ?
OH... SURE, ALVIN!
I'LL DO WHAT HE ASKS, JUST AS LON AS HE DOESN'T COME OVER HERE!
WELL, ALVIN, I OPENED THE WINDOW!
WHAP!
A BUNDLE... OF CLOTHES...
I'LL TAKE THOSE, LULU!
ALVIN!
THEY FLEW THROUGH THE AIR SO FAST THEY HARDLY GOT A DROP ON 'EM!

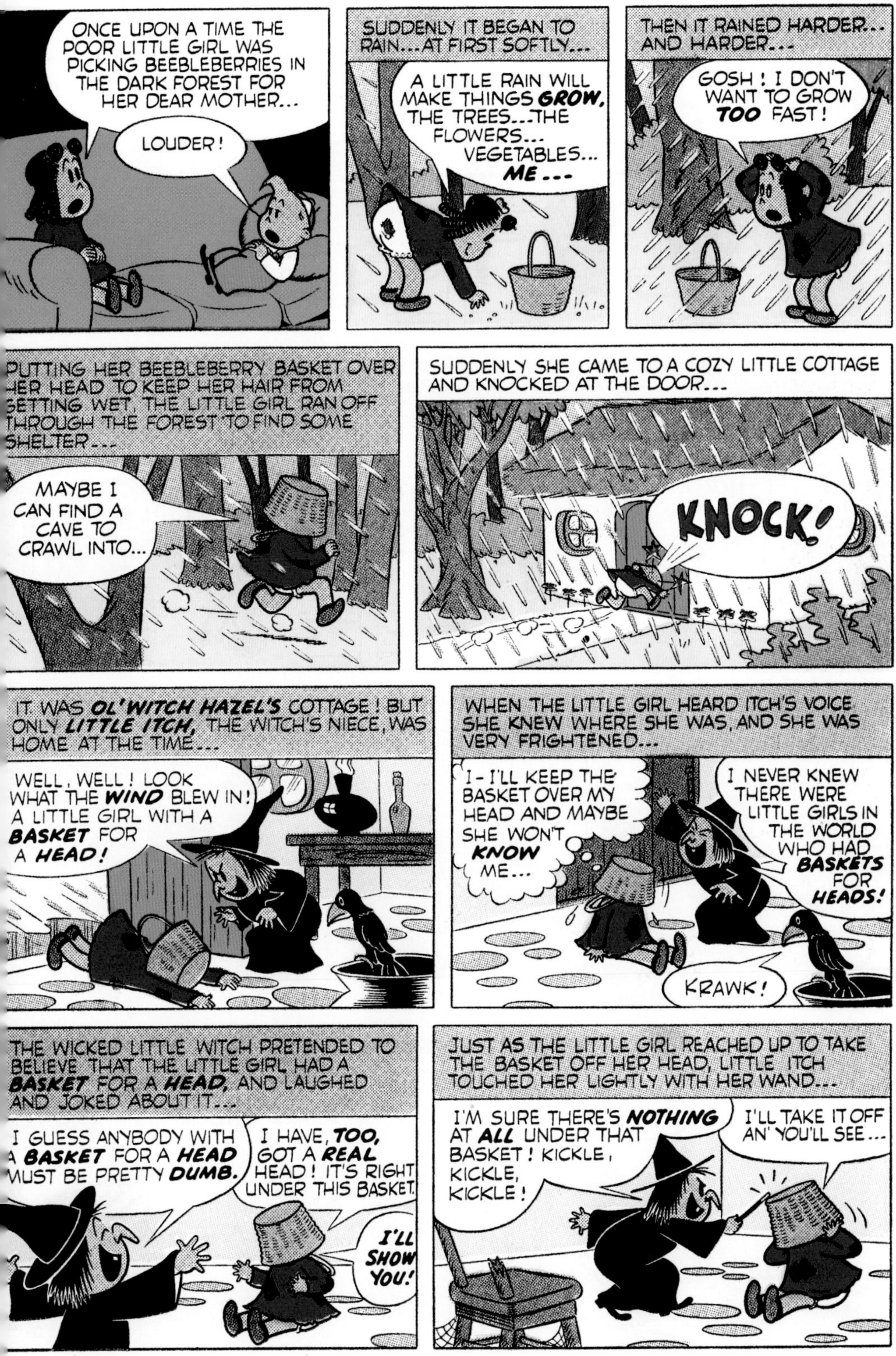
ONCE UPON A TIME THE POOR LITTLE GIRL WAS PICKING BEEBLEBERRIES IN THE DARK FOREST FOR HER DEAR MOTHER...
LOUDER!
SUDDENLY IT BEGAN TO RAIN... AT FIRST SOFTLY...
A LITTLE RAIN WILL MAKE THINGS GROW, THE TREES... THE FLOWERS... VEGETABLES... ME...
THEN IT RAINED HARDER... AND HARDER...
GOSH! I DON'T WANT TO GROW TOO FAST!
PUTTING HER BEEBLEBERRY BASKET OVER HER HEAD TO KEEP HER HAIR FROM GETTING WET, THE LITTLE GIRL RAN OFF THROUGH THE FOREST TO FIND SOME SHELTER...
MAYBE I CAN FIND A CAVE TO CRAWL INTO...
SUDDENLY SHE CAME TO A COZY LITTLE COTTAGE AND KNOCKED AT THE DOOR...
KNOCK!
IT WAS OL' WITCH HAZEL'S COTTAGE! BUT ONLY LITTLE ITCH, THE WITCH'S NIECE, WAS HOME AT THE TIME...
WELL, WELL! LOOK WHAT THE WIND BLEW IN! A LITTLE GIRL WITH A BASKET FOR A HEAD!
WHEN THE LITTLE GIRL HEARD ITCH'S VOICE SHE KNEW WHERE SHE WAS, AND SHE WAS VERY FRIGHTENED...
I-I'LL KEEP THE BASKET OVER MY HEAD AND MAYBE SHE WON'T KNOW ME...
I NEVER KNEW THERE WERE LITTLE GIRLS IN THE WORLD WHO HAD BASKETS FOR HEADS!
KRAWK!
THE WICKED LITTLE WITCH PRETENDED TO BELIEVE THAT THE LITTLE GIRL HAD A BASKET FOR A HEAD, AND LAUGHED AND JOKED ABOUT IT...
I GUESS ANYBODY WITH A BASKET FOR A HEAD MUST BE PRETTY DUMB.
I HAVE, TOO, GOT A REAL HEAD! IT'S RIGHT UNDER THIS BASKET.
I'LL SHOW YOU!
JUST AS THE LITTLE GIRL REACHED UP TO TAKE THE BASKET OFF HER HEAD, LITTLE ITCH TOUCHED HER LIGHTLY WITH HER WAND...
I'M SURE THERE'S NOTHING AT ALL UNDER THAT BASKET! KICKLE, KICKLE, KICKLE!
I'LL TAKE IT OFF AN' YOU'LL SEE...

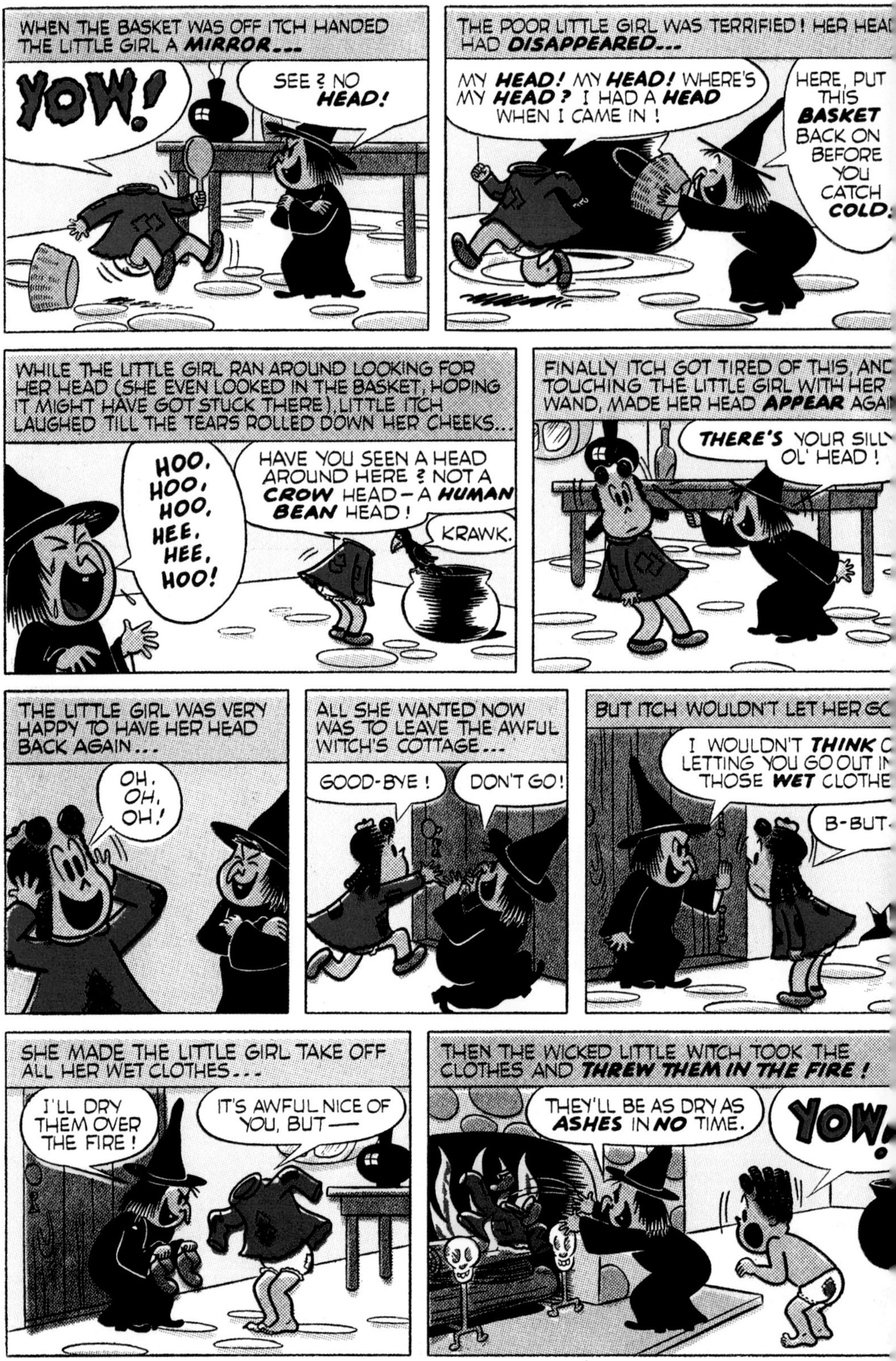
WHEN THE BASKET WAS OFF ITCH HANDED THE LITTLE GIRL A MIRROR...
YOW!
SEE ? NO HEAD!
THE POOR LITTLE GIRL WAS TERRIFIED! HER HEA
HAD DISAPPEARED...
MY HEAD! MY HEAD! WHERE'S MY HEAD? I HAD A HEAD WHEN I CAME IN!
HERE, PUT THIS BASKET BACK ON BEFORE YOU CATCH COLD
WHILE THE LITTLE GIRL RAN AROUND LOOKING FOR HER HEAD (SHE EVEN LOOKED IN THE BASKET, HOPING IT MIGHT HAVE GOT STUCK THERE), LITTLE ITCH LAUGHED TILL THE TEARS ROLLED DOWN HER CHEEKS...
HOO, HOO, HOO, HEE, HEE, HOO!
HAVE YOU SEEN A HEAD AROUND HERE ? NOT A CROW HEAD — A HUMAN BEAN HEAD!
KRAWK.
FINALLY ITCH GOT TIRED OF THIS, AND TOUCHING THE LITTLE GIRL WITH HER WAND, MADE HER HEAD APPEAR AGAI
THERE'S YOUR SILLY OL' HEAD!
THE LITTLE GIRL WAS VERY HAPPY TO HAVE HER HEAD BACK AGAIN...
OH, OH, OH!
ALL SHE WANTED NOW WAS TO LEAVE THE AWFUL WITCH'S COTTAGE...
GOOD-BYE!
DON'T GO!
BUT ITCH WOULDN'T LET HER G
I WOULDN'T THINK O
LETTING YOU GO OUT IN
THOSE WET CLOTHE
B-BUT-
SHE MADE THE LITTLE GIRL TAKE OFF ALL HER WET CLOTHES...
I'LL DRY THEM OVER THE FIRE!
IT'S AWFUL NICE OF YOU, BUT—
THEN THE WICKED LITTLE WITCH TOOK THE CLOTHES AND THREW THEM IN THE FIRE!
THEY'LL BE AS DRY AS ASHES IN NO TIME.
YOW

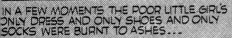

IN A FEW MOMENTS THE POOR LITTLE GIRL'S ONLY DRESS AND ONLY SOCKS AND ONLY SHOES WERE BURNT TO ASHES...

BUT I CAN'T WEAR **ASHES!**

HOO, HOO, HOO, HEE, HEE, HEE!

THE LITTLE GIRL FELT AWFUL...THERE SHE WAS, TRAPPED IN THE WITCH'S COTTAGE, WITHOUT A THING TO WEAR...

I CAN'T GO HOME LIKE **THIS!**

OH, **I** CAN FIX **THAT**, DEARIE!

THEN LITTLE ITCH TOOK OUT HER WAND AGAIN AND LIGHTLY TOUCHED THE LITTLE GIRL...

PRESTO, WHACKO!

**OW!**

SUDDENLY THE LITTLE GIRL WAS DRESSED FROM HEAD TO TOE IN THE MOST **BEAUTIFUL CLOTHES** SHE HAD EVER SEEN...

WOW! A **REAL MINK COAT** AN' **SILK STOCKINGS** AN' **GOLD SHOES!**

A LITTLE BETTER THAN THOSE **RAGS** YOU CAME **IN** HERE WITH, EH?

FLINGING OPEN THE DOOR, THE LITTLE GIRL HAPPILY DASHED OUT INTO THE RAIN...

HEE HEE!

OH, I CAN'T WAIT TO SHOW **MOTHER** MY NEW CLOTHES!

BUT AS SOON AS THE RAIN TOUCHED HER CLOTHES THEY **DISAPPEARED!**

**YOW!**

**SLAM!**

SHE TRIED TO GET BACK INTO THE COTTAGE, BUT SHE FOUND THE DOOR CLOSED AND LOCKED...

LET ME IN! I CAN'T GO HOME LIKE **THIS!**

CAN I HELP IT IF YOU'RE SO **HARD** ON CLOTHES? KICKLE, KICKLE!

FEARING THAT SOMEBODY WOULD COME ALONG AND SEE HER WITHOUT ANY CLOTHES ON, THE LITTLE GIRL PLEADED WITH ITCH TO LET HER IN...

*PLEASE LET ME IN!* PLEASE! PLEASE!

BANG! BANG!

GO AWAY OR I'LL TURN YOU INTO A **TOAD!**

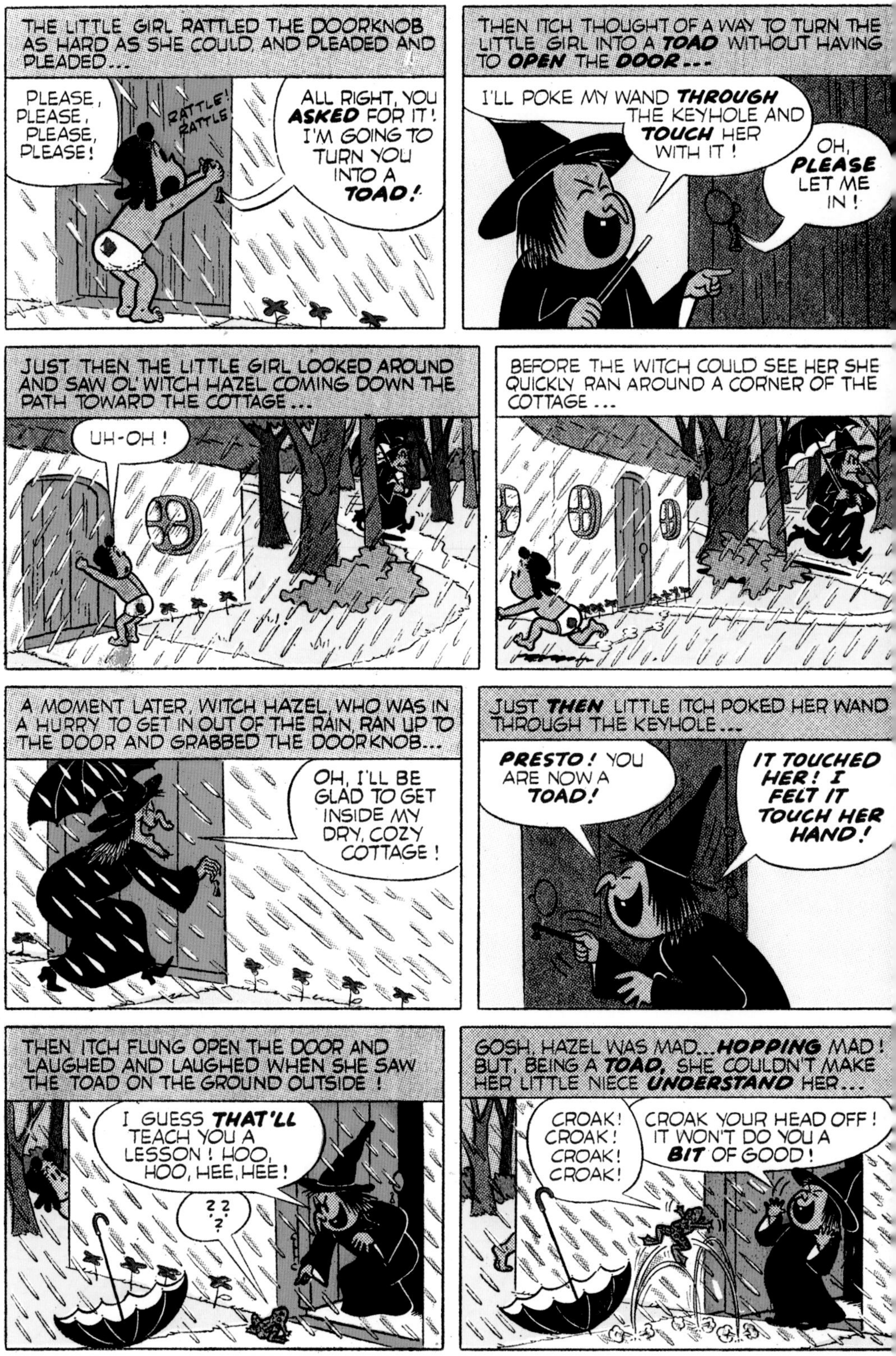
THE LITTLE GIRL RATTLED THE DOORKNOB AS HARD AS SHE COULD, AND PLEADED AND PLEADED...
PLEASE, PLEASE, PLEASE, PLEASE!
RATTLE! RATTLE
ALL RIGHT, YOU ASKED FOR IT! I'M GOING TO TURN YOU INTO A TOAD!
THEN ITCH THOUGHT OF A WAY TO TURN THE LITTLE GIRL INTO A TOAD WITHOUT HAVING TO OPEN THE DOOR...
I'LL POKE MY WAND THROUGH THE KEYHOLE AND TOUCH HER WITH IT!
OH, PLEASE LET ME IN!
JUST THEN THE LITTLE GIRL LOOKED AROUND AND SAW OL' WITCH HAZEL COMING DOWN THE PATH TOWARD THE COTTAGE...
UH-OH!
BEFORE THE WITCH COULD SEE HER SHE QUICKLY RAN AROUND A CORNER OF THE COTTAGE...
A MOMENT LATER, WITCH HAZEL, WHO WAS IN A HURRY TO GET IN OUT OF THE RAIN, RAN UP TO THE DOOR AND GRABBED THE DOORKNOB...
OH, I'LL BE GLAD TO GET INSIDE MY DRY, COZY COTTAGE!
JUST THEN LITTLE ITCH POKED HER WAND THROUGH THE KEYHOLE...
PRESTO! YOU ARE NOW A TOAD!
IT TOUCHED HER! I FELT IT TOUCH HER HAND!
THEN ITCH FLUNG OPEN THE DOOR AND LAUGHED AND LAUGHED WHEN SHE SAW THE TOAD ON THE GROUND OUTSIDE!
I GUESS THAT'LL TEACH YOU A LESSON! HOO, HOO, HEE, HEE!
? ? ?
GOSH, HAZEL WAS MAD...HOPPING MAD! BUT, BEING A TOAD, SHE COULDN'T MAKE HER LITTLE NIECE UNDERSTAND HER...
CROAK! CROAK! CROAK! CROAK!
CROAK YOUR HEAD OFF! IT WON'T DO YOU A BIT OF GOOD!

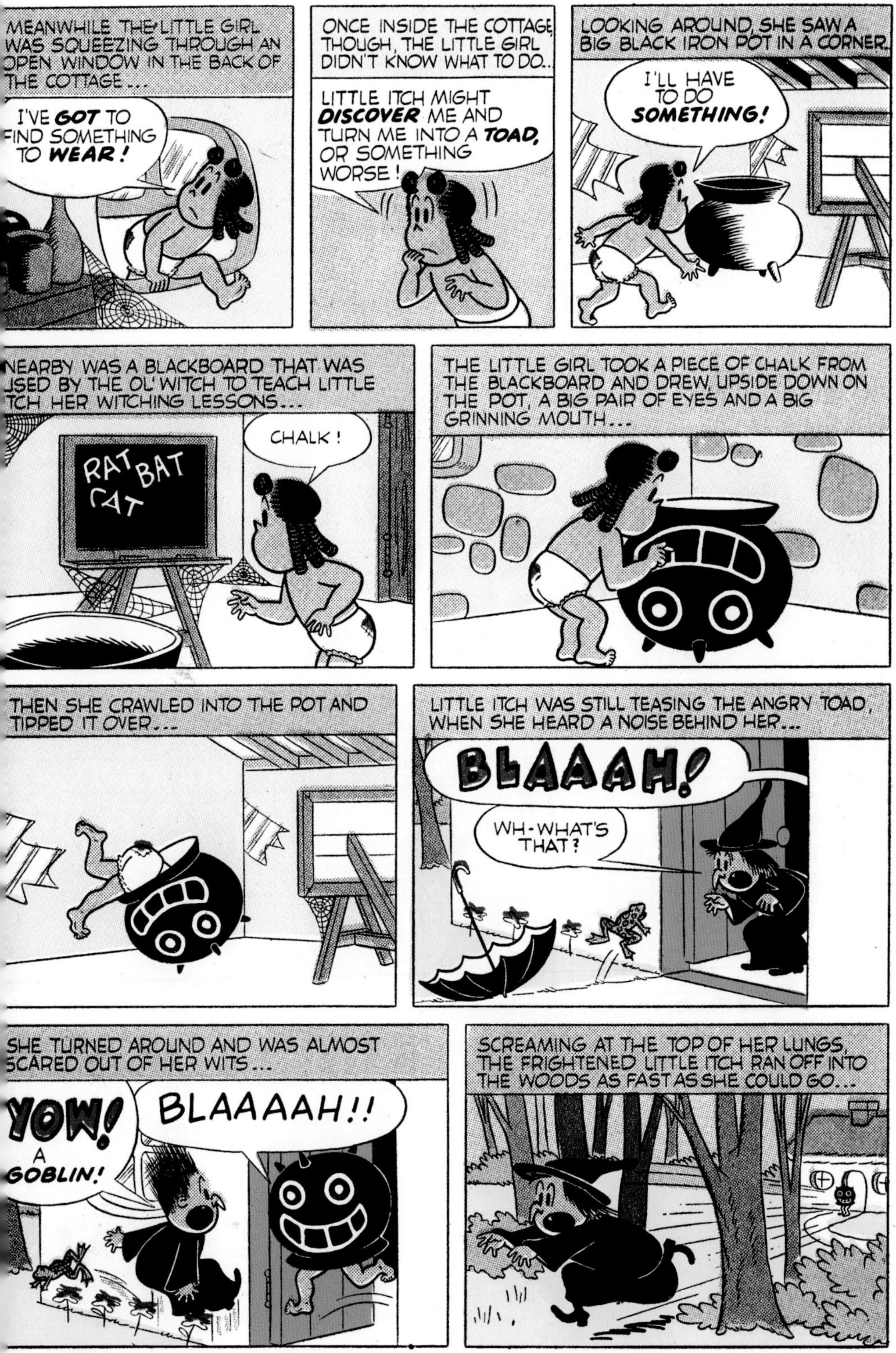
MEANWHILE THE LITTLE GIRL WAS SQUEEZING THROUGH AN OPEN WINDOW IN THE BACK OF THE COTTAGE...
I'VE GOT TO FIND SOMETHING TO WEAR!
ONCE INSIDE THE COTTAGE, THOUGH, THE LITTLE GIRL DIDN'T KNOW WHAT TO DO..
LITTLE ITCH MIGHT DISCOVER ME AND TURN ME INTO A TOAD, OR SOMETHING WORSE!
LOOKING AROUND, SHE SAW A BIG BLACK IRON POT IN A CORNER.
I'LL HAVE TO DO SOMETHING!
NEARBY WAS A BLACKBOARD THAT WAS USED BY THE OL' WITCH TO TEACH LITTLE ITCH HER WITCHING LESSONS...
RAT BAT CAT
CHALK!
THE LITTLE GIRL TOOK A PIECE OF CHALK FROM THE BLACKBOARD AND DREW, UPSIDE DOWN ON THE POT, A BIG PAIR OF EYES AND A BIG GRINNING MOUTH...
THEN SHE CRAWLED INTO THE POT AND TIPPED IT OVER...
LITTLE ITCH WAS STILL TEASING THE ANGRY TOAD, WHEN SHE HEARD A NOISE BEHIND HER...
BLAAAH!
WH-WHAT'S THAT?
SHE TURNED AROUND AND WAS ALMOST SCARED OUT OF HER WITS...
YOW! A GOBLIN!
BLAAAAH!!
SCREAMING AT THE TOP OF HER LUNGS, THE FRIGHTENED LITTLE ITCH RAN OFF INTO THE WOODS AS FAST AS SHE COULD GO...

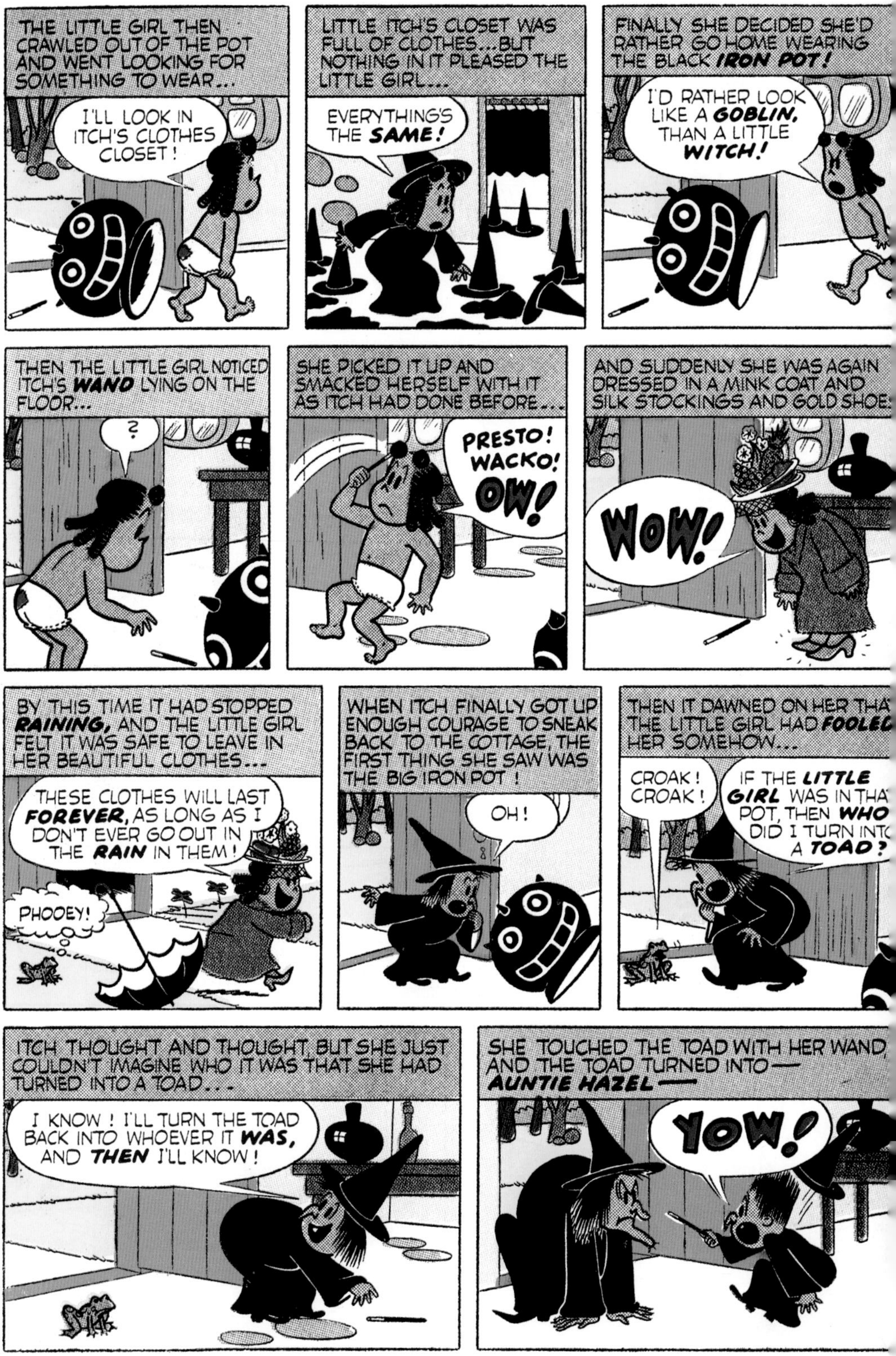
THE LITTLE GIRL THEN CRAWLED OUT OF THE POT AND WENT LOOKING FOR SOMETHING TO WEAR...
I'LL LOOK IN ITCH'S CLOTHES CLOSET!
LITTLE ITCH'S CLOSET WAS FULL OF CLOTHES...BUT NOTHING IN IT PLEASED THE LITTLE GIRL...
EVERYTHING'S THE SAME!
FINALLY SHE DECIDED SHE'D RATHER GO HOME WEARING THE BLACK IRON POT!
I'D RATHER LOOK LIKE A GOBLIN, THAN A LITTLE WITCH!
THEN THE LITTLE GIRL NOTICED ITCH'S WAND LYING ON THE FLOOR...
?
SHE PICKED IT UP AND SMACKED HERSELF WITH IT AS ITCH HAD DONE BEFORE...
PRESTO! WACKO! OW!
AND SUDDENLY SHE WAS AGAIN DRESSED IN A MINK COAT AND SILK STOCKINGS AND GOLD SHOES
WOW!
BY THIS TIME IT HAD STOPPED RAINING, AND THE LITTLE GIRL FELT IT WAS SAFE TO LEAVE IN HER BEAUTIFUL CLOTHES...
THESE CLOTHES WILL LAST FOREVER, AS LONG AS I DON'T EVER GO OUT IN THE RAIN IN THEM!
PHOOEY!
WHEN ITCH FINALLY GOT UP ENOUGH COURAGE TO SNEAK BACK TO THE COTTAGE, THE FIRST THING SHE SAW WAS THE BIG IRON POT!
OH!
THEN IT DAWNED ON HER THAT THE LITTLE GIRL HAD FOOLED HER SOMEHOW...
CROAK! CROAK!
IF THE LITTLE GIRL WAS IN THAT POT, THEN WHO DID I TURN INTO A TOAD?
ITCH THOUGHT AND THOUGHT, BUT SHE JUST COULDN'T IMAGINE WHO IT WAS THAT SHE HAD TURNED INTO A TOAD...
I KNOW! I'LL TURN THE TOAD BACK INTO WHOEVER IT WAS, AND THEN I'LL KNOW!
SHE TOUCHED THE TOAD WITH HER WAND, AND THE TOAD TURNED INTO— AUNTIE HAZEL—
YOW!

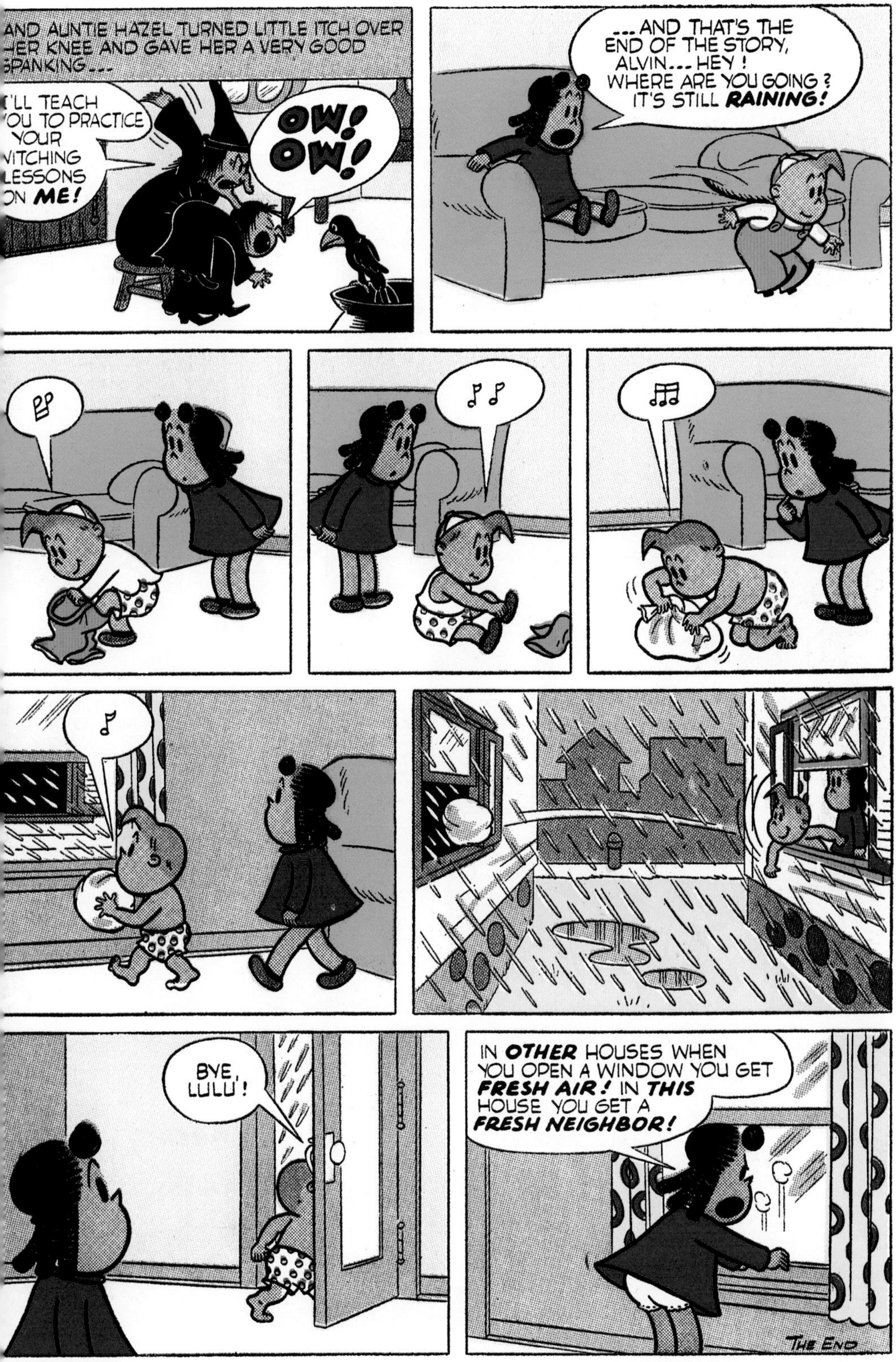
AND AUNTIE HAZEL TURNED LITTLE ITCH OVER HER KNEE AND GAVE HER A VERY GOOD SPANKING...
I'LL TEACH YOU TO PRACTICE YOUR WITCHING LESSONS ON ME!
OW! OW!
...AND THAT'S THE END OF THE STORY, ALVIN... HEY! WHERE ARE YOU GOING? IT'S STILL RAINING!
BYE, LULU!
IN OTHER HOUSES WHEN YOU OPEN A WINDOW YOU GET FRESH AIR! IN THIS HOUSE YOU GET A FRESH NEIGHBOR!
THE END

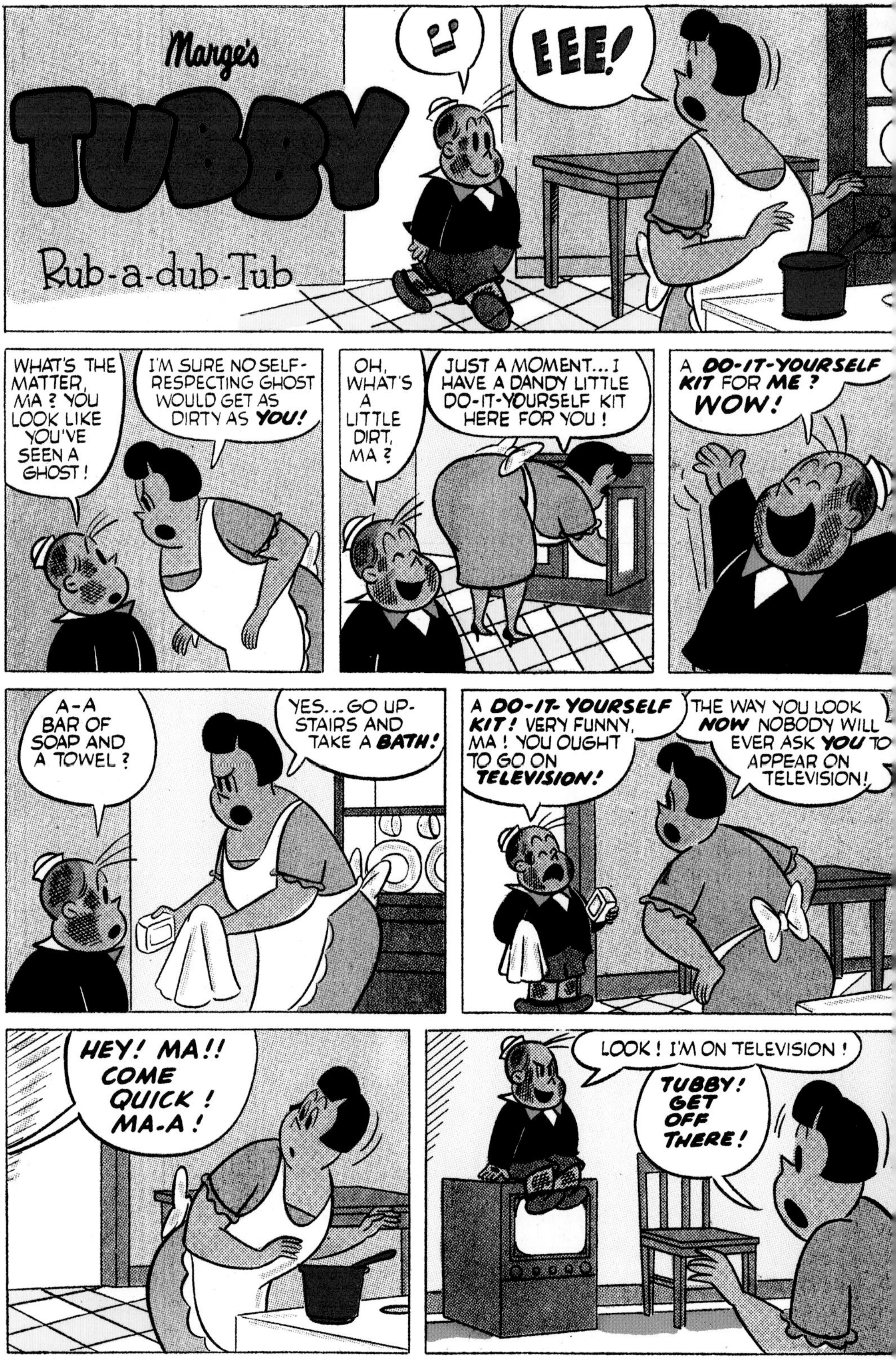
Marge's
TUBBY
Rub-a-dub-Tub
EEE!
WHAT'S THE MATTER, MA? YOU LOOK LIKE YOU'VE SEEN A GHOST!
I'M SURE NO SELF-RESPECTING GHOST WOULD GET AS DIRTY AS YOU!
OH, WHAT'S A LITTLE DIRT, MA?
JUST A MOMENT... I HAVE A DANDY LITTLE DO-IT-YOURSELF KIT HERE FOR YOU!
A DO-IT-YOURSELF KIT FOR ME? WOW!
A-A BAR OF SOAP AND A TOWEL?
YES...GO UPSTAIRS AND TAKE A BATH!
A DO-IT-YOURSELF KIT! VERY FUNNY, MA! YOU OUGHT TO GO ON TELEVISION!
THE WAY YOU LOOK NOW NOBODY WILL EVER ASK YOU TO APPEAR ON TELEVISION!
HEY! MA!! COME QUICK! MA-A!
LOOK! I'M ON TELEVISION!
TUBBY! GET OFF THERE!

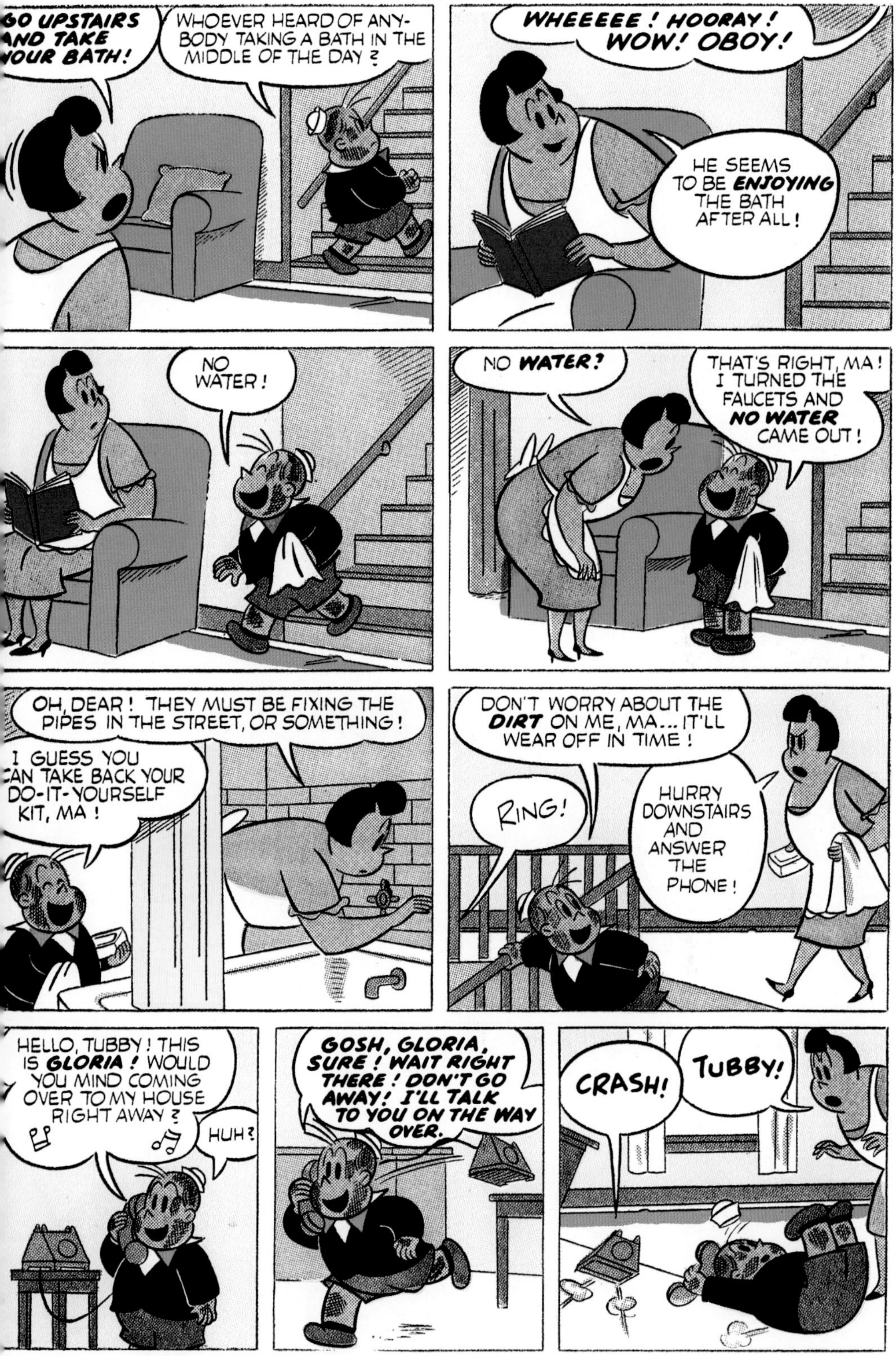
GO UPSTAIRS AND TAKE YOUR BATH!
WHOEVER HEARD OF ANYBODY TAKING A BATH IN THE MIDDLE OF THE DAY?
WHEEEEE! HOORAY! WOW! OBOY!
HE SEEMS TO BE ENJOYING THE BATH AFTER ALL!
NO WATER!
NO WATER?
THAT'S RIGHT, MA! I TURNED THE FAUCETS AND NO WATER CAME OUT!
OH, DEAR! THEY MUST BE FIXING THE PIPES IN THE STREET, OR SOMETHING!
I GUESS YOU CAN TAKE BACK YOUR DO-IT-YOURSELF KIT, MA!
DON'T WORRY ABOUT THE DIRT ON ME, MA... IT'LL WEAR OFF IN TIME!
RING!
HURRY DOWNSTAIRS AND ANSWER THE PHONE!
HELLO, TUBBY! THIS IS GLORIA! WOULD YOU MIND COMING OVER TO MY HOUSE RIGHT AWAY?
HUH?
GOSH, GLORIA, SURE! WAIT RIGHT THERE! DON'T GO AWAY! I'LL TALK TO YOU ON THE WAY OVER.
CRASH!
TUBBY!

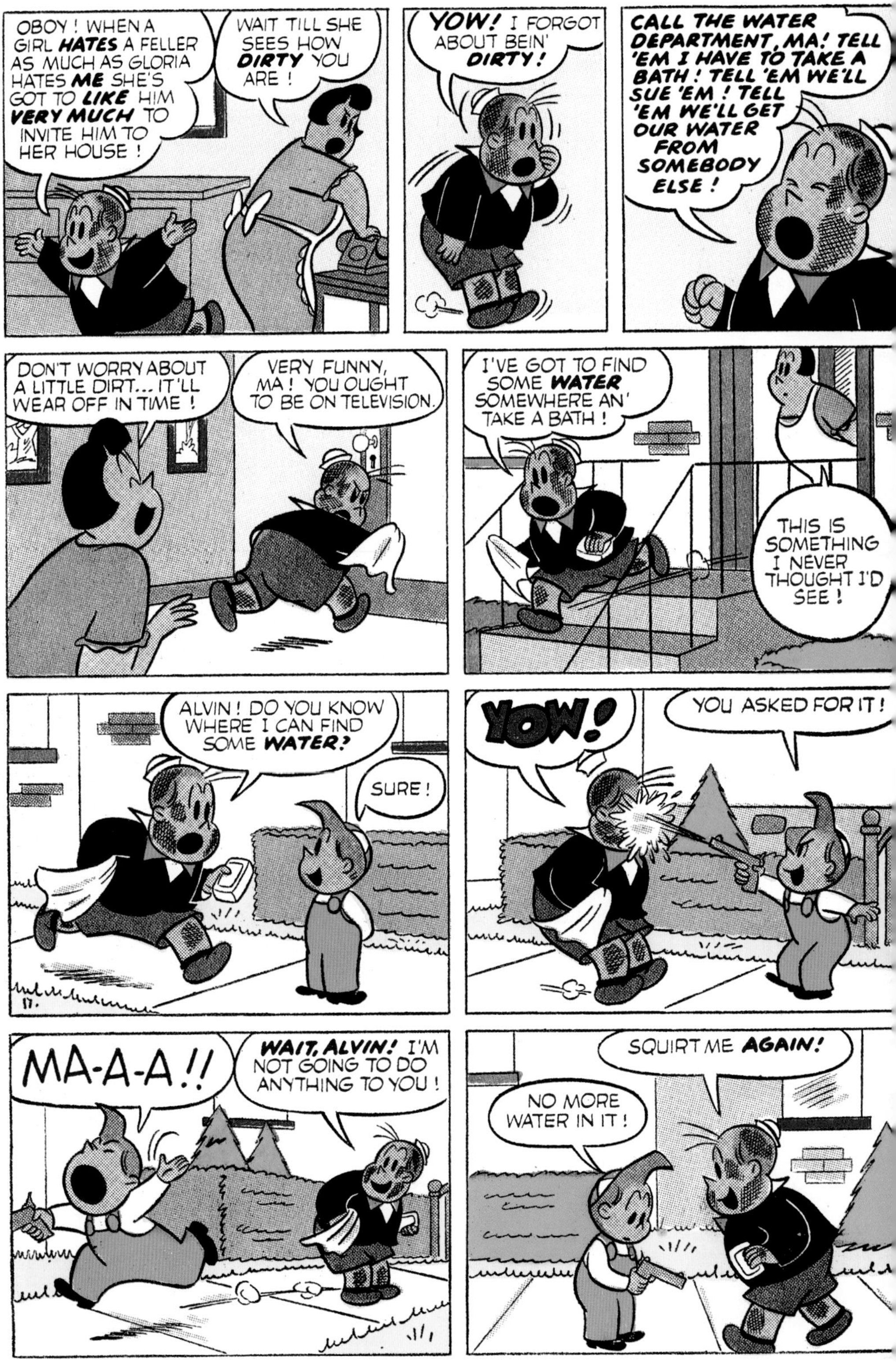
OBOY! WHEN A GIRL HATES A FELLER AS MUCH AS GLORIA HATES ME SHE'S GOT TO LIKE HIM VERY MUCH TO INVITE HIM TO HER HOUSE!
WAIT TILL SHE SEES HOW DIRTY YOU ARE!
YOW! I FORGOT ABOUT BEIN' DIRTY!
CALL THE WATER DEPARTMENT, MA! TELL 'EM I HAVE TO TAKE A BATH! TELL 'EM WE'LL SUE 'EM! TELL 'EM WE'LL GET OUR WATER FROM SOMEBODY ELSE!
DON'T WORRY ABOUT A LITTLE DIRT... IT'LL WEAR OFF IN TIME!
VERY FUNNY, MA! YOU OUGHT TO BE ON TELEVISION.
I'VE GOT TO FIND SOME WATER SOMEWHERE AN' TAKE A BATH!
THIS IS SOMETHING I NEVER THOUGHT I'D SEE!
ALVIN! DO YOU KNOW WHERE I CAN FIND SOME WATER?
SURE!
YOW!
YOU ASKED FOR IT!
MA-A-A!!
WAIT, ALVIN! I'M NOT GOING TO DO ANYTHING TO YOU!
SQUIRT ME AGAIN!
NO MORE WATER IN IT!

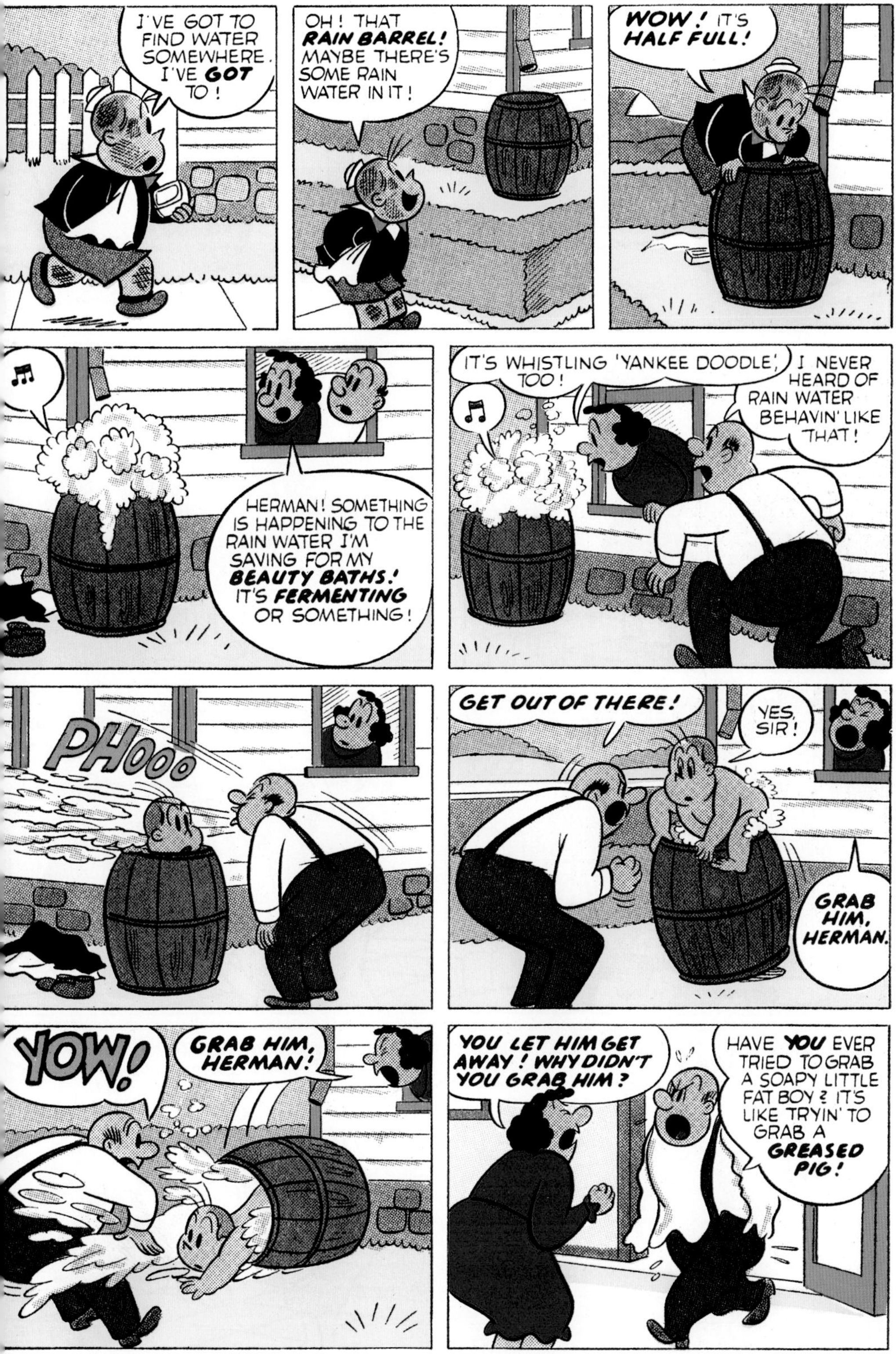
I'VE GOT TO FIND WATER SOMEWHERE. I'VE GOT TO!
OH! THAT RAIN BARREL! MAYBE THERE'S SOME RAIN WATER IN IT!
WOW! IT'S HALF FULL!
HERMAN! SOMETHING IS HAPPENING TO THE RAIN WATER I'M SAVING FOR MY BEAUTY BATHS! IT'S FERMENTING OR SOMETHING!
IT'S WHISTLING 'YANKEE DOODLE,' TOO!
I NEVER HEARD OF RAIN WATER BEHAVIN' LIKE THAT!
PHOOOO
GET OUT OF THERE!
YES, SIR!
GRAB HIM, HERMAN.
YOW!
GRAB HIM, HERMAN!
YOU LET HIM GET AWAY! WHY DIDN'T YOU GRAB HIM?
HAVE YOU EVER TRIED TO GRAB A SOAPY LITTLE FAT BOY? IT'S LIKE TRYIN' TO GRAB A GREASED PIG!

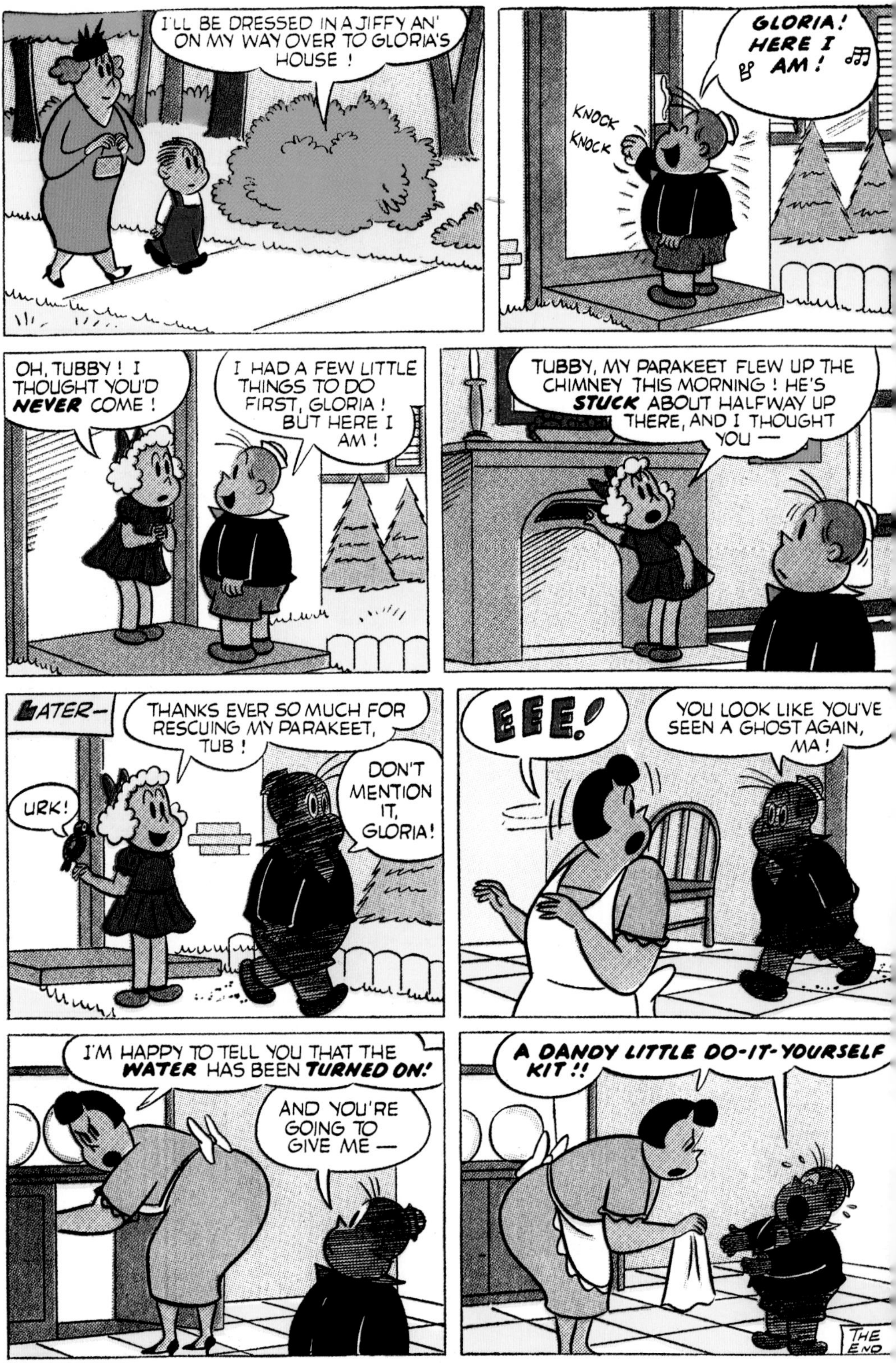
I'LL BE DRESSED IN A JIFFY AN' ON MY WAY OVER TO GLORIA'S HOUSE !
GLORIA! HERE I AM!
KNOCK
KNOCK
OH, TUBBY ! I THOUGHT YOU'D NEVER COME !
I HAD A FEW LITTLE THINGS TO DO FIRST, GLORIA ! BUT HERE I AM !
TUBBY, MY PARAKEET FLEW UP THE CHIMNEY THIS MORNING ! HE'S STUCK ABOUT HALFWAY UP THERE, AND I THOUGHT YOU —
LATER—
THANKS EVER SO MUCH FOR RESCUING MY PARAKEET, TUB !
URK!
DON'T MENTION IT, GLORIA!
EEE!
YOU LOOK LIKE YOU'VE SEEN A GHOST AGAIN, MA !
I'M HAPPY TO TELL YOU THAT THE WATER HAS BEEN TURNED ON!
AND YOU'RE GOING TO GIVE ME —
A DANDY LITTLE DO-IT-YOURSELF KIT !!
THE END

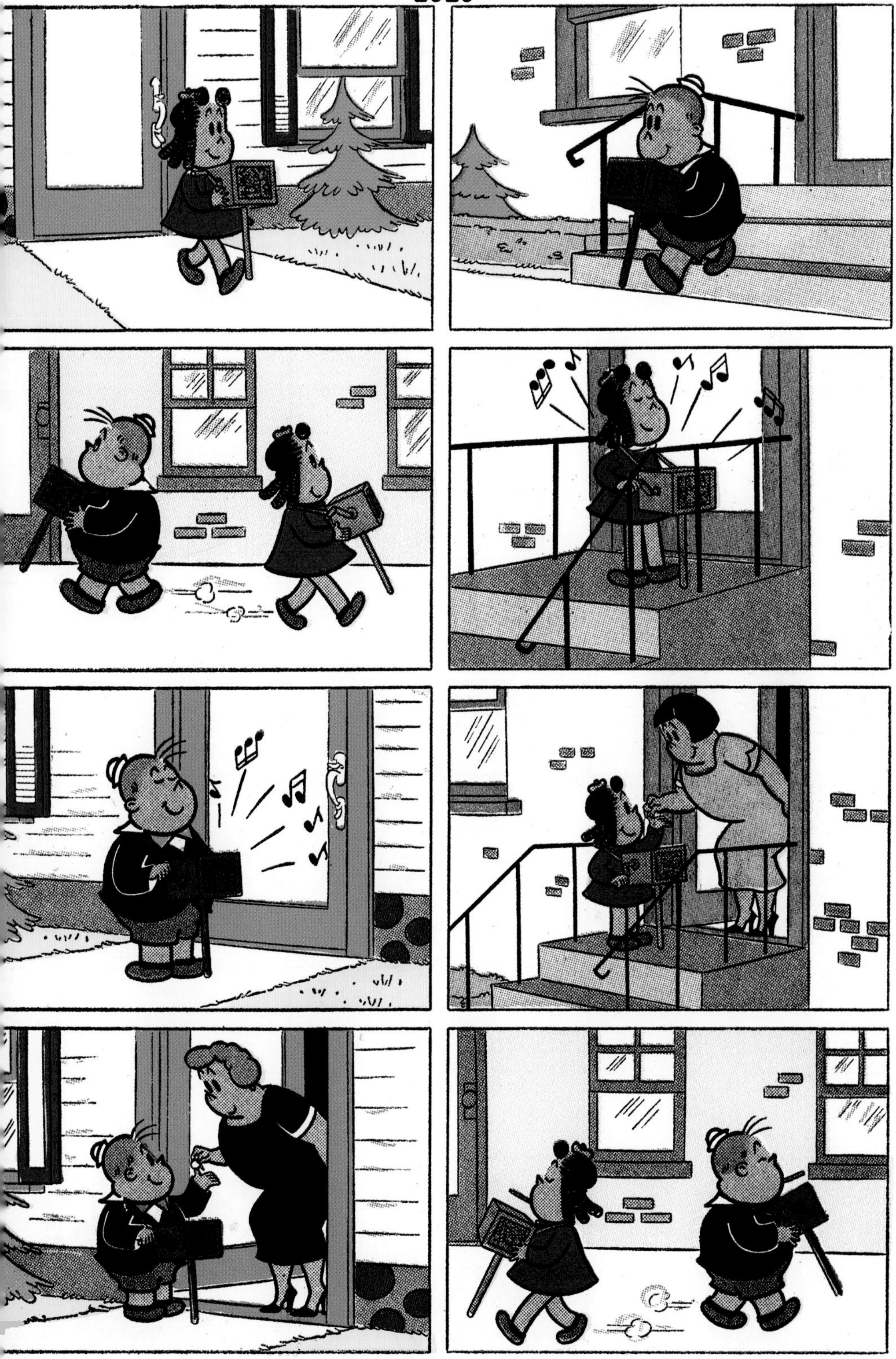

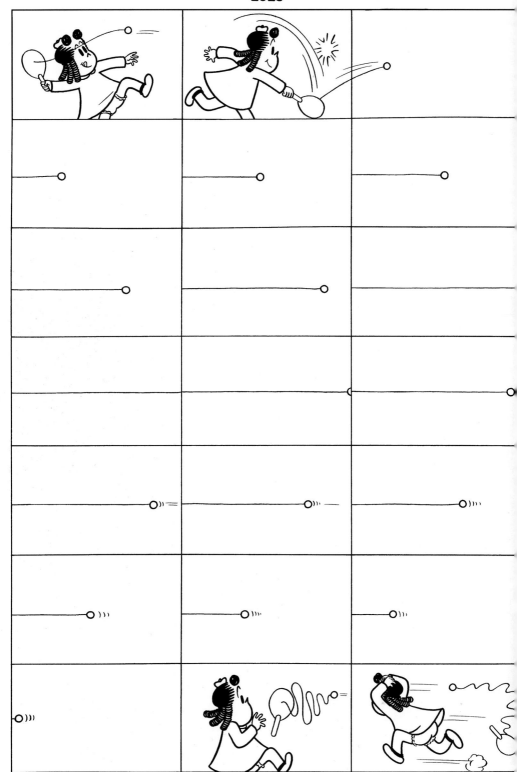

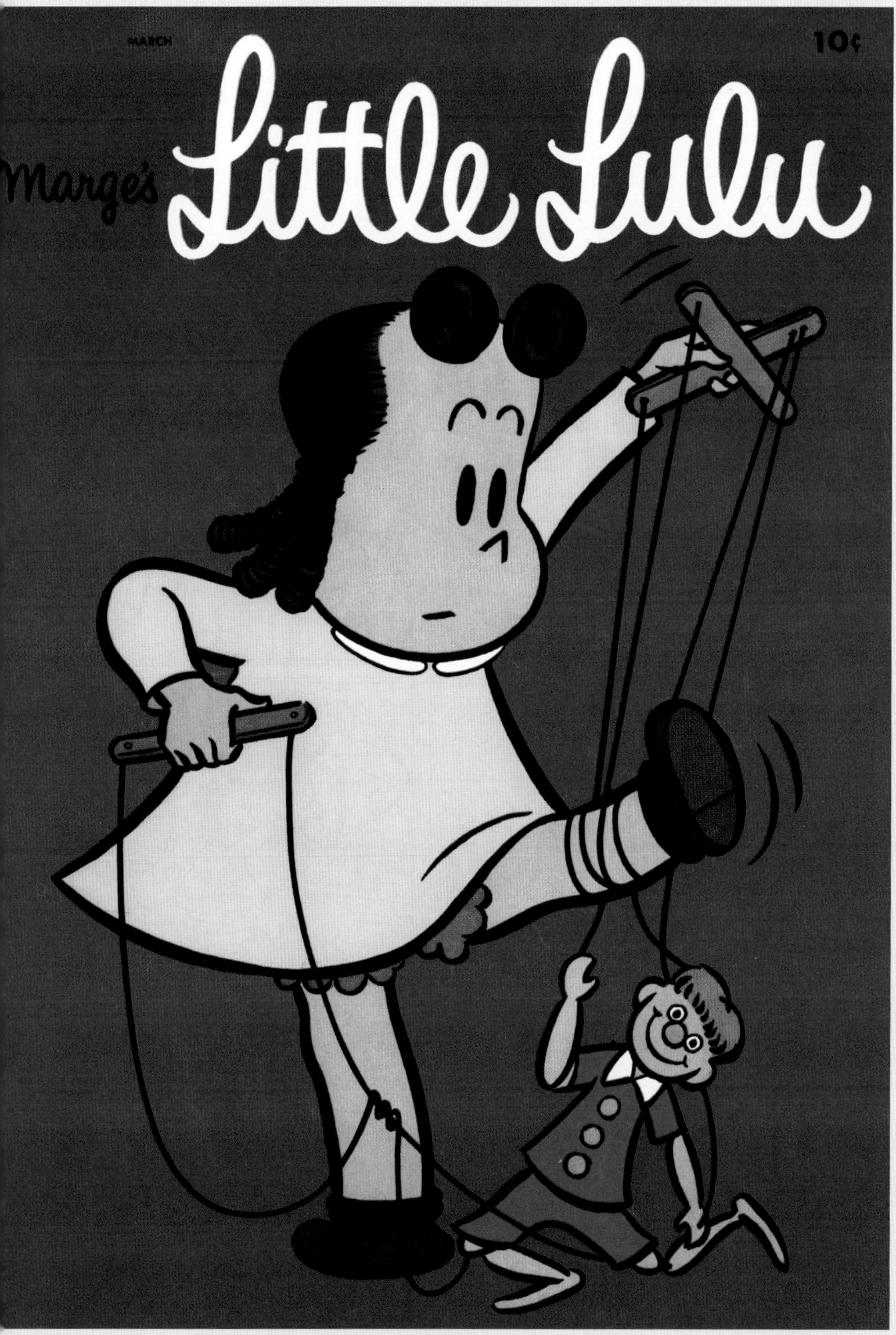
MARCH
10¢
Marge's Little Lulu

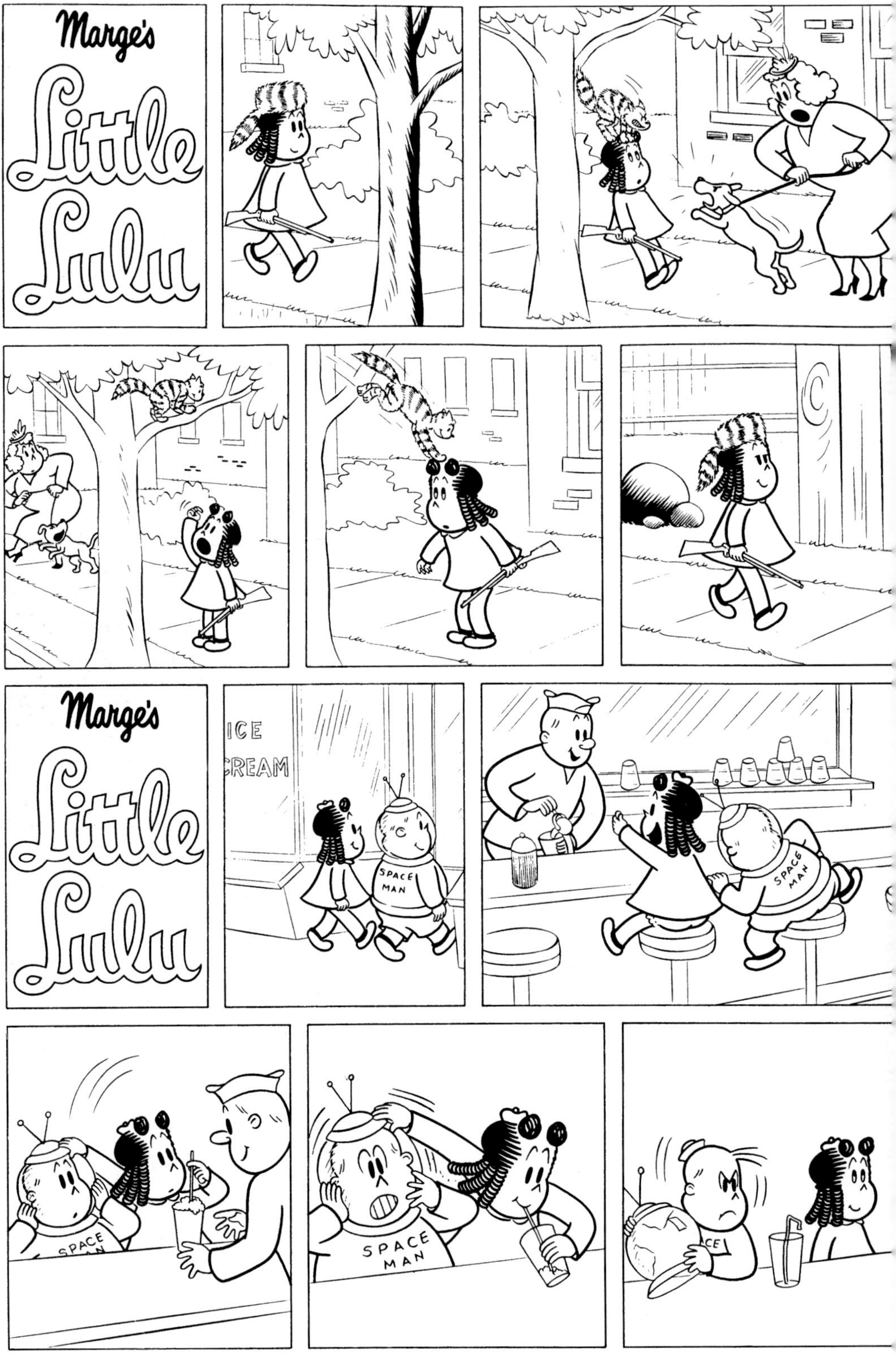
Marge's
Little Lulu
Marge's
Little Lulu
ICE
CREAM
SPACE MAN
SPACE MAN
SPACE MAN
SPACE MAN

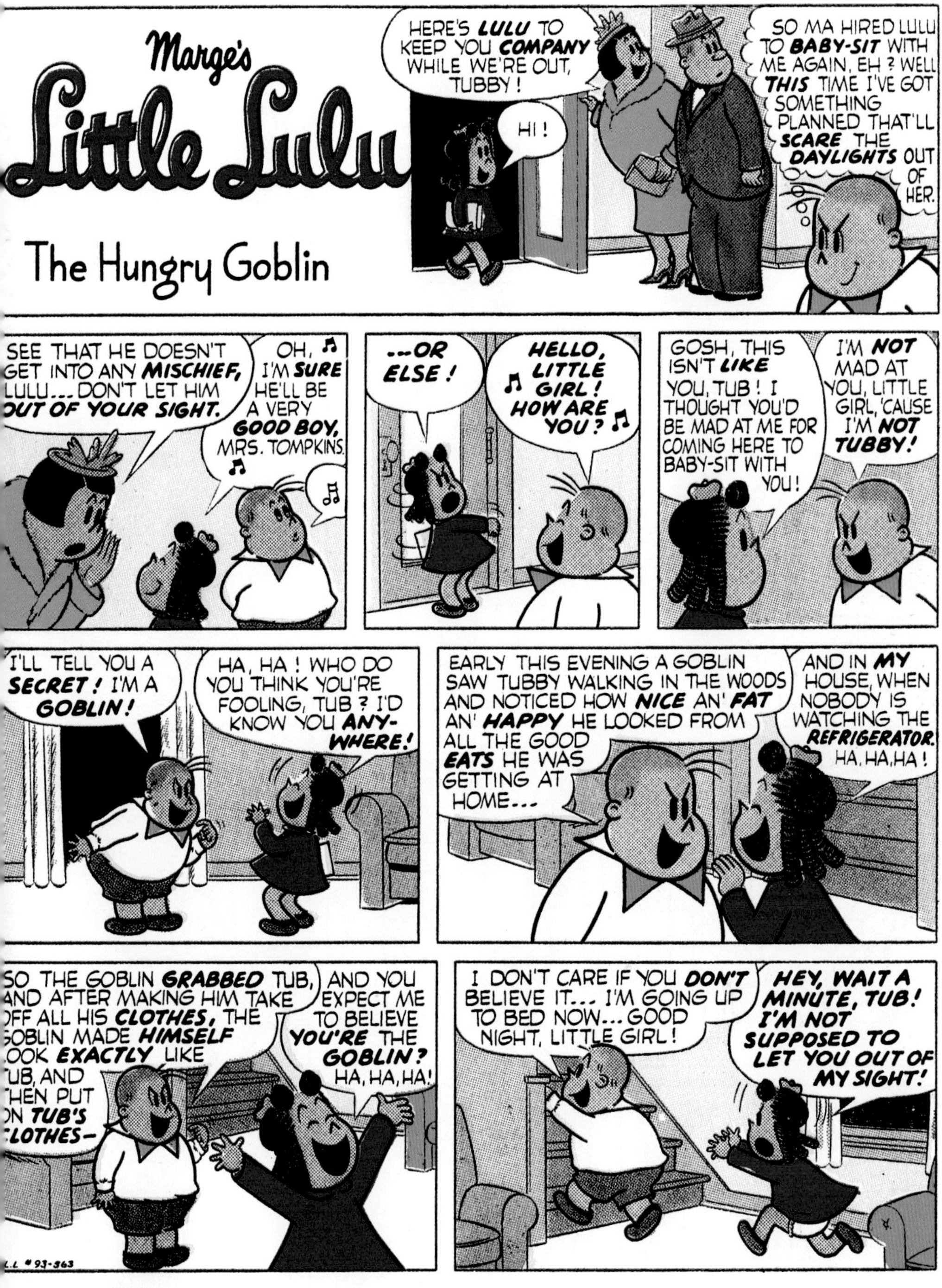
Marge's
Little Lulu
The Hungry Goblin
HERE'S LULU TO KEEP YOU COMPANY WHILE WE'RE OUT, TUBBY!
HI!
SO MA HIRED LULU TO BABY-SIT WITH ME AGAIN, EH? WELL THIS TIME I'VE GOT SOMETHING PLANNED THAT'LL SCARE THE DAYLIGHTS OUT OF HER.
SEE THAT HE DOESN'T GET INTO ANY MISCHIEF, LULU... DON'T LET HIM OUT OF YOUR SIGHT.
OH, I'M SURE HE'LL BE A VERY GOOD BOY, MRS. TOMPKINS.
...OR ELSE!
HELLO, LITTLE GIRL! HOW ARE YOU?
GOSH, THIS ISN'T LIKE YOU, TUB! I THOUGHT YOU'D BE MAD AT ME FOR COMING HERE TO BABY-SIT WITH YOU!
I'M NOT MAD AT YOU, LITTLE GIRL, 'CAUSE I'M NOT TUBBY!
I'LL TELL YOU A SECRET! I'M A GOBLIN!
HA, HA! WHO DO YOU THINK YOU'RE FOOLING, TUB? I'D KNOW YOU ANYWHERE!
EARLY THIS EVENING A GOBLIN SAW TUBBY WALKING IN THE WOODS AND NOTICED HOW NICE AN' FAT AN' HAPPY HE LOOKED FROM ALL THE GOOD EATS HE WAS GETTING AT HOME...
AND IN MY HOUSE, WHEN NOBODY IS WATCHING THE REFRIGERATOR! HA, HA, HA!
SO THE GOBLIN GRABBED TUB, AND AFTER MAKING HIM TAKE OFF ALL HIS CLOTHES, THE GOBLIN MADE HIMSELF LOOK EXACTLY LIKE TUB, AND THEN PUT ON TUB'S CLOTHES—
AND YOU EXPECT ME TO BELIEVE YOU'RE THE GOBLIN? HA, HA, HA!
I DON'T CARE IF YOU DON'T BELIEVE IT... I'M GOING UP TO BED NOW... GOOD NIGHT, LITTLE GIRL!
HEY, WAIT A MINUTE, TUB! I'M NOT SUPPOSED TO LET YOU OUT OF MY SIGHT!
L.L #93-363

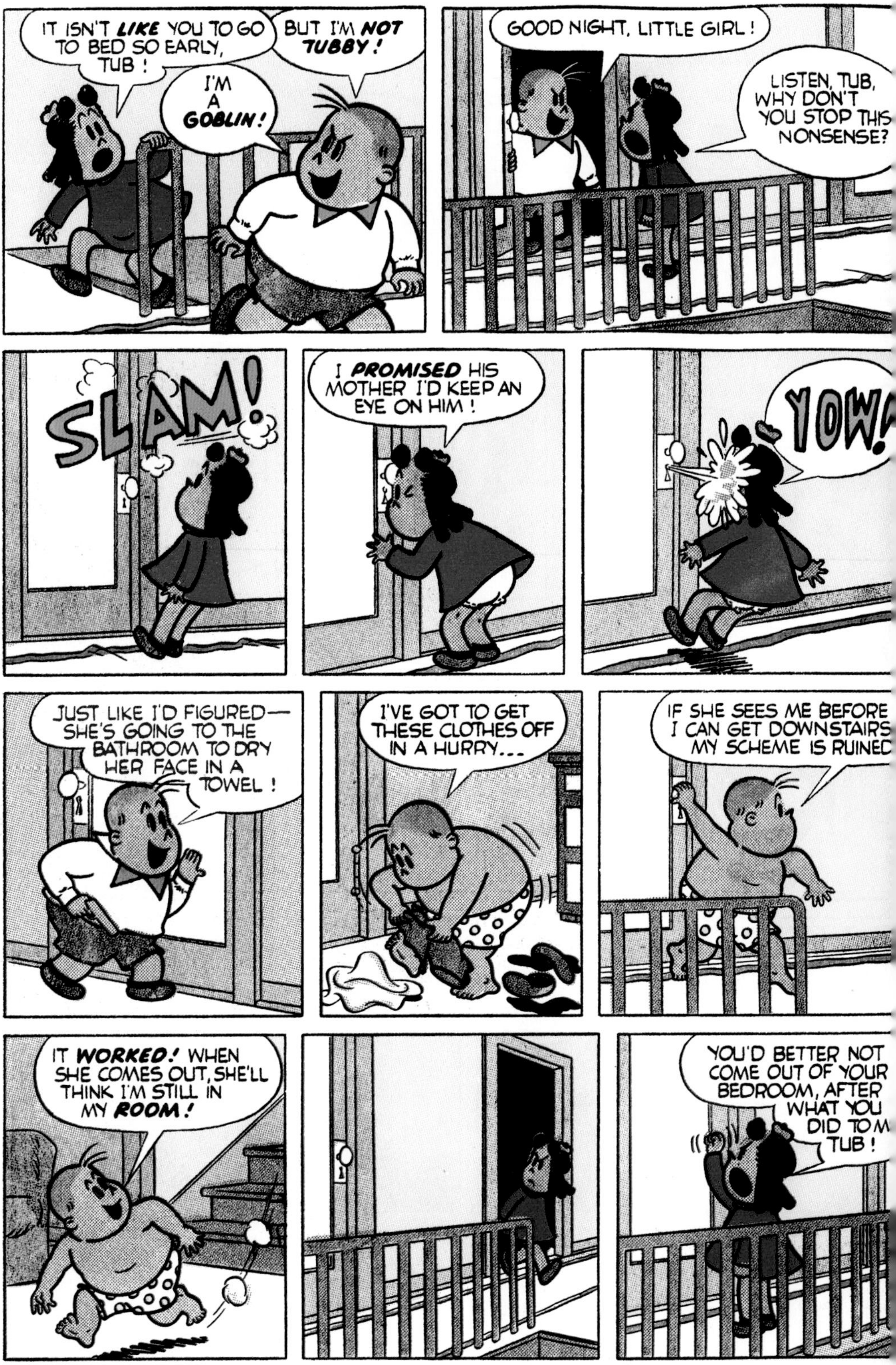
IT ISN'T **LIKE** YOU TO GO TO BED SO EARLY, TUB !
BUT I'M **NOT TUBBY !**
I'M A **GOBLIN !**
GOOD NIGHT, LITTLE GIRL !
LISTEN, TUB, WHY DON'T YOU STOP THIS NONSENSE?
SLAM!
I **PROMISED** HIS MOTHER I'D KEEP AN EYE ON HIM !
YOW!
JUST LIKE I'D FIGURED— SHE'S GOING TO THE BATHROOM TO DRY HER FACE IN A TOWEL !
I'VE GOT TO GET THESE CLOTHES OFF IN A HURRY...
IF SHE SEES ME BEFORE I CAN GET DOWNSTAIRS MY SCHEME IS RUINED
IT **WORKED!** WHEN SHE COMES OUT, SHE'LL THINK I'M STILL IN MY **ROOM !**
YOU'D BETTER NOT COME OUT OF YOUR BEDROOM, AFTER WHAT YOU DID TO M TUB !

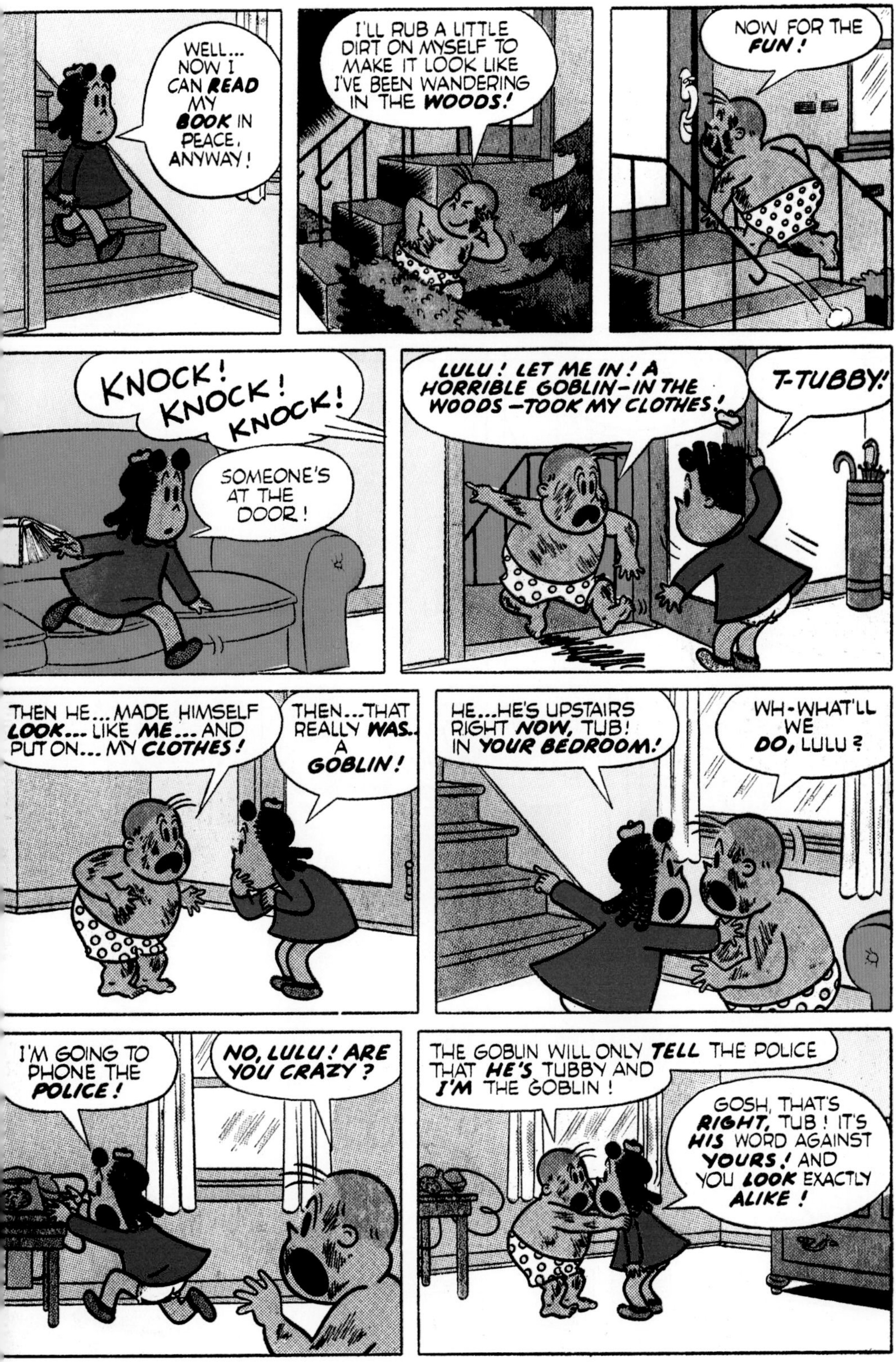
WELL... NOW I CAN READ MY BOOK IN PEACE, ANYWAY!
I'LL RUB A LITTLE DIRT ON MYSELF TO MAKE IT LOOK LIKE I'VE BEEN WANDERING IN THE WOODS!
NOW FOR THE FUN!
KNOCK! KNOCK! KNOCK!
SOMEONE'S AT THE DOOR!
LULU! LET ME IN! A HORRIBLE GOBLIN—IN THE WOODS—TOOK MY CLOTHES!
T-TUBBY!
THEN HE... MADE HIMSELF LOOK... LIKE ME... AND PUT ON... MY CLOTHES!
THEN... THAT REALLY WAS.. A GOBLIN!
HE... HE'S UPSTAIRS RIGHT NOW, TUB! IN YOUR BEDROOM!
WH-WHAT'LL WE DO, LULU?
I'M GOING TO PHONE THE POLICE!
NO, LULU! ARE YOU CRAZY?
THE GOBLIN WILL ONLY TELL THE POLICE THAT HE'S TUBBY AND I'M THE GOBLIN!
GOSH, THAT'S RIGHT, TUB! IT'S HIS WORD AGAINST YOURS! AND YOU LOOK EXACTLY ALIKE!

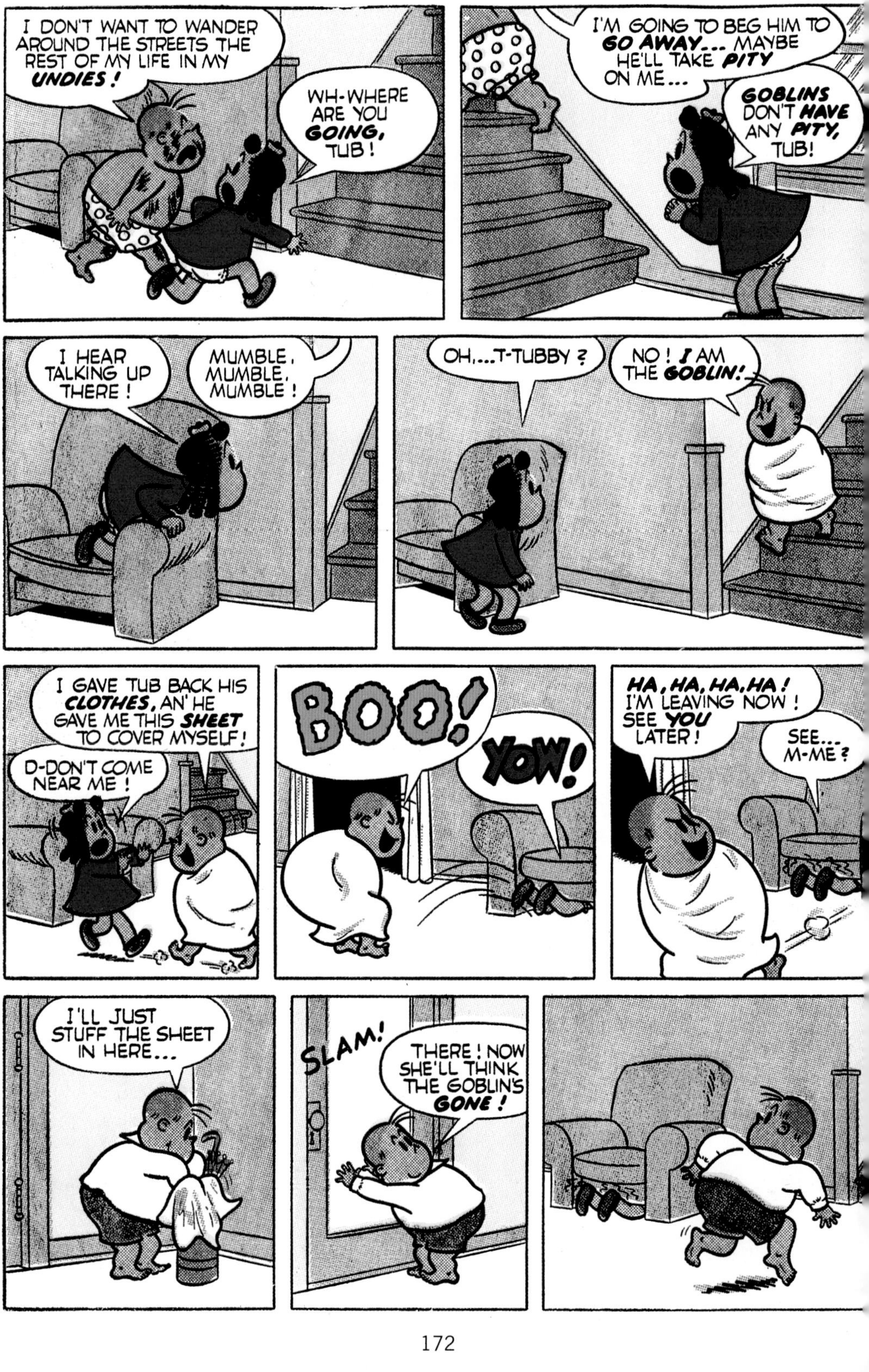

I DON'T WANT TO WANDER AROUND THE STREETS THE REST OF MY LIFE IN MY **UNDIES**!
WH-WHERE ARE YOU **GOING**, TUB!
I'M GOING TO BEG HIM TO **GO AWAY...** MAYBE HE'LL TAKE **PITY** ON ME...
**GOBLINS** DON'T **HAVE** ANY **PITY**, TUB!
I HEAR TALKING UP THERE!
MUMBLE, MUMBLE, MUMBLE!
OH,...T-TUBBY?
NO! **I** AM THE **GOBLIN!**
I GAVE TUB BACK HIS **CLOTHES**, AN' HE GAVE ME THIS **SHEET** TO COVER MYSELF!
D-DON'T COME NEAR ME!
BOO!
YOW!
**HA, HA, HA, HA!** I'M LEAVING NOW! SEE **YOU** LATER!
SEE... M-ME?
I'LL JUST STUFF THE SHEET IN HERE...
SLAM!
THERE! NOW SHE'LL THINK THE GOBLIN'S **GONE**!

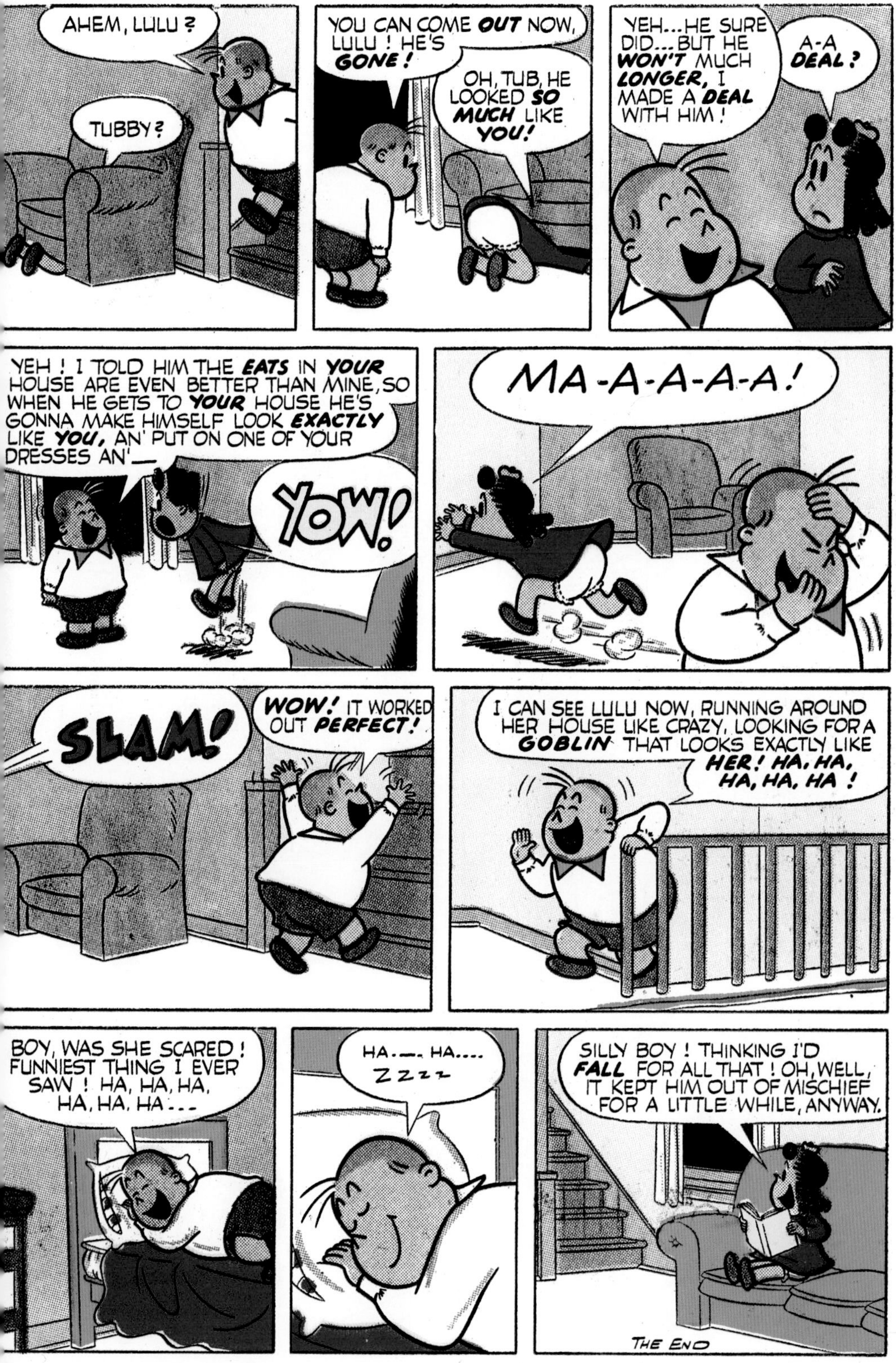
AHEM, LULU?
TUBBY?
YOU CAN COME OUT NOW, LULU! HE'S GONE!
OH, TUB, HE LOOKED SO MUCH LIKE YOU!
YEH...HE SURE DID...BUT HE WON'T MUCH LONGER, I MADE A DEAL WITH HIM!
A-A DEAL?
YEH! I TOLD HIM THE EATS IN YOUR HOUSE ARE EVEN BETTER THAN MINE, SO WHEN HE GETS TO YOUR HOUSE HE'S GONNA MAKE HIMSELF LOOK EXACTLY LIKE YOU, AN' PUT ON ONE OF YOUR DRESSES AN'—
YOW!
MA-A-A-A-A!
SLAM!
WOW! IT WORKED OUT PERFECT!
I CAN SEE LULU NOW, RUNNING AROUND HER HOUSE LIKE CRAZY, LOOKING FOR A GOBLIN THAT LOOKS EXACTLY LIKE HER! HA, HA, HA, HA, HA!
BOY, WAS SHE SCARED! FUNNIEST THING I EVER SAW! HA, HA, HA, HA, HA, HA...
HA.—.HA....
ZZZZ
SILLY BOY! THINKING I'D FALL FOR ALL THAT! OH, WELL, IT KEPT HIM OUT OF MISCHIEF FOR A LITTLE WHILE, ANYWAY.
THE END

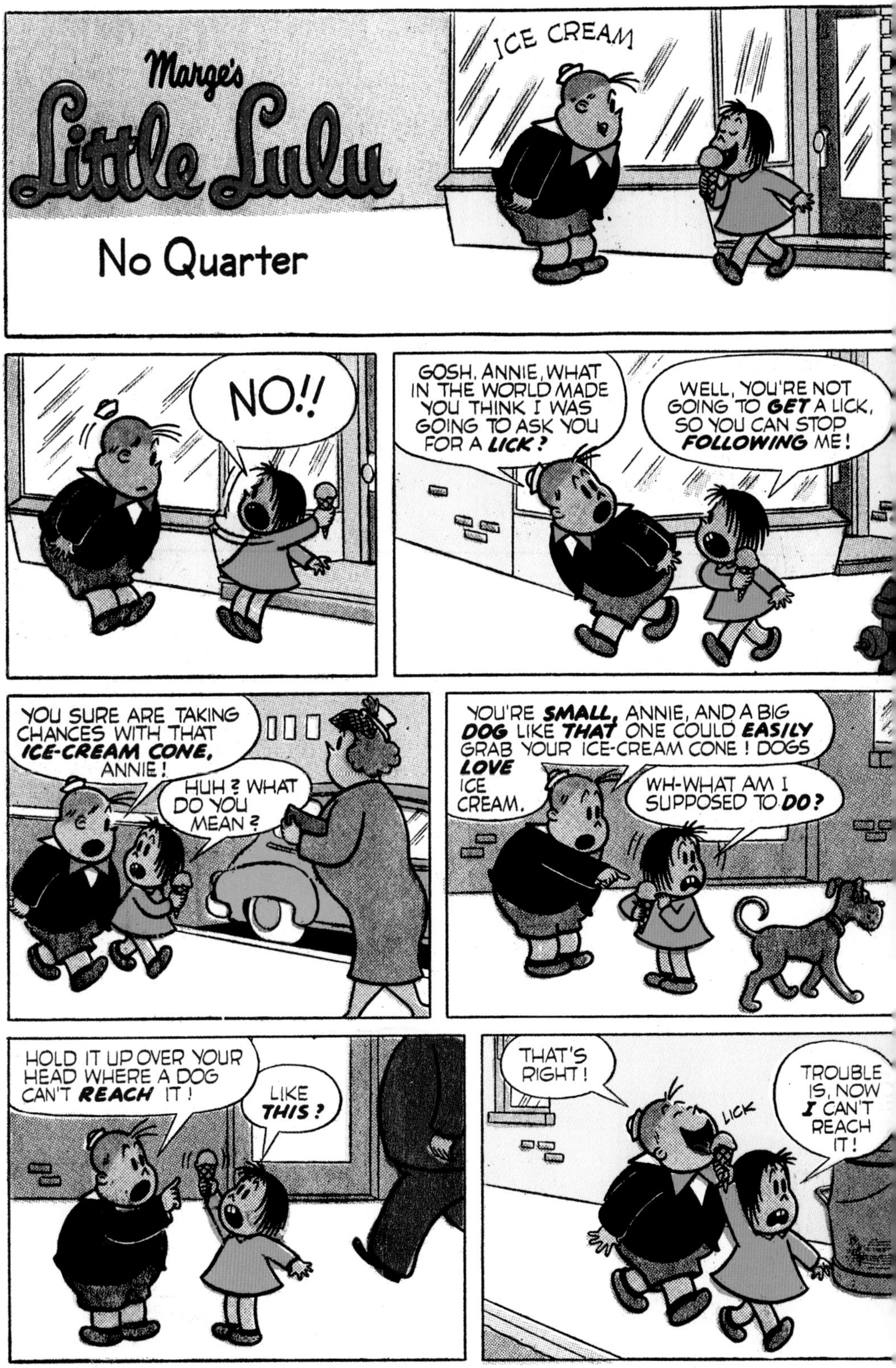
Marge's Little Lulu
No Quarter
ICE CREAM
NO!!
GOSH, ANNIE, WHAT IN THE WORLD MADE YOU THINK I WAS GOING TO ASK YOU FOR A LICK?
WELL, YOU'RE NOT GOING TO GET A LICK, SO YOU CAN STOP FOLLOWING ME!
YOU SURE ARE TAKING CHANCES WITH THAT ICE-CREAM CONE, ANNIE!
HUH? WHAT DO YOU MEAN?
YOU'RE SMALL, ANNIE, AND A BIG DOG LIKE THAT ONE COULD EASILY GRAB YOUR ICE-CREAM CONE! DOGS LOVE ICE CREAM.
WH-WHAT AM I SUPPOSED TO DO?
HOLD IT UP OVER YOUR HEAD WHERE A DOG CAN'T REACH IT!
LIKE THIS?
THAT'S RIGHT!
LICK
TROUBLE IS, NOW I CAN'T REACH IT!

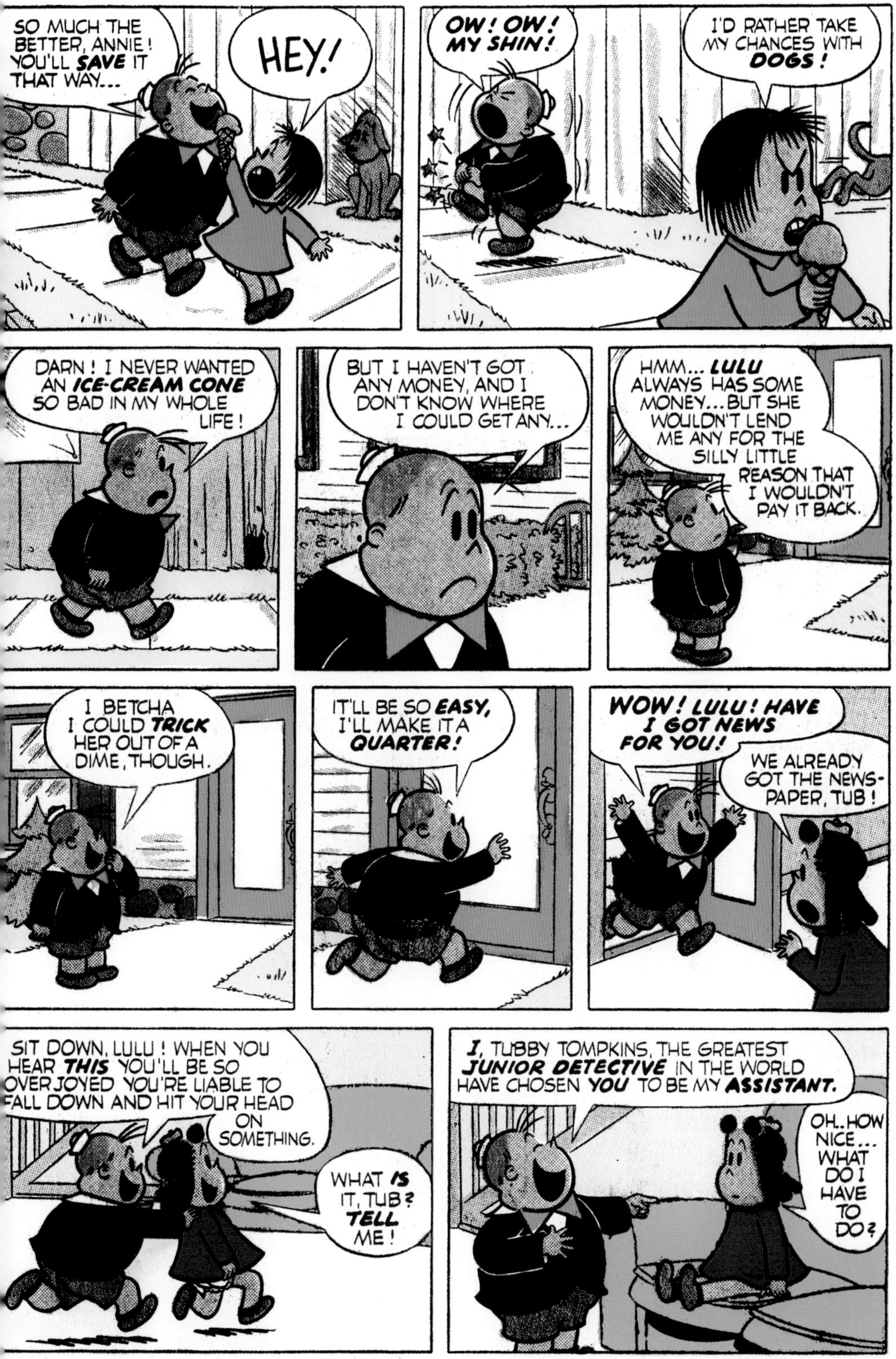
SO MUCH THE BETTER, ANNIE! YOU'LL SAVE IT THAT WAY...
HEY!
OW! OW! MY SHIN!
I'D RATHER TAKE MY CHANCES WITH DOGS!
DARN! I NEVER WANTED AN ICE-CREAM CONE SO BAD IN MY WHOLE LIFE!
BUT I HAVEN'T GOT ANY MONEY, AND I DON'T KNOW WHERE I COULD GET ANY...
HMM... LULU ALWAYS HAS SOME MONEY... BUT SHE WOULDN'T LEND ME ANY FOR THE SILLY LITTLE REASON THAT I WOULDN'T PAY IT BACK.
I BETCHA I COULD TRICK HER OUT OF A DIME, THOUGH.
IT'LL BE SO EASY, I'LL MAKE IT A QUARTER!
WOW! LULU! HAVE I GOT NEWS FOR YOU!
WE ALREADY GOT THE NEWS-PAPER, TUB!
SIT DOWN, LULU! WHEN YOU HEAR THIS YOU'LL BE SO OVERJOYED YOU'RE LIABLE TO FALL DOWN AND HIT YOUR HEAD ON SOMETHING.
WHAT IS IT, TUB? TELL ME!
I, TUBBY TOMPKINS, THE GREATEST JUNIOR DETECTIVE IN THE WORLD HAVE CHOSEN YOU TO BE MY ASSISTANT.
OH..HOW NICE... WHAT DO I HAVE TO DO?

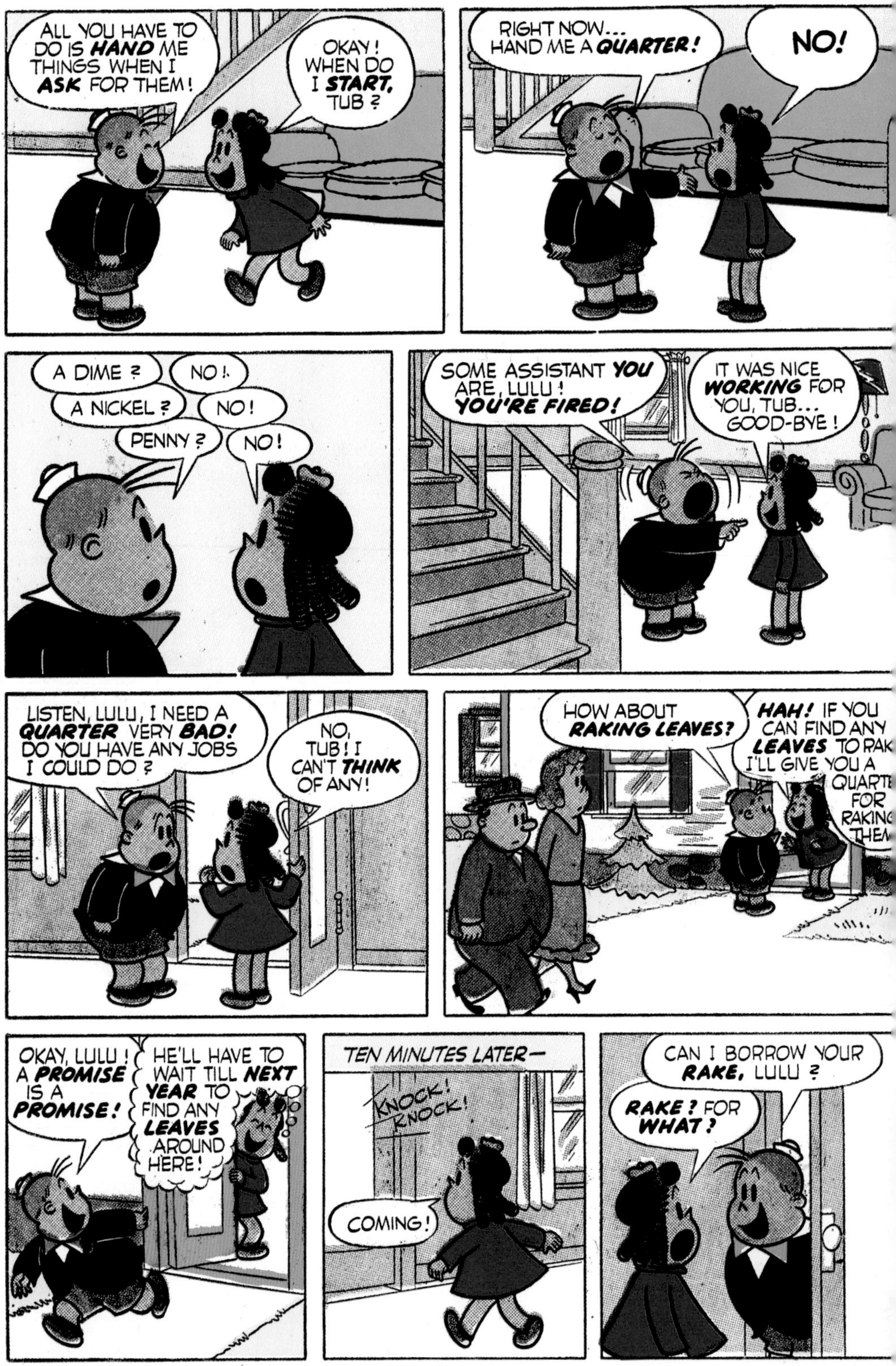
ALL YOU HAVE TO DO IS **HAND** ME THINGS WHEN I **ASK** FOR THEM!
OKAY! WHEN DO I **START,** TUB?
RIGHT NOW... HAND ME A **QUARTER!**
NO!
A DIME?
NO!
A NICKEL?
NO!
PENNY?
NO!
SOME ASSISTANT **YOU** ARE, LULU! **YOU'RE FIRED!**
IT WAS NICE **WORKING** FOR YOU, TUB... GOOD-BYE!
LISTEN, LULU, I NEED A **QUARTER** VERY **BAD!** DO YOU HAVE ANY JOBS I COULD DO?
NO, TUB! I CAN'T **THINK** OF ANY!
HOW ABOUT **RAKING LEAVES?**
**HAH!** IF YOU CAN FIND ANY **LEAVES** TO RAK I'LL GIVE YOU A QUARTE FOR RAKING THEM
OKAY, LULU! A **PROMISE** IS A **PROMISE!**
HE'LL HAVE TO WAIT TILL **NEXT YEAR** TO FIND ANY **LEAVES** AROUND HERE!
TEN MINUTES LATER—
KNOCK! KNOCK!
COMING!
CAN I BORROW YOUR **RAKE,** LULU?
**RAKE?** FOR **WHAT?**

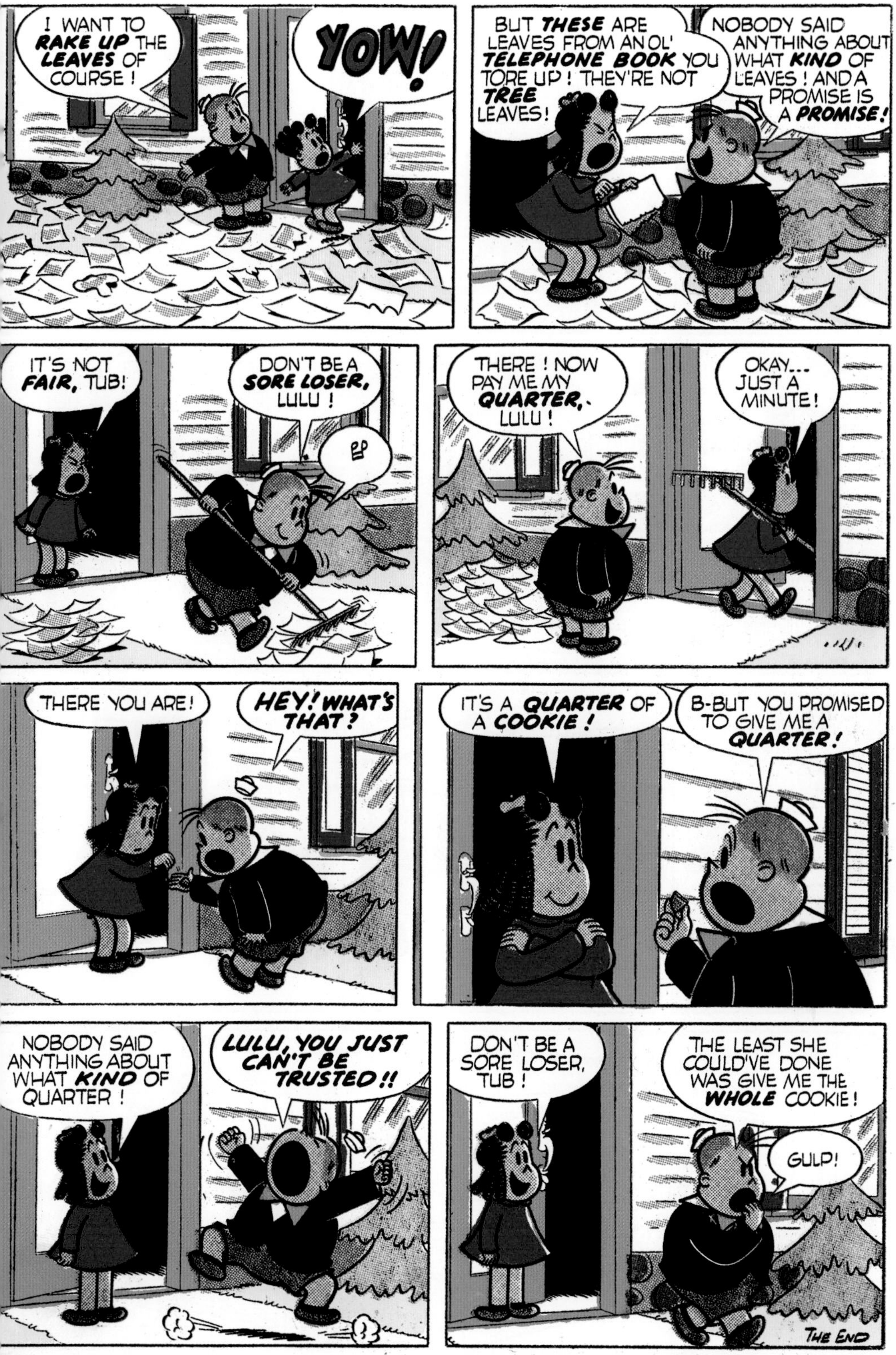
I WANT TO RAKE UP THE LEAVES OF COURSE!
YOW!
BUT THESE ARE LEAVES FROM AN OL' TELEPHONE BOOK YOU TORE UP! THEY'RE NOT TREE LEAVES!
NOBODY SAID ANYTHING ABOUT WHAT KIND OF LEAVES! AND A PROMISE IS A PROMISE!
IT'S NOT FAIR, TUB!
DON'T BE A SORE LOSER, LULU!
THERE! NOW PAY ME MY QUARTER, LULU!
OKAY... JUST A MINUTE!
THERE YOU ARE!
HEY! WHAT'S THAT?
IT'S A QUARTER OF A COOKIE!
B-BUT YOU PROMISED TO GIVE ME A QUARTER!
NOBODY SAID ANYTHING ABOUT WHAT KIND OF QUARTER!
LULU, YOU JUST CAN'T BE TRUSTED!!
DON'T BE A SORE LOSER, TUB!
THE LEAST SHE COULD'VE DONE WAS GIVE ME THE WHOLE COOKIE!
GULP!
THE END

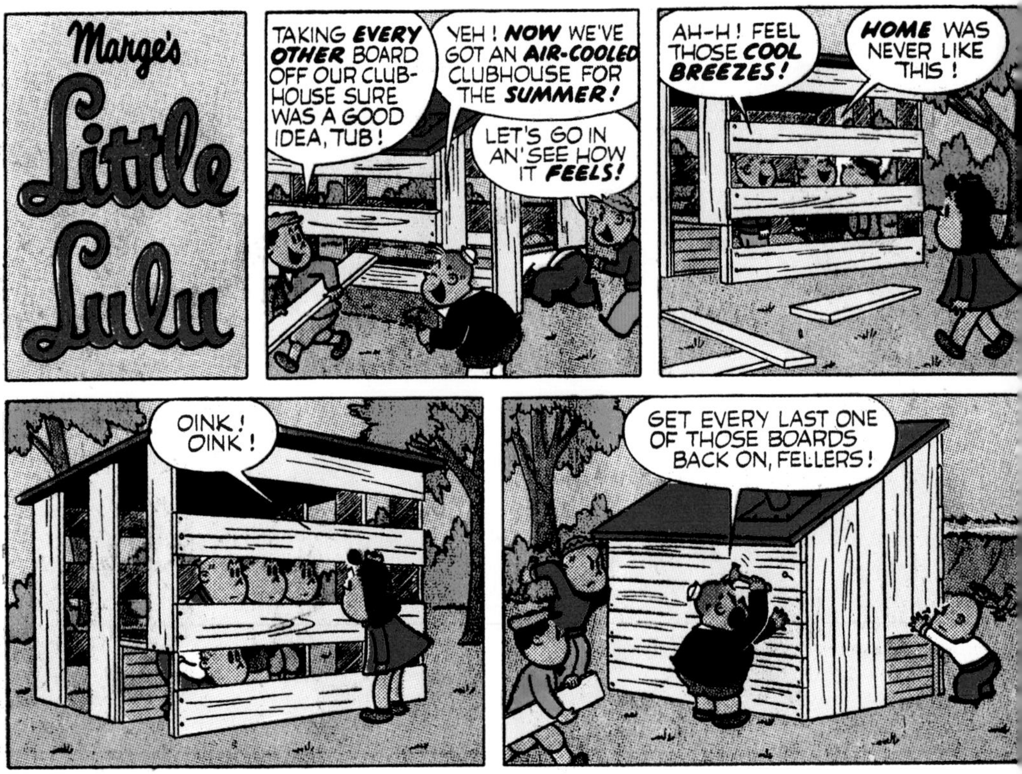
Marge's
Little Lulu
TAKING EVERY OTHER BOARD OFF OUR CLUB-HOUSE SURE WAS A GOOD IDEA, TUB!
YEH! NOW WE'VE GOT AN AIR-COOLED CLUBHOUSE FOR THE SUMMER!
LET'S GO IN AN' SEE HOW IT FEELS!
AH-H! FEEL THOSE COOL BREEZES!
HOME WAS NEVER LIKE THIS!
OINK! OINK!
GET EVERY LAST ONE OF THOSE BOARDS BACK ON, FELLERS!

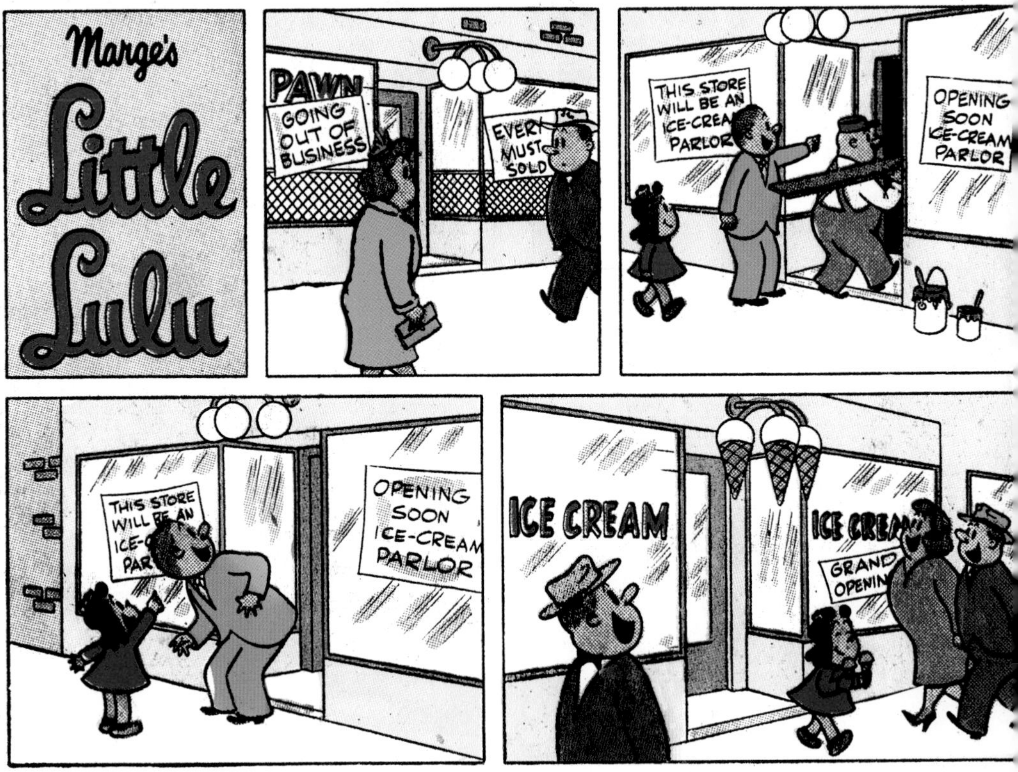
Marge's
Little Lulu
PAWN
GOING OUT OF BUSINESS
EVERY
MUST
SOLD
THIS STORE WILL BE AN ICE-CREA
PARLOR
OPENING SOON ICE-CREAM PARLOR
THIS STORE WILL BE AN
ICE-
PAR
OPENING SOON ICE-CREAM PARLOR
ICE CREAM
ICE CREA
GRAND OPENIN

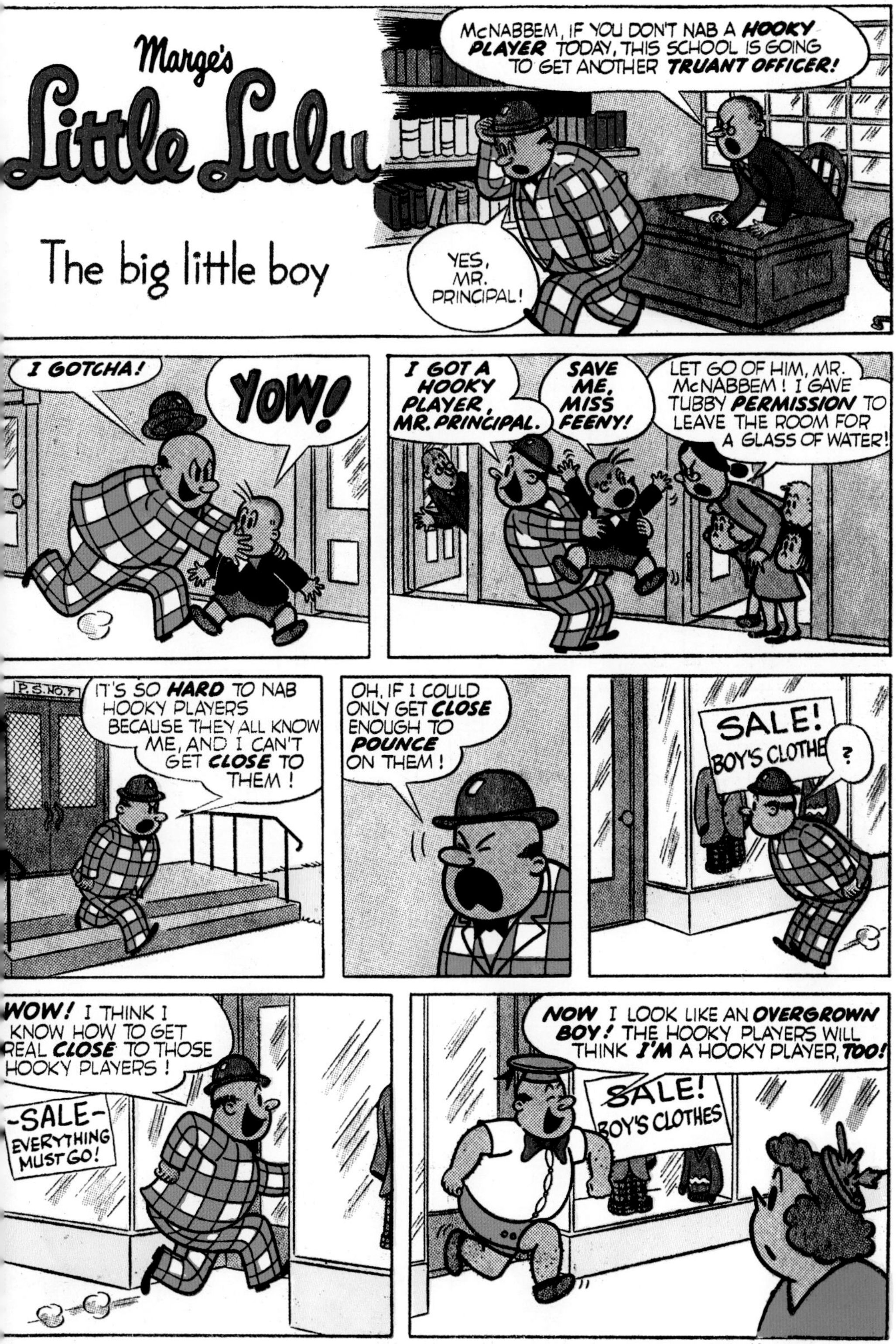
Marge's
Little Lulu
The big little boy
McNABBEM, IF YOU DON'T NAB A HOOKY PLAYER TODAY, THIS SCHOOL IS GOING TO GET ANOTHER TRUANT OFFICER!
YES, MR. PRINCIPAL!
I GOTCHA!
YOW!
I GOT A HOOKY PLAYER, MR. PRINCIPAL.
SAVE ME, MISS FEENY!
LET GO OF HIM, MR. McNABBEM! I GAVE TUBBY PERMISSION TO LEAVE THE ROOM FOR A GLASS OF WATER!
P.S. NO.7
IT'S SO HARD TO NAB HOOKY PLAYERS BECAUSE THEY ALL KNOW ME, AND I CAN'T GET CLOSE TO THEM!
OH, IF I COULD ONLY GET CLOSE ENOUGH TO POUNCE ON THEM!
SALE! BOY'S CLOTHE
?
WOW! I THINK I KNOW HOW TO GET REAL CLOSE TO THOSE HOOKY PLAYERS!
-SALE- EVERYTHING MUST GO!
NOW I LOOK LIKE AN OVERGROWN BOY! THE HOOKY PLAYERS WILL THINK I'M A HOOKY PLAYER, TOO!
SALE! BOY'S CLOTHES

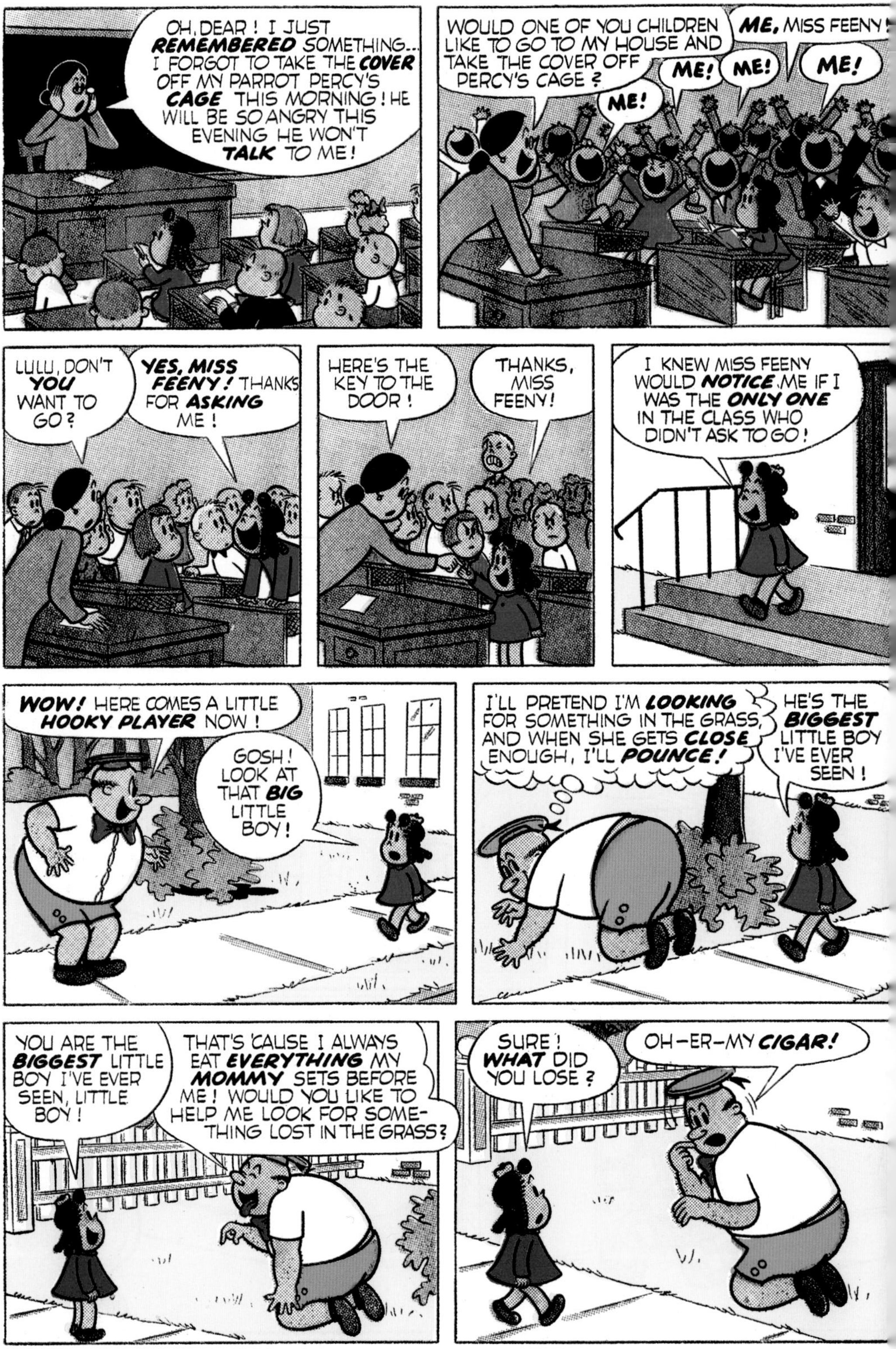
OH, DEAR! I JUST REMEMBERED SOMETHING... I FORGOT TO TAKE THE COVER OFF MY PARROT PERCY'S CAGE THIS MORNING! HE WILL BE SO ANGRY THIS EVENING HE WON'T TALK TO ME!
WOULD ONE OF YOU CHILDREN LIKE TO GO TO MY HOUSE AND TAKE THE COVER OFF PERCY'S CAGE?
ME, MISS FEENY!
ME!
ME!
ME!
ME!
LULU, DON'T YOU WANT TO GO?
YES, MISS FEENY! THANKS FOR ASKING ME!
HERE'S THE KEY TO THE DOOR!
THANKS, MISS FEENY!
I KNEW MISS FEENY WOULD NOTICE ME IF I WAS THE ONLY ONE IN THE CLASS WHO DIDN'T ASK TO GO!
WOW! HERE COMES A LITTLE HOOKY PLAYER NOW!
GOSH! LOOK AT THAT BIG LITTLE BOY!
I'LL PRETEND I'M LOOKING FOR SOMETHING IN THE GRASS, AND WHEN SHE GETS CLOSE ENOUGH, I'LL POUNCE!
HE'S THE BIGGEST LITTLE BOY I'VE EVER SEEN!
YOU ARE THE BIGGEST LITTLE BOY I'VE EVER SEEN, LITTLE BOY!
THAT'S 'CAUSE I ALWAYS EAT EVERYTHING MY MOMMY SETS BEFORE ME! WOULD YOU LIKE TO HELP ME LOOK FOR SOMETHING LOST IN THE GRASS?
SURE! WHAT DID YOU LOSE?
OH—ER—MY CIGAR!

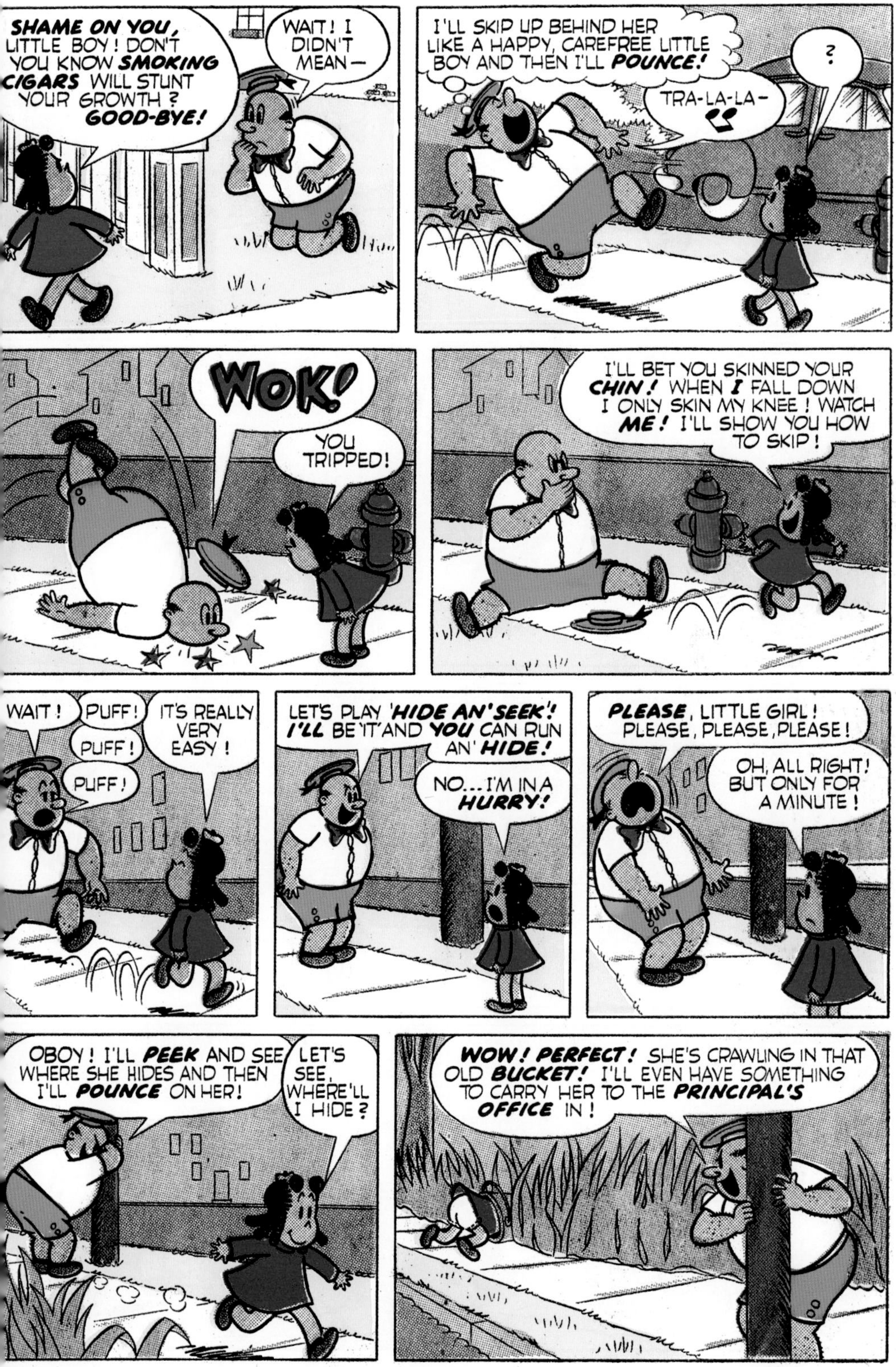
SHAME ON YOU, LITTLE BOY! DON'T YOU KNOW SMOKING CIGARS WILL STUNT YOUR GROWTH? GOOD-BYE!
WAIT! I DIDN'T MEAN—
I'LL SKIP UP BEHIND HER LIKE A HAPPY, CAREFREE LITTLE BOY AND THEN I'LL POUNCE!
TRA-LA-LA—
?
WOK!
YOU TRIPPED!
I'LL BET YOU SKINNED YOUR CHIN! WHEN I FALL DOWN I ONLY SKIN MY KNEE! WATCH ME! I'LL SHOW YOU HOW TO SKIP!
WAIT!
PUFF!
PUFF!
PUFF!
IT'S REALLY VERY EASY!
LET'S PLAY 'HIDE AN' SEEK'! I'LL BE 'IT' AND YOU CAN RUN AN' HIDE!
NO...I'M IN A HURRY!
PLEASE, LITTLE GIRL! PLEASE, PLEASE, PLEASE!
OH, ALL RIGHT! BUT ONLY FOR A MINUTE!
OBOY! I'LL PEEK AND SEE WHERE SHE HIDES AND THEN I'LL POUNCE ON HER!
LET'S SEE, WHERE'LL I HIDE?
WOW! PERFECT! SHE'S CRAWLING IN THAT OLD BUCKET! I'LL EVEN HAVE SOMETHING TO CARRY HER TO THE PRINCIPAL'S OFFICE IN!

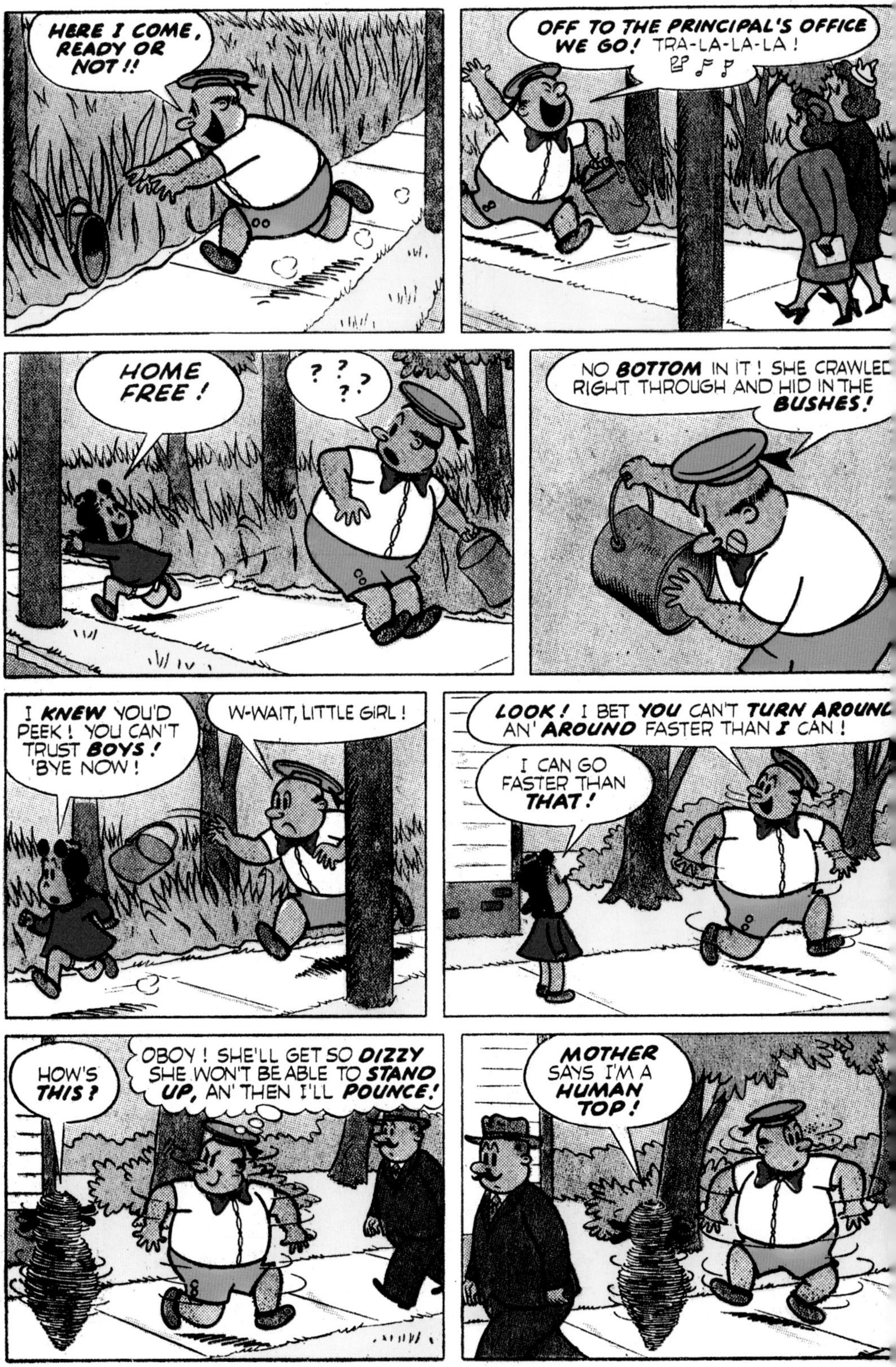
HERE I COME, READY OR NOT!!
OFF TO THE PRINCIPAL'S OFFICE WE GO! TRA-LA-LA-LA!
HOME FREE!
? ? ? ?
NO BOTTOM IN IT! SHE CRAWLED RIGHT THROUGH AND HID IN THE BUSHES!
I KNEW YOU'D PEEK! YOU CAN'T TRUST BOYS! 'BYE NOW!
W-WAIT, LITTLE GIRL!
LOOK! I BET YOU CAN'T TURN AROUND AN' AROUND FASTER THAN I CAN!
I CAN GO FASTER THAN THAT!
HOW'S THIS?
OBOY! SHE'LL GET SO DIZZY SHE WON'T BE ABLE TO STAND UP, AN' THEN I'LL POUNCE!
MOTHER SAYS I'M A HUMAN TOP!

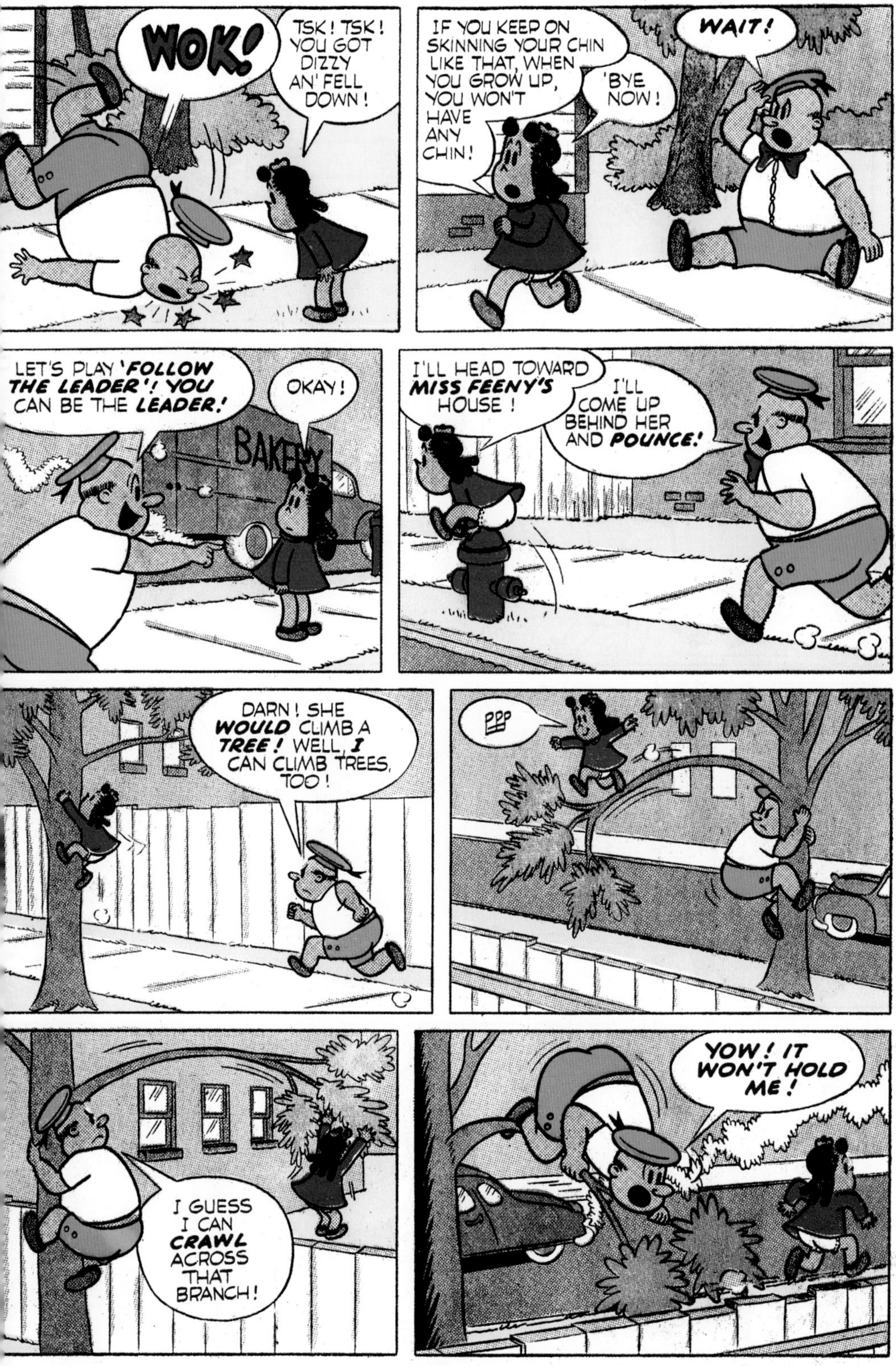
WOK!
TSK! TSK! YOU GOT DIZZY AN' FELL DOWN!
IF YOU KEEP ON SKINNING YOUR CHIN LIKE THAT, WHEN YOU GROW UP, YOU WON'T HAVE ANY CHIN!
'BYE NOW!
WAIT!
LET'S PLAY 'FOLLOW THE LEADER'! YOU CAN BE THE LEADER!
OKAY!
BAKERY
I'LL HEAD TOWARD MISS FEENY'S HOUSE!
I'LL COME UP BEHIND HER AND POUNCE!
DARN! SHE WOULD CLIMB A TREE! WELL, I CAN CLIMB TREES, TOO!
I GUESS I CAN CRAWL ACROSS THAT BRANCH!
YOW! IT WON'T HOLD ME!

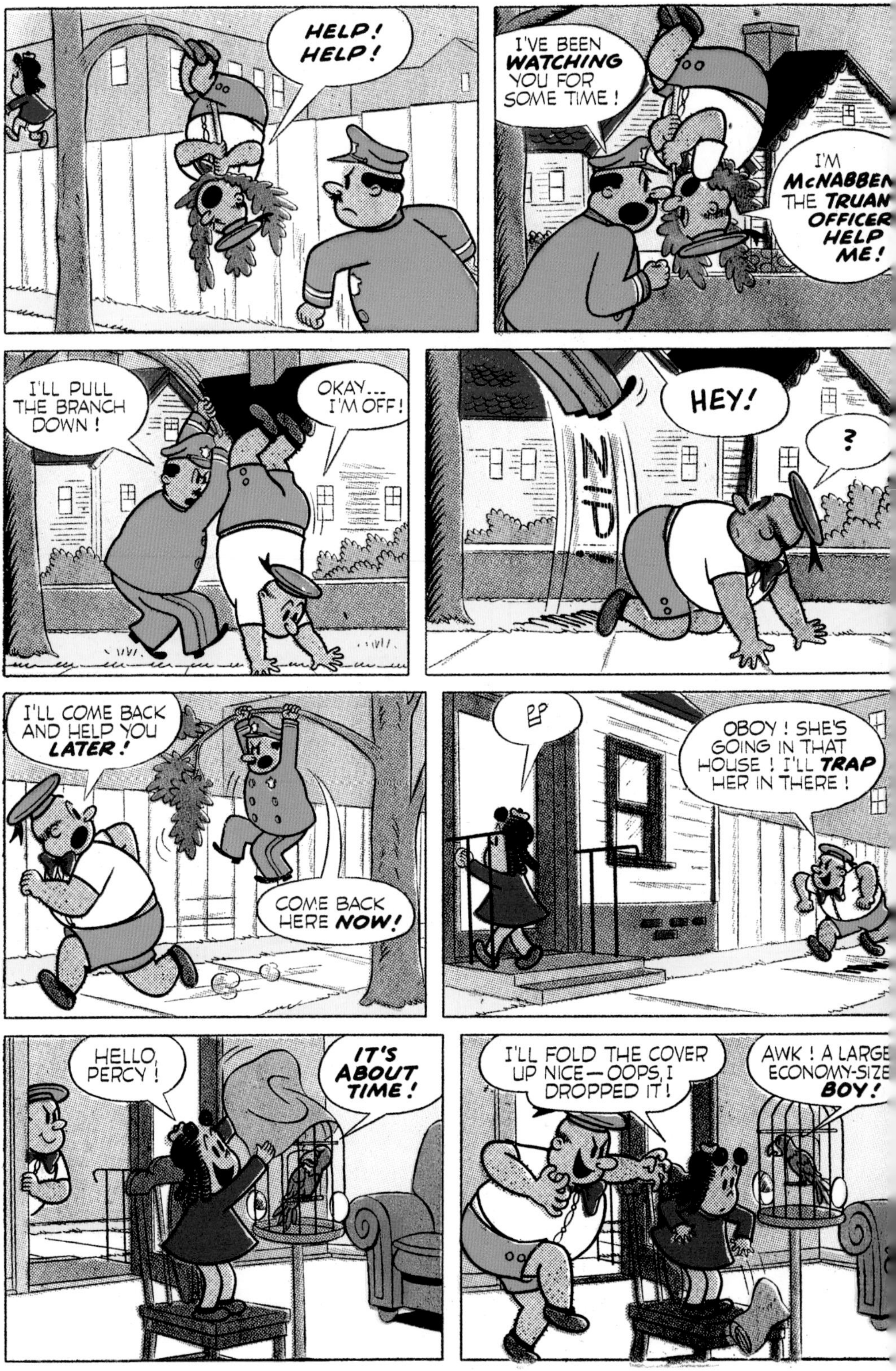
HELP! HELP!
I'VE BEEN WATCHING YOU FOR SOME TIME!
I'M McNABBEN THE TRUAN OFFICER HELP ME!
I'LL PULL THE BRANCH DOWN!
OKAY... I'M OFF!
HEY!
ZIP
?
I'LL COME BACK AND HELP YOU LATER!
COME BACK HERE NOW!
OBOY! SHE'S GOING IN THAT HOUSE! I'LL TRAP HER IN THERE!
HELLO, PERCY!
IT'S ABOUT TIME!
I'LL FOLD THE COVER UP NICE—OOPS, I DROPPED IT!
AWK! A LARGE ECONOMY-SIZE BOY!

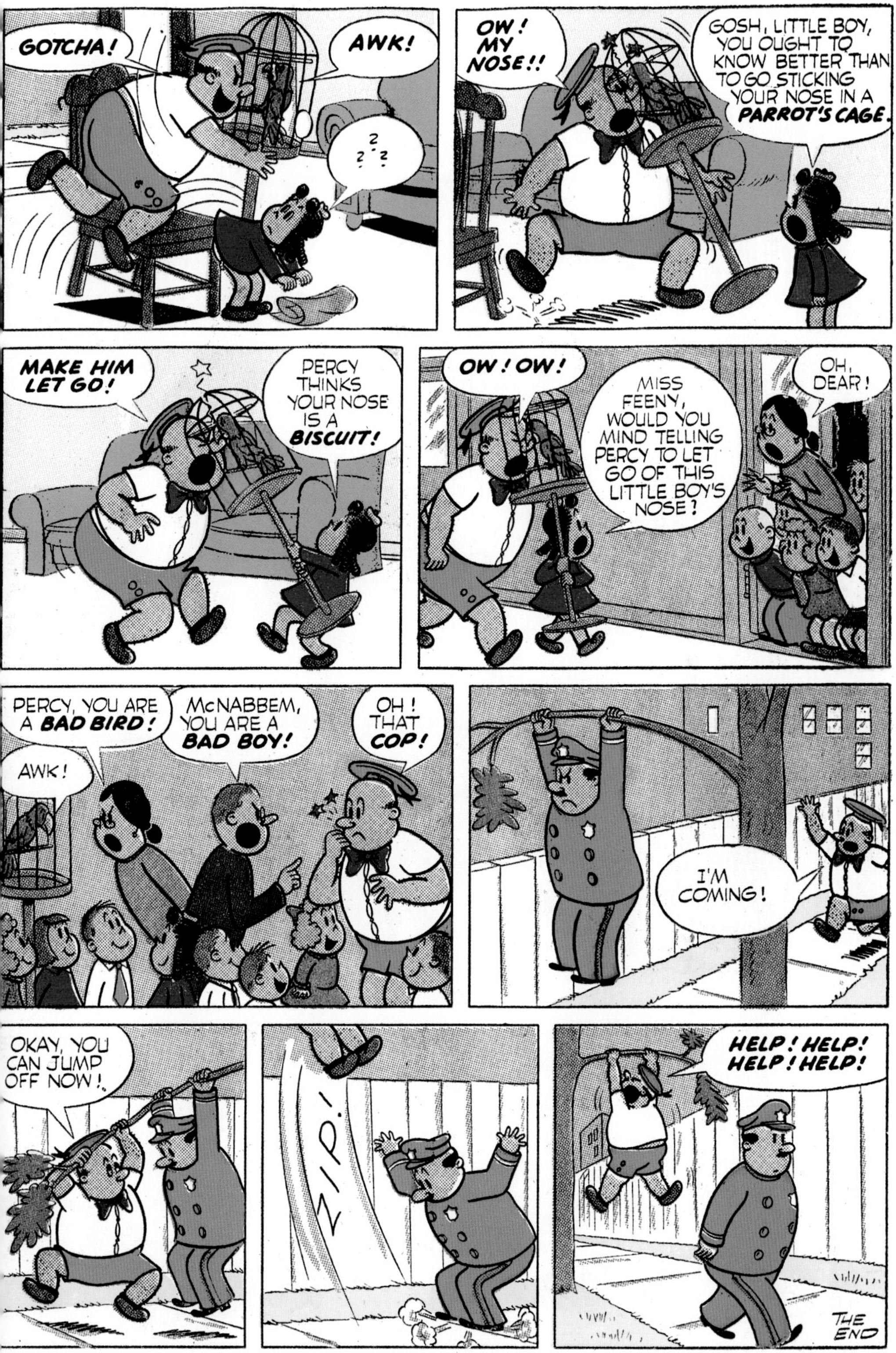
GOTCHA!
AWK!
Z Z Z
OW! MY NOSE!!
GOSH, LITTLE BOY, YOU OUGHT TO KNOW BETTER THAN TO GO STICKING YOUR NOSE IN A PARROT'S CAGE.
MAKE HIM LET GO!
PERCY THINKS YOUR NOSE IS A BISCUIT!
OW! OW!
MISS FEENY, WOULD YOU MIND TELLING PERCY TO LET GO OF THIS LITTLE BOY'S NOSE?
OH, DEAR!
PERCY, YOU ARE A BAD BIRD!
AWK!
McNABBEM, YOU ARE A BAD BOY!
OH! THAT COP!
I'M COMING!
OKAY, YOU CAN JUMP OFF NOW!
ZIP!
HELP! HELP! HELP! HELP!
THE END

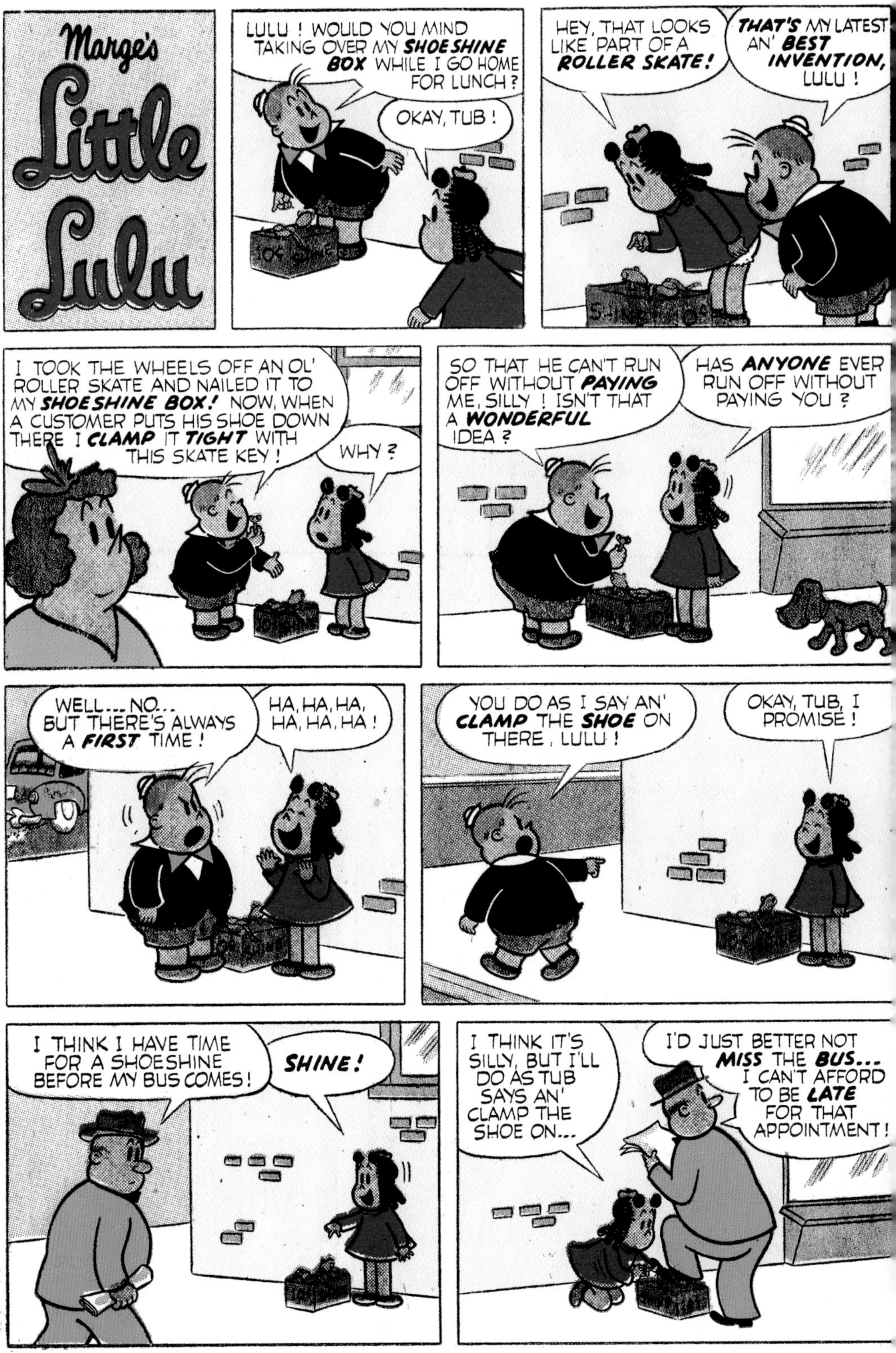
Marge's Little Lulu
LULU ! WOULD YOU MIND TAKING OVER MY SHOESHINE BOX WHILE I GO HOME FOR LUNCH ?
OKAY, TUB !
HEY, THAT LOOKS LIKE PART OF A ROLLER SKATE !
THAT'S MY LATEST AN' BEST INVENTION, LULU !
I TOOK THE WHEELS OFF AN OL' ROLLER SKATE AND NAILED IT TO MY SHOESHINE BOX! NOW, WHEN A CUSTOMER PUTS HIS SHOE DOWN THERE I CLAMP IT TIGHT WITH THIS SKATE KEY !
WHY ?
SO THAT HE CAN'T RUN OFF WITHOUT PAYING ME, SILLY ! ISN'T THAT A WONDERFUL IDEA ?
HAS ANYONE EVER RUN OFF WITHOUT PAYING YOU ?
WELL... NO... BUT THERE'S ALWAYS A FIRST TIME !
HA, HA, HA, HA, HA, HA !
YOU DO AS I SAY AN' CLAMP THE SHOE ON THERE, LULU !
OKAY, TUB, I PROMISE !
I THINK I HAVE TIME FOR A SHOESHINE BEFORE MY BUS COMES !
SHINE !
I THINK IT'S SILLY, BUT I'LL DO AS TUB SAYS AN' CLAMP THE SHOE ON...
I'D JUST BETTER NOT MISS THE BUS... I CAN'T AFFORD TO BE LATE FOR THAT APPOINTMENT !

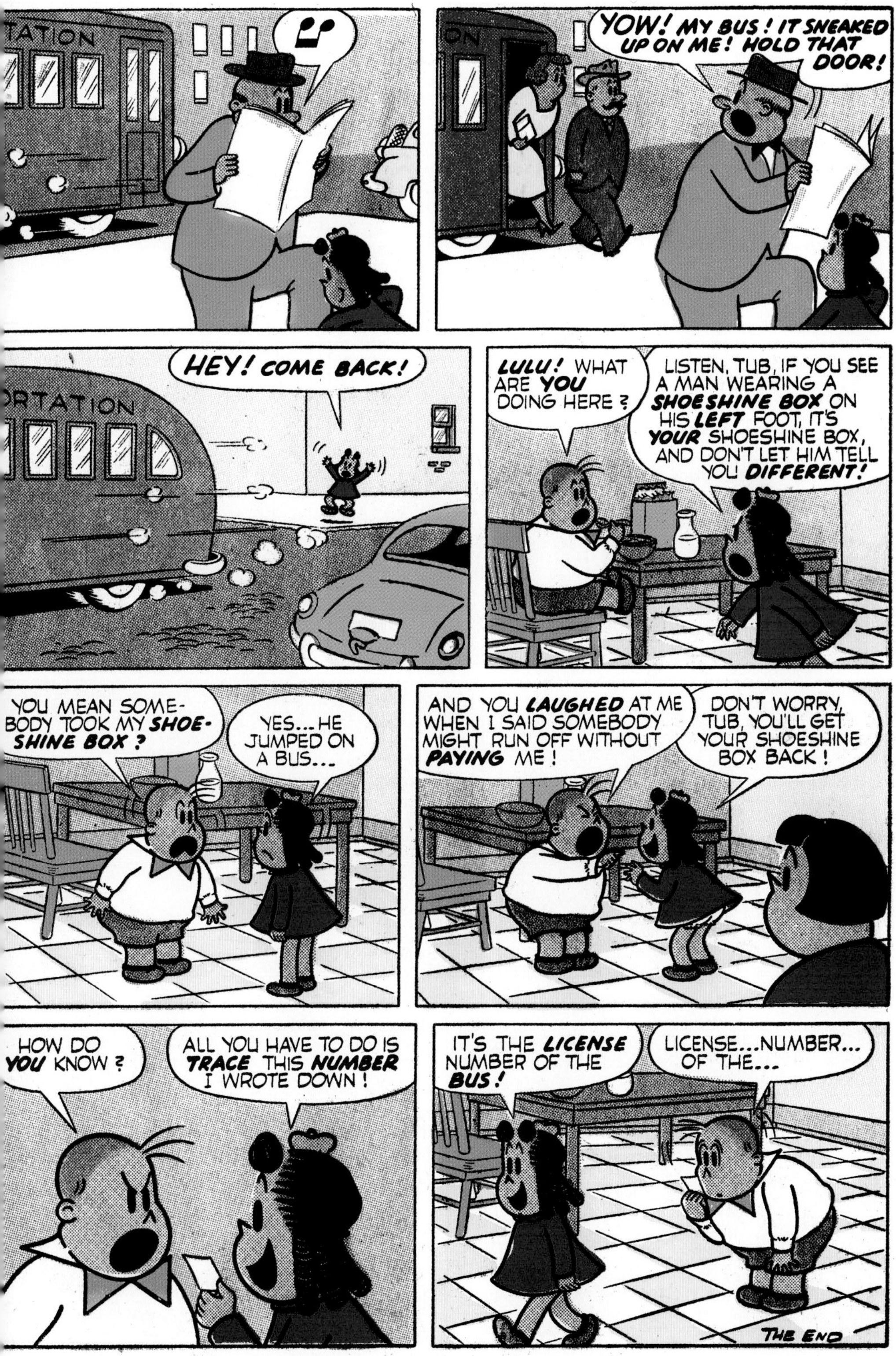
TATION
YOW! MY BUS! IT SNEAKED UP ON ME! HOLD THAT DOOR!
RTATION
HEY! COME BACK!
LULU! WHAT ARE YOU DOING HERE?
LISTEN, TUB, IF YOU SEE A MAN WEARING A SHOESHINE BOX ON HIS LEFT FOOT, IT'S YOUR SHOESHINE BOX, AND DON'T LET HIM TELL YOU DIFFERENT!
YOU MEAN SOMEBODY TOOK MY SHOESHINE BOX?
YES... HE JUMPED ON A BUS...
AND YOU LAUGHED AT ME WHEN I SAID SOMEBODY MIGHT RUN OFF WITHOUT PAYING ME!
DON'T WORRY, TUB, YOU'LL GET YOUR SHOESHINE BOX BACK!
HOW DO YOU KNOW?
ALL YOU HAVE TO DO IS TRACE THIS NUMBER I WROTE DOWN!
IT'S THE LICENSE NUMBER OF THE BUS!
LICENSE...NUMBER... OF THE...
THE END

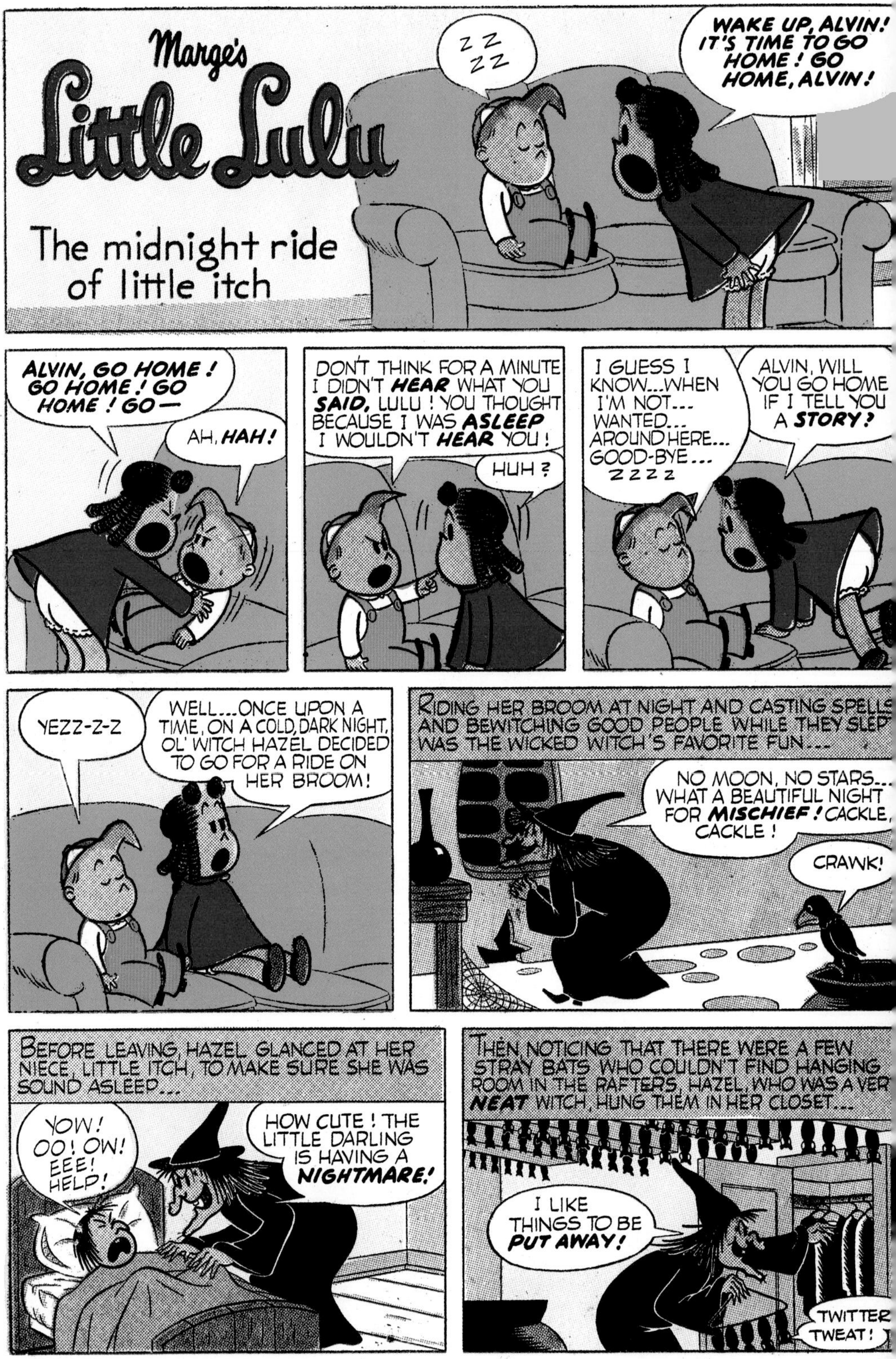
Marge's Little Lulu
The midnight ride of little itch
Z Z Z Z
WAKE UP, ALVIN! IT'S TIME TO GO HOME! GO HOME, ALVIN!
ALVIN, GO HOME! GO HOME! GO HOME! GO—
AH, HAH!
DON'T THINK FOR A MINUTE I DIDN'T HEAR WHAT YOU SAID, LULU! YOU THOUGHT BECAUSE I WAS ASLEEP I WOULDN'T HEAR YOU!
HUH?
I GUESS I KNOW...WHEN I'M NOT... WANTED... AROUND HERE... GOOD-BYE... ZZZZ
ALVIN, WILL YOU GO HOME IF I TELL YOU A STORY?
YEZZ-Z-Z
WELL...ONCE UPON A TIME, ON A COLD, DARK NIGHT, OL' WITCH HAZEL DECIDED TO GO FOR A RIDE ON HER BROOM!
RIDING HER BROOM AT NIGHT AND CASTING SPELLS AND BEWITCHING GOOD PEOPLE WHILE THEY SLEPT WAS THE WICKED WITCH'S FAVORITE FUN...
NO MOON, NO STARS... WHAT A BEAUTIFUL NIGHT FOR MISCHIEF! CACKLE, CACKLE!
CRAWK!
BEFORE LEAVING, HAZEL GLANCED AT HER NIECE, LITTLE ITCH, TO MAKE SURE SHE WAS SOUND ASLEEP...
YOW! OO! OW! EEE! HELP!
HOW CUTE! THE LITTLE DARLING IS HAVING A NIGHTMARE!
THEN NOTICING THAT THERE WERE A FEW STRAY BATS WHO COULDN'T FIND HANGING ROOM IN THE RAFTERS, HAZEL, WHO WAS A VERY NEAT WITCH, HUNG THEM IN HER CLOSET...
I LIKE THINGS TO BE PUT AWAY!
TWITTER TWEAT!

SATISFIED THAT EVERYTHING WAS IN ORDER, HAZEL JUMPED ON HER MAGIC BROOM AND FLEW OUT INTO THE NIGHT!

I'LL TERRIFY THE TOWN TONIGHT! CACKLE, CACKLE!

NO SOONER HAD HAZEL DISAPPEARED, WHEN LITTLE ITCH, WHO HAD PRETENDED TO BE ASLEEP, LEAPED OUT OF BED AND QUICKLY PUT ON HER CLOTHES...

WHY SHOULD **AUNTIE** HAVE ALL THE FUN?

**I'M** GOING OUT, TOO!

TREMBLING WITH EXCITEMENT, THE LITTLE WITCH JUMPED ON HER OWN LITTLE MAGIC BROOM...

I'LL GET BACK EARLY AND AUNTIE WILL NEVER KNOW I'VE BEEN OUT!

THEN, LIKE AN ARROW SHE SHOT OUT THE WINDOW...

TWITTER!

ZIP!

OW!

A SECOND LATER SHE WAS LYING FLAT ON THE GROUND, WITH A BIG LUMP ON HER HEAD...

**DARN TREE! WHY DID YOU HAVE TO GROW IN MY WAY?**

WHEN SHE FINALLY CLIMBED BACK ON HER BROOM, LITTLE ITCH WAS IN A VERY UGLY MOOD INDEED...

I CAN'T GET **EVEN** WITH A **TREE**, SO I'LL FIND A **HUMAN BEAN** TO GET EVEN WITH!

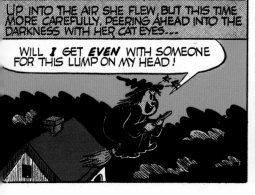

UP INTO THE AIR SHE FLEW, BUT THIS TIME MORE CAREFULLY, PEERING AHEAD INTO THE DARKNESS WITH HER CAT EYES...

WILL **I** GET **EVEN** WITH SOMEONE FOR THIS LUMP ON MY HEAD!

SILENTLY, HIGH ABOVE THE TREETOPS, SHE FLEW TOWARD THE DISTANT SLEEPING TOWN...

I'LL FIND A LITTLE GIRL ABOUT MY OWN SIZE... NO, A LITTLE **SMALLER**.

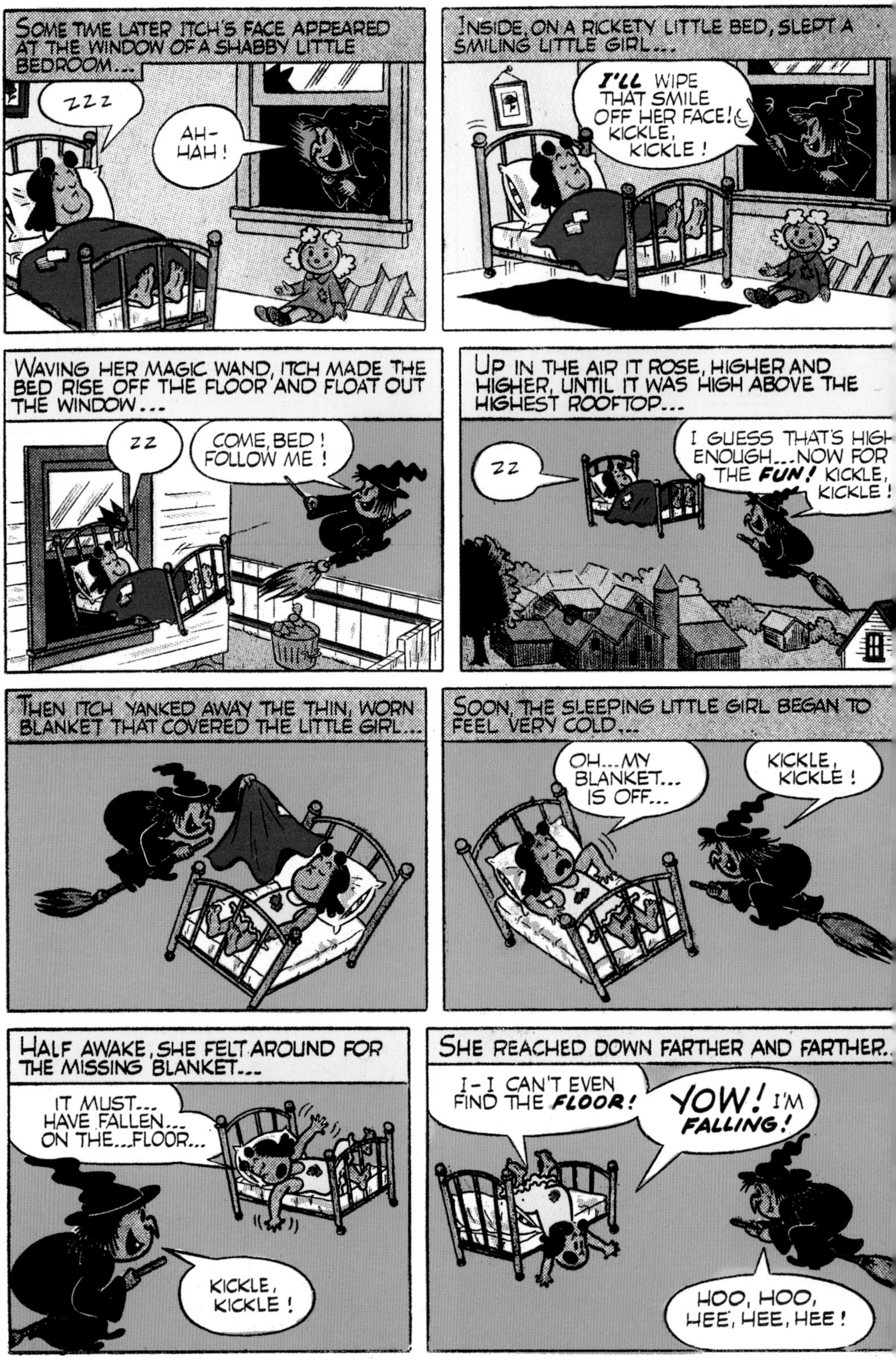
SOME TIME LATER ITCH'S FACE APPEARED AT THE WINDOW OF A SHABBY LITTLE BEDROOM...
ZZZ
AH-HAH!
INSIDE, ON A RICKETY LITTLE BED, SLEPT A SMILING LITTLE GIRL...
I'LL WIPE THAT SMILE OFF HER FACE! KICKLE, KICKLE!
WAVING HER MAGIC WAND, ITCH MADE THE BED RISE OFF THE FLOOR AND FLOAT OUT THE WINDOW...
ZZ
COME, BED! FOLLOW ME!
UP IN THE AIR IT ROSE, HIGHER AND HIGHER, UNTIL IT WAS HIGH ABOVE THE HIGHEST ROOFTOP...
ZZ
I GUESS THAT'S HIGH ENOUGH...NOW FOR THE FUN! KICKLE, KICKLE!
THEN ITCH YANKED AWAY THE THIN, WORN BLANKET THAT COVERED THE LITTLE GIRL...
SOON, THE SLEEPING LITTLE GIRL BEGAN TO FEEL VERY COLD...
OH...MY BLANKET... IS OFF...
KICKLE, KICKLE!
HALF AWAKE, SHE FELT AROUND FOR THE MISSING BLANKET...
IT MUST... HAVE FALLEN... ON THE...FLOOR...
KICKLE, KICKLE!
SHE REACHED DOWN FARTHER AND FARTHER...
I-I CAN'T EVEN FIND THE FLOOR!
YOW! I'M FALLING!
HOO, HOO, HEE, HEE, HEE!

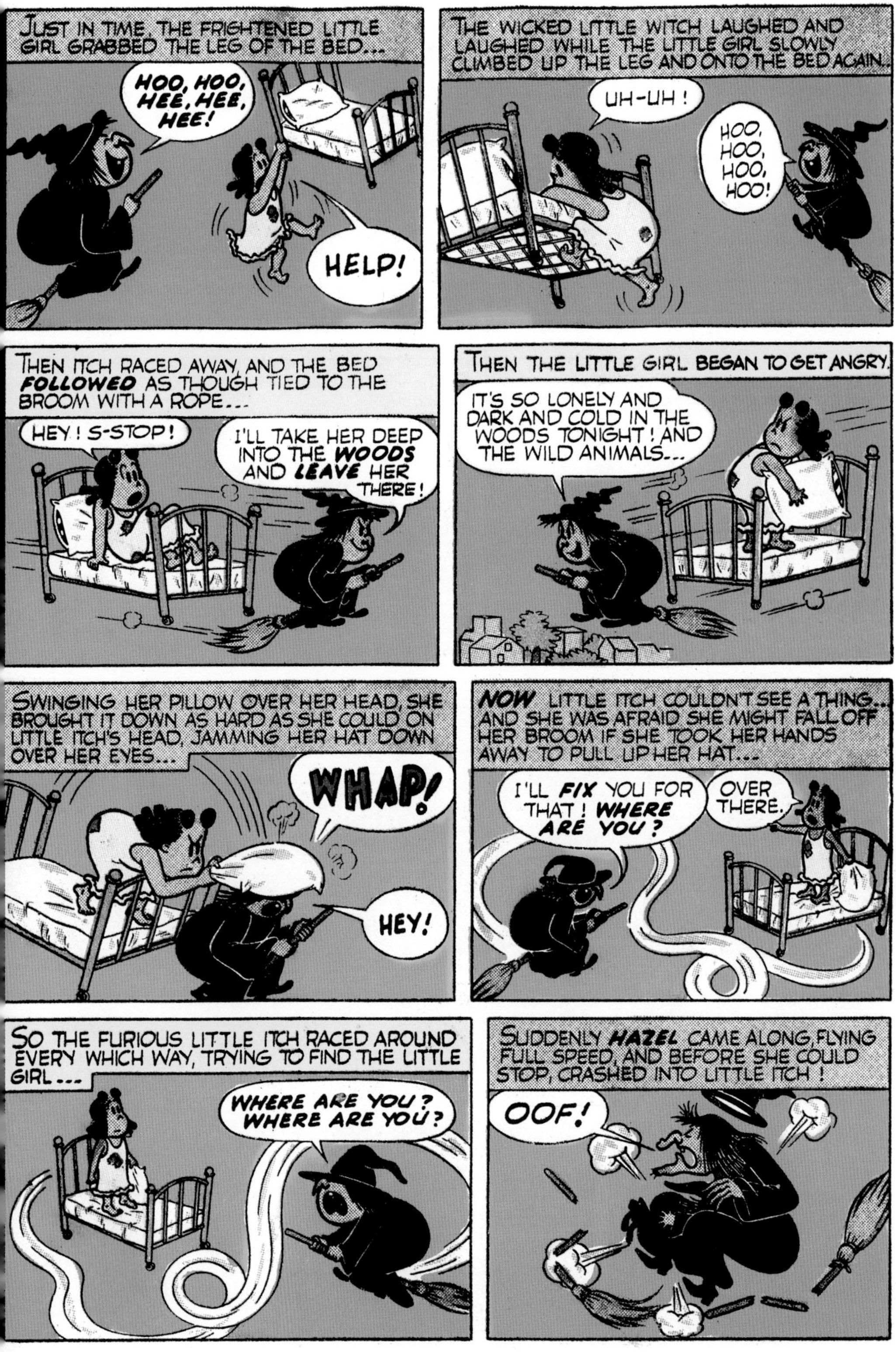
JUST IN TIME, THE FRIGHTENED LITTLE GIRL GRABBED THE LEG OF THE BED...
HOO, HOO, HEE, HEE, HEE!
HELP!
THE WICKED LITTLE WITCH LAUGHED AND LAUGHED WHILE THE LITTLE GIRL SLOWLY CLIMBED UP THE LEG AND ONTO THE BED AGAIN...
UH-UH!
HOO, HOO, HOO, HOO, HOO!
THEN ITCH RACED AWAY, AND THE BED FOLLOWED AS THOUGH TIED TO THE BROOM WITH A ROPE...
HEY! S-STOP!
I'LL TAKE HER DEEP INTO THE WOODS AND LEAVE HER THERE!
THEN THE LITTLE GIRL BEGAN TO GET ANGRY.
IT'S SO LONELY AND DARK AND COLD IN THE WOODS TONIGHT! AND THE WILD ANIMALS...
SWINGING HER PILLOW OVER HER HEAD, SHE BROUGHT IT DOWN AS HARD AS SHE COULD ON LITTLE ITCH'S HEAD, JAMMING HER HAT DOWN OVER HER EYES...
WHAP!
HEY!
NOW LITTLE ITCH COULDN'T SEE A THING... AND SHE WAS AFRAID SHE MIGHT FALL OFF HER BROOM IF SHE TOOK HER HANDS AWAY TO PULL UP HER HAT...
I'LL FIX YOU FOR THAT! WHERE ARE YOU?
OVER THERE.
SO THE FURIOUS LITTLE ITCH RACED AROUND EVERY WHICH WAY, TRYING TO FIND THE LITTLE GIRL...
WHERE ARE YOU? WHERE ARE YOU?
SUDDENLY HAZEL CAME ALONG, FLYING FULL SPEED, AND BEFORE SHE COULD STOP, CRASHED INTO LITTLE ITCH!
OOF!

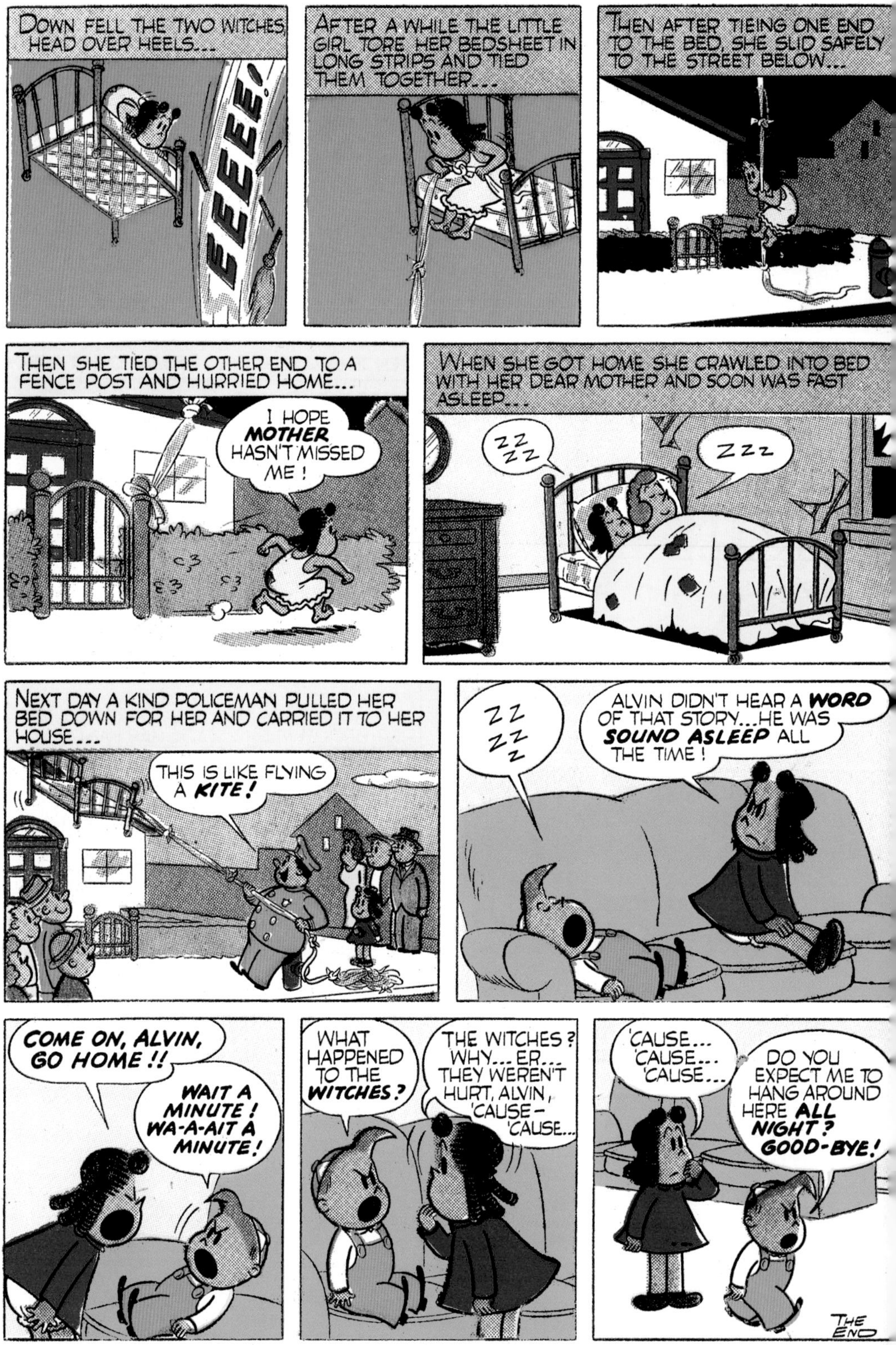
DOWN FELL THE TWO WITCHES HEAD OVER HEELS...
EEEEE!
AFTER A WHILE THE LITTLE GIRL TORE HER BEDSHEET IN LONG STRIPS AND TIED THEM TOGETHER...
THEN AFTER TIEING ONE END TO THE BED, SHE SLID SAFELY TO THE STREET BELOW...
THEN SHE TIED THE OTHER END TO A FENCE POST AND HURRIED HOME...
I HOPE MOTHER HASN'T MISSED ME!
WHEN SHE GOT HOME SHE CRAWLED INTO BED WITH HER DEAR MOTHER AND SOON WAS FAST ASLEEP...
Z Z Z Z
Z Z Z
NEXT DAY A KIND POLICEMAN PULLED HER BED DOWN FOR HER AND CARRIED IT TO HER HOUSE...
THIS IS LIKE FLYING A KITE!
Z Z Z Z Z
ALVIN DIDN'T HEAR A WORD OF THAT STORY...HE WAS SOUND ASLEEP ALL THE TIME!
COME ON, ALVIN, GO HOME!!
WAIT A MINUTE! WA-A-AIT A MINUTE!
WHAT HAPPENED TO THE WITCHES?
THE WITCHES? WHY... ER... THEY WEREN'T HURT, ALVIN, 'CAUSE— 'CAUSE...
'CAUSE... 'CAUSE... 'CAUSE...
DO YOU EXPECT ME TO HANG AROUND HERE ALL NIGHT? GOOD-BYE!
THE END

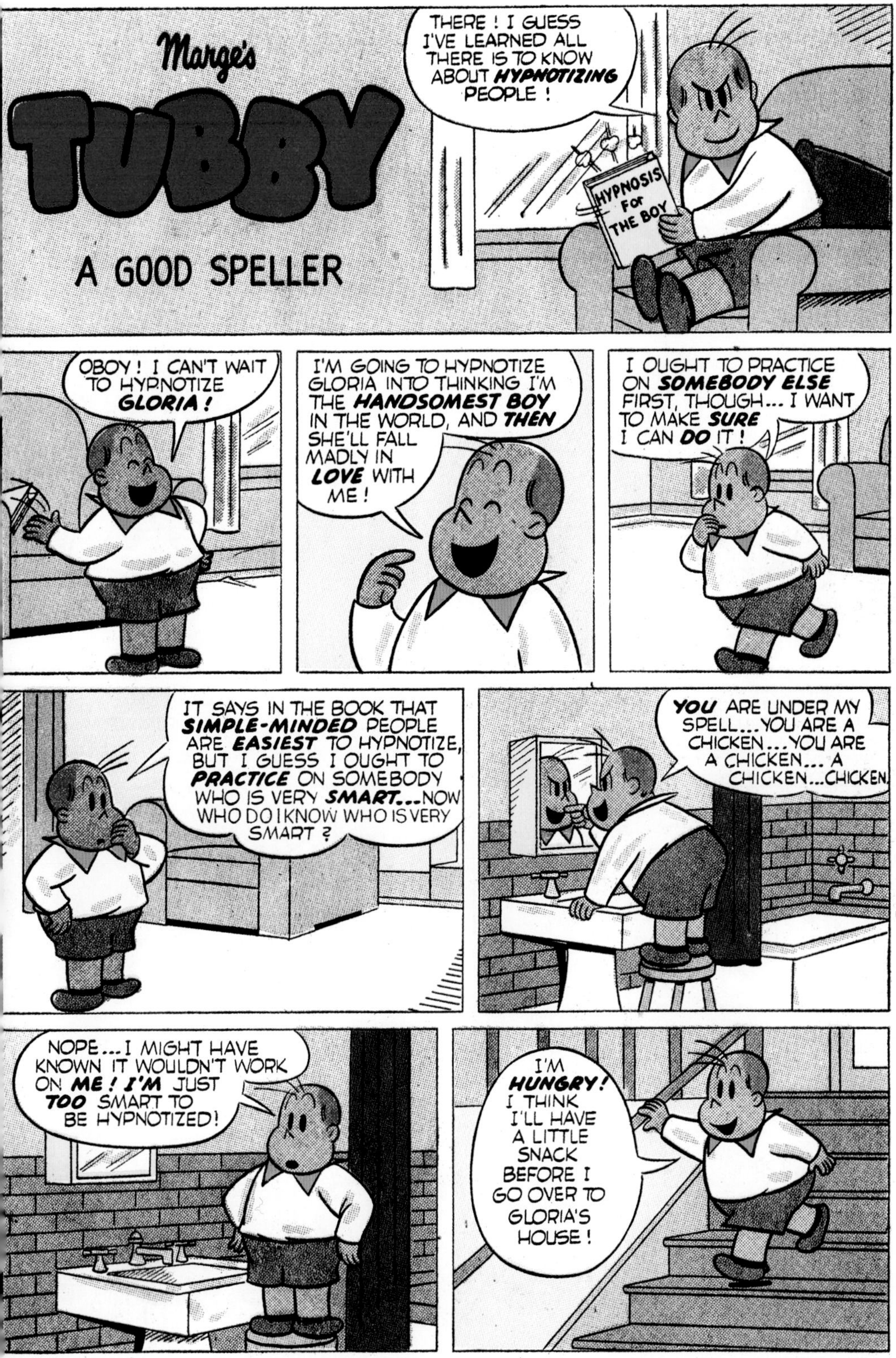
Marge's
TUBBY
A GOOD SPELLER
THERE! I GUESS I'VE LEARNED ALL THERE IS TO KNOW ABOUT HYPNOTIZING PEOPLE!
HYPNOSIS For THE BOY
OBOY! I CAN'T WAIT TO HYPNOTIZE GLORIA!
I'M GOING TO HYPNOTIZE GLORIA INTO THINKING I'M THE HANDSOMEST BOY IN THE WORLD, AND THEN SHE'LL FALL MADLY IN LOVE WITH ME!
I OUGHT TO PRACTICE ON SOMEBODY ELSE FIRST, THOUGH... I WANT TO MAKE SURE I CAN DO IT!
IT SAYS IN THE BOOK THAT SIMPLE-MINDED PEOPLE ARE EASIEST TO HYPNOTIZE, BUT I GUESS I OUGHT TO PRACTICE ON SOMEBODY WHO IS VERY SMART... NOW WHO DO I KNOW WHO IS VERY SMART?
YOU ARE UNDER MY SPELL... YOU ARE A CHICKEN... YOU ARE A CHICKEN... A CHICKEN... CHICKEN,
NOPE... I MIGHT HAVE KNOWN IT WOULDN'T WORK ON ME! I'M JUST TOO SMART TO BE HYPNOTIZED!
I'M HUNGRY! I THINK I'LL HAVE A LITTLE SNACK BEFORE I GO OVER TO GLORIA'S HOUSE!

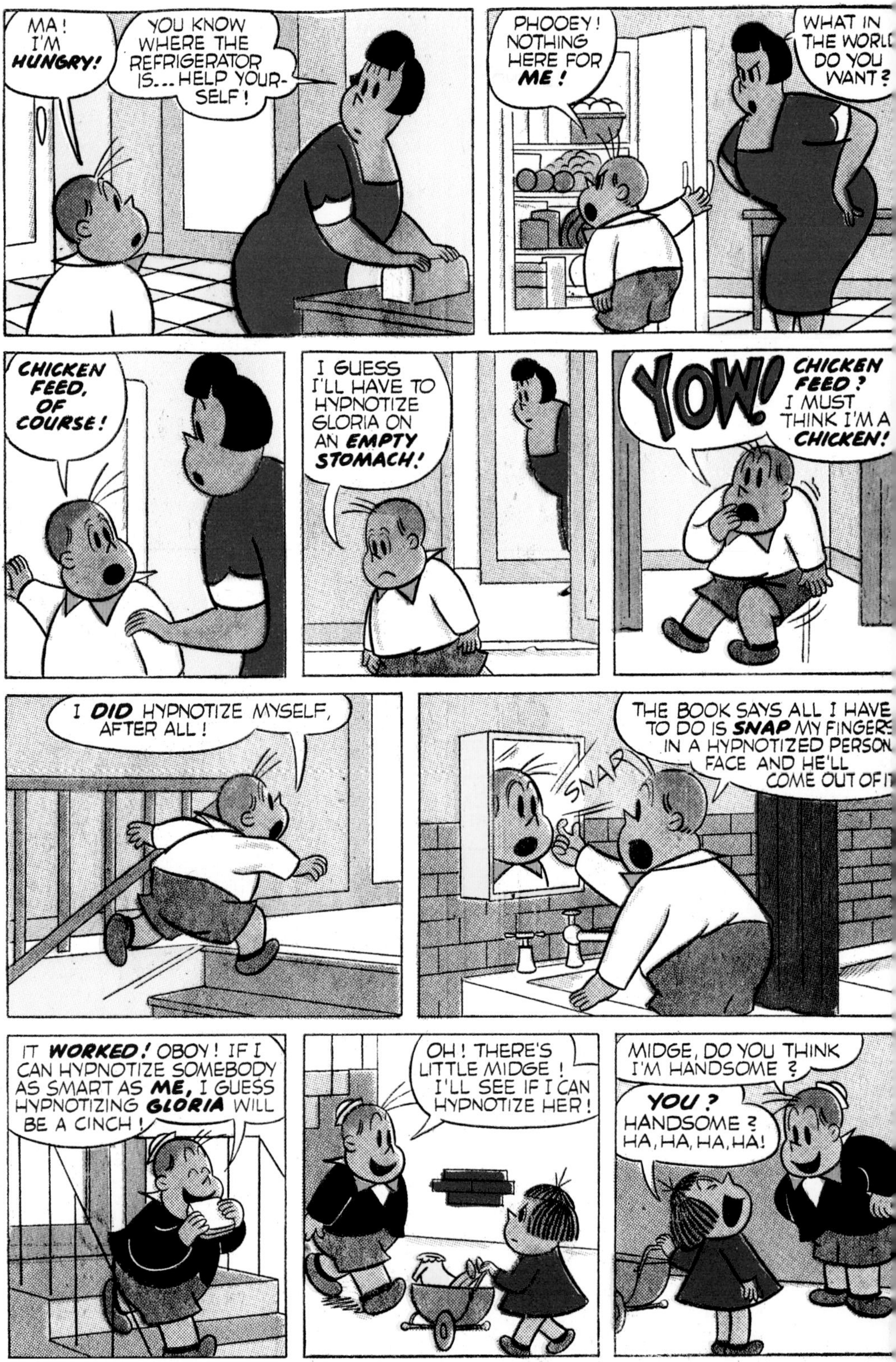

MA! I'M HUNGRY!
YOU KNOW WHERE THE REFRIGERATOR IS... HELP YOURSELF!
PHOOEY! NOTHING HERE FOR ME!
WHAT IN THE WORLD DO YOU WANT?
CHICKEN FEED, OF COURSE!
I GUESS I'LL HAVE TO HYPNOTIZE GLORIA ON AN EMPTY STOMACH!
YOW!
CHICKEN FEED? I MUST THINK I'M A CHICKEN!
I DID HYPNOTIZE MYSELF, AFTER ALL!
THE BOOK SAYS ALL I HAVE TO DO IS SNAP MY FINGERS IN A HYPNOTIZED PERSON'S FACE AND HE'LL COME OUT OF IT
SNAP
IT WORKED! OBOY! IF I CAN HYPNOTIZE SOMEBODY AS SMART AS ME, I GUESS HYPNOTIZING GLORIA WILL BE A CINCH!
OH! THERE'S LITTLE MIDGE! I'LL SEE IF I CAN HYPNOTIZE HER!
MIDGE, DO YOU THINK I'M HANDSOME?
YOU? HANDSOME? HA, HA, HA, HA!

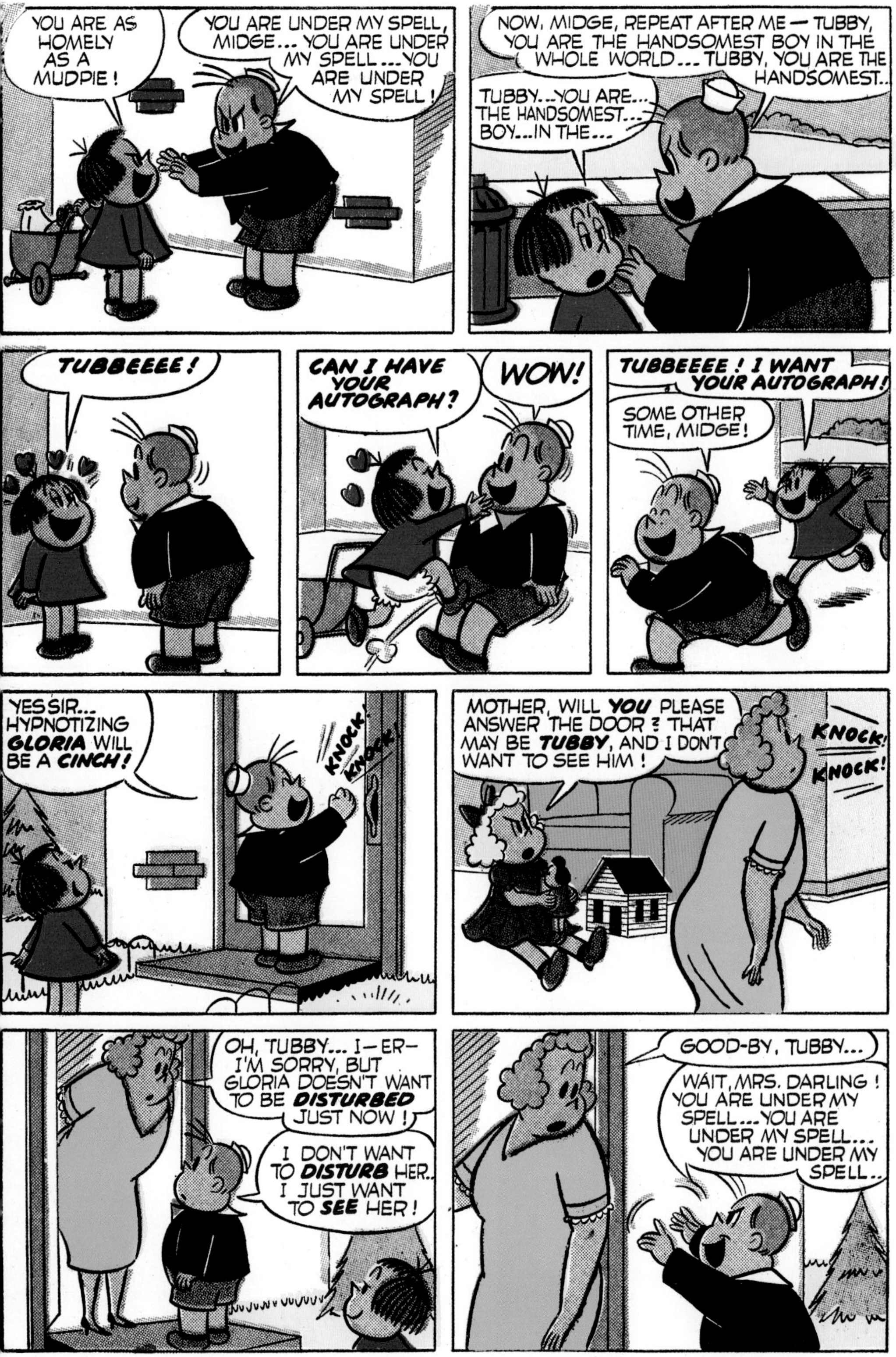

YOU ARE AS HOMELY AS A MUDPIE!
YOU ARE UNDER MY SPELL, MIDGE... YOU ARE UNDER MY SPELL... YOU ARE UNDER MY SPELL!
NOW, MIDGE, REPEAT AFTER ME — TUBBY, YOU ARE THE HANDSOMEST BOY IN THE WHOLE WORLD... TUBBY, YOU ARE THE HANDSOMEST..
TUBBY...YOU ARE... THE HANDSOMEST... BOY...IN THE...
TUBBEEEE!
CAN I HAVE YOUR AUTOGRAPH?
WOW!
TUBBEEEE! I WANT YOUR AUTOGRAPH!
SOME OTHER TIME, MIDGE!
YESSIR... HYPNOTIZING GLORIA WILL BE A CINCH!
KNOCK! KNOCK!
MOTHER, WILL YOU PLEASE ANSWER THE DOOR? THAT MAY BE TUBBY, AND I DON'T WANT TO SEE HIM!
KNOCK! KNOCK!
OH, TUBBY... I—ER— I'M SORRY, BUT GLORIA DOESN'T WANT TO BE DISTURBED JUST NOW!
I DON'T WANT TO DISTURB HER.. I JUST WANT TO SEE HER!
GOOD-BY, TUBBY...
WAIT, MRS. DARLING! YOU ARE UNDER MY SPELL... YOU ARE UNDER MY SPELL... YOU ARE UNDER MY SPELL..

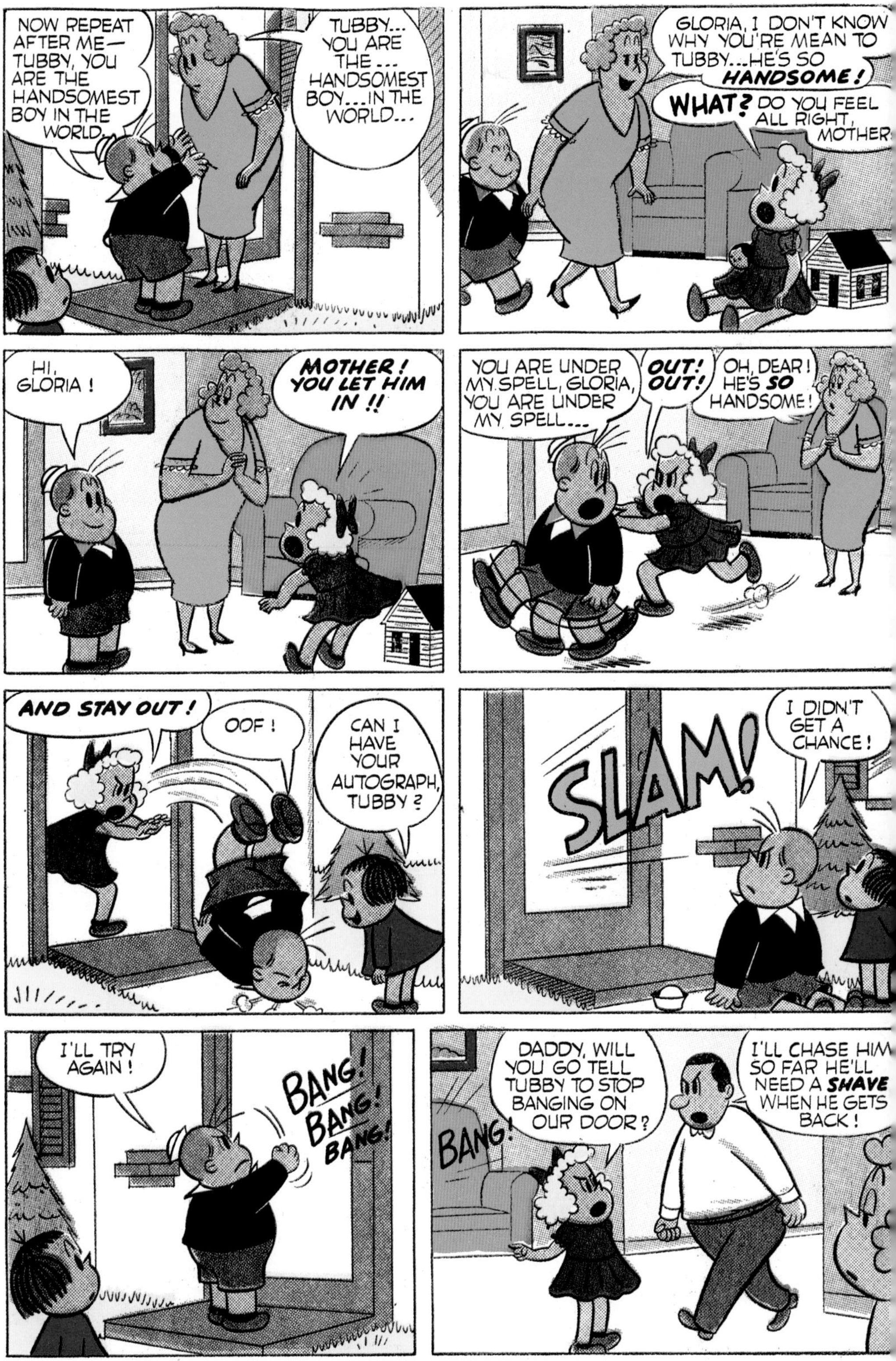
NOW REPEAT AFTER ME— TUBBY, YOU ARE THE HANDSOMEST BOY IN THE WORLD.
TUBBY... YOU ARE THE... HANDSOMEST BOY... IN THE WORLD...
GLORIA, I DON'T KNOW WHY YOU'RE MEAN TO TUBBY...HE'S SO HANDSOME!
WHAT? DO YOU FEEL ALL RIGHT, MOTHER
HI, GLORIA!
MOTHER! YOU LET HIM IN!!
YOU ARE UNDER MY SPELL, GLORIA, YOU ARE UNDER MY SPELL...
OUT! OUT!
OH, DEAR! HE'S SO HANDSOME!
AND STAY OUT!
OOF!
CAN I HAVE YOUR AUTOGRAPH, TUBBY?
SLAM!
I DIDN'T GET A CHANCE!
I'LL TRY AGAIN!
BANG! BANG! BANG!
BANG!
DADDY, WILL YOU GO TELL TUBBY TO STOP BANGING ON OUR DOOR?
I'LL CHASE HIM SO FAR HE'LL NEED A SHAVE WHEN HE GETS BACK!

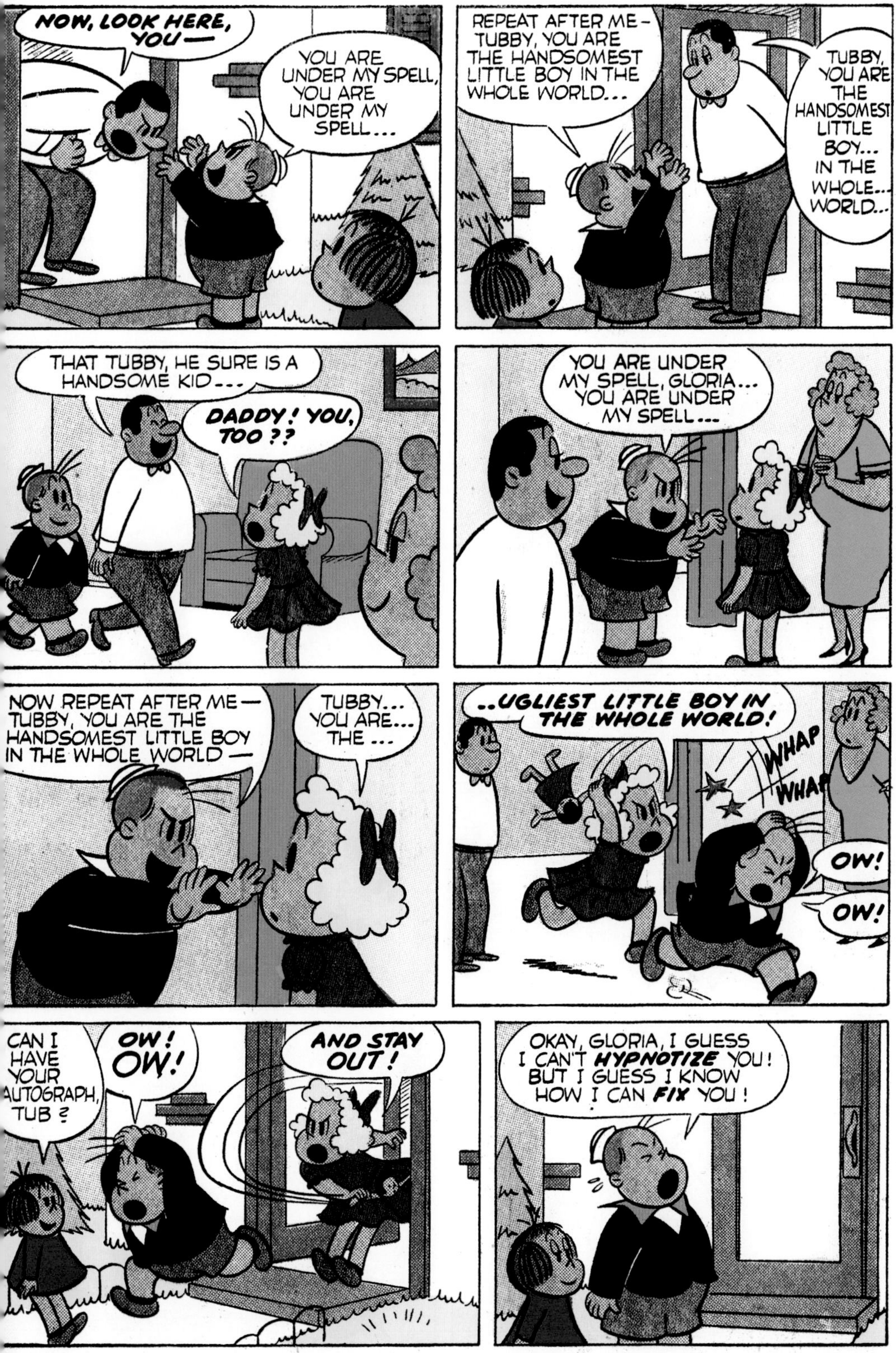

NOW, LOOK HERE, YOU—
YOU ARE UNDER MY SPELL, YOU ARE UNDER MY SPELL...
REPEAT AFTER ME— TUBBY, YOU ARE THE HANDSOMEST LITTLE BOY IN THE WHOLE WORLD...
TUBBY, YOU ARE THE HANDSOMEST LITTLE BOY... IN THE WHOLE... WORLD...
THAT TUBBY, HE SURE IS A HANDSOME KID...
DADDY! YOU, TOO??
YOU ARE UNDER MY SPELL, GLORIA... YOU ARE UNDER MY SPELL...
NOW REPEAT AFTER ME— TUBBY, YOU ARE THE HANDSOMEST LITTLE BOY IN THE WHOLE WORLD—
TUBBY... YOU ARE... THE...
..UGLIEST LITTLE BOY IN THE WHOLE WORLD!
WHAP
WHAP
OW!
OW!
CAN I HAVE YOUR AUTOGRAPH, TUB?
OW! OW!
AND STAY OUT!
OKAY, GLORIA, I GUESS I CAN'T HYPNOTIZE YOU! BUT I GUESS I KNOW HOW I CAN FIX YOU!

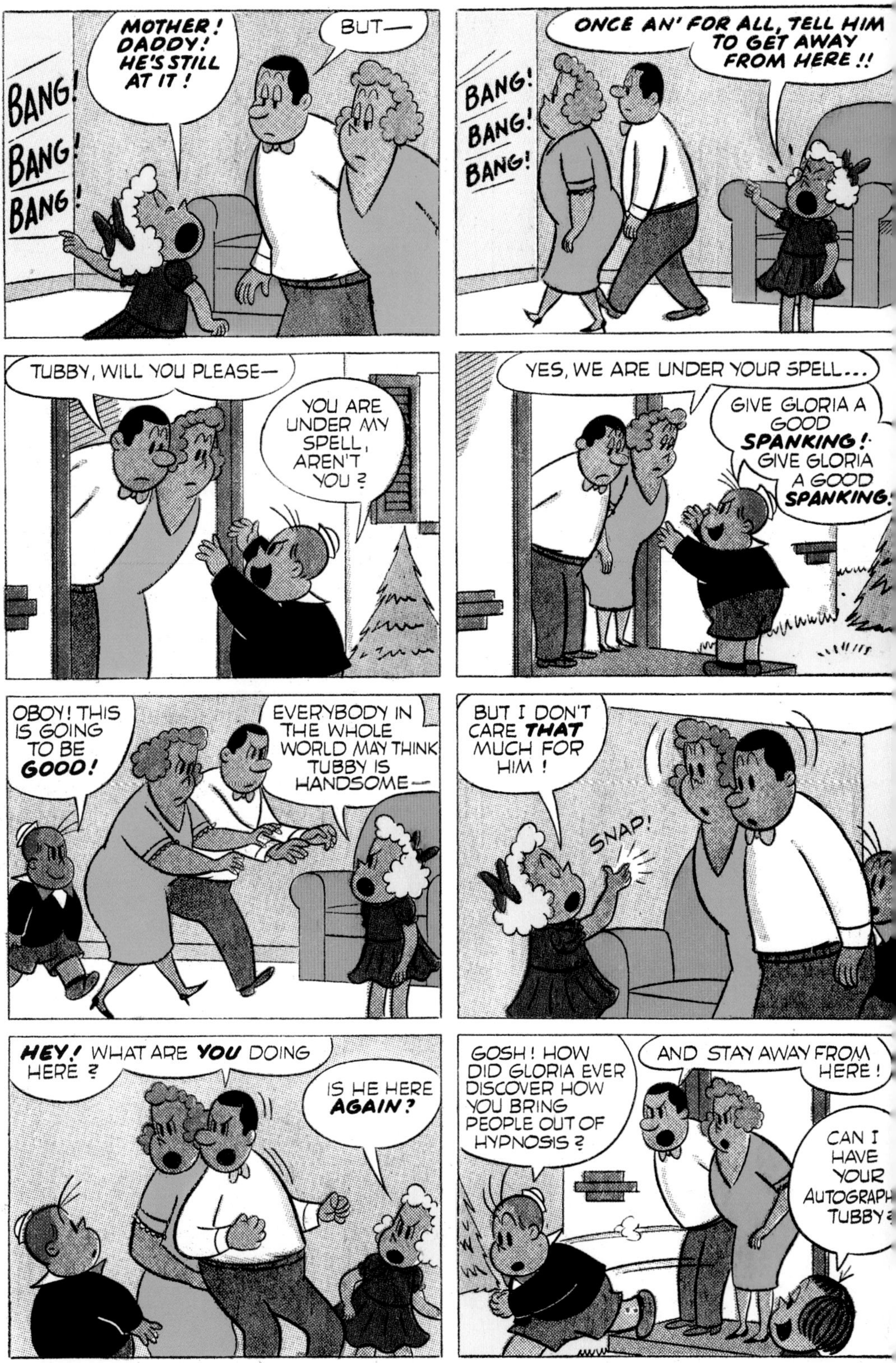
MOTHER! DADDY! HE'S STILL AT IT!
BUT—
BANG! BANG! BANG!
ONCE AN' FOR ALL, TELL HIM TO GET AWAY FROM HERE!!
BANG! BANG! BANG!
TUBBY, WILL YOU PLEASE—
YOU ARE UNDER MY SPELL, AREN'T YOU?
YES, WE ARE UNDER YOUR SPELL...
GIVE GLORIA A GOOD SPANKING! GIVE GLORIA A GOOD SPANKING!
OBOY! THIS IS GOING TO BE GOOD!
EVERYBODY IN THE WHOLE WORLD MAY THINK TUBBY IS HANDSOME—
BUT I DON'T CARE THAT MUCH FOR HIM!
SNAP!
HEY! WHAT ARE YOU DOING HERE?
IS HE HERE AGAIN?
GOSH! HOW DID GLORIA EVER DISCOVER HOW YOU BRING PEOPLE OUT OF HYPNOSIS?
AND STAY AWAY FROM HERE!
CAN I HAVE YOUR AUTOGRAPH TUBBY?

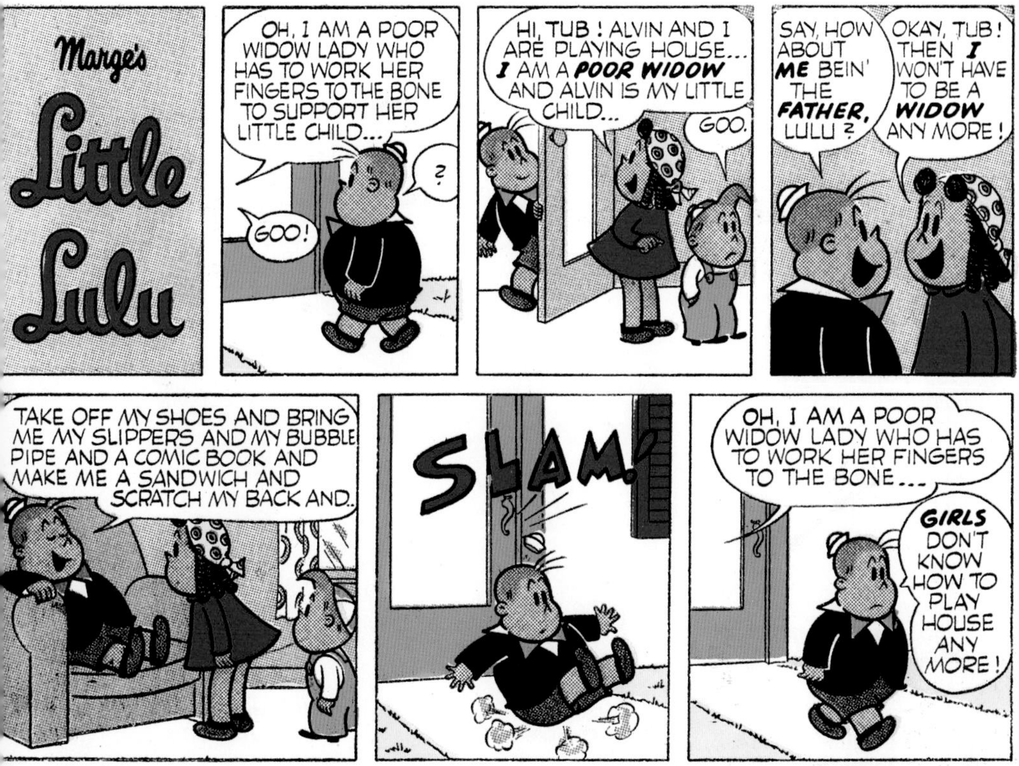
Marge's Little Lulu
OH, I AM A POOR WIDOW LADY WHO HAS TO WORK HER FINGERS TO THE BONE TO SUPPORT HER LITTLE CHILD...
?
GOO!
HI, TUB! ALVIN AND I ARE PLAYING HOUSE... I AM A POOR WIDOW AND ALVIN IS MY LITTLE CHILD...
GOO.
SAY, HOW ABOUT ME BEIN' THE FATHER, LULU?
OKAY, TUB! THEN I WON'T HAVE TO BE A WIDOW ANY MORE!
TAKE OFF MY SHOES AND BRING ME MY SLIPPERS AND MY BUBBLE PIPE AND A COMIC BOOK AND MAKE ME A SANDWICH AND SCRATCH MY BACK AND..
SLAM!
OH, I AM A POOR WIDOW LADY WHO HAS TO WORK HER FINGERS TO THE BONE...
GIRLS DON'T KNOW HOW TO PLAY HOUSE ANY MORE!

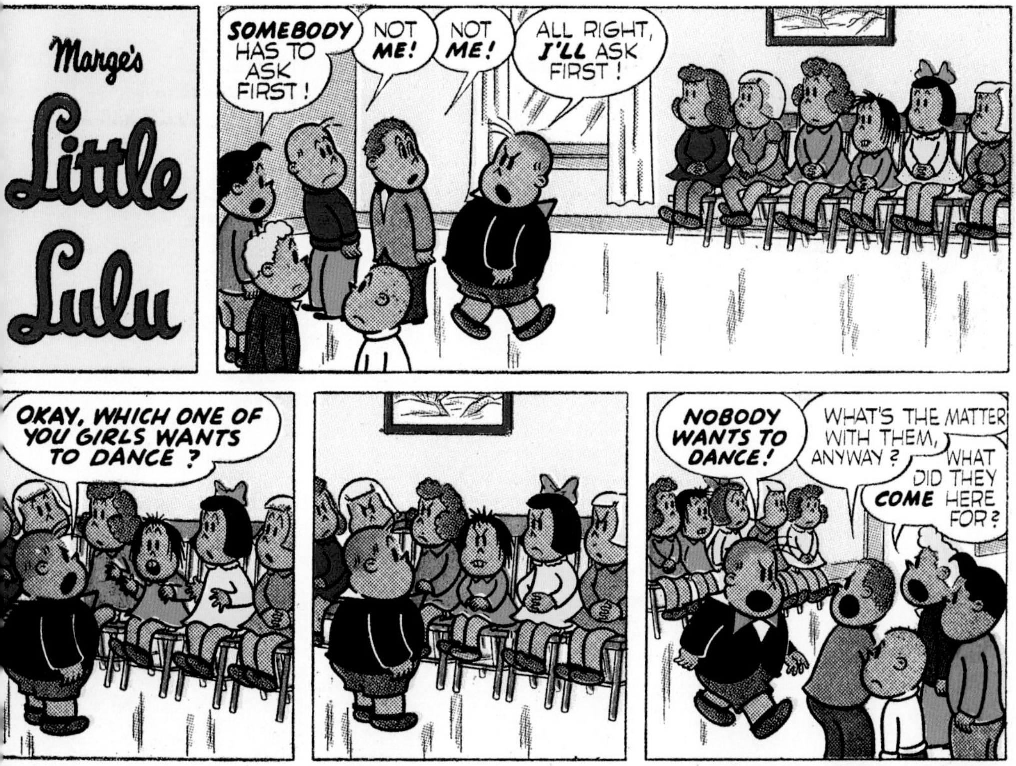
Marge's Little Lulu
SOMEBODY HAS TO ASK FIRST!
NOT ME!
NOT ME!
ALL RIGHT, I'LL ASK FIRST!
OKAY, WHICH ONE OF YOU GIRLS WANTS TO DANCE?
NOBODY WANTS TO DANCE!
WHAT'S THE MATTER WITH THEM, ANYWAY?
WHAT DID THEY COME HERE FOR?

# Little Lulu®

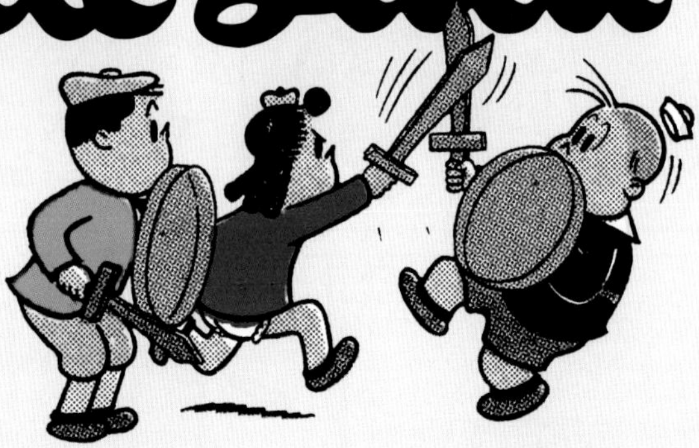

**Volume 1:**
**My Dinner with Lulu**
ISBN 978-1-59307-318-3
$9.95

**Volume 2:**
**Sunday Afternoon**
ISBN 978-1-59307-345-9
$9.95

**Volume 3:**
**Lulu in the Doghouse**
ISBN 978-1-59307-346-6
$9.95

**Volume 4:**
**Lulu Goes Shopping**
ISBN 978-1-59307-270-4
$9.95

**Volume 5:**
**Lulu Takes a Trip**
ISBN 978-1-59307-317-6
$9.95

**Volume 6:**
**Letters to Santa**
ISBN 978-1-59307-386-2
$9.95

**Volume 7:**
**Lulu's Umbrella Service**
ISBN 978-1-59307-399-2
$9.95

**Volume 8:**
**Late for School**
ISBN 978-1-59307-453-1
$9.95

**Volume 9:**
**Lucky Lulu**
ISBN 978-1-59307-471-5
$9.95

**Volume 10:**
**All Dressed Up**
ISBN 978-1-59307-534-7
$9.95

**Volume 11:**
**April Fools**
ISBN 978-1-59307-557-6
$9.95

**Volume 12:**
**Leave It to Lulu**
ISBN 978-1-59307-620-7
$9.95

**Volume 13:**
**Too Much Fun**
ISBN 978-1-59307-621-4
$9.95

**Volume 14:**
**Queen Lulu**
ISBN 978-1-59307-683-2
$9.95

**Volume 15:**
**The Explorers**
ISBN 978-1-59307-684-9
$9.95

**Volume 16:**
**A Handy Kid**
ISBN 978-1-59307-685-6
$10.95

**Volume 17:**
**The Valentine**
ISBN 978-1-59307-686-3
$10.95

**Volume 18:**
**The Expert**
ISBN 978-1-59307-687-0
$10.95

**FULL COLOR VOLUMES!**
**Volume 19:**
**The Alamo and Other Stories**
ISBN 978-1-59582-293-2
$14.95

**Little Lulu Color Special**
ISBN 978-1-59307-613-9
$13.95

DARK HORSE BOOKS

AVAILABLE AT YOUR LOCAL COMICS SHOP OR BOOKSTORE!
To find a comics shop in your area, call 1.888.266.4226. For more information or to order direct, visit darkhorse.com or call 1.800.862.0052. Mon.–Fri. 9 A.M. to 5 P.M. Pacific Time. *Prices and availability subject to change without notice.